"Here we see how a millennium-old nation ruled by a monarchy that had lasted a good three centuries fell apart *in three days*. Book 2 of *March 1917* powerfully reveals how a decent if flawed political and social order collapsed 'with incredible alacrity,' as Solzhenitsyn writes elsewhere."

—*The New Criterion*

"Although *The Red Wheel* is fiction, Solzhenitsyn prided himself on the historical accuracy of his work. [His] decision to write the novel in vignettes, ranging from several pages to several lines, opens the book to a variety of readers and approaches to reading."

—*Choice*

"It's the style, the story, the characters, the form, the way with words, the invention, the humor, the ideas, and the attitude the work contains that appeal, plus such things as escapism, confirmation of beliefs, upending of positions, expression of inchoate feelings, and the desire to be astonished and informed."

—*3:AM Magazine*

"'Revolutionary truths,' Solzhenitsyn writes, 'have a great quality: even hearing them with their own ears, the doomed don't understand.' It's too late for the millions who will be subjected to lifelong suffering because ideologically enthralled intellectuals hammered away at society's foundation until it collapsed. After Lenin comes Stalin. He always does."

—*The American Conservative*

THE RED WHEEL
A Narrative in Discrete Periods of Time

NODE I
August 1914 (Books 1–2)

NODE II
October 1916 (Books 1–2)

NODE III
March 1917 (Books 1–4)

NODE IV
April 1917 (Books 1–2)

The Center for Ethics and Culture Solzhenitsyn Series

The Center for Ethics and Culture Solzhenitsyn Series showcases the contributions and continuing inspiration of Aleksandr Solzhenitsyn (1918–2008), the Nobel Prize–winning novelist and historian. The series makes available works of Solzhenitsyn, including previously untranslated works, and aims to provide the leading platform for exploring the many facets of his enduring legacy. In his novels, essays, memoirs, and speeches, Solzhenitsyn revealed the devastating core of totalitarianism and warned against political, economic, and cultural dangers to the human spirit. In addition to publishing his work, this new series features thoughtful writers and commentators who draw inspiration from Solzhenitsyn's abiding care for Christianity and the West, and for the best of the Russian tradition. Through contributions in politics, literature, philosophy, and the arts, these writers follow Solzhenitsyn's trail in a world filled with new pitfalls and new possibilities for human freedom and human dignity.

Aleksandr Solzhenitsyn

MARCH 1917

THE RED WHEEL / NODE III
(8 March –31 March)

BOOK 3

Translated by Marian Schwartz

UNIVERSITY OF NOTRE DAME PRESS

NOTRE DAME, INDIANA

Published by the University of Notre Dame Press
Notre Dame, Indiana 46556
www.undpress.nd.edu

Library of Congress Control Number: 2017006656

ISBN: 978-0-268-20170-8   (Hardback)
ISBN: 978-0-268-20172-2   (WebPDF)
ISBN: 978-0-268-20169-2   (Epub)

∞*This paper meets the requirements of ANSI/NISO Z39.48-1992*
(Permanence of Paper).

Publisher's Note

March 1917 (consisting of books 1–4) is the centerpiece of *The Red Wheel*, Aleksandr Solzhenitsyn's multivolume historical novel on the roots and outbreak of the Russian Revolution, which he divided into four "nodes." *March 1917* is the third node.

The first node, *August 1914*, ends in the disastrous defeat of the Russians by the Germans at the Battle of Tannenberg in World War I. The second node, *November 1916*, offers a panorama of Russia on the eve of revolution. *August 1914* and *November 1916* focus on Russia's crises, revolutionary terrorism and its suppression, the missed opportunity of Pyotr Stolypin's reforms, and the souring of patriotism as Russia suffered in the world war.

March 1917 tells the story of the beginning of the revolution in Petrograd, as riots go unchecked, units of the army mutiny, and both the state and the numerous opposition leaders are incapable of controlling events. The present volume, book 3 of *March 1917*, is set during March 16–22. It will be followed by the English translation of the final book of *March 1917*, describing events through March 31, and the two books of *April 1917*.

The nodes of *The Red Wheel* can be read consecutively or independently. All blend fictional characters with numerous historical personages, usually introduced under their own names and with accurate biographical data. The depiction of historical characters and events is based on the author's extensive research in archives, administrative records, newspapers, memoirs, émigré collections, unpublished correspondence, family records, and other contemporary sources. In many sections the historical novel turns into dramatic history. Plots and subplots abound.

The English translations by H. T. Willetts of *August 1914* and *October 1916*, published by Farrar, Straus and Giroux in 1989 and 1999, respectively, appeared as Knot I and Knot II. The present translation, in accordance with the wishes of the Solzhenitsyn estate, has chosen the term "Node" as more faithful to the author's intent. Both terms refer, as in mathematics, to discrete points on a continuous line. Node 2 was published under the title *November 1916*; future editions will seek to restore the title *October 1916*, according to the author's wish that each Node's title be uniform across languages.

In a 1983 interview with Bernard Pivot, Aleksandr Solzhenitsyn described his narrative concept as follows: "The *Red Wheel* is the narrative of revolution in Russia, its movement through the whirlwind of revolution. This is an immense scope of material, and . . . it would be impossible to describe this many events and this many characters over such a lengthy stretch of time. That is why I have chosen the method of nodal points, or Nodes. I select short segments of time, of two or three weeks' duration, where the most vivid events unfold, or else where the decisive causes of future events are formed. And I describe in detail only these short segments. These are the Nodes. Through these nodal points I convey the general vector, the overall shape of this complex curve."

Dates in the original Russian text were given in the Old Style, according to the Julian calendar used in Russia until 1918. In the English translations these dates have been changed, in accordance with the author's wishes, to the New Style (Gregorian) calendar, putting them thirteen days ahead of the old dates. The March 1917 revolution thus corresponds to the February Revolution in Russian history (Old Style), just as the revolution that placed the Bolsheviks in power in November of that year is commonly referred to as the October Revolution.

In the "screen" sequences in this book, the different margins represent different instructions for the shooting of a film: sound effects or camera direction, action, and dialogue (in italics). The symbol "=" indicates "cut to." Chapters numbered with a double-prime (") show newspaper headlines of the day.

* * *

The English translation was made possible through a generous anonymous donation to the Solzhenitsyn Initiative at the Wilson Center's Kennan Institute, which is gratefully acknowledged.

The maps and the Index of Names have been adapted and revised from the versions in the French translation, *La Roue rouge*, Troisième nœud, *Mars dix-sept*, tomes 1–3, with the kind permission of Fayard and approval of the Solzhenitsyn estate.

Contents

CONTENTS / ix

CONTENTS / xi

SATURDAY, 17 MARCH

CONTENTS / xiii

SUNDAY, 18 MARCH

CONTENTS / xv

CONTENTS / xxi

16 MARCH
FRIDAY

[354]

How could you not light up at the thought that you were taking part in Russia's moments of greatness! While Russia's future was diving in and out of the hidden swell of negotiations in the Tsar's train car in Pskov, the engineer Lomonosov was pacing from office to office, from telephone to telephone—taking tiger-claw steps, his boot seeming to grab a piece of the floor each time it separated from it—but mostly to the telegraph, which was still connected to Pskov. Sitting at the other end was a railway inspector who had traveled with Guchkov to secure the road and who was recounting various minutiae from his observations.

This moment—dreamed of, longed for, by so many generations of the Russian intelligentsia, so many revolutionaries who had gone into exile or emigration, this fantastic, unattainable moment—here it had come and was passing in muffled obscurity inside a shuttered train car at the half-dark Pskov train station. How could the former little cadet and student railroader Yuri Lomonosov have imagined that he might be the first man in the Russian capital to catch—snatch—the news of the despot's abdication and cast it on the waves of a free and exultant Russia! (And would people remember his service?) Right now, Yuri Vladimirovich was reveling in each look, each move, each joke of his, each grasp of the receiver, each fingering of the streaming tape.

In the Tauride Palace, people were terribly agitated, waiting, but they had no direct connection to Pskov. Rodzyanko ordered that the act of abdication, as soon as it appeared, be transmitted by telegraph in code to the Ministry of Roads and Railways and from there by telephone to the Tauride Palace.

While Bublikov, badly wounded over not having been appointed minister, and maybe even especially for that reason, ordered that the first substantive tape from Pskov be delivered to him in his office first.

And so, after Pskov reported that the deputies had left the imperial train, Bublikov stood by the telegraph to await what was to follow.

Another half-hour's anguish ensued. No tape. He'd refused? Hadn't abdicated? There, in Pskov, they already knew but weren't reporting anything. Or they were encoding.

At last, it came! Bublikov took it and carried away the secret. Without opening his door, without sharing—he himself would be the first to transmit

1

it to someone in the Tauride Palace. Finally he shared it with Lomonosov as a reward. It was a brief telegram from Guchkov to Rodzyanko: "*Assent obtained*"! But until the Manifesto itself came in, mum's the word.

So there would be no chance to cast it on the Russian waves, except to whisper to loyal colleagues like Rulevsky or Sosnovsky. Lomonosov didn't get to strike.

Sic transit . . .! Here he'd been the emperor of a great country, and now in the blink of an eye he'd become a *former* emperor and no longer would elicit obsequiousness, respect, or regret in anyone.

The tape started flowing again, not encoded, but not about abdication at all. Pskov was asking, on Guchkov's instruction, to assign the imperial train a route to GHQ.

Lomonosov exploded. They've lost their minds! How can an abdicated despot be allowed to go to GHQ? And have the entire army handed over to him? This was another coup!

"Aleksandr Aleksandrovich! This is beyond comprehension! What is Guchkov doing? Inform the Duma!"

Bublikov felt like he'd been scalded with boiling water—and he grabbed the receiver.

However, he established distance: neither Lomonosov nor anyone else could continue to be present during his telephone conversations. All they could hear was that he was objecting harshly, practically shouting.

He stepped out on his office threshold, disappointed:

"The order is to let him go to GHQ. And they're pressing for the Manifesto. Ask why it hasn't been sent."

"There, in Pskov, it's been submitted to the military commandant for encoding. And they're refusing to transmit over our lines. They want it to go over military lines, to the General Staff."

Yet another disappointment: they'd been shunted away from the main nerve center, sidelined as a ministry.

"Complain to Guchkov!"

"Guchkov said it doesn't matter."

They'd been cast aside.

Bublikov hung his head and went to his office. But scarcely to sleep.

While Lomonosov, not losing his tiger step, paced and paced—and came up with something! He called the Duma, the Military Commission:

"So you're going to get the Manifesto, but where do you intend to print it?"

After all, the Duma didn't have its own printing press. The state printing press and all the others were dispersed and on strike.

"But we can do it at the Ministry of Roads and Railways press! We have employees in place."

Over there they hadn't even thought about this, the scatterbrains. Over there they were glad for the suggestion. Although they were still putting on airs:

"But you realize this is a matter of great secrecy. It has to be printed in such a way that it doesn't get out prematurely."

Lomonosov exulted over the receiver, and with military intonations:

"We have an excellent organization! It will not get out! And our own security. We can let all our unoccupied employees go and place a guard at the press."

They agreed. Excellent! He had cheered up Bublikov, who had been dispirited. New possibilities.

But now Pskov was putting on the brakes: the military commandant was encoding incredibly slowly. And then it still had to be transmitted over a military line. And then a colonel at the General Staff would decode it. A long business, another quarter of the night.

Bublikov decided to get some sleep, instructing Lomonosov, as soon as the decoding was complete, to send an automobile to this colonel with two soldiers and take one copy to the Duma for reading and a second here for printing. That would be morning already, and the press employees would have assembled.

Bublikov lay down in his office—but now Lomonosov certainly wouldn't lie down tonight, would not let his destiny slip. Nights like this come only once! He paced and paced, summoning clarity.

Right then Cavalry Captain Sosnovsky appeared, very red and loud and extraordinarily cheerful. Evidently he'd had a good sip there, in the minister's quarters.

Some wine! That was an idea. If there was anything one felt like, it was some good wine!

"Captain! You must bring a bottle of good wine to me on duty."

The cavalry captain grimaced slightly. The hour was late and his upbringing told him not to, but friendship and service, all for one. He smiled mischievously. He went and brought a bottle of excellent Madeira.

Now duty became much more cheerful. But impatient thoughts arose, too. For some reason the Manifesto had gotten hung up at the General Staff and still wasn't ready, was still being decoded. Then, one passage couldn't be decoded and required a second transmission.

Very strange. Very suspicious. Was there some monarchical conspiracy here? To detain the Manifesto at headquarters—and meanwhile something would happen, someone would help? . . .

Yes, of course, this was a conspiracy of sinister forces! That was clear. They wanted to hide the Manifesto and organize a counter-coup.

"So, colonel, can I send a motorcar for the document?"

"What motorcar?"

"To take it to the Duma."

"Forgive me, professor. I don't understand. Where do you come in here? The Pskov telegram is addressed to the Chief of the General Staff. Right now I'm finishing the decoding and I'll be reporting it to my superiors."

Was that so? It was perfectly clear, then! A counterrevolutionary officers' conspiracy!

His first thought was to cut all this colonel's telephone lines to keep him from reaching any agreements. The Pskov line was in our hands, through the Northwestern Railroad. And the municipal telephone? We could call the municipal telephone station and tell them, in the name of Commissar Bublikov, to turn off Colonel Shikheev's telephone.

Bublikov slept, and Lomonosov's fantasy drifted, warmed by the wine.

Fine. Now, ask Minister of Justice Kerensky for permission to arrest the colonel who wants to conceal the abdication.

Kerensky was known to stay awake around the clock. And his consent was immediately obtained.

That's it! Drive a truckful of soldiers to the General Staff, seize the colonel and all the copies of the document somehow—and take them to the Tauride Palace!

[3 5 5]

Admiral Kolchak was a decisive man in the extreme. Not only was he capable of bold decisions, but he was incapable of any other kind. In no month of his stormy life, in no service, could he have simply been static or apathetic. He sought always to reveal and carry out the loftiest mission, at the upper limit of his powers.

He always endeavored to take part in whatever was hardest. As a naval cadet he was already working at the Obukhov factory studying artillery, mines, and factory management. (His father worked there.) On his very first voyages as a lieutenant he began studying oceanography and hydrology. Even then he had such faith in his own star that he held as his goal discovering the South Pole! But he did not get on the South Pole expedition. Then, however, Baron Toll suddenly invited Kolchak to join an Academy of Sciences North Pole expedition as hydrologist and magnetologist. His father and brothers were all naval men, as were all the family's acquaintances, but 1899 was peacetime, so Aleksandr obtained leave from the military and went into scientific service. He spent time studying with Nansen, who built them a ship. (Polar sailors are all brothers.) Their three-year expedition could not get through the ice, though. From the New Siberian islands, Toll sent Kolchak and his collections up the Lena to ready another ship from Petersburg, while he himself persisted north—and vanished. In St. Petersburg in December 1902, they were trying to decide how to rescue Toll, but they couldn't sail until spring. Kolchak proposed and set about implementing a desperate winter plan. He persuaded four Arkhangelsk Pomors experienced in sailing through ice and immediately, at the height of winter, dashed all the way across Siberia to the mouth of the Yana, using dogs to drag the best whaleboat from Toll's hemmed-in ship over the snow from Tiksi—and thus, before the ice broke, made a dash for the New Siberian Islands. When the ocean briefly opened up in July, Kolchak and the Pomors on the whaleboat set off between the ice floes toward Bennett Island—where he found both Toll's note and his last collections. The note made it clear that Toll and his companions had starved to death. But Kolchak managed to return to the mouth of the Yana on the whaleboat without losing a single man. Exhausted by three years of expeditions, he reached Yakutsk in January 1904—and immediately learned about the outbreak of war with Japan. Not one minute more in the Academy of Sciences! No leave or rest! He had to return to the navy and the front. It was hard, but he wrested permission. Admiral Makarov knew about Kolchak and his oceanographic works—and before Makarov's death Kolchak already led the *Indignant* torpedo boat in the Yellow Sea, and later he saw the explosion of the *Petropavlovsk*, and himself torpedoed the Japanese cruiser *Takosado*, receiving the golden sword. But he had misjudged his powers. The North Pole took its revenge: a month with pneumonia and then brutal rheumatic arthritis. Just then the fleet came to a standstill and all actions were moved to dry land. Kolchak asked leave to be commander of the naval battery at Port Arthur and, overcoming his rheumatism, remained there until the day of surrender. He spent six months in captivity, was deemed an invalid, was among those magnanimously released home by the Japanese, and spent another six months submitting academic reports of his polar expedition. But the shamefully lost war burned inside him. The fleet had been built and led ignorantly, and the ships did not know how to shoot. So Kolchak, whose heart drowned with each Tsushima ship, drew a group of young and energetic naval officers together to elaborate scientific foundations for the fleet's organization so as to revive it in powerful form. They were able to create a Naval General Staff—and Kolchak was put in charge of the Baltic theater. The group reached for the sky! But Minister of the Navy Voevodsky undermined the entire shipbuilding program and delayed the fleet's restoration by two years, and there were also conflicts with the Duma. Impatient, Kolchak dashed back to the Artic Circle, on the steel *Vaigach*, which could withstand the icc's pressure: from Vladivostok, through the Bering Strait, to skirt all of Siberia to the north. But before that, the minister recalled Kolchak, and in the fall of 1910 he returned to his former post on the Naval General Staff.

Kolchak had no connections or acquaintances in higher places, but due to his outstanding abilities he kept being promoted. In 1913, he became flag captain for operations at Baltic Fleet headquarters, Commander Essen's right hand. The fleet was being built at a furious pace now, but they didn't make it in time for the war, which had been expected in 1915—but broke out in 1914! They had no dreadnoughts or submarines ready. (A day before the war started, Kolchak began without permission to lay minefields in the Gulf of Finland to protect their weak fleet—at which point an order reached him from the ministry to do so immediately!) A year later, already an admiral and in command of a mine division, he beat back the Germans' coastal offensive against Riga. In July 1916, he suddenly received a telegram saying that he had been appointed to command the Black Sea Fleet—at forty-three! His father, Vasily Ivanych, had been a naval gunner in Sevastopol in 1855—and here his son was on his way to that same immortal Sevastopol!

He understood this as a challenge and a demand for himself: What should he accomplish now? His primary objective was to keep the Black Sea calm from attacks and make sure that the sea supply for the Caucasus front did not get mired in the wild, dense mountains. The very night of the fleet's change of command—knowing and taunting him?—the fast-moving *Breslau* appeared out of the Bosphorus—and in those very first hours Kolchak rushed to drive her back. Then, he personally supervised the laying of minefields at the Bosphorus that were impassable both on and under the water and kept torpedo boats there on watch so that the Turks couldn't clear the mines. And so he held on as master of the Black Sea, moving all the more irrevocably and easily toward his historic objective: to seize the Bosphorus and the Dardanelles! Also during his journey south, Kolchak received approval for this landing from the Emperor ("based on your qualities, you are best suited of all for this"), and also apparently from General Alekseev—and he claimed this as his fervent objective.

He saw his task illuminated by such an undeniable light that he actually found it odd to encounter objections and disagreements in Russian minds. Once Turkey had entered the war, how could we not seize this opportunity? The war itself had unfolded in such a way as for us to realize our ages-old objective. Why had we been waging this war anyway? It held no other objectives for us. For an entire century, people had been talking and thinking about the straits—so why not take them now? We had frightened Europe unnecessarily by promising a cross atop Hagia Sophia—but were waiting to receive the straits like a present from their Allies. The simple, direct, and sole objective of the war being waged was dissipating in diplomatic shuffling and in GHQ's unnecessary efforts on land, along a thousand versts of front. It was perfectly clear that the Allies had absolutely no interest in giving us the straits, and England had always been the main obstacle—so we had to take them with our own forces. Today, England couldn't get in the way, and by the time a peace had been concluded we could control the straits in a real way. That was what Skobelev had said: Take Constantinople *before* peace is concluded, otherwise they won't give it to us. Taking control of the straits now would mean bringing the war's end closer.

The matter was perfectly practical and required merely assiduous preparation and silent swiftness, which were already streaming in Kolchak's breast and actions. Now his calculation was as follows: of the forty-five Turkish divisions, nearly all were on the Caucasus front and in Mesopotamia, Arabia, and Syria. In the Dardanelles there were two weakened divisions; in the Bosphorus, just two weak ones, and also two in Macedonia, but they could not be deployed quickly. The Germans would not be able to come to the Turks' aid in less than two weeks either, and the powerful German cruiser *Goeben* was in dry dock. Our agents had established that the Bosphorus field fortifications were in a state of neglect and unprotected, their artillery had been moved to the Dardanelles, and even on moonlit nights our torpedo boats could approach the Turkish shores unimpeded. All this gave them the opportunity to disembark right by the strait: clear the approaches at night, at dawn land a division on either side of the strait, begin to set up a barricade of mines, and meanwhile land a third division with heavy artillery and then send the transport flotillas back to bring two more divisions. The difficult moment would be just before the caravan's return with the second landing party, while we were chained to a narrow strip of coastline. But in the morning, the sun rising behind our backs would blind the Turks at the moment our offensive began. And by evening our fleet should enter the Bosphorus—and the path to Constantinople should be free!

Kolchak kept enough ships fitted out for one division at all times. He began arranging for two more divisions that winter, so as to be ready by May. The operation could only be carried out in June and July; after that, the weather was uncertain, and then came the storms, and supplies for the landing troops would be cut off. Since the previous November, Kolchak had been forming the first landing division. (He conferred on it naval banners, an anchor on their epaulets and sleeve, and named the regiments the Tsargrad and after the heroes of Sevastopol—Nakhimov, Kornilov, and Istomin!)

But GHQ, the earthbound, untrusting Alekseev, began to resist with all his strength, objecting that this was too risky—disembarking directly in the strait; that they should land much farther away and in numbers, and that meant with the forces of four corps, and that meant it was impossible because there was nowhere to take them from. (Just take them from the Caucasus Army! Are they really better deployed in mountain impasses?) Finally, any landing at all was complicated, and we have seen the disgrace of the Allies' Dardanelles operation. Finally, there has never been such an undertaking in the history of the world—so how can we dare it? . . . (That winter, when Alekseev was being treated in Sevastopol, Kolchak saw him and tried to persuade him. But it was pointless. However, he did get a good look for himself and saw that Alekseev was incapable of daring, he was not that kind of military leader. He thought inside the dogma of the concentration of superior forces and could not believe in a daring operation with lesser forces. Moreover, he was devoted to the "continental ideology," which said that this war's entire fate was to inflict a blow on the Germans, and for that, the Baltic fleet was more important. He was also eclipsed by the rote hands-off political doctrine, which said that the Bosphorus would "take itself" after Germany's fall, as if the keys to the Bosphorus were in Berlin.)

So Kolchak had readied the fleet and the means of transport and could have gotten by with just the Caucasus divisions—but he did not have the final order from GHQ.

Apart from the Bosphorus, all Kolchak had were the operations on the Asia Minor coast, in concert with the Caucasus Army Group. A few days before, Kolchak had gone to Batum on a torpedo boat—to meet with Nikolai Nikolaevich—who also refused support for Kolchak's Bosphorus landing.

He practically had the Bosphorus in his teeth! But he couldn't take it.

Before he left Batum, on the 13th, Kolchak received a telegram from Minister Grigorovich in Petrograd: "Decode personally." It reported major disturbances in Petrograd, saying the capital was in rebel hands and the garrison had gone over to their side, although, "at present the upheavals are quieting down." Kolchak showed it to the grand duke, who shrugged, who didn't know anything of the sort, but who released him to return quickly.

As one who makes swift and imperious decisions, Kolchak secretly ordered via telegraph, while still in Batum, that the commandant of the Sevastopol fortress stop any postal or telegraph communications between the Crimean peninsula and the rest of Russia and transmit only telegrams for the Commander of the Fleet and his headquarters. That same night, though, his torpedo boat picked up from Constantinople, from a powerful German wireless station, in a corrupted Russian-Bulgarian dialect, that there was revolution in Petrograd and terrible battles were under way. So what was there to hide? Telegraph operators on duty on all vessels were picking up all wireless.

Arriving in Sevastopol on 14 March, Kolchak received a telegram from Rodzyanko saying that the Provisional Committee of the State Duma had found itself compelled, for the good of the homeland, to take the restoration of state order in hand and was calling on the population and army for help, to prevent complications.

Restoring state order was always good. And the Duma was a sufficiently authoritative organ. Generally speaking, Kolchak sympathized with Duma figures (and they in turn considered him their great hope, as they did Nepenin). Russia had to be developed, and there was much that was ossified getting in the way. Developed—yes, but by bright minds, not in bloody outbursts.

For now, much remained unclear.

They got in touch with naval headquarters at GHQ and learned only that the Emperor had left for Tsarskoye Selo, the situation was unclear even to them, and no directive to Admiral Kolchak was to follow.

Kolchak had to decide for himself whether or not to continue the news blockade. And what stance to take.

After that, new telegrams kept coming in, not from agencies but from Rodzyanko himself, saying that all government power had passed to the Duma Committee and the former Council of Ministers had been removed. That the Duma Committee was asking the army and navy to maintain total calm and nourish the full conviction that the war would not be allowed to let up for a minute, and every officer, soldier, and sailor must perform his duty. . . .

Yes, that would be good. In a way, self-appointed—and in a way wholly loyal. But was a shakeup like this feasible during time of war?

GHQ couldn't seem to get anything ordered, advised, or explained. And had received nothing from the Emperor.

In his cabin on the *Saint George*, a command battleship at mooring anchor whose military campaigns were behind it, Kolchak assembled his senior officers. He told them everything he knew. There had already been new wireless from Constantinople reporting the absurd idea that there had been mass beatings of officers in the Baltic Fleet and the Germans were advancing swiftly at the front. (But if it were true?) In the face of this nonsense it had become clear that you couldn't hide the news much longer. He decided to send an order through the fleet that laid out the Petrograd news—and immediately to call over the wireless for his entire fleet and all ports to carry out their patriotic duty with intensity. And to believe their officers, who would report all the accurate information received, and not to believe outside agitators, who wanted to sow chaos in order to keep Russia from victory.

This was what was frightening, that this was happening in none other than time of war.

What a shame to be at the height of one's powers, at the head of an entire fleet, an entire sea and its ports, and at the same to be left in ignorance and not know what to do.

The moment Kolchak's ban was lifted, the news of the Petrograd uprising gushed into Crimea.

Seemingly nothing bad happened there, though. Service continued as usual without any violations anywhere. Here, on the Black Sea, they had not been preparing for any kind of mutiny.

And yesterday, a telegram from Alekseev had finally reached Kolchak—and it was astonishing. It said that the situation permitted for no solution other than the Emperor's abdication, and *if* the admiral shared this view, would he be so kind as to telegraph his loyal request.

But Kolchak did not know the true situation. Why didn't it permit a different solution? Alekseev hadn't told him. What was the admiral to do if he did *not* share this view? Nothing had been said. No other view was even contemplated.

Alekseev may have been a very experienced general, but he was a dug-in bureaucrat, lacking fresh air or movement. He'd undermined the Bosphorus, and now he was dragging Kolchak toward the Emperor's abdication.

Yes, Russia did need to develop. And dark webs of favoritism should not have been woven around the regime; the views had to be clean. But Kolchak had never understood or shared Russian society's ire over the lost Japanese war—against the government and Emperor. We were all to blame, our admirals, our staffs and officers, for our ignorance, negligence, laziness, ostentation, and utter lack of technical organization. In no way does the state order prevent cannons from firing well. Politics could not affect the quality of naval education. There could be different forms of government—if only there were a stable Russia. But if we begin now, during time of war, by toppling the Emperor, then what abyss will this creep toward? It could mean sudden and disastrous collapse.

And what was this strange, sinister, absentee council of the commanders-in-chief, with no explanations provided?

Naturally, Kolchak was not going to respond in any way, thereby demonstrating his disdain for this form of behavior.

However, he did understand that during these hours something irrevocable was unfolding at GHQ, in Pskov, or in Petrograd. But Kolchak was unable to find out, and unable to intervene—and this was the most frustrating of all because only in actions did his nature, his swift, nervous intelligence, defuse. He loved practical work, he loved danger and war and couldn't stand party politics. The stench of which was now wafting over.

Short, lean, slender, and nimble, with deft and accurate movements and a sharp, precise profile to his shaved face, the Tatarish Kolchak paced nervously through the flagship, flew up to the bridge, cast a well-aimed eye over his ships, and squinted at the sunlit sea as if a decision might rise up from it like smoke.

He began to regret that his meeting in Batum with Nikolai Nikolaevich hadn't been scheduled for three days later. They might have discussed whether to join forces—although it's difficult to join forces with grand dukes, who keep themselves at a distance.

The entire South was in the hands of the two of them. Kolchak's navy and the grand duke's army group comprised a separate, declinate, stand-alone wing of the armed forces. No matter what happened 2000 versts away in Petrograd—here, by joining together, they might create a bulwark and opposition to any events.

Nikolai Nikolaevich was the best of the grand dukes, the only one qualified for the Supreme Command, and his authority was recognized throughout the army. But was he prepared to stand firm? For all the grand duke's provocatively martial exterior, his prodigiously tall warrior figure, for all his aristocratic appearance, his long, thoroughbred face, the handsome cut of his eyes, and the almost theatrical effect from his many tours in high command—Kolchak, unfortunately, did not sense in him the reliability of an irreproachable ally.

There was also the Romanian front, Sakharov. Should he attempt to reach an agreement with him?

The day to its end, and the evening to its end, stretched out without incident.

In the night, though, a telegram arrived from GHQ: the Emperor's abdication!

An abdication wrested from him—as yesterday's questioning would suggest.

And why not the legitimate heir?

Petrograd was in the hands of a band, that was clear.

Kolchak had everything thought out. Serving under him was a first lieutenant, the Emperor's aide-de-camp, the Duke of Leuchtenberg, Prince

Romanovsky—Nikolai Nikolaevich's stepson. Lots of titles, but a young man prepared to execute orders, and even the designer of an anti-ship bomb. Immediately, that night, Kolchak summoned him and ordered him to prepare the *Stringent* torpedo boat for a mission.

The roused young man appeared, alert, a fire in his eyes.

Kolchak gave him nothing on paper: steps of this kind were taken orally.

The lieutenant stood at attention. The admiral barely knew any other position for himself.

"You will go right now to see the grand duke, your stepfather, and convey to him the following from me. Memorize this! The Emperor has abdicated the throne."

The lieutenant staggered, as if from an electric shock.

"The abdication is coercive in nature. I propose that the grand duke declare himself military dictator of Russia, and I'm putting the Black Sea fleet at his disposal."

[3 5 6]

As in the best historical legends and fairytales, where princes of the blood wait years for their predicted accession, so, too, Grand Duke Nikolai Nikolaevich had awaited the restoration of his Supreme Commander regalia.

He and his spouse Stana of Montenegro, and her sister Militsa and her spouse—his brother Pyotr Nikolaevich—and other close, sympathetic individuals who had long been distressed by Nicky's manner of rule, his whole chain of stupidities, mistakes, and foolish appointments, the omnipotent hand of his hysterical spouse, the undignified perversions in the state's rule, and the foul villain Rasputin, and the financial operators profiting around him. One thing had been chivalrously pure and lofty in all his rule—the Supreme Command led by Nikolai Nikolaevich. Encouraged by his envious wife and deceived by a naïve notion of his own military abilities, though, Nicky had made the fateful and unfortunate decision to take on the Supreme Command himself and send Nikolai Nikolaevich to a notorious place of honorable exile as Viceroy of the Caucasus. Such was the ill-concealed intrigue by sinister forces.

Nonetheless, Nikolai Nikolaevich overcame the insult and despondency, did not lower his tall head, but carried over even here as a symbol and a beloved leader, now of only one army rather than twelve, with its commander, Yudenich. Yudenich essentially stayed with the army, on its marches, and on its sally deep into Turkey and Mesopotamia, while Nikolai Nikolaevich spent his time in the Viceroy's palace in Tiflis, in the middle of the Caucasus, adored by the entire population of the region he ruled. Thus, although in reduced proportions, he remained himself.

From here, from exile, he watched painfully all the new mistakes of imperial rule and the disenchantment and despair of society, the splash of whose continued love, on the contrary, he sensed all the way here across the Range. And he said nothing. And only last November, on his sole visit to GHQ and at his sole meeting with Nicky after his removal, did he express himself frankly to his autocratic cousin about his perfidy, about his willingness to trust the suspicions and gossip which said that his uncle supposedly wanted to occupy the throne, and about the dark abyss of the decline of state authority. And Nicky? As usual, he took it all with indifference.

But just before the New Year, when Tiflis's mayor, Khatisov, returned from Petersburg and in a private audience secretly conveyed to the grand duke a secret invitation from Prince Lvov—to lend his name to a possible palace coup—Nikolai Nikolaevich became unprecedentedly agitated, shaken that matters had gone so perilously far. He took some time to think. These were days of intense and tortuous thought. He realized he could save the country. He knew how much more valuable, needed, and suitable he was for Russia than his first cousin once removed. But a grand duke or monarch's path must be chivalrously straight and cannot include a link of treason. At his next meeting with Khatisov, having called in General Yanushkevich, his chief of staff, for added measure, the grand duke firmly refused.

He refused—but a week later realized that he was now mixed up in this plot anyway, inasmuch as he had not brought it to the Emperor immediately! This awareness of complicity dug at him like a splinter—the unease, the constraint, the embarrassment—but each passing day or week shut off more and more tightly the possibility of clearing himself. In this way the grand duke—after refusing and maintaining his honor—became a threatened conspirator!

But that same honor would not allow him to break the ring and betray people well-disposed toward him, the same Prince Lvov. Ever since, though, he had done everything he could to avoid Khatisov.

Suddenly, at a meeting in Batum, Kolchak showed the grand duke a telegram about the upheavals in Petrograd and even saying that the capital was in the rebels' hands. The grand duke rushed to Tiflis. Right then, a certain trusted individual secretly told another that a certain Georgian newspaper had received a prearranged telegram from Petrograd implying the start of major events! By 15 March, agency reports had begun emphasizing the stunning revolutionary events. Naturally, the grand duke would not allow them to be published, but he proposed assembling the nobility of Tiflis and Kutais provinces so that he could apprise them. He himself was tremulously beginning to sense that his time had come. Those forces which had risen up in Petrograd were his sympathizers and allies.

The pressure of the news on the dam of military censorship mounted by the hour. So far, nothing had been printed openly, but everyone in essence already knew. Especially worried were the newspaper publishers and editors. On 15 March, Nikolai Nikolaevich deemed it appropriate to invite them to one of the spacious halls in the viceroy's palace, come out to see them under arms, and declare that he had always lent the press great importance and hoped that by its righteous word the press would promote calm. The viceroy believed that present events would end to the good of our Fatherland. Any hour now, instructions would arrive from GHQ on what to do about publication.

Indeed, that afternoon such permission from GHQ did arrive—but even before noon an invitation was received from Alekseev that froze the grand duke, sent him into a joyous fever. It said that the *dynastic question had been posed point blank*—so believed both the State Duma President and GHQ—and the situation evidently permitted no solution other than abdication in favor of the son. For the sake of Russia's salvation, Alekseev asked him to telegraph His Majesty in Pskov post-haste.

In the immediacy of this point-blank range, Nikolai Nikolaevich felt that he was being elevated to his own great, perhaps greatest moment. Who else of the Commanders-in-Chief was as authoritative and as lofty of status— and the sole august one!—to give the errant Nicky decisive and energetic counsel? Nicky did love Russia, after all! So, joining with him in their love for Russia, should he advise? Ask? No, *plead* for abdication!

The fruit was overripe. It could not hang on. Nicky had made too many mistakes, and *she* had made the most mistakes of all.

(Simultaneously: he was a grand duke—and not a speck of any conspirator! He was loyal but sensible.)

Irrevocably, this would restore the Supreme Command to Nikolai Nikolaevich! No one else could be appointed.

Nikolai Nikolaevich did not delay with his answer, although GHQ sought it more and more nervously and faster—he selected only the loftiest and holiest expressions in order deliberately to shake Nicky's soul. Dear, loyal Yanushkevich was right nearby, at the telegraph, and he helped.

During those very same hours, though, the agitated and grateful grand duke could not deny himself the joy of issuing from his Tiflis solitude a volley, from an ally to those friendly forces in the capital. Right there, at the next table, with Stana's participation, a telegram was being composed with a joyfully leaping pencil, a telegram his service did not require but the leanings of his heart did, a telegram to Rodzyanko confirming that, yes, the Viceroy had already sent a loyal plea to the Tsar: "for the sake of Russia's salvation"—to express himself more wisely in an open telegram, he couldn't write "abdication" when there had been none—but "to take the decision that you"—that is, Mikhail Vladimirovich Rodzyanko—"have recognized as the sole solution given the fateful conditions that have come about."

And all of a sudden, unusually quickly, a telegram arrived from the Duma president! Unfortunately, though, it was by way of reproach, not reply. Evidently, someone in Tiflis had complained about the interception of communiqués, and the Duma president had majestically confirmed that power had definitively passed into the hands of the Provisional Committee of the

State Duma and the president hoped that His Imperial Highness would lend his full assistance—and immediately ease censorship conditions.

An agonizing conflict between duty and conscience might have arisen, but fortunately GHQ had already given its permission.

On the other hand, GHQ had been totally quiet about the abdication's progress. Hour after hour, at first ecstatically, then worriedly, wound up and tense, Nikolai Nikolaevich, surrounded by his closest circle, was waiting for a decision there, in Pskov, for the liberating reply to arrive. Sometimes, losing patience altogether, he would order Yanukevich to send an inquiry to Alekseev, to find out.

GHQ promised. And again there was a delay. And again they inquired on behalf of the most august Commander-in-Chief. Just before midnight, GHQ promised once again.

Something was amiss in Pskov. Some inauspicious twist.

Gloom set in. They spent all evening in a state of tension. Between one and two in the morning, Stana went to bed. So did Yanushkevich. It seemed everything had been put off to tomorrow.

But Nikolai Nikolaevich had the feeling that—no, that wasn't true, it wasn't! And he sat in his uniform in his office with no thought of sleep.

At three in the morning, the duty officer ran in from the telegraph room—and handed the vigilant Viceroy a *most faithful* telegram from General Alekseev that contained a mountain of news.

By order of His Majesty, His Imperial Highness had been appointed Supreme Commander!

It had come to pass! The long-awaited hour, in reward for his loyalty and service.

And Prince Lvov was the head of government. Good.

And the Emperor had deigned to sign the act of abdication!—but passing the throne to Grand Duke Mikhail Aleksandrovich.

A joke. A bad joke.

Who on earth was Mikhail? Worthless and incapable. While here, in Caucasus exile, towered the most prominent and glorious of Nikolai I's grandsons.

Tar added to the honey. They had spoiled everything. . . .

This time, though, no one had asked his opinion. . . . Alekseev merely asked respectfully when he could expect His Imperial Highness's arrival at GHQ. Would His Imperial Highness see fit to grant Alekseev temporarily the rights of Supreme Commander? And would the Caucasus army group be handed over to someone or would Yudenich alone remain?

Having lost all desire to sleep, without waking or summoning anyone, pacing his formal palace study, wrestling contradictory emotions, Nikolai Nikolaevich overcame the cruel wound of the latest news and returned to his duty and dignity as Supreme Commander. (Although he could not imagine how he could serve under Misha.)

He replied to Alekseev: Until my arrival, take charge of military operations and staff and administrative orders.

. . . In extraordinary circumstances, I command you to address me immediately for commands. . . . I should like to remain Viceroy of the Caucasus as well. This is absolutely essential. . . .

But that wasn't all. It was clear that upon his assumption of powers, the new Supreme Commander would be required to issue an encouraging decree, an order to his troops.

Order No. 1.

This had to be the authoritative, mighty voice of a divinely chosen warrior responsive to the Russian heart and alien to any revolutionary raving.

Write it immediately, in the spaciousness of the night!

. . . By the Lord's inscrutable ways, I have been appointed Supreme Commander. I cross myself and fervently pray to God. . . . Only with God's omnipotent assistance will I gain the strength and reason to lead us to a final victory. . . . Wondrous heroes, most valiant knights of the Russian land! I know how much you are prepared to sacrifice for the good of Russia and the throne. . . .

*　　*　　*

Mad tyrants have trampled Russia's honor and dignity. . . . Savage defenders of the autocratic yoke. . . . Cruel, greedy half-men. . . .

RSDRP [Russian Social Democratic Workers Party]

*　　*　　*

[3 5 7]

Late the previous evening, the new government had ascertained that Guchkov had reached the Tsar in Pskov. So! Caught! Now they could expect the abdication at any moment.

That is, once again it made sense to wait in the Tauride Palace rather than disperse to their homes to sleep—for the fourth night now? And why did all the main events happen overnight? Their strength was failing them, but it was worth the wait. The few principals—Milyukov, Kerensky, Nekrasov, and somber Lvov—stayed to doze in armchairs and wait.

And Rodzyanko. In anticipation of the abdication, he now coveted it practically more than anyone.

They were all waiting for this final legitimization of the new government. Once this final legitimacy was achieved, their authority would be definitively established.

Actually, Milyukov wasn't dozing, he wasn't wasting the hours of this latest nighttime wait. He was sitting at his desk and to the general conversation patiently composing an address to "Everyone, everyone, everyone," all people and all countries, an address that should now be sent over the wireless in order to explain the situation in Russia. Who would see to this if not the Minister of Foreign Affairs? Not only would this be the first act of the as yet inactive government, but the form in which the world learned of our revolution depended wholly on this telegram. Stable sympathies for the new government and every material assistance—Milyukov had a good sense of Western society—depended on this.

They waited. The Tauride Palace had no direct connection to Pskov, but the General Staff did with Northern Army Group headquarters, as did the Ministry of Roads and Railways along its own lines. Bublikov was constantly calling Rodzyanko and trying to offer help and advice. He was the first to tell him about the end of the negotiations in Pskov and first to make the complaint that Pskov was requesting permission for the royal letter trains to proceed to GHQ. Was it really all right to let them go?

But those in government felt that this was actually more convenient. Here, right outside Petrograd, the former Tsar was rather an impediment. And simple decency demanded that they not refuse a personal request when the Tsar had abdicated the crown.

After two in the morning, communication arrived from Guchkov, albeit short, saying that the Emperor had abdicated, but in favor of Mikhail Aleksandrovich. The text of the Manifesto itself was being encoded in Pskov and would follow.

So much was this *almost* the same thing that at the very first they didn't grasp the point: in favor of Mikhail Aleksandrovich? How was that? Not as regent, but the throne itself to Mikhail?

As soon as they did understand, they were thrown into turmoil. They were flabbergasted! How could Guchkov? After all, they had an agreement! It was one thing to give the throne to a minor, Aleksei, that is, to go without a Tsar altogether in a way, and to saddle Mikhail with a regency council— because only in this way could constitutional rule be consolidated here irrevocably. But Mikhail as omnipotent Tsar? That was all wrong. It was unacceptable! Utterly unacceptable! Yes, he was army brass, and yes, so so foolish—but once he latched onto power, wouldn't he begin pressing? He was no minor, after all!

An abdication like *this* could blow up the entire government. And where, if you please, was Prince Georgi Lvov, the principal? Only now did they realize he was gone. They sent people out to search the rooms.

What would the Soviet of Workers' Deputies say? They had replaced one Tsar with another. Where was the tread of Revolution? How could this be justified to the masses?

Especially since the Soviet didn't want any kind of monarchy at all.

Kerensky (feeling himself more and more like the embodiment of the Soviet inside the government) leapt up—and declared categorically and even boldly that he was ready to fight them all:

"In no event will the Soviet of Workers' Deputies allow this!"

There! The government could not enter straightaway into conflict with the Soviet.

This turn with the abdication threatened to sweep them all away.

But Milyukov was especially discouraged. Unlike his colleagues, he found grounds here not for rage but for great concern. The past few hours he had been bashed for the monarchical principle itself. They'd compelled him to renounce it, to concede that it was just a matter of his "personal convictions." But didn't *this kind* of handover of the throne make the picture significantly worse? Didn't it look more like a concession to imperial authority? Given this maneuver, it would be even harder to defend a constitutional monarchy.

Hadn't they and the Soviets inserted a point about a Constituent Assembly? And how could he now press for the monarchy?

The fate of a major political figure. As on 30 October 1905, when everyone had exulted at the Manifesto, Milyukov had had the courage to reject it irreconcilably, so too now he had to have the courage to support the monarchy in its wreckage against the general flow.

But Prince Lvov was nowhere to be found in the palace. That meant he'd left to get some sleep. Summon him immediately! They called his apartment and woke up everyone there: No, he hadn't come to spend the night. Then where was he?

They had an idea. Might he have hidden at his friend Shchepkin's? They called there—and found him. Immediately! Immediately to the Tauride Palace! What a sly boots! He'd wanted a nap!

Meanwhile, after three in the morning now, from the General Staff, where they were decoding the Manifesto, they were able to extract the motivation clause over the telephone: "Not wishing to be separated from Our beloved son, We bequeath Our heritage to Our brother."

A fine kettle of fish! Milyukov had always had limitless contempt for this Tsar, but right now he felt bitterly offended. Even in departing, with his final action, he had spoiled the public cabinet! He was unwilling to risk his son! As usual, he was putting his family above all else! He was unwilling to risk his son! What had he been thinking before? Why had he kept him his heir? He preferred risking his unprepared brother. And the new government. And in the end, Russia itself!

And now Milyukov was going to be reproached most of all. . . .

Although the answer was clear to everyone—"no! no! no!"—but before formulating any decision, they had to put a stop to the Manifesto with utmost speed, that's what! So it couldn't leak! Of course, someone would start transmitting it from Pskov or GHQ now, without asking the government. They had to gain time to think this through! It had to be stopped in both places!

They'd been in a hurry and driven the abdication forward, but now— they were to stop it!

What would that take? An urgent telegram? No, a conversation with Pskov and GHQ.

Milyukov: moreover, clarify the possibility of changing the Manifesto back in favor of Aleksei!

Who was most impressive, and proper, and convincing to do all this if not Rodzyanko?

Here they had removed him entirely, but a new moment of decision had come, and once again only he would do!

And he, magnanimous, was prepared! He forgave them for pushing him out!

He was prepared right now.

Right now! Immediately!

It would be improper to send him and not send anyone from the government—but here came Prince Lvov. Here he was at last!

He squinted blandly. He displayed no embarrassment for hiding.

Go to change the Manifesto? Yes, he could.

Those who stayed were now drawn deeper and deeper into sharper and sharper arguments.

The neat, narrow-headed Kerensky dashed around the small room (but did not run off to his people in the Soviet!) and belched more and more flames to the effect that the sound decision dictated itself: total rejection of a monarchy of any kind! Mikhail's immediate abdication as well! Don't stop the Manifesto. No! Instead, quickly wrest an abdication from Mikhail as well—and immediately proclaim a Constituent Assembly!

Even Nekrasov became unprecedentedly agitated, came forward, cast gloomy glances around—and sat down to sketch out a draft of Mikhail's abdication.

Which meant the immediate proclamation of a republic!

While somber Lvov paced on the diagonal and quietly seethed with clenched fists.

Had it turned out that Milyukov alone remained in *favor* of a monarchy?

But the more radically his companions cast about, the soberer Milyukov became and the more firmly planted. The awkwardness of yesterday's concession already weighed on him. Why had he recognized the monarchy with his own personal opinion when it was there in the program of the Kadet party? It was wrong to retreat so quickly. That can unsettle the ranks.

And now Milyukov was insisting more and more: Oh no! The monarchy must be! If only for a while. There must be visibility for the legitimate handover of authority, without which we cannot proceed to act. Mikhail? Mikhail. So be it. For now.

A republic? No, we're not ready. We cannot take that leap.

They talked more and more nervously. They argued.

While the night passed. . . .

And Rodzyanko and Lvov had not returned.

After four o'clock, the necessary action became clear to them. It was inevitable now that they all go see Mikhail that morning. And tell him—what should they tell him?

The majority opinion!

No, both contending points of view! If Pavel Nikolaevich was not given the chance to present his point of view to the grand duke, he would quit the government altogether!

And Milyukov knew how to argue—not in front of a crowd of common soldiers, of course—with exquisite doggedness. Now he might not sleep or eat, he might argue them flat—but he would prove that only a monarchy was acceptable and not a republic.

They decided to go see Mikhail collectively and present both points of view.

Milyukov became angry in debate, picked up steam, and insisted even more that no matter what decision was made, the *other side* had to quit the government!

That is, he proposed, under a republic he would leave the government this very day, the government he had announced yesterday with such pride and love.

But under a monarchy—he would remain the sole minister for now? . . . (He was confident of quickly finding others.)

Such was the intensity reached.

Kerensky and Nekrasov exchanged winks, confident of victory.

Here is what Kerensky came up with: It was already after five, there was no point in Mikhail sleeping too long, and what if he went somewhere? We must call him right now and appoint our arrival! (Rodzyanko had already told them where Mikhail was hiding, in whose apartment.)

But set a time so that we can get some sleep.

Naturally. And also wait for Guchkov.

Kerensky rushed to phone. It had to be him, only him!

"Aleksan Fyodych! Just don't explain to him what this is about. Don't prepare him!"

It took some time to wake the grand duke and for him to come to the telephone. When he heard his utterly vapid, sleepy voice, Kerensky, anything but tired, but gaily, lively, asked, to make sure:

"Your Imperial Majesty? Do you know what happened yesterday evening in Pskov? No? Well, we will come see you and tell you, if you will allow us."

But he did not set a time.

[3 5 8]

A mistake was made at the General Staff, and the duty officer failed to warn the porter to open up. They had to drum on whatever first-floor windows they could. They woke up the yardman, who woke up the porter, who opened up.

Then they went upstairs and passed down the long corridors toward the direct line. For the third night in a row.

Then something went wrong with the connection to Pskov, then headquarters didn't answer, and Rodzyanko shouted, "Tell them it is the President of the State Duma calling! I will put them all under arrest!"

All this time, Prince Lvov was mostly silent, and Rodzyanko went off into the boil of his own thoughts; he had no great desire for conversation. He was the principal figure, it was up to him to talk and decide, and what was Lvov anyway?

After these terrible days and the entire puzzling complication, after two attacks and threats to kill him, naturally him first—his heart now wanted calm and his head clarity. One cannot live under constant threat of death, nor can one live in this kind of muddle. But now the Soviet was not going to recognize Mikhail as Tsar—and what would that spark? Civil war!

Rodzyanko was increasingly sure that the situation could be saved only by Mikhail's abdication, unfortunately.

And then, it followed, by a Constituent Assembly.

Until the Constituent Assembly, Rodzyanko would remain at Russia's head. That was just how it was. Or else his Committee would become a kind of regency council.

And the Constituent Assembly? Here was the hitch. It was quite possible, more than likely, that our Orthodox people would not want to live under any republic. And that meant there would have to be the selection of a new Tsar and a new dynasty—by the Constituent Assembly or nation-wide.

And whose first candidacy would come to everyone's mind? Yes! Of course. The actual present head of state, the universally admired President of the universally admired State Duma.

He imagined this breathlessly. Be the one to start a third Russian dynasty? Indeed, Russia had no political figure more suited for this, more prominent, more powerful.

What should be done if circumstances fell out this way against Nikolai II? And against Mikhail?

Rodzyanko began with Pskov—out of habit now, as he had the previous night. Everything had worked out so well with Ruzsky yesterday. Calculating that the Manifesto might not yet have leaked to GHQ.

On the other end, chief of staff Danilov had picked up. Rodzyanko demanded Ruzsky himself.

Finally, not right away: Ruzsky. By now it was shortly before six o'clock. Now Rodzyanko spoke (standing), the telegraph operator printed, and the tape went out:

"Greetings, your excellency. It is extremely important that the Manifesto on abdication and the handover of authority to Grand Duke Mikhail Aleksandrovich not be published until I inform you to do so, the issue being that we have managed to hold the revolutionary movement within more or less decent bounds only with great difficulty. The situation has still not righted itself, however, and civil war is quite possible! They may have reconciled themselves to the heir's accession and the grand duke's regency, but his accession as emperor is absolutely unacceptable! I beg you to take all measures in your power to bring about a delay."

He said everything most important. The telegraph operator understood that now the other high-ranking visitor would speak, and he tapped out:

"Rodzyanko has stepped away. Standing by the telegraph is Prince Lvov."

But first of all, Rodzyanko had not stepped away. Secondly, Lvov, although you could see the effort on his face, said nothing for he didn't know what else to say.

A pause ensued. In this time, a tape came in from Ruzsky:

"Fine, the instruction will be carried out. But how much the dissemination can be halted, I would not undertake to say in view of the fact that so much time has passed. I deeply regret"—one could picture his forever dissatisfied face frowning—"that the deputies sent here yesterday were not sufficiently settled in this role and in general what they had come for. At the present moment I beg you to illuminate for me now with full clarity the entire matter—what has happened and the possible consequences."

What had happened—Ruzsky would not understand that anyway since he hadn't witnessed the local bedlam. And the *possible consequences*, that time was needed for Mikhail's abdication—this, Rodzyanko sensed, was not to be told to the army groups.

Drawing Lvov aside, Rodzyanko once again took over the telegraph:

"Again, the matter is such that the deputies cannot be blamed. A soldier mutiny flared up that none of us expected and the likes of which I have never seen. Of course, they are not soldiers but ordinary men taken from their plows who have now found it effective to present all their common demands. All we heard in the crowd was Land and freedom! Down with the dynasty! Down with the Romanovs! Down with officers!"

His head was ringing like an agitated bell, and mixed up in this din was what he had heard in the Ekaterininsky Hall, and the party slogans hung up there, you didn't dare remove them, and relentlessly before his eyes the Emperor's bayonet-ridden portrait in the Duma hall—and what he'd heard by way of complaints from the private individuals who came running, and the opinions of members of government, and flickerings before his eyes were all the approaching soldier formations and the innumerable red flags and the endless blowing of the bands.

". . . Officer beatings began in many units. Workers joined in, and anarchy reached its apogee"—he did not shy from prevaricating for the sake of argument. "After long talks with the workers' deputies, only by nighttime today were we able to reach any agreement—for a Constituent Assembly to be convened soon, for the people to be able to express their view on their form of government—and only then did Petrograd breathe freely and the night pass relatively calmly. Little by little, over the course of the night, the troops are being put in order."

The night seemed to be ending, and without any massacres. But what was to come was terrible to contemplate:

"A proclamation of Grand Duke Mikhail Aleksandrovich as Emperor would be pouring fuel on the fire—and lead to the merciless annihilation of everything that can be annihilated. We would lose and give up our hold on any authority, and there would be no one to appease the people's unrest. It is advisable that basically until war's end the Supreme Council should continue to function—along with the Provisional Government now functioning with us. I am fully confident that, on these terms, speedy pacification is possible, there will certainly be a surge in patriotic feeling, everything will begin working at an increased rate, and a decisive victory will be assured."

After a delay at the other end, the following dribbled in:

"All instructions given. But it is extremely difficult to promise that we will be able to prevent dissemination. The intention was specifically for this measure to give the army a chance to shift to a state of calm. The imperial train has left for GHQ, and the center of further talks has to be shifted there. I ask you to install Hughes wires wherever the new government convenes—and inform me of the course of affairs twice a day."

Well, this was good. But Rodzyanko looked even further ahead:

"A Hughes wire will be installed. But I ask that, should the news of the Manifesto break through to the public and army, you at least not rush to administer the oath to the troops!"

Ruzsky, however, turned out to be even more prudent:

"I gave an instruction yesterday, in Pskov, to refrain from administering the oath."

This was wonderful! Without Petrograd he had figured out that they needed to wait?

". . . I will immediately inform the armies of my front of this, as well as GHQ. I think Prince Lvov was by the telegraph? Does he wish to speak with me?"

What was Lvov going to say! Rodzyanko held onto his place, lightly dismissing him. The State Duma Committee was above the government.

"No, everything has been said! Prince Lvov has nothing to add. We are both firmly relying on Divine assistance, on Russia's majesty and might, on the army's valor and steadfastness, and any obstacles notwithstanding, on the war's victorious conclusion!"

Rodzyanko had noted many times—both in Duma speeches and in conversations—that a stream of vigorous words makes you yourself more vigorous. Brisker. We have successfully delayed things, at least along the Northern Front!

As he was about to order a line to GHQ, the telegraph started tapping again:

"Mikhail Vladimirovich! Just to be sure I understood you correctly. This means for now everything remains as of old, as if there had been no Manifesto. Does the same go for the order to Prince Lvov to form a ministry? As for the appointment of Grand Duke Nikolai Nikolaevich by separate decree of the Emperor, I would also like to know your opinion of this. These decrees were reported tonight quite widely—all the way to Moscow and, of course, the Caucasus."

Ruzsky was quick on the uptake, perhaps too quick. Even Rodzyanko wasn't prepared for a countermand *like that*, especially with Lvov sitting right beside him. And Nikolai Nikolaevich wasn't in anyone's way.

"Today we've formed a government with Prince Lvov at its head. All will remain as before: the Supreme Council, a responsible ministry, and the legislative chambers—until the Constituent Assembly. We have no objection to the decree appointing Nikolai Nikolaevich Supreme Commander. Goodbye."

But Ruzsky latched on again:

"Tell me, who is at the head of the Supreme Council?"

His own words came back on the tape—and the enchantment wore off:

"I misspoke. Not the Supreme Council, but the Provisional Committee of the State Duma, under my chairmanship."

But it would remain Supreme. What could be higher?

And he began to wait for a line to GHQ.

There was not the same favorable disposition to speak frankly with Alekseev. An aftertaste remained from his mistrust of the night before last.

Meanwhile, a telegram from Evert was delivered to Rodzyanko from another telegraph.

It announced the Manifesto to the Western Army Group in his charge—and raised a prayer to the Almighty for the health of Tsar Mikhail Aleksandrovich . . . greeting in your person the State Duma and the new state order . . . in the firm hope that with God's help . . .

Ugh. Teach a fool to pray to God and he'll crack his brow. What was all the rush? . . .

[3 5 9]

Since the advice he gave the Emperor yesterday to abdicate the throne, General Evert had been beside himself. His big head had fallen into unfamiliar work, and he himself into an unprecedented, anything but military, mess. In all his sixty years of life and forty years of service, nothing of the kind had battered his big bones like this before.

How dare he express such advice to the Emperor? Where did he get the nerve? He barely recognized himself and was horrified: a brief moment, rushed, in haste. After all, all the commanders-in-chief had expressed this unanimously!

He had relied on common sense. GHQ's arguments seemed to have weight.

But he should have held back, bided his time, asked the army commanders, shared at least some of this intolerable burden of deciding the fate of the Russian crown! After all, this was not just an episode or a tactic for a few months on the best way to win the war. Now, after the fact, Evert understood that in two dynasties and six hundred years no one in the ancient Russian land had ever abdicated the crown—and this step now could have centuries-long consequences as well.

Evert began rereading his own advice-reply through the Emperor's eyes—and now could not read it otherwise than as a betrayal of his oath. Were the Emperor to reject such advice and tomorrow return to GHQ, he would have every right to dismiss Adjutant General Evert from all posts and strip him of all titles!

But his advice had already flowed irrevocably down the lines, and since that moment GHQ had demanded and asked nothing more. Somewhere, in secret and silence, a deed was being done. Abdication? Not abdication? . . .

Evert shut himself up in his bedroom and stretched until his spine cracked. He wanted somehow to straighten out his large body, for some step—but he couldn't think of one and no one had proposed anything. He couldn't reach out to the Emperor in Pskov and express his own obedience.

Nothing had come in from Pskov, but a bandit "deputation" of disorderly soldiers was storming around Polotsk and had disarmed the railroad guard. Such was the political nature of the moment, though, that they couldn't be arrested as ordinary bandits—GHQ had to be asked for permission. The Western Army Group had mobile reserves guarding the roads, but GHQ had forbidden sending them in, keeping them at the ready in case of need.

Evert agonized and agonized in his solitude, as if in captivity, until sometime after one o'clock Kvetsinsky brought him the first news of the abdication.

Whether this was good or bad—a block had fallen away!

And then the Manifesto itself. He read it from the tape—and what devastating words! A large tear fell on the tape's backing.

And although from the service standpoint this was a relief—after falling in step with all the commanders, he now remained in his post—nonetheless a stone lay on his heart, that he himself, with his own utterly loyal hands, had pushed the Emperor off the throne.

At three o'clock, GHQ ordered the Manifesto sent out to armies and units without delay.

That was it then. It had come to pass.

It had come to pass. He made his peace. And went to bed.

But sleep eluded him. Remorse had receded, but worries had drawn nigh. Somehow he had to find a place for himself under the new government. Anyone who knew Mikhail Aleksandrovich understood that he would be a very weak Emperor. The new government would exercise all power and leadership. Of all the commanders, Evert was obviously going to be unpopular with the new government because he was a "reactionary." Whereas society was just fine with Brusilov, Ruzsky, and Alekseev. But Evert was a *reactionary*. That's how those mangy newspapermen stuck a nickname on you—so that you'd never wash it away until the day you died. As if in soot: "reactionary."

No, his head was not inclined to sleep. His head lifted—somehow he had to show himself in a positive light and at that small price preserve the post he'd held so dear. Compose and send some kind of appeasing telegram? To Rodzyanko, obviously. Rodzyanko *was* raging Petrograd; the army groups and country respected no other name.

He turned on the light and sat there trying to compose something, but his pen couldn't do anything. And he himself had to compose this. Well, first that he had announced the Manifesto. And then, about raising prayers for the new Emperor. And now, along with all the troops entrusted to me, greeting your State Duma . . . no, in your person . . . And the new state order . . . And in hope that the homeland would find new strength in the people's unity, for victory, glory, and prosperity. . . .

He wrote in his large stick letters, a few sentences on three full pages. . . .

He was embarrassed to consult with Kvetsinsky, so he wrote it himself. He was also embarrassed to send this through Alekseev, but there was no other direct line. He himself took it to the telegraph room. Let it skip through in the night, while everyone was asleep.

It was nearly six o'clock. The night had ended before it had ever begun.

Nonetheless, he lay down. But the moment he drifted off, Kvetsinsky knocked: orders from GHQ. Immediately delay the announcement of the transmitted Manifesto!

What was this? Evert leapt to his full enormous height. So the abdication had not happened?

Oh no! What a disgrace! And what had he sent to Rodzyanko? What a disgrace!

Couldn't he get it back? If they'd halted the entire Manifesto, couldn't they retrieve one little telegram? . . .

[3 6 0]

That night General Alekseev again did not sleep long. At six in the morning, the duty officer was already tapping him on the shoulder: Rodzyanko was summoning him urgently to the telegraph.

His malaise had not yet passed, his back was killing him, and he was annoyed at this Rodzyanko. For two days he hadn't been able to get through, and now here he was in the night. Not only without washing up, but without properly waking up, still groggy and weak from his brief interrupted sleep, Alekseev began reading the tape with sticking eyes.

"Events are far from settled, the entire situation is alarming and unclear."

What was this? Hadn't complete calm ensued? Alekseev treated this Rodzyanko like a bad scout. But there weren't any other scouts. He was blindfolded.

"I emphatically beg you not to circulate any Manifesto until receipt from me of considerations that alone can immediately halt revolution."

That shook him from his drowsiness! But also out of any wish to talk. What a mad, fussy, and conceited man! First he alone knew: give us a responsible ministry and everything will calm down. They gave it. Then: too late! But now, again, he and he alone knew for certain: give us abdication and everything will calm down. They had done the impossible, they had crossed a mountain, they had achieved the abdication! And again, too little, too late! But once again, he alone knew the considerations that alone would halt revolution.

Which meant what now? Having compelled abdication from the Emperor, hold onto the Manifesto? But why? Who had that right?

Alekseev replied that the Manifesto had already been communicated to the commanders and districts because the total lack of information had raised questions regarding what line to toe. The army required clarity. If all this fails to correspond to your views, please clarify.

Conceal the Manifesto! Concealing the Manifesto now would make the shock even worse! An inquiry about a new oath had already been sent to Prime Minister Lvov, but who the devil could tell which of them there was senior, Lvov or Rodzyanko?

Rodzyanko replied that promulgating the Manifesto might start a *civil war*! Because Mikhail's candidacy as emperor was acceptable to no one!

So that's how it was! Wasn't it one day ago that this Samovar had threatened civil war if Mikhail did *not* become regent? General Alekseev was accustomed to thinking the military way, and he had no good grasp of these political whirlwinds, and on top of that he had a sick and unslept head. He was beginning to get angry.

Fine, he would issue delaying telegrams. But he was worried the Manifesto would become known in the armies anyway.

"I would prefer receiving guidance from you beforehand, in order to know what line to toe."

Rodzyanko replied at length and very chaotically, saying that some sort of truce had been established with someone. And a Constituent Assembly was to be convened. More news! Until that time, acting in addition to the Council of Ministers was some Supreme Committee—and besides that the two legislative chambers as well. *This* was why he was asking the Manifesto not be made public. (What was the connection here? . . .) The combination of the heir Aleksei and the regent Mikhail had already brought significant calm.

And so? Alekseev managed just to think and not to ask. Did they want to go back to that combination? Redo the Manifesto? Persuade the Emperor? Apparently so. The Rodzyanko tape did not break off.

". . . Nothing can quench the resentment and indignation against the existing regime. The Constituent Assembly's decision does not preclude the possibility of the dynasty's return to power. On the contrary, the combination expressed could guarantee a tremendous surge in patriotic feeling, an unprecedented surge. . . ."

Alekseev understood less and less. What "combination expressed"? The Aleksei-Mikhail combination or the Supreme Committee-cabinet-Duma-State Council combination? And what about the Duma's Provisional Committee now?

". . . a surge in energy, perfect calm in the country, and a brilliant victory over the enemy. The troops, consisting of peasants, have calmed down only at this combination and have decided to return to their officers and to submit to the demands of discipline and the Provisional Government. *Only today*, upon hearing this decision, did Petrograd begin to calm down somewhat."

If all these sentences were connected by anything, then it was the continuousness of the long and narrow tape. And only that. It had become harder and harder to understand. When did Petrograd begin to calm down—the day before yesterday or just today? Had Petrograd begun to calm down, or did the situation threaten civil war? How did which peasant forces learn about the abdication in favor of Mikhail if it hadn't yet been announced anywhere? And why and by whom had a Constituent Assembly been assembled that could return the dynasty to power, when the dynasty had no intention of going away anyway? And what kind of implied but concealed truce was it, in what other unknown talks, with someone? With whom? Extreme leftist parties, evidently. Who else?

Cursed be the day and hour, yesterday and the day before, when Alekseev got mixed up in these politics. Politics rose up like a blur, a burn.

But how could he not have? He stuck out where he was like a block of wood.

Abandoned by the Tsar.

In any event, at least now he had to put an end to this game with these politicians—and express the army's firm point of view.

Fine, I will take measures to delay the Manifesto with the commanders and in the districts. However, everything you have told me is far from gladdening. The concealment of what is going on and the Constituent Assembly are two dangerous toys when applied to the field army. The Petrograd garrison, having tasted the fruit of treason, will easily repeat it. That garrison is now detrimental to the homeland, useless to the army, and dangerous to the new regime. I wish to receive from you as soon as possible something final and definite—so that the army can turn solely to the war and turn away from the painful internal state of a part of Russia.

"I am a soldier, and my intentions turn in the enemy's direction."

There was the feeling of wanting to step away from this filth and be cleansed of it.

But Rodzyanko went on babbling for some reason, saying that the country was not to blame, that it had been wracked by disruptions and the people's self-esteem had suffered repeated insult. It would be at least six months until the Constituent Assembly, and by that time the war could be brought to a victorious conclusion.

Alekseev started to speak and forgot to ask about that band in Polotsk. And who was sending these bands? GHQ had done everything Petrograd demanded. Why weren't they stopping the banditry?

Alekseev had given the order to halt the abdication Manifesto back during the negotiations, and by their end, the officers in three army groups had already given orders. Now he had signed a general telegram to all commanders-in-chief—and one separately to the new Supreme Commander in the Caucasus.

By seven in the morning, all this had been dealt with.

And somehow they had missed their chance to go to bed.

Meanwhile, life plodded along, and they kept bringing him telegrams from other telegraphs. Here was a predawn telegram from Evert to Rodzyanko. And look! This one already announced it! . . . Alekseev had not anticipated such delight from Evert or such unnecessary obsequiousness toward the new regime.

Here was an early morning telegram from the grand duke in the Caucasus that had crossed his en route. So. The new Supreme Commander had temporarily entrusted Alekseev with military operations and staff and administrative orders—but nothing more. Under all extraordinary circumstances, he commanded Alekseev to address him, the grand duke, immediately.

So. Alekseev's freedom was immediately restricted. But that was even better. That meant he really did not have to talk to Rodzyanko. Let him deal with the grand duke. But after all, the extraordinary quality of these extraordinary circumstances—how could he not stop the Manifesto and deal with the Caucasus instead?

The grand duke's reply began coming in immediately. Annoyed:

"It never occurred to me to inform anyone of the Manifesto's content, since it had not yet been published according to legally established procedure."

And in fact, the grand duke was right! How did Alekseev and all the smart politicians make this blunder? What kind of proclamation of the Manifesto could there be before the Senate had published it according to law?

At least it was legal that they'd delayed it.

Not only could he not lie down, not only could he not take five minutes to think about the conversation—there was no time to drink a glass of tea. They kept bringing him more and more telegrams.

Ah, here it was. From Rodzyanko: no deputation had been sent to the army group.

Did that mean it was just a revolutionary gang in Polotsk? Too bad they hadn't detained them. They were afraid of spoiling their relations with the Duma.

And then two in a row from Nepenin in the Baltic Fleet. The first, saying he was trying to delay the Manifesto where that was still possible, but in Reval it had already been pasted up and received broad publicity—although the disturbances had stopped (despite Rodzyanko's scare . . .). And the second, half an hour later, saying that even in Sveaborg it had been partly proclaimed, but he saw nothing wrong in that. What difference did the Manifesto's form make? He asked for guidance. Where was the difficulty?

Alekseev himself hadn't understood from Rodzyanko what the problem was. Where the difficulty lay.

And what was the point of delaying the Manifesto if it had already come out in Reval, Sveaborg, and the Western Army Group?

Documents – 12

GHQ, to Adjutant General Alekseev

Vyritsa, 16 March, 9:25

Telegram received from Rodzyanko about the return to Mogilev. Please confirm where to send the St. George battalion.

Adjutant General Ivanov

[3 6 1]

The view from the observation point was more usual and familiar than the one from your own window. Every unnamed hillock, every depression, had been picked out by the eye and etched in memory. The old ones were all white, filled with snow, while the new missile craters had a black spray and afterward would be covered in white. Poking out of some depression was a poker, bent branch, or arm of a former person, your eye couldn't tell which, but through the stereoscope you could tell precisely. Up ahead, not far, our rusty wire barriers were stretched on small columns and bent stakes, sometimes trestles. Also around the stakes were pickets wrapped in barbed wire and spikes, like hedgehogs. Another couple hundred yards beyond that—German ones just like them. A rag that tore off someone fleeing had snagged on their wire fence and now fluttered at every gust of wind. And beyond that were the zones of the German firing line, where knowing all the embrasures and machine-gun nests depended on your steady eye. And then—the bluish smoke from the small trench stoves, which the understanding was no one fired on.

There had been no movement or change for a long time—this whole morbid landscape just grew dark and light with the march of the weather and the sun's daily rotation. Very rarely a shell would pelt down and open up a new crater. The rare bullet would strike close in the snow—which would hiss and send up a burst of steam.

The past few weeks there had been completely languid firing, not a single attack, not a single operation, just the revision of ranging marks, and at aerial balloons, and if somewhere Germans got to stirring too openly. A day's duty on observation sometimes passed without a single shot fired.

So, too, last night Kostya Gulai hadn't been disturbed once. He'd slept through it on the straw, on a raised bench in the chilled bunker, wearing his boots, greatcoat, and tall fur hat, tightly belted, and got up only once to relieve himself and keep his eye sharp—and hadn't even glanced into the scope, into the dark of night.

In the morning he was still sleeping soundly when he was woken up by Vanka Evgrafov, the duty telephone operator, a restive fellow, with spunk, who without an officer around didn't mind looking through the glasses to see what the German was up to. Now he touched the second lieutenant lightly on the leg, and cautiously, impatiently:

"Sir . . . sir . . ."

His voice held no alarm, and Gulai grunted discontentedly, sleepily:

"Well?"

"Sir, take a look at what the Germans have set up, eh?"

"What have they set up?"

They might have set up a weapon or some new machine, and maybe we should shoot.

There was already plenty of light through the bunker's observation slit, and Gulai saw Evgrafov's toothy grin, such as he always had out of curiosity, he liked to be in the thick of things.

"Oh, it's really something what they've set up, it's hard to describe. Go see for yourself!"

Gulai raised his body, battered from the rather hard bench, cursed at no one in particular and went to the slit—the peephole, as the soldiers called it.

The day was beginning clear. Bands of blue sky, a piece of cloud, a side-long, diffuse, sunny light—and everything—the crosses in the Catholic cemetery, the grove, the Ruchka River—still heaped with the white bulk from the day before yesterday's abundant snow.

The second lieutenant leaned toward the stereoscopic viewer, while Evgrafov next to him pressed up to the slit.

Directly opposite, along the line of the second guidepost, ahead of the German trenches, a plywood board, three by five feet, had been set up against their wire, on a stick stuck in the snow, and on the board, paper, and written on the paper in soot, in large letters, in Russian, in poorly calculated lines, spaced out here, squeezed in there:

Petersburg – revolushn!
Rus kaput.
Stop fight!

Is that so. What was this?

Gulai, the sun shining conveniently behind his back, looked and looked, enough to read it ten times over—now not at the words themselves but around them, to the right, to the left, to see what kinds of other movements and changes the Germans had made. None whatsoever, anywhere, and no one poking their noses out.

"What is it?" Evgrafov's curiosity was piqued.

"It's a joke. We'd find out about something like that before them."

A revolution? Out of the blue? It's a joke.

Nonetheless, he ordered Evgrafov to get the field telephone and call the sector command point. Evgrafov promptly buzzed them and asked for an officer—and Gulai could already hear in the receiver the thick, rough voice of Staff Captain Ofrosimov. Kostya himself had the very same rasp; his rough front-line voice had grown up so you couldn't hear the former schoolboy.

"Captain, did you see it?"

"Yes"—bristly.

Ofrosimov himself was like that, "shaggy," as the officers called him; indeed, his entire chest was covered in curly black hair.

"You haven't seen anything anywhere else? This is the only one like it?"

"The only one. Shoot the damn thing down, Gulai!"

"Um . . ." Gulai faltered, "You haven't heard anything?"

"What are you blathering about? Shoot it down this instant."

Ofrosimov was all decisiveness, and the longer he was at the front, the more Gulai respected men like that. That's how he himself saw life now.

He telephoned his senior battery officer, Captain Klementiev, who didn't come to the phone right away, or had just gotten up, or happened to be drinking his tea.

He listened and with sang-froid:

"What's the date over there? Not the first of April yet?"

Based on his calm voice, at least, nothing of the kind could have happened.

"The infantry's asking. Maybe I should shoot it down?" Gulai said.

"Fine, shoot it down." The senior officer liked artillery assignments. "But try to hit it on the first shell, okay?"

"I'll try," Gulai laughed.

He calculated the barrel's gradations from the ranging mark, and then on paper: the angle of divergence, the correction for distance. It would be interesting to shoot it down in one.

Evgrafov called the battery.

"First gun, action!" Gulai barked at him, and he repeated it back.

While they were preparing—

"Deflection . . . aim . . . level . . . shell . . . a single shell."

The battery reported their readiness.

"Fire!" and he went to the stereoscope.

And curious Evgrafov, having shouted "fire," dropped the telephone and skipped over to an observation slit.

There it was, and the whistle that went with it. It whistled and wailed not far above his head and crashed, raising a fountain of snow-earth several feet to the left of the board.

The air cleared—and the board was gone, blown away.

"Thank him." Gulai nodded at the telephone.

Evgrafov smiled, showing his teeth.

Right then, his gunner came in from the trench and brought him a breakfast in two pots, now getting cold.

First he sat down to the telephones, while Evgrafov darted over to the little stove, to light it and heat the kettle. And to pour some of it in a spur of the trench with untrampled snow, so the second lieutenant could wash up, his cheeks and nose.

They started eating, Evgrafov on the straw, Gulai on a billet of wood, the kettle on a low table. Ivan was chattering on about this and that, trench news—Gulai wasn't listening.

He thought, And what if it were the truth? After all, don't some people's lives run into events like this?

Right now, at the front, Kostya had been through so much and aged so much, but before he'd have taken it like a young man. Any unusual, even dangerous, even disagreeable event attracted him, just so it happened! His fearless body actually felt like brushing up against danger. (And surviving it, of course.)

Revolution! That whirling, flame, fantasy—right? Actually, there could hardly be an experience stronger than being under a good bombardment.

They drank their tea, nibbling on sugar to sweeten it.

Before, Evgrafov would probably have gone to tell the battery about the sign. But now he eagerly went on about the Skopin factory girls. (He himself had been a merchant's clerk in Skopin.)

Gulai busied himself a little with records and observations. There wasn't really anything to do. You could sleep all day, even read a book.

The buzzer sounded—and Evgrafov held out the receiver to him:

"Brigade headquarters."

The voice in the receiver was so reedy and delicate, you could take it for a woman's. Ah, that was him calling, that little prince at headquarters, Captain Volkonsky. He asked—and gave away his concern—was this the same second lieutenant speaking to him who had seen the German sign? Not about how dashingly they'd struck it down with a single shell, but what exactly had been written there.

Gulai had seen this little prince a few times: delicate of face, delicate of lips, with playing fingers, and the self-confidence that comes from noble breeding had ticked him off. Blue blood had always made Gulai seethe. It infuriated him that someone thought nature made him higher born and elected. Even if someone like that carried himself simply, Gulai still picked up on it, the way he expressed himself and arrogantly knew his own inborn superiority. Captain Volkonsky had a singing, mistrustful tone, slippery and vapid sentences—as if to say he couldn't talk seriously in this company, he had people who understood him elsewhere.

But now—he was nervous!

Gulai couldn't help but answer him more and more rudely and ponderously than he himself had understood the morning's incident. Basically, he'd taken it for a joke, but for some reason he now reported it to Prince Volkonsky not as a joke.

He heard Volkonsky's voice drop. Did he maybe know something coming from our side?

But Gulai wouldn't stoop to questioning him.

He put down the receiver and stepped away, but he felt something rising in him.

Was it truly something? . . . Something like revolution?

Things really had rotted away here. One good shake—and it would be cleansed, only better.

So, you pleasure-seekers, has this got you worried? What were you thinking these last hundred fifty, two hundred years? How could you be so nonchalant about having slaves—and not let that bother you? Was all you did develop your refined arts? And laugh in your drawing rooms? And assemble in shimmering mansions for balls? So-and-so's carriage is here! Beauties would flutter, clutching their gathered silk hems and not letting any outsiders into their palaces, except that the servants saw everything. How did you get to be chosen like that? Why were you lifted out of the universal suffering—to those azure coasts? Every Volkonsky, Obolensky, Shuvalov, Dolgoruky—may you be raked to shreds—you've had a good time, but what have you given Russia? What good have you ever done anyone? You never gave as much as you took and took—and you thought you wouldn't feel the heat? Well, if not today, then later, but just you wait: you'll feel the heat!

Then there were all those von Traubenbergs, Jungersburgs, Kaulbarses, Carlstedts, and Silberkranzes. How many of them have settled, crowded, populated all the top levels? And we have to teach soldiers to pronounce all those names? How do you free your collar from them?

Something rather cheerful started playing his chest—and Gulai actually started regretting that all this was just the German infantry's clumsy joke.

[3 6 2]

The whole day, the whole course of the day is set by how you wake up, whether your blood has gone to your head or not. There are different forms: either the pressure can stay with you all day, or you can tell it will disperse. An infirmity you don't want to tell anyone about: it concerns you alone, and it's up to you to complete its entire fragile course.

Sleep's influence had been utterly transformed over the years: from a firm, joyous absence where the beginning and end almost met up in forgetfulness, sleep dragged out into long hard labor, with groans in its tossings and turnings, then with drilling in your joints, with dreams, dreams, a twilight awareness, tormenting visions—and the faltering morning always lower than the dispersed evening. In the evening, you feel like an energetic person, pleased even with the day just past—and by morning all that has been overturned, sunk far down, and flat on your back, and you wake up in insignificance, scarcely believing that your powers might once again stir—and once again gather momentum for a useful day.

Inching up a little higher on the pillows every five minutes—just a little higher, finally half-sitting up, Varsonofiev anxiously tried to sniff out what kind of order was setting in there today, in his mind. Would things remain heaped up, with unexamined corners of his brain that couldn't be brought into his thinking and thoughts that couldn't mature—or would things gradually spin out, clear up, the way the sky clears up (helped along by coffee)? Would he once again feel and propel the former power of his mind and pen?

But sometimes he felt faint of heart and unsure. Getting up made no sense at all. For it to make sense, he had to find something sustaining and pleasant, say, a good letter that was supposed to come today. Or—we're going to heat the water heater today.

At this difficult morning hour, one's awareness of outside events streams undifferentiated over the surface. In the inert, defenseless moment of awakening, as he tries to rise from the ashes, each time not knowing whether he will—the first bitterness and burden a person is forced to accept is his own small life, which no one knows or cares about, a life even he himself considered insignificant and unimportant in comparison with all his scholarly activities. He returns to powerless memory and slogs through, slogs through.

Lyoka. Here she was, after ravaging him for years, unwilling to let go even now. He dreamed of her, and so expressively: first putting, squeezing, several large axes into her vanity drawer and trying to shut it, but it kept twisting and cracking. Then, standing next to a baby carriage, mumbling, old, she demanded he come close, but when he did, she turned out to be lying in the carriage, fitting somehow, but also grown-up. And the dream's secret gripped his heart with horror.

Now, if she was fated to die before Pavel Ivanovich, then she would start coming to him *from the other side* even more insistently.

And his daughter? How did he miss that? Why didn't he guide her? So many successes with his students—with other people's children—but his own? How could he have failed to safeguard her from this godless consciousness, this contemptible milieu?

Hadn't he himself gone through the same? . . .

And in general, there seemed to have been so few outward, factual events, yet the caverns of memory weighed on him. The older Pavel Ivanovich got, the more distinctly he recalled his early years. Utterly forgotten guilt, guilt he had never understood, was revealed to him and began to burn, starting with his mother and father—guilt before those who had passed away or scattered to the winds long since, so there was no finding them to ask forgiveness and make amends.

Why was it that a man's whole life, upon closer examination, consisted of almost nothing but mistakes? Why are we never allowed to take correct and luminous decisions in time and are only given to weave our life together—and only with an old man's debilitated glance make out what was missed? Each new time we're convinced we're right, and each time we're wrong.

Most surprising was that he sincerely never had seen any of this in time. The simplest moves of ravishing youth and the blindness of middle age, so distinct now—why hadn't he made them out before?

Sixty-one years old! That was a lot. That was a very long life.

As before, he liked what he did, but somehow not the way he used to. No longer did it afford him the same tempting delight, and so to fortify himself, Varsonofiev had to think not just about its essence but about what answer and deflection he would offer his opponents. His worldly resolve solidified more and more on his opponents. He needed to deflect them. To correct false moves. To convey his spiritual experience to young people. Everything we have accumulated but not passed on will perish with us fruitlessly, after all.

So little strength and time is given a man just to cope with his own heart and his own thinking. But doesn't someone have to make an effort to advance public life?

Quite recently, Pavel Ivanovich learned of the death of two of his peers—due to no perceptible cause. Does that mean it was just age? What a powerful impact this has: your peers are already parting with this world. The road is ending. A road inevitable for all.

But to look back from a certain time, a great many close, sympathetic people tied to you in multiple ways have already passed on to the *next* world. And you feel lonelier and lonelier here and in a way beside the point: you understand the newcomers poorly, and they you.

Sixty years was a full life that could well slam shut right there. But for some reason he had been given extra above and beyond, extra compared with the dead. A merciful gift, in addition. To think things through. And to make corrections where possible. To correct old mistakes if their loose ends haven't been lost.

Most of the time they've been dropped and lost, though. How he would like to start afresh and hew closer to the correct line!

And you almost knew in advance that that was impossible.

Not only mornings but entire days could be spent this way, days of expansive contemplation about who knew what, something not found early in the morning, but you just wish you could sort through your past life and something else, in conjunction. The feeling that this was productive and something would be found. Only don't hurry, don't even set yourself a task.

So he sat, propped up by tall pillows, his legs stretched out under the blanket—although downstairs, in the mailbox, his newspapers awaited him with more incredible, leapfrogging news.

So it had come! Petersburg and Moscow were shaking. Something ought to shake out of this; things could scarcely calm down smoothly now. Rodzyanko telegraphed Mrozovsky in Moscow, saying that the government no longer existed. Mrozovsky rushed to clear himself: "I'm an old soldier who has risked his head in many a campaign"—and over the telephone he twice tried to talk Chelnokov into coming and accepting his capitulation, but he wouldn't even do that! The Moscow city governor was arrested at the train station fleeing. Somewhere heaven knew where the Tsar was thrashing and casting about. Even when he was no longer young, a mere fifteen years ago, Varsonofiev had so awaited this! How he would now have seethed, how his legs wouldn't have stayed planted but would have dashed across this street morass and sought a way to talk himself hoarse and apply himself somewhere. It was for that public life alone, it seemed, that he had nurtured the summit of his consciousness.

But after ten pre-old years, something in him had ripened.

These days he spent going over the sporadic newspapers and the individual leaflets proclaiming extraordinary events. And he listened to Epifanovna about how in the taverns people had taken food without paying, hauled inventory out of the colonial shop on Bolshaya Nikitskaya, robbed the bakery on Tishinka, and stormed the watch store on the corner of Bolshaya Gruzinskaya and Tverskaya. And about the apartment searches by armed soldiers. He himself had walked one time from Maly Vlasievsky to the Prechistensky Gate, and another time to Arbat Square, but even outside, in the intoxicated crush, he couldn't shake the feeling that all this going on outwardly wasn't the main thing.

Pavel Ivanovich could discern and understand the main thing from his own apartment, which had known better days, without going outside or even reading the newspapers—merely by freeing room for his thoughts and reading the carved ceiling.

One needed the ability to understand life in its most basic, simplest features. That may be old age's best gift.

In states, as in the life of the individual person, everything comes and goes in waves. One's possessions are countless, and suddenly there's nothing. A person lives and a state lives in apparent health oblivious to the fact that they are already on the brink.

At one time, he too thought that if only they could establish a republic, a liberated state system—and—and what? What could the daily political fever change for the better in the true life of men? What kind of principles could it offer that would bring us out of our emotional sufferings, our emotional evil? Was the essence of our life really political?

So, too, his former public activities had been one big mistake, then.

And would he eventually understand his present mistake?

How could you remake the world if you couldn't figure out your own soul?

Right then he heard: a bell ringing? . . .

Not the ringing of a specific church. And not the measured, mournful, Lenten summons to morning service—not that it was the time for that. And not the Church of St. Vlasi nearby, which was silent. Not the Assumption on Mogilnitsy, not St. Nicholas in Plotniki, not the Protection on Levshinsky—Pavel Ivanovich could tell them all apart even with the window closed, from their sound and direction.

But the powerful bell ringing continued. The striking bell was no less than the Ivan the Great tower.

It was unusual. Entirely out of season. Pavel Ivanovich lowered his feet into his slippers and put on his robe from the back of the chair. He walked up to and opened one small window, and a second.

Yes, it was the Kremlin striking. Striking many bells. And as always, the Ivan stood out among them.

After sixty years's living at a single location in Moscow, hadn't Varsonofiev come to know the ring and peal of every bell? But this was not only out of season, unexplained by the church calendar—on a Friday morning in the third week of Lent—it was like a foul-mouthed man among decent people, like a drunk among the sober. The strikes were many, and incoherent, and quick, and weak—and without any harmony, elegance, or skill. These were strikes not by bell ringers.

First excited. Then too much. Then quite languid and intermittently silent.

These were strikes—as if Tatars had climbed the Russian bell towers to tug away at them.

Pavel Ivanovich stood at the small window—and listened in amazement. One could guess how these bell ringers had broken into the bell towers at an agreed-upon time and what they were trying to express so discordantly. But how did this sound to a native Muscovite?

The small churches nearby hadn't joined in, not a one. But of those farther away—some had. Varsonofiev stood there for ten minutes or so—and the main bell of Christ the Savior boomed. Followed by a rattling tinkling. Just as pointless.

Pavel Ivanovich stood and stood and stood. And not only became thoroughly chilled but was enveloped by a great melancholy.

Devastation, even.

As if the cheeky revolutionary peal was guffawing, mocking all his remorse, reflection, and weighing.

Now even less could be understood in Russia's journey. And his own life.

[3 6 3]

Just yesterday the sun was hers.

But not today. It had gone away.

All the wonderful excitement, all the overabundance of delight had gone away—only to be covered up by longing and resentment in exchange.

No, no, Likonya wasn't heavy-hearted! After all, she'd had those oh so impossible six days. And those could not be taken away.

Even the pain that came after him was beautiful.

But what happened to her? Apparently, she wasn't herself.

She didn't remember the encounter at all.

Everything she'd wanted to explain—and she hadn't. Next to *him*, her whole past was suddenly shallow and unneeded. Next to him, she couldn't remember her own disappointments and sufferings.

She got lost.

Instead, he was by her side and filled everything.

She was an insignificant little girl compared to him, and he would be right in not appreciating her, disdaining her.

Without having understood her.

Abandoning her.

This had already happened once in her life: she had brought everything, but none of it was needed.

No, it was her own fault! She'd gone numb, she wasn't herself.

And in the end he was just amusing himself? . . .

And now would they even be together one more time, to set things right?

While outside there was this whirl of a crowd, this wild red and songs, everyone glad at something.

While the dark theaters were like funeral halls.
Indeed, would they be together one more time?
Darling! Don't leave! Darling! Be with me one more time!
I'll embrace you as never before!

[3 6 4]

God, what a night! . . . Never could there be two such nights in a person's life!

No sleep all night, but what an elevating, memorable, thrilling night for the happy conclusion of the Great Russian Revolution!

By nightfall it was clear that something was being decided in Pskov. Nepenin sent his telegram through GHQ in support of abdication, and even exaggerated, in the opinion of his staff, that he was having tremendous difficulty keeping the fleet loyal—the greater part of the fleet was behaving calmly and nobly—and that only abdication could fend off a catastrophe of incalculable consequences.

He sent his telegram—and everything drowned in the night's silence, and it was hard to believe that things would turn out for the best. After two in the morning, when they had talked everything over and over and dispersed to their beds, a telegram arrived saying that the Tsar had signed the abdication Manifesto!

And so, without a night, the day, the next day, started in straightaway. The crews were asleep, and small duty lamps were lit on the dark ship hulls. The portholes of the dreadnaughts and battleships were not lit, the crew of the *Krechet* was asleep, too, as was anyone the telegraph operators themselves hadn't awakened—but Prince Cherkassky and Rengarten went to Adrian's cabin to congratulate him! They would have summoned Shchastny, who was entirely one of them, too, but the evening before he had gone to Petrograd as the fleet's representative.

Nepenin found a bottle of champagne. The three of them drank it in the cabin, making no noise, with voices overwrought but not loud. To the new Russia! To the new era! What a blinding dawn to a free, expansive, and great Russian life!

How fantastically quickly and easily it had all been resolved! They had only just been searching for how to act, who to topple, how to give Duma members pushes from without—but everyone had behaved so excellently, and everything had proceeded so smoothly!

Adrian, too, was down to earth as never before, there was no barrier between them, although despite the threesome's gaiety his face seemed concerned. Yet they spoke as one.

About who to replace with whom. Remove the hard-liners and refresh the staff. How everything was going to look! And sound! About Russia's innumerable possibilities.

My God, how easily it all came about, though!

Right then they brought a tape from the new government with an order for the admiral to immediately arrest Finnish Governor-General Seyn and one other prominent Tsarist official.

Fair-haired Nepenin raised his eyebrows. A police order, inappropriate for his position and service. But there was also this reverse side, a natural feature of revolution.

They would have to be detained. And isolated from the city. On a ship. And taken to Petrograd.

He ordered an automobile and escort and left for town to make the arrest.

Meanwhile Cherkassky and Rengarten waited for his return in the headquarters chancellery. They speculated on how the operation would go. They discussed everything again and again. They were simply burning, they couldn't sit still. Rengarten would jump up and pace, in that cramped space, two and a half paces.

They also devised a cell for Seyn—the flagship mechanic's vacant cabin—and ordered it made ready, and right then, soon after, steps were heard in the hall, and Cherkassky went to meet them and show them the way. Seyn, who was moving like an inflated, astonished scarecrow, stepped in obediently and let himself be locked in. He had already given his saber to Nepenin back in the palace, not having moved a muscle to object or resist.

This was an indicator and symbol, that it went so smoothly. So it—everything!—would continue like this!

Nepenin said that he had invited Finnish figures here to the ship for the day. After Seyn's arrest, it was natural to establish friendly contact with them and promise broad rights to the Finnish Sejm.

They left Adrian to rest and themselves went to pace the deck some more. Dawn had not yet broken. A light frost, a light westerly, the whole starry sky open, pressure 764. It would be a clear morning.

And it was coming soon. There was no point going to bed. Better to greet it awake.

Here's what they and the prince came up with. Together they would tidy up and systemize all the telegrams and documents from the past few days connected with the revolution. How many days? All of four! But a great deal had accumulated, and later it would all get jumbled up and lost.

They worked with interest, never ceasing to be amazed at the tread of history across their own heads.

The morning blazed up bright and sunny, festive, and the white icy expanses made them squint.

The text of the Tsar's Manifesto had arrived in these past few hours. (Cherkassky found it to be written in amazingly noble language. Who had composed it for the Tsar?) An unslept Nepenin assembled the flag officers before seven o'clock—not for a meeting but having them stand in formation in his saloon—and read them the Manifesto.

They amiably shouted "hurrah" to Emperor Mikhail II! All this was much more cheerful and brighter than yesterday's ominous indeterminacy. Apparently, there were no discontented faces this time. A new emperor, and the Russian Empire continues!

Barely had the flag officers dispersed to announce this to their ships, though, than the *Krechet's* telegraph received from Alekseev at GHQ Rodzyanko's request to take all measures and means to delay announcing the Manifesto reported that night! In view of special conditions that would be explained later.

Like thunder! What did this mean?

But it had already been sent out! In Reval and here, too. . . . Our principle had always been to inform the sailors as quickly and honestly as possible!

What was this starting up again? What was this? The revolution had turned back? The Tsar was rescinding his abdication? . . . Betrayal?

A pall fell over everything despite the brilliant morning.

What had already been achieved, what the heart had already lived and absorbed so tremulously, could not be parted with!

The Colonel could not be allowed back on the throne!

[3 6 5]

General Ruzsky somehow had already withstood yesterday's predawn blow from Rodzyanko, who'd said that his victory was not a victory, and events were taking longer strides. Yesterday he had once again gathered all the forces of his intellect to prevail upon the Tsar—and once again he had prevailed! By nighttime he was once again fired up, dining with Guchkov and Shulgin and seeing them off later on the train, while he himself took a motorcar to town, to headquarters. He was intoxicated by the role he'd played and felt himself equal to the grandiose Events.

But when today, at five in the morning, barely slipping into sleep, he was awakened once again to come to the telegraph, and again Rodzyanko with crude, uncalculated movements wiped off the board all the winning figures set up there, Ruzsky felt he'd been punctured and all the air inside him had started to escape, leaving him to shrivel up. Shriveled, huddled, and small, he fell on his bed, after six by then—and tried to fall asleep, but no longer to any benefit, a sour sleep, without refreshment, occasionally starting awake— even sleep eluded him—limp, battered—after how many days of superhuman tension? Could it really be fewer than two? Impossible to believe. It felt like more than a week.

He had stretched to keep up with events, to lead them even—but no, evidently he was too old for that kind of stretching, sixty-three years old. Quite a repulsive, slobbery condition. It was unbelievable the enthusiasm that had reigned just a few hours before at dinner with the deputies.

What kind of deputies were they? What were they worth, even the famous Guchkov? They themselves didn't know what they'd been after. They'd been totally unprepared.

It was still flattering that they'd telegraphed Ruzsky first rather than Alekseev. Of course, they were counting on finding greater understanding from him. Under the new government, he might be the Supreme Commander. What was Nikolai Nikolaevich? A figure for parades and photographs. They were hardly going to approve him. And Alekseev was to blame for 1915, the mind behind the clumsy Carpathian escapade who had then succumbed to the psychosis of retreat. Would he really make a good Supreme Commander? But the government was behaving as if it had gone mad.

Petrograd events seemed not to have had a coherent flow, where a subsequent event flows out of the event previous. Rather, they would pop up suddenly, like a magician's puppet, and the magician was Rodzyanko. He could present—in the next conversation or five minutes later—first an unprecedented soldier mutiny and then total calm. More than likely, they themselves hadn't understood the populace's mood and what was going on in Petrograd. But when Petrograd was in Ruzsky's charge, he had always known the city's mood. So all these past few days, then, both the members of the Duma and public figures had been playing a desperate, risky game—and now, out of weakness, had let it all slip. Given this kind of instantaneous changeability of the Petrograd situation, though, how could the Northern Army Group exist and be stationed right next door?

Ruzsky managed to tell Rodzyanko as much as he could. On the other hand, Rodzyanko was pressing his own powerful figure even through the telegraph, so evident was it how he had sidelined the meek Lvov there, not letting him make a peep. Through this eternal self-promotion of his, Rodzyanko had kept them from finding out what other people there were thinking and doing. One would have liked to hear from the head of the new government, but he was mute, and instead of him Rodzyanko burst through with his monologues—and not just as the Duma president but as the chairman of some unheard-of Supreme Council—as under Anna Ioannovna—whose role alongside the government had been by no means clear; but after the repetitions and requests to repeat, it turned out that there was no Supreme Council whatsoever, it was just a slip of the tongue. Quite a slip of the tongue—printed out slowly, three times, on the tape!

How could one confuse things so badly? And what was going on in men's minds there? Ruzsky couldn't fathom the twists and turns of the Duma politicians. At first he reluctantly approved their order to hold back the Manifesto and sent them to talk with GHQ. But if one thought that matters were heading toward a Constituent Assembly, then, obviously they were heading toward a republic, too, right? In that case, naturally, Nikolai's Manifesto definitely had to be held back. And most important, stopped, so that no one anywhere swore an oath to Mikhail.

In the next room, Danilov had already coughed several times, evidently calculating that Ruzsky would wake up but reluctant to rouse him. He felt broken and wasn't going to be able to fall asleep. Without rising from his bed, Ruzsky summoned him.

The sturdy, hale Danilov exuded a daytime vigor. The ban on distributing the Manifesto had to be repeated categorically one more time, in the name of the Army Group commander, and most important, under no circumstance let it lead to an oath. Here it was ready, here was the pen.

Propping himself up with pillows, Ruzsky signed on a cardboard backing.

Some kind of guideline had to be sent out for clarification. Why had the Manifesto been held back? Because there was going to be a Constituent Assembly. And confirming the appointments of Lvov and Nikolai Nikolaevich.

But on this point Ruzsky realized that this could not be! The grand duke's position would become shaky now as well.

"GHQ has confirmed it, Nikolai Vladimirich."

"Well, then, send it out," Ruzsky conceded listlessly.

He shouldn't have chased after all this, he shouldn't have taken part. . . .

And now Danilov had also brought some telegram for approval. To all commanders of the armies, the Dvinsk District, and reserve militias and army communications officers. Saying that checkpoints had to be set up on all railroads and the patrol and cordon service added to in order to isolate the troops from any possible penetration by agitators and to prevent the formation in the rear of gangs of looters and tramps.

"No general decree from GHQ?"

No.

Alcksccv was a fine one! How could he stoop so low? Trying to please the new regime.

Not stirring anything but his hand, which picked up the paper, and reading it a couple of times, Ruzsky, the back of his head on a pillow, got to thinking. In this decree, which was natural for the army and seemingly internal, nonetheless an abyss had split open. At dinner it had seemed easy to get along with the new regime. But this telegram reminded him that it wasn't. Here a deputation-band had arrived yesterday in Polotsk, and had it taken a course slightly more to the right it would have ended up not at the Western Army Group but at the Northern. The Northern was next to the capital, and all the tests would be made on it, and all the bands would be sent here before anywhere else.

Alekseev had not taken that step—so it was up to Ruzsky. All of Ruzsky's convictions and moods fit in with being friends and getting along with the new government. These were all cultured people, not the dull, narrow-minded autocracy. But it was already evident that they were going to be incapable of stopping these bands.

And if these bands were to get a free hand, there was no Ruzsky as army group commander, there was no army group at all, and there was no active Russian military. And then it would have made no sense to start all this.

Being a general, he did not have a choice. And with a bitter wrinkle, he told Danilov:

"Yuri Nikiforovich, add that the Northern Army Group commander has ordered that the most draconian measures be taken against these gangs."

And he handed back the document and continued to lie there in his debility.

[3 6 6]

They slept briefly, but like the dead, not feeling the train car's jolts, making up for the sleep lost before in the Tauride Palace. They barely dragged themselves to consciousness at the last switch points. It was hard to get up— and the memory of the Petersburg chaos immediately struck them, this being after the night's Pskov fairytale.

They never had washed up.

They never had met up with General Ivanov en route, though there was no need for that now.

Gloomy, looking sick and old, Guchkov, also unshaven, thought and decided:

"Perhaps the Manifesto will be safer with you. I'm on view, I . . ."

He took his wallet out of an inside pocket and from it the secret folded pages and handed them to Shulgin.

Shulgin willingly put them in his own wallet and into his same pocket. His headache had dulled if not faded altogether.

It was an early frosty morning. The rising sun had turned the high-walled brick church near the Stockyard pink.

Three days before, the head of these very same Northwestern Railroads, Valuyev, was executed and torn up by a crowd near this very place, close to the Warsaw Station. Now Valuyev's replacement, whom Bublikov had appointed, quickly entered their train car. He had no wish to be torn apart like Valuyev and could not refuse the crowd anything. But he warned the deputies that the mood was very agitated, people knew of their arrival and were waiting—and he advised them not to go to any rallies whatsoever. But he didn't dare refuse for them.

Returning with a heavy "Tauride" feeling, the deputies went out on the train platform and descended the stairs. They had, after all, secretly slipped away from the Soviet—so how would they now be met? A crowd had already converged on their train car, more than a hundred—soldiers, young officers, the general public.

Guchkov was the first to trudge down, while Shulgin remained slightly higher up on the train car platform. The faces of the public that he saw were sullen—and like lightning, an idea flashed in him: Why hide it? Who was it a secret from now? He was going to gladden and defuse them here and now.

Before he could consult with Guchkov, still on the platform, from his semi-elevation, he gave a sweep of a light hand and shouted in his reedy, not very loud voice:

"The Emperor has abdicated! Due to the heir's illness, Emperor Mikhail Aleksandrovich will ascend to the throne!"

Was it astonishment that flickered across their faces? Agreement? A "hurrah" was heard, but a quiet, thin, disjointed one.

And right away the jumble of the fully free crowd intensified around the deputies. Someone invited them, someone demanded and pulled—in several directions at once, and they were expected everywhere. Before he could have a word with Guchkov, they'd been separated.

But Shulgin liked this kind of excitement. In any case, the Russian masses were not indifferent to politics, as they'd been slandered. So had they always been drawn in this way? Or had they been provoked over the past few days?

Shulgin strode cheerfully behind his escorts. His mind was devoid of simple ordinary clarity but had a fantastic elation—higher and stronger than himself, as he walked down the platform—drawn to give a speech for which he had never prepared. His legs didn't feel like his legs, his tongue like his tongue—they had been given him only partially as he sailed wholly through the air. The pages of the imperial abdication in his pocket were like a special reward, secret from everyone.

It was his special fate specifically to carry at his chest those two weightless pages that overturned all Russian history!

The sight on the platform of young officers with combat-uniform epaulets standing together and the fresh, sobering air revealed to Shulgin, right then, as he walked, one more important argument as to why it was essential to accept the abdication: in this way the oath would be lifted from excessively loyal officers and their lives would be saved from retribution.

He was led into the ticket hall, where an infantry unit had been lined up in four ranks forming the letter "П"—and obviously, Shulgin understood, for no other reason than in anticipation of him and to listen to him.

The fourth, free side was closed off by the station crowd. He could not avoid delivering a speech.

Commands rang out, palms slapped gunstocks, rifle butts clattered on the floor—and silence fell. Shulgin was standing in the open area of the floor—not at all higher than them, lost among them.

He saw those gray ranks and was suffused with an awareness of his responsibility—and how unprepared he was. If they had waited for him here for just fifteen minutes, they were already better prepared for this meeting than he was by his entire political life and all his speeches. He sensed that whatever he told them now would not be equal to the moment.

But he had the Abdication itself in his pocket! Why must he hide it away?

In front of everyone, he took it out of his pocket, out of his wallet, unfolded it—and immediately began reading what was still warm from the nighttime signature, immediately and out loud to the waiting people.

"In the days of the great struggle against a foreign foe . . . It has pleased the Lord God to send down on Russia a further painful trial . . ."

His voice had always been weak, but especially for a hall holding several thousand people. So quiet were they, though—they seemed not to be breathing even—that the words covered the length and breadth of the hall unimpaired.

". . . We have deemed it a duty of conscience to facilitate Our people's. . . . For the good of the country . . . We have considered it desirable to abdicate the throne of the Russian State and lay down the Supreme Power. . . ."

For the second year, from the time he joined the Progressive Bloc up until last night's negotiations, Shulgin had been listed and sat seemingly in opposition to the Tsar. But now, in possession of these sheets of paper, he seemed to have merged with the Tsar. He uttered these words as if they were his own, wholly radiating the Tsar's pain:

". . . Our heritage to Our brother the Grand Duke Mikhail Aleksandrovich, We bless his ascension to the throne of the Russian State. . . . All faithful sons of the Fatherland to fulfill their sacred and patriotic duty . . . in obeying the Tsar at the painful moment of national trials. . . ."

Shulgin finished, swallowed, looked up mournfully from his papers—and saw bayonets seem to sway, tilt, and rock. A ruddy young soldier he could see well—was crying.

And another, farther back in the crowd, apparently, judging from the sound.

There were no other sounds in the hall. No one had shouted out anything impudent or contradictory.

Or approving.

This understanding between the Tsar and the people made Shulgin shudder, and he began to speak easily, from his own private thoughts, only not coherently:

"Did you hear Emperor Nikolai the Second's last words? He showed us, and all Russians, how we must be able to forget ourselves for Russia. . . . Will we, of different ranks and estates, officers and soldiers, noblemen and peasants, rich and poor, be able to forget everything for the sake of what alone unites us—our homeland, Russia? . . . Unless we all act as one, our implacable foe will crush us. Everyone—gather around your new Tsar! Render him your obedience. He shall lead us!"

Straining his voice, now breaking off, now pushing off from the stream of his own speech:

"To our Tsar—Mikhail the Second—I proclaim—hurrah!"

And "hurrah!"—loud, fervent, undisturbed by anyone—filled the hall!

In that instant Shulgin sensed that the monarchy was saved and all would be done properly! They had extracted one miserable monarch—but had saved the monarchy and Russia!

Drained but happy, his head spinning, Shulgin walked—no, was led—down a corridor. Not for another speech, surely?

Led. And some railway clerk told him he was being requested on the telephone. By the Duma. Milyukov.

He was led into a room where the lifted receiver awaited. Milyukov's voice was so hoarse and strained, you could tell over the telephone:

"Aleksandr Ivanych? . . . No? Vasili Vitalich? Here's the thing. Under no circumstances are you to announce anywhere or show the Manifesto!"

"How's that? I've already announced it!"

"To whom?"

"To everyone here. . . . Some regiment. . . . To the people in general! And they took it marvelously. They shouted hurrah to Emperor Mikhail!"

"Oh, you shouldn't have! Shouldn't have! In no case should you have done so! You don't know, the situation has taken a sharp turn against the monarchy. Here, among our neighbors, the mood has been strongly exacerbated. . . . We've received the text by telegraph, and this text does not satisfy them at all. . . . They are demanding that we, it's essential—mention the Constituent Assembly. Please, don't take any steps with the Manifesto of any kind. That will only bring greater misfortunes."

Shulgin was flabbergasted. What did all this matter if the people were receiving it with hurrahs and tears?

"That's too bad. . . . Too bad. . . . But people are receiving it marvelously. . . . Then I'll go warn Guchkov. He's evidently announcing it somewhere, too. . . ."

"Go stop him! And then both of you go straight to 12 Millionnaya Street, to Prince Putyatin's apartment."

"What for?"

"There's going to be . . . a continuation. We're all on our way there right now. Please, hurry."

Shulgin hurried, but he found out that Guchkov was at a workers' rally in the railway workshops, where things were not shaping up so auspiciously.

Then he started worrying about the text at his chest and he faltered, not knowing what he should do.

But they were already summoning him, dragging him to yet another telephone. It was a call from engineer Lomonosov in the office of the now famous Bublikov. And very much to the point: if the deputy wanted to convey *the act* safely, engineer Lebedev would approach him right now at the train station. (Just how many Lebedevs were there?)

Just like that, to a stranger—and surreptitiously? . . . The great act of Abdication? . . .

[367]

Bublikov was asleep, so the wakeful Lomonosov answered the call from the Duma. It was Rodzyanko himself on the telephone, despite the early hour. His question was:

"Where is Guchkov?"

Lomonosov had no connection to this, apparently, but did actually know, for an inspector of his from the Warsaw Train Station had called him.

"He arrived half an hour ago."

"So where is he?"

"You mean he's not there? I have no way of knowing. I'll check immediately."

"Check, my friend. We're very worried. We need the original of the act. We fear it might get taken away from them there. Times are such!"

After the failure that night to seize the Manifesto, Lomonosov swiftly realized the advantages:

"I understand. . . . Do you want us to rescue it? . . . I'm commencing the operation. I'll report upon completion. How about the printing? We're ready."

(Not entirely ready yet, not even ready, but the employees would be assembling in an hour.)

"The printing . . . ? The printing"—Rodzyanko faltered—"has been delayed."

"But we're ready!"

"Good. Stay that way."

"The operation is under way!"

Lomonosov, apparently, had become the most military man in Petrograd in these past few days. Why the delay in printing? What hesitation? But there was no time to ponder. They had to seize the original of the Manifesto. Possession is power!

Sitting on duty by the telephones was Lebedev, his long-time associate in locomotive experiments whom he'd called in the day before yesterday. Bellicose, poised to swoop down—Lomonosov liked choosing men like that.

And here was a bellicose objective: to the Warsaw station, and fast! Find the deputies there, tell them you're from Bublikov—that's a name people know—on orders from Rodzyanko, and have them slip you the Manifesto discreetly. No one knows you, so you can take it away. And bring it here!

Lebedev broke off. Lomonosov manned the telephones himself. This was no time for sleep, a critical battle! He was pacing like a tiger, quickly figuring. A revolution can only be made in the night or pre-dawn hours! Actually, it was already light, after eight. The Duma kept calling, hovering, pressing to know where Guchkov was—and where was the Act? How helpless they were. Without Bublikov and Lomonosov, they would have been asleep at the switch for the whole revolution! Call the Warsaw station, call the Warsaw station. One, another, a third telephone—either no answer or no way to summon them. This is the Ministry of Roads and Railways calling. On instruction from Commissar Bublikov. Find one of the two deputies immediately. They're there at the station, and summon them to the telephone. This is urgent. This is in the name of the revolution. Do this immediately!

They did.

What days and hours! They made it worth being born. Without waking Bublikov, pacing around the room, his feet positively digging, dragging new schemes out of the floor. The greatest document in all Russian history! Seize it! The Duma kept calling, trying to get through? I'm so sick of them! We're doing this!

"Who is this? . . . Deputy Shulgin? Good morning to you. This is a call from Commissar Bublikov, on instruction from Rodzyanko. Are you having difficulties there? Our engineer will go find you right away. His name is Lebedev and he's absolutely loyal. You can *hand it over* to him. Do you have it with you? And your hands will be free. . . . You're welcome! We serve a free Russia!"

Back to pacing around the room, in a hunter's fever. First they'd chased down the imperial train, then Ivanov, and now the abdication. Quite the days!

Nearly ten o'clock. Bublikov woke up as well, all crumpled, disheveled, upset. But one spark from Lomonosov was enough to convey to him their task—and he was instantly in motion and rubbing his hot palms together.

"Why hasn't Lebedev telephoned? He couldn't have been caught there, too, could he? Why don't you get over there, Yuri Vladimirovich, and I'll stay by the telephone myself."

Oh well, that made sense. Put on someone's leather railway jacket and a railway cap. Down the stairs—and into the motorcar on duty.

But the frost, it grabbed him by the ears! Meanwhile the sun was coming out. Good weather for a stroll.

There was hardly any distance to go: a short way down the Fontanka and then past the Izmailovsky companies. Right where they'd begun the overthrow of Peter III. Izmailovsky Prospect strewn in red. And the people. The people! The disorderly soldiers, the civilians, all of them thronging down the pavement! It would have been faster on foot here.

The closer to the station, the denser it got. The motorcar wasn't armed, they hadn't thought to put soldiers on the fenders, and people weren't letting them through that easily. They barely maneuvered the bridge across the Obvodny Canal. And on to the station.

Good thing—he glimpsed Lebedev in the crowd. In his dandyish fur coat with the raised collar—walking like a grand gentleman. Dressed inappropriately—he could have been harassed.

He shouted, waved to him, and Lebedev indicated with just his head: keep going.

The task now was to turn around again in this mass. The crowd cursed, displeased. Lomonosov briskly explained to them it was a necessity.

And back across the same bridge (where they'd bumped off Valuyev).

This, apparently, was where they'd finished off Pleve, too. Quite the location. He picked up Lebedev, who climbed onto the seat, pulling up his fur coat. And in a whisper:

"Here." Thrusting the pages at him. "But Guchkov's been arrested by the workers!"

"What? What for?" Lomonosov was aghast. That was the last thing he'd expected.

The swing of Revolution. They're all like that!

Just so they don't grab us en route, too.

Fontanka. The ministry. Bublikov's office.

"Get out for a minute, gentlemen. Sosnovsky, don't let anyone in!"

The four of them remained: Bublikov, one other commissar, Lomonosov, and Lebedev.

They put it on the table, leaned over, fixed their eyes on it.

"Nikolashka's got what he was asking for!" Bublikov said emphatically.

They read it greedily, silently.

Bublikov was the first to crack the puzzle:

"What a crafty Byzantine! Why a dispatch and not in proper form? Just in case—grounds for appeal? . . . And why abdicate for the heir? Under what law? Aha! To lift the odium from his son during the riots. Mikhail's in a morganatic marriage, so who's the next heir? Aleksei again! Splendid!"

[3 6 8]

There was a big, thick, black crowd of workers in the enormous depot with the glassed-in, steel-latticed roof—but by no means to work, as there had been no work anywhere these past few days; and there were many more than could have worked here. A locomotive engine under repair should have been right here—but they'd taken it away. All that remained was a narrow, high-ascending ladder with a dog-leg platform—evidently for repairing the engine's upper parts—and that is what Guchkov had had to clamber up. Instead of steps, the ladder had round iron bars, which were awkward for galoshes, to say nothing of his sore leg, and the handrail was of the same bars, dirty and sticky with oil. Guchkov's whole capacious and expensive fur coat constricted his climbing and twice got caught underfoot, which to an onlooker must have seemed funny. His pince-nez nearly broke, too, and that would have been a total disaster. He paused to put it in his pocket. When he got to the platform—he placed it back on the bridge of his nose.

It wasn't very wide here and he was a little afraid of falling off. Fortunately, iron rod railings enclosed him. The droning black crowd below made it even more unpleasant. Everyone was simply talking with everyone else, but all this combined and rose up like a menacing rumble. This assembled crowd and its uncontrolled rumble far below reinforced the sense of a burst-open revolution. He had been too late in extracting the abdication. Too late! It hadn't forestalled anything. The masses that everyone had always feared awakening—here they were, awake.

Standing with him now, on the platform, were a few men. He didn't have a chance to examine them and understand who they were. He couldn't even see their faces because they had stepped forward, toward the edge. All he saw were shoulders in plain coats or worker's jackets, two raised collars, two turned down, plainly shorn napes, and the backs of service caps and hats. Naturally, Guchkov was expecting them to turn around to face him and invite him to speak, expecting them to announce him—but none of the four turned around, not even the one who had given him a hand on the last step up—but one did say:

"And who do they have there in the new government, comrades? Now, with waves of popular anger crashing more and more furiously at the palace walls, do you think they asked anyone from the laboring people?"

And Guchkov realized that all of them here had gathered not to listen to him, that they had started their rally before and had just watched him silently as he walked through the depot and clambered up.

". . . Prince Lvov! I dare say—his estates spread out over ten provinces. A prince! Oh, a different Lvov, also a prince, I dare say, could be that one's cousin. And the textile manufacturer Konovalov! He has half the textile industry in his pocket, and now he's going to be minister of all industry!"

Guchkov couldn't see their faces, but their accent was educated, pretending to be genuinely working-class. Down below, though, people were buzzing excitedly, indignant.

"And the Minister of Finance is Mr. Tereshchenko! Who is this Tereshchenko? Anybody know? In Ukraine everyone knows him. He's the most famous sugar manufacturer, he's got a good twenty sugar factories! and thousands of acres of land! And how many millions of rubles! And now the people's money is getting handed over to him and the two piles are going to mingle together."

The sea of people below buzzed menacingly. Oh, how untowardly it had all begun. They'd knocked him off-track—and where was he to pick up now? And that solid, impregnable last phrase! Could you really object to that in a rally speech?

"Their Duma's reactionary! Against the people! Bourgeois! All of them in the Duma are capitalists and landowners! They chose just the same kinds for the new leadership, for the new deception of the people! And here *the gentleman Guchkov* has come to see us!"

This exclamation, like a direct blow to the belly, made his insides collapse. The speaker turned around for a second—and the undoubtedly Social Democratic agitator's face flashed.

"Oh, now he's going to tell you that he collaborated with the working class, that he's your friend. Now he's going to tell you that he safeguarded and led the Workers' Group under the War Industry Committee. That's right! Collaborators! That's who he gathered! How best to turn us into bloody flesh! How to feed us down that endless pipe our brothers can never return from! The Duma wants to wage war without end!"

Meanwhile, the thought had flashed in Guchkov's mind of somehow starting with the Workers' Group, exploiting that connection—and now they'd cut him right off. And with this break, like that sudden blow to the belly, half a step from the precipice where you come crashing down—you don't get up alive, and Guchkov felt himself getting flustered. Here they were about to let him speak and he didn't know what to say. Yes, he knew the generally polite and tame Workers' Group, but he'd never known this working mass, only theoretically. You couldn't make out a single face, a single voice—it was a mass! And a calculating hand had just tossed out bait for the crowd to snatch up? Princes! Landowners! Capitalists! Millionaires! . . . How could he climb over that?

That night, Guchkov had entered the green-leather royal salon car with gravitas as the representative of the people. And here in the oily engine depot he had climbed up awkwardly—as the representative of despised gentlemen. While the people were far below.

He hadn't felt flustered in the Transvaal under English shells, or in Manchuria under Honghuzi bullets, and Guchkov had voluntarily stayed back with the wounded in the encirclement outside Lodz, but here—he was frightened! This abyss gaped—physically, directly at his chest—between the gentleman tossed high up who no one understood and the riled crowd that had no wish to understand him.

How was he to address them? "Gentlemen?" They'd take that for mockery and he'd lose everything from his first word. "Comrades?" That would be toadying.

"What did he and the Tsar agree to there? Let him tell us that now!"

It was all cut off. The war, the people's heroism—cut off. The meeting in Pskov—cut off. Yet it was time to begin speaking. They looked around at him, gave him a little tug—or push—toward the terrible edge—they might push him off in jest—but how to address them:

"Fellow citizens!" That was bad, too, but he'd said it. He himself could hear how hollow it was, out of Roman history, not quite right, but he had to go on. He was compelled to go on. Maybe his voice was wrong, his words, too, but the training of dozens and dozens of speeches delivered meant something: the well-worn paths of basic ideas, and each word familiarly drawing ten more right ones behind it.

"Our ferocious enemy, our common enemy, is on our Russian land and wants to enslave us all—peasants, landowners, workers, and factory owners alike. Yes, I worked with your best activists, and they helped our defense— and that's how it is in all countries. Because they are Russian people, and that's how it should be. But the war could not be won as long as a rotten government stood at its head and shady men were scurrying around the Tsar. Now we have forced the Tsar to make room for a people's government! And he has agreed to concede the throne! So that nothing impedes our Russian victory!"

He didn't have the text, not that this was the setting to read it, but he repeated its main patriotic arguments . . . And then, speaking louder than he could:

"Tonight in Pskov, Emperor Nikolai the Second abdicated the Russian throne! And passed it on to his brother, now Emperor Mikhail the Second!"

"Saddled with a second?" someone shouted harshly. "Down with him, too!"

A few more voices, but very insistent, all from the same spot:

"Down with him, too!"

"We don't want him!"

"Nobody told you to!"

"Landowners!"

And the previous speaker, next to him, straining:

"They reached an agreement behind our back! The princes!"

A few of these shouts suddenly raked the dark surface of the crowd, which started buzzing hostilely, a glowering, gathering storm.

Guchkov realized all was lost. There was no bringing or holding them back. He fell silent.

Such a defeat he had never experienced in his entire oratorial life.

"Arrest him, the dear man!"

"See what he's made of!"

The Social Democrat had already grabbed him by the shoulders, arresting him.

Even simpler to push him off from here.

But from somewhere else, not where these were shouting as a group, a sonorous, powerful voice of deliverance rang out:

"Let him go, let him go! He came here as our guest. What are we—savages?"

And again a wave passed through the crowd, but now of relaxed, amiable talk.

[3 6 9 '']

(FROM THE NEWSPAPERS)

NEW GOVERNMENT. Made up of . . .

A national government has finally been created through the heroic efforts of the entire people! Joyous news like conciliatory church bells, like "Lord, now lettest". . . . The mad gallop of ministerial changes is over. . . .

RUSSIA'S RENEWAL . . .

DIGNITARIES IMPRISONED IN THE PETER AND PAUL FORTRESS.

The State Bank and all private banks will be open today for two hours to carry out all operations.

STATEMENT BY KERENSKY AND CHKHEIDZE. Minister of Justice Kerensky and Soviet of Workers' and Soldiers' Deputies Chairman Chkheidze have authorized us to announce that any decrees in which soldiers are called on not to obey officers and not to carry out orders of the new Provisional government are malicious provocation.

ROUT OF THE MOSCOW OKHRANA
ROUT OF THE CRIMINAL INVESTIGATION DEPARTMENT . . .

ORDER No. 3 FOR THE CITY OF PETROGRAD
All prisoners who have languished in prisons for their political convictions have been released. Unfortunately, criminals, too, have been given their freedom along with them. These murderers, thieves, and robbers have changed into the uniforms of lower ranks and are boldly breaking into private apartments, robbing, raping, and inspiring terror. I order all such persons immediately arrested and dealt with harshly, up to and including execution. . . .

M. Karaulov

Greetings from the Socialist Revolutionaries to A. F. Kerensky.
. . . in your person, Aleksandr Fyodorovich . . . a staunch and indefatigable fighter for democracy, leader of the revolutionary people . . .

GENERAL BRUSILOV HAS RECOGNIZED THE NEW GOVERNMENT.

The quarters of the Union of the Russian People on Likhov Lane in Moscow has been eliminated. Banners, proclamations, and pins have been confiscated.

FOOD ORGANIZATION. The old government's multiple attempts to procure grain did not have success due to the population's lack of trust in the old regime. . . . Now the population will meet the new regime halfway. . . . Immediately begin to requisition grain from its owners. . . . The Food Supply Commission, appealing to the honor and dignity of each citizen, requests that you limit yourself in the consumption of food. . . .

. . . A gray-haired old man picked up the *Revolutionary Bulletin*, crossed himself, and said: "I'll put it inside the icon."

According to rumors, former Council of Ministers Chairman **Stürmer** died en route to the Peter and Paul Fortress.

COMMISSARIAT OF ROADS AND RAILWAYS. State Duma Commissar Bublikov has sent telegraph instructions down the lines. . . . Thanks to these instructions, the removal of members of the gendarme police will not create any difficulties whatsoever. . . . Commissar Bublikov has received dispatches from all corners welcoming . . . The universal readiness to double efforts at repairing rolling stock.

FOOLISH RUMORS. For the past few days, rumors of an obviously provocative nature and spread by persons unknown have been circulating about major failures of our army on the Riga-Dvinsk front. All these rumors lack any and all foundation.

PROCLAMATION FROM THE PEOPLE'S FREEDOM PARTY . . . Citizens, put your trust in this regime, all to a man, and let the new government complete the great deed of Russia's liberation . . . May it rise up . . . may it strengthen . . . may it ignite . . . The dawn of freedom has begun to glow . . . Show the greatest self-possession . . . Let each man offer his sacrifice . . . Let all who work the land bring grain . . . Let the tradesman open his storehouses . . . Let the working class with doubled energy . . . Let old insults be forgotten in the common surge! . . .

VOICE OF DEPARTMENT OFFICIALS. During the present historic days, we, ministry employees . . . permeated with a profound awareness of the importance . . . joyfully greet and express . . . in the name of the Fatherland's free development . . .

. . . Police officers imprisoned in the State Duma have been allowed to receive bed linens from home. They have openly stated that they hadn't expected such attentive treatment.

Employees and servants of the **Winter Palace** have sent a deputation to Minister of Justice Kerensky . . . to express their feeling of solidarity with the liberated people . . .

Moscow. All gendarme officers of all Moscow railways have been arrested. On the Aleksandrovsky R.R., a clerk arrested all individuals in charge of the traffic department.

At the Khitrovy market. . . . Having learned where the vodka was, Khitrovians tied up the disguised policemen, led them to the Duma, and declared: "Here is our gift to the new government. Even we Khitrovians understand the supreme triumph of the great revolution. Maybe, if this had happened twenty years ago, we would have been among the people's

elected." The Khitrovians were invited to stop by the Duma, but they refused: "We'll go protect our corners, or else the weak will fall for alcohol
without us there."

Tver Governor Bünting was killed after offering resistance to the revolutionary movement. . . . He was an ardent reactionary.

ARREST OF RENNENKAMPF, suppressor of the revolutionary movement of 1905 . . .

TELEGRAMS OF GREETING . . . in fairly large numbers . . . From public organizations, zemstvos . . . from the Tsaritsyn garrison . . . from the clergy . . .
from the explosives factory . . . from the Bar.

ARREST OF Cnt. KOKOVTSOV. This morning, Count Kokovtsov, the
former prime minister, showed up at one of the Petrograd banks and presented a check for a fairly large sum of money . . . The detained man
protested his arrest, explaining that he had been issued a free pass for the city
and his apartment had been exempted from searches. Despite his protests,
Count Kokovtsov was delivered under convoy to the city duma. The commissar did not deem it possible to release the count and asked the State
Duma for instructions.

English operations in Mesopotamia . . .

TESTIMONY. A rumor is circulating among the Petrograd populace to the
effect that machine guns have been removed from the Cathedral of the Transfiguration . . . Because of this, the cathedral has been subjected to gunfire
several times. As the priesthood requires, I testify that there have never been
any machine guns atop the cathedral, and this has been confirmed by multiple searches by university students and soldiers. Citizens, rumors can lead
you down a path false for the fatherland. The clergy is far from any thought of
going counter to the present popular movement. Long live the renewed Russia and may all its domestic and foreign enemies be scattered.

Archpriest Adrianovsky

[3 7 0]

Kutepov was sitting up in a compartment, having failed to get a sleeping berth.

His neighbors, overflowing with the Petrograd events, were bringing them
along to Moscow—and since they couldn't sleep, due to this overflowing,
and to the crowding in the train car, they spent the entire evening and night
in lively discussion. The public sitting there was from the well-to-do class,

but, Kutepov noted, no one expressed sympathy for the Emperor's situation. They were only worried that the revolution might move on to brigandage. Everyone saw the Emperor as doomed, and they discussed the advantage over him of Grand Duke Mikhail Aleksandrovich, and what a fortunate outcome it would be if the throne passed to him because the destructive revolution would end immediately. But one gentleman turned out to be a supporter of a republic—and a long debate arose about the advantages of a republic versus a monarchy. An old lady in mourning objected, saying that after all, under a republic, couldn't Jews become officials or officers? That was beyond imagining. Another gasped that there would be no Corps of Pages, and would that mean that her son, a page, wouldn't graduate? What were the pages to do?

All of them and all their conversations nauseated Kutepov, so he pretended to sleep sitting up.

But he couldn't fall asleep all night.

He'd been convinced that there was nothing he could do in Petrograd—and only wanted to get back to his regiment as quickly as possible.

The trains were dragging, stopping, moving with great delays. They did not get to Tver until dawn.

Kutepov went out on the empty platform and stretched his legs, creaking on the snow.

Suddenly, two men walked quickly toward him.

Both were soldiers, and they were holding bared revolvers.

They approached more and more swiftly, and closer, and one cried out: "Hands up!"

There was no way he could have anticipated this. He'd been strolling in peaceful drowsiness. But he had ingrained in him a front-line persistence of nerves—ever ready for a shell to fall, or an explosion—and a physical impossibility of being frightened by anything unexpected. He merely straightened up. Naturally, he did not put his hands up. And, as he understood the event, he responded calmly and with faint mockery:

"What's the matter? Perhaps you think I have a gun? There have been so many searches, not a single officer does."

(His own revolver, fortunately, was not at his waist but in his traveling bag; he'd just not had time to get it out and put it on.)

But the soldier said:

"People on the train here are saying you fired on the people in Petrograd."

Revolvers were aimed, and there was no way to sidestep them. But if it was "people are saying," that meant they themselves weren't from Liteiny and someone else had identified him.

In his unhurried, calm bass, Kutepov answered:

"You can't believe every rumor you hear."

Right then the station bell rang abruptly—and Kutepov realized there hadn't been a second, they'd rung three right away! The caprices of revolution.

The engine whistled in response.

If they themselves had seen him on Liteiny, half a second would have been enough to riddle him with bullets then and there.

But they hesitated, and their train car was far away, there was no time to explain—so they rushed off headlong, lowering their revolvers.

A jerk passed through the train car—and they were moving.

But Kutepov's car was right there, and its platform was empty, not even a conductor.

Kutepov quickly hopped on and passed quickly through the corridor. What there couldn't be was his things in any way discomposed: front-line tidiness, everything on him, and his traveling bag buckled.

He swished past his neighbors, grabbed it, and hopped out.

The train had already picked up speed—but he managed perfectly well, jumping off while it was in motion and still even with the platform.

Without even slipping. The train pulled away.

And on this platform, which had nearly been the end of his life—no, the end was not yet in sight, in mind, no one is given to foresee it!—Kutepov walked a little more to calm down (it turned out he was far from calm) and went to see the station chief and noted the stop on his ticket.

He went to the restaurant and ate a leisurely breakfast. (While Liteiny Prospect and everything Petrograd scrolled through his mind.)

He went to the ticket office and found out that the Petrograd-Voronezh express was expected.

He punched his ticket for that.

From Voronezh he could transfer to Kiev, and to the front.

And then we'd see!

And he strolled up and down the same platform.

Documents – 13

APPEAL TO SOLDIERS
from the elected commander of the Preobrazhensky Reserve Battalion
16 March 1917

Yesterday, at a general meeting of delegates, soldiers resolved to elect: as battalion commander, Second Lieutenant Zaring; as battalion adjutant, Lieutenant Maksheev . . .

The named officers are confident that they will be given the soldiers' full trust and themselves promise to work with them amicably and as one.

. . . .

I propose that the battalion committee discuss whether they agree to call up the following officers:

—Captain Skripitsyn
—Second Lieutenant Rausch von Traubenberg
—Ensign Holthoer

. . . .

I propose releasing to their apartments without being called in to work in the battalion:
— Second Lieutenant Nelidov
— Second Lieutenant Rosen
— Second Lieutenant Ilyashevich . . .
. . . .
I propose arresting pending investigation:
— Colonel Pr. Argutinsky-Dolgorukov
— Captain Priklonsky
. . . .

Commander of the Preobrazhensky Battalion
Second Lieutenant Zaring

[3 7 1]

Vorotyntsev stepped onto the Kiev platform already knowing that his train to Vinnitsa wasn't due until after dinner. But he had to learn the news right away! Get fresh newspapers even before stamping his ticket.

He rushed past the strapping rail gendarmes (in Moscow they'd already disappeared, but along the way they were at their posts, and here, too) and to the newspaper kiosk. There was a stack of fresh newspapers being snatched up avidly. From the conversations he realized that before tonight Kiev had known nothing reliable, and all telegrams about the events had been detained. But yesterday evening, representatives of the Kiev press had been invited to see the Military District commanding officer, who announced that General Brusilov had given him permission to publish all telegrams about the upheaval. Now, vying through headlines and fonts, the newspapers had published dozens, clusters of news items, both Petrograd and Moscow ones.

Right while he was walking—as he never did and as he despised—Vorotyntsev opened one and then another and read by the ticket window and finished up on a bench he came across.

Kronstadt had gone over to the side of the revolution. . . . The Provisional Government . . . Half the names were unfamiliar, but here were Guchkov and Shingarev. That's not bad. But where was the Emperor? What was his relationship to this self-generating government? . . . The Allied powers had recognized the Provisional Government. . . . They'd been in a very big rush. . . . But where was the Emperor? Ah, here: the royal train had arrived in Pskov. . . .

And that was it. No other explanations of any kind.

But that was not so bad, then. The Supreme Commander was at Northern Army Group headquarters, that meant he was with the troops.

But the lack of clarity between him and the unauthorized government was too strange. Shouldn't it be either chased out or recognized? If the government wasn't reckoning with him anymore, then what had happened to the Emperor?

And the Kiev news. Today had been the first day of the Kiev authorized revolution, and Vorotyntsev was bringing revolution with him, as it were. The executive committee of public organizations was led by a doctor, now cobblers would be baking pies—and maybe even commanding armies? And the obliging Brusilov—knowledgeable army men called him the *Fox Commander*—had already managed to send a telegram to this doctor assuring him that the *entire Army had recognized the new government!* What idiocy was this, and how could he know it, that the Army had recognized it? *When* could it have recognized it if there had yet to be any telegrams about it here? . . .

And what about the Romanian Army Group and Sakharov? Not a word anywhere. Nor was there about any other generals. It was Brusilov's parade alone.

What was going to happen with the army group now? What was this all lurching toward?

It was puzzling, incomprehensible.

And now in Kiev, in agreement with the military authorities, the provincial Gendarme Administration and the Okhrana had been abolished, their cases and archives transferred, of course, to the Bar association, while the garrison officers . . . were permitted to create a city militia and join the Executive Committee.

Vorotyntsev sat with the newspapers in his lap, disheartened.

One thing was clear: back to his 9th Army as quickly as possible! Right now, when things were so unstable, if someone was going to act sensibly and correctly, it was General Lechitsky.

Lechitsky was one of the Russian army's most victorious generals, the only one who had been able to win in the Japanese War and to go on the offensive that awful summer of '15. While falling back, using frequent counterattacks, he took more prisoners and trophies than he had lost, and at the end of the withdrawal his was the sole army to remain on enemy soil. In the offensive of '16, our 9th had taken more territory and prisoners than any of the four advancing armies. Only Lechitsky had never promoted himself, the way Brusilov had, and the newspapers didn't shout about him. And now he was rotting away in Romania.

The most thoughtful and independent general. If anyone could sort this out and determine what to do now, it was he.

To be by his side!

[3 7 2]

Sasha had plunged into the revolution! He was never home, could not tell day from night, slept at the commissariat, and then was always awake, never did one thing continuously but kept being called away, pulled away, sent away on something else, didn't wash, ate whenever—only with youth and enthusiasm can anyone take pleasure in bearing up to all this.

Then there was jealousy: two other ensigns, Pertik and Voloshko, were acting on the Petersburg side with their detachments, but independently of the commissariat—and even of each other, although both were from the same Military Commission and had warrants from it to institute order at their discretion. How could three forces be acting on the same Petersburg side—and each at its own discretion? Sasha went to seek out those ensigns, and argued with them—but they showed him their credentials and were adamant, and then at practically the exact same time went off somewhere—both of them, with their detachments.

Meanwhile there were fewer and fewer guards; people were asking for them from everywhere. Sasha never had enough for his own detachment, and he began attaching to it freshly minted policemen with white armbands—university students, his usual merry public, and it was strange that Sasha had now risen above them like some high official.

But it was true. He felt that he now had acquired a military bearing, and voice, and appearance—all in just these past few days of revolution—and both students and workers listened to him willingly.

Then they had to patrol and conduct searches in suspicious homes and apartments. But it quickly became clear that they were again being rivaled on the Petersburg side by other patrols made up entirely of soldiers, and time and again residents would run to the commissariat to complain that they'd been robbed. The simpleton Peshekhonov was certain these were robbers dressed in soldiers' uniforms, but there weren't that many uniforms lying around anywhere, and Sasha, who had come closer to the matter, was assured that these were genuine soldiers who were thronging from the barracks, stealing, and leaving. They had to be hunted at night, and they had to go in armored cars to withstand their armed rebuff. Someone brought them an armored car just like the one Sasha had ridden in to take the Mariinsky Palace. From residents' reports, he figured out which apartment one gang had brought their loot to—and swooped down there at night, seized two orderlies, a dozen rifles and revolvers, more than sixty purses and wallets, all already cleaned out of money, and lots of timepieces—watches, pocket watches, and alarm clocks—bronze statuettes, lengths of fabric, silver spoons.

Because of these generally rather tame occupations, Sasha missed something very interesting that had also passed through their commissariat but gone to someone else: the gathering up of documents kept at the routed and half-burned Okhrana! There it was—revolution on a large scale, like the taking of the Mariinsky Palace—and Sasha had missed it. So frustrating!

Sasha managed to change guards by the commissariat and make sure no one got in without a pass—there's a lofty revolutionary occupation! But even here, when a crowd came trying to barge in and demanding guns, Sasha was away trying to catch those gangs.

Right then, a rumor spread through Petrograd that some *black automobile* had started racing through the city at night, would not let itself be stopped, and was shooting madly in all directions, inspiring terror. Sasha burned to stop that black automobile! If it was racing all through the city, then it couldn't avoid Kamennoostrovsky Prospect and would get caught!

At his five-way intersection he set up a full ambush—and lay in wait all night and stopped every single car, but there was no Black Automobile.

Suddenly, in one stopped automobile next to the driver, the lantern light picked out Motya Ryss wearing a squirrel cap and a thick red-checked scarf painstakingly wound.

"Where are you going at two in the morning?"

"An assignment," Matvei said significantly, enigmatically. They did have a pass, from the Soviet, but it said nothing about the trip's purpose. He felt the pull of envy that here Matvei was taking part in mysterious affairs—while Sasha was tromping around on an idiotic patrol.

"Well, we're here so we might as well talk for five minutes"—and he invited Matvei to the commissariat.

They turned the automobile and went in.

They still knew very little about each other. They'd only met that winter and there was a tone between them—of not wanting to cede primacy. Matvei had become more pompous and did not express the slightest surprise at Sasha's command status. He had always been more taken up with himself (which made Sasha feel bad for Veronika). His large, moist lips now pursed with disdain even. He wouldn't admit the purpose of his trip but asked:

"Did you read the leaflet?"

"Which one?"

"Against officers. My leaflet."

"What do you mean, 'yours'?"

And an argument broke out. A week before, Sasha might have read that leaflet with malicious glee—have at them and their gold epaulets! But over the past few days . . .

"So how do you see it? Can the revolution really wage battles without officers? Not trust even those who came over to its side? Not even trust me?" Sasha raised his voice at him.

Matvei remained unperturbed and sulked.

He never did reveal where he was going or why—he just left. He praised his Interdistrict men highly and said that only they and the Bolsheviks were doers.

But Sasha still felt that digging splinter, and he stopped the nighttime automobiles less assiduously, all the time continuing his argument with Matvei. This encounter had made it clear to him that he couldn't go on flailing around over nonsense. He had to do something major. He was wasting his time here.

Right then the snatches that had been floating around coalesced for him. These past few days, he had been flailing so much, almost without sleep, that he hadn't even been reading the only two newspapers. Nonetheless, in yesterday's newspaper he hadn't missed the appeal by Matvei's own

Psychoneurological Institute and the three Socialist factions—Russian, Polish, and Jewish—saying, *The revolution has not been brought to completion!*
Marvelously said! This seemed highly significant, foreboding, to Sasha! Not
brought to completion! Oh, so much more was going to happen, and so
many other individuals were going to appear, and these, today's, would
wane. These students had figured correctly! Everything still lay ahead, and
we would still proclaim our young, triumphant word!

There was another appeal, in *Izvestia*—to *Socialist officers*—to come to the
working class's aid in the organization and military training of its forces. In the
afternoon, Sasha was so sleepy, he'd read this with a languid eye, but now, after
his clash with Matvei, it suddenly became clear to him: *Socialist officer!* That
was what he was! And there weren't that many such men, maybe a dozen in
all Petrograd. Something along this line was exactly what was needed! Exactly,
in defiance of Ryss's leaflet—honest revolutionary officers needed to set about
the military organization of the masses. Here was Sasha's path!

There never was a Black Automobile. They lifted the ambush and went
to get some sleep.

[3 7 3]

*   *   *

In Reval, Nikolai II's abdication manifesto had been announced early in
the morning, but the disturbances hadn't let up in the least. A crowd had
gathered at the city prison demanding the release of prisoners supposedly
immured in a cell (a legend that had been going around for years). A delegation was admitted and found nothing. Nonetheless, they started rampaging.

The Reval fortress's commandant, Vice Admiral Gerasimov, an old Port
Arthur man, rode around the city, from rally to rally, assuring people that
the Baltic Fleet was marching in step with the people's government. He ad-
monished them very gently nearer to the prison, too. They responded with
a rock to his head. He was carried away unconscious.

*   *   *

In Kronstadt, more and more bands of sailors kept coming to the Naval
Remand Prison searching among those arrested for officers to execute.
Other sailors came, too—searching for their own mates to liberate.

*   *   *

In Petrograd, since early morning, a rumor had been going around that
the Tsar had abdicated the throne, although it wasn't in the newspapers.

There were still no streetcars running, no fancy carriages or fancy motor-cars (requisitioned, they were driving military men around). Cabs were rare. The crowd on Nevsky had lost its elegant Petersburg look. Lots of idle, merrymaking soldiers. In the manner of these revolutionary days, people were lounging not only on the sidewalks but in the thoroughfares, too, when they didn't have to move over for demonstrations.

The demonstrations, made up of whoever gathered, went on without a clear goal or route, simply rejoicing. They carried red flags and posters like religious banners, some with drawings of the terrible black hydra of counterrevolution.

People watched them from the sidewalks, pressed close together—ladies in fur collars and common women in knit scarves, men in bowlers and ordinary ear-flap hats. On their faces—joy, curiosity, bewilderment.

More officers on the streets than the night before. Without their swords.

At intersections, where there used to be policemen posted, there were now student-militia wearing white armbands. Occasionally they checked automobiles' passes. If they didn't stop, they would shoot in the air.

There were far fewer trucks with armed soldiers.

Many expensive shops were closed. But flowers and sweets were being sold.

*   *   *

Some students went around to shop stalls and told their owners that by order of the Executive Committee they had to sell eggs at no more than 40 kopecks for ten and butter for 80 kopecks a pound. Fearful of the new orders and regime, the tradesmen obeyed. Later, though, they learned that the Soviet's Executive Committee had given no such order—and they went back to the old price. Then the public got angry and there was nearly a pogrom against the shops.

In the lines: "Freedom be hanged, we still have to cool our heels."

*   *   *

Red fabric was in short supply. To make the now-mandatory red banner, yardmen were tearing the blue and white stripes off the old Russian flag.

Around the neck of the monument to Aleksandr III—a huge red tie.

In one courtyard, a female student donated her own red blouse—and it was immediately torn up into emblems of freedom.

*   *   *

The imperial coats of arms were taken off the Filippov coffeehouse on Nevsky. As were the illuminated imperial monograms with electric lights from the balcony of the building next door. People smashed crowbars against the clamps so the huge monogram broke off its railings—and fell full weight to the sidewalk, its lights shattering.

The public scattered—and was drawn back to admire it.

* * *

On the major corners there were small crowds of twenty, fifty, one hundred people, and when someone got on a barrel, a pedestal, a solid snowpile—it would become a rally. The speakers could be a student, a civilian in a worn coat, or a soldier with an unbuttoned greatcoat and under it a grimy tunic.

And of course, on the squares—at the corner of Sadovaya and Nevsky, near the Cathedral of Our Lady of Kazan, or on Senate Square, under the very hooves of Peter's horse.

"Hurrah, comrades! There is no going back to cursed autocracy!"

Here someone climbed up and argued that Aleksei and Mikhail should reign now. Educated voices answered him:

"How can you? . . . What Romanovs? . . . There should be a republic! You're a provocateur!"

And on another corner a speaker threatened:

"Comrades! You've only just managed to win great freedom, and they already want to take it away under the pretext that your freedom has to be protected!"

Shouts from the crowd:

"Liar! Nobody's taking it away! Let 'em try!"

* * *

At one such street rally, an actor from the Aleksandrinsky Theater tried to explain what a responsible ministry was. They shouted at him:

"Provocateur! Arrest him! To the Tauride Palace with him!"

* * *

The dead look of Frederiks's dark red home, burned down two days before by an angry crowd, was dispiriting. Fire had gutted the building. Its charred columns poked out of the black sockets of rubble piles. Frozen streams from firefighting had formed icicles like stalactites. Women were digging in, searching through the rubble in the courtyard. A fellow wearing a lambskin cap was squatting in the cellar, unscrewing the tap from a copper boiler.

People on the street were gawking at the burned home. Someone wearing a mangy sealskin cap: "All the good lost here, my God. Why set fire to it?" "And who are you? A disguised copper or something?" People drew round: "Search him! Bayonet him!" He started shaking and took out his passport. "Liar! Spy! How much did you get?" They let him go. He moved away with shaky steps and started running at his peril. Both the crowd and some chance soldiers rushed after him with a whoop and a whistle, loading their rifles as they went. They caught up to him on a narrow little humped bridge over a canal and pinned him to the grating: "Pity the baron, do you? Beat the bourgeois! Into the drink with him!"

*   *   *

Rumors going about town said that both Wilhelm and the Crown Prince had been killed and the German army was already laying down its weapons. People were saying there'd been more upheavals in Kronstadt today. People were saying two colonels had been killed on Vasilievsky Island.

*   *   *

Somewhere in the cellar of some police station they found confiscated *literature*, which was seized and taken to the State Duma to be turned in, but there they said there was nowhere to put it. Then they took it to the Gurevich High School on Basseinaya, where lots of different meetings were going on. They handed it out there.

*   *   *

A short, old general came up to passing soldiers on the streets and tried to convince them that they had to salute, for saluting was a symbol of the unity of the entire military family. And not saluting would destroy the army.

The soldiers grinned and didn't argue. He was a general, after all, if slightly nutty.

A military driver explained saucily to the general:

"It's saluting the epaulet, and the Tsar established the epaulet. No Tsar— no epaulet or salute."

The general:

"Do you recognize money with the Tsar's portrait?"

"But that's money."

*   *   *

Lena Taube's mother went to the State Duma to find out about her husband. She hadn't been able to get through to Kronstadt for more than two days, but a telegram had come from there saying he had been arrested. What for? Maybe he was killed? . . .

But no matter who she asked, everyone was in a hurry. They said it wasn't their responsibility, they didn't know, no list of killed and arrested officers had come in from Kronstadt.

*   *   *

A column of high school students arrived at the Tauride Palace to greet the Provisional Government. They were let into the Ekaterininsky Hall. Right then, soldiers were carrying in on their shoulders a perspiring Chkheidze, who was wiping the sweat with his handkerchief. From the height of soldier shoulders he reproached the students for welcoming the Provisional Government and not the Soviet of Workers' Deputies, which was making sure the government didn't appropriate too much power. The students applauded him.

Meanwhile, the rally in the hall continued. A Caucasus man mounted the staircase, waving his dagger, and promised to drive the Germans from Russia. They applauded him stormily.

[3 7 4]

All day yesterday it had been impossible to get to Gatchina, and he had nowhere to go from Princess Putyatina's apartment.

Then late yesterday a note had arrived from Rodzyanko. Rather than gladden, it burdened him even more: Mikhail could not avoid being regent! And Rodzyanko himself might be hanged at any moment.

And that was all. Not a sound, not a line more.

Poor fatman! . . . Quite the situation in the city . . .

But Mikhail hoped it would all work out and all the threats were exaggerated. That was his nature: not to agonize overmuch, to calm down quickly. He discussed the situation with his secretary Johnson—and fell asleep.

At six o'clock in the morning, the telephone rang in their corridor. Princess Putyatina summoned the secretary, who woke up Mikhail Aleksandrovich. Deputy Kerensky was insistent. People said he was a great power now, so now members of the dynasty were supposed to come to the telephone.

A clamorous, excited voice rang out in the receiver. He asked whether the grand duke knew what had happened yesterday in Pskov. No, I don't know anything. What happened? (Mikhail had known since the evening that the Emperor was in Pskov. Was something wrong with him?)

Kerensky didn't explain anything, but he asked permission for several members of the Provisional Government and several members of the Duma's Provisional Committee to come to the apartment.

Mikhail asked the princess. She gave her permission, fine.

As soon as he'd put down the receiver, he realized that Kerensky had not set a precise time. Soon, obviously, since he had called with such urgency when it was still dark. The hour was indecently early, but events were too unusual.

There was no going back to bed. They started moving into the daily routine while it was still dark, changing clothes, drinking coffee.

At seven o'clock, though, they still weren't there.

The drawing room had been readied. Mikhail put on his uniform with lieutenant general epaulets, the Emperor's monogram, and adjutant general aiguillettes. He sat down in the middle of the large sofa, ready to receive.

But they didn't come.

What could have happened there in Pskov? It had begun to look ominously as though the throne was being handed over to Aleksei, as Buchanan had prophesied. And Uncle Pavel.

But what extreme could have compelled Nicky? . . .

And they would foist the regency on Mikhail. Oh, they were depriving him of any kind of life! Regent? All was lost . . .

As before, there was no telephone with Gatchina. How unfortunately he and Natasha had parted, and in these days in particular! She always kept current on what was being published, written, and pronounced there. . . . Mikhail could only try to construct her attitude toward a regency, knowing that she had always been very much in favor of the Duma. Therefore, if the Duma was going to ask him to accept it—obviously, he should?

But even at eight o'clock no one had come. Or telephoned. No one had explained. He had to wait.

Nine o'clock—and still no one. He started getting sleepy, since he hadn't finished sleeping.

They drank another cup of coffee.

The long wait had somehow diminished the event's importance— whether or not to consent. He was tired of waiting.

He paced across the large drawing room carpet, clearing a passage for himself between armchairs. He languished.

Fate was toying with him! He had, by his brother's will, been excluded from service and stripped of his colonel's rank and had had property guardianship established over him. He had commanded a brigade and a division and eventually was inspector for the entire cavalry. And now they were offering him all Russia? He wasn't used to such scope; he was used to living within more constraint.

What there wasn't now was any kind of joy.

And what's more, hostility and envy would start up among the grand dukes.

Only just before ten o'clock did the front doorbells ring. Mikhail was so unaffected that he wanted to greet the visitors one by one and begin talking, but the princess insisted he go to his room and only afterward come out to those gathered. (There was room for all this. The Putyatins' apartment had as many as ten rooms, not counting the servants' wing, which ran crosswise into the courtyard.)

At Johnson's invitation, Mikhail tugged at his uniform and went out to his visitors, embarrassed that he had made such prominent men wait for him as for a lordly personage.

He then went around with even greater attentiveness, shaking the hands of those who had come. Some of the names he was hearing for the first time, and he knew no one by face except Rodzyanko. Prince Lvov made a very dear impression. While Milyukov, with his wide, powerful neck, shook Mikhail's hand in a peculiar way, detaining it while looking firmly through his glasses. Kerensky looked like a nimble youth who had sat in one place too long. And he didn't know why there was a Cossack captain, a swordsman, among the Duma members.

The grand duke invited everyone to sit. A Voltaire chair had been placed for him more or less in the middle of a semi-circle, and the guests took seats on its two flanks, on sofas and in armchairs. All the furniture here was French. Rodzyanko sat down next to the grand duke, in a similarly mighty chair, as did the head of the new government, Prince Lvov.

Joyous, springtime sun streamed through the lace curtains on the three tall windows.

First, Rodzyanko told the grand duke that the matter had gone much further than anticipated. He had not been appointed regent but had been conveyed the throne as Emperor!

Mikhail nearly jumped out of his chair. What was this? Nicky had not only abdicated? But also . . . ? Though he knew perfectly well Mikhail's distaste for matters of state!

Rodzyanko suggested they discuss what to do.

Mikhail was stunned. They had not allowed him to prepare for news such as this. And to discuss it now, right away, in front of everyone? All these worthy, educated, well-known men had come to see him—to discuss this? While he—he hadn't yet dared even think about the dimensions of his new position.

Confused, he asked them to explain. What now? To share their thoughts.

First in importance, prominence, and volume to speak was Rodzyanko. Mikhail listened to him with respect and trust. Rodzyanko began by saying that the decision would depend on the grand duke. He could give a perfectly free answer. There would be no pressure on him. But he had to give his answer now.

The Duma president spoke a little hoarsely, perhaps, but that did not diminish the significance. He wasn't expressing his own opinion but pointing out the one indubitable thing: how things had to be. He explained that the very conveyance of the throne to the grand duke was irregular. According to law, the reigning emperor could abdicate only for himself but not in anyone's favor, and the conveyance could come about only according to the line of succession, that is, in this instance, only to Aleksei. The act of abdication did not say that his son was abdicating the throne. Thus, the entire conveyance of the throne to Mikhail Aleksandrovich was temporary and could only give rise to brutal legal disputes.

That was how the grand duke understood it, too. Why had his brother conceived of such a thing? Why had he done this?

This ambiguity would give legal support to those individuals who wanted to bring down Russia's entire monarchy. Given such a shaky foundation and the mounting revolutionary mood of the masses and their leaders, in this troubled, alarming time, accepting the throne would be insanity on the grand duke's part.

Mikhail thought so, too.

He would reign for a matter of hours, perhaps, Rodzyanko explained—and tremendous bloodletting would begin in the capital and then civil war would break out. The grand duke had no loyal troops at his disposal, and he himself would be killed, as would all his supporters. Leaving Petrograd was impossible; they weren't letting out a single automobile or train.

Actually, it was Rodzyanko who had urged him to come to Petrograd; had he stayed in Gatchina, he could have left freely.

Who would dare and what right did he have to ignite a civil war when there was a war with a fierce foreign enemy under way? On the contrary, in this terrible moment we should all be striving not to arouse passions but to assuage them. Assuage the agitated sea of the people's life.

Rodzyanko spoke authoritatively and at length, restating the same thing in new words and covering the same ground, but even if it had been much less, Mikhail had been convinced from his first words and did not reproach Rodzyanko for turning around since the day before, that he himself just yesterday had tried to convince Mikhail to take full responsibility, whereas now he was advocating for the opposite. He should not take the throne—and praise God! Before he could master that terrible thought, Mikhail learned with even greater joy that it was invented and false. What was there to say? Can a mind really withstand all this political confusion? Away! Away! Stop! To the front!

Movement began. Brought from the antechamber—some man brought from somewhere—was a manuscript copy of the Emperor's Manifesto certified by the Commissar of Roads and Railways. They gave it to the grand duke to examine. A stranger's handwriting altogether, though legible, but the words were Nikolai's, and Mikhail tried to imagine why he had written in someone else's hand. He started reading. He already knew what it was about—but it was all new. He couldn't consider it carefully, but what stung and struck him was this:

"Not wishing to be separated from Our beloved son, We bequeath Our heritage to Our brother."

There was something offensive here. He'd thought about but hadn't asked his brother. He guarded his son like the apple of his eye—and didn't spare his brother, foisted the throne on him. And—

". . . We to Our Brother to administer the affairs of state in full union with the national representatives. . ."

Fine to bequest that. So why didn't he himself do that? Mikhail wasn't insulted, but it was insulting nonetheless.

Meanwhile, Prince Lvov started talking on the other side of Mikhail's chair. Rodzyanko had a hoarse, damaged voice, but the prince's was quite untouched, all bright and cleansed. He himself was so handsome, so roundly combed and cut, and looked and expressed himself so well-meaningly—a marvelous, calm man who he would never want to insult with an objection or disagreement. But it was also very hard to understand from his rounded phrases what opinion the prince himself held. Accept the throne or not?

Lvov's speech was lulling, and Mikhail's attention bogged down.

Mikhail noticed that some deputies, having settled into the upholstery, were practically dozing off, struggling. But twitchy Kerensky quickly turned his head at each person's words. And also one foppish young man whose name Mikhail couldn't recall startled every time the door opened, at every sound in the front hall, and sat high in his chair.

Still, from what he could catch from Lvov's smooth speech, he was of the same opinion as Rodzyanko.

After Lvov, they exchanged glances. Maybe there was no need to say more? Why had they spent so long trying to convince him?

No, now Milyukov wanted to speak. He stated so imperiously from his sofa and coughed for reinforcement. No one objected, least of all Mikhail.

Milyukov's face was sullen and had become so tense as to wrinkle. He made a major effort and filled his chest so that he looked like an angry gray-haired teacher, and his voice was so husky, it was as if he had shouted himself hoarse in ten unruly classes. From his very first words he spoke angrily and demandingly:

"Your Imperial Highness! There can be no question of your not accepting the throne! Not even a thought! Your responsibility to your birth, to your three-hundred-year dynasty, to Russia! . . . Emperor Nikolai the Second has abdicated for himself and his son, but if you abdicate as well, that will be an abdication for the entire dynasty. But Russia cannot exist without a monarchy. The monarch is its center! Its axis! It is the sole authority known to all. The sole concept of authority. And the basis for our oath. Preserving the monarchy is the only possible way to preserve order in the country. If it cannot rest on that symbol, the Provisional Government simply will not survive to a Constituent Assembly."

Mikhail listened in amazement. Milyukov. He knew that name. He was the throne's chief critic. And now—to be saying this? There had to be something behind this! And what a grave thing he had said: Russia cannot exist without a monarchy! And it was true. Of course it couldn't. That much Mikhail understood.

But if Nicky had abdicated anyway, who else was there to accept it? And if Mikhail, too, abdicated—what then?

Milyukov added:

"Civil war will not begin if you accept the throne, but it will if you *don't*! And that will be deadly given the foreign war. Total chaos and a bloody mess will ensue. . . . But you—you hold Russia's simple salvation in your hands. Accept the throne! This is the only way our new regime can gain a foothold. We must all cling to tradition, stability, and the monarchy, which is the only thing the people know and recognize!"

This Mikhail understood! He just wanted all this to gain a foothold without him. He hadn't expected this of his brother. But if there was no other solution, how could he not come to the rescue? If the situation turned out to be so ominous and desperate, then he had to come to the rescue, didn't he? It was a kind of military duty, then, wasn't it?

Meanwhile, two new people joined the gathered eight: Guchkov, whom he knew; and with him a rather lightweight fop with a pointy mustache.

They did not introduce themselves or greet anyone, merely bowed to the grand duke, but apparently were known to all here. To Milyukov's ponderous speech, they silently took chairs in the closed circle directly opposite the grand duke. Milyukov did not miss a beat with their arrival.

"Your Imperial Highness! If you do not accept the throne now, there will be a new Time of Troubles in Russia, and possibly one even more devastating and lengthy. *That* is bloodshed we must fear—more, perhaps, than the temporary and minor bloodshed right now. Mikhail Vladimiro-vich has correctly drawn the capital scene here, indeed we have all seen it, but I definitely do not agree with his conclusion. Yes, right now, here in the capital, it is difficult to find a loyal unit for support. But they do exist in Moscow, I think. They exist throughout the country. The entire field army is a loyal force! You must go there immediately—and you will be invincible."

The experienced old politician's powers of persuasion had a strong effect on Mikhail. Indeed, the entire army was at the Emperor's disposal. He had only to go to it.

Oh, why had his brother's abdication found Mikhail not at the front? Had he stayed with his Native Division, he could have taken lead of the troops immediately.

But even now slipping out of Petrograd was probably not that hard. There wasn't a solid cordon around the city. He could wait for tonight, at worst, change clothes, and in the night—in two automobiles? Or even on foot? Mikhail found slipping away as a cavalry mission understandable and not difficult.

And yet, his brother had been with all the troops, with full authority—but he had abdicated.

He was once told a prediction—he didn't believe it or take it seriously—that he would be Mikhail II and the last Russian emperor.

"Your Imperial Highness!" Milyukov pressed on without stopping, constantly spinning the same thing in a new way. "We are the first who won't survive this stormy time without you. We **beg** of you, both for help . . ."

The sun lit the room so powerfully, that it made whoever it fell on squint.

[3 7 5]

How General Alekseev wanted a conclusive and final regime! How he wanted that today there not be any new shake-up. After all, things seemed to have fallen into place. A Supreme Commander had been appointed and wholly legitimately, by the will of His Majesty the Emperor, who had not yet abdicated at the time. Just as legitimately, a prime minister had been appointed. And he had selected the necessary complement of ministers, which had been announced today both in Petrograd and in the Moscow newspapers. It was natural now for General Alekseev to compose a circular telegram-decree informing all troops about the appointments that had taken place.

He now also had the freedom to give orders against the gangs. Since they were definitely not deputations from the State Duma, he could now send the Western Army Group a categorical military order to initiate energetic actions against that gang in Polotsk, or wherever it was, and against other such purely revolutionary, unbridled gangs as would try to seize control of the railways or to infiltrate the army itself. Should such gangs appear, it was advisable, rather than disband them, to try to arrest them and, if possible, immediately appoint a field court-martial and carry out the sentence immediately.

Nothing terrible had happened in Petrograd itself, it turned out. He had spoken that morning with the Naval General Staff, where the captain on duty had reassured him that everything was coming to rights in the capital, there was no slaughter of officers going on, nor had there been, that was all nonsense, and all the officers were alive and well. The Provisional Government was strong and its authority was unshaken.

Go judge for yourself. And here he had believed Rodzyanko.

But GHQ did not have eyes on the ground to see for itself what was happening in Petrograd. The Petrograd situation was so puzzling, it might as well have been the moon.

From all the way in Odessa the district commander had sent a telegram: Release all political prisoners by way of appeasement? And saying that just such an instruction from the Minister of Justice had already arrived in Kherson. Perhaps. But why wasn't all this appeasement and calming preceded by a formal announcement of the new Emperor Mikhail II? Why must his name be hidden from the people and why not call on the army to swear an oath?

For Alekseev, this was completely incomprehensible, and even more alarming with each passing hour.

Here, even Evert had telegraphed energetically about this alarm. When could he expect to receive instructions? Shouldn't it be announced to the troops that there was a Manifesto but it had been delayed? And what were the reasons for the delay?

Brusilov asked for guidance as well.

How could Alekseev respond to all this? He himself was increasingly baffled. He had even begun to suspect some sort of intrigue. He was making his way through a strange, impassable forest and getting scratched, ill-equipped as he was for this political gossip, where topographical maps, compasses, and military commands were of no use. Politics was binding him hand and foot with its creeping vines.

If Petrograd was calm, what was Rodzyanko so afraid of? What was compelling him to negotiate with leftists, and why was he intent on making concessions to them? How many nights had he repeated that the new regime had been recognized by all, established and unitary, which was why he had dictated so imperiously to the front. But there were soldier mutinies each and every night?

All of a sudden a sharp, unpleasant suspicion struck Alekseev. Had the Samovar *simply fabricated* this for his own political purposes? Why had he contradicted himself and been contradicted by others so many times?

And why had Alekseev put so much trust in him? It was simply that he'd heard from no one else from Petrograd these past few days. And Rodzyanko had stated everything so confidently.

Right then (why not earlier?) he received a copy of the same conversation with Rodzyanko from Ruzsky. It turned out that Rodzyanko had telegraphed Ruzsky an hour earlier about delaying the Manifesto. (He'd gotten into the habit. What was this new manner of bypassing GHQ and addressing the army group commanders?) He spoke with Ruzsky much more candidly, saying Mikhail's ascension as emperor was *totally unacceptable*! That talks had been held with the workers' deputies—and had settled upon a Constituent Assembly, which—this is how it could be understood—*would determine Russia's form of government*?

Oof! It felt like a bayonet had been thrust between his ribs. Here it was! This is what it was about! Alekseev, the simpleton, hadn't understood why Rodzyanko had mentioned the Constituent Assembly. This was why!

Was this also why Rodzyanko had delayed the Manifesto? Had he been digging under Emperor Mikhail? And even, apparently, under the entire dynasty? . . .

Wasn't this why the new Emperor was in their way? They wanted to extend this indeterminate condition, didn't they? And during that time end the dynasty? Oh, the scoundrels! They'd conspired with the leftists—about what? Overthrowing the dynasty? There was a phrase there: "does not preclude the dynasty's return." As if it had already been dispensed with.

So Rodzyanko might well be the chief republican? The revolution's leader? . . . Or at least a pawn in the leftists' hands?

And Alekseev had listened to him—and collected the abdication from the commanders? . . .

So General Alekseev had fallen into a trap! . . . A trap! Had Rodzyanko deceived him, taken advantage of him?

How could he have supposed such guile in him?

This pinned Alekseev down in his hard chair. Such a fool, such a fool—he couldn't remember ever in his life having been set up . . .

The disgrace! The disgrace!

He had never allowed tribulations to get the better of him, though. He had always felt and stated that a commander's touchstone was to preserve clarity of mind and calmness of spirit in the face of failures. He had to act. If the Supreme Commander had been at GHQ now, Alekseev would have gone and honestly admitted his full disgrace.

But now, while he was in Tiflis? Right now Alekseev himself had to decide on a measure against Petrograd.

But did all his military experience and all his strategic knowledge give him no hint as to what he could undertake against this garrulous company? Troops had already been sent and recalled. He had been misled in telegraph conversations. It was an unusual situation—and he couldn't come up with anything. Except to report to Tiflis, to the Supreme Commander.

Not that he was going to decide anything before he got here. And that might well take more than a week.

Nearby were only Lukomsky and Klembovsky—who wouldn't do.

Suddenly, Alekseev had a thought. Yesterday, when the need had been to incline the Emperor toward abdication, he had gone to all the army group commanders. He had borrowed this idea from Rodzyanko, who had been bombarding the commanders with telegrams. Now, too, all the commanders besides Ruzsky were in the dark, asking questions, and waiting for answers. Why had the Manifesto been delayed? Some explanation was due them in any case. An honest exposition of what had happened had to be composed, everything as it was now understood—in restrained words, of course, without giving vent to emotion. Composed and sent out. That would also serve as his report to the Supreme Commander.

Alekseev had never known a military situation that could not be summarized and then resolved with a single, terse, practical document. Just composing the document helped him bring clarity to his thoughts and calm his spirit. The act itself imposed discipline.

He sat down then and there to write the circular telegram to all the army group commanders. That this was in clarification of their questions about the Manifesto's delay. This morning the State Duma president had requested this delay from GHQ, but the reason for his insistence was more clearly laid out in his conversation with the Northern Army Group commander. Rodzyanko had been dreaming and trying to convince them that the Emperor's accession could be put off and they could wait, with the Provisional Duma Committee and a responsible ministry, for a Constituent Assembly. But the

Manifesto had already become known in some places and keeping an act of the highest importance secret was unthinkable. Apparently there was no unanimity in the State Duma or its Provisional Committee, and the leftist parties were putting powerful pressure on them. Rodzyanko's communiqués held no candor or sincerity. His basic motifs might prove incorrect and aimed toward inciting military leaders to join in decisions made by radical elements as if it were an inevitable fact. The troops of the Petrograd garrison had been thoroughly propagandized and were both harmful and dangerous for everyone. A danger had been created for the entire field army.

All this was so. It was laid out intelligently and not at length—and with a few emphases concerning Rodzyanko. But what had he written all this for? And what did he propose undertaking against the danger?

Obviously (after waiting for instructions from the Supreme Commander), to demand that the Duma president implement the Manifesto!

But if he didn't? And more than likely he wouldn't . . .

He grasped at an idea, and it took shape: repeat the Rodzyanko maneuver and collect the commanders' opinions. Yesterday they had been more powerful than the Emperor himself.

Only GHQ could make this even more persuasive: assemble the commanders themselves! A conference.

Yes! Now it was clear to Alekseev. Then they would decide everything. But without Nikolai Nikolaevich, he did not dare order them to assemble and could not order a date to be scheduled. That was beyond his rights. All he could do was *propose* such a conference to the commanders. If the grand duke was still not in Mogilev then, then they would assemble no later than 21–22 March.

In conclusion:

"The collective voice of the army's highest ranks and their terms must become known to everyone and exert influence on the course of events. I request that you express your opinion as to whether you deem such a congress in Mogilev appropriate."

This is how we will assemble and stand up to the tottering, inconsistent government.

But then, the commanders-in-chief were also just a handful, and if they were truly to consult, then let's follow Evert's idea:

"Perhaps you will deem it necessary to inquire also of the commanders of the armies."

He finished it—and took the telegram to the telegraph room on his own two feet.

As long as he was writing it, he was in action. But when he parted with it, the action ceased.

And he was left alone with his remorse.

What on earth had transpired? . . .

[3 7 6]

The Manifesto had been delayed in the Western Army Group—although here and there it might have gotten through to the troops, but then what?

They delayed it—but that was no solution, not indefinitely.

They delayed it—but they had to avoid a slip-up like that. Stop the twitching, and behave with dignity.

And what was the reason? What unknown things were changing there at the top?

GHQ delayed it and said not a word. And Evert had them send a telegram asking when it could be announced. The Manifesto's delay was highly undesirable! Otherwise, then, he needed to announce the chief of staff's telegram about the delay to the troops. And to know the reasons. Tell us!

The GHQ's reply: Be patient! The chief of staff is composing another telegram.

But they didn't send it.

Meanwhile, feeling a surge of confidence, Evert now told GHQ in a new tone that it could be this Manifesto or some other one, but it had to be announced to the troops with full solemnity and a divine service performed for the health of the newly ascended monarch. The Western Army Group commander was waiting for the necessary instructions to be given to the military clergy.

The great act of a new Russian monarch's ascension could not be reduced to the clicking of Hughes wires.

Meanwhile, although the Emperor was being hidden away, civilian telegraphs had already informally brought the new government's roster. You mean the government could exist without a monarch? Apparently it could, since they had transmitted this. And since yesterday they had let the Petrograd news get through, there was no sense holding back this news. Come to terms with it and let it through.

Actually, should a military general be so concerned about what kind of government there was in Petrograd? They had changed before. His business was obeying GHQ. And maintaining the dignity of a commander-in-chief.

Just try to maintain it, though! Had anyone ever indicated where the limit to this dignity lay? Through civilian telegraph offices, an instruction from Kerensky, the new Minister of Justice, reached Evert's headquarters on the release of all political prisoners in Minsk Province! And on the fact that a new military commandant with *special* authority was on his way to Kaluga (Western Army Group zone)!

So that's how it was! What was to be done now? Resist? Submit? There was no other choice.

The new regime had immediately shaken him and grabbed him by the throat.

Evert felt troubled and vile. As if he had let slip all the might of his Western Army Group. As if the entire army group had remained in place—but was no more.

Suddenly! Joyous news. Alekseev himself telegraphed saying that the deputations were pretenders, that these were simply unbridled revolutionary gangs—and he should take the most energetic measures!—and seize them and try them in a field court martial!

So there it was! That's our way! Language like that raised no doubts! It was long in coming!

Evert had been tossed back and forth for two full days, from hot to cold and back, but *this* return was joyous and his strength had returned! An energetic Evert gave immediate orders to assign parties under firm officers to the main hub stations now without gendarmes. They had to hurry and make up for the two lost days.

Everything could still be made up for!—and those regiments turned back to Petrograd, twofold, and threefold!—if His Majesty Emperor Mikhail II so commanded!

But for some reason he was hiding and had allowed his ascension to be hidden.

Meanwhile, bald and imperturbable Kvetsinsky with the shaggy eyebrows brought Alekseev's new and very long telegram. Alekseev explained to the commanders that the men in Petrograd and Rodzyanko had been deceiving them all! Even here he did not explain why the Manifesto had been delayed up until now—but there was some Petrograd conspiracy involved. Alekseev, however, was going to insist.

Well, at last! Not a firm tone, but at least firm notes. Why hadn't this kind of sober speech come from Alekseev yesterday? Had there not been this whole blanking out by weak-kneed generals, might there not have been an abdication?

Alekseev was now proposing calling a conference in Mogilev of the commanders in order to establish unity. And in this way exert influence on the course of events.

Hang it all, yes, twenty times yes—of course, that was the way! Evert's response was Yes! Yes!—the natural response of a general in the field army, unless his command had weakened.

But they allowed him, as he had requested, to consult with his army commanders. Another two or three hours wouldn't be a loss at this point, so consult he would.

[3 7 7]

The entire journey back from Pskov, the simplest thing somehow never occurred to Guchkov: what if Mikhail refused? For some reason, he hadn't imagined such a thing. Only when they were shouting at the engine depot and wanted him either dragged out, or arrested, or worse—did this notion occur to him, that Mikhail might not even last as Tsar?

The depot had shaken Guchkov. He knew the cold hatred of duelists facing off, but mass crowd fury was much much worse! How could he counter it? He was powerless. Deafened. Back from death's door.

When he had stepped into the heavy air of the meeting on Million-naya, Guchkov had started to realize that, if Mikhail refused, nothing could be done.

Only then did he feel a stab of guilt over having carelessly accepted the Tsar's abdication. For some reason, he hadn't anticipated this step from Nikolai (but for Nikolai it was so natural to save his son for himself; there could have been no other step). Guchkov had been flustered and in Russian style had made a generous gesture—he had given him his son.

And now the entire throne had begun to totter.

With even greater sympathy did Guchkov now listen to Milyukov's inexhaustible speech. He knew Milyukov's exceptional ability to plant himself firmly in an occupied position, vary his arguments, and stay put—but today even he was amazed at the inexhaustibility of the Milyukov argumentation in his speech, which seemed endless, at least an hour long. The inexhaustibility lay in the fact that, after going through all his arguments on how to encourage Mikhail's decisiveness, he revealed a new set of arguments for convincing his skeptical colleagues that there was no other solution for them, either. And then he covered it with another new roof, saying that there was no other solution for anyone, for Russia itself.

Understandably, he argued with that kind of conviction not only for pre-serving the monarchy in general but also, in the general interest, for the preservation of a weak, power-averse monarch with whom it would be easy to govern. But if they, the rest of them, did not understand this, then he was going to starve them out.

Guchkov himself, still under the impression of his failure at the depot, having tested the popular waters in real life, was now discovering more and more distinctly how all their Dumas, speeches, committees, and groups so far had been for naught. If a firm authority did not hold over everyone in Russia, they would be swept, washed away in an instant.

He even espied this promise in Milyukov's remonstrances (only it could-n't be said out loud): if a force were assembled sufficient to defend Mikhail, then a Constituent Assembly wouldn't be needed, right? And yesterday's humiliating agreement with the Soviet could be disregarded?

More than that, according to Guchkov, they could arrest all those ras-cals, that Executive Committee?

Tall, gaunt Mikhail, very youthful, indeed ten years younger than the ab-dicated Tsar and not burdened by imperial cares—seemingly rather weak, though, despite his agile, military figure—tried to listen and then evidently got distracted. He held himself quite simply, easily changed relaxed positions in his chair, and occasionally cast his eyes over all those present—not the most expressive faces—seeking sympathy and decision. Surprise never left the upper part of his face. There was even something feminine in his habits. No, he wasn't up to it!

Gray-haired Milyukov kept repeating that the monarch was Russia's sole unifying center fully recognized by the people—and the decision being taken now should be such as not to leave Russia without a monarch. The scale of the shock to the popular psyche if the Russian peasantry suddenly was left without its Tsar was unimaginable. The Provisional Government was a fragile boat and would drown in the ocean of popular upheaval. The borderlands would start to fall away and Russia would fall apart. No one present could be certain he would survive in this great collapse.

More than anything, Guchkov was struck by the purport of Milyukov's speech. Soon it would be fifteen years that they had been sparring in the public arena—and never had he encountered in his opponent such dazzling insight, never had he heard from him such brilliant speech, never had he experienced such a pull to join forces with him. It was amazing how Milyukov had suddenly managed to rise above his unvarying political sympathies—and see Russia unobstructed in its entirety, exactly as it was.

But Guchkov surveyed the circle of men sitting there—the darkly wide-eyed other Lvov, the foolish dandy Tereshchenko, the sham and enigmatic Nekrasov—his recent associates, to say nothing of the unbearable contortionist Kerensky, and saw that they were in an unassailably joyous mood and were not at all frightened by Milyukov's scary words.

Milyukov's face turned deep red and his mustache bristled. He was now insisting not so much for Mikhail as he was trying to convince his colleagues that the foundations of Russia's state order had to be observed. That the continuity of the state machinery had to be preserved without question. That if the old machinery were suddenly to cease to exist, a new one would not take hold. That the leap from autocracy directly to a republic was too great and such experiments in history never ended well. He tried to convince them that in their hands right now was the happy chance to ensure the monarchy's constitutional character. In this way, their government would be constitutional, not provisional. The danger of hastily assembling a Constituent Assembly during time of war would fall away.

But to whom was he proposing all this? For whom was he laying out his historiosophical conceptions? Who among them could understand and appreciate them? Guchkov surveyed the faces and was filled with despair. The self-intoxicated, corpulent, flabby Rodzyanko was an Octobrist who had joined up with the leftist Kerensky, who was also intoxicated with himself and was, moreover, an instigator with a theatrical flair. Mellow Prince Lvov. And again that unbalanced idiot Vladimir Lvov, and yet another dolt—the big Cossack Karaulov. And another unbalanced one, the romantic Shulgin, though that one at least understood ideas.

Rodzyanko's position—against accepting the throne and for abdication—was especially surprising. Right now he was acting against his own convictions—after all, he was an ardent monarchist—and even against his personal interests, for he was close to Mikhail.

Right then there was not only no one to speak out with authority, there was no one to listen and understand intelligently. Tereshchenko, obviously frightened, was worriedly turning his head from side to side. Had Guchkov really encouraged this man and the ambiguous Nekrasov to join a coup plot? What good were they anyway?

Remarkably enough, Milyukov did finish.

They moved on now to the protests and debates, but decided to take a break. The grand duke went out, but everyone wanted to hear from the new arrivals about Nikolai's abdication. Milyukov approached point-blank, though, and harshly reproached him (you could hear his bitter triumph over his rival): How could he have accepted the abdication in Mikhail's favor so carelessly? Everyone on all sides reproached him, saying this was not in his remit, and how could Guchkov have agreed?

But he could not admit out loud that he'd made a bad mistake (all the more frustrating because he himself realized this) and could not defend himself. He himself didn't understand how this had slipped through his fingers, and he couldn't admit he'd taken pity on the Tsar's fatherly feelings. In the thick of things this went unnoticed. He had taken the wrested act into his hands like the victory of a lifetime—and this was where he'd blundered.

This was why even talking with Milyukov, despite his sympathy for his position, was unbearable.

On the other hand, Shulgin, always eager to paint a picture, ran on with his story. As if the events of the street and the Tauride Palace had left room for this, everyone wondered, How exactly? In what building? How had Nikolai behaved? Objected? What had he looked like when he was signing?

But a no lesser action was taking place right now, and they could not delay any longer. People had been scorching Milyukov in the corridors, everyone was against him—and now it was time for the session. They summoned the grand duke and everyone resumed their seats.

The grand duke's face was pure, carefree, almost childlike, except for the blond mustache. And innocent blue eyes. It was unimaginable that just now, there, in the next room, he was struggling to make a choice for the state.

Now Kerensky came forward to speak, having been in the first rank these past few days. His jerky, self-confident manner had intensified drastically. He bore himself with the aplomb that he alone here represented the revolutionary masses and he alone knew the popular wishes exactly. His moment had come, and victory rang out in the passion of his speech.

"Your Highness! Gentlemen! In coming here, to this meeting, I have forgone party principles! My party comrades would *tear me to pieces*, comrades, if they knew. But inasmuch"—with all the fire of his voice—"as I have always consistently implemented the will of *my party*, they trust me. Just yesterday. Just yesterday!"—he exclaimed, reveling in the thought uttered and the uttering voice—"there might have been an agreement on a constitutional monarchy. However"—and his voice became ominous, as did his eyes—"after the *machine guns from the churches*! fired on the people! the indignation was too great!" He himself was exhausted from this indignation but recognized the justice of it. "Your Highness! In accepting the crown, you will be laying yourself open to popular indignation and"—he craned his narrow head and lowered his tone—"you yourself may perish." And even lower: "And we shall all perish with you. . . ."

They shrank. Kerensky had convinced them more than Milyukov had with his theoretical scheme.

But Mikhail looked at him calmly, as if he were even a half-absent listener. He face was open and his expression pure of heart.

Whereas Kerensky, of course, was concerned for himself. If there was a monarchy, how could he account for himself to the Soviet of Workers' Deputies? And—he would have to leave the government. The deft orator left out only that he would be the first, along with the Soviet of Deputies, to prevent Mikhail from joining the troops. He skipped agilely from one sensitive string to the next quivering one. And he acted his part, as on the Duma tribute, gasping for air, letting his voice swoop:

"Your Highness! You know, everyone knows, it's no secret, I have always dared talk about this: my convictions are republican. I am opposed to a monarchy. . . ." And a pause after these, so recently terrifying words. "Right now, though, I don't want to touch on my own convictions. I am even disregarding them. . . . I have come here—for the good of the fatherland! . . . Therefore allow me to speak to you in a different way. As one Russian to another. . . . Pavel Nikolaevich Milyukov is wrong. By accepting the throne, you will not save Russia. Quite the contrary! You will destroy it! Russia can be appeased no more. I know the mood of the masses, the workers and soldiers! The workers of Petrograd will not allow your accession. Right now, there is drastic discontent everywhere—specifically against the monarchy, monarchy in general, monarchy as such! It is the attempt to preserve the monarchy that would be the impetus for a bloody drama! And in the face of a foreign enemy, as you yourself know, Russia must have complete unity. Will a bloody civil war ensue? What a horror! Does Your Highness really want to occupy the throne at such a price? . . . No! I am certain of it! Therefore, I appeal to Your Highness . . . as one Russian to another . . ."—he was gasping for air and on the brink of tears—"I implore you, implore you! Make this sacrifice for Russia! For Russia's sake, for the sake of its serenity and integrity. Renounce the throne!"

He had no more emotional strength to speak. In any case, he had said everything, laid it all out.

Oh, the scoundrel! Guchkov would have to speak. (How everything had changed. Milyukov and Guchkov, the leader of the opposition and the chief conspirator, had become the main pillars of the throne. Only recently, who would have believed it?) Had the deputies reached an agreement without him that one would come out in favor, another against, and that was that? Oh no!

Guchkov was not of the same manner or age as Kerensky. It was indecent to show off like that when the actors were together backstage. Guchkov spoke without any ornamentation, as succinctly as he could, and his voice truly was weary and ragged—from all the speeches, all the trips, Vyazemsky's death, and the depot today.

On the other hand, he spoke with full conviction, the conviction that the weary look of an elderly man gives, saying how everything was bad and the one way all might be saved. By accepting the crown, naturally. Out of his love for Russia, indeed, as a Russian, the grand duke must accept it. He had to saddle himself with the difficult role of national leader in the new Time of Troubles that had already begun. Some were saying that this was risky even for his own life, but this argument, of course, could mean nothing for a man as valorous as the grand duke. Finally (Guchkov had come up with this in the last hour), there was another solution. If the grand duke could not bring himself to become Emperor, let him accept the regency for a vacant throne, "ad interim regent of the Empire." Let him act as "the nation's protector." He could even limit himself more and promise formally that upon the war's conclusion he would hand over all power to a Constituent Assembly. Just so he accepted this authority now, just so he created an instantaneous and stable continuity of supreme authority in the state. How could one fail to see, who could fail to agree, that *without this* Russia was done for?

Guchkov spoke in hopes of convincing him without fail. Of dispelling, overpowering the Petrograd intoxication to which people succumbed only in that city. He spoke, all the while looking at the forty-year-old grand duke, an unquestionably fine, pure, modest, and delicate man, weak-willed, unfortunately, but also possessed of military courage. Such was the combination. And Guchkov hoped he would accept his arguments and accept his tone and hoped the outcome would be good. Guchkov sensed only this one shortcoming in his speech: he should have proposed some decisive, practical action for the next few hours, but he couldn't think of one. He realized that an action lay somewhere on the surface. He rummaged and searched—but could not find one.

Of course, he assumed the grand duke's secret flight from Petrograd—to Moscow or the front—but it was inappropriate to say so out loud.

And he also had to verify whether the Petrograd garrison was entirely in the hands of the Soviet. Might he perhaps base himself in Petrograd, too?

At first, no major debates were planned. But after two such decisive speeches in favor, the low rumbling "against" got stronger. And not speaking coherently, one and then another tossed out individual phrases, not fundamental considerations for Russia, but in essence the same fear. They were frightening themselves and the grand duke, saying that accepting the throne was perilous, ruinous. And at the head of all these cowards was Rodzyanko. (So frightened by the soldiers?) Even the exhausted Shulgin suddenly, out of some enthusiasm, joined this chorus. He had taken a long step away from monarchism! Someone even expressed the thought that if the grand duke accepted the throne, he would immediately redden it with dynastic blood, for in Petrograd they would immediately slaughter all the members of the dynasty who were there.

No one spoke at length, but it became clear that everyone here except Guchkov and Milyukov was against him accepting the throne.

No one spoke at length, but a solid front emerged—and Milyukov became indignant and demanded the floor again and fought for it with his hoofed insistence.

A din of objections rose up: you can't a second time! Kerensky objected resoundingly and very freely. But Milyukov's authority had loomed over the majority of Duma members for years, and they didn't dare forbid him to speak.

Guchkov supported this, of course. The throne had to be salvaged no matter how hopeless, as on Devil's Bridge over the abyss. For both of them, there was now a fork in the road: either remain in the monarchical government or leave the republican one. Whoever was defeated now had to leave the government and not get in its way.

Speaking, Milyukov was now sterner, sinister even. His mustache still had a streak of black, but his smoothed head was entirely gray, and all his features had become sharper in response to the willfulness of these youngsters who didn't understand their own good. Everyone could see what was happening in Petrograd. Nothing could be done without shoring up the public order, and doing that required a strong authority. But a strong authority could rest only on a symbol familiar to the masses. And if one were to lay claim to joining the government, one had to have a concept of the Russian state and its traditions. Without that, without the monarch, the Provisional Government wouldn't last even until the Constituent Assembly convened: before that could happen, total anarchy would break out and any sense of statehood would be lost.

No one dared interrupt Milyukov except for Rodzyanko, who was sitting there looking dazed—but Milyukov cut him off, as if he himself were President. And kept on speaking. He spoke for a long time, as if afraid to stop. As long as he was still talking, the monarchy would continue to exist in Russia; the moment he stopped, it would end.

Yes! he insisted, insisted desperately, accepting authority threatened great risk both for the life of the grand duke, and actually for the ministers, too—but they had to take that risk for the fatherland's sake. Even if the odds of success were one in a million, they had to take the risk! This was our shared responsibility, our responsibility for the future. However, Milyukov thought, outside Petrograd matters stood not badly at all—and there the grand duke would be able to assemble a military force. For example, in

Moscow, according to fresh information, there was total order in the garrison, and an organized force would be found there.

And then, three energetic and popular men prepared for anything—on the throne, at the head of the army, and at the head of the government—might still save everything.

That is? . . . Mikhail? Nikolai Nikolaevich? And, then, Milyukov himself? . . .

While Mikhail listened and listened, and no matter how hard he tried to remain calm, he began to be agitated. Saddle himself as well with putting down a portion of his subjects by force of arms?

How much easier it would be if they were all talking in some one direction! As it was, the choice was very obscure.

This is what he thought: all of them here, other than the two—whether members of the Provisional Government or the Duma Committee—everyone wanted his abdication. If so, then how could he rule with them? Who could he rely upon? All these men had fought so hard against his brother's rule and had defamed the throne. And toppled it. And now they were to be his government?

No, politics was intolerable! He wished he'd never come into contact with it.

But now the time had come for the grand duke to speak. To respond and decide.

But he wasn't ready!

"Gentlemen," Mikhail Aleksandrovich made a weak go of it. "If there is no unity among you, then how can I? It's difficult for me. . . ."

He hesitated. Everyone hesitated.

The grand duke made a proposal. Might he not now speak separately with . . . with someone, by order of rank with the Duma President and, evidently, the Prime Minister?

Prince Lvov? The prince, with his pure, semi-beatific look, had no definite opinion. He could speak, by all means. Or he could not.

Large, self-contained, and seemingly omnipotent Rodzyanko was troubled. (Why with him specifically? Was it going to look like a conspiracy with the monarchy behind the public's back? . . .) He replied that everyone here was part of a single whole, and no one could have a private conversation.

He cast a fearful sidelong look at Kerensky.

Oh, how that scoundrel had grown in power! Wasn't he now chief among them? Here he was unconstrained, he was the freest man here, and he gallantly consented:

"Our moral duty, gentlemen, is to provide the grand duke with every opportunity for a correct and free decision. Just so there are no outside influences or telephone conversations."

No telephone? The grand duke agreed.

Milyukov might have objected: an unfavorable combination? But on the other hand, he himself had spoken twice.

While Guchkov—Guchkov, if they had allowed him a tête-à-tête for two minutes, he would have offered the following thought: "Your Imperial Highness, you mustn't try to decide in half an hour, and don't let yourself be driven into a wedge! Demand a day. Two! Why hasn't the Emperor's abdication been published? Let Russia learn of it, and you and Russia will think together! Demand two days, and in that time you could even be at GHQ. Your true place is there! . . ."

No! Guchkov could not convey his mind to Mikhail in front of everyone, in front of Kerensky. And he couldn't in any case. Mikhail himself was the wrong man. His coming to power would be beneficial but obviously impossible. Even Guchkov was not himself and suddenly felt his powers depleted. Had he traveled and talked himself out yesterday?

Meanwhile, Kerensky barred the way for the grand duke:

"Promise, Your Highness, not to consult with your spouse!"

"She isn't here." Mikhail smiled sadly. "She is in Gatchina. . . ."

The grand duke, Rodzyanko, and Lvov went into the next room.

While there they walked around and discussed, and someone still argued with Milyukov, who hadn't risen from the sofa. Guchkov said to Nekrasov and the other Lvov, the blockhead:

"You are pushing the country toward ruin. And I will not join you on this path."

To Shulgin he said:

"I hadn't expected this of you. You're simply barreling along."

But he and Milyukov did not confer, either.

Tereshchenko walked around and looked out the windows at Millionnaya Street—at the people strolling there with red bows and to see whether there wasn't a crowd coming here, to this building, to lynch them all.

Hirsute Efremov, who had arrived late, showed Guchkov that day's issue of *Izvestia of Workers' Deputies*. In it was an ominous article against Milyukov's words of the previous day about a regency.

Due to his travel, Guchkov didn't know about that speech in the Ekaterininsky Hall or anything over the previous evening.

Indeed, the situation had been so neglected that the only *way back* was by civil war. Evidently, starting with the arrest of the Executive Committee.

Was Guchkov ready for this? If they were to concede to these menacers, it would only be worse.

Right then he recalled that Masha had heard nothing about him since the previous day. He went to ask where the telephone was.

In the dining room, two maids were setting the table for breakfast for all the guests, in the presence of the princess. The telephone was in the hall.

But no sooner had Aleksandr Ivanych lifted the receiver than next to him appeared a nervous, twisty Kerensky. He stared.

"What's the matter with you?" Guchkov asked in a voice that made no attempt at courtesy.

Not the least flustered, Kerensky did not even say but confidently stated: "I want to know who you're going to speak to!"

"Why might that interest you?" a scowling Guchkov barely deigned to ask.

"Perhaps you wish to summon a military unit and impose Mikhail by force?"

Once a fool . . . How they had all been taught the lessons of Western revolutions.

Actually, he ought to.

"No, my wife. Leave me alone."

Kerensky stepped away but so that he could hear from a distance, the boor.

Why he had secluded himself with those two, Mikhail himself didn't know. Simply to play for time, to think?

He had no hopes for Lvov, but he had always relied on Rodzyanko. Perhaps now, behind closed doors, he would suggest something clear?

But Rodzyanko, that high-and-mighty Samovar:

"We have nothing to rely on, Your Imperial Highness! Neither you nor I has an armed force. The only thing I can guarantee is that I will die by your side."

"I thank you." Mikhail smiled.

It had come to pass that if he was to accept the throne, he had to start by deceiving them all? Flee them all—in secret? Without having had a chance to consult with Natasha? Ask to put it off until tomorrow and flee tonight? Was he even going to have to do this in secret from the guard posted here for him?

Rodzyanko, as if guessing:

"And no one can take you out of Petrograd. All automobiles are being checked."

No, this was the wrong moment to leap onto a horse. This wasn't an army attack. He was alone.

"I thank you," Mikhail said quietly. "If you will allow me, now I would like to be entirely alone."

The grand duke entered the drawing room timidly. Not regally at all.

It was obvious that all this debate had exhausted him.

He began to speak standing—and so no one else sat down but heard him out standing. His voice was cameral and even gentle:

"Gentlemen. I would have no hesitations if I knew for certain what was best for Russia. Even among you, however, there is no unanimity. You are the people's representatives"—he spread his long, delicate fingers—"and you know better what the people's will is. Without the people's permission, even I deem it impossible . . . to accept. . . . So that obviously . . . the best thing . . . is to abdicate. . . . So shall we table this until . . . the Constituent Assembly?"

That was it.

They were silent.

But the overfree Kerensky immediately thrust himself forward:

"Your Highness! History will value your action for it breathes of nobility. I see you are an honest man. Henceforth I will always state as much. And we, Your Highness, will hold the sacred chalice of authority so that not a single drop of this precious moisture is spilled before the Constituent Assembly!"

Mikhail Aleksandrovich smiled.

No one said anything.

[3 7 8]

As arranged the night before, Peshekhonov stopped by the House of the People today, early in the morning, for the billeting officers of the 1st Machine-gun Regiment, to choose quarters. Once again, he had trouble getting past the strict self-selected guard—but once inside he learned that the machine-gunners no longer wanted to move.

And why was that?

It turned out, the committee had ordered an automobile sent for eight o'clock and it hadn't been sent—and this showed disrespect for the regiment and intent against it, and now they trusted no one and wouldn't budge.

However, the plumbing at the House of the People had failed and urine was already flooding the hall in one area and the wall was getting soaked. In the regimental committee's room, Peshekhonov worked hard to persuade the comrade delegate soldiers. Someone else might not have succeeded, but Peshekhonov had a very common look—a petit bourgeois man with a round, sheared haircut and a mustache that fell into his beard—and the soldiers let themselves be convinced. The committee chairman himself, an ensign in the war, also of common background, agreed to accompany him in the automobile, as did one bumptious soldier.

They got into the back seat, and still not trusting Peshekhonov, lest he twist them around his finger somehow, they themselves said to go right, and left, and stop near some building (every big one)—and had Peshekhonov explain to them why this building was out of the question or inconvenient.

Peshekhonov had the anguished thought that he needed to attend to his commissar affairs, but as it stood he would be riding around with them all day. Occasionally they didn't believe him and went to check for themselves but took him along as hostage so he wouldn't leave.

He couldn't control them! He himself had no idea where he would tell them to go anyway. No one place was big enough for them all, and they didn't want to go to separate places.

They ended up riding all the way to the Botanical Gardens on Aptekarsky Island.

"What's that building?" One caught their eye.

It was the famous Herbarium, the pride of Russia, not many like it in the whole world. Though from the outside the building really did look like a large barracks.

Peshekhonov took fright and started explaining to the ensign that they couldn't here—and made no impression. The ensign's education left something to be desired. . . .

They had to go look. They found one guard, and there was no research staff, no workers of any kind, which was even worse, because the white coats might have scared them off. But inside there was cleanliness, all spit and polish, it was bright and warm. The billeting officers liked it right away:

"Here's where we'll put ourselves!"

Peshekhonov threw up his hands:

"You can't, gentlemen! These are very rare collections!"

"What do you mean?"

Then he got craftier:

"Look, small rooms. No facilities for a residence and nothing to make bunks out of."

"We'll go on the floor! The floors here are cleaner than your bed."

"So how many of you can fit here? Two or three companies? There aren't enough washrooms either."

He barely managed to drag them away. They didn't want to leave. They continued through the Botanical Gardens. The hothouses. They liked it there, too.

"How will you ever sleep here? There's unctuous soil everywhere, and damp, and you'll start getting sick right away."

They hesitated. They wanted to go back to the Herbarium.

Right then one garden employee said that nearby there were some completely empty and perfectly suitable buildings—ministerial dachas.

"What kind? . . . Ministers'?"

Oh, they were lusting after that! Live where ministers were booted out? Very much! Give it a try!

"Take us there!"

What kind of dachas? Why, the neighboring plot was the very dacha of the Minister of the Interior where Stolypin was living in 1906, where he was bombed.

"There are annexes there, too."

There was a break in the fence right there for a shortcut, the snow was trampled, and off they went.

The annexes were abandoned, untended, and unheated, and there was disarray and trash everywhere, but the furniture was in place. One room was hung and spread with rugs, and there was a working telephone on a table, as if someone had just been living here. (The employee explained that Protopopov had come here to relax at Christmastime.)

Although the spaces were totally unsuited for soldiers, after this room the billeting officers were satisfied—they'd take it. They'd probably marked this one for the committee.

"You've seen for yourself," Peshekhonov turned it to his advantage, "there are no suitable spaces on the whole Petersburg side. You were wrong to leave Oranienbaum."

"Well, mebbe, mebbe"—and they sniffed. "But now we're going to live at the ministers'."

They went through the courtyard and came out toward the Nevka embankment. On the spot of the once-bombed dacha now stood a monument to Stolypin—not a big one, not one for a square, but nonetheless larger-than-life-size, bronze, and on a pedestal.

"Who's this, do you know? Why's it here?" Peshekhonov asked.

They didn't know anything—not Stolypin's name, not what kind of bombing.

"He was a big assistant to the Tsar!" the commissar explained. "He was cruel to revolutionaries. He put down the first revolution."

Peshekhonov thought to himself with glee that they would knock down the monument first thing, of course.

The soldier blew his nose onto the snow and wiped it:

"Leave him be. He's no bother."

[379]

Vorotyntsev experienced a distinct feeling for every Russian town he visited (and there were many) and noted what was special about that town—the people he'd come to know, the look of the streets and boulevards, the cliffs above the rivers, the churches placed high up, and also the many peculiarities, like in Tambov—the unpaved passages alongside the streets for cavalry, in Zaraisk—its incommensurately large kremlin—and in Kostroma, the proximity of the Ipatiev Monastery and Susanin country. Everywhere, too, there were favorite places, Crowns, Ramparts, where inhabitants customarily gathered, heard the news, and talked. Other than the countryside, what was Russia if not fourscore such towns? The diversity of their faces comprised the combined face of Russia.

An especially distinct feeling for Kiev. No matter how quickly he rode through it or how preoccupied he was, here Vorotyntsev, like each of us, no doubt, felt he was stepping on special, ancient ground blessed by the cross of the enormous St. Vladimir over the Dnieper. This piece of ancient Rus' towered immortally, the first capital, in fact, not the third. Any day you came to Kiev, any day you walked through it, always felt like a special day.

Not only that, Kiev had a special softness, whether from the south, or from its Ukrainian rhythm, or from something else? It was softer than those two capitals.

Vorotyntsev had nearly half a day to spend in Kiev—and what better than to leave his small suitcase at the train station and set out idly through the city? No addresses where he might go came to mind.

The air was very springlike. The jackdaws were racing. On the train station square, cabbies—sleighs and wheeled—were waiting in turn. On the streets alongside the footways streams gurgled, and the discharge from drainpipes ran across the sidewalks. The rather slippery sidewalks were in some places sprinkled with coal cinders, while in others yardmen had scraped them clean. After the whole stormy onslaught, the snowmelt was overwhelming. Lots of snow piles had been shoveled up, intensifying the closed-in feeling of a city already full with carriages, carts, streetcars, and the usual traffic.

Streets as far as the university's Botanical Gardens were their daily selves, as if they knew nothing. Behind the garden railings there was a snowy peace. But with Vladimirskaya the agitation and revels began. Here Vorotyntsev saw the red lapel bows he already knew, the red ribbon pinned to a coat or a cap. How had this fashion been picked up and communicated so quickly? Had they guessed rather than seen it? Not as thickly as in Moscow, though. But faces still bore the same perplexed and joyous bewilderment.

There were no policemen at any intersections. But no arrested policemen were being led away, either. Was it just that the police had disappeared, or had they changed clothes?

There was this, though: not a single vagrant, dissolute soldier with a rifle, as in Moscow. Unarmed singletons were walking modestly, as if on leave, saluting smartly. And officers responded easily, all of them armed, not hounded as if they were suspects . There was no foul complicity in any villainy as in Moscow. A strict armed detail passing by; it was different indeed.

Apparently, everything here was still in order. Maybe the capitals' outrage wouldn't get here in that form. Hopefully not!

Kiev was a rail hub for the Romanian as well as the Southwestern Army Group. If Kiev went crazy and supplies got interrupted, that was when the Germans would strike, wasn't it?

A great concentration was seething near the university, spilling out onto the pavement. To avoid it, Vorotyntsev made a detour diagonally across the square.

Several broad red flags were already hanging on wealthy Bibikov Boulevard, on its enormous apartment buildings. As if these rich owners needed revolution most passionately of all. Right here there was even more of the reveling public, not common folk but urban and educated, and they were cramming the entire boulevard so they didn't fit on the sidewalks.

Oh well, "freedom" is a word dear to everyone. They'll celebrate—and calm down? Subside?

At the intersection of Bibikov Boulevard and Kreshchatik, at the police-man's vacant spot, two university students stood importantly, trying to direct traffic.

While the streetcars went their way.

Vorotyntsev had noted earlier that there were no marches—but on Kresh-chatik he saw the first, made up of young people, carrying an unfurled red canvas with a slogan about a democratic republic. They were singing and shouting.

And carrying this so unceremoniously, as if it were something decided and clear to all. Who had decided this, that it was a "democratic republic"? Was that really something to decide on the street?

Truly, though, what kind of situation was this? The old authorities had vanished. Committees of some kind had appeared. And the Tsar was silent.

As if the orb of his power were tottering on a mountain's single peak.

Well, suppose the new government was a fact. Ultimately, what of it? Guchkov. Shingarev and Milyukov. Men of state, not out of nowhere.

On Kreshchatik's sidewalks, the crowd was like a vice, and sometimes it was impossible to move in it at will and one could only flow with it. All the in-habitants seemed to have tumbled out onto the streets to flow aimlessly, with exclamations, hailings, and congratulations. Of course, there was more cu-riosity than anything. But the genteel public had joy as well. Petty bourgeois women, on the other hand, peered guardedly from under their kerchiefs.

He thought that in the past few years, after all, Kiev had been the most loyal of the three capitals. All the deputies from here were rightists, and be-fore the war the masses' monarchism had manifested itself here more than anywhere. Was everyone now flowing through the streets really so content? But there were no gloomy faces to be seen. No matter how many enemies of the coup there were here now, it had been quickly established that dis-content could not be expressed. The power of the crowd! It had swept everything up in a single day and there was no shouting against it. People may have been hiding their feelings, pretending, but they walked amid the joyous exclamations.

What was not to be seen, fortunately, were any disgraceful, disorderly military marches with red flags.

Two university students, a high school boy, and two girls with red arm-bands raced by in a cab with crazed howls and arm waving. The students had clumsily and flashily strapped on guns; the high school boy, a sword.

Other young people thronged the pavement, arm in arm, as if out for a stroll, and they sang—not love songs but these songs, mutinous songs.

Yes, things were gentler in Kiev, but it was as if his same long, agonizing Moscow day was continuing. The revolution had already begun to seem fa-miliarly endless; he had seen it all, seen it and seen it again.

At one point he was hemmed in and stopped for a quarter of a minute by the steps of a newspaper office. Standing on the steps were two intellectuals—

one wearing a tilted hat and willy-nilly scarf, and the other having stepped outside without a coat, but he looked like a newspaper rat, his spectacles on the tip of his nose. And he said quietly to the other:

"We have precise information at the office that he abdicated yesterday! But for some reason there haven't been any agent communiqués."

But an opening formed and Vorotyntsev moved on before he realized what had singed him. There was no turning back, though, no asking, it was rude to eavesdrop. The opportunity passed.

But it couldn't have been about anyone else: **abdicated**.

Abdicated?

The final puzzle was ending. A chance phrase, unproven—but its accuracy had struck him. Yes! There was no other possibility! Why else could he be stuck and saying nothing—in Pskov?

Ay-yai-yai!

Abdicated? Well, he'd come to grief.

Could he really have fought it?

Among the troops! And he'd abdicated?

But how could he have failed to think of the Army? And the war, which he himself, he himself had waged so persistently and recklessly? And all of a sudden . . .

Under Aleksei the situation would be completely unstable. *Who* had everything in his hands? Where were those hands?

Events were spilling away—like this crowd—and you couldn't stop them or bring yourself to take part. His own loathsome, pathetic inaction. Vorotyntsev was subdued, aimless and powerless, and didn't know what to do.

The crowd flowed away. Suddenly he recalled that capricious Kadet lady at the Shingarev apartment and how she had predicted the fascinating sensation of us flying into the abyss. Although today there was no storm, or blizzard, or earthquake, or eruption—but in this warm, overcast, slippery bottom, Vorotyntsev felt the Russian bulk slip and tumble down! Even more terrible was that this was inaudible and amid smiles.

See how Brusilov had made haste to publicly bow and click his heels. But Vorotyntsev had fought for a year with Brusilov in the 8th Army—and understood what an opportunist he was.

What about the Romanian Army Group, though? Sakharov was silent, at least that much.

Abdicated? So now he wasn't the Supreme Commander, either? We have to stand on our own feet all the more.

Russia was wobbling, convulsing!

Up ahead, where Kreshchatik widened, a large new gathering could be seen, its droning audible. In the middle there was a tall object, and people were there on top, and waving.

Cut off from it all by his thoughts, Vorotyntsev didn't look closely right away or discern that this was a monument, and people had climbed onto the base by the figure and were clinging to it. Approaching it in the human current, cut off by his thoughts, he still didn't realize what monument this was. Or what kind of rope had been thrown around the figure—while below people were pulling to whoops, whistles, and laughter. Volunteers' many hands were tugging this rope, evidently trying to topple the figure—although it would crash directly onto them, onto the crowd without reaching out—head first, feet last, the way people fall full-length in extreme grief or extreme despair.

Vorotyntsev let himself be borne past the City Duma with the Archangel Michael on its long, slender spire. From the broad balcony they were reading out telegrams from Petrograd (but not about the abdication) and shouting speeches. Further skirting the monument. Only then did he see clearly and remember: it was Stolypin! They'd put him up, right here, after his murder, before the war.

However, he stood much more firmly than they'd thought on his parallelepiped base, carved into which were a Russian warrior, a weeping boyar's wife, and his phrase, "You shall not frighten us!"

"We can't take it down this way!" people shouted from below.

But up top, several efficient youths had grabbed hold of the figure's feet and were working intrepidly. One, without a cap, a fiery redhead, managed to fling another small rope around Stolypin's neck, bring both ends forward, and now in redhead delight shouted down:

"We're tying a Stolypin tie!"

The crowd guffawed.

What could Vorotyntsev do? Wave his sword? He could not stop this filth.

Constrained like a helpless log, he felt that if this revolution had staggered him in Moscow, here in Kiev he now detested it.

[3 8 0]

Given his speechless lowly commander-ensign, Stankevich now had to think for his whole sapper battalion. He couldn't restart training the soldiers, as they were still inflamed by the uprising. However, he did have to make a concerted search for a path to understanding with them, otherwise the battalion would fall apart.

A government had been formed! Evidently, he had to hurry to discuss this with the soldiers, give them explanations, make them understand.

So Stankevich started going from company to company. He didn't line them up but assembled them, like during seated lessons, in the barracks, without their greatcoats and caps, and delivered short speeches. He had been planning to talk only about names, who had taken which post, how he was connected with the people, and how long he had fought for their interests, but the first two speeches—and all the rest thereafter—did not go very well. In front of the silent soldiers, Stankevich suddenly felt the need to justify himself in some way—justify the fact that there should be a government in the country at all, why it was essential. And it turned out that even this was not so easy to prove, at least he obviously failed to convince his listeners. (The thought occurred to them that if he had spoken in defense of the Tsar, they would probably have understood it, for it was familiar. Here was what was probably not clear to them: What was this thing called "a government"? What about the Tsar, then?)

The ministers' names made no impression. Seemingly, Prince Lvov's Zemgor fame had been widespread throughout the country—but in none of the companies had any of the soldiers, to a man, heard of him. No one nodded and no one smiled. Whether Stankevich spoke about the contributions to the army of the new Minister of War Guchkov or about the crushing blows the current Minister of Foreign Affairs had inflicted on the old regime, he read no gratitude or recognition on their faces. The others they knew even less, and Stankevich himself couldn't find words to convince them of what they had accomplished. Something snapped in him. And he began talking with an even greater, final hope about his friend Kerensky. Here, satisfaction appeared on men's faces, but not all—just on locals, the Petersburgers', who had rubbed up against, read, heard of him. And then the approval was not because he was a minister but in spite of the fact.

Stankevich returned from his tour of the companies devastated.

He liked thinking and formulating everything through to the end. And he tried to do so now. The suddenness and ease of the coup had stolen everyone's proper sense of measure and criticism. Apparently, if the regime had fallen so easily, a regime that was considered indestructible, then from now on everything would go successfully and happily all the more. But in fact, what might the Provisional Government attempt to do? Just restore an organization of authority that wholly recalled the old. It was incapable of digesting the inrush of the revolutionary element; the ministers' very minds couldn't fathom this. The Duma Committee had vanquished the front to the revolution's benefit and had handed over to it the entire officer class—but would not earn its gratitude. Because in revolution you must **advance quickly**. You must develop and move faster than the revolution itself. Only then can you take it in hand.

Stankevich castigated himself for his distress on the morning of 12 March. He knew, he had agreed with Gustave Le Bon, that what the popular majority needs is order, not revolution. Therefore, a revolution would never be made by the people, but by a random crowd in which no one knew clearly why they were shouting and rebelling. A crowd is led by destructive elements with a criminal mentality—who psychologically infect them and unify the mass of inert elements. A revolution can be defined as the moment when there is no punishment for the crime.

Now, finding himself at the center of the whirlwind, *how* was he to control it, guide it?

Even in the Tauride Palace, the Duma Committee and Provisional Government were scarcely noticeable. By now, the leader of the revolution was undoubtedly the Soviet's Executive Committee. It already controlled the entire army, though the officer class was not on its side. It was in control because the soldiers were drawn to it precisely because they could feel the anti-officer force in it.

But a regime founded on this is dangerous, and the Executive Committee itself might explode into anarchy. Stankevich had already heard disgruntled comments from Kerensky about the Committee's leaders not understanding the significance of their authority and being prepared to undermine everything irresponsibly. Kerensky, who had succeeded better than anyone in riding the advance crest and in his heart had been in the new government for several days, was one of the first to begin to sense this dangerous vacuum around the regime.

Stankevich considered this tactic of being on the advance crest correct. What he had come up with in the past hour or so was that the danger of anarchy had to be fought in its very nest! He had to join the Executive Committee itself—just the Soviet for starters and move on from there. And how to join the Soviet? As the delegate from the officers of his battalion. It was very simple. The Soviet was considered to be made up of soldiers' deputies, but pull this apart, break down this concept: the officers, too, had to have their own representatives there, and this way they would feel a connection and everything would stabilize.

In the meeting room, the battalion officers were sitting idle in a distraught cluster. They didn't dare summon the soldiers to training and didn't dare take advantage of their idleness to go home. It was simply amazing, the officers' utter uncertainty in the face of all that had happened: the powerful military system developed over centuries had fallen apart in a few days. Stankevich himself would certainly have been thrown as well had he not had a populist-socialist upbringing and party ties.

Now he was offering himself as a delegate to the Soviet—and the officers agreed hopefully and without a murmur. No need even to vote.

They drew up a mandate, according to form, and Stankevich, not wasting any time, headed for the Tauride Palace.

It was a ruddy, sunny day. There was still a light frost, but spring already permeated the light and air. Red flags hung on apartment buildings. Many were out and about. Stankevich took the alley to Fuhrstadtskaya and continued down its narrow boulevard. Near Potemkin Street, he ran into Kolya, his nephew twice-removed, who was in his last year of high school.

Amid the general animation, Kolya's face looked frankly sad. That was very odd for a high school boy these days. He was a thoughtful boy.

"Well, how goes it, Kolya?" Stankevich asked.

Kolya looked at him almost with fear:

"Oh, Uncle Volodya! Very badly."

[3 8 1]

Kolya's father was something of a writer and because of his name was often confused with Stanyukovich, a famous author of maritime stories who had died, a radical intellectual who had spent time in exile for his ties to the People's Will. Kolya's father, on the other hand, had never had any connections with any parties, but the gentleman was liberal and, like everyone, always sympathized with any freedom movement.

With the outbreak of this war, also like everyone, he had accepted it patriotically, and the previous year, as a senior reserve officer, had volunteered to command a militia battalion. He was at the front to this day, and Kolya was living on Fuhrstadtskaya with his stepmother, an energetic woman significantly younger than his father. In her youth she was on the verge of becoming an SR, had nearly joined the party, and sympathized greatly with them. Her marriage bathed her in a comfortable, well-off life, but it turned out she had not forgotten her old sympathies—and during these revolutionary days those sympathies had swelled up and she had followed events breathlessly.

That's how it was in all the adult society around them: enchantment at the revolution, general enthusiasm, bright faces for each other, and a kind of sacred seed sprouting in everyone. You'd think youthful hearts would burst from joy all the more.

But no. Like several other boys in his class, Kolya had immediately perceived the revolution as a filthy mutiny—from the very first street scenes.

There had been arguments these past few days between stepmother and son. Placing her palms to her golden temple curls, she responded so ecstatically, she was simply afraid to believe that this happy liberation had at last come upon Russia. While Kolya replied insistently that it was brigandage and theft. (No one had come to search their apartment, so he could show no proof.) For the past few days their arguments had been over the Tsar. Did Russia need a Tsar? Could it go on without one? His stepmother had reared up: where did we get such conservatives behind our school desks? She considered the monarchy medieval. The people, which had matured, needed a parliamentary republic, as in France. She said "*we*": our revolution, our victory!

Relations between stepmother and stepson were such that she never compelled him to do anything, merely suggested that he might want to. This was how she spoke now, too:

"Might you go to the Saburovs', Kolya? They've organized a dining room for soldiers. I've cooked something for them there, too. Grab it and take it there?"

Kolya was friends with the younger Saburovs and was happy to go.

In the familiar marble front hall of their home he saw smears and clumps of mud on the white floor and the rugs, which they obviously hadn't had time to clean up. All the hooks in the coatroom were hung with soldiers' greatcoats. In the large room, soldiers, more than thirty men, were sitting around an enormous table that was expanded for maximum ceremony and was set with many platters and plates, expensive dishes, and filled with the most exquisite food: caviar, salmon, the best smoked sausage, to say nothing of kulebyakas, turnovers, and salad. Shaven-headed soldiers in tunics—it was actually hot in the hall—were sitting and eating a lot, mostly silently, but looking around at everything with curiosity. They sniffed and wiped their noses with their fists. The young Saburovs, high school girls and university girls and boys of friendly families carried, served, laid out, and ran to the kitchen for more—and were cheerful, noisy, and generally animated by their activity.

Kolya took his stepmother's donations to the kitchen and returned. Apparently, he was supposed to rejoice that their unenlightened, insulted *little brothers* were sitting like humans, respectably, in a refined atmosphere, and eating delicious food. But to him it all seemed terribly false. The excessive generosity and even elegance of the table, the feeding in the very best room adorned with bronze, porcelain, and lacquered furniture, and the melting dirt under their boots, and the smears on the white tablecloth, and the soldiers' loud belching, and their far from well-meaning looks around—and the twittering young ladies bending over backward for them, and just the misguided animation of the young people. Even when the soldiers, one and then another, got the urge to smoke their cheap tobacco right there—they were invited not to get up and were brought marble ashtrays for their newspaper-rolled smokes, red fragments of burned tobacco falling on the carpet or tablecloth.

Kolya did almost nothing. The scene offended him, it was awful, humiliating—and pointless as well because all soldiers could not be fed in this way every day. And why these specific reservists, who had been called up toward the end of the war? Many had yet to get a whiff of gunpowder—whereas his fifty-five-year-old father had volunteered to fight, and his older cousin, who attended the Tenishev commercial training school, rather than dodge the draft to continue his education, had also gone voluntarily.

The hypocrisy was agonizing.

On the other hand, among the young ladies he saw one he didn't know, older than he was, the age of a university student, but shorter and dark-haired, with enigmatic eyes he couldn't tear himself away from. Kolya fastened his eyes on her with the hopelessness of a younger man and couldn't look away. She was also serving, but not a lot, and slowly, with a degree of reluctance and almost without a smile, as if acting a part foisted on her. Her name was Likonya.

Then she stood up to the wall, her hands folded behind her back, and stood like that a ways off. There seemed to be a grin on her lips—and those lips! A beauty!

All this put together led Kolya to make up his mind and approach her, stand next to her, unintroduced, and say softly:

"What a disgrace. How we're humiliating ourselves. Oh, we'll come to regret it."

She bestowed her dark gaze on him and made a very very light, kind of sideways twisting movement—with her head, or shoulders maybe—and with this alone expressed more than he could have had the nerve to express. But she also replied:

"Yes. One should never lose oneself."

What an idea! And the voice! Simply an astonishing young woman. And what sad, magnetic eyes. And she herself—like one of the figurines set out in this room.

Soon after, she disappeared. Kolya didn't notice when. Disappeared as if she'd never been. And that made him anxious. He wanted to see and hear her again. He left hastily, in hopes of catching up to her.

Not seeing him, two soldiers stood behind the coatroom closet smoking. One said:

"Oh, how these stinkers live! They're scared. You can't buy us off with caviar, though. Pretty soon we'll take care of these goody-goody shits . . . And these students . . ."

. . . All this he told his Uncle Volodya when they met.

[382"]

(FROM *Izvestia of the Soviet of Workers' and Soldiers' Deputies*)

A REGENCY AND CONSTITUENT ASSEMBLY. . . . The Provisional Government does not have the right to develop any permanent form of administration. . . . Does Milyukov fear a Civil War? On whose part? Who's going to take up arms in favor of the "royal family"? Only the Black Hundreds. . . . This is the Black Hundreds dressed in soldier greatcoats, simulating our revolutionary patrols, robbing inhabitants. . . .

OFFICERS AND SOLDIERS. . . . Order No. 1 puts officers in their place. . . . The soldier becomes a citizen and ceases to be a slave. . . . the committees, under whose control are all weapons, which are not issued to officers even at their demand, for weapons are the property of all soldiers and all citizens. Henceforth, soldiers are a self-administrating group that runs its own affairs absolutely independently. . . .

FATEFUL DATE (13 March 1881–14 March 1917). . . .The execution of Aleksandr II by a bold group of revolutionaries . . . Tsarism set in motion only the whip, bullet, and gallows. . . . What our isolated comrades were unable to do in unequal battle has now been brought about. . . .

AMNESTY. Up until now, the entire nation has been shackled in chains. . . . Comrade exiles, comrade convicts! In the name of the entire democracy, we welcome you as freed hostages. . . .

ALL JEWS ACCEPTED INTO THE LEGAL PROFESSION. The decision has been made to accept into the legal profession all Jews who are lawyers' assistants.

GREETINGS FROM THE ENGLISH ARMY. A representative of the English army has told the new Minister of Justice Kerensky that he has been empowered by the English ambassador to welcome the Soviet of Workers' Deputies and the Committee of the State Duma.

CITIES JOIN. The following have joined the revolutionary movement in full: Moscow, Nizhni Novgorod, Kharkov, Saratov, Vologda, Kursk, Orel.

WHERE ARE THE TSAR AND TSARITSA. Rumors notwithstanding, Nikolai II has not been arrested. The Empress is at Tsarskoye Selo, in complete safety.

. . . General Sukhomlinov's maid was sent immediately under convoy to the State Duma.

ON THE SEARCHES. Over the past few days, patrols have been carrying out searches, looking for any remaining policemen, spies, and hooligans. . . . In the course of this useful work, unfortunately, there have been more than a few violations of military discipline. We know that during these searches there have been instances of outright theft. From one of our comrades . . . The patrols must remember that the great work they are doing . . . Therefore, when entering someone else's residence, they must be conscious of their sacred duty . . .

CITIZENS! A great deed has been accomplished. The old regime, which destroyed Russia, has fallen apart. . . . The army and populace must be fed. Make haste to sell your grain to authorized representatives, give them everything you can. . . . Make haste to deliver your grain as assigned, the homeland is waiting . . .

Rodzyanko

TO THE COMRADE WORKERS AND CITIZENS OF PETROGRAD. The Soviet of Workers' Deputies calls on you not to impede the transport of food shipments through the city. The outcome of the revolution depends on it. Flour must be distributed to the bakeries so that we have bread. . . . Already today, 14–16 million pounds have to be brought from the Nikolaevsky Train Station.

[3 8 3]

But once the grand duke had agreed to everything, it turned out that the abdication itself was not even ready. The zealous republican Nekrasov had taken up its composition in the night. And had brought it in his pocket. But now when they looked over his draft—this man had not the slightest notion of legal-governmental concepts or the deliberateness of each word in such texts.

Actually, the others were unable to compose it without error, either.

Right then Princess Putyatina invited everyone to breakfast.

They began making telephone calls and summoning constitutional lawyers Nabokov and Baron Nolde, telling them to make sure to bring the legal code.

The grand duke did not come to the table.

Unable to bear his defeat, Milyukov refused breakfast and left.

So did Guchkov.

The rest at the table animatedly discussed Nekrasov's draft, and what in it needed to be changed, and what a mountain had been crossed, and what valleys now lay spread out before them.

But Nabokov and Nolde arrived and immediately disappointed them: the laws of succession did not provide for "abdication" of any kind. Except formally, perhaps, if they were to equate abdication with death? But then, all the more so, the throne was surely supposed to be conveyed to the normal heir. By abdicating, the Emperor could not deprive another person of the throne because the throne was not his private property. Thus, the very conveyance of the throne to Mikhail was illegal, and now it was impossible to know on what grounds Mikhail was supposed to abdicate. To say nothing of how to write an abdication for him.

Furthermore, who was Mikhail from yesterday to today? Emperor? Or regent?

But there could be no regent without a bearer of Supreme Power.

So they were in quite a tangle.

A manifesto from a nonexistent emperor?

Clever Nabokov realized, though, that the matter ultimately was not about formalities. What was important now was to compose the Manifesto in such a way as not to shake the popular psyche but rather to strengthen the power of the Provisional Government in the eyes of the population, especially that part of it for whom Mikhail held moral significance—to formally secure the fullness of power of the Provisional Government and its successor connection to the Duma. And through the Constituent Assembly to envision succession for both a constitutional monarchy and a legitimate permanent government. And in doing so conceal and not play up the fact that Prince Lvov had been appointed by the former Tsar: in today's atmosphere, this would be a weakening.

After breakfast, everyone dispersed for the time being, while Nabokov and Nolde remained, and to assist the lawyers Shulgin imposed himself to take part in the great historic event to its completion.

The composers secluded themselves in the Putyatin children's classroom, sat and worked there.

They revised and revised and gradually something began to emerge: "A heavy task has been entrusted to Us by the will of Our brother. . . . Animated by the same feelings as the entire nation, that the welfare of Our country comes above all, We are firmly resolved to accept the Supreme Power only if this should be the desire of Our great people, who must . . . through their representatives in the Constituent Assembly establish the form of government and new fundamental laws of the Russian State . . ."

But if Mikhail did not accept Supreme Power, then what right did he have to give binding instructions, including about a Constituent Assembly?

Each word seemed infinitely important. How would Russia react? How would the legally intelligent West?

"We enjoin all citizens to obey the Provisional Government . . ." gave rise to a new debate as to how to qualify the Provisional Government. Everyone had the urge to write "which arose at the will of the people." But back at breakfast, Kerensky had bluntly protested, saying he could not allow a government of the wealthy classes to arise at the will of the people. Rodzyanko wanted "set up at the initiative of the State Duma," as Shulgin insisted as well. It was very difficult to come up with a third serious suggestion.

Nabokov sat down at the Putyatin girls' desk and rewrote the draft in his superlative handwriting.

Then they invited the grand duke into the classroom. They anticipated no objections from him.

He leaned on the desk and read it without picking it up.

He asked disconcertedly to replace the royal "We" with a simple "I." And to replace the word "enjoin" with "request."

And then . . . where is God mentioned here?

The composers' minds had been otherwise occupied. They had not just been in a hurry, they had simply forgotten. God? Yes, there had to be God.

They inserted: "invoking God's blessing . . ."

That meant they copied it out once again, two copies of it. On school paper, lined school paper.

The room was already dimming, soon it would be time to turn on the light.

Returning right then were Prince Lvov, Rodzyanko, and Kerensky, who wished to follow this through to the end.

Once again they called in the grand duke.

He picked up the pen of Putyatin's high school son, sat down at the small desk, and signed:

"Mikhail."

Everyone was instilled with the moment's significance.

Now for certain he was not Emperor—and Rodzyanko embraced him with his paw-like hands, kissing him.

While Kerensky exclaimed once again:

"Your Imperial Highness, you are a noble man!"

[3 8 4]

Go on rebelling? Or not? Overthrow the bourgeois government or not? And if yes, then now, before it could take its first breath and the ministers had not yet taken their seats? Or bide our time while we collect more weapons and forces?

Yesterday's leaflet, so passionately composed with the Vyborg District Committee—"all power to the Soviet!"—had not only not been approved by the Executive Committee but had been banned by its own Petersburg Committee of Bolsheviks. Shlyapnikov had definitely not expected that!

He had demanded a decisive session of the Petersburg Committee by this afternoon. For now, he himself rushed to the Tauride Palace. Let's discuss at the EC yesterday's behavior by Kerensky! Let's call out that harlequin! No, the Mensheviks were too cowardly to put it on the agenda. Instead, they assigned Shlyapnikov to duty for the EC—to receive delegations and visitors. Now he wouldn't even be on time for the start of the Petersburg Committee's session. He sent Molotov and Zalutsky ahead to make a report for the Bureau of the Central Committee. They agreed to keep to the following: even if we don't call for an immediate uprising (although we should!), then at least no trust in a government of the major bourgeoisie! Agitate for the creation of a truly revolutionary government!

For now, he himself was on duty for the EC, and whoever was on duty had the right to respond without consulting with the Executive Committee. People came from the Ozerki and the 1st Pargolovo neighborhoods: Can we create a separate militia? Of course, create them. Where can we get guns? Requisition them where you can. Don't expect them from the Soviet. When work starts up again, can we walk out? Go ahead. But who's going to pay for our day? We'll make the capitalists!

Then he rushed to the Labor Exchange and the Petersburg Committee. He had to enter from the side street through a plain shop door, cross through the store, then go up a dusty staircase to the very top floor, almost the attic, and also walk through several musty office rooms under a low, slanted ceiling—and only then reach the meeting room seized by Politikus for the PC. This downtrodden, pathetic, dusty space itself demonstrated just how timid, powerless, and sidelined the Bolshevik party was. This was especially striking after the ferment in the Tauride Palace and the expansive will of the street crowds.

What kind of leaders were they here? It was as if their place really was here, in the attic. They were sitting around a long, uncovered table and on benches against the slanting walls. There were about fifteen people there. Gray-haired, gray-mustached Stuchka, a decent but grumpy man. Feodosi Krivobokov, also known as Nevsky—his hair looked whipped up and his gaze like a sheep's. Cross-eyed, self-confident Schmidt. And the orderly-minded Politikus presiding and feeling very good and even jesting gaily now.

Molotov's report was over, and now bland Avilov was tediously offering up Menshevik nonsense in the debates, saying that we were living through a bourgeois revolution and so the proletariat's task was to wholly and honestly support the Provisional Government. He kept quoting Marx and Engels—and the one thing you felt like asking him was, And where were you when we were being chased by detectives through Petersburg and rumbling in a general strike? Now you've taken a seat here safely beside them: support the Provisional Government, "insomuch-insofar" as its actions are going to correspond to the interests of the proletariat. (But of course they're not!) He was saying it makes sense to kill the cow without milking it first.

As far as the cow goes, that's fine, but you're not getting the point.

Only Shutko, the youngest, although balding, merrily demanded they take armed action, and immediately! We'd collected so many guns on the Vyborg side—and they were all with the workers! The Moscow Battalion would join us, too! We could sweep aside the Provisional Government now faster than we did the Tsar! In Novaya Derevnya they were already tearing up the Soviet's *Izvestia* and shouting that they were a bunch of collaborators and we needed to go arrest and kill Rodzyanko and Milyukov!

Skinny bespectacled Kalinin from the Aivaz factory, with his spade-beard, you couldn't tell whether he was sympathetic or not. Pretty crafty.

But here's what! It turned out, Molotov did not make a militant report. The fight had gone out of him, and he had started to take the PC's side: the government and Soviet had more troops, nearly the entire army behind them, and the correlation of forces was not in our favor.

Shlyapnikov sensed the rightness of an immediate uprising, but he couldn't express it convincingly to this dusty assemblage. Look here, this is all our fault! he said. Yesterday at the Soviet, when it came to voting not to support the bourgeois government, in the entire hall only fifteen firm hands went up, and that included the Interdistrict men, while the Bolsheviks on their own had the numbers, but they turned tail and let themselves be made fools of. These Bolsheviks—what ilk were they? If our own ranks were falling apart, who was going to respect us? What about the Soviet? We're in a minority there and can't seize power through it. To them, we were "calling for anarchy." Before our very eyes, they were drawing workers into the deception of "nationwide brotherhood" or "an alliance of the entire revolutionary democracy"—and we couldn't bring ourselves to destroy it. What kind of brotherhood can there be with the bourgeoisie? What kind of alliance with defensists? Is this what we won our victory on the streets for, only to establish bourgeois law and order? To hand over power from one clique to another?

But a resigned conciliation had overpowered them. What was especially troubling was that even Mitya Pavlov, who was sitting right there, had also swung back and favored the moderates. If Pavlov thought that way, that meant many qualified workers wanted peace now, too.

Although Shlyapnikov was chairman of the Bureau of the Central Committee, and the only Central Committee member here, and answered personally to Lenin for the entire party line, and could order the militant Vyborgers to rise up even without this timid PC — how could he when he was almost alone against all of them? He didn't have the confidence to pound his fist and shout: This is how it's going to be!

He felt the unrepeatable days slipping away, days when the Provisional Government had nothing to hold onto and knocking it aside was a simple matter of nudging an elbow.

[3 8 5]

First as a joke and then in earnest, the members of the Executive Committee decided that they all needed a break from "Soviet plenums." Not only could the EC get no work done because someone was constantly being called away to the Soviet, but you couldn't even squeeze from room to room to get through the palace of the revolution — that's how many of these workers' and soldiers' deputies were packed in, and the confusion was simply intolerable. And there was no sense to be had from them — absolutely none. You couldn't discuss a single issue with them — not that anything should be solved there. All the ongoing and important work, all the political tasks, had been laid upon the Executive Committee alone. No, to hell with this permanent rally. A way had to be found to put an end to this daily multitude. Every day new "deputies" kept being added, and they kept pushing and shoving. Go try and disband them now! Who could and would dare!

So many of these delegates had accumulated — today, apparently, more than thirteen hundred — that now they'd thronged into the Duma's White Hall. But even in the White Hall, never more than five hundred Duma members had met, and the deputy chairs had armrests, which meant you couldn't squeeze two in together. Everyone who hadn't grabbed a seat was now just sitting on the steps of the amphitheater aisles and densely packing the floor below, standing, as well as the public galleries. There were even several soldiers still toting rifles. Gratifying for them.

Naturally, Chkheidze went there to fill the time with a solemn speech in the morning, while he still had the strength. He climbed onto Rodzyanko's presidential tower, where he would not have thought to go before, and from there proclaimed: Let the Duma of 16 June (no one understood the term) look in — and it would see who was in charge here now. And he indicated — climbed down—where Markov the Second had sat and where Chkheidze himself had—while soon deputies from the national Constituent Assembly would gather here. Because the banner of the world proletariat had already been raised high—and long live this moment!

Then began a string of greetings to the Soviet—from Golutvin and Kolomna, from Saratov, from various regiments—and by then Chkheidze himself had lost all desire to linger and left hastily for the Executive Committee. Nor did Nakhamkes have any wish to preside. However, they still had to send out someone who could shout, someone energetic. They persuaded Bogdanov, the Menshevik, and he took it up.

Today, too, the Executive Committee moved to a new location—a room near the White Hall, on the way to the Semi-Circular. In part because everyone knew where the old room was, even behind the curtain, and they prevented it from meeting, especially on secret matters. In part because in previous rooms the EC office was now at work—household staffs and added volunteers, and starting today they were going to be serving hot dinners and suppers to their own people. It was the right thing to do—spread out through the Tauride Palace, gain a foothold, and not let anyone move the Soviet of Deputies to any other building.

There was also a concern about where to put the tens of soldiers whom Sokolov had selected so hastily and brought to the Executive Committee. Sitting and seriously discussing anything with them was impossible. True, they'd been selected for just three days, which meant tomorrow was their last day, but they weren't going to leave voluntarily, were they? For today, they'd been convinced that their place was in the White Hall, where all the soldiers were. And off they'd gone. Phew.

In the Executive Committee's new meeting room, another nice institution had been established: set out on a separate table by the wall, piled up, was butter, cheese, sausage, preserves, loaves of luscious white bread, and two-pound sacks of granulated sugar in abundance—which distracted them because sugar had been rationed for several months and there wasn't always money for white bread, either. It was long since time to institute this because the EC members were drained, worn out, spending ten to twelve hours at a time without leaving the palace and then having to worry about where to get something to eat.

Now the very appearance of the meetings had changed, as if moisture had been added to their former dryness. There hadn't been a minute when everyone sat around the meeting table without two or three or four always standing next to that food table, usually with their backs to the people meeting, and rustling something there. What they were lacking here was serving dishes: no plates, no spoons, no forks—just tin mugs, some of them rusty. But such intoxicatingly sweet tea can be stirred with pencils or writing pens! All the rest they cut up and took, even the preserves, with their penknives, helping with their fingers.

One of the issues of today's EC discussions was the Romanovs' fate. But that issue was resolved more easily than any other, almost without debate: the Romanovs found no defender or sympathizer here. Nikolai's abdication manifesto aroused only laughter in the EC. Was this the full power of the Tsarism that had oppressed us so? The staging of a decorous voluntary abdication when he had been spontaneously deposed! The revolution was rolling on its merry way, and nothing depended on the conduct of the Romanov gang.

The baseness and duplicity of the franchised classes was another matter. Only today did EC members get to the bottom of all this double-dealing. While insincerely conducting talks with the EC, the franchised gentlemen had secretly outfitted an expedition to go to the Tsar in an attempt to save the dynasty and the monarchy! How did you like that? Could you believe them at all? (Some members were simply beside themselves.) Bourgeois perfidy and proletarian gullibility! (But how did we ever let their trip slip past us? That had been exactly the time when Rulevsky, who reported to the Soviet everything happening at Bublikov's Ministry of Roads and Railways, had stepped out.) Oh, those franchised villains! Irresponsible, underhanded talks! True, they hadn't gained anything in particular. But there was also that bald-faced sentence by Milyukov yesterday in favor of the monarchy. And today he and Mikhail had been pottering around together. The sooner the dynasty was isolated, the calmer things would be. There would be no restoration.

This was decided in principle. Arrest everyone. First the men. The Military Commission would have to work out the mechanics of the arrests.

What was infuriating was something else: the behavior of comrade Kerensky! That was what needed discussing. (He himself, of course, wasn't here; he saw no need to attend the EC.) Circulating there, in the bourgeois nest itself, he couldn't help but know about the plutocracy's attempt to save the dynasty. Why hadn't he protested? Why hadn't he told us?

If they were talking about Kerensky, the outrage over him ran broader and deeper—it was his shameless backstabbing yesterday: jumping out in front of a senseless crowd and demagogically dragging an agreement out of them.

They were all angry, but they also understood that Kerensky had reached heights where their discussion no longer affected him.

He himself did not show up for the meeting but had the audacity to send to them—from room to room!—a demand: order one of the Soviet's members to go to the Peter and Paul Fortress, where an assault was under way on the weapons stores under the Bolsheviks' leadership—whereas all weapons now belonged to the Provisional Government exclusively.

Shlyapnikov was a fine knave, too. Even to his EC comrades he always turned an impenetrable face, as if he was even now under police surveillance: clean-shaven, smooth cheeks, eyes impassively calm, mustache perfectly still on his upper lip, hair smoothly combed, hands most often interlaced on his chest. You might think you saw a smirk, but you'd never catch him laughing outright. All the comrades from all the parties came to the Soviet as if they were coming home, only the Bolsheviks were insincere. They always had their own conspiracy.

Even though right then Shlyapnikov had an innocent look, he went to call and check, but clearly he knew, and more than likely even, he was secretly guiding the whole weapons grab. He returned with the following explanation: nothing needed doing. There was no looting going on. The workers were living in great friendship with the Peter and Paul soldiers, who were generously giving them some of their own weapons. There was nothing bad in arming the workers. The Soviet would be even better ensured of protection.

Meanwhile, whenever the doors to the White Hall opened, they heard nothing but shouts and greetings, shouts and greetings.

Finally, the Executive Committee was now obligated and able to put its own work in order. Up until now, it had been shredded by members' contradictory instructions. Everyone was in charge of every question, and whether or not they knew it, certain instructions canceled out others. Today, while the soldiers were gone, they divided up into eleven commissions and elected as their secretary the punctilious and polite Kapelinsky, so that now they would have minutes, too.

Actually, they met here calmly for just a few short hours. Their new location leaked out, and petitioners with emergency and urgent petitions started to find their way in.

While their own issues were left up in the air. The franchised classes raised a great fuss about Order No. 1, and the Military Commission demanded to know how to understand it and what row to hoe. Truly, the devil himself couldn't understand what they'd ordered there. Not even everyone on the EC knew about this order (it was good they'd at least managed to do away with the election of officers). Also, to *whom* had they issued the order? The Petrograd garrison alone? But it had gone on to the entire army in the field, they hadn't taken that into account.

Now the majority, even those who did know, started hedging, saying that they didn't know about this order. Fine. Instruct the Military Commission to issue clarifications for Order No. 1.

But then that forced even more the question as to what they all felt about continuing the war. They had always been too busy to talk about that.

Next door the large hall was abuzz.

Comrades! Close the door. We can't listen to them. We have our own issues!

Their principal issue was this. Complete victory for the revolution would occur with the revival of Petrograd's normal life. While the factories would take time to sort out, the most visible and most essential matter for everyone was starting up the streetcars. This would be a relief for the revolutionary inhabitants and a symbol of the restoration of order under the revolutionary regime. It was one thing, though, that over the days of revolution the street-car tracks had been packed deep with snow, which had been trampled and frozen into ice, so that clearing them would require crowbars, and on a Sunday, when you wouldn't be able to find people to work now even on a weekday. The Municipal Board was in total disarray and was asking for assistance from the Executive Committee. (It never would have occurred to anyone to expect assistance from the Provisional Government.)

Clearing the tracks—somehow they would, but the most acute question was what to do about the soldiers. After all, now, taking advantage of the revolution's gains, they would all make their way to the streetcars, and not to the back landing but inside, alongside the ordinary people—and naturally they wouldn't want to pay the ten kopecks and would board for free, even for one or two stops—and in that way pack the streetcars so that neither the old, nor the small, nor women would be able to board or even get close to a streetcar. The streetcar system would go broke and would be serving not the inhabitants but hauling only soldiers—and there were fifteen hundred of them in the garrison. Locusts!

The question had gone from technical to highly political! It made sense to force the soldiers to pay at least half-fare—five kopecks. But the Executive Committee couldn't publish that statement without losing its revolutionary face! The masses had wrested themselves from slavery and won their freedom—and they wanted to enjoy it! The garrison had to be dealt with extremely delicately.

They decided to leave soldier transit gratuitous.

The Municipal Board also asked them to call on the populace to return the streetcar levers and other fixtures. At an acute moment in the street upheavals this had been an impudent find, it had been the key to the Revolution—taking streetcar levers away from conductors.

But now, these same levers had become the key to returning to a peaceful situation.

Documents – 14

EXECUTIVE COMMITTEE OF THE
SOVIET OF WORKERS' AND SOLDIERS' DEPUTIES

From the minutes of 16 March:

RESOLVED:

1) . . . arrest the Romanov dynasty . . .

2) With regard to Mikhail, carry out an actual arrest, but formally declare him merely subject to actual surveillance by the revolutionary army.

3) With regard to Nikolai Nikolaevich, in view of the danger of arresting him in the Caucasus, call him to Petrograd preliminarily and en route establish strict surveillance over him.

Carry out the arrest of the women of the House of Romanov gradually . . .

[3 8 6]

SCREEN

Coat of arms of the Russian state.

A band plays a military march, "The Grenadier"—how fancy! All those wreaths! All those laurels!

Closer —

How much sharpness on all sides! Sharp feathers on strong eagle wings.

Getting even closer —

The force and tension are actually curving the top feathers like claws. And two joined eagle heads, with crests like sharp scales.

Even larger —

Tongues poking out like stingers.

Slightly curved beaks.

This was drawn in obscure antiquity, to frighten neighbors to death. These are the majestic Byzantine eagles, and their ferocious eyes, one apiece, keep us from penetrating their unseen designs.

Two heads—two halves of the Great Roman empire.

"The Grenadier"! How festive, how it flaunts its garlanded splendor. The sounds even admire themselves.

But since then—they've changed, changed this coat of arms, lowered the wings, then lifted them and stretched them out, then gathered up the tail, then spread it wide. So much time they put into these eagles since Peter's reign! Molded them to the banners of all units, to the tops of banner shafts, to belt buckles, to every greatcoat button.

There are marches when your feet barely touch the ground. Like the Paris march of 1815, the march of the world's unselfish victors. Oh, we need none of that, we'll take a look and leave.

To the eagle's black and green body, cast on its spread wings, lighter, the eight coats of arms of the realms, and the soldered center covered with the large shield of

St. George, slaying the dragon from his white steed.

And atop the two crowned eagle heads are two small crowns; they carry above themselves—by nothing, by a light ribbon—one large crown uniting them.

It sails above the coat of arms—on nothing, on the ribbon.

Regiments, regiments, regiments pass somewhere down below, under this coat of arms hanging in the sky.

Moving away —

> Again—the entire coat of arms whole. Now we see its under-
> pinnings. Across the necks and the soldered double body, their
> energies pass to the claws, their whole strength is in those
> claws,
>
> and one claw holds the scepter and the other claw the orb—for
> that other, upper, crown.
>
> Nature does not display such as this to us. But it is firmly articulated.

Each march, meanwhile, has its own sorrow.

> To each his own. You can't get enough of it—but it's frightening.
> And strong. It can hold on and hold on . . .
> But a hammer enters the frame, on a handle, from invisible hands,
> hung on the side at the top—

A blow!

> A blow!—and—
> and no crown! And gone is one of the heads!
> Roman, Byzantine, Russian or otherwise –

A blow!

> hammers it!
> hammers it!
> And there is no orb, it's been broken off!

A blow!

> A blow! And there is no second head and wing, broken off along a
> jagged line!
> And what is left—a soldered body covered by St. George's shield,
> and a solitary scepter in a solitary paw,
> extended now to no one knows who,
> And it holds on by no one knows what –
> but one more blow and it's smashed to bits!
> = And we watch the fragments fly
> past the hammerer on the ladder –
> past the "Pharmacy" sign —
> down to the sidewalk,
> where the previous wooden splinters lie.
> = A handful of people with red scraps on their chests and caps stand
> and watch.

A loud march—"The Joy of Victory"! We won to this march, we stepped to
this march, knowing no bounds. What gaiety there was before! Ah, and
here it is again!

> = And again the eagle coming out from the sign,
> and again a blow of the hammer!

"The Joy of Victory"! over the accursed past. As the trumpets sing and
promise!

> = Nevsky Prospect, one side.

So many of these eagles, they hadn't noticed how the prospect was
    hung with them, not just on the pharmacies—
on the signs of offices,
purveyors to the court,
other merchants . . .
=   People don't hesitate to find tall ladders and prop them up,
    or drive a truck onto the sidewalk: it's easy to knock them down
      from a truck bed.
    And take a hammer to it, the accursed thing!
=   Or a rifle butt!
=   Or paint over what's drawn there with a black brush.
"The Joy of Victory"! It could not have been merrier than before, but it is!
    You couldn't make quicker work of it, but here . . .
=   Fragments piled up. And entire eagles.
    They finish them off with rifle butts on the snowy sidewalk.
    Break and trample them with their feet.
The guffaw of the crowd and the cries—let 'em have it!
=   While the yardmen sweep and sweep . . .
    Sweep energetically, perhaps not merrily, but leaning into it.
    In the broom's sweepings—eagle heads, crowns, orbs, scepters.
=   In front of the Anichkov Palace,
    in front of its two stone gates
    on the sidewalk, on the beaten snow
    they've dragged, collected, a pile of these fragments and—
=   it's burning! A merry activity! Now this is merry!
    They clap their hands, elbow each other in the side,
    show others, watch.
But even this march has an amazing melodiousness in places,
and it modulates imperceptibly to another march, "Longing for the
    Homeland."
=   tongues of fire repeat the bonfire flights of eagle feathers,
    their never-divined bonfire doom!—
    even before, the eagle was aflame, only the flame was black and green!
"Longing for the Homeland"?—are regiments marching somewhere far
    away? And when—when will we go back again? . . .
=   A soldier with his bayonets shoves the fragments of coats of arms,
      the orbs, the crowns into the bonfire
    snags them and tosses them into where the fire's thickest.

[3 8 7]

    That morning, the telephone rang for the celebrated lawyer Karabchev-
sky, chairman of the Petrograd Bar, at his apartment. The voice, which even
in the receiver was young and vibrating, announced:

"Nikolai Platonovich! Speaking with you is Minister of Justice Aleksandr Fyodorovich Kerensky." He introduced himself in the third person and very highly. "As you know, a Provisional Government has formed, and I have taken the minister of justice portfolio in it."

If he hadn't been a member of the State Duma, Kerensky would still be a small-time lawyer, a preparatory-class lawyer who didn't even know the entire Criminal Code. But now the relationship had changed drastically:

"I congratulate you, Aleksandr Fyodorovich!"

"Thank you very much." And straight to the point: "Nikolai Platonovich! I intend to place justice in Russia at a towering height!"

"A superb goal!" Karabchevsky could only be astonished.

"I want," the little-boy voice rang out from his end, "I want to thoroughly reconstitute the Ministry of Justice personnel. And the Senate's. All of this, naturally, to come from the legal estate. Might you, today—the matter can suffer no delay—assemble your comrades from the council? So that I can consult with you and select all the candidates."

"Alas," Karabchevsky could only despair. "As you know, our council's building perished in the fire of the building of Judicial Determinations."

Kerensky would not relent:

"Would you be willing to receive me and the council at your home?"

His onslaught was like a storm you couldn't resist. And he probably should get in step with events and the new minister's rise. They arranged to meet after three o'clock. No matter what your feelings about attorney-at-law Kerensky, everyone was curious and needed to get a good look at this grandiose turning point in history.

By three o'clock, everyone had gathered in Karabchevsky's large study and taken their places in the armchairs and on the sofas. Here as in no other milieu there were many "definite leftists," and they were exultant. They had been celebrating for the past few days and were now this minute, too. Portly Karabchevsky himself and the other respectable lawyers viewed events with restrained enthusiasm (Karabchevsky felt some resentment at the outrageous seizure of his motorcar, which had yet to be found), but they considered themselves obligated all the more to help justice maintain its high standards even in this revolutionary upheaval, the speed of which stunned the imagination.

Everyone found it unusual to see right here as minister not a pretentious imperial official but an accessible colleague from their estate.

At exactly three o'clock, the door in Karabchevsky's office swung open, but in walked not the expected minister but the bulky, clumsy, guilty-looking Count Orlov-Davydov, whom Karabchevsky knew well, having directed his case at one time. The count announced, on behalf of Aleksandr Fyodorovich, that Aleksan Fyodich was slightly delayed, he'd been detained in the Duma, and he, Orlov-Davydov, asked permission to wait here. Karabchevsky led him into the next room.

As they waited for the minister, they discussed what was going on, what had and hadn't happened. It turned out that in the District Court fire **all** the notarial documents of Petersburg had burned up! A rumor had gone around that the members of the Duma Committee, while declaring their authority, all had poison on them—and if government forces came, they would all kill themselves. (Karabchevsky didn't believe it. What could threaten them that gravely?)

Suddenly movement was heard in the front hall. The porter zealously opened the office door—and a skinny, well-proportioned young man with a short crewcut of fair hair walked in quickly, half at a run. He was wearing some kind of black workers jacket (although waisted) whose standing collar enveloped his narrow neck so high—and whose lapel was buttoned to the top, and whose sleeves were tight at the wrists—that not a glimpse of his white shirt was visible anywhere, as if the jacket had been donned over his naked body.

No one in society dressed like that. There was something military-campaign-ish in this attire and something immediately unusual that set the new minister apart from mortals.

Hurrying behind him was another young man wearing a military uniform, but they recognized him—another lawyer. With an easy sideways movement of his left hand, Kerensky let it be known that this behind him was the minister's aide.

Orlov-Davydov's large head poked out indelicately from the other door, observing but reluctant to enter.

Everyone stood up, and Kerensky threw his head back and stopped short, awaiting greetings. He was very smoothly shaven, but the impression was as if nothing grew on his face yet. However, his shining, exalted look expressed such fiery faith that they dared not laugh.

Karabchevsky, with his luxuriant leonine head (the lion of the Beilis trial) and the gravitas of an old lawyer in possession of magniloquent gestures and a velvety voice, delivered the expected, albeit brief, speech to the boy-minister. Saying that the Petrograd Bar hoped the new Minister of Justice would be the staunch keeper of the law that Russia, tormented by lawlessness, so badly needed.

Still in the same frozen, thrown-back position, Kerensky heard him out and then flung both his light arms to the side, wishing to embrace everyone at once—and with a bullet's speed and an appealing sincerity, wholly emanating sincerity, said:

"My dear teachers! Dear comrades! I have not yet accepted the ministry—and here I am already with you! If there is something truly worthy and fine, and perhaps the only something worthy and fine, in Russia after all, then it is undoubtedly the legal profession. Who else has always stood watch over the law and freedom? And here I am with you in the very first hours of my activities! I have come to ask you to take as much part as feasible in raising justice to a height that corresponds to the importance of the historical moment!" Naturally, he might have said much much more, but his emotions would not let him go on. Instead, he rushed to embrace and bestow a kiss on all the lawyers present, beginning with Karabchevsky.

This happened so quickly and abruptly and with such a flood of emotions that when he had bestowed his kiss on everyone and they had seated him in an armchair, he was close to fainting. His narrow face, pale, too youthful, and his too-thin neck, and that short hair, cut like a little boy's, suddenly exposed how puny and defenseless he was.

His hands were cold. His pallor was deep, his head leaned against the chair back, and his eyes were barely looking.

Karabchevsky took serious fright that the minister was about to die in his apartment. He instructed strong wine be served and quickly.

The minister barely showed any movement. Everyone, stunned, held their breath between life and death. Orlov-Davydov, who looked like a very big, very sad dog, had squeezed wholly through the door and was reassuring them that this happened with Aleksan Fyodorych—due to excessively deep emotions, due to overexhaustion—and would pass soon. He needed a sniff of ammonia.

But Karabchevsky had already raised a glass of wine to his lifeless lips. Kerensky's lips responded immediately and he took a few sips.

He continued to lie there, leaning back, but already coming around. Color returned to his skinny face. His features were no longer so doomed.

"I'm tired . . . terribly terribly tired," the minister said weakly. "Four nights without any sleep at all. . . ." But pride returned to his gaze: "On the other hand—it has come to pass! What we didn't dare expect has come to pass!"

Everyone took their seats, and hirsute Orlov-Davydov squeezed back into the adjoining room.

The reviving minister did not fail to sympathize with the fact that the fire had deprived the lawyers of such a beautiful and well-appointed building.

Karabchevsky objected politely in response:

"Yes, it's sad that our old comforts have perished, but it is significant that our tie to the old court has been broken in this way and we are no longer dependent on it but are called upon to correct the evil it has done."

Questions rang out—to learn from the minister about the details of the new government's formation.

Growing steadily easier and livelier, Kerensky began to speak more and more easily and rapidly. His narrow head was moving freely, and his hands were now dancing on the armrests.

"Gentlemen! I have accepted this post for the sake of our homeland's salvation! Cognizant of the full importance and full responsibility . . ."

He listed the principal ministers, but rather offhandedly, not one of them with respect. He also said quite frankly that the most striking and most radical minister was, naturally, he himself—and in the position of Prosecutor-General, in addition. And now in the matter of Russian justice there would be no place for any compromises with reactionaries whatsoever. He guaranteed it! Now—his look became menacing, and yet schoolboy-ish—the justice system would see a most thorough *purge*!

Yes, they objected, embarrassed, but after all, judges and senators were lifetime appointments by law, and this was an important gain of Aleksandr II's reforms. . . .

Yes! Yes! Naturally, Kerensky highly prized the principle of judges' permanence and was especially deeply devoted to this sacred principle, and we have all defended it against the claws of autocracy. Yes! But it's impossible not to remove them! We must clean house! We're going to have to find ways to compel some to leave voluntarily.

"Ah, but look"—he turned to address one of the council members present—"you're going to be able to arrange this for us, isn't that so? Right now I am appointing you director of the staffing department. I hope you'll agree? . . . Gentlemen, I hope you approve?"

No one said a word against it, although they were baffled. The man appointed was known only for his leftist party predilections, but otherwise only for his laziness and inefficiency.

The minister hastened to pass out more positions, and it was evident how proud he was that this was happening so simply, so amicably, among peers and in a private apartment, as it could not have been under the ossified Tsarist regime. He made the appointments with a light, homey touch, not writing anything down.

He needed a prosecutor for the Petrograd High Court. Someone suggested Pereverzev, who had defended the *Potemkin* sailors, had conducted himself gloriously in the Beilis trial, and not just the one political trial, and was now at the front as a food supply inspector. Karabchevsky objected:

"But he's racing around there on a horse. Let him."

But Kerensky liked this immediately.

"Then let him race around on a horse here! The prosecutor of the revolution—and on a horse! Magnificent! I'm appointing him!"

But he got to thinking about Karabchevsky:

"Nikolai Platonovich! What about you? Do you want to be senator of the criminal appeals department? Agree! My firm intention is to appoint several lawyers as senators! By the way, you know," he recalled or even had always remembered, "They were sorting through cases in the Ministry of Justice criminal department and they found Protopopov's report on opening a criminal prosecution against your humble servant—for one of my speeches in the Duma. How do you like that?" He cocked his head to the side, perhaps a little coquettishly despite that strict black jacket. "If it had gone a little further, if the revolution hadn't happened—I . . . unfortunately. . . . You and I would not be meeting here like this. . . ."

Nonetheless, Karabchevsky was not convinced by the generous offer. This was some frivolous game. Such offhand appointments couldn't possibly be for real. He asked that he be left as he was, a lawyer.

And what kind of lawyer he was—everyone knew that. Who in the Russian legal profession could forget his stormy defense of Sazonov, who had killed Pleve! He had gone above and beyond all a lawyer's limits. He was not defending Sazonov, he was accusing the murdered Pleve, who had hung this person, imprisoned thousands of others, mocked the intelligentsia, strangled Finland, squeezed the Poles, and incited men to massacre Jews! . . . The judge had tried to stop him, but Karabchevsky had gone on like a magnificent lion: "What I mean is that Sazonov understood it this way, that Pleve was a monster! Killing him meant freeing the Russian people. It was a good deed!" Ah, how many immortal speeches have been delivered in Russia. No, this will never die. This will yield a hundredfold harvest of freedom!

So it was now.

"I will still be of use to someone as a defender."

"Under the new regime? To whom?" Kerensky wondered with a roving, distracted smile. "Not to Nikolai Romanov?"

"And why not?" Karabchevsky proudly accepted the challenge. "Even for him. If you make up your mind to try him."

Kerensky leaned back pensively, his eyes searching somewhere above those gathered. Then, in the general silence, he ran his index finger across his own neck—and briskly jerked his finger up.

Everyone understood the sign: hanging!

There was no way to understood it otherwise.

Kerensky cast an enigmatic glance over them all, still listening for something:

"Might two or three sacrifices be essential?" He was consulting with them, or perhaps informing them of the indubitable.

"No!" Karabchevsky made bold to object during this sepulchral silence. "Anything but that. You must forget about the French Revolution. Better to forget it! It's shameful to follow in its bloody tracks. We are in the twentieth century."

Other voices rang out, asking the death penalty not be invoked.

"Oh yes! Oh yes!" Kerensky assented quite easily, in a new outburst. "A bloodless revolution had always been my dream! Just wait! We will astonish the world with our magnanimity no less than with we have with the painlessness of the coup!"

And he began speaking heatedly about how many legislative commissions were to be created immediately, how the laws would be reviewed decisively. How the country would receive, in the very first decrees, the gifts of full and equal rights for the Jews! and equal rights for women!

"However!" And he raised his finger ominously, and his youthful voice acquired a metallic edge. "One of our very first actions will be to create an Extraordinary Commission of Inquiry for handing former ministers over to the court! Dignitaries! High-level officials! And I shall appoint as chairman"—he gave a hearty laugh but then sternly again—"Moscow attorney-at-law Mu-ravyov! Eh? The same last name! Let it remind people of Muravyov the hangman, Muravyov the minister—and make them tremble! Eh?"

Tea was served.

[3 8 8]

Poisoned, all poisoned. Work ablaze—and it had fallen from his hands.

Hour after hour, locked up in the minister's office, Bublikov remained glued to the telephone, conducting negotiations with Rodzyanko and others—to remain Minister of Roads and Railways. Rodzyanko had already yielded and promised that Nekrasov could move over to the Ministry of Education. Could Bublikov himself come in for talks? . . .

"I have no desire to talk to him! My foot will not remain here for a minute under Nekrasov; he comes in one door and I go out the other!"

He had put the victory and all of Russia at their feet! They couldn't appreciate that, the swine!

Bublikov had the idea that every hour he was still here was his gain. He had to issue a storm of orders and impose reforms, if only to leave behind an indelible revolutionary memory.

He drew up directive after directive and sent them down the lines.

Cancel all instructions from the former committees on railway security.

Release everyone arrested or punished by those committees.

Announce to all railroaders that Russia's rebirth into a new, free existence instills a firm hope in everyone selflessly fulfilling their duty, so that no punishments will be required anymore.

They reported from the Vindava railway that soldiers were smashing up stations and lunchrooms.

That's all right. You can't make an omelet without breaking eggs.

He and Lomonosov began discussing what kind of government this really was. It was shameful. Who there was a specialist? They'd spent fifty years winning their freedom just to put together this gaggle of ninnies. It was simply unbearable for an expert to watch.

Meanwhile Lomonosov had already assembled the typesetters (Cavalry Captain Sosnovsky had posted a guard at the press), but he hadn't been able to start printing the Manifesto all day because the Tauride Palace hadn't given the go-ahead. The perfect clarity of the situation notwithstanding, they hadn't! Idiots! What were they waiting for? It was clear that the faster it got printed, the faster we'd be done with Nikolashka.

For now, they handwrote a copy of the abdication, and certified it themselves. This was what was sent (instead of sending the precious original through the dangerous streets) at the government's demand, for some reason to 12 Millionnaya Street.

While that was dragging out, he discussed with his own people here what they should want. A parliamentary monarchy? The entire dynasty's deposition perhaps? That would be much handsomer and more revolutionary, wafts of gunpowder smoke! But in time of war? . . .

Finally his man Lebedev called from Millionnaya, where he had remained to reconnoiter: Hurrah! One more abdication in favor of a Constituent Assembly! Nabokov had sat down to write the document.

Stunning! Like a golden dream. The sacred old words: Constituent Assembly!

But when would they bring it to print? Damnation! Why weren't they allowing it? They were destroying the whole revolution!

The dynasty would turn around—and take it all back.

And the Soviet of Deputies—they beat us out, the scoundrels! Without having the texts, they released a flyer through the streets with the headline: "Nikolai abdicates in favor of Mikhail and Mikhail in favor of the people!"

Finally the order arrived from the Duma: print the first Manifesto.

But where was the second?

For some reason, Prince Lvov had taken the second to the Duma and would send it on afterward.

Lomonosov went down to the press and there, reveling in his voice, read out Nikolai's abdication.

The two old typesetters crossed themselves devoutly, as for someone deceased.

[3 8 9]

Lev Tolstoy's former, and last, secretary, Valentin Bulgakov—still a young man, these past few days traveling for the Union of Zemstvos, where he had spent the war years—had ended up in Petrograd. Now, seeing everything going on here, the final victory of the new regime, which meant, presumably, an imminent broad amnesty, he felt a responsibility and concern. How could he deliver from the prisons the Tolstoyans, Malevannians, and Subbotniks who, because of their convictions, had refused to perform military service and had done time at hard labor or in prisoner companies? His concern was that they were listed as criminals rather than religious, so an amnesty composed in revolutionary haste might not include them. Meanwhile, as the young Tolstoyan realized, these were the best, the purest people, whose moral consciousness was centuries ahead of the consciousness of modern humanity, and their entire guilt lay in the fact that they were above those who had remained at liberty. There were a few hundred such people in all Russia, and he had to hurry to free them.

But to whom should he turn? And how? Obviously, directly to the new Minister of Justice, Kerensky. Famous for his fairness and impartiality, the young minister, a bold friend of freedom, would not fear being reproached for Germanophilia and would resolve the matter quickly and favorably. And he had to hurry, before the amnesty was published. But each of the previous days Bulgakov had tried and failed to get into the Tauride Palace. Just in case, he had first written the minister a letter laying everything out and sealed it.

Today it wasn't hard to get to the palace and the open space in front of it, but on the front steps they checked very strictly and demanded his pass.

He thought of showing all the guards his envelope, which he had to put in the minister's hands personally. They started advising him on how to obtain a pass. They let him through the first door, to the commandant's office. They wouldn't issue him a pass but sent him to the duty officer unit, where they told him they didn't know anything. At the entrance to the Ekaterininsky Hall, the student monitors sent him upstairs, to the Military Commission, for a pass.

More corridors, recesses, recesses. There were guards with rifles at some doors (but they were smoking at their posts). A spiral iron staircase nearly to the attic. Low ceilings, smoke everywhere, lots of officers, and also soldiers, and everyone pushing, and squeezing through, and talking. A sign on one door, on a scrap of paper in blue pencil: "War Ministry." A cultivated sailor asked those entering:

"What are you here for?"

Bulgakov showed him the envelope, and the sailor let him through.

In the small, low-ceilinged room filled with tobacco smoke and people and all spat upon and soiled, he spotted two or three tables with papers. At one table sat a soldier and a red-faced young lady wearing a thin white blouse who was fanning herself with her handkerchief. Bulgakov started repeating what he had said and taking his Union of Zemstvos papers out of his pocket in order to confirm his identity—but the soldier didn't even look and quickly filled out a blank typed on a Remington: "Certificate. Issued herewith to (name) the right to free entry and exit from the State Duma as working in the Military Commission. For the head of the general office . . ." Seal of the Duma Committee.

In just that brief time the sweat had started pouring off Bulgakov. He rushed downstairs with his document. Now everything was open to him.

He found himself in a corridor where there were fewer people and they were speaking softly, couriers gave out information on where to find whom, and no one went through any doors without being announced first. At the right door they told him that Kerensky was not in the Tauride Palace just then.

Wouldn't you know it. The good it had done him. He decided to try something else:

"And Vasili Alekseevich Maklakov?"

"I'll check." The courier didn't go through the door, though, but toward a long coatrack right there in the corridor and started going through the fur and woolen coats.

"No, Maklakov's not here either."

So ended his contemplated petition. Bulgakov couldn't think of anything else and so went to the Ekaterininsky Hall to hang around the Duma for a while.

A rally was under way there. From an open, elevated staircase that led to the galleries of the Duma hall of sessions, an officer read Nikolai's abdication once and then once more. Then people started buzzing and shouts rang out: "What about Mikhail?" More shouts demanding a member of the new government come and report.

The crowd, not too dense, was shifting from foot to foot and droning away. Cigarette peddlers and candy sellers jostled. While others started talking, small rallies. Close by, a youth of the Jewish type with burning eyes called on people to follow not the Provisional Government, and not the landowner Rodzyanko, but the Soviet of Workers' Deputies.

After ten minutes or so, a gentleman went up on the landing and announced that he was State Duma member Lebedev and he had been delegated to inform those gathered that Grand Duke Mikhail Aleksandrovich's refusal of the throne had indeed taken place.

People started applauding. And shouting "hurrah!"

Meanwhile, some young cadets entered the hall with a tromping of boots that could be heard even through the noise and, independently of the rally, immediately formed up along the length of the hall, by the columns, in two rows. They said they wanted to present themselves to the new government. Everything was here. Everything was in this hall!

But not a single free or willing government member was to be found, rather the gray-haired honorable Duma member Klyuzhev, a specialist in popular education, went out to the cadets and started talking in his old man's voice—first calmly, about all the great principles from the eighteenth century on which humanity stands and about our Mother Russia, and about the precepts of the great Suvorov, and how the young officers would become the soldiers' teachers, and then—agitated now, the old man's voice even started to shake—how the officers would become the conduits to the people, through the soldier, of education and those great ideas put forth by our revolution.

A young lady standing near Bulgakov began protesting loudly:

"It's a lie. A lie! What's this nonsense he's saying! It's wrong! . . ."

In an hour here, Bulgakov had discerned a number of these extremely forward and rather disheveled young ladies who had packed in here, taken up nearly all the chairs, formed a semi-circle opposite the tribune, and made more noise than anyone deciding whether or not to give their approval. Who gave them this authority? Whose representatives were they? Each behaved as if she were the voice of the revolution itself. More than likely they had familial ties, connections to figures, and that way had obtained entrance passes—and now as a mass were expressing the correct opinion, drowning out anything and everything else.

One cadet nearby objected to the young lady. She shrilly defended her position, unintimidated by the speaker.

Right then people came out on the same staircase landing and announced that the rally in this hall had to stop because it was interfering with the session of the Soviet of Workers' Deputies in the main Duma hall.

The cadets made a sharp turn and exited in formation, the rest wandered off, and some of the young ladies abandoned their chairs. Bulgakov, too, started wandering around the hall—and only then did he see in the far left corner another separate group of people, gathered tightly and cordoned off from the public by a chain of armed soldiers. What was this? They turned out to be arrested policemen and constables who were being transferred from building to building but had been detained and shunted to the side in the Ekaterininsky Hall by the rally—and so had involuntarily taken part in it.

The majority of the policemen were in civilian dress and looked on aloofly, others frowned—while idlers went up to them to gawk, some with curiosity, some with hatred.

Bulgakov went back and asked for Kerensky again—not there. He despaired and was about to leave when suddenly he saw in the aisle of the Cupola Hall the characteristic lumplike, elephant-headed figure of Prince Pavel Dolgorukov, chairman of the Kadet Party's Moscow Committee. Here was luck! Such a prominent man, the conscience of the Kadet party, and an acquaintance: he had been at Yasnaya Polyana and at Moscow meetings of the Tolstoy Society. Here was his rescue! Bulgakov hurried to intercept him. The prince recognized him.

"Dear friend! What brings you here?"

Bulgakov told him, with great agitation, about his business. He was now counting on Dolgorukov seeing this all through, going all the way to Milyukov if he had to:

"Pavel Dmitrich! Why, at such a time, should the purest, most moral people remain in prison?"

"Yes." The prince slackened and hung his head slightly. "It's a ticklish question. . . ."

"But Pavel Dmitrich, but why? Would you have thought this way a month, a week ago? It is a straightforward matter. These are pure prisoners of conscience! What has changed? The revolution can only bring their swifter release!"

"Yes, my dear man," the prince was thinking and stalling. "Exactly, the situation has changed. Under the Tsar, not one of us would have doubted. . . . But if in the present situation we were to announce release for all of them? Well, think for yourself. . . . It's dangerous! After all, so many malingerers would be drawn after them. Who would go on fighting? You know, I would strongly advise you not to raise this issue right now. . . . It might seriously complicate the new government's position."

[3 9 0]

Betrayal undercuts us worse than any external calamity. It drains the main forces from our heart, a draining for which no means can compensate.

The entire previous night, the betrayal of the Guards Crew, which had somehow been pushed back by the string of the day's events, had returned and had burned—seared—her heart. There was also the betrayal of those generals or whoever was close to the Emperor now—instead of supporting him they had continued to hold him trapped. She didn't know whose betrayal it was, but it had to be a betrayal by many if all help had flowed away and those close and loyal to him were no more—whereas there were always plenty of strangers and enemies. Even Sablin—what *surveillance* was he under that he couldn't come after changing clothes, as Apraksin had?

What was happening with Nicky? Why had he spent a second night in Pskov? Why wasn't he moving this way with troops?

To people of great energy such as Aleksandra Fyodorovna was, the impossibility of acting or even knowing events is enervating.

She barely fell asleep for an hour and a half just before dawn. In the morning she looked at herself in the mirror. How much thinner and older she had grown in just a few days! Her heart had swollen painfully even more, as if it had shifted. Her legs hurt and she could barely walk.

Even the children had gotten worse: their ears had become inflamed and hurt badly, and their measles promised to develop with serious complications. Only the heir was at ease, and Marie was still holding out.

The unstable atmosphere between the palace and Tsarskoye Selo garrison continued even after the Duma deputies toured the garrison. Naturally, though, the palace's defenders could not have withstood a storm, and bloodshed could not be allowed! So they patrolled near the palace wearing white armbands, like a neutral service. While the hero General Groten sat under arrest in the town hall. Such a defender was no more!

What was going to happen to the palaces of Pavlovsk, Gatchina, Peterhof, and Oranienbaum? At any moment they could be smashed and looted—and there were no forces to prevent that.

Nothing new had trickled in. Events seemed at a standstill. Toppled, Petrograd could no longer bring good news, just more and more arrests. The telephones were silent. No friendly messengers had come.

The day went on, and the day went on—and not one line more from Nicky in Pskov. The officers had left—had they reached him? Oh, if only she had one sentence from him! A telegram!

It was easier since she'd started discussing everything frankly with the children.

And the weather was sunny, pristine, not a cloud, not a breeze! That meant: believe and hope.

They found a good outlet for these wearying hours. They brought the large icon of the Mother of God into the green bedroom where the children lay, and the priest came from the Church of Our Lady of the Sign and led a marvelous service and acathistus. Very heartening!

God is above us all and we must live by limitless faith in Him. We do not know His ways, or how He will help, but He will hear all prayers.

Then they carried the icon through all the rooms with singing and censing. They carried it into and walked all the way around the courtyard, song and incense rising to the sky, the icon's gold under the sun. They carried it to Anya's wing.

Right then the Empress learned that an officer's wife was planning to go to Pskov—and they agreed that she would take a letter for the Emperor.

What a relief for her heart! She could write!

But she couldn't write too much or too clearly. What if the woman were searched en route? Everyone had lost their minds now.

My beloved, the soul of my soul, my little one! Oh, how my heart bleeds for you! I'm going out of my mind, knowing nothing but the most vile rumors, which could lead a person to madness and rend her heart. Oh, my angel! God will have mercy on you and will send strength and wisdom down upon you! He will reward you for these unbelievable sufferings. Everything has to be fine. I do not waver in my faith. We are all holding on. Each conceals his alarm. I have too much in my soul and heart, I cannot write . . .

I am holding on only by my faith in my martyr and am myself not intervening in anything. I have a fear of harming something by a wrong action, since there is no news from you. Of *them*, the Duma men, I have seen no one and asked about nothing, so do not believe it if they tell you such a thing. Now everyone is lying.

And right then—as if in confirmation that everyone was now lying incredibly, a downcast and embarrassed Benckendorff arrived and asked permission to convey a sinister, unbelievable rumor.

"What now?" The Empress clutched her heart.

By way of routes unknown and from he knew not whom, the absurd rumor had come that the Emperor had given up the throne altogether, wholly.

Well, this was so far beyond wild that the Empress did not even get upset. She went on writing her letter.

But at dusk, before she could finish and send it off, she was informed that Grand Duke Pavel had arrived.

She rejoiced. A break in the silence, to speak with someone fresh and generally well-disposed.

And immediately—his face struck her. On his last visit he had tried to bear himself with pompous importance, defending himself. Now he bore a solicitous expression, as if he were approaching an invalid's bed.

He fell to the Empress's hand with a long kiss. He straightened up—and still said nothing.

Only then did the Empress take fright.

"What? What's happened to Nicky?" she asked brokenly. (She thought, Is he alive?)

"Nicky is fine," Pavel hastened to right himself. "But I wanted to be by Your side in this difficult moment. . . ."

"What?" the Empress exclaimed.

"You don't know?" he said, amazed.

He took a scanty printed leaflet with large, pale black letters on crummy paper out of his pocket. It was folded, and he began unfolding it.

This was the emergency communiqué about the Emperor's abdication of the throne—both for himself and for the heir. Just this—no text, no details.

"This cannot be! Deceit! Forgery! They're forging everything now!" she exclaimed and she stamped her foot.

But for whom? Where would this leaflet have come from, rolled and rolled and rolled out by printing presses?

Under no circumstances whatsoever! Nicky would rather die than sign such a thing!

But the gray-haired, majestic Pavel stood there dolefully.

The paper's very dirtiness, its filthy grayness, its repulsiveness denied any possibility of arguing.

Truth shows itself to us in impossible vestments.

"It's all over," said Pavel. "Russia is in the hands of the most terrible revolutionaries."

His look, though, was not entirely in keeping with these words. He had sent his own idiotic manifesto to the Duma, after all, recognizing the new regime.

And now he was also talking rubbish about how he'd written to Rodzyanko today imploring him to return a constitutional throne to the Emperor.

Oh no! Oh, not that!

As the soul flies out of the body at death, so the Empress's consciousness flew out of her and up, high up, to the sky, to the very pinnacle of existence, seeking explanations for what had happened.

And there, in the heavenly height, she understood her adored husband: he had remained true to himself. He had been compelled to yield—but not in the main thing. He had not signed anything that contradicted what he had sworn to at his coronation. He had not inflicted harm on the crown itself, had not divided it. He had not sworn an oath to any vile constitution. He had saved his own holy purity. He had sworn to pass it on to his son. But he couldn't pass on to him less than full power. That was what this was about! Meanwhile, Aleksei was a minor and could not swear an oath to a constitution.

No sooner had she returned from her flight than her legs buckled. She dropped into an armchair and wept.

Pavel stood before her solemnly and sorrowfully.

He seemed to be ready to console the Empress for a long time. But she had no need of him and soon let him go.

It was easier for her to grind and digest the full weight that had come crashing down by herself.

He advised her something at the end—but she didn't hear it or take it in. Only an hour later did she recall what he'd said. He had suggested she make an inventory of her jewels and surrender them to the Provisional Government for safekeeping. What nonsense.

But Pavel had the best intentions. It turned out, as he left, he also addressed a crowd of soldiers not in formation by the palace approach:

"Brothers! Our beloved Emperor has abdicated. In the palace that you guard, there is neither Empress nor Heir but rather a nursemaid and her sick children. . . . Promise me, your old superior, to keep them healthy and unharmed."

They promised dissonantly.

Was she really just a nursemaid?

No, the Empress could not yet feel herself that. But her head and heart could not keep up with what she had learned.

The Judas Ruzsky! This was all his doing, of course!

She went to share the news. With Lili. She didn't speak English, with her she spoke Russian.

"Your Majesty, I love you more than anything in the world!" Lili exclaimed through tears.

"I know that. I see that, Lili."

Lili ran for Dr. Botkin, who came with medicine.

Marie, the first of the children to learn the news, sobbed bitterly, curled up in the corner of her large sofa.

But she couldn't bring herself to tell the sick ones. And there was no point.

She also had to console old Benckendorff.

But at what emotional impasse, in what despair and impotence, could Nicky have signed such a thing? Everything that had been built these twenty-two years—and even earlier by his father—and even earlier by his grandfather—and great-grandfather—to destroy everything with one stroke of the pen?

No, anything but reproach him now. This was hardest of all on him.

What if she sent—along inoperative lines—into nowhere—a hopeless telegram?

Oh, I shall not let anyone touch your radiant, righteous soul!

[3 9 1]

The most august Supreme Commander did not rejoice for long over the previous night's news. Just before morning he sent GHQ his solemn Order No. 1—and had barely lain down, in his boots, on the sofa, imagining what happiness awaited Stana upon awakening—when half an hour later he himself was tapped on the shoulder and told not to announce the Tsar's Manifesto, to delay it!

What had happened? Dread filled his heart! And . . . and . . .?

No, the Supreme Commander's appointment was not being stopped.

Thank God. Russia, in any case, was saved.

But what had gone on there in Pskov? What had Nicky been doing—wavering, resisting, clinging? . . .

Perhaps he should be allowed to remain? He was in no way worse than Misha. But what about Alix then? . . . And all the squabbles again from the beginning? . . .

So the present day stretched on in harrowing uncertainty and there still was no perfect joy.

Almost no one knew the fateful secret, the swinging of history's weights—and outwardly Tiflis exulted. Since last evening, the newspapers had been erupting with streams of revolutionary news. The crazily joyous Mayor Khatisov rode in for his appointment—and was received kindly. From here he hurried to send out to all cities that there had been no clashes in the Caucasus between the regime and the populace. And then to the emergency session of the City Duma to report on his meeting with the Viceroy. That the Supreme Commander had declared that anyone in government service who dared not recognize the instructions of the new government would be immediately removed. The populace was presented with full freedom of assembly! He also ordered political prisoners released from the Baku prison.

The eastern streets of Tiflis, especially Erivan Square, and near the Kura, and the entire city basin under wide, sheltering Mount David with its white church on its slope and its funicular to the top, were filled with exultation and there was red everywhere. At the railway settlement of Nakhalovka, a joyous rally was held.

They didn't know what a heart-rending struggle was going on under cover!

The most august Supreme Commander was heart and soul as one with this popular exultation and the new regime. He stepped out on the palace's broad balcony. He sent a telegram to Prince Lvov, who had always been so well-disposed, requesting that His Excellency, as of this moment, keep the grand duke informed about the state of affairs in the Empire, for only in this way could the Supreme Commander fulfill his duty to lead the armies.

But the Manifesto was teetering, the throne was teetering—and the Supreme Commander might teeter as well. While here, in Tiflis, his post was reliable and worthy.

And—would that the telegraph help and overtake our desires!—send Prince Lvov one more telegram encoded and top secret:

". . . It is with satisfaction that I can attest that the peoples of the Caucasus Territory regard me with trust. The appointment of a new Viceroy right now would be extremely dangerous. I would deem it extremely desirable for the common cause for me to retain the title of Viceroy. For the duration of the war, I could leave my deputy here. . . ."

Meanwhile, a confused and dangerous telegram arrived from Alekseev in the middle of the day. It seemed to have as its goal explaining the Manifesto's delay to the commanders, but he was in fact advancing a plan for how to resist the State Duma and its President, and, perhaps, even the new government. A secret meeting of commanders akin to a conspiracy?

Oh no! With God as his witness, Nikolai Nikolaevich's attitude toward the new regime had not been clouded by anything and he wanted to keep it pure. He would not allow any conspiracy, which went against his chivalrous nature!

He replied to Alekseev with the frostiest insistence, saying that the role of expressing the Army's opinion was entrusted to the Supreme Commander solely—although, of course, he would inquire as to the commanders' opinion. Our sacred duty is to fulfill our duty in battle with the enemy. It would be a few days before the grand duke could leave for GHQ, so for now he would be issuing the appropriate instructions from here.

Although Nikolai Nikolaevich was prepared to spread his wings and immediately fly across the Caucasus range to Mogilev, the Caucasus viceregency was not a mere needle to be tossed aside so easily, especially given the populace's boundless love for you. The circuitous rail journey extended the travel time even more.

But the handover of the throne to Mikhail concerned him greatly. This would inevitably incite carnage. At the same time, the next heir had not been indicated. Who would it be *after* Mikhail? It was important to know the Prime Minister's opinion on this—he was right there in the cauldron of events.

Once again, Adjutant General Nikolai sent Prince Lvov what was now a third telegram—encoded and top secret.

. . . It is essential that I learn immediately your opinion on the matter of the Manifesto. Personally, I worry that abdication in favor of Grand Duke Mikhail Aleksandrovich will intensify the confusion in the people's minds, especially given the unclear wording. Who is heir to the throne? At the same time, I have received reports of an impending agreement with the Soviet of Workers' Deputies on calling a Constituent Assembly. As Supreme Commander responsible for our armies' success, I must state categorically that this would be a great mistake threatening Russia with ruin. Not for a minute have I doubted that the Provisional Government unites around itself all patriotically minded Russian people. For the general calming of minds, a formal oath by the Emperor to a constitutional form of governance will be essential. . . .

How willingly, how freely and consciously would a Nikolai III now give such an oath!

*　　*　　*

Traitors to the people's welfare. . . . Perennial thieves of the Russian land. . . . All these owls from the sinister monarchical forest . . . The hard-of-hearing old regime. . . .

*　　*　　*

[3 9 2]

Responses from the army commanders began arriving at Western Army Group headquarters.

From Nesvizh, Second Army Commander General Smirnov replied that if it had been decided to acquaint the army with the situation inside the country, then they must speak only the naked truth. If the soldiers' faith in the explanations of their immediate superiors were undermined, that would be terrible. We must not betray instability in our decisions: retractions and changes provoke disorderly thought.

All this had the ring of truth for a military man, so that it was actually shameful to hear from his subordinates, who insisted on firmness, no ambiguity, openness, and nothing else! Evert scarcely needed to ask his subordinates about this. Since yesterday, instead of all this unrelated correspondence, he had had to take the decisions of a commander. Alekseev could not head up the Army; that was clear. But where was the grand duke, and how long would it take him to get here?

From Dombrovitsy, Third Army Commander General Lesch replied that the army was calm for now. But postponing the meeting to 21–22 March was too long. Rumors would get through and could lead to disturbances. Since the Manifesto had been announced in some places, it was better to adhere to it and announce its implementation.

From Molodechno, Tenth Army Commander General Gorbatovsky replied that conveying the throne to Grand Duke Mikhail Aleksandrovich would not lead to the country's pacification. The best solution was to pass the throne on to the Heir Apparent, to whom the army and people had already sworn an oath, and establish as regent Grand Duke Nikolai Nikolaevich as the most popular among the troops and the people.

This was beginning to look like a parliament: three voices and there was already disagreement. This was why military life required decisions by a sole leader! Who to give the throne to, who the regency—that was for them on top to decide, not a matter for our minds. But Gorbatovsky went on to write correctly that the decision could not be delayed for a single day!

Evert himself thought the very same thing. He pictured the oh-so-quiet Alekseev and his trifling, inexpressive face with slits for eyes. What was he capable of venturing? A conscientious staff clerk, that's what he was, and no kind of commander-in-chief. What bad luck that he was all they had standing at the head of the Russian army during these critical days! . . .

Reporting to GHQ and summarizing all three commanders' opinion, Evert concluded by expressing his own thoughts:

". . . Delaying for a day, for an hour, is inadmissible! We must give the troops an absolutely definite . . ."

A definite what? If everything had already been decided and signed in Petrograd anyway, the army couldn't go counter, could it?

". . . a definite explanation about the new administration and regime . . . The troops might attribute the absence of an official explanation to leaders' reluctance to make peace with the new situation, their opposition. . . ."

That was where the danger lay. Dangers on all sides, in fact.

". . . The creation of the Provisional Government and the holding of elections for the Constituent Assembly will plunge the country into a prolonged period of anarchy. The troops will also demand the right to vote and undoubted upheavals will begin."

But a solution could be seen, nonetheless, and Evert suggested it to Alekseev. Repeat the previous day's device—a collective statement by the commanders, only now with respect to the State Duma. Demand the immediate announcement of the supreme Manifesto legitimately published by the Senate. And in the name of the homeland's salvation, reject a Constituent Assembly, which would lead to upheavals in the country and army, to havoc and devastation.

But what if the Duma didn't agree?

". . . Failing this, ask for our replacement by men who are capable of leading the troops to a victorious conclusion even amidst the devastation."

A kind of concession? But a sarcastic concession that made them laugh. He would like to see those victorious generals of the Provisional Government!

". . . And this declaration must be made no later than tomorrow morning. Postponing the congress of commanders until the 21st is out of the question, so quickly is the situation developing!"

He signed his sticklike signature. He would have liked to see the slits of Alekseev's eyes narrow.

Evert livened up, fortified, over this reply. Indeed, what kind of blind obscurity had confused him and them all yesterday? Why had they lost their military voice? Why had they lost their firm footing? How had they dared instruct the Emperor so disrespectfully—but wouldn't dare instruct the Duma? Why had they gotten mixed up in this at all? But since they had . . .

If the commanders felt so abandoned, though, how must all the officers and soldiers of the Western Army Group feel, especially given this rumor about a banned Manifesto?

"Here's what, my dear Mikhail Fyodorych," he told Kvetsinsky. "You sit right down and write an order for the army group."

Evert's thoughts matured ponderously, just as he himself was ponderous, but with persistence and depth.

"Write in the spirit I like. Not a decree but more like a fatherly admonition from me. Say they shouldn't waste their time and nerves on a pointless discussion of domestic governance. Let order in the rear be the concern of those invested with it. The troops should be looking ahead, in the enemy's eyes, not back."

The order was indisputably clear, and bald Kvetsinsky willingly went to compose it.

But while he was composing, GHQ just would not respond. It had come to a standstill. What were they deciding there? Meanwhile, the hours were passing.

GHQ had not responded, but the quartermaster general now brought the local Minsk news. This evening, in the city duma, there was going to be an unauthorized emergency meeting of the zemstvo, the city duma members, and cooperative members—and they wanted to elect a "committee of public safety."

What was to be done? Oh, what was to be done?

But what was to be done? If Petrograd was wavering, if GHQ was wavering, how could Evert take it upon himself to disband the city duma? Or ban a gathering of public representatives?

Oh, this was a delicate matter. How far things had gone!

Kvetsinsky brought the requested order, the fatherly admonition, cleanly typed—but Evert wouldn't sign it. He was plunged in doubt.

[3 9 3]

Having sent his inquiry to the commanders-in-chief of the army groups, Alekseev waited impatiently for replies. As impatiently as he had yesterday.

The first reply was not long in coming. Just before three o'clock a telegram arrived—from whom? From Sakharov, who yesterday it had taken longer to squeeze a reply out of than anyone and who now replied briefly and clearly that he deemed a congress of commanders desirable and was entering into discussion with his own army commanders.

Evert's idea had caught on. But wouldn't it be too broad a consultation if all fourteen army commanders were brought in? What would come of this talk shop?

Right then, an unexpected one arrived from Kolchak. They hadn't even sent the inquiry to him. But he'd simply broken his silence: the mood in the fleet, troops, and population remained calm. But for this to continue, it had to be announced who the legitimate government in the country was now and who the Supreme Commander. The admiral had none of this information and requested that he be informed.

The only remarkable thing about all this was that the Black Sea fleet was calm. In all the rest, Kolchak had made a proud and impenetrable face, not only had he apparently not received yesterday's inquiry about the abdication but last night his telegraph operators had not brought him any Manifesto. It could not even occur to Kolchak that there could be a change of Emperor in this country. He was only asking haughtily what kind of government it was now fumbling around there, and, damn it, ultimately, do we have a Supreme Commander one might talk to instead of you?

He could just see Kolchak's hooked nose and frank face, his keen eyes and imperious lips. There had long been a deep quarrel between them over the Bosphorus. Now it had deepened.

A telegram arrived from Nikolai Nikolaevich, but also not the expected reply but something strange. The Supreme Commander, who had not yet been announced everywhere, from his seat in Caucasus exile, seemed to be complaining to his chief of staff about some civil engineer who had ordered security removed from all the railroads of the Trans-Caucasus. To which the grand duke had replied that this was absolutely impossible. Given conditions in the Caucasus and the war, the struggle against espionage required continuity, revolution or no.

Also correct. But who else could he telegraph about this? Why, the Prime Minister.

Right then Alekseev was summoned to the direct line by Brusilov. From this ever at-attention, responsive general, Alekseev expected to receive consent to the conference in his first sentences, just as Brusilov had decisively agreed yesterday to the Tsar's abdication. But nothing of the kind. The conversation somehow took quite a different turn.

Brusilov reported that in order to hasten the Manifesto's appearance, he had sent a private telegram to Rodzyanko, who was his old messmate in the corps, and in a comradely way had asked for him to try to influence the leftist elements.

It took Alekseev some time to process this. Was he to take this to mean that communication between the Commander of the Southwestern Army Group and Rodzyanko might exist apart from GHQ, without its knowledge or permission? As for the bitter words of disenchantment spoken by Alekseev to the effect that Rodzyanko had not been candid or sincere and might even be pulling for the leftists—this was skirted as unsaid and even impermissible with respect to a messmate. The suggestion being that you can't reach agreement with me? Brusilov was quick, too quick perhaps, and not always in a direction useful to the service. So what about the conference of commanders? Clumsy Alekseev did not get to ask this, as Brusilov's tape was gushing.

No answer had come in from Rodzyanko, and it was too long to wait for the gathering of commanders (and that was *all* he said about the conference). The troops' patience could be tried no longer. And so, Brusilov proposed, announce that the Emperor had abdicated the throne, that the Provisional

Committee of the State Duma had taken up the country's governance—and proceed to call on them to safeguard Mother Russia and not interfere in politics.

So this was how things stood. He himself and Rodzyanko would maintain a secret correspondence and let Alekseev give his consent to disrupt Rodzyanko's request and announce the Manifesto.

Instead of the commanders' desirable unanimity, there was a diffusion in all directions. As clear and amicable as they had been yesterday about persuading the Emperor to abdicate, that's how murky and divided everything was today. Unresolvable circumstances had thickened, and Alekseev felt lost, deceived, and out of place. He tried to fend off the attack and explain things to Brusilov.

. . . After all, he had inquired of Petrograd several times—Rodzyanko and others—and no one had come to the telegraph, as if they'd all died. There was no one to whom he could report! About the impossibility of playing any further into their hands and hushing up the Manifesto. Whereas for the Supreme Commander the Manifesto didn't exist until it had been published through the Senate. . . .

The grand duke there in his Caucasus was in no danger whatsoever, was in no hurry to go anywhere, and was prepared to wait calmly. Here, though, the land was burning up, and what was Alekseev to do? . . . Right here, right now, over the Hughes, over the tape on its way to Brusilov! The universal lack of understanding was offensive, the disdain, his own sense of abandonment. Forgetting to see the egotistical grin on Brusilov's quivering, responsive face, Alekseev in his simplicity complained to him even more:

"The hardest thing has been establishing any accord with today's evasive government."

He could not express himself more harshly over the official telegraph!

Whereas Brusilov did not accept his candor, but then, poised, he shifted: he was listening, he would expect an order by evening, he had the honor to bow . . .

Thus ended the conversation. Only afterward did Alekseev see that Brusilov had cleanly dodged the question of whether or not the commanders should meet.

How all those Petrograd politicians had been searching for Alekseev in previous hours—and now they'd all gone missing. The day was slipping away—and everyone was silent! Which of them should he seek out? Rodzyanko? His soul turned away. Lvov? He'd already asked him about the oath and about the lifting of railroad security. His invisible excellency had remained silent.

He was in despair. Everything had twisted around in less than twenty-four hours. Just yesterday at this time he had firmly held the reins, and everything everywhere in the theater of military operations was under his control, except for Polotsk, and all that was needed for a general and final pacification was the Emperor's abdication.

And now they had the abdication—and things were fraying further.

If the Germans attacked the Russian army, there would not be the slightest doubt or hesitation as to whether we should fire back. But because the attack was coming from behind, in the form of anarchical bands encouraged by someone from Petrograd, if not the government itself, then it had become unclear whether they really could use arms. Wouldn't this spoil their relations with the government? Wouldn't this give rise to internecine strife, which was to be avoided above all else?

Although, what was an army worth whose rear could be destroyed? He ordered his own telegram to Evert on the revolutionary gangs sent out to the remaining army groups except for the Caucasus.

But what about the conference of commanders? Finally Ruzsky's long-awaited answer arrived. However, in its form and tone it was a methodical reprimand, as if Ruzsky were senior in rank. Yes, the Manifesto had to be announced. But the commanders-in-chief must each stay where they were, as each of them was the sole authoritative power. They must not assemble, at least not until the Supreme Commander took up his post.

That is, he declared that under Alekseev he would not let them assemble. Well, Alekseev never took offense at those kinds of caustic remarks.

But Nikolai Nikolaevich was still silent. He hadn't said a word about the conference.

Brusilov suddenly sent another separate rejection of the meeting—and in Ruzsky's exact words (had they been in contact?): they had to stay in place, at their posts.

And it was true, they did. But that meant not letting the commanders-in-chief merge into a single force.

The telegraph operators had also brought Rodzyanko a copy of the Nepenin telegram, just two hours before: in Reval, where the abdication had been announced that morning, before they could rejoice that the situation had calmed down, troops had refused to obey even the Duma members who had arrived, and the disturbances in Helsingfors had barely stopped.

Alekseev decided—this was already about six o'clock in the evening—to appeal to Petrograd not for the first time. Of course, he was unable to summon Rodzyanko this time either. Lvov he didn't try, not seeing the point. On the other hand, Guchkov turned out to be at the ministerial residence and came to the telegraph.

Still taking Rodzyanko to be the man in charge, Alekseev was not actually addressing Guchkov or the Council of Ministers but was asking them to pass it on to Rodzyanko, saying that concealing a manifesto of such great importance, as Rodzyanko had requested, made no sense. The rumor had already seeped into the troop milieu, and there could be ominous consequences. The Manifesto had to be promulgated without delay in accordance with established procedure.

It seemed so clear! Why did this have to be proven to the Petrograders? How could they make a game of this most significant of documents? Did

Mikhail himself for some reason not want to announce it? Or were they wavering again about returning the throne to Aleksei? Or even Nikolai?

The details of the state system could be worked out later, after the country had calmed down. But right now—publish the Manifesto! Five million armed men were waiting for an explanation of what had happened!

Having finally taken command of the line and reached a listening Petrograd ear, Alekseev now would not let him reply and hastened to speak his mind while someone was listening.

Secondly. Preferably, the new government would address a fervent appeal to the army in the field to fulfill their sacred duty. Thirdly, I insist that all communications between the government and the armies be conducted only through the staff entrusted to me.

When Alekseev had finally said everything burning in him and had let Guchkov respond, he read in the very first sentences of the reply something inconceivable: Mikhail Aleksandrovich had also decided **to refuse the throne**. Both Manifestos would be promulgated this coming night.

Alekseev was shocked. This he could not grasp! Why had all this been done then? What was the point of yesterday's abdication? And who would remain? . . . **Who**? . . .

The Provisional Government would remain in power, led by Prince Lvov. Until the Constituent Assembly, which would decide the state system. The date had not been decided.

This meant there was *no one* on the throne?

An offensive, humiliating awareness—betrayal!—crushed Alekseev in its slashing grip, making him gasp. He'd been betrayed—like a fool. Led by the nose!

Meanwhile the tape was cheerfully delivering answers to other important questions. An appeal to the army? Without delay. Communications with the army? Yes, through GHQ and the commanders-in-chief. Did General Alekseev have anything else to say?

Oh, did he! Oh yes! His miserable weak head was splitting there was so much he needed to say at once. Nothing was squaring with anything else, everything had flown off and come crashing down, and there was nothing firm left! Instead of a minor reshuffle on the throne, the throne itself had fallen?

But Alekseev could only complain pathetically:

". . . Couldn't they convince the grand duke to take power at least until the Assembly? . . . And how would the army now receive this new Manifesto? Wouldn't it see it as *imposed from without*? . . . The present army had to be protected—and protected from any passions in domestic issues. Too heavy a task lay on the army, and it had to be eased, not . . ."

But why had he typed all this? Who now were these belated arguments for? They had not consulted with him at the proper moment. They had just told him to keep quiet and not announce it! . . .

Guchkov, it turned out, agreed with Alekseev. He himself, and Milyukov as well, had believed that the throne must surely be occupied by someone. But these arguments had convinced no one. And the grand duke's decision had been free and irrevocable. He would have to obey and attempt to consolidate the new order—and prevent any damage to the army. With this intention, Guchkov had accepted the post of Minister of War.

Alekseev walked from the telegraph room back to his office as if blinded, unsteady on his feet.

Lukomsky was alarmed and approached:

"What's the matter, Mikhal Vasilich? Feeling poorly again?"

Alekseev was glad to stop. He gave Lukomsky a look, even more squinting and frowning than usual. Always slightly dissatisfied, distrustful, his dense sergeant face was now even sharper. As if he himself were searching for what was wrong.

"*I'll never forgive myself,*" he replied in a slow and muffled but creaky voice, "*for trusting certain people's sincerity.* For sending that unfortunate inquiry yesterday to the commanders-in-chief."

[3 9 4]

Spineless ditherer! Milksop! How could Mikhail abdicate?

And now came the laws of democracy! If your point of view differed from the majority's, you had to resign.

Outrageous! Pavel Nikolaevich had been aspiring to this post his entire life. All his abilities had led him here! This post had been marked out for him long ago both by Russian public opinion and by the opinion of all his party comrades, and even by the opinion of the Allied countries. Who was more prepared for it than Milyukov, with his historical erudition and his actual personal knowledge of Europe, and America, and especially the Balkans, the most entangled place. On any question—Finland, Poland, Serbia, Bulgaria, the Straits, the war's goals—Milyukov had an opinion worked out in advance. Of all the present members of the Provisional Government, Milyukov alone had come to his ministerial seat not as a novice but as a master.

This became very clear to everyone when three days ago, before any government had formed, the director of the Chancellery of the Ministry of Foreign Affairs telephoned the Tauride Palace and summoned none other than Milyukov to the telephone, asking him to send a guard to protect the secret archives. And Milyukov did, thereby safeguarding the continuity of state secrecy.

And now, because they hadn't succeeded in convincing Mikhail, all this had come crashing down? And he had to resign? Due to the hot-headed condition among the ministers (he himself had proposed it) that whoever's opinion was rejected would have to resign and not be an obstacle?

But was Milyukov any obstacle to the government's actions? He was its foundation, he was its spirit, it was he who had assembled its entire framework. He had also conducted the most difficult negotiations with the Soviet. Right now, bypassing the unimpressive Lvov, he was the de facto leader. To whom was he to yield this seat now?

He pictured Kerensky and Nekrasov rejoicing. He already had a presentiment: this boy Kerensky had the winding flair, the thrust, and the grasp to snatch the top spot in the government.

Allowing that was unthinkable!

But who else could stop it? Such was the government that had formed.

The second genuine leader was Guchkov, but he too had to leave now, according to the same rule.

As he was leaving Putyatina's apartment, Milyukov announced once again to the remaining colleagues that now according to their agreement and the sense of the matter he was leaving the government.

No one had made him say it, no one had reminded him, he was simply acting honestly according to the rules of democracy.

But no sooner had he gotten into his motorcar than he regretted it. Why had he repeated it this time?

What had Nikolai done! What a wretched man! Owing to his personal attachments, he had shaken the entire monarchy! At such a moment!

They'd already put the Constituent Assembly in writing. It was evident from everything that the monarchy's chances were slim.

It was painful! Bitter! Who had prepared the whole revolution if not Milyukov and the Progressive Bloc? If not his 14 November speech?

And now, on the first day of victory—leave? . . .

How bitter.

He told the driver: Basseinaya. After four sleepless nights and the downfall he'd suffered, he wanted to go to bed. All was lost.

But they rode up to the Summer Garden and he realized he'd made another mistake: he was right next to the Pevchesky Bridge! Why in these final hours, while he was still minister—why not enter the ministry building this once as its master? . . . How many times had he mentally entered this building this way—and now for the first time he could do so in reality.

Was it really for the last time? . . . This was so frustrating that he didn't even want to think about it.

On the other hand, it was good he hadn't gone there right away. That would have been noted on Millionnaya and interpreted unfavorably. Now he could go there anew and from the other direction.

He told the driver to wait near his home, since he didn't have anything to do now, except to take some revolutionary riffraff from the Tauride Palace.

While he was having his breakfast, he thought, how was it that he, the leader of the Kadet party, could leave his post without the approval of the party leadership? The idea came to him to invite Vinaver in to consult. He picked up the telephone.

At that moment their relations were complicated. Vinaver himself claimed to be the Kadet party's top leader and could not shake the thought that Milyukov occupied his place.

Maksim Moiseevich replied he would have to think about it. In any case, though, it seemed like nonsense to him: the monarchy was no grounds for resignation.

Milyukov felt better.

He called the ministry, that same chancellery director, and announced that he was coming over right now to meet the ministry's leading officials.

And he went.

Everything in Pavel Nikolaevich was singing when, met by the chancellery's comrade minister and director at Palace Square, he entered this solemn building where the fates of war and peace, the Russian Empire, the Balkans, and the East had been decided for so many years. He walked. He walked through the formal passageways and halls with their grandiose mirror windows on the square and on the Aleksandr Column. And reached his magnificent office.

Now, at last, he was where he should be! And now leave this?

He assembled the department directors and section chiefs. Milyukov came out to them—they stood—and delivered a brief, calm, and clear speech about the situation that had come about in the country and asking all employees to continue to perform their duties.

Foreign affairs were a delicate fabric and there could be no revolutionary upheavals here.

They asked him whether the government could cope with the masses' stormy mood.

Milyukov replied:

"I hope we are able to divert it into a calmer channel."

He also spent some time in his office. Oh, how fine! And this view on the imperial square! To direct Russia's sovereign course from here!

And receive envoys here.

A pity!

He went home to Basseinaya.

He thought he might nap, but he was racked by frustration and alarm.

Anna Sergeevna implored him not to leave in any event! Dear Nabokov called, still not having finished writing Mikhail's abdication.

He argued heatedly:

"Pavel Nikolaevich! Your departure would be a catastrophe! Who would conduct foreign policy? Europe knows only you! It would create the impression of dissension in the government from the very first steps. It would be a blow to the party and the remaining Kadet ministers. For Russia's sake and the party's, you must remain!"

He was a clever man, you see, an outstanding lawyer, and he knew what he was saying.

Soon after, a delegation led by Vinaver arrived from the Central Committee. The very dear Maksim Moiseevich, although younger than Milyukov, was balding, aging, and wore an ingenuous beard:

"No, no, Pavel Nikolaich! What little boy antics are these? You should be ashamed! And over what? The monarchy? Leaving your post now would mean betraying both the revolution and freedom."

Vinaver argued convincingly that there had been no casus for any mistrust in Milyukov on the part of any faction. That practical disagreements inside a government were an ever-present and inevitable attribute of its activities. And inasmuch as Pavel Nikolaevich was satisfied with the principles that lay at the base of Mikhail's abdication text, he had every legitimate right to remain in his post.

A flexible, powerful mind, a subtle analyst, one had to admit. Yes, exactly: Pavel Nikolaevich was wholly satisfied with the abdication text. One might even harbor the hope that Mikhail would use this abdication to win wide popularity and the future Constituent Assembly would choose him as their monarch.

He looked at Vinaver with sympathy. How much they'd achieved together, after all. What a long and glorious journey! He recalled Vinaver's extreme rage when, eleven years ago, standing by a dusty piano, they together sketched out in pencil the first draft of the Vyborg Appeal, and Vinaver rejected Milyukov's draft for lacking elemental, indignant force, saying they had to add a general political strike as well!

But now—such a clear mind.

And Pavel Nikolaevich agreed. He realized he did not even have the right to refuse and abandon the great cause begun and his party's line at the very outset and the most important moment. Right now things seemed shaky and gloomy. But perhaps the republic, or the heretofore undefined state system, might yet gain a foothold.

He drove to the Tauride Palace, where Prince Lvov met him with the brightest smile.

"Pavel Nikolaevich! You must stay. Guchkov is another matter. They say the army doesn't like him. But you! . . ."

No, Guchkov was not another matter. Now, convinced he should stay, Pavel Nikolaevich had to convince Guchkov to stay, too. Guchkov was not bound by the nighttime dispute or by any compact, but obviously the same implacable democratic principle loomed over him as well.

Milyukov started out through the Tauride Palace to find Guchkov, who was probably in his office at the Military Commission, upstairs.

Yes, destiny had linked them firmly and bizarrely! Always opponents, rivals, and here they were harnessed together, to the same chariot. Now, today, only these two, who had shaken the Romanov throne—only these two were standing for the monarchy!

Right now in the new government, the only person Milyukov understood as on a level with him in terms of strength and political experience was, of course, Guchkov. In this cherished public cabinet to which Milyukov had led Russia via the Bloc—in this cabinet his sole rival, Guchkov, was now his true ally.

Upstairs, in a stuffy room under a low ceiling, he found Guchkov hunched over papers and surrounded by military men.

He called him out and they went somewhere else, to another room.

Guchkov was sullen and tired, and there was nothing joyously ministerial about him.

They were left alone and sat across a table, and Milyukov said:

"Aleksandr Ivanych, our lawyers believe that there are no formal grounds for your resignation or mine."

"What formal grounds?" Guchkov glowered askance.

"In the sense of trust not shown you or the impossibility of collaborating under a monarchy-free status."

"So what can be done now?" Guchkov shrugged. "What and how can be done now to hold together and retain it all? . . . Russia itself. It's not about the formal grounds, but that there's nothing to retain Russia with. All is lost."

The light had gone out in him. He was dark, old, exhausted.

But Milyukov tried to convince him with restored confidence and a firm voice:

"We'll cope, Aleksandr Ivanych! Together—we'll pull through. Just don't lose heart. Don't resign! You alone can help us organize a strong authority and a strong army. Without you—I can't envision . . ."

Although he could envision just that, it would be difficult indeed. Guchkov sat there just as extinguished. Broken even.

"I just don't understand. . . . While I was traveling, you were in such a hurry to announce the government, such a hurry to announce the agreement with the Soviet. But those are in fact shackles on our feet. What did you promise them? What were you thinking? Not taking troops out of Petrograd. How could you have, without me? I thought you'd wait for me, wait for the act of abdication. And now—what is this maneuver here? I don't understand. I'm a monarchist. Where do I come in now?"

"But for your part, Aleksandr Ivanych, you were in a hurry to accept an ill-considered form of abdication. That wasn't what we'd agreed. And didn't you lead us to an impasse?"

But why torment each other for nothing? On the contrary, it was time to close ranks, reach agreements.

Guchkov had no desire to leave the government, either. Nor could he imagine abandoning Russia without leadership.

[3 9 5]

In all the photographs, Varya's expression was that of a skinny failure, which she tried to hide with a proud or even triumphant look.

Sometimes seeming gayer than she was, waving her arms about more confidently than she felt—while underneath, in a narrow space, deep down, she was alone, alone. . . .

A Pyatigorsk orphan, she had, beyond her wildest imaginings, lived in Petersburg for four years now and completed the Bestuzhev courses, but her life never had filled out. All that head cramming just had not conveyed to her heart. She had completed the Bestuzhev courses and was about to go somewhere, to the back of beyond, as a teacher, and there Petersburg's deceptive lambency would end.

During her Pyatigorsk period, Varya had sung purely, she had loved to sing—and where else to sing if not in church? It was unpleasant, joining the forces of ignorance, but where else could she sing? At first she'd gone to Petersburg specifically to study singing; people had gotten her hopes up that if her voice developed successfully she might even end up on the stage. But meager male attention, her girlfriends, and the mirror quickly revealed to Varya that she was not destined for the stage. So perverse was this type of human activity that singing wasn't enough for the stage; she also needed so-called beauty. She was forced to concede to this stupid universal conspiracy and abandon her singing courses.

As if someone could prove, could define in precise words, what beauty did or did not consist of. Plekhanov argued convincingly that this concept had changed radically over the ages, and what was once considered beautiful in time came to be deemed not beautiful, and vice versa. For sensible men, a flexible notion of female beauty should have absolutely no real significance. The line of a nose can be straightened; they say there are devices for that. . . . Meanwhile, Varya's feet were light and delicate enough for the ballet.

Thus Varya moved, studied, argued heatedly, and among her friends was known for her love of justice and standing every inch of ground. Inside, though, a sadness sprawled that soon she would be twenty-three and her life had not worked out.

In a stunning whirlwind, this Revolution had swooped down! How everything had changed and begun to shine! First of all—Justice! For all people in everything at once, thundering Justice! Secondly, the eddy, the round dance of thousands which you could dive into and join.

For the first few days, back before the actual revolution, they started bringing bread directly to the courses for the female students and teachers so they wouldn't have to stand in line—and Varya took efficient charge of this. Then there was the day of the main whirlwind—Monday, when everyone ran in circles like crazy people, and on the evening of that day, appeals were tossed out of passing automobiles to the inhabitants: to give hot meals to homeless, frozen soldiers!

The same way this very leaflet was picked up by a street draft and tossed up lightly, that was how Varya was picked up and spun: this was for her! How much energy, organization, precision, and practical calculation was needed right then! But she had all these qualities, and with such joy, such skill she would apply all this!

Indeed, it had worked out marvelously. She found a few older and younger women, obtained a free space on Malaya Posadskaya, and with a good stove—and started collecting utensils, tables, stools, dishes, food, and money from the surrounding inhabitants. Everyone donated everything willingly. And then they simply set up a small table outside the entrance and a plate—and into that passers-by put their change, so that quite a lot was collected. They called this the tearoom, but then they cooked dinners for the soldiers, and there was also a large, dark adjoining room, like a store-room, which they swept and heated and there, right on the floor, put thirty or so men recently made homeless, with and without rifles. There was no sign, and at first they called out to passers-by, but then people started thronging, they knew.

What support this was! To seat a hungry revolutionary soldier, worker, or sailor weary from hours of wandering and warm him with a glass of sweet hot tea with halva or cocoa, which they had never seen in their lives, and with sandwiches, though it was early still, before dawn, though it was late into the night, the tearoom barely closed for the night, just as the whole city barely slept. In the daytime they served cabbage soup with corned beef, and noodles, and buttery porridge. And when the men left, they were each given a pack of good cigarettes. And the most unruly soldiers off the street became kind here.

Varya raced among the tables, among all of them—happy, cheerful, feeling even thinner and better, and everyone called out to her, called her "little sister Varya." She was embraced jocularly and clapped on the shoulders, and in response she felt boundless love for them all, rough, clumsy, and dirty as they were, their tall fur hats dropped in their lap, scratching their heads or in the heat not knowing how to blow their noses neatly. She loved them in the way everyone in the city loved one another during those great days—that universal brotherhood that one had only dreamt of, that others would get to see, but here it had come, sincere brotherhood! This unexpected multitude of male strength, so much in one place, the wonderful harsh smell of tobacco and boots and something else, and all this strength needed her, called to her, asked and thanked her. Varya had never dreamed of such happy days. All her past torments seemed never to have been. (But these days were going to end, the feeding stations were going to end—and it would be a pity to part with them.)

She put more of her effort into this than anyone, went to more trouble than anyone, even spent the night here—and naturally came to be in charge of this tearoom. Meanwhile, on the Petersburg side, a commissariat had been created—and had announced that those tearooms (and quite a few had appeared throughout the city) which submitted reports would receive food from the commissariat at reduced cost. Although the reports were an added chore, obtaining food was simpler, and there was more of it, and they could feed more people, so Varya took on the task and they registered. Late every evening she ran there, to the Elite cinema, to the food department, with her reports and to submit her collections to the till.

Everything would have been marvelous during these shining days of a renewed Russia—but people could not yet sustain that high level of brotherhood. The day before, toward nightfall, a young man with a face covered in blackheads had suddenly appeared in the tearoom, volunteer military, who declared that he had been appointed commandant of the Petersburg side and ordered she surrender the daily take to him. Varya sensed something untoward, thrust her fists into her apron pockets, and asked him to show her his authorization. But he did that, and it was written there that, yes, such-and-such volunteer had been appointed by the Provisional Committee of the State Duma and the Soviet of Workers' Deputies to be commandant of the Petersburg side and all citizens were required to carry out all his instructions.

Varya was put out, but dodged by saying that the collections simply could not be turned over in less than two hours, so he should tell her where. The volunteer replied that he himself would wait here and would gladly have some tea.

That strengthened her suspicions all the more! She ordered him served tea while she herself ran to the commissariat. There they told her not to give him the money under any circumstances and that he himself should come to the commissariat. Varya went back and told him this. He replied that it was too late for him to go, but she could take his authorization to the commissariat. Varya put the authorization in her pocket and ran to the commissariat wearing a light blouse and scarf, as if she had nothing else to do. There she was received by old Peshekhonov himself, with the droopy mustache. He twirled the authorization around and said it was a fake. The seal was illegible, the signatures were illegible, and it was an impossible instance that the Duma Committee and Soviet of Deputies would give anyone a general instruction jointly. He ordered the collection brought here and that person told to come here, if not today then tomorrow.

Varya returned worked up for a clash but knew she wouldn't give in and would let him have it. She was fiery in arguments!

In that time, though, the pretender had fled.

They also stopped putting the collection plate outside, as people had started stealing from it.

Today after dinner someone new showed up—drove up in an automobile. Tall and pale, he immediately presented a document saying he was such-and-such a doctor appointed by the State Duma Committee as commandant of all tearooms on the Petersburg side, and he and his aide—volunteer so-and-so, yesterday's surname—had been instructed to collect all money on hand in all tearooms immediately for the till held in common for all. There was a stamp now from a certain committee and perfectly distinct, and the signature was clear—but Varya was surprised. The commandant of the *whole* Petersburg side was an aide to the commandant of just the tearooms? It was clearly an attempt to rob them, and she wasn't going to let that happen. Her bile rose most of all at this outrage against brotherhood.

But she restrained herself and did not start quarreling, instead saying they would have to go see the commissar. All right, the doctor offered her a seat in his motorcar.

Now she took him directly not to the food department but to Peshekhonov, who admitted that he knew that sprawling signature—Duma member Karaulov. He told the tall, pale doctor that he fully recognized his authority, but the question of handing over the tearooms to his supervision was complicated by several factors, for the clarification of which he asked the doctor to go with him immediately to the State Duma Committee, now in the commissariat's automobile.

The doctor agreed to go but ceremoniously refused to get into Peshekhonov's motorcar and would follow in his own.

Peshekhonov asked, "But where is your aide?" He had left his aide somewhere else.

They left, and Varya headed back.

Apparently the attempt had been beaten back, but Varya felt terrible. They had spat on something pure and good, they wanted to take it away, there were new hands now, and their whole tearoom no longer seemed to her such a glorious feast.

She also noted that some of the soldiers were eating regularly there three or four times a day and had stayed for the night for three nights already, without their rifles. They were just living there, the deserters.

[3 9 6]

*   *   *

In Moscow that morning they set fire to the Okhrana and the Criminal Investigation Department on Gnezdnikovsky Lane, and to the city governor's chancellery. Wooden archive storehouses burned up. Files and registers flew out the windows of the burning main building. The crowd tore them up, shouted, encouraged more be thrown out, and started bonfires on the street and in the courtyard. They wouldn't let the firemen through to put it out.

That was also when the volunteer bell ringers were ringing the Kremlin bells, including the Ivan the Great—in honor of the revolution.

Lab dogs escaped from the Moscow Women's Medical Institute: they were not being fed anymore or locked in. The emaciated animals prowled around, some near pharmacies, where they were reminded of the same familiar smell.

Young militia men went to the Convent of Martha and Mary to arrest Grand Duchess Elizaveta Fyodorovna, the Empress's sister. She refused to go: "I am a nun." (She had spent twelve years here as a nun, since her husband's murder.) They telephoned from the cloister to inform the Committee of Public Organizations, which replied: "Neither Chelnokov (the mayor) nor Kishkin (the commissar of Moscow) have given orders for an arrest." The grand duchess also forced the militia men to attend the prayer service and only then let them go.

General Mrozovsky wrote Chelnokov from house arrest: "I have the honor to bring to your attention the fact that I have joined the popular movement and recognize the new government."

Policemen showed up to arrest the mitred archpriest Vostorgov, a former favorite of the Emperor, a known arbiter of church affairs, and chairman of the Union of the Russian People in Moscow. But he said: "I wholly recognize the new regime and request to be left under house arrest."

*　　*　　*

In the afternoon, a rumor arose that Evert himself was advancing on Moscow—or else he was sending the corps of some insubordinate general. The telephone lines were ringing off the hook in all editorial offices. Panic flared in the Committee of Social Organizations, the City Duma, and the Soviet of Workers' Deputies.

But in general, the revolution went quickly and easily in Moscow. The riding around in trucks ended, and by nightfall the crowds were fewer. There still were no streetcars, but cabbies had appeared and stores were open. Militia were riding around in automobiles, calling on the people to return to their peaceful occupations.

In the evening, all the theaters opened.

But by nightfall, there was widespread fear of the criminals who had escaped the Butyrskaya Prison.

*　　*　　*

In Reval, the disturbances reached the *Peter the Great* and *Bayan* right at the head of the pier—and rallies were seething alongside these ships, with workers demanding the sailors join them and go with them to the city. However, Rear Admiral Verderevsky convinced the sailors that if they did so the crowd would loot the ships and their food supplies. That was effective. Not a single sailor went.

*   *   *

In Petrograd, many cafeterias and cafes were turned into feeding stations for soldiers; other members of the public were not allowed in.

Sailors showed up in restaurants—and there was a new fashion: being powdered. They paid their checks—everyone had money.

The brothels could not keep up with servicing the soldiers. They all paid legally, with the loot of those days, some with jewelry, some with knick-knacks, even silver service.

But the Petrograd theaters were all closed. Notices on the doors: "Performances postponed until special instruction." "At the behest of the Provisional Committee, entrance to this building is prohibited. No arrests, seizures, inspection of papers . . ."

Those arrested were held in manèges and cinemas; there weren't enough places. The buildings weren't equipped and people lay on the floor. In Kresty there was no more heating or lighting. They kept them that way, since it was temporary.

*   *   *

Servants ran to rallies and, returning, told their employers:

"They're talking about some *old dredgeen* . . . . And all the pearly chariots from all the countries gathering together."

A maid was friendly with a propagandized clerk from headquarters and considered herself educated. She ran to the Duma to listen to speeches and brought back to her employers:

"Wilhelm is a smart tsar, not like ours."

Marina, the Karabchevskys' maid, was sharp-tongued. She'd seen Count Orlov before, when her employer had defended him. Now she said:

"What they're saying on the street is that now it'll be the princes and counts sweeping the streets instead of the yardmen. That's why our little count made up to Kerensky himself as his driver. . . . He didn't feel like picking up a broom. . . ."

*   *   *

The public roaming the streets had started nibbling on sunflower seeds more and more, even on Nevsky. Now no one was preventing them from spitting on the ground. Shells and more shells on the snow.

Under the Anichkov Bridge, toppled heraldic eagles—metal eagles that wouldn't burn—lay smashed on the ice.

*   *   *

Before sunset, a female student with a Red Cross armband was walking with a university boy along the frozen Neva, following the path between the

Trinity and Palace bridges. To their left floated the cupola of St. Isaac's; to their right, they could see the mosque's blue cupola.

The university student, pointing to St. Isaac's:

"Still standing, that synodic institution."

The female student, to the mosque:

"And that one over there, poking up doing nothing."

*   *   *

Toward day's end, a truck moved slowly down Nevsky, and from it someone was reading out something. Then they started to move on but weren't allowed to go far, and people shouted again:

"Read it again! Not everyone heard!"

The vehicle stopped again, and the crowd gathered tightly around it. A ruddy young shaved gentleman who looked like an actor, wearing a black fur cap and a coat with a black fur collar, stood full height in the truck bed surrounded by several amateurs. He wiped his lips with a bright white handkerchief and, with a look of happy assurance, read again—distinctly, loudly, in a beautifully pitched declamatory voice:

"Abdication from the throne! Deputy Karaulov appeared before the Duma and announced that Emperor Nikolai II had abdicated the throne in favor of Mikhail Aleksandrovich! Mikhail Aleksandrovich, in turn, abdicated the throne in favor of the people! The most grandiose rallies and ovations are under way in the Duma! The ecstasy is beyond description!"

"Hurrah! Hurrah!" people shouted here, too.

An intoxicating feeling: now we were all for one. There were finally honest, sensible people in power.

"The Tsar was only getting in the way of the smart generals at headquarters. Now the war will go better!"

"Now you'll see. In a week there won't be a single monarchist left in Russia."

*   *   *

On Nevsky, in the *Evening Times* window, they had posted the latest telegrams about the abdications. Two cavalry guardsmen walked up wearing full-length greatcoats. The older, with his sergeant's stripes, told the younger:

"Read."

And the younger clearly read out the Emperor's abdication.

"And then?" the older exclaimed impatiently. "Anything?"

"Grand Duke Mikhail Aleksandrovich also ab—"

"That can't be! Read it again."

The younger read it again.

Very quietly, the older man said:
"It's all over. Let's go."

*　*　*

In the St. George Community Infirmary, the wounded wept when they learned of the Emperor's abdication. One with two amputated legs, always cheerful and patient, now sobbed inconsolably:
"What did I give my legs for? The Tsar's gone now. All is lost!"

*　*　*

Overnight, residents formed a guard in Petrograd apartment building entrances, whoever happened to join, all ages—old men, ladies, high school boys.
On the night of 17 March, a snowstorm swirled over Petrograd.

*　*　*

On the night of 17 March, confined to the ministerial pavilion, Vice Admiral Kartsev, head officer of the Sea Cadet Corps (dubbed "Longbeard" by the cadets consistent with his appearance), the son-in-law of the untouched Minister of the Navy Grigorovich, crazed by his vain attempts to get some fresh air (and by all the journalists who had come to scoff, and by the new officials, and by Kerensky, and recalling the desecration of his corps?), lunged at a sentry and wrenched away his rifle. Another sentry in the room fired twice and shot him straight through the shoulder. A third sentry fired and hit a colonel sitting right there in the neck. In the adjoining room, a sentry fired without hitting anyone. Sergeant Kruglov ran in with his Browning raised and a whistle in his mouth. Had any of the arrested men moved, he would have whistled, the command for all sentries to fire.
But Kartsev wanted to commit suicide. When they bound up his wound, he tricked the medics and lunged at yet another sentry and managed to wound himself in the chest with his bayonet. He was screaming. They took him to the hospital.

[3 9 7]

Peshekhonov arrived at the Tauride Palace—but the self-appointed commandant doctor did not follow. He disappeared. Too bad Peshekhonov hadn't taken away his authorization with Karaulov's distinct signature! All the same, though, he had to go yell at Karaulov.

However, before he could find him or anyone else, for that matter, he was handed, as were all takers here, a large, half-blank sheet of paper—the half-blankness constituting its solemnity: an emergency supplement to *Izvestia of the Soviet*, and dirtily printed on it in five-inch letters was the following:

"ABDICATION FROM THE THRONE
Deputy Karaulov appeared before the Duma and announced . . ."

What? This was Karaulov, too?

Life in Petrograd was seething, there was real work in the commissariat—but here they had their own concerns. "Abdication from the throne"? Peshekhonov understood that this was major and he had to take it in, but his head, spinning from commissariat affairs, refused.

". . . in favor of Mikhail Aleksandrovich, and Mikhail Aleksandrovich in favor of the people . . ."

This was tremendous, of course, and impossible to grasp at once. What did that mean: in favor of the people? A republic?

The leaflet went on to assert that "in the Duma, the most grandiose rallies and ovations are under way, and the ecstasy is beyond description." However, standing right in the middle of the Ekaterininsky Hall, Peshekhonov saw neither ovations nor ecstasy. People were taking the leaflet quite calmly, and the bustle was even much less than in their commissariat because here it was much roomier and people moved around more freely.

Finding Karaulov would have been a task if he weren't peculiar for his Cossack uniform and also his tall black Terek fur hat. With his mustache twirled as far to the sides as they would stay, he strode around as if on parade, feeling that here, as well as in Petrograd, and in the whole revolution even, he was the most central person. Indeed, whose orders thundered through the city more than anyone else's if not his (albeit canceling each other out)? Indeed, who was it who had brought the abdication communiqué to the Duma? With the two brother Tsars, none other than Karaulov went down in history as the third! Not the appropriate moment to give him a dressing-down. Peshekhonov pulled him away from the other contenders and began trying to convince him—and Karaulov took offense. His generally kind face maintained its bearing. He remembered no such doctor, but if he'd signed it, that meant it was right. He had to sign thousands of slips of paper now. How could you delve into each one?

In certain respects, Karaulov had the same roots as Peshekhonov. He was a stranger here. For all his newspaper editorship, Peshekhonov, like Karaulov, remained a simple man; despite Karaulov's Duma membership and his former philology education, he was still a Cossack swordsman.

Now that Peshekhonov had arrived at the Tauride Palace, he decided to see to other matters that had accumulated. He'd begun here four days before and had left voluntarily to enter into real life in a city district—and the people here had fallen into a stupor. All the Tauride life and turmoil now seemed shadowy for some reason, made up, inauthentic.

This impression got even stronger when he learned from acquaintances that Milyukov and Guchkov, the main members of the government declared just yesterday, were today already resigning!

His head was spinning! A government of shadows.

The true authority was, of course, the Soviet of Deputies. Peshekhonov needed to go there, first to the motor department. There was a department like that in the commissariat, too, and somehow there seemed to be a sinister linkage between the two departments. Perhaps they were stealing automobiles. He decided to swoop down then and there, without warning his people, with oversight questions.

Then he needed to find Kerensky and hand over to him, as Minister of Justice, the list of provocateurs—not the main ones—discovered in Okhrana papers. However, he was unable to find Kerensky anywhere. He thought he might be at the Soviet's Executive Committee, which was in continuous session. But no, they told him he was never there and had moved over entirely to the government.

On the other hand, they gave out a hot supper there, so, opportunely, he ate. Sitting at the table were his comrades, all men he knew, sweating from all their debates. Peshekhonov had a small matter of his own, too. He sat down at the table among them and asked Zeitlin what nonsense they were going on about, saying that people were coming to the commissariat and asking for permission to start up a print publication. Was that really necessary?

"What do you mean?" Zeitlin said. "Of course. There was a resolution. Only with EC permission."

This riled Peshekhonov. But he restrained himself and asked for permission—for himself, for his beloved magazine *Russian Treasures*.

"Just a minute," Zeitlin said, "we'll arrange it."

He reached over—prepared blanks for this turned out to be lying on the table already—wrote in *Russian Treasures*, signed for the secretary—and held it out to Nakhamkes to sign for the chairman.

He did.

Peshekhonov felt himself swelling up inside. He picked up one more blank, moved over, wrote in another, new title for his magazine, *Russian Notes*, on his way gave it to Kapelinsky to sign for the secretary and went up to Chkheidze, who was presiding, and quietly asked:

"Nikolai Semyonych, please sign."

Chkheidze glanced down and signed without saying a word.

And then, in a flood, Peshekhonov shouted out to the entire session, interrupting it:

"What is wrong with you, comrades? Are you trying to deprive us of the gains of 1905? Since '05, even under Tsarist rule, permission has not been required for periodical publications! Whoever wants to can publish. And now—you're . . .?"

The session was silent. Someone's voice pleaded, embarrassed:

"There's nothing to be done for it, Aleksei Vasilich. What kind of revolution would it be if any rightist newspaper could just come out?"

[3 9 8]

Immediately after the emancipation of the serfs, Elpidifor Paramonov arrived in Rostov-on-Don from Greater Russia, from the north, on foot, wearing bast shoes. Fifty years later, his sons Pyotr and Nikolai were among Rostov's richest men, wheeler-dealers in many businesses, especially flour milling, and the Paramonov brothers' five-story mill rose up on the banks of the Don, equipped according to the latest word. The Paramonov home on Pushkinskaya, known to all Rostov, was like a palace or even a castle, behind a high stone wall. Nikolai could rouse himself in the middle of the night on the basis of a sudden hunch and race off in his motorcar to make a new deal. (His wife rebuked him: "Don't we have enough?") But the brothers' energy did not go solely into being millionaires. Pyotr was chairman of the Rostov stock exchange committee, and when in the middle of the war Guchkov was creating war industry committees all over, Nikolai Elpidiforovich became chairman. Even more than his brother, he treasured his fame as an opposition progressivist, but also as a patron of the arts, and wanted to become the southern Russian Tretyakov. He was famous throughout the South and even published banned books, for which he served a brief sentence — which only added to his luster among the intelligentsia. Time and again, the Paramonov brothers' names had turned up throughout the southern Russian press, and last year Kostrichin, a member of the Rostov Municipal Board and leader of the local Union of the Russian People, in his nasty *Rostov Sheet*, called Pyotr Paramonov a "marauder of the rear and a plunderer," referring to the fact that he had kept flour in his storehouses in order to speculate, ratcheting up the price — and the Paramonov brothers took Kostrichin to court for libel. During the trial, another accusation arose that the Paramonovs were selling flour to Germany, but this dangled without evidence; however, gossip had it that the Paramonovs lost the case (and swore to flatten this Kostrichin like a pancake). All the progressive Rostov public and press were behind the Paramonovs. There was sympathy for them even among authorities like City Governor Meyer. The Paramonov brothers, with their might, which was also corporeal, being of hefty size, grew into major figures opposed to the Petersburg regime.

And then the revolution came, and at just the right time!

After its stormy success in Rostov, on the evening of 15 March, in the Melkonov-Ezekov mansion, Paramonov and Zeeler, the head of the local Zemgor, constituted a Civil Committee for the cities of Rostov and Nakhichevan. In order to include representatives from all the principal public organizations and strata of the population, it would eventually swell to more than fifty. Late in the evening, representatives from a student revolutionary committee and a workers' group arrived as well. But these last immediately demanded a separate room in the house, met separately, and declared that they did not wish to unite with capitalists. A surprise! And they would have their own separate Soviet of Workers' Deputies.

Paramonov didn't believe in that nonsense, but tomorrow, of course, we'd persuade them, what were they without us? Also rolling in that night was new information from Petrograd saying that not any Duma Committee, nor Rodzyanko, but a stable Provisional Government was in charge—and this put the objective of the Rostov structure in a new light. By the morning of 16 March, they had made an appointment with City Governor Meyer, saying they were coming to see him for a new conference and he should assemble the main officials.

Very concerning was the situation in Novocherkassk, the Cossack capital. But in the morning, the Don's official paper came out with a full complement of news, and Grabbe, the district ataman, had also submitted to the revolution! Now this would all pass through the Cossack villages, enlightening even those dull Cossack brains. Hurrah! The Cossacks had been rendered harmless!

After sleeping half the night, Paramonov now strode through the city governor's office like the city's Master, jealously eyeing who Meyer had assembled here. With him in his suite once again were Zeeler, two mayors, and a few leftist city councillors. (There was also the issue of how to purge or entirely disband the Rostov City Duma. There were only two rightist dumas in all Russia—Odessa and Rostov. Nowhere else did such an outrage persist.)

And so, our task was the painless fortification of the new regime. Did the administration recognize all instructions from the Provisional Government as binding?

Meyer was the first to state that he did entirely. But the garrison chief, Lieutenant General Kvanchkhadze, dodged a direct answer. He was merely a soldier and it was not his business to discuss the government. He would carry out the ataman's orders, whatever they were. Then the district court prosecutor expressed himself to the effect that he was not competent from a strictly legal standpoint. This very much upset those present, for it was looking like a conspiracy. The Nakhichevan mayor added to their alarm, saying that he could not make any commitments without a general decision of his duma.

The fate of revolutionary Rostov was tottering! But City Governor Meyer, with great tact and persistence, tried to convince each of them in turn that by their actions of the previous evening they had already stepped away from their principles and they had no choice but to persist.

They relented. Then Zeeler proposed sending an ecstatic telegram to the Provisional Government, but Kvanchkhadze dug his heels in—and they had to limit themselves to an inexpressive, bureaucratic text.

Paramonov demanded that the city governor immediately arrest Kostrichin and the entire leadership of the Union of the Russian People. Meyer promised that in any event he would render them harmless and put them under house arrest. He agreed to seal the Okhrana immediately. He promised to give the police precise instructions not to show a lack of tact toward demonstrations anywhere, such as might be interpreted as a protest against life's new order, and if the demonstrators drove a policeman from his post, then without question he had to leave. (It was perfectly clear to everyone that the police force was doomed, and it did not have long to live. The population could not trust its sincerity. And these instructions of Meyer's were some of his last. The militia that was arising needed a base—and for that it would be good to clear out the Union of Russian People from the municipal garden rotunda. Fine.)

Paramonov thought he had anticipated everything. But he returned to the Civil Committee and a member, a lawyer, Shik, expressed concern and convinced him that they needed to send a commission immediately—without confiding in Meyer—to seize all the secret correspondence from the city governor's chancellery. They did.

Meanwhile, all Rostov was overflowing with jubilation! No one was working or trading or studying anywhere. The streets were flooded with people—and it was spring, too! The streetcars, which had come out in early morning, couldn't move and dragged off to the depot. Demonstrations thronged down Sadovaya, down Taganrog, down Pushkin, down Bolshoi— especially young people and intelligentsia, some with raised arms, some waving handkerchiefs, some even carrying flowers. Their galoshes kneaded through the slush, fell through, and took on water—but how gay they were! Bands showed up, too, and marched toward the French and English consulates. Rallies were held in military barracks, where civilians slipped in. City policemen remained at their posts, having fastened red ribbons to their uniforms. Then, volunteer militia started standing near them here and there, while elsewhere police were driven from their posts altogether.

In fact, though, the situation was not all that joyous. The Civil Committee, forty-five people already, sat the entire second half of the day and all evening but could not finally take shape because the Soviet of Workers' Deputies, which occupied rooms right there, kept rejecting their outstretched hand and not only didn't want to unite with the Civil Committee but stated that it was forming a militia itself, would put food matters into the hands of cooperatives and workers, and did not recognize the Civil Committee's food commission. Several times, Paramonov went to sit with them for talks, but always without result. It was offensive that their leaders were not workers at all but intellectuals, they had just the one worker Petrenko as chairman, for show—but here they were setting themselves apart deeply and irreconcilably, tearing down the entire civic cause in Rostov. The police chief who showed up went not to the Civil Committee but straight to the Soviet to convince them that without police, crimes would be committed and taxes would not be collected. Even worse, the soldiers had started to form their own organization, and they, too, refused to recognize the Civil Committee, but were going to send their own emissaries to all the police precincts. Paramonov rode around trying to convince the soldiers' ringleaders—and failed to convince them of anything either.

So what were they to have? Chaos rather than sensible freedom? Was that what our best aspirations had been leading to all these years?

Right then yet another blow struck Nikolai Elpidiforovich. While he was riding around, the Civil Committee's mood changed as well, and suddenly they chose as their chairman not him but Zeeler.

This was too . . . What the hell was this?

[399]

In the evening, a blizzard swirled over the ice and snowdrifts of the Helsingfors anchorage with the black silhouettes of ships. Snow dusted the decks. Sentries wrapped themselves up to their heads in sheepskin coats.

Lieutenant Bubnov, head of watch on the lead battleship *St. Andrew*, did not immediately notice that there was a red battle light hanging on the mast of the neighboring battleship *Emperor Paul I*, and one gun turret—yes! it had turned this way! toward the *St. Andrew*!

He glanced up at his own mast—and saw on his own mast ball the same red lantern.

But he hadn't ordered it raised! What was this?

He went to the bridge to find out. From up top the petty officer on duty rushed toward him.

"Your honor! It's mutiny on the ship! The crew is seizing the weapons!"

He sent the petty officer to see the senior officer, gave a command from the bridge that the watch be called up top—and himself descended to the deck.

The watch quickly ran out with bayonets pointed.

But already, in the flickering of snow and wind, under the deck lights, a crowd of armed men who were not his sailors thronged across the deck.

He shouted to them:

"Halt!"

The crowd halted.

To the watch:

"Load!"

Oh, not loaded yet! They ran on, slipping, this way.

But the watch hesitated and did not load.

Bubnov wrested away one rifle—to load it himself—but a shot flashed from the spar-deck—and the lieutenant fell.

The *St. Andrew*'s commander, Captain First Rank Gadd, who had just escorted to fleet headquarters the commander of the battleship squad, Rear Admiral Nebolsin, descended to his cabin and sat down to drink tea under a green-shaded table lamp.

But had he heard—a bugle? Yes. Yes. He put down his glass and listened again.

And a rifle shot perhaps? More than one?

He put on his service cap and went out into the corridor.

Running down the corridor were a boatswain and a petty officer with a bloodied head.

"The crew is shooting! . . . They killed the head of watch!"

Outside!

No way to get out. They were shooting at the exit.

Down, to the officer cabin.

Here were about ten officers.

"We'll hold out together, gentlemen!"

With what? Our revolvers. . . .

"Guard the entrance!"

And to the telephone. He was able to report to fleet headquarters, on the *Krechet*.

The officers massed together at the entrance with their revolvers.

While the sailors started firing at the officer cabin—from above, through the deck portholes.

They wounded a midshipman and killed an orderly.

Bullets were whizzing and clattering. The entire floor was covered in glass shards.

They put the midshipman on the sofa and the doctor bandaged him up.

Above they could hear the sailors' frenzied obscenities.

They turned off the electricity to the officer cabin.

Captain Gadd exclaimed:

"We just have to make them see sense! Who is with me?"

And into the corridor! But the firing kept them from going on deck again.

Shouts came from there:

"Midshipman R.! Up top!" (The crew liked him.)

The captain let him go:

"Maybe you'll be able to calm them down."

But the siege of the officer cabin did not abate. In the darkness, the shots kept crashing—and bullets kept penetrating the thin bulkhead. One more officer was wounded.

Then the captain, alone, hurtled out, under fire.

He wasn't hit. And swiftly, fearlessly, in the light of the infrequent lamps, he walked into the crowd:

"Sailors! I'm here alone. It would cost you nothing to kill me. But hear me out!"

"Bloodsucker! We don't want to!" one man shouted.

"You starved us with fish! The officers wouldn't let us come to you to complain!"

"That's not true! Every month I went around to the entire crew. And I always said, come to me if there's a problem. Right?"

"Right! Right!"

"We don't have anything against you . . ."

"He's lying!"

The hoarse captain first rank stepped up to a higher spot—to talk.

But a new and frightening crowd ran up the gang-plank—it was the sailors from the *Paul*, who had already finished up there. And now, at full tilt, seeing the captain on the higher spot:

"Run him through!"

Some gave way to them, while others closed ranks in the captain's defense.

And the *Paul* men stepped back.

Then midshipman R. shouted:

"How about it, boys! A hurrah for our commander!"

And they lifted him on their shoulders.

But took him—to the casemate: "You'll be safer here."

From the casemate, the captain telephoned the officer cabin and ordered the officers to surrender their weapons and go to the casemate.

One young midshipman was guffawing, loudly and crazily. He was led off to the infirmary, but the sailors couldn't stand the guffawing and shot the midshipman on the way.

All over the ship, here and there, dying wails rang out: re-enlisted NCOs and petty officers were being caught and killed.

[4 0 0]

Yes, something had begun at the in Helsingfors anchorage. In the afternoon, there was a sailor demonstration in the mine defense district. Nepenin went there to calm them down.

He gave an order for all ships not to give sailors shore leave.

The day, which had begun with such a joyous burst, was now flowing agonizingly. A rumor arose from somewhere that there were going to be riots on the ships. But why would there be? Hadn't the admiral's frankness helped, his daily disclosure of all events to the sailors? No, it hadn't. Rather, it had done harm. Now, knowing everything, they were expressing themselves openly and harshly on the foredecks.

Officers from different ships told each other that they could feel the sullen accumulation of sailor ill will.

But almost nothing obvious had happened in the past day. The crews on the ships had been training. The day had been brilliantly sunny. But their souls had grown so dark, such alarm had gripped them, that at twilight Captain Rengarten, a bundle of nerves, said to Prince Cherkassky:

"Misha, I think we're on our way to ruin. Only a miracle can save us."

"Surely not! Don't exaggerate!" Cherkassky stood his ground.

Sixteen hours before, they had greeted this blessed day with champagne — and had anticipated anything at all, just not this turning, both within and without. Then, that spirited night, they could not have imagined they would fall into such melancholy by evening. Now they could not imagine why they could have been so overjoyed the previous night.

Overcoming their anguish, they thought to compose a new order to all crews explaining today's new situation. Which they themselves didn't understand.

But they didn't finish. Their vague presentiments proved accurate.

No sooner had darkness fallen than *Paul I* raised a red light and turned its gun turret on the *St. Andrew*, which was next to it.

A little while later, the *St. Andrew* raised its red battle light.

Major gestures by major ships, so threatening and expressive at maritime distances.

The *St. Andrew*'s captain managed to telephone: mutiny!

Rifle and revolver shots were heard on both ships.

Who could they be exchanging fire with if not the officers?

Into the air?

It seemed there was a "hurrah."

Then, in the column of the 2nd squad, the battleships, the *Glory*, which was moored next to those two, also raised a red lantern.

It was on these battleships that the crews still didn't know their officers well, weren't used to them, hadn't been in battle with them.

Responding from a distance, from the column of the 1st squad, the dreadnoughts, the *Sevastopol* and *Poltava* raised red lanterns.

But the *Petropavlovsk* and *Gangut* didn't.

Isolated, malevolent red eyes looked at each other through the darkness. What did they mean?

There were no wireless communications, and from the *Krechet* one could only guess what irrevocable thing was happening there.

If the crews were mutinying, what about the officers? Where could officers go on a mutinied ship?

Firing. . . . "Hurrah" . . .

When they reported to Nepenin about the mutiny, he swelled up inside. He hesitated and adjusted:

"Which of the dreadnoughts could open fire on the *Paul*?"

But he immediately checked himself:

"No, I'm not going to shed blood."

What was happening? *It had come* here. . . .

A stunned Nepenin ordered the *Krechet* crew to line up on deck, in the blizzard.

He delivered a speech to this small formation—in a heavy voice, with all his candor. Saying he wanted to be straightforward and sincere in everything—but certain scoundrels were muddling the crews. Saying he loved and served only Russia, and along with the people had joined the people's government. What else? But only scoundrels could mutiny, while standing against the Germans.

"No matter who it was!" burst from him. "The devil could govern the country! But we have to stand against the Germans and defend Russia! That's all I have to say. I am here entirely, before you. Whoever is with me, remain in place. Whoever is against—two steps out of formation."

Someone shouted:

"Hurrah for the admiral!"

And others:

"Hurrah for the admiral!"—

and the formation dispersed, rushed toward Nepenin, picked him up, and started tossing him.

When they had calmed down, Nepenin addressed them:

"Are there any among you willing, able to speak? Who will go from ship to ship and explain? Two steps forward."

This time many took those steps. Everyone was enthusiastic. Nepenin said:

"Divide up into groups of five. Go from ship to ship. Repeat everything I've said. And tell them that after you I'll be coming myself!"

Meanwhile, machine-gun clatter reached them from some ship.

Were they really firing? At our own? . . .

Everywhere there was seething and killing—in the darkness you couldn't tell, under those red lights hanging from the mast balls.

Crowd "hurrahs" flew in from different vessels.

The firing stopped.

Had they killed off whoever they'd wanted to? . . .

The shouts rose and were cast from ship to ship.

The emissaries from the *Krechet* had only just come on shore when crowds thronged from other ships, and everyone headed this way—toward the *Krechet*.

Here it was! Somewhere in Pskov the Tsar might abdicate, and somewhere in Petrograd the Provisional Government might hold sway, but here, on a March night, in a snowstorm, on the dark and icy sea, which had already taken its first bodies of officers, in the desolation of the anchorage, under red lanterns and narrow rays of light along masts—here they had their own law, their own justice, their own revolution of the brink and ruin.

The approaching sailors formed a large crowd in front of the *Krechet*. For a rally.

Only gunfire could keep them on the gang-planks, and then not for long.

But not only did Nepenin not want to shed blood, he was most offended that he was the first of the major military leaders to have been prepared for this revolution even before its beginning, who had forestalled its progress with his support—and now he and his officers would face retribution from their own sailors?

Turning the vessel's lanterns on the shore crowd in their black pea-jackets and seaman's caps, the admiral sent invitations to the *Krechet* for five deputies from each ship.

The shouts in the crowd intensified: send deputies? who exactly?

Meanwhile the battleships had signaled to the dreadnoughts to arrest the officers!

The *Krechet*'s crew asked for permission to raise the red light to them, too. And the admiral gave it. . . .

The red lantern climbed up and up. The admiral's vessel had joined the mutiny!

And firing could be heard from the mine division.

Now the *Paul I*, which had started it all, radioed: "Speakers, don't speak into the air. The German will hear!"

Deputies came onto the *Krechet*. They lined up on the command deck, and the admiral spoke with them.

His staff Decembrists found him a pitiful sight—so tired was he, so beleaguered, trying so hard to curb his anger. He tried to hold composed talks and find out what it was they wanted. The deputies explained one after another: that a sailor be addressed formally and treated with respect; that a sailor be allowed to smoke on the street . . .

Only that? . . .

They had murdered officers and NCOs on battleships just now and thrown them overboard for that?

Rage for the ignorant, stupid formation tore Nepenin apart. Battered, solid, and round-headed, he became enraged and started shouting.

"The people who killed officers are swine! And swine lit the red lights! And out of cowardice pointed their fire into the air! I despise cowardice! And I'm afraid of nothing! I am calling on my fleet to stand against the Germans! The revolution can be made in Petrograd without us!"

The deputies stood stock-still. Stood well. Listened.

Right then Kerensky's long socialist telegram was delivered to him and appropriately read aloud. At the end it called for obedience to Nepenin, inasmuch as he had recognized the Provisional Government.

The telegram calmed down the deputies greatly.

The admiral allowed meetings of the crews to be held on their vessels and, later, a meeting of the crews' deputies in the carpentry shop on shore.

The deputies dispersed. One of them said:

"He's not going to do anything he promised."

Rengarten grabbed him by the sleeve and started explaining, choking on his own vehemence.

Oh brother-nation, the prejudices that bind you! How can anyone break through to your heart? And shine a light on your reason! Why can't you tell who your friends are?

(This was understandable. The lower ranks of the Baltic Fleet were taken from Petersburg workers, who could more easily be taught the machinery. And in the fleet they earned less than in the factories—and just what they got inculcated with in the machine sections and stoker crews! . . .)

A handful gathered around them. Rengarten spoke and spoke—and was stunned by their muddle-headed, seemingly incoherent and even senseless answers. Even their dull faces. He couldn't catch their logic and inwardly shied away. Was it really with these sailors that they were equal Russian citizens?

He went hoarse. His clerk stepped in to help, having returned from exhorting the other crews.

In the end, perhaps they could persuade, clarify relations, and understand one another. But it took so many words! What a gap!

After the deputies' departure, Nepenin immediately let go, sat down, and lost both his anger and his strength.

They sat in total distress and spoke listlessly.

Some ships were able to radio in how many officers had been killed and exactly who. Who had been bayonetted. Whose skull had been smashed with a sledgehammer. Only then did they learn that Rear Admiral Nebolsin had been shot on the ice.

They had listened to the admiral's speech—and hadn't told him! Nepenin had exploded in front of them—and they had already killed Nebolsin! . . . (He'd lived through Tsushima—and now this . . .)

Together with the Kronstadters they had lost what would soon be half as many officers as died at Tsushima.

Here, on the *Krechet*, they had fought them off—for a night? half a night? two hours?

He had to request support. Duma members sent over.

They sent a telegram to GHQ and the Duma:

"The Baltic Fleet as a military force has ceased to exist."

[4 0 1]

In those very minutes when General Alekseev was finishing his conversation with Guchkov, Grand Duke Nikolai Nikolaevich's telegram came in on the other Hughes.

It was a reply, five hours in coming, to Alekseev's circular telegram proposing that the commanders meet. Today the grand duke was in no hurry, as he had been yesterday. After all, he was now Supreme Commander. The telegram's tone immediately put Alekseev in his place:

"In communications with the government, the expresser of the unified opinion of the Army and Navy must be I, albeit not of the commanders' collegial opinion."

So that was his response to the Alekseev plan.

How easy it had been yesterday to bring together the commanders—and how out of reach today.

The Supreme Commander had imposed his powerful hand—and Alekseev was forced to moderate his initiative. But that was even better. Alekseev was tired. . . .

As for the Manifesto, Nikolai Nikolaevich anticipated the throne's handover to the Heir Apparent. The handover of the throne to Mikhail Aleksandrovich announced this morning would inevitably incite carnage.

Was that so? That was astonishing. Why would Mikhail's name incite slaughter? Only uncertainty and confusion can incite slaughter. What made Nikolai Nikolaevich see such a thing from the Caucasus? Did that mean we should now rejoice at Mikhail's abdication?

Or had Alekseev really failed to understand something? (Not that he had to understand, it was easier on the mind.) Or the grand dukes had their own score and their own understanding between them. Fine.

This was no time to ponder that, though: Petrograd was summoning him back to the telegraph. They'd been absent the whole day and then in the evening had suddenly come to life.

Had something new happened? Alekseev went there alarmed, lightly scuffing his spur-less, undandyish boots across the floor.

The telegraph informed him that Rodzyanko was busy with urgent matters. (Fine. He was no longer needed.) And that Guchkov had submitted his resignation as Minister of War! And that whoever was now standing at the telegraph was handling military matters. Did General Alekseev think it would be possible to speak with him?

Alekseev felt as though he'd been struck in the forehead with a stick. His eyes popped. Could such a thing really come about in thirty or even forty minutes? What kind of madhouse was this? If you permit:

"I have just finished a conversation with Guchkov. He did not say a single word about resignation. On the contrary, he indicated he would devote all his efforts to the army's benefit."

Nonetheless, it was so.

Did that mean the entire conversation with Guchkov had already gone to hell? And if there was that kind of instability in the government—what was the field army to do?

"If you could bring it to the Prime Minister's attention, then I would ask that I be kept informed as to the course of affairs. Because it is impossible to give instructions blindfolded."

"An hour ago, government member Nekrasov informed me that Guchkov had resigned."

That is, when he was speaking with Alekseev, he had already resigned and hadn't said anything about it?

"Well, maybe he took his resignation back. If you were talking with him after six o'clock? . . ."

Definitely after six o'clock.

Possibly. But there had been three summonses from GHQ—either for Rodzyanko or for Guchkov.

". . . But Guchkov wasn't at the Duma, so I took leave to go personally to the telegraph room so as not to detain you."

Ah, so that was it. It wasn't they who'd summoned Alekseev but Alekseev's own summons that was still in effect. . . . It was bedlam. They were running around, not seeing or listening to each other.

"Do you have anything else to say?"

"No, nothing. I would ask you to note your name on the tape."

"State Duma member Colonel Engelhardt." Alekseev had never had the honor to hear that name. What was going on in the new government? And what should GHQ be doing? With whom had he cut a deal? . . .

Now that the meeting of commanders had been buried, Lukomsky as if to mock him brought Evert's reply with the survey of the army commanders. Evert agreed and was hurrying to assemble the commanders as quickly as possible.

Yes, they could have united some of them somehow. But it had all been let slip.

During these days what was striking was how many events were fit into a brief period of time. First he was talking with the war minister, then he was no longer minister and you couldn't get from the telegraph to your office and sit down to think things through and recover yourself. Then, in an hour he would be meeting with the former Emperor—and how uneasy he felt. How could he withstand his trusting gaze? What words could he use to explain? And here came a new telegram from the sailors. From Nepenin.

Brief but piercing. Mutiny on several large vessels! Admiral Nebolsin killed! . . .

". . . The Baltic Fleet as a military force has ceased to exist."

It was as if his arm had been chopped off with a single stroke! The commander himself had admitted this about his fleet—still a mighty fleet yesterday—that it had **ceased to exist**!

Alekseev crossed himself.

My God. My God. Save Russia!

Here they were supposed to have protected the armed forces. . . . An entire menacing fleet—and in one fell swoop it *had ceased to exist*! . . . What had gone on? How?

The telegram was brief, three lines in all, and Alekseev still could not bring himself to read it to the end. But the end was the most stunning. As if he had lost his reason and last courage, Admiral Nepenin had asked GHQ:

"What can I do?"

It was unthinkable to express oneself this way in a military telegram. A military man would not dare utter such words. Unless he had lost his mind.

In any case, it was not General Alekseev who could give advice from here. Alekseev had to go meet the Emperor.

His soul resisted mightily. A lack of clarity and an awkwardness had arisen between them such as had never been.

Why, why had the Emperor left? . . .

And now—why had he come back again? . . .

It was so difficult to explain all the steps taken these past few days—especially since they had been rewarded with disappointment. Deceit, even.

Rout, even.

How much easier it had been just fifteen minutes ago, before the Nepenin telegram!

He very much dreaded this meeting.

One piece of *advice* Alekseev did issue was to the foreign representatives: not to go to the train station, whereas all headquarters officials—everyone could go who wanted. The more, the better.

He put on his greatcoat—and was brought another telegram. From that blockhead Ivanov: Was it true he should return to Mogilev?

He was greatly needed here. Except by whom? . . .

He had already gotten into the motorcar and was about to pull away when they ran up with yet another consolation from Nepenin:

"Mutiny on nearly all vessels."

[4 0 2]

It was a long road on a rocking train car for Nikolai after what he'd been through in Pskov.

He felt scorched. Only today had he felt how much. Sleep had not helped it pass. Nor had his book on Caesar.

A marvelous sunny and frosty day was passing outside his windows. But it was not cheering his soul.

From the train he sent his brother a telegram.

"To His Majesty the Emperor Mikhail."

An unusual formulation. But written by his own hand.

"Events of the past few days have compelled me to decide irrevocably on this extreme step. Forgive me if I have grieved you and for not managing to warn you. I shall remain forever your faithful and devoted brother. . . . I fervently pray to God to help you and our homeland. Nicky."

May the Lord send him a more successful reign!

He also sent a telegram to Mama in Kiev. Summoned her to GHQ.

Over the course of the day he had spoken briefly with Frederiks, Voeikov, and Nilov—but still had not untensed. Somehow they had misunderstood him.

Voeikov reproached him. He had told the Emperor that he should keep the guard in Petrograd—and so he should have. And nothing would have happened.

But there had been no way to do that. Was that really not clear? Had he kept the guard in Petrograd, in safety, then that preference would have been an insult to the rest of the army! That would have been impossible!

It would have been just as impossible and ugly (they advised, too) to recall second-tour soldiers from the army and form them into police battalions.

The hours went by. The day was now overcast, too. But not only did the scorching not pass, but yesterday's grew, it grew in significance.

Yesterday, Nikolai had made his decision more easily than he was apprehending it today.

Might he not have abdicated? . . . Simply said: No! And that's that! Dug his heels in. And what? . . . What would they have done?

He was left with a nasty aftertaste from the tone Ruzsky had used with him over these past few days. How Nikolai now regretted it. Why had he given in to Grigori's remonstrances and returned Ruzsky to command the front after the dissatisfaction and displacement? He had elevated him so, only to have him reverse the Empire's destiny.

Maybe, just maybe he could have done something differently yesterday. But that was not the first day a tight shroud had covered his head, and even if there had been something simple and available, it wasn't evident. Yesterday he hadn't seen it.

Maybe there had been a very simple solution, but it had not revealed itself.

Who was Nikolai now? Except for his distant youth, he remembered himself always as emperor, and only that. And all of a sudden—he wasn't. . . .

But he also wasn't just a private person unknown to anyone. That would have been much easier. Now he was a particular cold nothing set up for shame and ridicule by all who had known him in his former life.

Most shameful of all was envisioning how he would meet the foreign representatives at GHQ. It was before them, perhaps, that he felt most ashamed. After all, to them he had been Russia itself. How would they look at him now?

The feeling was as if he'd been disrobed or smeared with dirt. Very humiliating somehow.

And how would he meet the staff? . . . if it was so hard even with his suite. (Everyone expressed it with their eyes.)

Why had he gone to GHQ anyway? . . . Better to have gone straight to Tsarskoye!

His eyes slid over Julius Caesar—but inside him he saw it going by, still going by: his reign. Such a long reign, it seemed—but now short and incomplete.

For twenty-two years he had striven to do only what was best. Had he really done something that wasn't?

Descendants would judge. They would condemn his every step.

This train car rocking had promised to continue on until the evening, apart from life, pushing back everything unpleasant.

But here he was deceived. In Orsha, sleek Bazili, head of GHQ's diplomatic chancellery, who had composed the first draft of abdication, boarded the train. He had come in order to discuss en route with the Emperor what documents to draw up for advising the Allies of what had happened.

He reopened the wound, a few hours early. And tactlessly touched upon the sore spot:

"We were in despair, Your Majesty, that you hadn't passed your crown onto the Tsarevich."

Nikolai sighed:

"I could not part with my son."

Didn't they understand? . . .

So the day came to an end, a free day; but it had passed bringing not peace but rather something even worse. A feeling of being crushed.

Now, in the darkness, they were pulling into Mogilev.

Nikolai became agitated over the upcoming meetings, each of which would humiliate him.

Actually, at the station he anticipated only a few people, the usual greeters—Grand Dukes Sergei Mikhailovich, Boris, perhaps Sandro, if he was here, and a few of the senior generals. However, coming in and peering through the iced-over window he saw on the platform a long, stock-still formation of officers—more than there had ever been, along with officials, and the end not in sight.

Shivers ran across the top of his head. Was he afraid? Yes, he was. It was as if they were honoring a dead man, despite everything!

Tears pricked his eyes: proudly, for the army's honor!

He felt sorry for himself. Was he now somehow excluded from the army's honor? Had he remained a colonel? Of what regiment? . . . .

Hesitation gripped him. How was he to appear before everyone at once? With what step? After all, he would have to control himself, so that tears . . . .

While he was lingering, into the train car walked Alekseev himself to his rescue. Thank goodness!

As ordinary as ever, not overly wise, squinting slightly—"my squint-eyed friend." . . . He had made missteps these past few days, and yesterday he had grieved Nikolai. But right now, Nikolai saw his unpretentious, serviceman's face—and warmth bathed his heart, and his irritation at him passed. Loyal army souls! He embraced him emotionally, touching mustaches, slantwise.

They stood in the very same light green salon car where yesterday, at about this time, Nikolai had received the Duma deputies. And by chance they had sat at the very same little table, Nikolai in the same seat and Alekseev in Ruzsky's.

Alekseev's eyebrows nearly covered his eyes. It was hard for him to start.

"That's all right." Nikolai touched his sleeve.

They sat for a minute in silence.

"It's all right," Nikolai reassured him.

Then Alekseev bitterly inhaled and bitterly said:

"Your Majesty. I have just learned from Guchkov . . ."

Nothing good could have come from Guchkov. Yet another misery? Haven't all miseries been exhausted? . . .

". . . that Grand Duke Mikhail Aleksandrovich, now I no longer know whether this is true or not . . ."

"What is it?" Nikolai exclaimed with alarm.

". . . has abdicated the throne. . . . Not accepted it."

Misha? Not accepted it? My God! How could that be?

"And—who then? . . ."

Alekseev himself nearly wept. Never had the Emperor seen him so grief-stricken:

"No one. The Provisional Government. Or a Constituent Assembly maybe. There's still no document. . . ." And he complained: "Couldn't he have accepted it for at least six months? . . ."

My God! Everything Nikolai had upheld for so many years! Misha had thrown it to the dogs? . . .

Now the blow had hit home! Nikolai dropped his head in his hands.

[4 0 3]

Svechin had always known and been firm in his motto, "To serve." But very strange days had come when "to serve" had come to mean distancing oneself from taking action. Up until now there had been an inspiring accumulation of ammunition. The spring offensive promised to proceed with an abundance of our gunfire. These past few days, however, GHQ's official activities had shifted from logical, scheduled actions to the secret scurrying about of a few leading persons—Alekseev, Lukomsky, and Klembovsky—who were not inclined to share very much even with other GHQ generals, and the documents they wrote, sent, and received were also excluded from the normal paperwork, leaving their GHQ colleagues to guesswork and tense observation.

The Emperor, having spent all of five days at GHQ, had suddenly left, and in the night, as never before. And then every half-day became unusual, and every night, but information about them was not conveyed to GHQ officers, was not discussed at any meetings or in the GHQ officer dining room, and now was dug up little by little by each department—operations, military shipments, the duty general—either when events concerned their competence or when their officers were put on telegraph duty. Lukomsky had also let something slip to someone in the Quartermaster General's department. And since GHQ officers were accustomed to exchanging opinions and amicably discussing everything of interest, they basically did grasp the course of events, albeit with some delay.

Svechin's first emotion during those days had been frustration and shame such as he had not experienced even after this war's bitterest operations. The entire Supreme Command of the Russian Army—including the Tsar, the troika of main generals, and anyone else in charge of administration—was an assemblage of the enfeebled. Instead of mastering the situation and show-ing strength, as befits military men, they all bent over backwards to find ways to step back and yield. From the military standpoint, what was mutinous Pet-rograd? A chaotic, hungry, unarmed, disorganized mass that was also in the most disadvantageous, geographically constrained position. The rebellious reserve battalions were a flabby assemblage of untrained half-soldiers who had nothing more than half a rifle for every four men, and then didn't know which end to load. The army in the field had not just superiority over Petro-grad but incomparability. The deeply calm status of the front allowed them to immediately remove from it up to half a million soldiers, but even thirty thousand would have been more than enough.

Despite all this, the Supreme Command had thought only about retreat and surrender. It was a panopticum of weak and incapable men—both in Petrograd and in Mogilev. For a long time there had been an outstanding procession of talentless and bland appointments—and here at once it came together in paralysis. This could not be only the Emperor's poor judgment of people. Even acting totally blindly, probability theory would have him occa-sionally making a mistake and appointing worthy men anyway. One had to be an unexampled master to place an old ruin at the head of the govern-ment, a cocooned general as the Minister of War, a scoundrel to be the Min-ister of Interior, a blockhead as District Commander, and send an overly cautious coward to be dictator. This was more likely a mistake of the doc-trine—the training and the spirit—in which the command had been reared, like Schlieffen in reverse: how to let yourself be surrounded and dismem-bered and to capitulate as quickly as possible. And the unfortunate weapons of this anti-Schlieffen doctrine were above all the Emperor and Alekseev. Al-though Alekseev had led the masterful withdrawal of 1915, his frowning face alone, the face of a semi-literate sergeant, betrayed the fact that this sergeant could not be entrusted personally with Russia's fate. In the past year and a half, a bold thought like Kolchak's landing in the Bosphorus had not been able to get through his slumbering breast. His entire method was gradual arithmetic accumulation, but right now, in the face of an angry Petrograd, he was losing his arithmetic bravery, too. What a misfortune that he had re-turned from his illness at this inopportune time! Had Gurko stayed a bit longer at the head of GHQ, he wouldn't have spoken with Petrograd that way and this entire revolution would not have sped off.

With each day, the feeling of humiliation in Svechin did not pass but deep-ened. What was all his—and their—military appearance for, their military language, their military way of thinking, the sword at their side, the pistol at their waist, if in the power of decrepit milksop-generals they were doomed to carry documents from desk to desk and wait for decisions from windbags in Petrograd and couldn't even defend their troops from the breath of decomposition?

An officer in the active troops can be mighty because of his orders and can be insignificant because of his subordination. The epaulets on his shoulders give a lot and take away a lot.

From the very first day, Svechin had believed that the uprising should be crushed, that all these delays, concessions, and transitory pacifications were only to the detriment of the army and Russia. Just yesterday morning, though, he could not have predicted how catastrophically far it would go. There had been no way to predict that frowning old man Alekseev would contrive a bloc of commanders-in-chief for the Emperor's abdication and that this bloc would come together so easily and swiftly, even including Evert. That the abdication from the throne of the Russian state would be achieved in a matter of hours, without a single shot fired, without bringing out a single battalion. This was something no normal person could ever have predicted.

But Svechin was no less amazed at his own turn toward the Emperor over these past two days. Throughout this war, he had forgiven him neither that he personally assumed Supreme Command nor, even more, his lapses in it. Svechin saw and remembered a dozen major and a dozen minor mistakes, all of which the Tsar could have stopped or corrected had he not been at some kind of indulgent remove. It was his timidity, weakness, and military mediocrity that Svechin could not forgive—and he thought he would never budge even five degrees on this.

And then all of a sudden, as night was falling yesterday, he turned nearly ninety toward him. This happened the moment Lieutenant Colonel Tikhobrazov brought to the Operations Section the intermediate Pskov telegram, Danilov's reply to GHQ's urging. The telegram said that they were awaiting the deputies, but in the meantime, in an extended conversation with senior generals of the Northern Army Group, His Majesty had stated that *there was no sacrifice that he would not make for the true good of the homeland.*

This was so unbusinesslike, so unmilitary, so incommensurate with the Emperor's commanding height, or with the true correlation of forces, or with where the sacrifice was needed. This was a cry of pain, when a hand is heartlessly flattened—but it was this guileless cry that had cut through. In this sudden cry, his very core poured out as it was, in this cry it was impossible to lie. This cry made clear to everyone that their distant, reserved, incomprehensible Emperor in fact had only one thing in his soul, that he was prepared to sacrifice himself for Russia.

Only he didn't know how.

And had done so in the worst possible way.

While incapable of vindicating him for his mistakes, ending with this one, Svechin suddenly lost the zeal to blame him. The Tsar was guilty, guilty, guilty—but he didn't see, didn't know, didn't understand, and that meant it was as if he were innocent. At the summit of power, which he occupied not through ambition but through bad luck, he had taken missteps, made mistakes—and here he had made a mistake for all of Russia—but Svechin did not have the cruelty to castigate him.

He felt sorry for him.

This feeling held and even intensified when for several hours of the night, they—half a dozen officers and the scathing Grand Duke Sergei Mikhailovich—sat and sat in the room adjoining the telegraph room awaiting the fateful decision, while Pskov kept putting them off, saying that "there were no telegrams for GHQ in the telegraph room." Then the tape about the abdication finally started coming in. Followed by the abdication itself. Several voices exclaimed: Mikhail!

The abdication itself was a similar cry of pain. Considered not from a statesman's viewpoint but with the protective movement of a father "not wishing to be separated from our beloved son." . . .

Having safeguarded his son for the throne for so many years—and now to save his son *from* the throne?

What was the point of this whole abdication if those who had demanded it immediately demanded that it not be, that it be concealed?

And how was this all left up in the air now? What next?

The day of 16 March thickened, overfull with mysterious events that did not reach GHQ. In Mogilev there were already rumors among the inhabitants. And now the first newspapers had broken through and were going like hotcakes, including today's *Russian Word* from Moscow. The drunken, rowdy "Order No. 1," and not from some colonel at least but some "Soviet of Workers' Deputies"—any civilian rube can write an order, but are military men supposed to carry it out? And then Nikolai Nikolaevich's Order No. 1—that day they had clashed at GHQ: one "order" to destroy the army, another to laud the knights of the Russian land. Meanwhile the abdicated Emperor was still traveling back to GHQ for some incomprehensible purpose. There was not a single matter that he had to hand over to someone; everything was moving along without him. Like an extracted tooth, like a torn-off finger, he longed to return to his former place, where he could no longer take hold.

Yet due to the obvious futility of his return and the swiftness of the former Emperor's distraught fall—although there was no order to meet him and no one was obligated to go meet the abdicated Emperor, the resigned Supreme Commander, and it was not their custom to go meet him—nonetheless, many went from every department, including the modest ranks. And Svechin, of course. Who could have shown such baseness as not to meet him?

About 150 men came.

It was minus 12 degrees, and a cold, biting wind blew the fine snow, there was no standing on the platform, and the train was late. They waited in the pavilion until its approach. When it left the last halt—they moved to the "military" platform, which was lit with lanterns—and formed a very long line, single file, according to seniority of rank. They barely fit on the platform.

Standing separately was a cluster of civilians, including the governor.

Finally the train's triangle of lights appeared in the darkness, in the distance. Closer and larger—puffing away, shafts working, large red wheels slowly turning.

The swinging light, the swaying lantern posts—ten dark blue train cars with the royal monogram, snow-swept, icicles stuck from the roof, ice coating the windows.

The train slowed funereally. And came to a halt.

All the generals and officers stood at attention.

Brake steam burst out noisily and escaped between the train cars. Two burly Kuban Cossacks hopped out of one train car, pulled a red-carpeted gangway toward the door, and stood stock-still on either side.

The train platform fell perfectly silent.

They were waiting for the Emperor's exit. But he didn't come.

So then the hunched-over Alekseev entered the train car.

They did not appear for about five minutes. The biting wind blew. Everyone stood there, but no longer at attention, warming their ears.

Important words were being spoken there in the train car right now. Then the Emperor appeared in the train car doors—wearing the uniform of the Kuban foot scouts and a tall sheepskin hat. He descended to the platform. With a faint smile, he saluted the entire formation and bowed to all at once.

Following him out were Alekseev, the tall, bent, and silver-mustached Frederiks, and Voeikov, his head ridiculously upright.

Without pulling himself up, without preparing himself for the moment, the Emperor crossed with his ordinary, unexaggerated step. As if nothing were wrong.

Always awkward, he doubtless felt ten times more awkward today: to appear before his subordinate officers as nobody, nothing.

The Emperor shook the hand of the first general in the formation. (Lukomsky had stayed back at headquarters.)

After that those in formation started removing their gloves.

The Emperor slowly moved along the front of officers, shaking hands.

Occasionally saying something trivial and apologetic in order to fill the awful silence.

Occasionally he simply lingered for a second, eye to eye.

Once or twice he threw his head back sharply and strangely.

Nearby there was a lamp, and Svechin, standing in the second stretch of ten, could see that the Emperor was making this movement to toss back his tears, so that the wind would carry them off and he wouldn't have to wipe them away.

Svechin had seen the Emperor up close more than once and in full light, and he had attended, when it was his turn, the highest-level dinners, where there was also a similar passing through the ranks, and the Emperor had shaken his hand and stood face to face—but it had all been cold, formal, and insignificant.

Now, though, in the lantern's weak light, Svechin saw the abdicated Emperor's thinner, older, yellow-gray, even sallow face and the bags under his eyes—and he looked deeply into his eyes, sympathetically and firmly, and shook his hand strongly and fully, giving him belated courage.

[4 0 4]

Rodzyanko again! Urgently demanding General Alekseev!

"Lieutenant General Lukomsky at the telegraph. If the State Duma president can convey the communication to me, I can receive it."

He laid it on immediately:

"Situation difficult."

Oh, what's happened now, for God's sake?

No:

"When will General Alekseev return and come to the telegraph?"

"General Alekseev is meeting His Majesty. I can't say when he's going to return. But I am kept informed on all issues and can respond."

Oh well, Rodzyanko was amenable and ready to talk. It turned out, matters were not only not difficult but actually quite favorable—or had something turned around in the last minute?

"I can tell you that this day has passed more calmly. Evidently, everything is coming more or less right."

. . . Yesterday they had to enter into an agreement with the leftist parties. Secure their promise to halt the disturbances at the cost of a few general points, so to speak. Or else—downright anarchy would have ensued, significantly more irrepressible than in 1905. . . .

"The disturbances were already so great that they threatened to turn into total slaughter and an all-out brawl between the population and the soldiers."

(A hair-raising picture—for all of two-million Petrograd to be bashing one another! How could that be? Civilians against soldiers or among themselves, too?)

. . . And now, in order to avoid nonstop bloodshed, it was decided to enter into an agreement with the leftists. Their main point was the necessity of a Constituent Assembly. Well, and a few other demands for various freedoms. The Russian people have fully earned them with the blood they've shed on fields of battle. And now:

"Today has been significantly quieter. The soldier mutinies are being neutralized, the lower ranks are returning to barracks, and little by little the city is regaining its usual look. I hope that soon we will start working on defense and on organizing the essential victory."

While the telegraph was pouring all this out, in walked a gloomy Alekseev with a pained face, already picking up and reading the tape.

It remained unclear where the summons's urgency lay and what Rodzyanko wanted.

. . . The government had no other choice.

"The Emperor's act of abdication has been met calmly, although, at my request, has still not been published." And here was more:

"Be so kind as to give an order for its immediate publication and along with it simultaneously the act of abdication of Grand Duke Mikhail Aleksandrovich. . . ."

Here was the full text.

"Although these acts have not been published, rumor of them has gone everywhere and been met by the population with universal exultation. A 101-gun salute to the new government was made from the fortress."

Tomorrow Rodzyanko would transmit the text of the new oath that would be so good as to put into effect. And now, what news from the front?

If he hadn't interrupted himself with a question, one could go on reading and reading him until midnight.

"General Alekseev at the telegraph. The front is fine. . . . However, over the course of the entire day rumors have reached the troops' ranks causing bewilderment and could end badly." And . . .

". . . the Baltic Fleet's status is dismal. Mutiny on nearly all vessels. The navy's military force has evidently vanished."

How could he get this into his rock-hard head?

"In the spring we will have to fight without the Baltic Fleet, and this could be ruinous. And this was all the result of delays: the essence of the act of 15 March was not explained to the fleet's personnel."

However, Alekseev had already come out of his syncopal submissiveness of these past two days and, on the contrary, had felt exasperated from his meeting with the Emperor and his kindness. Now he was able to send Rodzyanko something even slightly insulting:

"The condition of the Petrograd garrison troops is sad and hopeless. They have been thoroughly corrupted by the workers' propaganda, against which evidently no measures whatsoever have been taken."

. . . The contagion is gradually affecting other reserve regiments around them as well. Troop leaders will need to make great efforts in order to save the field army from the disgraceful contagion of military betrayal. . . .

"Military betrayal," not their "freedom," that is how he should put it.

"All the infected reserve regiments are lost to the homeland. We are nearly on the eve of the start of military operations, and we are losing considerable strength. The government must put a limit on the propaganda. Stern measures must bring those who have forgotten discipline to their senses. . . ."

He dictated all this, but somehow little hoping, and then not hoping at all, that the State Duma president would understand him. And then his heart pushed him beyond practical arguments:

"For now I can add nothing more, other than these words: *God, save Russia!*"

Rodzyanko's face could not be seen, nor his voice heard, but bass roulades of unhinged mockery broke from the tape:

"I sincerely regret that your excellency is in such a sad and despondent mood. This hardly serves as a favorable factor for victory. Whereas now all of us here are in a cheerful and decisive mood! Yesterday we received a telegram from the Baltic Fleet commander saying that all had calmed down in the Baltic Fleet, all the mutinies had been neutralized, and the fleet was welcoming the new government."

His gay tone came through sacrilegiously. And this was the man Alekseev had been obeying like a sheep these past few days!

Meanwhile, he asked Lukomsky whether there was anything else from Nepenin.

Rodzyanko, in turn, wanted to make fun even more insultingly somehow:

"Preferably, under the influence of our valorous leaders of the army groups and armies, this same mood will be conveyed to us from the entire front. So that the entire people and the army can finally take up retribution against the accursed German in a unified, amicable way, without reservations or mutual suspicions!"

For some reason he had warmed to the topic, for some reason he now had time, though he hadn't before at all.

"Here, we too are exclaiming, God, save Russia! Little by little, everything is calming down here, and very soon we will take up work for the defense with redoubled energy!"

Finally he broke off. And Alekseev was able to dictate to the telegraph operator in a broken, muffled tone:

"Please be so kind, your excellency, to hear out two telegrams. Helsingfors. Seven-thirty in the evening: 'mutiny on the *St. Andrew, Paul,* and *Glory.* Admiral Nebolsin killed. The Baltic Fleet as a military force has ceased to exist.' Second: 'mutiny on nearly all vessels.' Signed, Nepenin. You see how one has to be cautious in assessing events."

Again he failed to find the full harshness. But finally giving back what he had been putting up with these past few nights:

"Regarding my mood, I would never allow myself to *mislead those on whom lies responsibility to the homeland.* Be well."

However, Rodzyanko wasn't struck by any of it, neither the entire Baltic Fleet nor the direct insult.

"Your excellency, do not be angry with me. These past few days I've forgotten to inquire about your health and whether your stay in Sevastopol brought you sufficient benefit."

* * *

SOMEONE ELSE'S FOOL IS A JOKE,
YOUR OWN FOOL A CALAMITY

* * *

[4 0 5]

They printed Nikolai's abdication—and stopped there, since the people at the Tauride Palace themselves didn't have Mikhail's abdication; Prince Lvov had gone missing somewhere with it. Meanwhile the Council of Ministers needed to have the first abdication and see it in the original.

It had to be taken there, it was an important matter, and Bublikov, clearly, was not going to go and did not want to see them—so Lomonosov willingly agreed to rush it there. He wanted to have a look at these sowers of Russian fields.

And he left with the precious deed.

He'd overlooked something. He should have had Cavalry Captain Sosnovsky ride next to him and the two soldiers with rifles put on the wings, to push through better. They raced the automobile—and people barely jumped out of the way. They did well slipping down the Fontanka and then mistakenly turned onto Vladimirskaya. A narrow street, a few soldiers with bayonets were blocking it. A university student with a red armband ordered:

"Get out! The automobile is needed for an urgent matter!"

Immediately, in a decisive snarl, Lomonosov:

"I am on an exceptionally urgent matter! I am the aide to the railway commissar! I am on my way to the Council of Ministers session!"

"Exactly what matter?"

Damn it, can't say! And damn it, can't go and carry around this deed on foot. A turning point in Russian history is in your pocket.

Snarling even more:

"This is none of your business, comrade! You will answer for the delay! Communication with Moscow could suffer!"

That worked.

"All right, check the motorcar pass."

They did, and let him through.

They raced down Liteiny, along the streetcar tracks.

In front of the Tauride Palace—automobiles, a crowd. They got inside easily, the guard being away.

And there—despoiled halls covered with spat-out sunflower husks. Hundreds of people walking, standing, and sitting. Vendors had gathered here, too, and were selling cigarettes, sunflower seeds, and poppy seed buns.

Where could a Council of Ministers be meeting amidst all this? He was directed here, there, and somewhere else. Finally, down the left corridor, at one door, cadets were standing watch. Here.

They wouldn't let him in. A deputy escorted him through.

In two small, adjoining rooms people were sitting, pacing. Ministers? No? What an overtaken, frightened look on them. Lomonosov stiffened in his dignity.

It was proclaimed that the Manifesto had been brought—and immediately they craned to see, the curious or the ministers.

Nekrasov moved up; he wanted to take the abdication himself since he was the minister over Lomonosov. No, we're no fools: either the Prime Minister or the Prosecutor-General.

But Milyukov sternly pushed everyone aside—and began to examine it directly, and for some reason in the light, as if he had arcane knowledge about historical manifestos, had held many in his hands, and was expecting watermarks here.

But Lomonosov drilled through them with his darting eyes. No, the titans of the revolution should not be like this! Blunderers!

And still no Lvov. And they had to wait for the second Manifesto to print. He sat and waited. But now there was a discussion about how tomorrow Kokoshkin had to be brought from Moscow to Petrograd, but he wasn't going to make the last train today. And they gasped, the muddlers, not knowing what to do.

Lomonosov hastened to show the ministers what genuine administration looks like. He picked up the receiver and sent an order to the Nikolaevsky Train Station to schedule a special train tonight from Moscow consisting of one first-class train car.

They looked with sanctified respect. Once the egg's been stood on its tip— it looks so simple.

At last, Prince Lvov showed up with his oh-so-blissful face and told some muddled story about why he had been delayed.

The ministers crowded together with the same curiosity to examine the second Manifesto, too. Lomonosov also elbowed his way through, among them.

This one was written in ink, in a calligraphic hand, on a piece of ruled notebook paper.

Only then did everyone see that there was no heading! What was it to be called upon publication?

A scholarly debate broke out! A philosophical debate!

Nikolai had lent his document the form of a telegram to the chief of staff, and that remained. But anything at all could be added in Nabokov's hand to Mikhail's abdication.

. . . By God's grace Mikhail II . . .? . . . we declare to all our subjects . . .?

You're forgetting, though, that he never reigned!

No, why, he was emperor for nearly a full day!

Since there had been no real authority, however, there had been no reign, either. . . .

From the shaven melon of his head, Lomonosov brilliantly and archly glared at the ministers, not hiding from them his astute mind. But hiding the contempt in his chest, and—frustration, his frustration.

[4 0 6]

In his entire life, Alekseev probably had not had a day like the one just passed. There had been the few sleepless days of the Sventiany Offensive, but that was a purely military objective, and he had had the means of defense in his hands—and it had ended in victory. But now bricks were falling on his bare defenseless head—and there was nothing to ward them off. The deception with Mikhail Aleksandrovich had happened without him. The Baltic Fleet was perishing without him. Not only this, though, but also an agonizing new uneasiness was rending his breast—regarding the Emperor, especially because he had not reproached Alekseev for his failures but had looked so trustingly and brightly and had even reassured him. This added to the unspeakable shame he felt. Alekseev understood he had made a major mistake.

Now, tonight, he could not avoid seeing the Emperor. First he had brought him, at the governor's residence, Mikhail's abdication. And the Emperor had read it in his presence. While Alekseev stood to attention awaiting a reproach.

They hadn't seen each other for four days and three nights—but so much had happened. And how the Emperor had aged.

However—there was no reproach. The Emperor grieved to the point of moaning:

"What has he done? Who put him up to this? What Constituent Assembly? What filth!"

But now, too, he did not look badly at Alekseev.

And Alekseev wholly shared his reaction. What Constituent Assembly during time of war? Blather.

The second time, after one in the morning, he went to see the Emperor again—now without great need but to console him with a telegram that had just arrived from the Northern Army Group from the Adjutant General the Khan of Nakhichevan, commander of the Guards Cavalry Corps.

". . . I cast at His Majesty's feet the limitless devotion of the Guards Cavalry and their readiness to die for their adored monarch."

The Emperor read it with movement in his face and took the telegram to his room.

That was still the middle of the night. But how to behave the next afternoon? Alekseev found himself in a situation of delicate, shaky imbalance. The Emperor had expressed his desire to come tomorrow, as usual, to the morning report. And although there could not be any kind of report now, for he was not the Supreme Commander, and it would look strange from the outside and perhaps be reported to Petrograd and to the grand duke in Tiflis—Alekseev did not have the emotional strength to tell the Emperor no to his sad, large, imploring eyes.

The imbalance was so sensitive and responsive that, angry though he was, at the end of the conversation Alekseev sent soothing words to Rodzyanko. After all, he had inquired about his health, and this was a kindness, so he was grateful, and he rectified his error, but defects remained that hindered his work.

An imbalance so delicate that even now, what was the right thing to do with the Manifestos? They could not be held up for so much as an hour. They had to be sent to the army groups. But he didn't dare take such a step without the Supreme Commander's approval—and mightn't the whole night pass before consent arrived from Tiflis?

Alekseev simultaneously sent to Tiflis both the text of Mikhail's Manifesto and a respectful inquiry as to whether the grand duke gave his permission to promulgate both Manifestos. And simultaneously he wrote to the army groups a cover letter to the Manifestos saying that they should be immediately announced to the army and civil authorities and, moreover, indicating to the troops that Russia's entire existence depended on the war's results, and all warriors must be permeated by a unified idea. . . . There could be no internecine strife whatsoever. . .

At two in the morning—he sent it out. But all night he still couldn't calm down, couldn't go to bed, until a telegram of permission arrived from Nikolai Nikolaevich. And then—once again telegraph the army groups that the Supreme Commander had given his approval.

Right then, though, another delayed telegram from Prince Lvov came in—more as a reminder that here was yet another authority over General Alekseev.

But the multitude of these authorities did not chafe at him as did his terrible self-consciousness before the Emperor. A terrible tension: how was he to address him? Without causing him excessive pain—but also staying within sensible bounds, being respectful but not letting himself be put in an intolerable position. What from the past was all right now and what wasn't?

Alekseev had worked amicably and obligingly with the Emperor for so many months. But only today had he felt how intimately connected they were.

Painfully so.

Fatefully so.

[4 0 7]

These past few days at Special Army headquarters outside Lutsk, as at all the armies' headquarters, long telegrams with unfathomable news kept pouring in. It had always been natural to see Russian letters crawling out of the telegraph and forming into sensible army communiqués. But these past few days they had formed at first into not quite ordinary words and then into incredible sentences. No one could have predicted these sentences, to say nothing of the entire flow of events that had fallen out of a clear blue sky. The waiting along the front had been so peaceful this winter, the arms and equipment had accumulated so steadily, and the war seemed to have reached a mountain pass from which they could see its end—and all of a sudden revolution had come crashing down!

A major general, the quartermaster, with the tapes wound around his hand like uncut macaroni, went to report, to show them first to the chief of staff and then to General Gurko himself.

Vasili Iosifovich, always stern, over fifty, and with quick turns of the head and a gaze ready for surprises, read all the tapes himself abruptly and quickly, held them out with his fingers, and his decisive mouth under his youthful dark mustache compressed lopsidedly.

An astonishing situation! Behind the back of the vast field army, an inopportune, nonsensical turmoil had begun, a worm had gnawed at the insides of the rear—while the generals stood at the head of superb armed forces and kept watch over the dozing foreign enemy—and they didn't have the choice to turn around, the choice to intervene, and no one had even asked their opinion, as if they were superfluous and alien! The condition of a paralytic: his mind works, his awareness is keen, but he can't move a finger.

Gurko was in an especially vexing state because it was between *his* fingers that it had spilled, through *his* energetic grip. Oh, if only he had still been at GHQ these past few days! He would have given that riffraff a good slap in the face! Will, firmness, and swiftness of mind—all this General Gurko possessed in abundance, and had he been chief of staff for the Supreme Commander now, he wouldn't have let the matter waver and float for a minute and in the Emperor's absence would have been even freer. How was this? By order of the Emperor they'd dispatched three Guards regiments to embark from the Southwestern Army Group—and all of a sudden the order was canceled? Who could cancel it if the Emperor was en route?

When in early November Gurko had been called into GHQ to replace Alekseev during his illness, he had been very much surprised. He had never expected that kind of promotion. (He had already been promised leave for a calm three weeks, and he had been planning to go to his beloved Kislovodsk.) He was younger than all the army group commanders and many army commanders. He hadn't expected the promotion, but he immediately told the Emperor: I will apply all my forces in these duties, too, but I will always speak to you frankly, only the truth in each serious matter, and I will conduct myself as if I were in a permanent rather than temporary post. He established himself instantly. He was not timid about telling the Emperor something unpleasant and did not try to hide his connections with Guchkov, and by knocking down the gossip, himself opened the conversation: Our group wants to make Russia wholly independent of the Western states in the conduct of any war, and that is all. The Emperor merely shrugged, as if to say, That is my constant desire as well. Gurko: Your ministers definitely do not understand this objective. He established himself—and the ministers began coming to see him at GHQ, and he got Rittikh to agree with Shakhovskoy, Shuvaev, and Krieger, so provisioning would continue, because they were at sixes and sevens. It was Gurko who was the first in Russia, and before the Allies, to compose a swift and harsh rejection of the clever German peace proposals, so that Germany would not hope to end the war as arbitrarily as it had begun it—and brought it to the Emperor for his signature. He insisted to the Emperor that the Poles should be given not autonomy but full independence. Gurko also held a December meeting of his commanders, conducted his own reform of the divisions from sixteen to twelve battalions, an additional seventy divisions were promised by late spring, and he could already feel in his grasp the victorious campaign of 1917. It was also he, representing Russia, who had held the February Petrograd conference of Allies, who had revealed their total ignorance of the status of Russian military affairs. He had shamed them and insisted that they share material resources equally and not only demand of us efforts above and beyond their own, while giving us only their surplus equipment. Immediately after this, a telegram arrived unexpectedly from Alekseev in the Crimea saying that he was sufficiently well to return ahead of time, on 5 March. Well then, so be it. Gurko himself mastered his own inertia: he left GHQ as easily as he'd joined it—and left for the Special Army on 7 March.

So everything would be as it should. But before he could get to Lutsk, the Petrograd events began. And this jerking around of Guards regiments. (He now remembered how Khabalov in February had refused the two cavalry regiments.) Who was **there** now? Oh, vest-pocket Belyaev!

Here, beleaguered after a major winter acceleration, Gurko now suffered from worse nerves in inactixon than at the height of a big battle. For some reason he was waiting for events to call on him again! When yesterday they had called up Kornilov, a corps commander, to take over the Petrograd District, Gurko, although it was beneath his position, envied him. He himself was prepared to break through there right now and quickly set everything to rights.

But no one had called on General Gurko or his troops to go anywhere. GHQ was in hiding, and there'd been a pause in the wires, when suddenly last night, just before morning, a tape arrived such that they woke up the commander, he snatched up this twisted rustle—and in front of his headquarters generals openly clutched his head:

"It's all over now."

So clear had it become to him in that instant that it was all over and the war was lost!

The Emperor had abdicated.

The handover to Mikhail would not go smoothly.

Immediately he ordered his corps commanders assembled; there were eight of them in his large army. Two hours later they had assembled. No sooner had Gurko begun to consult with them about what to do and how to announce this than they handed him a new telegram: Delay the first telegram!

Excellent! Hope. Had the current somehow shifted there, in Pskov and Petrograd?

The corps commanders dispersed.

The current had shifted—but how to intervene? How to help? No one was calling for assistance.

Gurko became even more spent over the course of this fruitless day.

Early that night he was awakened again.

Gurko emerged from his bedroom wearing his yellow camel's hair pajamas. Though just now awakened, he bore no traces of sleep and was immediately ready for action—and he cast a keen glance at the tapes, not anticipating any good from the white loops. And sat down for some reason on a table rather than a chair.

He took the hank and unwound it. The colonel from the quartermaster unit, who had bypassed the chief of staff with the tape, did not help the commander read it, did not head him off with words, knowing that he liked to do everything himself.

One Manifesto. . . . Another Manifesto. . . .

Gurko's eyes scanned the tape, and even his tense, nervous face yielded to astonishment.

Was he to believe the dynasty had come to an end?

And with it the monarchy in Russia!

He threw his head back and squinted.

He gave the colonel a look, as if to dress him down for an offense. He handed back the twisted tape and did not order anyone woken for now.

He had to think.

Left alone, he banged on the table a few times—painfully for his hand. He dashed around the room and banged again with the flat of his hand. Without sitting down, he propped his head on his arms on the table.

What a helpless, idiotic situation! You couldn't get into a mess like this in any battle. He had a full force, all the Guards and also non-Guards corps—and he couldn't do anything.

He cursed himself for having waited for something these past few days without attempting anything. . . .

But—what?

Well, Belyaev was a puppet. But he was amazed at Alekseev. He had all the power in his hands, all the forces. How could he have allowed this?

How on earth had he not intervened?

Now, given over to chaos, given over to windbags—Russia would drown in blood.

But Gurko hadn't been able to find his own missed opportunity. He'd searched for it, even fearing to find it (and then not forgive himself)—but honestly hadn't. While he had been in Petrograd, while he had been at GHQ—there'd been no inkling of anything like this.

Now all his opportunities consisted of exchanging comments through Brusilov. This was like rolling up his sleeves for a fight and starting to mix shit up to his elbow.

But how could Alekseev, who was running a fever, be allowed back to service?

He went and plopped down on the bed so hard that the netting squeaked.

A few times he turned over with a bounce, searching for a solution.

But didn't find one.

Nor did he find any mistake or oversight of his own during these days.

That meant it was over, and he shouldn't torture himself.

Actually, he knew his own nerves and that he wasn't going to get any sleep that night.

The thing was—his omnipotence had so recently been so palpable.

His speech to the ministers, to the Emperor, to the Allies had burst out in a stormy stream. He had the directness to dazzle anyone he liked and they were compelled to hear him out. While the Protopopov secret police were following the movements through Petrograd of the Supreme Commander's chief of staff, his private meetings, and of course rushed to inform the Tsar—Gurko wasn't trying to hide and willingly met with sensible and independent Russian people. However much he had seen the Emperor this winter, not once had he bowed to him obligingly but rather had defended his opinions to the point of a raised voice, a shout even, a threat of resignation—and the Emperor had always yielded. If he was busy, Gurko could himself postpone an audience scheduled for him by His Majesty. Unable to tolerate the Empress, he declined to appear before her and only once spoke to her at an Allied dinner. For years on end, Gurko had been the most independent of generals, unbearable for his independence, and was even considered the leader of the meticulous "Young Turks"—but he simply could not merely serve out his time without attempting to fix things. They had also brought his brother to justice and humiliated the name Gurko—so couldn't he rejoice just a mite at today's revolution?

But he knew this was the end for Russia.

Yes, this winter he had nearly shouted at the Emperor.

But now his anger had played out. Now he was experiencing a rush of pain for that weak man who had ruined us all.

Now, with each minute, he pitied him more and more. He pictured how all those he had been kind to and drawn close would turn away from him, betray him, flee to all their burrows. . . .

No, there was no falling asleep. He didn't even try.

He went to his desk. Read papers, correct orders? That didn't work either.

Summon the corps commanders again? Let them get some sleep. There might be another directive by morning.

One thought kept swirling in his head. Right now, along with the two Manifestos to the divisions, he could send out a secret inquiry for information to be gathered on how the lower ranks and their district's population felt about the acts of abdication.

In any event, it would be useful to know. (What if, perhaps—he could do it over again?)

But inside, something unconscious was growing, and Gurko himself had yet to heed it.

He read papers and underlined.

Suddenly it became obvious: now that the Emperor had been overthrown, humiliated, and abandoned—now was the time to extend him support.

Write a letter?

Right away, when everyone would be tottering back, saying they'd never been monarchists, to assure him, even exaggeratedly, that he was a monarchist and a loyal subject.

The suddenness of the thought did not surprise him. That is how ideas always come to us, in a flash or else not at all.

Were the fates of letters shaky now? They might not be passed on to the Emperor or he might be under blockade.

Send it with a loyal officer. One of his Grodno Hussars. (Gurko had begun his service there.)

And if he was going to Mogilev anyway—why not send Alekseev a letter? If he didn't know how to hold on to the reins of state—let him at least intercede, so that well-known people weren't raided in Petrograd and the elderly weren't put under arrest.

This grew so much inside him that he had no desire, no yearning, to do anything else now but to write a letter to the Emperor.

Although Gurko himself had yet to understand what he should write. Propose a path to salvation, a path of action? He couldn't. But that could be the sole genuine meaning.

Simply to express something. That these difficult days for Russia could not be so lamentable to anyone as they were to His Majesty. That writing here was not he but the millions of loyal sons of Russia, who understood that the Emperor was animated by Russia's good and preferred the magnanimous deed of taking all the consequences on himself rather than subject the country to the horrors of internecine strife or yield it to the triumph of enemy arms. The people's grateful memory would appreciate this self-sacrifice of a monarch who was both a servant and a benefactor of the country, on the example of his crowned ancestors.

General Gurko could not find the words to express his admiration for the sublimity of this sacrifice.

His abdication on behalf of the Heir was perhaps inspired by God. Four years hence he would not be able to take the reins of governance into his own, still weak, hands. Once he had received a proper, unhurried upbringing to a more mature age, having thoroughly studied the state sciences, and acquired knowledge of people and life—he might one day be called upon by right-thinking people of Russia to accept his legitimate heritage.

It could be predicted that the country, after the bitter lessons of domestic upheavals and the experience of a state governance for which the Russian people were historically and socially unprepared, would once again turn to a divinely anointed Emperor. The history of nations teaches us that there is nothing unusual in this. But the conditions in which the coup d'état took place in the capital, so unexpected for the army, which was constrained by the enemy's proximity, give us grounds to hope for such a return.

General Gurko could encourage his Emperor with nothing more: in good conscience, he saw no help coming soon.

It was easier to assess the value of the Provisional Government, which was releasing from the prisons people condemned for political activity—and simultaneously imprisoning the Emperor's former loyal servants, who had acted within the framework of existing laws. Could those arrests be called a manifestation of the freedom written on the usurpers' banners?

But those who in the future would form the nucleus around which men would close ranks, those who would pursue genuine development and the steady rise of the Russian people . . .

What would this letter be about, without anything practical, scattered into fractional thoughts? Never in his life had Gurko written such nonpractical letters. But only as he was finishing it did he sense he was recuperating.

Permit me, Your Majesty, to draw Your attention to all this. Recalling your kindness toward me over the course of the few months I spent at your will as Your close aide, I allow myself to hope that You will also accept favorably the outpourings of my heart, which has been gripped by sorrow during these days that threaten the life of Russia. Believe me that I have been guided only by my sense of loyalty to the Russian autocrat, a sense I inherited from my ancestors, who always possessed the courage and honesty to express to their Tsars only the genuine truth.

17 March
Saturday

[408]

The previous night, the naval Decembrists had burned with happiness; tonight, with suffering and fear. The mind refused to picture what the fleet was now. How could it continue to be run by murderous sailors? And what would happen to them themselves by the time morning came?

Rescue from the State Duma, in the form of a speaker or two, could not come before the daytime hours. But last evening—such were the freedoms now—the machinist-deputy Sakman went to the *Krechet* for a direct conversation with the government. It turned out, Kerensky at his end replied that he was asking the sailors to immediately cease their rout of the Russian fleet and reminded him that Vice Admiral Nepenin had openly recognized the authority of the Provisional Government and submitted to it unconditionally, and so the sailors should trust his orders. Then again, Kerensky simultaneously assured the sailor-deputy that the Provisional Government was guaranteeing to sailors, as to all citizens, full freedom of agitation and propaganda.

The present day would have to be survived. The Baltic Fleet at anchor was a separate world, and nothing going on in Russia could be brought here across the icy expanses.

Except by radio. That Mikhail had abdicated.

And this most certainly did not add stability here.

However, just before dawn, Adrian Ivanovich, who since yesterday seemed to have gone entirely limp, summoned his trusted circle with glittering eyes and the restored liveliness of his impressive face. Solidly put together, he was filled, like a bomb. And he spoke through his luxuriant mustache:

"A journey once begun must never be abandoned! There is nothing worse than roamings and trawlings. It would be a mistake right now for us to betray our convictions or our method. All these bloody forms which the revolution is assuming are, to a certain extent, then, inevitable. We are continuing our method—an open appeal to the sailors. Right now, before they wake up. Come, let's finish the text."

They finished it, and before daybreak, at five o'clock, Rengarten brought to the wireless Admiral Nepenin's appeal to all crews.

So that no misunderstandings would arise, it said there, the Commander of the Fleet was once again announcing to officers and sailors his steadfast decision to firmly support the authority of the new government. He was demanding that all ranks of the fleet work as one to support order. He believed

184

in the complete unity of officers and sailors, who were responsible with their honor to the homeland for its future.

He could not be more direct, honest, and open!

The battleships were nearly dark, with rare lights, but with the same ominous, stark, lonely crimson lamps on their mast balls.

The admiral's confidence was conveyed to those close to him. They went to have some hot, strong tea before the start of a difficult day.

But before they could finish drinking, a frightened wireless operator ran in and brought a reply from an unknown ship, from unknown, unsleeping people, out of the predawn haze.

"To Nepenin's wireless. Comrade sailors, don't believe the tyrant! Remember the order to salute! No! We will not get freedom from the vampires of the old regime! Death to the tyrant—and no faith whatsoever from the united democratic fleet organization."

The direct threat was made even stronger by the fact that the authors were anonymous. As in any ship-to-ship signal, there was the inscrutability of giants in this. It's hard to believe that this is ordinary people transmitting this, some wakeful telegraph operator—and not an invisible, gnarled monster moving his paw.

Insanity! Total breakdown! Such a sensibly conceived coup d'état, such a magnificently begun revolution—what it had turned into!

And all they could hope for was . . . a miracle?

There could be no lying down. There could be no calming down.

Drag this day around like a slave's yoke.

What was going to happen today?

Cherkassky tried to reassure him: according to the theory of oscillatory movement, repetitions of oscillations are inevitable, but they will go down.

Right then a wonderful thought came to Rengarten. Let the admiral issue a general order to remove portraits of the Tsar. This would make a good impression.

Nepenin consented. They sent a wireless telegram, to everyone.

[4 0 9]

The next relief, an ensign, was feeling under the weather, so the captain asked Gulai to stay on one more night at the observation post.

Again there was no gunfire, and Gulai slept just as heroically, but when he woke up, the water had boiled at the telephone operator's.

He slurped some.

It was completely gray in the bunker, an overcast day.

The telephone operator on duty was sullen, and just sat by his equipment without looking through any scope. But Gulai put an eye to the eyepieces—and in the very same place as yesterday, and even, apparently, on the same board, a new sign taunted them:

Tsar Nicolas kaput!
Soldiers—Go home!

Hey hey . . .

One bullet doesn't get shot twice. They weren't joking twice.

And again on high notes, like trumpeters playing, not really alarm but a youthful feeling of joy at the unknown rang out in Kostya.

Indeed, he wanted to experience an interesting change.

He woke up for good right away. And was even prepared to spend a second boring day at the observation post, if only to have someone to talk to.

But he didn't report to the battery because they'd just order him to knock it down—and for what? They were transmitting news to us, we should be grateful.

Let the news reach Prince Volkonsky.

What on earth could have happened, though, and why didn't we know anything?

An end to the war? That'd be pretty good. He was sick of the damn thing. But what on earth was happening in Petersburg and with the Tsar?

Here's what. Go to the infantry. This was a legitimate absence and there was no need to report. He taught the telephone operator how to answer, and made his way down the communication passageways.

The trenches were already trod everywhere underfoot, and the recent snow was flattened. And nothing was coming down.

There were no signs in the labyrinths of passageways, so anyone who didn't know every turn would get lost.

There was silence all around—complete silence. Not a shot fired, not a wagon thump, not a human voice. No inkling how very many men were dug in here in the burrows and breathing.

If it really was revolution—then what of the war? Wrap the war up. Good.

Revolution! There was, after all, something attractive and inviting in that sound.

He wondered what Sanya thought. Actually, Sanya kept pushing his porridge around his plate.

He got as far as the battalion command point. The door they had hanging wasn't of their own making but removed from somewhere in the village, with figurative panels.

Inside they had set up two areas: the first for the telephone operators and couriers; and beyond a partition, in the same bunker, another small officers room.

The soldiers were lying on straw, the telephone operator on a stump.

"Anyone in?" Gulai nodded to the second space and knocked there.

Because of the morning hour, he was thinking to find only the duty officer, who was in fact there, Ofrosimov again, but in addition to him, sitting at the little table, was the battalion commander—short, pointy-mustached Lieutenant Colonel Grokholets.

"May I, colonel, sir?" Gulai leaned over in the small door.

"Yes, yes." Grokholets nodded, preoccupied. He was sitting at the table without cap or greatcoat, his small head bald but with a brash, isolated fore-lock at his crown.

They had it heated here. Ofrosimov, morose, was also sitting without a cap, but his greatcoat was strapped with belts.

Grokholets nodded slightly for the second lieutenant to sit. The chairs here were all blocks of wood with cross-wise planks.

Gulai straddled one after removing his cap, too.

From the look of them he realized they knew. So he didn't ask.

Grokholets, known for his pointed jokes in front of soldier formations and in the company of officers, for which he was beloved by all, his jokes al-ways being spurring little lashes—now sat very small and pointed, but all the pointiness of his twisted mustache and piercing eyes was inert.

Gulai didn't ask—but they weren't surprised at his arrival and silence either. There had been this silence here before him. Which made things even clearer.

Ofrosimov, with his earthy strength, sat with his arms wrapped around himself, as if trying to keep himself from jumping up.

And this apprehensively anticipatory waiting checked the joyous percus-sion in Gulai—and he involuntarily picked up on their gloom.

"But what does Petersburg have to do with this?" Ofrosimov barely got out. "The army won't let them!"

"And what exactly is in Petersburg, gentlemen?" Gulai asked now in a full tone of apprehension.

"The educated people have lost their nerve," Ofrosimov forced out.

For all his wit, even Grokholets couldn't come up with anything more than he had learned:

"The Petrograd garrison has mutinied. Power has been seized by twelve Duma members. All the ministers have been arrested."

"And . . . the Emperor?" The question came immediately and involun-tarily. (It had been Gulai's former habit to say "Tsar," as did everyone in so-ciety, but among officers that sounded rude.)

"Nothing is known."

"So how do they know?" Gulai pressed, now referring to the German sign openly.

"Rumors." Grokholets shrugged his narrow shoulders. "But they've been spread over all the telephones and by all the soldiers."

"But if that's so," Gulai reasoned, "then why doesn't the command an-nounce it directly?"

Grokholets slowly directed his head in a nod, as if recognizing some-thing invisible that had arrived:

"Right now, the division chief is summoning all regimental commanders and . . . and?"—he was surprised to say this—"regimental priests."

That priests were sent was the most convincing thing—like at a funeral.

Ofrosimov sat there like a dark cloud.

By now it had been conveyed to Gulai quite seriously that no, there wasn't a whiff of amusement here. He, too, sat there like a sullen boulder.

And the slender, agile battalion commander, despite having his unit, armed, prepared for both battle and death, as always—yet what could he do? . . .

All his pointiness was poking into something dull and unknown.

Despite all their feelings and thoughts, everything depended not on them—but on what the leadership would decide.

[4 1 0]

It is during the tensest days that there is the least opportunity for restoring one's strength. Two nights in a row had been completely destroyed for Ruzsky. You couldn't rest even during the day. This third night they were threatening to wreck, too—but after two in the morning, the second Manifesto finally arrived, and the state crisis was apparently at an end. Ruzsky ordered Danilov not to wake him for anything, went to bed with a sedative, unwound, and fell asleep.

Danilov would have gladly taken a nap, too, but there was his position as chief of staff, and by constitution he was much stronger than Ruzsky, as well as younger.

All that remained, apparently, was the technical aspect of conveying to their three armies, and to the Karelian isthmus, and to the Baltic Fleet all the above-received documents—Nikolai's abdication again, Mikhail's abdication, and Nikolai Nikolaevich's Order No. 1—and with that over and done you could go to bed. But this was not to be.

A telegraph summons followed from an unusual connection: the Western Army Group. Kvetsinsky was summoning Danilov. He communicated that the Western commander was in a state of great alarm and mistrust (he didn't explain whom he didn't trust, but it seemed to be GHQ), pointing out that Mikhail's Manifesto did not bear any validating signature and was probably void. Evert didn't want to publish it until he received the decision of the remaining commanders-in-chief.

Right then it dawned on Danilov: Truly! Nikolai's Manifesto had been validated by Frederiks, but Mikhail's not by anyone. Was this laxity? Ineptitude? Or was there some point here? . . . Evert was getting very cautious. . . . However, Danilov could not take it upon himself to awaken Ruzsky. Let the Manifesto stay with Evert for a while.

Although, for example, all the upheavals in the Baltic Fleet were explained by both GHQ and the Northern Army Group headquarters specifically by the holdup of the first Manifesto. If they had announced it right away, there wouldn't have been any upheavals.

The transmission of the Manifestos by Northern headquarters began. GHQ assumed everything was proceeding properly. They sent a request that they be informed as to how the announcement of the acts was being taken by the troops and population.

But right then Boldyrev took a closer look and reported to Danilov that there was a sentence in Nikolai Nikolaevich's Order No. 1—"Knights of the Russian land! I know how much you are prepared to sacrifice for the good of Russia **and the throne** . . ."—but what damn throne now if we were transmitting Mikhail's abdication?

Indeed, it was absurd. Both Mikhail's Manifesto and Nikolai Nikolaevich's order had simply been marked with the same date of 16 March, but the times weren't noted—and now bewilderment was going to spread over all the troops.

Boldyrev suggested deleting "and the throne" and leaving only "the good of Russia." But Danilov, ever the loyal hand, retained his old respect for Nikolai Nikolaevich from their joint service. How could we abridge the Supreme Commander? We don't have the right. At the moment when the grand duke was writing, there was still a throne.

Awaken Ruzsky? Again, he couldn't. He decided to telephone Lukomsky. Maybe the grand duke's order could be held until there was clarification? Could the Supreme Commander himself correct it? Lukomsky was also at an impasse: We don't have the right to hold it back, but maybe we could interpret it that Mikhail's abdication, too, had come down to us from the height of the throne? "No! There would be grave misunderstandings everywhere. Who would understand these subtleties?" "Then," Lukomsky proposed, "shall we release the Supreme Commander's order significantly earlier than the Manifesto?" "But that moment has passed. We were in a hurry to communicate the Manifestos." And rightly so.

There was no solution. And Ruzsky could not be disturbed. Alekseev was not agreeable to abridging anything and demanded the Supreme Commander's order be sent out, too.

No, the Northern Army Group decided to wait. The night's end and the dawn hours were deciding nothing so they held onto the Supreme Commander's order. Finally the two of them, Danilov and Boldyrev, decided to rouse the Northern commander.

The room was half-dark: there was daylight outside, but there were curtains. Ruzsky woke up painfully, even with a moan. And a reproach. He heard them out.

"What nonsense. . . ."

Well of course it was an anachronism. Well of course the falsity of "and the throne" offended the ear.

While they were explaining to him—Danilov seated by the bed, Boldyrev standing behind him—his happy sleep slipped away irrevocably. But after stretching his legs out under the blanket, Ruzsky was also glad that he didn't have to get up and dress, didn't have to go to the telegraph. At sixty-three, that would all be nauseating. . . . He didn't take the document from Danilov to examine but rather examined it by ear, eyes closed.

An anachronism. . . . Not only in that "throne" but in Nikolai Nikolaevich himself, overblown in his capacity as Supreme Commander. The day
before yesterday, there had been so much struggle around the abdication
that Ruzsky hadn't been able to bring himself to speak up about this right
away. But, in fact, it was a helpless, pathetic move backward. They'd taken
a great historic step—and immediately wobbled like cowards.

There is was, the crow cawing—"and the throne"—while the cheese falls.
A strikingly incorrigible old fool, how could he fail so miserably at having a
feel for the times? Of course no kind of "throne" could go into the order.
They could have figured that out for themselves and not disturbed him.

And then there was Alekseev! . . . Oh, the assiduous clerk! How had he
found the nerve to call a conference of commanders? . . .

No, only by uniting with the new government were we going to hold
on now.

[411"]

(FROM THE NEWSPAPERS)

MANIFESTO OF NIKOLAI II

ABDICATION OF GRAND DUKE MIKHAIL ALEKSANDROVICH

DETAILS OF THE ABDICATION
"What am I to do?" the Tsar asked quietly.
"Abdicate the throne," replied the representative from the Provisional
Government.
The Tsar was immediately given for his signature an act of abdication
prepared in advance, and the Tsar signed it.

WIRELESS TELEGRAM ABROAD. To everyone, everyone, everyone. For
the purpose of averting total anarchy . . . In a brief period, with the unanimous mood of the entire army in favor of the coup . . . Were able to enter
into relations with the Soviet of Workers' Deputies . . . Attempts to send military units against the capital ended in the most utter failure since the
troops sent immediately went over to the side of the State Duma. . . . The
English, French, and Italian ambassadors have recognized the people's government, which has saved the country. . . .

The populace's enthusiasm regarding what has come about gives us full
confidence in the tremendous increase in the strength of the national resistance . . . for securing a decisive victory over the enemy.

. . . Each of us much now forget everything and give ourselves over entirely to the happiness of the homeland. Now, only traitors and people who
do not love Russia are fighting the new authority.

THE HOMELAND RESURRECTED. . . . Oh, great nation! The moment has come—and you have risen up, great, mighty, and splendid. Risen up like a giant—and your chains turned out to be but a spider web. No matter what happens now, we are consoled. This moment has repaid us for everything.

. . . The Romanov family is a clan of despots and degenerates. We must sweep this trash away down to the foundation. . .

. . . Naïve people fear that with the elimination of the monarchy, Russia's state unity might falter. But it is free political institutions that will strengthen Russian state unity. The new government arose not through self-appointment: on it rests the will of the people.

BEHIND THE GRAND-DUCAL SCENE . . . Now the curtain can be raised over this corner of Russian life . . .

THE HEIR APPARENT'S ILLNESS, as has been reported, has taken on an adverse character.

REPORT POGROMS. The Bureau of Information requests that it be informed at telephone no. . . .

PURISHKEVICH today toured all the regiments and called on officers and soldiers to submit to the Provisional Government.

AUCTIONS OF THE REVOLUTION. A few days ago in Petrograd there were no regular newspapers. Yesterday, no sooner had the Moscow train pulled up to the Petrograd train platform, than a crowd of porters rushed for the baggage car. A battle began that then moved toward the kiosks. A few minutes later, there were no Moscow newspapers left. Then, over the course of the day, they were quoted on Nevsky like stock certificates—at 100 and 1000 rubles per issue. At the Baker's Coffeehouse, a copy of *Russian Word* was sold for 10,000 rubles to Mr. Levenson, director of the Tin Company. Those who bought newspapers received an ovation and then were hoisted in triumph.

CABBIES. Carrier company owners brought a petition before the City Duma on abolishing the set rate. The Duma granted it . . .

Other auctions arose for revolutionary needs. At first, poems on the death of Rasputin were sold, and then partly burned documents of the Security Department.

IN THE SYNOD, 17 March. Metropolitan Vladimir, on behalf of all present, expressed his joy at the liberation of the Orthodox Church.

Duma member priests address a brotherly appeal to the Orthodox clergy of all Russia: immediately recognize the authority of the Duma's Provisional Committee and through their ardent pastoral word explain to the people that the change of authority has come about for their good and that only this way can the Homeland be led onto the path of happiness, prosperity and florescence.

One after another, the purveyors to His Majesty are hurrying to reject their honorary title.

Superfluous institutions. The military censorship commission has been disbanded. . . .

THE OFFENSIVE OF OUR CAUCASUS ARMY is continuing to develop. We have occupied the pass opening the road to Mesopotamia. In the Baghdad direction. . . .

ENGLISH SUCCESSES IN MESOPOTAMIA . . .

In the Moscow Soviet of Deputies. . . . A French officer's speech, saying that the revolution in France began in the exact same way, evoked much applause . . . The manufacture of ammunition must be accelerated.

Employees of Moscow savings banks have expressed their limitless joy regarding the coup that has come about.

. . . to raise the question of destroying passports as documents that demean human dignity. . .

Moscow hairdressers welcome the first citizen of free Russia, the State Duma president, and express their limitless joy . . .

REGARDING THE ESCAPE OF CONVICTS from Butyrskaya prison. . . . 1700 people have been detained. The majority were at the Khitrovy market and in eating-houses, and many surrendered voluntarily. A few were caught during a robbery. However, none of the gang of "Sashka the seminarian" or "Vaska the Frenchman" has been detained yet.

When the arrested policemen were led through the Moscow streets, the crowd could barely contain itself: "Rip their epaulets off!" "Kill them!" "Tear them to pieces!" The militia barely managed to restrain the crowd from mob law. For the entire brief journey, city police were the subject of the most malicious and entirely understandable ridicule.

JEWISH RALLY. In the next few days, Moscow Jews are organizing a rally.

The new Moscow Province administration. . . . The former vice governor has been sent to Butyrskaya Prison.

ELEPHANT-DEMONSTRATORS. Yesterday on Tverskaya there was an unusual procession: two elephants and a camel, with greetings to the popular representation on their horse-cloths, and behind them, standing on a chariot, the famous clown and animal trainer Durov, who suffered so much under the old regime.

[4 1 2]

The cold wind did not die down, and through the night and morning it blew, persistent and importunate, blowing something in.

When it had fully dawned, a view opened up as if the Emperor were not at GHQ: no paired sentries in front of the entrance to the governor's residence. No agents in civilian dress loitering in front of the palace. All that remained were two gendarmes by the palace railing.

A big red flag hung over the city hall across the square.

At eight o'clock, Lieutenant Colonel Tikhobrazov began his twenty-four-hour shift and occupied the duty room on the lower floor, next to the telegraph room.

He checked the codes. He did the rounds of the first and second floors.

From a second-floor window he observed a scene: a handful of civilians, probably merchants, had gathered in front of the palace railing. They were gesticulating energetically and, apparently, exclaiming, persisting in their effort to get inside, but the gendarmes wouldn't let them in. Then someone went to the governor's residence. He returned—and tried to persuade the people gathered. Finally, reluctantly and uncertainly, they dispersed.

In that time, headquarters learned what the scene was about: these were agitated suppliers coming and demanding money, worried that the Emperor would now go bankrupt and not pay them.

Tikhobrazov blushed as if it had been he himself coming with a demand.

Just so, while they were standing there, the Emperor didn't see them out the window and recognize this disgrace.

But from the windows of his study he could see, obliquely.

Tikhobrazov was worried. Would the Emperor come as usual at ten-thirty to hear Alekseev's report? It seemed impossible! But at the same time so familiar. And if he did come—what title would one use for him?

Tikhobrazov loved the Emperor. He considered him strikingly simple and responsive, as rarely happens with royal status. He was immeasurably happy to have shaken his hand yesterday, awkward as that bitter occasion was. After a year and a half, the Emperor knew everyone here, at GHQ, and called Tikhobrazov "the little captain," even after he was promoted to lieutenant colonel.

Just after ten, he stood on the second floor near a convenient window and watched to see whether the Emperor was coming.

Yes! He appeared exactly as always, but walking entirely alone, as he never had before—without the palace commandant or the duty convoy, just the aide-de-camp escorting him.

As yesterday, he was wearing a Circassian foot-scout coat, without a greatcoat.

With an officer's skill, Tikhobrazov precisely calculated his own exit—so that he would meet the Emperor outside, near the corner of the Quartermaster General's department.

However! He did not dare to look up as usual—so as not to see the royal loneliness. . . .

Two steps in front of the Emperor, when he himself stopped, Tikhobrazov did not dare look higher than the royal mouth, for fear of immodestly glimpsing, through his eyes, the unfortunate monarch's soul.

"Your Majesty!" he reported, but his voice was trembling. "There have been no incidents at the quartermaster-general administration during the shift! Lieutenant Colonel Tikhobrazov on duty."

And he turned at attention, yielding to the Emperor.

The Emperor lowered his hand from his visor and went into headquarters.

Thus he had managed not to see the Emperor's face.

Tikhobrazov followed two paces behind and left him at the bottom of the stairs leading up.

[4 1 3]

He had slept well again, and sleep had restored his spirit's health. He had slept well because no matter how crushed his soul—he had done nothing against his conscience. A terrible, devastating step—but not against his conscience.

It had become so much calmer in the evening for another reason, too: overcoming his distaste for the telephone, he asked them to try to connect him to the Tsarskoye Selo palace (this, obviously, now went not only through Petrograd but also through Duma oversight). It took them a long time to connect—but suddenly it worked. And Nikolai heard a voice—distant, weak, barely audible, dissimilar—but still the voice of his Alix. His heart fluttered, as it always did at each new meeting with her, and sank that she was going to bitterly reproach him. . . .

But Sunny Alix did not even hint at a reproach, she only wanted to reassure him and convey her love.

She also said that the Cossacks had not betrayed them at all and were at their posts at the palace. That was gossip.

His heart revived greatly at this. Nothing was so low as betrayal; nothing so uplifting as loyalty.

In Pskov, he had been betrayed. Ruzsky had betrayed him. Tied him in knots, made a fool of him. (And how he had trusted him! He had laid the failure outside Lodz and on the left bank of the Vistula on Rennenkampf. But actually Ruzsky had been to blame.)

Nikolasha had betrayed him. Brusilov had betrayed him. And Evert.

His thoughts could not turn to reproaching Alekseev as well. They had worked together so long and so well. Such a conscientious, unpretentious, honest man. He had simply gotten too worked up and had muddled things.

This morning a precious telegram had arrived from Alix, an encouraging one. From yesterday, after she'd learned everything.

The nighttime telegram from the Khan of Nakhichevan was very encouraging as well. Ah, his beloved Guards Cavalry! . . . Ah, how many loyal and beloved men he had left behind!

But why did encouraging voices always arrive late? . . . Why didn't they reach him in time? . . . Like that black October of 1905. . . .

And contrary to the weather, something rare: yesterday, on that clear and frosty day, his despair had stood immovable, a cold mountain. Whereas today, a despondent and windy one, his despair had softened.

Passed, even. Although such difficulty tangled in his breast—beyond expression. Still worse did he understand what had happened in Pskov.

The things a heart can withstand! Even that had passed.

He sent Alix a telegram saying that his despair was passing. To fortify her.

And soon his Mama would arrive from Kiev to share his grief and loneliness.

What he had not expected at all was that his abdication would not open the way to Tsarskoye Selo for him. He was now a private person. Why wouldn't they let him join his family? But now apparently they wouldn't.

He didn't know who had forbidden it, but he couldn't go. And he didn't know who to turn to.

First he had to go there, and the children had to get well. Then, evidently, while everything was being packed up and before the war's end, he would have to go to England. Quite recently, in February, Nikolai had written a good letter to Georgie, who would doubtless be happy to receive them all at Windsor.

Such was fate: his youthful intimacy with Alix had begun at Windsor, and here they were old, tired, and uncrowned, with five children—and they were going there once again.

But after the war, of course, they must return to Livadia. They would be left Livadia. It could not be taken away.

The day before yesterday the Emperor had not had the sense to demand the simplest thing of the deputies—safety and freedom of movement for his family and the entire dynasty.

Somehow, this had gone without saying.

After all, he had thought Mikhail would be Tsar. Who could have thought that Mikhail, too, would abdicate?

It was incomprehensible what kind of status Russia had now moved into. A republic?

A shudder tore through him at Misha's Constituent Assembly. What baseness—a throne in Russia no more!

But it was good that the disturbances in Petrograd had ended. If only that continued.

That meant his abdication was not without benefit. That meant it had been necessary.

This thought broke off painfully, though, when he recalled that his beloved Baltic Fleet had fallen ill, too.

God willing, though, it would recuperate.

On his desk he found a few delayed letters and telegrams. One of them was from the English military representative at GHQ, General Hanbury-Williams, practically the Emperor's friend. It had been sent from here three days before, meant to catch up with him, hadn't found him anywhere, and had been returned.

Hanbury wrote that he was an old soldier, and the Emperor knew his personal devotion, and it was for this reason alone that he ventured to give him advice. The advice itself was mild, nothing was fully stated, but apparently was the following: do not sent troops from the front against the disturbances, rather share the weight of the burden of power with the people.

A responsible ministry? . . . There, even a friend like that . . .

That was it. Now the weight had not only been shared but ceded altogether.

Nikolai was not going to be sitting at dinner with Williams and the others now. Yesterday evening, he and Alekseev in a rambling discussion tried to determine what the new protocol would consist of. They determined that no one would be invited to the royal table, including foreign representatives.

That made things easier. Even before, when there was darkness in his soul, this had taken so much effort before breakfast and dinner to make the ceremonial round of all the guests lined up in the hall, thirty or so: sixty efforts to say something other than the general dinner comments, sixty personal looks, sixty handshakes.

It was bizarre to see from his office window—on the other side of the square, on the town hall—a red flag. The flag that the Cossacks used to tear down, take away from illegal gatherings, was now snapping in the wind on the high spire above Governor's Square. Two pieces of red fabric hung to the ground at the zemstvo board entrance, as well.

A large piece of paper had been pasted to a wall near the city duma—and there was always a constantly changing crowd near it reading. Some would move away and others would step up. They exchanged voices, soundless across the windy square.

Abdication . . .

The Emperor looked at his own abdication as if from an ambush.

Meanwhile, the time was approaching for the usual report with Alekseev. Until Nikolasha arrived, wasn't it natural to continue to perform his duties? And didn't that mean going to the morning report?

He so wanted to! At least today, for the last time! He was so used to it! He couldn't give it up in one day. To the minute, as always, he went to the Quartermaster General's department, accompanied by only Mordvinov.

With utter devotion, the "little captain" reported to him at the entrance. Everything was as before, which was very cheering.

Downstairs, Nikolai exchanged greetings with the field gendarme and the doorman.

And Alekseev came down to meet him as well, as always, halfway down the stairs, although he did hesitate.

During the operations section of the report, the quartermaster-general was always present and then left, leaving the Emperor and Alekseev alone. But now, in the report room besides Lukomsky there was also Klembovsky. Why two? Both had come to GHQ recently, and Nikolai wasn't used to them. They constrained him. Today it would be better to be alone with Alekseev.

This was the room next to the operations department. It was called the "Emperor's office," although he came here only for reports. There was the armchair the Emperor always sat in taking report, a few Viennese chairs around a table covered in green cloth, and five large stands for the maps of the five fronts.

How Nikolai loved this quiet, paper-filled office, and this reliable disposition, this mandatory hour in his day, even on Sunday, which gave meaning to the remaining twenty-three. In a viscously creaky voice, as if he were displeased, never hurrying, methodically as ever, Alekseev usually listed the main events, main decisions taken, main movement of units, appointments of individuals, and provisioning progress and needs—and the Emperor would nod, approve, occasionally make slight corrections concerning individuals and their awards, and—remembered everything, due to the qualities of his generally tenacious memory, which was especially inclined toward military life.

Today, too, he sat down the same way, and Alekseev the same way, and the other two stood in the corners for some reason. It resembled what had been, but it felt like the last time. Alekseev didn't say, "Don't come anymore, Your Majesty," but in the brevity and vacuity of his sentences, emphatically separated by pauses—and given Alekseev's pointy eyebrows jutting out on his worried face—one got the sense that he found this report irritating.

Indeed, what was there to say about the front when not even isolated shots had been heard there, to say nothing of military actions. The Germans had not taken advantage of the revolution but had stopped still, letting it run its course.

Static titles and ossified military formulas alternated.

But Nikolai liked it anyway. This calm sitting and listening, and while he was sitting and listening, it was still as if nothing had happened, nothing had broken, cracked, fallen. When he stood up and left here, though, he would again fall into that incomprehensible, shameful emptiness.

He wanted, he wanted so much for the report to last longer. But out of modesty he could not make any move in that direction.

He looked with love at the guileless, unbrilliant, but honestly devoted Alekseev, so selfless in his labor. At his permanently furrowed eyebrows and

wrinkled forehead, bare to the crown—hardly any hair grew on his head—
his potato nose, and his spread and upturned sergeant's mustache.

He loved him. As his own choice, his own creation, one not everyone
understood.

Apparently, it was over, and he had to . . . He had to . . .

Nikolai rose very slowly from his armchair and said, anxiously:

"It is difficult for me to part from you, Mikhail Vasilich. It is sad to be at
report for the last time. . . . But God's will is stronger than mine. I believe
that Russia will gain victory."

He shook his hand firmly (barely refraining from a kiss).

Standing now, embarrassed, he posed his final question: To whom should
he turn, with whom seek consent regarding his passage to Tsarskoye Selo?
And, upon the children's recuperation—to Murman and England? But so
that, after the war, he could return to Livadia? . . .

[4 1 4]

News of the Emperor's abdication produced unexpected movement in
the Combined Guards Regiment and the defenders of the Tsarskoye Selo
palace. If the Emperor had abdicated, they were now not bound by their
oath. And if that was so, then they had to submit to the Provisional Government. And the officers couldn't argue. They themselves had begun to think
the same. (Even before this, they had been carrying on in a leftist tone.)

After this, the Empress could no longer argue either. She gave her consent for one officer and four lower ranks from the Convoy and the Combined regiment to be sent as "delegates" to the State Duma. Early that
evening, they left, and that night were received there—and, fortunately, it
was confirmed that they should continue their defense of the palace—but
could it have been lifted? . . . Actually, after this journey, the entire situation
had changed—invisibly and soundlessly. Now that they had registered their
loyalty to the new order (disorder), the palace was taken.

Today, the police and palace staff had rushed to send the same kinds of
delegations to the Duma.

But the chiefs of palace police and palace administration were arrested
anyway. Nor was General Groten released. They were all being held in the
Lycée, apparently.

Doctor Botkin was nearly arrested in Petrograd by a patient's side.

And something terrible was cooking among the Tsarskoye Selo Guards
riflemen, who had chosen their own commanders, were not saluting, were
smoking right in officers' faces, and were even arresting officers right and left.

Agitators from among them had already started wandering into palace
units to get a closer look.

Who now could tell where the line had been drawn? . . .

Sailors came from the Guards Crew—and collected their abandoned banner. And demanded their officers be handed over.

In this environment—this was now captivity—they were now to live for no one knew how long.

With a piercing pain, the Empress ordered the members of the Convoy to snip off all royal monograms.

"How is that, Your Majesty? The heart turns cold!"

"Remove it, remove it. I want no bloodshed. They would blame me for all of it again."

And also—Count Adam Zamoisky, who had so touched the Empress a few days before, asked to be received. Now—with the same independent, proud dignity, he declared that the abdication canceled his status as aide-de-camp, canceled his duty to be here—and asked to be released to GHQ. Now, moreover, he, as a Pole, had to put himself at the service of Poland.

Awful little newspapers had been brought to the palace, and now these vile *Izvestias* instead of all the former ones (also wretched)—and in it, filling an entire page was nothing but the two abdications of the two brothers, in large print, one after the other.

Now, when there was no longer any doubt that this was exactly what had happened and there was nothing to stop, one could give a close read to the worthy, noble sentences of Nicky's abdication.

Or wonder at Mikhail's strange decision to bow to the Constituent Assembly. Could a monarch, having been given the crown, really dispose of it like that? Oh, Misha, Misha, weak man.

But there was relief in all this, too. Poor Aleksei would not be given the crown, unfortunately, but on the other hand he was now spared all the tribulation, spared for his parents. Now he would be with them always.

Everyone spoke confidently—and there was a brief mention in the newspaper—about there being a revolution in Germany, too! Wilhelm killed and his son wounded!

To the extent the Empress since the previous day had decidedly not believed any rumors—to that same extent she now could not doubt them. What had begun in the world was a horrible period of disasters, and now it had befallen Willy as well. He would not get the chance to rejoice at the Russian revolution!

But what about Darmstadt? And her brother Ernie?

The whole world had turned upside down, the whole world was falling. And why so simultaneously? Or was this a Masonic plot? Unquestionably so. It was they who had ignited this war. They who had been undermining monarchies for a long time.

But the whole hurricane whirlwind of these days had taught Aleksandra her powerlessness. How she had striven and strained these past few years to steer the state! To appoint individuals to positions and tell them what to do.

But now it was revealed that all this had been for naught, all had been in vain, and man is powerless.

Did Nicky still have his plans and courage? But she herself would no longer make any statesmanly movements. Or stir. Or exist. She'd learned her lesson.

Late last evening she'd suddenly been called to the telephone—a direct line from GHQ. Oh, modern miracle, oh, relief—to hear her husband's direct voice, impaired though it was, as if under layers of earth heaped on his chest.

He promised that soon, soon he would return.

His voice, barely stronger than breathing, the shadows of words still distinguished by certain contours, but only the heart could guess at his dear, beloved voice itself, from its intonations.

But not his feelings. And what could they talk about now with everything being eavesdropped on?

How were the children? This was hard: Anastasia's temperature was going up, she had more spots, Olga had pleuritis, and Anya had pleuritis. The only joy was that Aleksei was better, cheerful.

Do the children know? No, she hadn't told them yet. . . .

She managed to warn him not to believe the Convoy's betrayal. That was all a misunderstanding!

And she managed to find out who exactly those two were—the swine!— who had come to extort the abdication.

Intentional, diabolical humiliation! To send that lout, that pig Guchkov, his personal, vindictive enemy. Yet more grief for his cup of suffering!

The conversation only embittered her. So much left unsaid.

But this morning a telegram from Nicky got through, from GHQ. He had received her telegram from yesterday. Oh, joy! Their connection was being restored! But there had been this sentence: his *despair was passing.*

Passing? Yes, thank God. But the fact that he, so exquisitely reserved, had brought himself to put that word in an open telegram flung the door open on the fullness of the abyss her husband had been through. An abyss even blacker than Aleksandra could have imagined.

This afternoon, in the green room, with its lowered curtains, where all the children lay, she finished writing her letter of yesterday. That officer's wife hadn't left yesterday, so Aleksandra could add to it. She had now decided to go even farther—to Mogilev—and deliver the letter.

I'm afraid to think what you are enduring. How are you there—completely alone? This is driving me mad. (Oh, would he guess meanwhile to send a letter to her this same way, with someone, with a courier?)

Oh! Better times will come, and both you and your country will be rewarded a hundredfold for all your sufferings. One mustn't lose heart. Christianity teaches us to believe until the final breath. Ahead everything is shining brightly, and God shall yet recompense the monarch a hundredfold for his ordeals.

There, Serbia has perished, torn to pieces—this is punishment for the fact that they killed their king and queen.

It cannot be that the Lord has sentenced Russia, too, to such a fate.

When there is a shortage of human imagination and human forces, lofty souls have their own way—the way to faith! Aleksandra knew how to give herself over to this exalting, heavenward impulse. The darker and more strained it was around her, the brighter the heavenly shaft shone above her. These were minutes—and hours—of mystical ecstasy, when she was given to see with a different, lofty vision!

He had abdicated—but perhaps this was exactly how he had saved his son's reign! The unstained crown would yet return to her son's pure head!

Good times were yet to come, a turn toward the light. Great and splendid times for all Russia had yet to come! Her heart sensed that all this would not end so simply and dolefully. God would send help from the heavens.

Not for nothing would the Veneration of the Precious Cross begin today!

When there is not sufficient human imagination, a path accessible only to the select understanding opens up: a **miracle**!

Oh, my hero! We shall see you on the throne once again, lifted up by your people once again. You will be crowned by God himself, in this land, in your country!

Here people are saying that since the abdication people are beside themselves with despair. A protest movement is beginning among the troops. They all adore their Emperor. I sense that the army will rise up! And lift you back up onto the throne!

[4 1 5]

Ground detachments had been drifting into port since early morning, wishing to see the admiral, wishing to have their own *soviet* of deputies.

Nepenin received the sailor deputies and heard them out. He ordered tea and bread prepared for their meeting in the joiners workshop.

Then he received the officers who had come with their ground units. He gave permission for the ground regiments to "organize."

Clearly, they had to wait a while for the new regime's beneficial influence to reach here. Duma deputies might even arrive today. In Petrograd, both Manifestos of abdication had been published.

But that last night the fleet had not held out! These murders (all the details of them, all the names, were not yet known on the *Krechet*) could not be pushed out of memory. This was not the moment to reproach the sailor deputies, though, or even to devise a punishment. Herein lay the tragedy of revolutionary murders: they cannot be tried or disputed and don't even require apologies. Someone was killed—yes, they were, that's it, bad luck.

One had to be big-hearted about the confusion of these ignorant people who had always been deprived of social justice, and someone's malicious, pre-dawn telegram threatening to kill the admiral himself—one had to see the whole broad picture of Russia's nascent liberation and keep the Baltic Fleet in this frame until a lucid moment came.

Most of all, Nepenin was astonished at this sailor outburst given the correctness of his own behavior. After all, he had made no attempt to deceive, he had announced everything to the sailors as soon as he himself found out, and he was the first of the major military leaders to recognize the revolutionary government—but everything had gone as though he had dug his heels in for the Tsar to the very last. Why? What had his officers died for?

Confident of its rightness, revolution never answers questions like this.

But Nepenin wasn't shaken in his sense of rightness, either. Or in the rightness of his ardent inner circle—Cherkassky, Rengarten, Dovkont. If anyone was wrong, then it was those who for so many years had dragged out their opposition to progress, free development, and all Russians coming together as equal citizens.

But this would all be corrected, if only they were given the time. Nepenin himself would correct things here in the fleet.

Yet how could he now face the sailors' formation—while suspecting a murderer in each man?

Suddenly, just after noon, a rumor went around—not a wireless message but a rumor, though how?—through orderlies, embarrassed that apparently . . . apparently . . . on the city square, they had named the mine defense chief, Vice Admiral Maksimov, to be the new Commander of the Fleet!

Rengarten, red in the face, reported this to Nepenin as utter nonsense.

Indeed, what nonsense was this? How was it that sailors in the city could name their new commander themselves?

But before they could wonder or ridicule—ten minutes later—an automobile with a red flag came driving down the embankment, and heading from it to the *Krechet* was the robust Maksimov himself, and by his side Nepenin's staff officer for warrants Captain 2nd Rank Lev Muravyov (a Decembrist surname!) and several sailors peering quite maliciously.

Thus, all as one, they barged in on Nepenin, the sailors with pursed brows and lips and their hands on their carbines, Muravyov with an entirely shameless, independent look, and Maksimov with a roving—or even mischievous?—smile on his big face.

The admirals were left alone, and Maksimov shrugged and explained with a strong Finnish accent:

"There you have it, Adrian Ivanych! A little while ago I was arrested, now I've been promoted to Commander of the Fleet, and tomorrow I'll be hanged."

He didn't relate how this was so, how he'd gone from arrest to commander. Had he promised them something?

"I did not consider refusal possible, not wanting to undermine the fleet's battle worthiness."

The sailors did not leave them entirely alone but stood on the other side of the door, looming.

Nepenin sat in total shock. Up until the day before yesterday, only the Emperor could have removed him. But now the Emperor had removed himself. Nepenin couldn't immediately picture to whom the Commander of the Baltic Fleet now reported. There was no such thing as reporting to the government or even the Minister of the Navy. The new government didn't even have a Minister of the Navy. Guchkov held both positions. Guchkov was generally of like mind with all the Young Turks, but there was no way right now to verify and support like-mindedness by telegraph.

But something had to be decided.

What could be decided, though, if the *Emperor Paul I*, where everything had begun yesterday, had already sent a wireless message to all ships to carry out only Maksimov's orders and not Nepenin's?

The *Emperor Paul* had a "central committee of ships' deputies."

No, Nepenin could not surrender his power—this was now the competence of . . . the Provisional Government?

But how could he prevent it?

No matter what Nepenin thought, he no longer had the authority.

Although he still had it weighing on his shoulders and heart.

First, he decided to report—not to GHQ but to the State Duma—about all that had transpired.

He wrote—and wanted to carry it to the wireless cabin himself. But the sailors at the door wouldn't let him in.

He was as if under arrest.

They read the telegram and then let his adjutant carry it off.

How could he not transfer his authority now? . . .

To avoid dual power, he and Maksimov decided to sign all orders jointly.

They decided that Maksimov, taking for his automobile not only a red flag but also the flag of the Commander of the Fleet, would go see the commandant of Sveaborg Fortress to establish unity of actions.

With him, the entire accompanying group of sailors left, too. The admiral returned to pace through his *Krechet*, where an agitated crowd seethed, blue Dutch sailor shirts interspersed with gray soldier greatcoats.

Staff officers proposed composing on Nepenin's behalf an order to the fleet saying that he welcomed the new regime.

It had already been written and announced both yesterday and today at dawn, but so what? One more time to hammer home the point, circumstances were such.

In the end, a nerve-wracked Rengarten came to tell him what was being printed at the fleet printing press "by deputy decision": thousands of leaflets with a transcript of the night's conversation between "deputy" Sakman and Kerensky. And Kerensky's declaration that sailors were ensured complete freedom to agitate.

Meanwhile, it turned out that not only was there a "committee of sailor deputies" on the *Emperor Paul*, but there were three of them in different places and of different opinions.

Cherkassky suggested that as long as there was communication, as long as Nepenin had access to the telegraph cabin (the *Krechet* crew was remaining calm), he should contact General Naval Headquarters in Petrograd and request that Kerensky come to the telegraph for a conversation.

Correct!

Cherkassky went to summon him.

Nepenin tried not to let his firmness dissipate. He had to make it through just a few hours!

Orderlies brought news that the assembly of the crews in the joiners workshop had chosen a new fleet staff! — and had also elected Nepenin as one of the staff.

Right then, a group of armed sailors entered from the embankment, about twenty men, while forty remained shy of the gangplank — and announced they were arresting all *Krechet* officers.

They were told that the admiral's vessel and headquarters could not be left without officers.

They droned a while and left a few — the flagship navigator, mechanic, priest, and several on the staff — Cherkassky, Rengarten, and Spolatbog — and ordered the rest to get off, arrested.

Including Nepenin.

There was nothing to be done. The admiral shrugged and obeyed.

The loyal Decembrists looked at him with breaking alarm.

And right away, the sixty or so men in a tight crowd led them down the embankment, toward the fortress.

*　　*　　*

Greetings to you, dawn of liberation
From base slavery under the executioners' yoke!
(*Russian Will*)

[4 1 6]

Yesterday at midday, the wrong time, a thunderous ringing of bells suddenly crashed over Moscow, as if it were Easter! First from the Kremlin, and then others started answering it, answering from other different places, rolling and droning over Moscow — for a good two hours.

Meanwhile, Ksenia and her high school friend Berta Land, who was also a Moscow upper course student now, happened to be out walking; as before, there were no classes. Many passersby and Berta delighted in how marvelously it had been conceived: to mark the holiday of Russia's revival with the ringing of bells. Some were walking and laughing, while others crossed themselves out of habit. True, they had heard that this ringing was somehow a spoof. Not only was it not all the churches, but phony bell ringers, evidently, had climbed into the bell towers to strike discordant strike after strike.

Many were delighted, but Ksenia was too shy to express the idea that this was inappropriate and even offensive: How could this be, during Lent? Not that she herself was observant.

Generally speaking, life had taught Ksenia early on where to say what and exactly what she had the right to like and not like. Since childhood, it had been impossible to live more differently than on their farm and at the Kharitonovs'. But Ksenia had mastered the art of not confusing the two different behaviors. She felt fine in both places. She was partly embarrassed by her Kuban life—both the great wealth and, with it, the ignorance. On the other hand, she wasn't the least embarrassed, since the wealth had come by honest means, through the energy and wit of her exceptional father, who, had he had an education, would not have been lost among Moscow's most prominent figures. Nor did she feel any immorality in the wealth itself— but rather an independence. To say this among her fellow students, though, was impossible, uncultured. Then, on the other hand, this ignorance and Ukrainian speech was dear to her, and touching, and it would have been ugly and demeaning to talk about it with an apologetic look.

So Ksenia walked past the Iverskaya chapel with Berta as if she didn't notice, while in fact she felt palpably split—and wished she could go up and stand there dutifully. These past few days of revolution, pilgrims had crowded here alongside the noisy duma crowd. They were mostly women, common people, and they'd taken turns going inside, where the usual multitude of candles blazed.

And then there was this drunken ringing. At that moment, nearly a thousand captive city policemen were led out right under it, from the basement of the city duma. They lined up meekly in a column and were led somewhere up Tverskaya. The crowd craned to watch them, but peacefully, not shouting anything hostile.

People drove all over the city calling on everyone to return to their peaceful activities. On the walls, they hung a proclamation from the new commander, Gruzinov: "The coup is over! Now it is the business of each person to go back to work. The gatherings are a hindrance, and anyone who stays on the streets is a conscious enemy of the homeland!" But everyone just laughed. They were on the loose, they'd developed a taste for this, although now they were on the sidewalks since the thoroughfare was getting cleared out.

Yesterday both the theaters and the movie houses had opened. Yesterday, one newspaper had spread joyous news: the murderer Sashka the seminarian had been arrested along with his gang, and Moscow had heaved a sigh of relief.

But today, in the newspapers, it turned out that that gang and also Vaska the Frenchman's gang were all at liberty. The newspapers had also run the Tsarist abdications, and the newsboys were all running around and shouting: "End of the House of Romanov! Sashka the seminarian at liberty!"

Down all the streets they were knocking off and removing coats of arms from pharmacies and institutions and painting over them on commercial signs.

Today they also buried the three soldiers, "martyrs of the revolution," killed on Kamenny Bridge. The funeral procession started in the center, went up Znamenka toward Povarskaya—and to Brotherhood Cemetery. Military officers carried a hundred wreaths, ladies bouquets of red tulips, and the procession strung out, stopping for speeches, and people said 100,000 men were at this funeral. Following the funeral wagon was a company of drivers and a band, a school of motorcyclists, and another band of cadets.

Ksenia and Berta weren't going that way but to Red Square, where a parade of troops was scheduled. By then, the public had taken the best spots, and the nimbler ones—this was not for young ladies—had climbed onto the Trade Rows roof and nestled between the Historical Museum's towers, on St. Basil's ledges, and on the trees along the Kremlin wall. But the High Place was a crush of bodies.

It was a splendid day, frosty and still. The sun peeked out from time to time through the spotty clouds, sometimes more, sometimes less.

Many of the public had come not on their own but in ranks, with banners no one had ever seen—of parties or organizations—and stood there with them. The crowd got thicker and thicker. While the troops stood in their ranks, many with red scraps hanging from their bayonets. The middle of the square was left empty, and on it were trucks with elevated tripods for cameras and film equipment.

The ceremony began next to Minin and Pozharsky, red flags having been stuck in Pozharsky's hand a day or two ago, with the inscription: "Morning of Freedom." Clergymen emerged from the Spassky Gate in their gold raiments (again not concomitant with Lent) and headed there in a procession, with gonfalons and a large chorus. The Kremlin bells struck, now in competent hands. The troops thrust up their rifles and froze, many men in the crowd immediately removed their caps, others made a move to but hesitated, and still others didn't budge. Indeed, there was something not quite ecclesiastical about it, although bishops were taking part and the clergy was moving in puffs of incense. All of a sudden, a powerful band—several bands at once—started playing a march that could be heard through the bells and interrupted the church choir. A small cavalcade of officers appeared from the Historical Museum: it was they who were being met with the march. In the lead, riding separately, evidently, was the new Commander Gruzinov—not all that dashing, and a languid face, but picturesque and dark-eyed. They rode there, toward Minin, and dismounted. The prayer service began, and once again something was wrong: one aeroplane and then another appeared over the square, distracting everyone. The second flew quite low, nearly catching on the towers, stealing all the crowd's attention. It also dropped on the square something white and red—it turned out to be a large bouquet of red tulips in a white wrapper—which was brought to the commander at a run. Only when the aeroplanes had flown off did the powerful bass of the famed Archdeacon Rozov go into force, reaching the entire square even. Service over, the clergy started back to the Kremlin, the bells were struck again, and the bands started playing "How Glorious," while Gruzinov struck a new mounted position, rising above the city's unmounted fathers, his left arm embracing the bestowed bouquet, and rode like that past the troop ranks and delivered a speech: "There can be no return to the past. The old regime is no more. Abide in peace!"

Then the wholly military part began: formation changes, commands, bands. The troops stood tall and began to march, red ribbons and patches on their chests, and this was going to take a very long time because they were standing as far back as Resurrection Square—nearly to the Moscow River Bridge.

They watched the cadets in front but then tired of it, and Ksenia dragged her friend to the Aleksandrovsky Garden. They threaded their way between formations and squeezed further down. There, along the garden fence, waiting their turn, stood militia units with green banners and "For Faith, Tsar, and Fatherland," only "Tsar" had a piece of red ribbon sewn over it everywhere.

Meanwhile here, in this long, narrow, picturesque garden just outside the looming ancient crenellated wall—notwithstanding and not knowing any revolution—lots and lots of children were playing and sledding with their nannies, mamas, and grandmas.

God, what more interesting and inexhaustible spectacle on earth than these inexperienced, defenseless tots with their colorful little caps and bonnets, every half-year of life its own generation. Their awkward or already enthusiastic running. Their awakening to the world of words and concepts. Their games, friendship, first quarrels, and quickly passing tears. And at every complaint and every joy—running to their protector.

What joy it was to hear them out, to reassure, help, and guide them.

It was with Berta during their high school years in Rostov that they used to stroll through the municipal garden, look closely at the playing children, and choose: "Which would you like to have?" That was their game.

And now Ksenia gazed with deep emotion and envy at one, another, a fifth.

Her entire life to this point, all her learning, all her entertainments could have only one meaning and one goal. That without question, without a doubt, the one thing on earth she wanted was a son!

There could be no greater happiness!

And it was very much time already! Twenty-two!

It no longer made sense. Why not now? In a year, she would leave Moscow and drown in the Pecheneg steppes.

[4 1 7]

Once again the grand duke was awakened before light. And once again by a sensational communiqué: Mikhail, too, had abdicated. The text of his abdication itself had come.

Nikolai Nikolaevich instantly understood it as good and even happy news. With an awareness that came quickly with his awakening he assessed that this abdication was a good for Russia (as Nicky's had been). Mikhail could not have coped with the responsibility of the crown, so it was better to abdicate at the very outset.

Now the Supreme Commander's fullness of power had been freed from subordination to this undistinguished boy.

However, there was a loathsomeness in the abdication—handing power over to a Constituent Assembly. To what? Why this Assembly suddenly? Why these French things for Russia?

Actually, that was a matter for the long term, after the war. For now, all the people's loftiest efforts would be headed up by the Supreme Commander. There was a profound and loyal monarchical popular feeling, which would, of course, turn to selecting a Tsar.

His heart beat vaguely, ardently, with a presentiment.

In the new situation, though, Alekseev had to be given immediate instructions. Nikolai Nikolaevich sent them immediately. Saying that now especially he was enjoining all troop leaders to explain to army and naval officers that they must calmly await the expression of the Russian people's will and for now obey their lawful superiors.

This came out marvelously subtly. Nikolai Nikolaevich had neither entered into conflict with the government nor risen up against that ungodly Assembly—but he had not bowed to it, either. *Expression of the Russian people's will*—that was exactly right, that would certainly come. But take it however you like.

The grand duke was so worked up there was now no point going back to sleep. His was too excellent a mood! Springy, ready, he traversed the sea of carpets through the palace halls. He was about to leave it behind, after all, and Nikolai Nikolaevich loved it very much. Everything here was luxurious in the Oriental fashion—and what luxurious receptions he had held here! Now he stopped by the botanical garden and walked under the palms. Now he stood in a hall next to an enormous mirror window—and gratefully looked at morning Tiflis, on the banks of the Kura, at the foot of the mountain— Tiflis, so docile and amiable toward him always.

The southern spring was already unfolding; he could scarcely believe that up north people were still wearing fur coats.

That up north, although the revolution was beneficial, awaited by all honest people—there had been some excesses and disturbances, about which Alekseev had complained. The Baltic Fleet disturbed him a little, too; something there had given way.

A separate telegram arrived from Alekseev as well saying that the abdicated Emperor (Alekseev still called him "His Majesty") had proposed remaining at GHQ for a few more days.

Was that so? And for what purpose? Why? Unclear.

But an important finding. The last thing he wanted right now was an encounter with Nicky. Under no circumstance.

But if he left Tiflis not in haste, the day after tomorrow, then another three days en route—Nicky would leave by that time.

He could not depart hastily. The Caucasus had its own tradition of expansive farewell ceremonies, and one had to know how to observe it lovingly. One had to retain the Caucasus's heart—and the Caucasus themselves could not be handed over to anyone. It was quite possible that, following Georgian custom, the city would give the Viceroy a farewell dinner—magnificent, deserved, abundant, and long, such as starts at midday and goes on into the night.

Right now an unusual audience had been scheduled in the palace. At the request of dear Khatisov, the grand duke was receiving him along with two prominent Social Democrats—Zhordania and Ramishvili. An odd audience, of course—a member of the royal family receiving socialists!—but such were the times.

They proved to be perfectly amiable, decent, and thoughtful men, not bomb-throwers of any kind. And with them Khatisov was so pleasant, and his piercing black eyes gleamed. They had a heart-to-heart conversation. The grand duke assured them yet again of his perfect loyalty to the new regime, while Khatisov emphasized that there was no need in Tiflis, as there was in other cities of Russia, to create any kind of new public organ with the functions of governmental authority. The grand duke's openhearted conduct had eliminated any suspicions or conflict.

Oh yes! Oh yes! Nikolai Nikolaevich declared himself once again to be a sincere adherent of the new regime. As he had promised, all officials who raised doubts about their loyalty to the new regime would be dismissed. All politicals had already been released. The gendarme administrations were all being disbanded. . . .

And what, the grand duke inquired of the Socialists, was the working class's attitude toward the war?

They assured him that the working class wished for victory over the enemy.

"Just as I thought," the grand duke fervently approved. "I know that you are for the homeland's defense. I am going to leave, and I am hoping that you here . . ."

Khatisov assured him yet again that the broad masses welcomed the grand duke's appointment as Supreme Commander, although . . . although many interpretations had been evoked by the circumstance that the order of his appointment had been made not by the Provisional Government but by the former Tsar, and at the very moment of his abdication.

Unfortunately, given the altered situation, this circumstance did indeed cast a shadow over the triumph for the grand duke himself as well. All he could say in response was that the appointment came before the abdication, and immediately afterward was sanctioned by the Provisional Government—so that it could be deemed an appointment by the Provisional Government.

Scarcely had the Socialists left—Stana had been impatiently awaiting her husband. Her son had arrived urgently from the Crimea, the grand duke's stepson Sergei, Duke of Leuchtenberg, Prince Romanovsky—and throughout this conversation she waited with him and now warned her husband of Kolchak's extraordinary and risky proposal!

Her son walked in, and his mother remained to be present.

What was this? The young man, who had raced here on two destroyers in succession (the *Stringent* had been rocked by a storm; from Feodosia the admiral had given the envoy a larger vessel, the *Ardent*) and then by special train from Batum—was carrying no document? The commission had not been one for paper. Formally accepting the order "attention," the lieutenant rapped out the few sentences entrusted to him. Admiral Kolchak considered the situation in Petrograd catastrophic and at GHQ dubious. None of the commanders of any of the western army groups were taking measures against the uprising. At the height of war, Russia was without a real authority. The admiral proposed that His Imperial Highness, for the sake of the country's salvation, declare himself dictator. And put at his disposal the Black Sea Fleet in order to close up with the Caucasus Army Group. This would be a solid, untouched force for Petrograd to reckon with. That was all.

So unexpectedly, such a blow—like a storm at sea into the lungs! Dictator? What audacity!

But what a military step!

Dictator? Was this even more than Supreme Commander?

"No, less. Less!" Stana fervently assured him. "This isn't from the government's hand, so it's less! How can one give way? He is calling on you to mutiny! You're already the Supreme Commander, what else? What is a dictatorship for? How can you turn now? And against hospitable Tiflis?"

For her, everything had been decided irrevocably.

"Yes, indeed," the grand duke came to his senses. "This is an uprising against the government. How can I betray Tiflis's trust? And the Socialists here? . . . Without losing face? . . ."

No, in reality, that kind of turn was no longer an option. It had been let slip. Let slip. (But it seared—as with Khatisov's proposal last winter to approve a coup d'état . . .)

With deep sorrow, the grand duke nodded:

"Alas, alas . . . You'll go to Kolchak and say . . ."

"He is not going to Sevastopol!" his mother intervened, having already thought everything through. "Even though you refuse, it's still going to look like dealings. You are the Supreme Commander, and you will command the lieutenant to accompany you to GHQ!"

Once again, she was right.

Why, indeed, had Kolchak—so audaciously, so unexpectedly . . .?

No. Oh, no! It was pointless, senseless to rebel against the government, against society, against all Russia! And—perhaps—against GHQ? He did not have that strength.

Stana was right.

Of course the grand duke refused.

But with inward regret and distress, as if what was most beautiful had suddenly been lost.

No, on the contrary! He should do everything he could to strengthen relations with the new government. It was odd that he had sent three telegrams yesterday to Prince Lvov—and not a single reply. Might they be displeased in some way?

[4 1 8]

_____

SCREEN

_____

Led like this: up ahead—no escorts (sailors do not know prison ways).
Up ahead—Admiral Nepenin! Alone.
A roundish, quick-witted, lively face, only his mouth covered by a
    mustache-beard.
But tensed. He hadn't expected this treatment!
Behind him, in step, his adjutant, a first lieutenant.
Also in step, at either side, two sailors.
Ribbons flutter over pea-jackets, which means they're walking fast.
You can tell from their shoulders, too.
Farther back, more sailors, it's like a horseshoe behind.
And in its span—more officers of various ranks.
Some impenetrable. Some obviously scared. No one expected it.
    No one was prepared. Who among us has ever been prepared
    for his life to be turned upside down?
In back, the edges of the sailor horseshoe merge into one dense
    sailor crowd.
There it is, a crowd of sixty or so, not in formation, not a convoy, but
    a packed and angry crowd, with carbines, barrels up and forward,
they're leading
a handful of officers in the middle,
unarmed, their sides free of daggers.
The sailors walk confidently, cruelly knowing where.

The uncoordinated, continuous tromping of feet.

    Is it the sailor uniform, is it the sailor life or the special way they're
        selected—but why do they seem so fierce and ruthless?

    Other faces are already beyond the limit of human expression.
        Where does so much malice come from?

    But the officers' faces—different stock? different ways?—despite the
        similar black uniform—maturity and refinement.

    And confusion now, and a lost look back.

    Oh, they can't live together! How can these two breeds live together?
    here, walking in the same frame.

    Walking where?

    The officers can guess. They know that that night on other ships . . .

    The sailors know, too.

    And won't falter in the least.

    If the sailors were walking in formation, it wouldn't be so awful.
        But now—in a crowd, shoulder to shoulder, practically jaw to
        jaw, barrel to barrel, walking, confidently moving forward!

Tramping over the snowy road.

Below

    just feet, by the ground.

    Now, in feet, in black trousers, the leaders and led look more alike.

=   The admiral, with a responsive, mobile face, feeling this press and
        speed behind his back, without turning around, feels them,—
    and walks just as confidently and hurriedly.

    As if leading them!

    Yes! As if it was he leading them, according to his admiral plan.

    Leading this handful, the way he led the whole fleet.

    His keen eyes, his luxuriant mustache tremble.

    How he explained to them, amenably and candidly! How he be-
        lieved in their souls! How he had hopes for them!

    Our sacred people!

    Sailors. Jaw to jaw.

=   There, in the last officer row—a flicker.

    A flicker, like someone falling.

The whole time we see up ahead—

    we see large and up close the admiral's face,

    not yet disenchanted even now,

    how he trusted and hoped.

    But there, behind, sailor hands are pushing officers aside, dragging
        them off.

    dragging them off to the sides, to the right,

    to the left,

    throwing somewhere behind them across the dark and beribboned
        sailor envelopment—

farther on—they're convoying them or throwing them out, we can't
see, all we see is officers disappearing from the envelopment one
after another,
and the envelopment gets closer and closer this way, toward the
admiral, jaws upon jaws.
On seaman's caps, whoever catches it, notices: *Glory, St. Andrew . . .*
And what is that terrible uniform on the sailors? What are those
ribbons, with their gentle fluttering, so unnatural on men's
heads,
with bestial heads,
those cruel ribbons?
= View of Sveaborg Fortress.
= Snowy banks.
= Trampled snow on the street down which they are leading
= the admiral with the lively, open face, who so believed in these heroes in black,
how he leads them now, without looking back.
= But in back they're throwing out the last officers,
and not one is shouting, it is a terrible silence, only the sailors' tramping,
and the admiral strides, confident that he is leading all the *Krechet's*
officers, the fleet's staff,
but all he has left is one little adjutant.
= Behind the admiral's back—the lead sailor in the envelopment, the
revolutionary sailor from the posters and frames we are going to
see and see and see.
= Two figures: the short, thickset admiral—and behind, the advancing
hulk of a sailor.
Now! It's happening now!
= Feet. Someone from behind strikes the other, delicate one—that
would be the adjutant—on the knee.
Losing his balance, the adjutant trips and bends over.
Up ahead
= The admiral! Still the same, confident of his rightness. The poster
sailor
tosses up his carbine!
= The admiral's back full screen and a barrel tip—
firing!
A shot!
= And back to the admiral's face!
simpler than ever, innocent—
only now having understood,
only now having learned the whole truth he'd been seeking!
= But he's already dropped out of the frame.
Fallen.

The sailors' envelopment stops.
They look down. With curiosity.
And finish him off, there, down.
A shot, a shot.

[4 1 9]

The abdicated Tsar's stay at GHQ hampered General Alekseev more and more palpably with each passing hour. Now for some reason to furnish the traditional report when on all sides events were swelling, straining—demanding all his attention. The Emperor himself had given up both Supreme Power in the state and the Supreme Command—and since yesterday all affairs had naturally flowed around the former Tsar, and Alekseev had to participate in this flow: not report his actions to him, send the necessary communiqués and orders to the army groups—all this now flowed by telegraph to the Caucasus, which was supposed to send its approval or disapproval of the decisions of the chief of staff. (It must be said that Nikolai Nikolaevich changed his orders with great agility: he had already dropped "throne" and inserted "expression of the Russian people's will," to wit, the Constituent Assembly. This kind of agility was instructive for Alekseev himself.)

But for the former Tsar and Supreme Commander, time had stopped. This last report weighed on Alekseev's heart, too. What were people going to say? How would people interpret this? Just in case, he had summoned Lukomsky and Klembovsky as witnesses. At the report itself he agonized over what to say. There was nothing to say! While he was informing the former Supreme Commander that there had been no military actions in the past week, officers were being murdered in the Baltic Fleet hourly. While they were shut away in a quiet little room, the telegraphs and adjoining rooms were filling with ominous news, demands, and inquiries.

The only matter of true interest to the former Emperor, which due to his timid manner he had expressed only at the end and in passing, was his petition for passage and departure. Although it was true that this seemingly had nothing to do with Alekseev, the Emperor had no other choice than to ask through the chain of command. It was awkward being cast as the Emperor's advocate, but there was no other way, and Alekseev did want the Emperor to leave as soon as possible. (The arrival of the Empress Dowager was also impending, after midday, and the old etiquette had him spending time to go meet her. He didn't want to offend the old woman, but why in person? He regretted the time.)

Evidently, he had to write a telegram to Prince Lvov. . . . "The abdicated Emperor is requesting my assistance. . . ." "Assistance" wasn't good, as if he were an accomplice. . . . "Is requesting that I contact you. . . . Unimpeded passage to Tsarskoye Selo to join his ill family . . . a safe sojourn there until the children's recuperation. . . . Unimpeded passage to Murman with persons escorting . . ."

All right, that was enough. This was not the time to talk about a later return to Russia, to Livadia. Not for Alekseev.

". . . I earnestly petition for the speediest decision . . . since prolonging the sojourn here of an emperor who has abdicated his throne is undesirable in consequence of . . ."

This was not his first telegram to Lvov. Alekseev had sent him, as the chief person in the state, the Supreme Commander's main injunctions. But Lvov had sent no reply. This gave the general staff chief a chill.

And now he had to send another telegram—but to whom? First the Western Army Group had complained and now the Northern—new bands. Armed delegates from the workers' party had arrived in Rezhitsa, freed everyone arrested everywhere, burnt the prisoners' files, disarmed the sentries, police, and officers, and threatened everyone with firearms. . . .

Who to address with this? Once again, the head of the government. Ask his excellency to put a stop to phenomena like these. Now, however, firmly:

". . . along with this, I have told the army group commanders that these types of gangs should be seized and handed over immediately to a field court martial. . . ."

Right then Lukomsky came in. They'd been expecting General Kornilov to pass through either that evening or that night, but he had gotten off at Mogilev and was here now. Wouldn't the chief of staff receive him?

In essence, Kornilov had been appointed without Alekseev's being consulted, and he was riding past, and he had no immediate business with him—but it turned out that Alekseev had to receive him.

General Alekseev had known General Kornilov only at a remove, from headquarters of the Southwestern Army Group at one time—as a division chief—and later seen him, but fleetingly, at GHQ, when he had been presented to the Emperor after his escape from captivity.

Withered and wiry, the Kalmykish Kornilov was relatively short, like Alekseev. He immediately exuded the fact that he was not one of those handsome soldiers, not one of those court sycophants, not even one of those cultured men—but came from ignorant brutes, as did Alekseev, which also linked them. (Little did Alekseev suspect that Kornilov might think him too bureaucratic.)

Looking at Kornilov's dark face, there was no sign that he was proud of his new appointment, but his swift, narrow eyes strictly picked out what he was after: how he was going to fulfill his next battle objective. On top of this, he was a man of few words.

Kornilov was passing through, a few minutes until his train, and Alekseev was in a swirl of papers, his head harassed, and Kornilov had nothing to do with his new position whatsoever and might not have stopped by—but suddenly, in this brief encounter and given their mutual simplicity, he had a revelation. Might he actually speak with him? Might he, on his way to Petrograd, now be the main and decisive person?

With piqued hope, Alekseev told him not to forget that GHQ had allowed this whole revolution only in order to keep the army inviolable, for the war. Could he attempt to keep Petrograd in line, so that the capital, if it wasn't going to help the war, at least didn't impede it? The entire contagion, after all, was flowing out of Petrograd, all these bands along all the railroads, aiming weapons right at people, breaking into institutions, robbing apartments . . .

In a show of trust, he even revealed to Kornilov ingenuously and perhaps recklessly that he should not put too much confidence in the civilian leaders, who could be quite insincere and evasive.

Kornilov's eyes flashed darkly. (Meaning he had known this?) He expressed nothing in words, but in his firm handshake. Meaning he would try.

And the carousel sent each on his way.

Perhaps his appointment wasn't the worst thing.

One didn't know where to expect bad news from now. People were reporting to Alekseev that today in Mogilev itself, here and there, certain *rallies* had flared up—that is, assemblies, about freedom and justice, and that soldiers in GHQ units were going there of their own volition. Should they be prohibited? Was it right to prohibit everything? . . .

This was what they reported: that among the lower ranks at GHQ there was great dissatisfaction with Voeikov and with Frederiks as a German. And that the soldiers were allegedly demanding that they be removed from Mogilev, and an outburst was possible.

Another affliction. The Emperor's sojourn at GHQ, with all his superfluous staff, had truly become burdensome and truly could taunt the soldiers' attention. In Mogilev itself, as nowhere else, excessive grounds for upheavals had to be averted. Perhaps it would be calmer for everyone if Voeikov and Frederiks left Mogilev quickly.

But right then, a new jolt: a report over the telephone from the train station that the same kind of detachment-band, with weapons and demands, allegedly from the Moscow soviet of deputies, had shown up there—but the station guard hadn't been flustered, had arrested three of them, and the rest had hopped onto a passing train.

Here, in Mogilev? . . . He could hardly go on. If they pushed through to Mogilev, this had ceased to be a mere specter. What could he do? Were they going to burst into GHQ itself?

No doubt about it! He summoned Voeikov and convinced him that in this revolutionary time soldiers had to make sacrifices, and better to offer this sacrifice voluntarily than be torn to pieces.

Then he went to see the Emperor and obtained his consent to order that these two immediately leave GHQ.

Impotence, as in a disease. The Tsar had abdicated, but he, the Supreme Commander's chief of staff, had not! And here people and events had ceased to obey him—an unfamiliar condition for a military man!

To his relief, Guchkov summoned him to the telegraph.

Summoned him, having just received an alarming telegram about the disturbances in Rezhitsa. Meanwhile, there were no grounds for being upset. The general calming of minds was going forward rather quickly in Petrograd. Guchkov was counting on this influence having an effect on the front, too, before too long.

Imagining their Petrograd was in no way possible! From one day to the next, there had been a calming, everything coming right, everything entering its proper channel! And from one day to the next, the corrupting influence lashed out stronger and stronger!

. . . But in Polotsk, seventeen men who were passing through from Petrograd had disarmed the gendarmes. . . . And right now, at Mogilev station . . . And yesterday in Smolensk touring artists from Petrograd and Moscow had arrested the district troop commander and the chief of staff. . . . Some of them had spread out to the villages and represented a danger for the rear expanse of the front, where there were no troop units. . . . Even if these were echoes of what Petrograd had already been through, here we had no choice but . . . And now Kornilov was on his way, and order had to be established in the units of the Petrograd garrison.

Guchkov, however, was in a hurry to get to the Council of Ministers and had to end their conversation. But he earnestly requested, earnestly, that GHQ not take harsh measures against the participants in these disorders. That would merely be pouring oil on the fire and hinder the calming in Petrograd.

Was that so. And here Alekseev had something simpler in mind: grab these gangs and shoot them . . .

[4 2 0]

How imperfectly we are made! One can prepare all one's life for some anticipated moment, and when it comes, fail to grasp it—and lose. How he was going to accept the Tsar's abdication—so many times had Guchkov tried that on! And then on his journey to Pskov, which ought to have been his life's crowning point—his insides gave way completely, he fell ill, and he lost his faith in his own powers. The irreparable had come to pass. Instead of straightening out and increasing the progress of the ship of state, he had knocked it over on its side, and it was taking on water.

Guchkov saw soberly; his vision was intact. This government he had been taken into had nothing behind it but a couple of dozen heated Duma speeches. Yesterday he had resigned not formally, because his opinion remained in the minority, but because all at once he had seen this whole government and his status in it as hopeless. Milyukov had persuaded him to remain. Assured him that there would be the broadest support from the intellectual class and the Allied countries. Only Milyukov would be dealing with the diplomats and their rosy hopes for an upsurge in Russian patriotism and bellicosity. While Guchkov would be doing so with the mutinied soldiers and rattled officers—and a garrison that had not been taken out of the city, a millstone around his neck.

While he was rushing after the abdication, here, in Petrograd, he had missed Order No. 1 from the Soviet of Deputies and its entire development. The "order" had appeared, it turned out, even before Guchkov boarded the train, but he hadn't read it and hadn't known about it, let alone stopped it. Only yesterday, as night was falling, after Millionnaya, did he read it with a heavy head—and still hadn't appreciated its danger, had lumped it in with the inevitable peripheral excesses of revolution that would be forgotten by everyone tomorrow—just so soldiers were not allowed to express hostility toward their officers.

Only this morning, when the "order" was a full two days old and a million copies had been distributed far and beyond Petrograd, did Guchkov read it with eyes wide open and was horrified. He realized that this was where he had to begin his ministerial work. From the first step he had been saddled with the Soviet of Workers' Deputies and its "order," like dogs that had sunk their teeth into him.

He had to begin with yesterday's telegram from Alekseev, which had shown him that anyone who cared to could insinuate himself and give orders to the front lines. The civilian Gruzinov, who had taken it upon himself to seize command of the Moscow District, had appointed a commandant for Kaluga, which was subordinate to Evert.

And with Kazan, where the commander of the Military District (ten provinces) was arrested by an excited crowd—and the Kazan burghers were now demanding his removal.

And with the request, a duty of honor, from Stolypin's widow, Olga Borisovna, who asked for protection after she had been tormented by searches and insults. And he'd sent a guard to her apartment for a few days.

Now Guchkov had arrived at the Moika, at the war minister's residence, to accept the legacy of the fled Belyaev. (Loyal clerks had besieged him with the information that on his last day Belyaev had burned important papers. Someone had obligingly submitted preserved drafts. Guchkov ordered them sorted out.)

Here, at the ministerial residence, there was a telegraph with a direct line to GHQ. Waiting at it was Alekseev's still fresh telegram about how revolutionary bands had shown up in various places in the Northern Army Group and were running riot. They spoke over the telegraph, too. But over no telegraph could Guchkov explain to Alekseev the full complexity of what was going on in Petrograd, the War Ministry, and Guchkov's own breast. He had to reinforce the honest general's well-being, not undermine it. He responded cheerfully. And—here was a situation!—the general asked him not to take harsh measures against these bands. Doing so would set off something in Petrograd the likes of which . . . It was important to keep the center calm.

He broke off, saying he was hurrying to the Council of Ministers. Indeed, the session was already under way and he had to go—but did he really? He pictured the circle of his colleagues. Who among them was a man? Or who among them could understand the full weight of the situation?

He didn't go.

The weather was gloomy, Petersburgish—dark, heavy clouds, slow flakes of snow.

There was another ecstatic telegram from Nikolai Nikolaevich in the Caucasus. Another ridiculous old man. Guchkov was worried about that appointment.

Right then, Bublikov telephoned, not having lost his explosive initiative. He was ringing the alarm, saying that the Tsar, having been allowed into GHQ, shouldn't be allowed to organize military resistance there. Guchkov shrugged this off, saying that Nikolai was utterly harmless.

They were afraid of a baby calf.

Guchkov ordered that he himself not be connected to anyone else.

Time had slipped away. He had to take on the ministry, decide, and act.

But before that there was already Order No. 1 everywhere—before the Minister of War had started his own count at one. And his own No. 1 was terribly boring, to the point of a yawning spasm. That he had entered into the ministry's administration; that all officials were to remain at their positions; that the entire existing routine for office work and sending documents was to be maintained; and how to go about it now without supreme approval. . . .

Addressing the army in full voice was something he couldn't do. Back on 14 March, late in the day, the proclamation he had written to the army (written just in time, before Order No. 1, he'd intuited the moment!) about war to victory had at the time been detained by the Soviet of Workers' Deputies and to this day had not been printed over the course of his entire journey. No one even knew where the text was.

For now he did or didn't do things, decided or didn't decide things—while in Petrograd battalions there were self-styled elections for commanders under way; other officers were dismissed by soldier vote, some even arrested.

Guchkov ought now to begin with some other order—a concession, a capitulation, yielding in something under the pressure of Order No. 1 because he could not pretend it did not exist. He inevitably had to approve something from Order No. 1—and issue it on behalf of the ministry, so the military system didn't break.

And so, the beginning of Guchkov's ministerial activity was to sit over the order from the Soviet of Workers' Deputies . . . and adopt it . . .

Committees in the units? That was something he could no longer touch. (For he could not cancel it.)

The troops' political subordination to the Soviet of Deputies? He couldn't cancel that. (But he could avoid it.)

Refusal to implement orders from the Military Commission? . . . (And his own orders now . . . He was afraid that would happen.)

The irony . . . At one time, striving for broad army reforms, Guchkov himself had proposed introducing collective discussion into the army. (Not this kind, of course. . . .) And Stolypin had replied that as soon as the army stopped obeying a single will it would immediately break down.

Weapons under the committees' control and officers not issued any? That was beyond the imagination! (But he also couldn't openly object.) Too wild even to consider.

Maybe point six: out of formation, soldiers must not have their civil rights impinged upon? Or point seven, abolishing officers addressing soldiers with the familiar "you"?

Now this was something he could accept. Recognize it. Reformulate it and issue it as his own order? No, that would be embarrassing, let it be as No. 114, the next order of the war department, continuing the Belyaev enumeration.

Delete the term "lower rank" and replace it with "soldier." Delete "your excellency" and "your honor," and instead: "general, sir," "colonel, sir," "captain, sir." Use the formal "you" with all soldiers in and outside of service. Cancel the ban on soldiers smoking in the streets, riding inside streetcars, sitting in the theater, visiting clubs, and participating in political alliances.

This he could not fail to accept. This had already forcefully taken hold. It made sense. And it corresponded to public ideals.

But what about not saluting? That he could not accept! Without saluting—that wouldn't be the army! But he also couldn't reject it; the situation did not allow and was too heated around it.

Discipline had to be maintained not by mechanical saluting but by the officers' professional superiority.

The army's frustrated chief reformer, was Guchkov now supposed to stifle overly impatient reform?

It was irritating how the Soviet of Deputies had beat him to it.

The whole revolution had beaten them all to it. The mob had wrested it from the intelligentsia's hands and now there was no taking back full power.

He decided to circumvent saluting for now. Saluting—he would have to ask GHQ's urgent opinion on that.

But because the war minister had repeated the tail of the Soviet of Deputies' order and had not banged his fist at all the rest, had not ordered the committees disbanded and weapons subordinated to unit commanders rather than the lowliest soldiers—hadn't that resulted in . . . the war minister tacitly approving Order No. 1 in full?

Yes, there was a paradox here unresolvable within the framework of the present day. But of course, with the passage of time—healing, sensible time—and under the influence of the brutal military situation at the front, this utopian military order from Petrograd civilian intellectuals would fall away of its own accord, wither away as absurd.

Oh, naturally, his heated words about needed improvements (to be introduced by the sensible, progressive men coming to power), his thundering from the tribune back during the Third State Duma, fulminating against the Empire's army and naval procedures and uttered to applause— those were for a different kind of improvements Guchkov had in mind. Most of all, he had pointed out back then that we would not see victories until we replaced a command structure selected according to the principle of protectionism and sycophancy. And until we had younger commanders.

Was this the dream he had imagined? The dream had been a series of sensible, fruitful reforms that would purge the military atmosphere and restore health to the entire military organism. Above all, clear all the fools or old men, useless and ruinous, out of high posts and install everywhere as officials the most talented, excellent, and suitable men the Russian army had. Eliminate everything harmful, and make over everything dilatory. Consistently carry out reforms of the conditions for appointments to positions, the conditions for performing service, and the systems of military training, reinforcement, and mobilization.

Today he had become minister—but could he tackle such a vast array? A war was in progress. The Soviet of Deputies pressed. Did he dare? Ought he now to tackle this general purge of the command structure and grandiose transformations of the army?

Perhaps he ought! And why not? Why were these reforms needed if not for the victoriousness of our army? When did we need victoriousness more if not during time of war?

We were being destroyed from the bottom up—but we would quickly heal from the top down!

But *with whom* to begin the reforms? Where were his impetuous Young Turks scattered along the distant front lines? When could Krymov get here? Khagondokov? What would Gurko think? Would he and Alekseev manage to pull together? (Actually, much more easily than he and Nikolai Nikolaevich.) The person he could rely upon closely, powerfully was Nepenin— absolutely his man, a progressive admiral. This was good. He would preserve the Baltic Fleet. And Kolchak the Black Sea Fleet.

While sitting in Petrograd itself, a quarter-mile away, at the General Staff, was the even more progressive, the even more consistently liberal General Polivanov, a smart man, a helper with whom much had already been discussed and thought through concerning this reform and who had no need of explanations.

He called him. Reached him. And immediately, heatedly: this could not be put off, events would not suffer delay, tomorrow was Sunday, shouldn't a start be made on the great reforms simply today? Assemble a few generals and a few colonels from the General Staff in a few hours at the ministerial residence? . . .

Convening—Polivanov agreed. But he doubted this could be done quickly or soon, without serious preparation.

"Now, what about . . . lifting ethnic and confessional restrictions on officer promotions. The prohibition had been maintained, essentially, against Jews. This step would immediately give us major support from the public. An effective and very visible act."

A few months before, Guchkov himself had been against this. But now this would be a reinforcing step. We would stand more firmly against the charge that officers were reactionaries.

They were agreed. They selected candidates for the commission.

Guchkov telephoned the Military Commission—and came upon Obodovsky.

A new idea! Here was who was needed! Here was luck!

"Pyotr Akimovich! Dear man! Serve Russia. Don't be stubborn! I am appointing you to a commission on comprehensive army reform."

"What do you mean, Aleksandr Ivanych? I'm no officer. I'm no military man at all."

"It's you, you we need most of all, you and your mind!"

Guchkov was silent now, but mentally he knew himself well enough. He himself, the war minister, with all his long experience as a volunteer in the Transvaal, Manchuria, or the Balkans—was he really a military man?

The idea of reform stirred him, gladdened him, and Guchkov began sketching out the main ideas for his opening speech at the commission's first session.

But right then he was brought a telegram from Helsingfors saying that Admiral Nepenin had been killed and torn to pieces by a crowd of sailors!

Guchkov felt as if he'd been clubbed. Black spots swam before his eyes.

[4 2 1]

Amusing things can happen in a revolution. Careers can shoot up or plummet almost fantastically. Yesterday after dinner, having played out his service at the Military Commission, the Native Division cavalryman Colonel Polovtsov, wearing his shaggy tall fur hat and Circassian coat, took encoded telegrams to the Chief Administration of the General Staff to be sent. By the General Staff entrance, he saw Engelhardt's automobile. That was good, no going back to the Tauride Palace on foot. He asked the door-man where the colonel was and learned he was on a direct line to GHQ. Was that so? Engelhardt was already talking directly to GHQ? He turned in his own telegrams—and waited for Engelhardt, who emerged soon after, quite flushed and pleased. They got into the automobile. He didn't have to ply him with questions. Engelhardt gushed, himself revealing, first, that Mikhail had not accepted the throne (ugh, Polovtsov's best patronage had been reduced to naught!). Second, Guchkov would not be war minister, he was resigning, and Engelhardt was to be war minister. That was what he was just talking about with Alekseev now. And also this: whether because they had worked side by side the past few days, or because they were side by side in the automobile, or because he realized what kind of officer Polovtsov was:

"You can spit on the Military Commission. What kind of institution is that, and not long for this world now. Move over to me, to the War Ministry, and be directly under me."

Instantaneous in deliberation, Polovtsov agreed, naturally. Having lost interest in the Military Commission, he soon went home—to get a good sleep and pull himself together so he was at his very best for the coming day.

That night there was a blizzard, the streets were in slantwise snowdrifts but somehow freshened from the revolutionary rabble. There'd been no loi-terers since early morning, and people were only out on business. It was gay, knowing one's own secret, which in an hour would be revealed to all.

But he arrived at the Tauride Palace—and a turnabout, disappointment. Guchkov had stayed on as minister and already established himself in the ministerial residence on the Moika. While Engelhardt, smiling embarrass-edly at Polovtsov, stayed on at the Military Commission, which had lost its spirit and meaning, and wrote an order for the garrison—for all units to sub-mit reports on their complement of weaponry, how much they lacked or had in excess, and how practical matters stood.

Bor-ing and so dull! Had this been worth Polovtsov quitting the Native Division, venturing an unauthorized separation—only to go stale here? . . . Suddenly, Polovtsov lost any interest in hanging around here, in the back halls of the third floor, with its low ceilings and trifling affairs. The true main arena had moved to the other part of the Tauride Palace and may even have slipped away from the palace altogether.

Musing, Polovtsov chose a scattered form of actions. Wearing his waisted undertunic, he walked through the palace once, and then twice, and learned the news. He met the comical Peretz, a colonel from journalism, very pompous, who had been thrilled to take over as palace commandant, and Polovtsov eagerly listened to his chatter.

Look, they'd started bringing prisoners even from provincial towns—"pending instructions"—and what to do with them? Some of the rooms near the galleries had had to be cleared of prisoners so that the Soviet could meet in the Great Hall. Some of the prisoners were herded to a high school.

Peretz uttered not in jest about the Tauride Palace: "Palace of Equality," "Citadel of the Revolution," and exalted his own service here. He admired the selfless workers helping everywhere. (It seemed he had even closer relations with one of the helpful female students.) Some enthusiasts, however, had cruelly disappointed Colonel Peretz. Some Chaadaev had started collections "for the aid of political prisoners," scooped up thousands of rubles, and then disappeared. Someone else helping the colonel in the quartermaster service had received an order for 2,400 pairs of boots from the quartermaster depot and then spirited them away. Then they found out he was a felon released from Kresty.

Peretz was disappointed most bitterly of all by his closest assistant, Dr. Overok. He had graduated from a foreign university. Showed up at the Duma the very first day, dashed about during the arrest of dignitaries, observed their strict detention—and suddenly was identified by some sergeant and then even further exposed as the fugitive company medic Averkiev, son of a Petersburg doorman sought by many investigators, who had looted in Petersburg, the Caucasus, and Odessa ("Count d'Overcq"), been tried in Harbin for marauding, arrested in Vladivostok, and brought to the capital for investigation—and then been freed by the revolutionary people! During those days of the revolution he had managed to steal 35,000 during apartment searches.

All these were amusing things, and Polovtsov was much amused by the stories. See how revolution plays with people!

But how was he to come right?

Obodovsky was nowhere to be seen, and Polovtsov was looking for him specifically, through his distraction thinking intensely about himself and realizing that irretrievable hours were slipping away. He stood briefly listening to a soldiers' rally through the open door to the Great Hall. The famous Duma hall floated in clouds of cheap tobacco smoke, and from their chairs, from the gallery, from the aisles, the soldiers were howling at the speaker, who was shouting that Order No. 1 was too little! That choosing committees was too little! And all commanders had to be elected, up to and including the commander of the people's army! Such a tumult arose that the Soviet's chairman couldn't outshout it and waved his fist for a recess.

But it was in that hall during the recess that Obodovsky was found. It was stuffy and smoky there, impossible to see faces—but Polovtsov looked sternly, imperturbably, and ignored the fact that soldiers were not saluting him. Obodovsky was walking slowly with a construction engineer, and they were evaluating the sagging of the floors. The hall of sessions and its galleries were intended for no more than one thousand people, and now two and a half had crammed in. The greatest danger was for the galleries, but the floors were loosening, too. While in the past few days as many as 15,000 at a time had crowded in the Ekaterininsky Hall.

But who could have kept this mass out? Who would have dared limit it?

Polovtsov caught Obodovsky and said:

"Pyotr Akimovich! Guchkov listens to you. Suggest to him that he needs a genuine military officer and intelligent military mind by his side. Let him take me on. He won't regret it."

[4 2 2]

The first day released from Kresty, Kozma thought: now we'll go back to the Workers' Group and together with the War Industry Committee, and the Military-Technical Committee . . . We'll make an all-out charge to save Russia and the army. The war's still plodding along, the war hasn't gone anywhere, has it?

But no! Not on your life! All Petrograd, all the workers, all the educated people had guzzled a frenzy potion—and no one could imagine going back to their jobs. They were celebrating, celebrating, celebrating, day after day, loafing, every last one of them. The longer the celebrating lasted, there'd be no interest in workdays, you couldn't put people back inside their old selves, they were going feral and were going to start down the brigands' line. But Kozma himself was thinking about work, about how to aid our freezing soldiers, and figured everyone was going to have the same thought. But no. Even Aleksandr Ivanych Guchkov himself was convening his important committee no more—and instead was racing around Petersburg, or after the Tsar's abdication. As capable as Pyotr Akimych Obodovsky was—he, too, had disbanded his committee and was circling right there, in the Tauride Palace. And there was no way to assemble the Workers' Group; that didn't even occur to anyone now. No one had called off the Workers' Group, no one had called off the Duma, no one had called off the war—but it had become impossible, and that was that. As if they didn't exist.

The fact that they'd chosen Kozma for the Executive Committee—at first he thought it was a hindrance, and he looked dazed and lonely here among the big talkers. But now it turned out there was nowhere else for him anyway. Everything was new—and everyone was in new places. No remonstrances he made or going around he did would make work resume in the factories: even less than before could he openly have dealings with his worker brothers. He could only try it here, through the Tauride Palace, through the Soviet.

So he was prepared to suffer the endless convening here, in hopes of using it to force a general return to work. But he turned out to be a kind of scarecrow here. What he was here for, from morning until evening, grinding away—that he understood less and less every day. Sitting on the Executive Committee were more than twenty of them (including comings and goings), not counting soldiers, of whom fewer than half had been elected at a noisy standing-room session of the Soviet—like Gvozdev, whom all working

Petersburg knew. More than half had appointed themselves, amongst themselves, but they were quite glib and clamorous and behaved as if they needed nothing else in life. Where there was seemingly nothing at all to discuss, they would hold forth: about capitalism, socialism, imperialism, internationalism. It was like a bag of trash lashing Kozma about the ears. But when a firm decision needed to be made—they snuck away. One thing was clear. It was time to get to work. We'd been reveling for a week, something even in peacetime one couldn't allow oneself. This way no one was going to be shod, dressed, or fed—and all the worse in wartime. Kozma felt constrained among them. He rose a few times and spoke, about factory work, but it came out rather clumsily and they stopped him. And when they voted, Kozma wasn't even once in the majority; his side was always outvoted. So that, if he weren't sitting here and raising his hand—no one would have noticed the difference.

Gvozdev waded in and stood in the crush of the Soviet itself. There they were saying the simplest words, and all from the heart—only everyone's heart had descended into jabber and idleness: they would climb up and carry on like drunkards, each in his own way. So this turbulence spread over men's shoulders and heads—and now, if someone were to stand over them and call them to their workbenches, they'd just guffaw and refuse to go.

Finally, just yesterday, the Executive Committee seemed to get down to business: dividing up into working commissions, by categories of work. But even these commissions were formed purely so they could wag their tongues, and the biggest loudmouths found their way here. But when work had to be done, they immediately assigned Gvozdev to three commissions: automotive, finance, and the commission for resumption of work that he had insisted on.

The Bolsheviks immediately barred that. It isn't time to go back to work! The revolution isn't over yet! Our main enemy the bourgeoisie is still on its feet. We still haven't won the eight-hour workday, or land for the peasants, or a democratic republic. There's no going back to workbenches, under no circumstance.

Thankfully, it was a small handful of Bolsheviks on the Executive Committee, but for them, if everything was in smithereens, all the better; they had no sense. No need for work or war or government. Drive everyone out! They'd boxed Gvozdev in before, and they were boxing him in now. Before, working was impossible because you'd be working for the Tsar. But now they were barring him again, saying it was impossible.

That was when Kozma suggested the following. At least let those factories that worked directly for defense go back to work. But even there the Bolsheviks disagreed. We are against separating the revolutionary army and the proletariat! We are in favor of the maximum conservation and development of revolutionary proletarian energy!

Even if you have to fight them again with stools, like at Ericsson. What was the resumption commission for then?

But even if you make a decision now—you aren't going to start to work right away. What about firing all the boilers back up? What about where pipes have burst? In the past few days, snow and blizzards have swept over factory yards and rail spurs. They needed to be shoveled, cleaned, fuel brought in, furnaces heated—even the workshops themselves had chilled off—it was going to be three full days from deciding to working.

He met Obodovsky in the corridor. Pyotr Akimovich grieved most about the streetcars. Ice had jammed the tracks in the past few days, when there'd been a brief thaw, and the wires had broken in sixteen places. In some places cars had been toppled and streetcar levers pilfered. Bringing the factories back to life—that meant starting with the streetcars.

Meanwhile, some regiments had woken up and started coming to the Tauride Palace with placards: "Soldiers to your trenches! Workers to your benches!" Good, this was support for us.

They knew Gvozdev at all the factories. His own people everywhere would answer the call. Every factory had serious workers who would have been back in their places long ago but had been bullied out of it.

Today at the Executive Committee, Gvozdev stood up more firmly and laid it all out for his comrade revolutionaries. If you counted it, this was the ninth or tenth day working Petersburg had been playing hooky. What were we doing playing hooky if there was a war going on? What would be left of Russia? No one was manufacturing shells or cartridges. You could only wonder that the Germans were still watching our revelry—but if they struck they'd cover the ground to Petersburg in a week. Either start work now or our whole talking-shop was going to come crashing down.

"Start on what terms?" the Bolsheviks, five of them sitting there, shouted. "Back to the old ones? After this kind of revolutionary victory?"

The others wouldn't object. The others vacillated. A risky business: they were always calling for strikes, and now for work? They were afraid even to bring the matter up with the Soviet. Who would bring it up, say it, only to get shouted down?

"I will," Kozma said.

"No-o-o," they buzzed. "We need a politically commanding comrade here."

They decided to meet again the next morning and discuss it again.

Toward the session's end, the previous day's Moscow newspapers were brought in, with all their full pages—two hours' worth of reading. Petersburg was seething with events, and Moscow was describing them.

Kozma took a newspaper. He skimmed:

"Death of Zubatov."

". . . On 2 March, the well-known Zubatov shot himself in his apartment on Pyatnitskaya Street, shot clean through from temple to temple, dying instantly. He left a note saying farewell to his son, not to blame anyone, he couldn't survive the destruction of the monarchical system . . ."

Kozma felt sorry for him. Despite his police rank—he had wanted good for the workers. He was right, though: you need a paycheck, not a revolution.

My, how he loved the monarchy.

[4 2 3]

Though Peshekhonov did "obtain" permission for his *Russian Notes*, and though he didn't forget about it (he ran it in Korolenko's absence), he couldn't even stop by the editorial office for five minutes but just telephoned and asked the employees to request an essay from Fyodor Kovynev in particular for the next issue. He wanted to preserve a vivid picture of these unrepeatable days, a picture someone who hadn't participated couldn't feel—but Kovynev knew how to describe.

All life was set in motion, but a most fanciful kind. This was a social chaos out of which there had yet to be created a new, worthy, civil society. History rarely produces these kinds of social experiments. Aleksei Vasilich was living through the rarest of moments, face to face with this chaos, in the very thick of it, unquestionably the most interesting period of his life. Given the little sleep and disorderly days, this awareness gave him much strength. Here he was in full swing with his beloved people, in its unpretentious sweep. What else could he wish for?

Even over these past four days, many of his colleagues in the commissariat had floundered and left, and others had taken their places. Peshekhonov couldn't keep up with all the names and didn't always recognize them by face, or know he was speaking with a colleague.

Especially since visitors, too, were trying to reach him through all the cordons, including the most unexpected.

Through the crowd, standing out in it, a priest pushed through.

"What's the matter, father?"

He had come from Finland:

"Look, I don't know what to do: do I name the Tsar and his whole family in the litany or not? . . . Given the circumstances now it seems not—but I fear skipping it all the same. And the higher-ups have no instructions. I've come to Petersburg and can't find anyone. What do you say?"

Or they came to complain that since the revolution there'd been no heat in their building. The building owner was called in to explain.

Or some petty bourgeois woman wouldn't listen to anyone but the most important commissar. And why? Because she needed firewood moved to a different apartment, so give her permission.

"Please, go move it. Who's stopping you?"

"Oh, no, sir, they'll take it away! You confirm this for me in writing."

"But who's going to take it away?"

"You just try to move it! There are a lot of people after other people's property, and each has authority."

Peshekhonov wrote it but had his doubts that the firewood she was moving was her own, and so sent a comrade to go to the place and take a look. No, all was in order.

People put it this way: "It's freedom, sure, but it's dubious."

And that "commandant of all tearooms" who had turned up so menacingly yesterday and then slipped away en route to the Tauride Palace—today he was found lying around in one of the tearooms, completely enervated. He'd turned out to be a morphine addict, though he really was a doctor, too.

The commissariat on his own Petersburg side was also going to have to do all it could to defend its authority—from pretenders and other authorities.

First of all, he learned that another commissariat was functioning, on Kronverksky. They verified this, that a self-appointed circle of intellectuals, observing the anarchy, had decided to organize an authority, primarily for food supply. This claimant turned out not to be dangerous, and Peshekhonov proposed they join him. They argued—and yielded.

But yet another separate commissariat declared itself, on Krestovsky Island. Peshekhonov wasn't opposed to Krestovsky splitting off. His district was already extensive. But rumors reached him that the Krestovsky commissariat had been out of line, carrying out requisitions and oppressing local tradesmen. They went to check, and it turned out that their commissariat had been elected by an assembly of local citizens and so had been formed more democratically than Peshekhonov's. However, while himself a democrat, Peshekhonov could not allow this kind of bifurcation of actions and forced them to submit and follow correct policy.

Then a denunciation came in saying that in one building on Kamennoostrovsky the superintendent had passed out forms for residents to fill out regarding who had what kind of and how many weapons. The denunciation raised the suspicion, of course, that this was being done for a counterrevolutionary purpose: it was a building with grand apartments inhabited by wealthy people. Peshekhonov summoned the superintendent, who confirmed that he had passed out those forms, not at his own initiative, but on instruction from the Petersburg side's commandant, who was lodging in their building.

What commandant was this? Peshekhonov wanted to see him right away. He appeared. And it turned out he was a real commandant, appointed by the Military Commission, an officer of the Grenadier Regiment, a polite prince with a French accent, and he had been commandant for three or four days already, but other than these forms, he hadn't actually done anything. Summoning up his menace, Peshekhonov told him he would not allow dual power.

So Peshekhonov was working energetically to establish single rule—but whose? Those who had sent him in the first place—the Soviet of Workers' Deputies.

But what about a government? Did we have one or not?

[4 2 4]

Petrograders could assure him all they liked that things were quieting down, but the contagion of anarchy had spread, especially to the nearby Northern Army Group.

The top generals had fulfilled their duty to the revolution and helped remove the Tsar painlessly—but the revolution had not fulfilled its duty to the generals: it had begun to destabilize the front itself.

No joyous communiqués from the Provisional Government could quell General Ruzsky's alarm. These bands, who had already skipped past Pskov, were already in the nearby rear of the Northern Army Group and were walling off everything else. In Pskov itself, some soldiers from a motor company from Petrograd had removed the city police. Local soldiers had begun roaming through Pskov in disorderly groups. In Rezhitsa—between army group headquarters and 5th Army headquarters!—an armed band of unknown origin had done as it pleased—raged in police stations, pointed guns at everyone, burned case and police documents, disarmed officers . . . Something like that in the army's rear? How were they to wage war? In all his military career, General Ruzsky had never encountered anything like it: microbes penetrating military barriers and instantly destroying its fabric. How were they to act against them? If they weren't destroyed at the very outset, they would bring down the entire army, the entire conventional subordination to senior ranks and to regulations on which the army structure rests. If that were destroyed, there would be nothing left.

Due to the complexity of the revolutionary situation, however, Ruzsky also could not bring himself to act independently, to capture and punish these bandits. However ungrateful and irresponsible the Petrograd figures were, General Ruzsky could not oppose them on his own, could not act alone in a punitive role. Society would not forgive him. Therefore he had to achieve unity of actions among all the commanders—and after the incident in Rezhitsa, Ruzsky had begun to regret that he had rejected a commanders' congress. Now all he could do was what, send a report to Alekseev? That he did.

But Alekseev lacked the talent and daring of a genuine commander. He would never issue a bold order. He of course would merely report to Petrograd, and that would take up hours, and days, and no one knew whether anything sensible would come of it. So that the telegram sent to Alekseev about the bands would be left hanging for a long time. After all, this contagion would take its time spreading to Mogilev, but here it had destroyed the very body of the Northern Army Group, and the commander himself and his headquarters were not protected. No guard could defend against that plague. Red scraps had already started to appear on the soldiers and at headquarters itself, even among the garrison troops. And he couldn't forbid it because even the Duma deputies had come to Pskov in the same company of agitators wearing bows.

All Ruzsky could do was enter into direct relations with one of his neighbors. Not Evert, of course. He was a dim-witted toady and a monarchist. But Nepenin, with whom Ruzsky shared social sympathies and progressive views. Their current positions were similar: things had boiled up for Nepenin even earlier and more. Together, he and Nepenin might now work out a tactful common approach.

Ruzsky gave some thought to how he could contact Nepenin most directly. Obviously, via Reval. He started drafting a telegram that could pass safely through the encoders' hands—and at the same time, as from one refined man to another, convey to Nepenin the full delicacy of his thoughts.

Right then Danilov, with his heavy gait, brought him a copy he had come by—a typeset leaflet, messily printed, of that most strange "Order No. 1" they had heard about but hadn't lent any significance. Somehow it was being disseminated among the lower ranks of front-line units! Although it had not been sent through any lawful channel.

Here it was. Danilov put the crumpled page on the table and flattened it with his heavy hand. They read it.

This seemed to be an order for the Petrograd District, but sent out disregarding the commander and all officers, not to their command structure but directly and solely to the lower ranks. Did this assume that military units were now supposed to obey not their commanders but the Soviet of Workers' Deputies?

Ruzsky could not believe his eyes. Only madmen could write this. This could not be allowed during time of war! Or had it been sent from Germany?

Utterly unheard of! These bacilli could kill off the army in a week.

The entire headquarters building started to teeter.

Danilov cursed. Ruzsky never used those kinds of expressions.

What should he do? . . . Telegraph GHQ immediately. What else? Send them the text of this order since they must not yet know it? The danger lay in the fact that there was a similar point in the telegram announcing the new government, saying that all restrictions had been lifted for soldiers in the exercise of their social rights. And if this had been declared so openly and was going to be implemented just like **this**? . . . Nothing but total chaos could flare up, internal dissension, and the army would perish!

That meant that inside the army itself a countervailing, disinfectant order had to be issued without a moment's delay! But could Alekseev's sluggish mind really find a solution here? All these past eighteen months were a misfortune due to Alekseev being made the Supreme Commander's chief of staff, but during these fateful days, that misfortune had been tripled.

How capably Ruzsky would have dealt with this had he been at GHQ! . . . Nikolai could not be forgiven his choice.

Here's what! Send a copy of the telegram to Guchkov. The war minister was now the only intelligent man with whom one could reach an agreement and work.

It was sent to Alekseev. It was sent to Guchkov.

Oh no, that still wasn't it! Ruzsky had a vague sense of something he hadn't understood even twenty-four hours before: in Petrograd the main force right now wasn't Rodzyanko or the Provisional Government but the Soviet of Workers' Deputies. He had to use supreme tact to establish relations directly with the Soviet, with regard to the revolutionary moment. This was not something just anyone could do, and not directly. Right now the Soviet of Workers' Deputies, of course, was possessed of tremendous vanity and tremendous bias against the former authorities. But Ruzsky was starting to see the outlines of such a possibility. Not only did he know how to be tactful as no other general could, but he should be helped by one fortunate circumstance: General Mikhail Bonch-Bruevich had served in close proximity to him since 1914. During Ruzsky's initial period, Bonch was right here as chief of staff of the Northern Army Group, was forced out soon after Ruzsky, and got deep into counterintelligence, but then the counterintelligence service ran into unpleasantness with society, especially over the Rubinstein affair — and Bonch returned to Ruzsky and henceforth was at the disposal of the Northern Army Group's commander. Under his General Staff epaulets, Bonch-Bruevich had quite freedom-loving sympathies. There was one problem. These past few days he had not been in Pskov. He had been traveling, in remote areas, on the incomplete lateral rail line — but he had to be summoned with all haste. This was because, people said, his brother, Vladimir Bonch-Bruevich, a longtime practically underground revolutionary, had now surfaced in the Soviet and was a prominent figure. Ties are ties, especially familial ones. They might prove the best in a revolutionary storm.

Summon Bonch immediately and give him some high post. We'll think of something.

That's it, that's it. But for now Ruzsky was choosing his words for his telegram to Nepenin. If only he could meet with him right now and come up with a common tactic. With him alone could he act intelligently and in concert.

He imagined Nepenin's expressive, inspired face and his quick way of understanding.

An officer ran in from the telegraph room and handed Ruzsky a telegram himself, as was done in extraordinary instances.

The letters formed into words:

"Vice Admiral Nepenin was killed by a shot from the crowd at the gateway to the Sveaborg port."

[4 2 5]

His afternoon visit with Mama, rather than the quiet anticipated joy of reassurance, crushed Nikolai. Barely had he entered her train car from the cold and windy platform and reached out to embrace her, seeking maternal

compassion in his misfortune, than he was struck by her stern and even pitiless look. He could not remember her so pitiless, perhaps only when he'd
wanted to dismiss Stolypin and she wouldn't allow it.

From her very first, confident words, Mama impressed upon him that he
had made the most terrible mistake. She was absolutely convinced that she
clearly understood everything. So greatly upset was she, she switched to
German and brought home to him that he simply didn't dare abdicate,
there were no grounds for doing so. He had no right whatsoever to abdicate
for Aleksei and didn't dare burden Mikhail with the sudden responsibility,
which he himself had relieved him of long ago. And now the entire dynasty
had come tumbling down! Tumbling down, destroying the cause of his
great father. And grandfather. And steadfast great-grandfather.

My God! Everything sank and burst inside Nikolai all over again. He had
only just begun to regain his life force, his ability to stand on his feet had
only just begun to return—and in a single blow it was all crushed, trampled
anew. He had hoped to derive strength from Mama, hoped she would help
him heal his emotional wound (and he would then help Alix)—and now a
new wound.

Destroyed the dynasty? He didn't think so. The dynasty could still return,
perhaps to Aleksei all the same, for God's wonders are inscrutable. Nikolai
seized on another aspect: through his abdication he had sought universal
reconciliation in Russia, a way to avoid bloodshed. . . .

But the Dowager Empress, with her own eye and that of his late Father,
saw only that he had brought down his Father's throne! Brought down the
dynasty! And Russia with it!

But not Russia! Not Russia! Nikolai implored. My God! The first healing film had only just formed around his lacerated heart—and now it was
all torn up again. He'd barely begun to crawl out of his despair—and now
was thrown back into it.

But they were deprived of the chance to sit, hear each other out, regain
their senses. The greeting party was standing on the platform by the train—
and it would be strange to wait too long to go out to them. After that, lunch
had been arranged in the governor's residence, and he couldn't change the
schedule. Everyone had to go there. Now their faces, emotions, and speech
were shackled for an hour and a half, and everything receded deep inside.

The wiry seventy-year-old woman, who had maintained both the slen-
derness of her narrow little figure and her enchanting smile, made the
rounds of those meeting them, and her son followed her unperturbed, with
light eyes, so that no one could penetrate their tragic state.

Then in the motorcars. And then at lunch. Speaking and smiling as he
should in front of strangers. But in his mind, a stormy tumult: What, then?
What now? . . .

What was terrible for us was not so much the events that had taken place
but how much we were to blame for them. The worst agonies stemmed

from our own guilt, not the misfortune. Now his Mama had revealed Niko-lai's guilt to him.

So—what now? God! Once again, Nikolai was tormented by the mistake he had obviously committed but could not yet grasp. Might he? Might he have remained the Russian Tsar? Had he himself, in an incautious, hasty action, thrown off his own crown? . . .

But how? What should he have done in Pskov? . . .

It was tearing him up.

Only after lunch were he and his mother left alone—back to this pain. Even worse—his obligation!

With her steady, intense power of persuasion, Mama now insisted that agonizing was the least of it. He was *obligated*. He *must* undertake to cor-rect this! He *must* restore the crown to himself or Aleksei!

Oh, smashing, pitiless duty! . . . But how was this possible? Now there was no way this was possible! . . .

Not for himself—then for Aleksei. He hadn't even attempted this step, after all. Why shouldn't it work? The throne was vacant, after all.

They sorted through the ways. Though they didn't find one. Mama be-lieved that at the very beginning, if he'd left GHQ, he should have gone straight to his Guard, to Lutsk, not Tsarskoye Selo. (A reproach.) Even now it wasn't too late. The Guard was loyal to him!

But how could he leave now? This was perfectly awkward!

They sat for a long time. No way was found. But one thing was true: as long as no one occupied the throne and no one laid claim to it, this goal was not unthinkable—restore the throne to Aleksei. Aleksei had not abdi-cated! He was the legitimate successor to whom the entire army had long since sworn an oath—and he had not abdicated! The entire army would be ecstatic! They adored the Heir! Even after Mikhail's refusal, this was an en-tirely natural step—to go to Aleksei again.

He and Mama parted until the evening. Nikolai remained, having promised her to begin this undertaking. Such a harsh wind, he didn't go for his usual motorcar drive, just walked around the little garden, pondering.

Oh, how the necessity of action weighed when he had so hoped to give his soul a rest! Even this morning, it seemed, he had been happy—by com-parison with the present misfortune of having to act!

And act *how*? How to even start? Who to turn to?

Nikolai's sole remaining tie with the world was General Alekseev. Only through Alekseev, then.

Here was how: he had abdicated via telegram, and he could correct that via telegram! That was all there was to it. Send a telegram to the head of the new government, Lvov, whom the Emperor had appointed, saying that he was rescinding his original decision and conveying the throne to Aleksei, not Mikhail!

A simple and legitimate change of decision! Since Mikhail had not ac-cepted, he would pass it to Aleksei!

He pondered some more as he returned to the residence. Undoubtedly so. Even quite simple.

From the packet of fresh telegraph blanks on the table he took one and wrote, to Prince Lvov, saying that he was changing his previously expressed will and would convey the All-Russian throne to his son Aleksei. And he signed it as he always had: Nikolai. Even after the abdication, there was only one Nikolai.

The more swiftly he acted, the better. Send this telegram—and instantly know he had done everything possible.

Without an escort, as he was already accustomed, and without putting on his greatcoat, wearing his Kuban Cossack batallion's hooded Circassian coat, Nikolai started for the quartermaster unit's building.

No one was expecting him and no one noticed him. No one greeted him now in front of the building. He opened the door himself and went in himself—though once he was inside the gendarme on duty shuddered and saluted—but Nikolai was already going up the staircase.

He was certain to find Alekseev. Alekseev was always sitting in his place in his office and writing something. So it was. Having unhooked his eyeglasses from his left ear and leaning his left eye very close to the paper, he was writing quickly.

Nikolai entered. Alekseev stood up and adjusted his eyeglasses.

Up until now it hadn't even been hard—but now suddenly it was: to hold out to this general, whom he had elevated to this seat, this ordinary, this dear, grumpy man, and in the room where they were alone together, eye to eye. Simply to hold out the written telegram for some reason was proving very awkward.

Nikolai hesitated. Meanwhile, Alekseev walked around the desk, closer. Bewildered.

Feeling himself smiling—and quite inappropriately—a pathetic smile, perhaps, Nikolai took out the blue blank folded in two and shyly held it out to Alekseev:

"Mikhail Vasilievich. . . . I—here I've decided . . . I've changed my mind. . . . Please send this to Petrograd. . . ."

Alekseev took the blank, unfolded it, put his eyeglasses back on, and began to read. And suddenly, from his sharp frown and stern gaze—it turned out he could have a very stern gaze—it seemed to Nikolai that Alekseev was angry.

Such a thing had never come between them, nor could it have, but right now—that was how it seemed. Nikolai's heart sank. In order to mollify the general, he hastened to be the first to say:

"I think this will be good, Mikhail Vasilich. This way we'll fix everything and everything will fall into place, firm up."

Alekseev looked out captiously, sternly, from his unshining brow, which was constantly clouded by thoughts. And narrowed his eyes very slightly. And said very very softly, so that the hoarseness of his voice didn't come through:

"This is in no way possible, Your Majesty."

"But why, Mikhail Vasilich?" Nikolai turned to him suppliantly. "After all, isn't it my right to whom I convey the throne?"

Without his usual courtesy, Alekseev looked Nikolai in the eye obstinately from under his frown. And said even more softly:

"But that moment has passed, Your Majesty. That would render us both ridiculous."

So unbending and glowering, so unpersuadable did he look that Nikolai made up his mind to express to him—not in words, just with his eyes—while they were looking so closely and directly. Express with his eyes the half-reproach that could not be expressed in fully voiced words: "But you know you're partly to blame in all this, too, Mikhail Vasilich. Let's fix it together."

They stood there silently—and looked at each other. But Alekseev did not blink, or soften, or look away. He kept looking unflinchingly, directly.

And since nothing had been put into words, he did not have to reply.

Nor could Nikolai come up with anything else. Everything he had thought of—he had just done. Now he looked for somewhere to put his empty hands—drop them, raise them, hold onto his belt.

They stood facing each other in a lost pause that they didn't know how to end.

Alekseev said firmly:

"Your Majesty. All your desires concerning Tsarskoye Selo, and Murman, and England—I've already telegraphed them to the head of government."

"Thank you."

"And forgive me, there was one desire I did not feel was possible to mention now, given the current circumstances: your return to Russia after the war. Right now, that would sound inappropriate. But when the time comes, then naturally . . ."

"Yes?" Nikolai rejoined or only wanted to make a rejoinder. Naturally? . . . Still, it hurt him that his own return to Russia was omitted.

On the other hand, why had they brought this up now, even if it was important? An obscuring change of topic had taken place, and it was now increasingly awkward to return to the main subject.

Increasingly awkward. But still they stood facing each other. Everything seemed exhausted, so he might as well leave. It seemed awkward to sit down for a conversation. But Alekseev still had the telegram. And it was good he did.

"So that's how it is," Nikolai said, because he couldn't not say something.

"Yes," Alekseev agreed.

Feeling dissatisfied, but no longer capable of doing anything, Nikolai walked to the door.

Alekseev respectfully accompanied him.

Below, on the landing, the duty officer was waiting, Lieutenant Colonel Tikhobrazov. He had missed the Emperor's entrance and was now waiting to give his obligatory report.

With a gesture of his hand, the Emperor declined the report and stood smoothing his mustache up and down with two fingers.

Alekseev stood, obedient as always, arms along his seams, one holding the telegram.

Nonetheless, the Emperor said in his kindly and abashed way:

"Mikhail Vasilich, why don't you send the telegram anyway."

"That is impossible, Your Majesty," Alekseev frowned sharply. "That would compromise both you and me."

The Emperor smiled weakly.

"But why don't you send it anyway, it's hardly any trouble . . ."

He smoothed his mustache again, with his thumb and middle finger. Waiting for but receiving no answer, he held his hand out to the general. And shook hands with the lieutenant colonel as well.

And slowly started down the stairs.

Unusually slowly, as if he wanted to go back and say something. Or hear something.

Not hearing anything, though, as of the middle of the staircase he moved off without hesitation.

Tikhobrazov followed him.

✳   ✳   ✳

FOR THE TSAR'S SIN GOD WILL PUNISH THE ENTIRE LAND

✳   ✳   ✳

[4 2 6 "]

(FROM Izvestia of the Soviet of Workers' and Soldiers' Deputies)

END OF THE ROMANOV-HOLSTEINS . . . PRISON for the supreme criminal, the ataman of the brigand gang! That is the voice of the people. Instead, they are still allowing him to issue manifestos, to hand us over to his brother like an inheritance!

ON RELATIONS BETWEEN OFFICERS AND SOLDIERS. Russian democracy will strive to have a people's militia take the place of the standing army and for the universal arming of the people. But in anticipation of that, rid the army of disgraceful customs immediately. All steps in this direction must be taken immediately. Order No. 1 states these first steps.

FROM THE SOVIET OF WORKERS' DEPUTIES. Citizens! Taking into account the fact that the situation with streetcar movement has entailed significant inconvenience for the populace . . . ordered to restore streetcar movement. Petrograd's populace is asked not to impede the proper movement of streetcars . . . regularly pay for tickets . . . immediately return the levers taken during the days of the uprising to the streetcar administration. . . .

PRISONS PRESERVED AS HISTORICAL TREASURE . . . An order has been given to preserve the remains of the political prison . . .

Resolution of the Polish workers of Petrograd. In the struggle against our common enemy—the Tsarist government, the bulwark of world reaction . . . for the final struggle of the reborn International . . .

. . .The Petrograd Committee of the Jewish Social Democratic Labor Party (Poale-Zion) . . . a general meeting at Gurevich High School.

The Petrograd Committee of the Jewish Labor Party of Socialist-Territorialists invites comrades to a general meeting . . .

Moscow. On 16 March, a demonstration of tailors passed down Sadovaya. On its banners, "Down with autocracy!" "Confiscate gentry lands." An anti-defensist mood. "Hurrah" shouted out several times in honor of the International's rebirth.

To all pharmacy workers. Current events demand our immediate participation. . . . Anyone for whom the interests of popular freedom are dear . . . on Sunday—to a general meeting of pharmacists . . .

To workers in the furnace trade. Comrade stove makers! The moment has come for us to take part in the creation of a new order. . . . In unified address we announce . . . on 18 March, at the Teremok cabaret theater . . .

Comrade pressers! Everyone is organizing and sending representatives to the Soviet of Workers' and Soldiers' Deputies to take part in the creation of a Free Russia. Are we really going to lag behind? We will meet at the women's Medical Institute and discuss our extremely difficult position.

PARADE POSTPONED. The parade for the troops planned for 18 March, which was supposed to be the celebration of our decisive victory . . . has been postponed.

[4 2 7]

The closer he is to the front, the more hardened and confident the front-line officer feels: here is our entire might, our entire home, away from your muddled life in the rear. Vorotyntsev found no cause for reassurance on this return, however. Everything inside him was now broken to bits and refused to come together.

But on the small platform at Ungheni, his fourth transfer already, it was hard not to recognize Krymov's sturdy figure from behind. He seemed too heavy for the army! But he gained something by the breadth of his shoulders, and any saber at his side seemed a little too short.

Vorotyntsev was tremendously pleased. He caught up and grabbed his arm above the elbow:

"Aleksan Mikhalych!"

He turned around and boomed:

"Ooh . . . Oh . . ."

They had a hearty handshake.

His beard was down to nothing, but his mustache was bigger, bushier, and black.

Although they were both in the 9th Army, they hadn't seen each other since autumn. Their army group had taken the 3rd Cavalry Corps into its reserve, at the rear, where it was easier to feed them, but they had nothing to do right now.

A mere five years older than Vorotyntsev, Krymov, however, was looking rather old after the fray. He'd seen more than his fill during the past few years. As had we all.

That autumn, Vorotyntsev had conveyed an invitation to Krymov from Guchkov, and apparently Krymov had made the trip to Petrograd. And now everything had collapsed from an unexpected direction, a shock beyond belief . . .

"So now . . ."

Krymov, a dense hulk, was not all that shaken, though.

"Well, and so." He smacked his lips. "Well and so. . . ."

Where was he coming from and going to?

He said nothing about Petrograd. He'd been in Moscow. And had had a look at Kiev. On his way back to the 9th.

Whereas Krymov was going to Jassy, to army group headquarters.

So they'd be traveling together? The train was in two hours.

But you couldn't drag words out of Krymov so easily. It took sitting for a while, having a smoke.

"All right, let's go," Krymov growled.

They'd used the familiar "you" with each other since Prussia.

But sitting at a separate small table in the little hall, taking up a cozy corner, was the same strapping Evstafi, and standing there was not a field bag but a small trunk. Krymov liked traveling in comfort. You could conveniently pack provisions in a trunk like that and put in a bottle and it wouldn't spill.

Evstafi stood up, saluted the colonel, and grinned. He'd recognized him.

The buffet at Ungheni wasn't much, but Krymov sent for something nice and hot, and the rest they would take from his trunk.

Besides the heaviness that drowsed in Krymov, there was a slowness, as if he felt no need to do anything faster than Mother Earth. He sat down firmly on the oak railroad bench, took a large case of Ussuri leaf tobacco out of his pocket, and started rolling a small curved cigar.

Vorotyntsev asked him to roll a quirly for him, too, instead of his own fat one. But a straight one. He had an army-issue case for a small cigar, too. On his capital trip he'd packed it in his suitcase, but as he'd approached the Prut he'd put it back in his tunic pocket.

The tobacco turned out to have a marvelous sweet strength.

Officers always said "Emperor"; only intellectuals said "Tsar," but now Krymov did, too, although he was no intellectual, rather more like a legendary Ilya Muromets who had a right to speak that way. As if he were not in the imperial service, as if he were his own separate element. He judged him with pity, as he would someone weak, not superior:

"And what could the Tsar do but abdicate? If you can't hang onto the mane, you're not going to hang onto the tail."

"Well, not the tail! He had all real military power."

Krymov looked past him with a steady squint. And took another drag. And let it out. And passed judgment:

"If a wheel jumps off, that means it was poorly set."

"What about Mikhail? How could he?"

"Well, about Mikhail you're right . . ." Krymov smacked his lips. And he got angry: "How could they let the Heir slip through their fingers? Our Cossacks are simply weeping. Now what? It's like the entire road's been wrecked, the bridge blown up."

"If only Gurko had been at GHQ these past few days!"

Krymov furrowed his thick brows:

"Well, Gurko wasn't appointed for some reason. They were free to choose."

He inhaled and expelled smoke:

"Why ever did he get sidetracked to Pskov?"

There was no sensible answer to the Tsar's muddled journey. He hadn't even attempted to turn to the army for support.

Krymov was slow and not generous of speech. Only now had their talk come to his own news:

"Today our Count Keller, Fyodor Artemych, broke his saber."

"How's that?

Krymov spoke about his corps commander Keller almost with disdain, as if he himself were in charge. But approvingly as well:

"He led one regiment to 'God, Save the Tsar' and announced: 'I can serve no one but the Tsar!' And broke it."

Even Vorotyntsev shuddered.

Count Keller—there wasn't another general like him in the Russian cavalry! What wonders he'd worked with the 3rd Corps. And how handsomely he did everything. If he did ride out, then it was with the banner of the Miraculous Image of the Savior. And with forty Cossacks. Each with four St. George crosses apiece. (While he himself had had both legs shattered.)

"Who is to lead the corps now?"

Krymov, who was still dozing gloomily, took the last drag on his hand-rolled and put it out:

"They want to appoint me."

Only now he said it! Without any show of pride or embarrassment, a corps was just a corps.

"Now they're summoning me to headquarters."

What a moment for Krymov to be going!

"Who does the Ussuri go to?" Vorotyntsev well knew this officer's painful separation from the unit that had been like family.

"Who else? Wrangel. Pyotr Wrangel."

Wrangel? They'd studied at the Academy together. Quick of mind, tall of stature. He hadn't stayed to serve in the General Staff—straight to the ranks.

Evstafi and the buffet girl spread a tablecloth and served an honest Ukrainian borsch loaded with vegetables and cooked with lard. Krymov and Vorotyntsev removed their service caps and moved over to eat. Each had a shot, from the bottle in the trunk.

Krymov's hair had thinned. Still the same hard head, hard face, and menacing expression. Yet somehow it conveyed a tottering of his former strength.

Vorotyntsev now not only grieved over the present day but recalled last year's autumn. He couldn't stop himself from asking about Guchkov. Had Krymov met with Guchkov? Where had they left off?

Yes, in the winter in Petrograd, Krymov and Guchkov had spoken separately, and then with everyone, at Rodzyanko's apartment. Even then they had been saying it—"coup"—out loud, but Rodzyanko forbade it: I swore an oath, not in my home! But the Duma members all 'round had decided that the Tsar was ruining Russia and there was no reason to spare him.

From Krymov's open speech, Vorotyntsev now saw clearly how far he himself had turned around since that autumn.

"I, too, Aleksan Mikhalych, thought nearly the same thing. . . ."

Krymov was just the figure for such a matter. Yes! What general would take it upon himself to remove his division from the front, unafraid of punishment, so that the horses would be fed! As he led his division out of the war, so he could also . . .

However . . .

"What Guchkov proposed then is none of *our* business. At the struggle's outset he confused his own plan with the Kadets', more for England."

But Krymov, once he did get going, you couldn't stop him easily either:

"I promised him. In late February. And prepared my leave accordingly. But while I was collecting myself, over there they had—already? . . . Wouldn't you know it. So now Guchkov himself is in the government. What is the point of going to see him? They have coped by themselves."

Coped? Oh, if only.

"But Aleksan Mikhalych! It's the very height of the war. And the German isn't going to doze and isn't going to give us time to organize."

"And what?" Krymov grumbled. "How is this government worse than any other? Here Guchkov is just about to take up the matter and drive all the no-talents out of the army. . . . I think that right now is when a great deal can be set right . . ."

"If only! But so could the whole opportunity go to waste! There, in Petrograd, people say, they're disarming all the officers, and even killing them."

"Well! Well!" He didn't believe it. "You weren't there. How do you know?"

"Officers in Moscow were talking about it, straight off the train!"

"Nonsense. What do officers have to do with this? Demonstrations? They'll go around kissing each other for two days, disperse, and work will begin. Ridiculous."

Yes, they could sit here firmly on the railroad bench. Indeed, anyone who hadn't seen it with their own eyes yet—how could he believe *that*?

Even Vorotyntsev himself hadn't seen the main thing. But recalling his own wobble, his wading through Moscow and Kiev:

"There—it's unlike anything, bear in mind. All the military commands cease to have effect, it's as if you had your hands turn to jelly. Right now the only full force we have left is the field army, here. Naturally, if the army were to turn around and give a good blow, this upheaval would vanish. But the abdication, and Mikhail—they're depriving us of . . . It's as if we've become nobody, too. No more legitimate than this government."

"Nonsense," Krymov rumbled. "This government will find its feet. But not in one day."

"You should have seen it! If you'd seen the way entire military units were marching with a red sheet, bowing to the bedlam!"

"They'll run around for a couple of days and settle down."

Krymov's belly was full of borsch and for now he lit up his quirly.

But the more a large mass accelerated, the harder it was to stop. As they'd once rolled down from the Carpathians.

"See here!" Vorotyntsev tried to disabuse him. "If everything comes crashing down, that's worse than losing the war. Here, let me tell you the whole story."

Fine, the dozing hulk was listening.

But was not convinced of anything. That Mrozovsky and District headquarters had lost their heads—just pathetic, sh . . . ds, who did they have there? And in Kiev? Seems as though nothing's happened there at all.

The new commander of the 3rd Cavalry Corps calmly smacked his lips. There was such power in that heavy, immovable figure that what was conveyed was that nothing was threatening the army! What scaredy-cat would think otherwise? . . .

[4 2 8]

Himmer's position in the revolution was so peculiar that it prevented him from getting involved with any party faction or engaging in the usual narrow party work. His position on the Executive Committee as well was so particular that he was burdened by the detailed work of the commissions. He had been roped into the intercity commission along with Rafes and Aleksandrovich. And to the commission on legislative proposals.

The intercity was an important commission. It was supposed to keep its finger on the pulse of all Russia and spread the now local Petrograd revolution throughout Russia. They could not limit their authority to Petrograd and its environs alone. The Executive Committee had to take on the role of the all-Russian center and direct the course of affairs in other cities. Over the past twenty-four hours, alarming news had come in that anti-Semitic agitation was under way in some cities! That had to be torn up by the root by sending commissars from the Petrograd Soviet.

But for all the clear importance of this task, Himmer's intellect was more drawn to the commission on legislative proposals, which he himself had suggested. He had to work only on the overall meaning of events, only lay out the revolution's overall path. (He had been doing this—but his comrades had used his results without understanding.) Each separate activity in each separate commission, no matter how urgent or important it seemed, was secondary and trivial. Objectives that had previously been formulated and named were no longer objectives, just technicalities. The revolution's true objectives, the most prominent features of its course, could be glimpsed through the fog of what was coming, groped for in the dimension of the future, and predicting them, incorporating them in the formula before they came to light—that was the theoretician's objective!

The Executive Committee's other members, having reached an agreement with the bourgeois government, were reassured that this agreement would now naturally go into effect. But Himmer was not like that! Gazing at Milyukov's polite but stubborn face, and the bulges on his forehead, and his chin, and with his keen, vigilant gaze—Himmer distrusted him from the very first signature, anticipating a brazen bourgeois trick. And he was right to! The Soviet's deputies, exhausted, went to get some sleep—and that very hour the enfranchised traitors violated the agreement by dishonestly and secretly sending Guchkov to see the Tsar—to preserve the stinking rags of wretched despotism. A correct and deft move by the monarchists! Fortunately, they failed. After all, for all the noise it made, democracy was scattered and weak—and now it could not have entered into a civil war against the closed ranks of a monarchic-military center.

One had to be all the more cautious and distrustful at every step!

Himmer decided for himself to continue systematically going to the Tauride Palace's ministerial wing and each time he came to pressure them, each time he inquired how the implementation of the government's promised program was proceeding. Without being delegated by anyone, he himself, personally, would establish oversight without any let-up whatsoever!

Unfortunately, this was not to be. The ministers removed their headquarters from the Tauride Palace and moved closer to the Chernyshev Bridge. Who was supposed to monitor them now? Kerensky? But Kerensky was behaving irresponsibly and even dishonestly. Not once had he reported to the Executive Committee as to how he was acting inside the government.

Now Himmer had to figure out how, while in the Tauride Palace, he could extend from here to their other building and gradually penetrate the organic work of the government and plant cells in its bowels—to develop there. This had to be done in two ways: first, through systematic, hypercritical oversight, sending his own representatives directly there; and second, by anticipating the government and elaborating draft decrees—and then applying the Soviet's pressure to foist them on the ministers. (This was why Himmer had come up with the commission on legislative proposals.)

Otherwise there was a danger that the enfranchised group would become an absolute cabinet, even worse than the Tsarist government! Their nature was ultra-imperialistic, and they had to be kept in check. They had to be compelled to carry out not their own foreign and domestic policy but the Soviet's! He had to advance on the wealthy classes without cease and strip them of everything possible. Not only was the revolution not over—it had only just begun!

Thus Himmer had correctly planned it all out—nonetheless Milyukov had proved quicker and cleverer! Before the government could take a single step, Milyukov had sent his wireless message "to everyone, everyone, everyone!" On Saturday the 17th, toward the end of the day and the Executive Committee's session, Sokolov flitted in bearing a telegram, whose significance he himself did not understand—and no one on the Executive Committee lent it its proper significance—or were they tired? . . . But meanwhile, this was the most outrageous falsification of the revolution's progress! It explained to Europe that everything had supposedly blazed up due to the dissolution of the Duma, which the regiments had defended from the Tsarist clique. What an unconscionable turn! The Duma had been borne over the waves like flotsam from a wreck—and now they were ascribing to themselves the leading role! Milyukov called the upheavals in the troops that had given birth to the revolution "alarming," "of menacing proportions," and the actions of the leftist parties "a serious complication." You don't say!

That alone choked Himmer with rage. But these were just the flowers. The berries were that Milyukov, without having reached an agreement with anyone (despicably exploiting the Soviet's tactful silence), had telegraphed a promise of further war (calling it "national resistance") and doing everything for a "decisive victory." Was that so! Our revolution, understood not as a blow against any war (as it in fact was) but as its reinforce-

ment! Instead of a denouement to the merciless class struggle throughout
Europe—flood it with the blood of armies! A gracious liberal-national coup
in favor of the Dardanelles ideology!

And this was transmitted over the wireless "to everyone, everyone!" as the
sole voice from Russia. The Western proletariat would hear it—and how
would they take it? With bewilderment and despair, the collapse of their
hopes for the Russian proletariat!

While the Russian proletariat, while Himmer did not have his own wireless station to refute him! He could write (and he did write, in one burst) an
article of refutation for *Izvestia*—and gave it to Nakhamkes. (But he didn't
print it!)

Himmer writhed and twisted like a corkscrew. What should he do where
he was? The Executive Committee dispersed wearily, indifferently. He
rushed to see Chkheidze:

"Nikolai Semyonovich! We can't just let this stand! We must publish an
appeal now to the European proletariat—in the name of the Soviet! In the
name of the Russian revolution! We are obligated to outline our position or
else the silence will distort the Soviet's position, too."

Chkheidze was weary, too. He looked at Himmer with puffy, sore eyes,
overjoyed by events:

"All right, then, write a draft."

He knew Himmer. Even if you didn't give your permission, he'd write it
anyway.

[4 2 9]

But what about the Don? His sister Masha was torn. With her adopted
Petya, she stronger than any mother for him—keeping an eye on the household in Glazunovskaya, not letting go of their father's homestead, that
warm nest for the two brothers and two sisters, here they'd added on gardens and outbuildings, and all this work done by plowmen, mowers, rakers,
sawyers, carters, and carpenters in the gardens, the vegetable patch, with
the animals, all of them hired; but now the foreman, Ergakov, had been
spoiled and wasn't keeping an eye on things or keeping up with the work,
and he was a liar. In winter there's much less work to do. Nonetheless, there
was a dam and three young horses, and now the old mare was supposed to
foal, and there had to be someone spending the night with her, and also the
five cows and five calves. As well as the hogs, sheep, fifteen or so geese, and
thirty ducks—these were for her dimwit of a sister Dunya with the mind of
a child who also fed the workers. In the winter, ice had to be hauled from
the Medveditsa; the last year's hay from the meadows and what had been
chopped down on the allotment in the public forest all hauled; soon now
they'd have to get in the firewood and cover the forcing frames; rabbits had

overrun the gardens and acacia there, and gnawed away; and also an agreement reached with the village ataman about when to bring the mare that winter to his English thoroughbred. People said Cossack women were like American women: independent and self-sufficient. Masha was a hammer, for the two women and the man, working harder than seemed humanly possible, even studying horticulture according to Schroeder (she had finished high school), with a spinsterly devotion to Fedya, who she considered brighter than the sun, and every fifth day dispatched a letter to him: Will you be angry at me for my many expenditures, for overpaying? Tell me, did I deal correctly with this, and this, and this? And now she was stopped in her tracks by Petya's illness, and should he continue the medication? Bring a new thermometer from Petersburg, as this one may be wrong. And—what was going on with people in Glazunovskaya itself, and how the co-op was doing, zealously instituted by Fedya, but he himself was gone; it began in stormy meetings—"what is its point?"—and now there was no one to go for goods, and the co-op had no kerosene, or sugar, or iron, but private traders were getting goods from somewhere. Fedya's Cossacks railed against him for the co-op. And this hurt Fedya—to tears, if he were one for tears; but until you went down there yourself, and made people understand— they just wouldn't believe you!

But now, the Petrograd doings made you drag your feet outside, made your eyes need to look and take it in, your fingers to write it down. It was good no one these days needed the institute library. The Mining students were now thronging either to the police or the patrols with the Finland battalion, they'd opened a cafeteria for the soldiers, and no one was interested in lessons. So that even Kovynev locked up the library and was gone to town for entire days.

He wasn't the only person drawn inexorably to the streets. Everyone was! Everywhere there was a bazaar-like gaiety, all the livelier for being spontaneous. This was the revolutionary psychosis (he wrote): man cannot exist separately, he has a physical desire to merge with the masses. And the mere act of pushing, exchanging glances, shouts, the general flow, made it seem that we were achieving something greater. Now we were all united; no need for parties anymore!

How the high school boys beamed at the intersections with their white armbands! What fun for them to direct the movement of adults. (Which meant, then, that you weren't going to get anyone to school.) Here we are—and now we'll get along without police. A new era! "Now the police bribe will disappear, too," Fyodor Dmitrievich overheard, and he wrote it down. However, as a worldly man, he thought it dubious.

His feet carried him, carried him all over town. He was drawn to be present everywhere, to see and hear everything. But when his memory was filled to the brim and couldn't hold all the words he'd heard, Kovynev shyly stepped into some lobby or entrance, or just simply turned away, pulled off his glove lined in homemade down, and hurried to write in his little book:

"A handful of women on the street arguing. A lady in a pince-nez and an elegant cloak trying to convince simply dressed women that they shouldn't kill people in the streets, that it was foolish minds that released brigands from prisons. One woman got angry: 'Foolish minds carry on like this one. On your way before the people mess up that scallywag of yours.'

"Somewhere else. Speaker: 'May there be a democratic republic with a responsible monarch!'"

Everywhere clusters debating—city coats and homespun coats, great-coats and female students. Beardless youths shouting: Off with Rodzyanko and Milyukov to the Peter and Paul Fortress as enemies of the people!

So much pressing audacity and tenacity these past few days, with firing in the air and searches, so much excess force when there was no resistance what-soever. Some young civilians riding around on officers' seized horses, sitting on them like dogs on a fence—evidently they'd never sat on one before—but what a triumphant look! And the horses? Hungry, sad, tormented eyes, as if they understood absolutely everything, not just that a ruffian had taken over the able soldier's saddle. Not just the horses! Even the automobiles were to be pitied, so befouled and spoiled, abandoned in the middle of the street.

Zinusha, he recalled, had once written: if you were suddenly confronted with complete freedom, you wouldn't know how to arrange your life.

Before, they'd always wondered when on earth the masses were going to get going. And now they may have gotten going too much. The rise of free-dom had not been drawn in these colors before.

And there wasn't anyone to stand up to the insolence. There'd been no *other side* in this Petrograd revolution at all these past few days, no one had been found arguing or even conversing timidly, no one had attempted to ex-press out loud even regret over what had passed. There were lots of stunned people, of course, but they were silent outside, or else hiding in their homes.

No, he'd heard that that morning in the 3rd Cadet Corps they'd read the Tsar's abdication in front of formation—and the young cadets had wept co-pious tears. The head officer ordered them to carry the Emperor's portrait out of the recreation hall—but the cadets wouldn't give it up and stood by the portrait with armed rifles for hours. Then the officer peacefully per-suaded them to carry the portrait out to the corps museum to the accompa-niment of a band playing "God Save the Tsar."

There'd been a scuffle at the Sea Cadet Corps on Vasilievsky, too. A crowd came in and started pulling the flags of St. Andrew off a large model of a military sailing ship and hanging red ones. The naval cadets couldn't stand it and drove the crowd out of the building and yard with their Japan-ese rifles.

But even their childish defense introduced a certain balance. Kovynev was not an admirer of the old regime in the least. However, if the old wasn't defended at all, nothing new could come of it.

Now everyone was waiting for news from the provinces. How were they? Would they rise up in the Tsar's defense?

In the early evening, Kovynev returned to his apartment exhausted, promising himself not to go anywhere the next day. In the morning, though, the uneradicated irritant drew him back to the streets. He wandered and recorded:

"In the next apartment all the silver taken away. Men with armbands.

"They surround the building and shoot. And there are small children here.

"A lady in a hat was just sweeping our stairs. And the very best! They've drunk our blood! And now the soldiers' wives can eat chalklit."

How many days was it idle scroungers had been pouring out on the street, spitting sunflower shells and grinning, as if nothing else lay ahead of wartime Russia under a free regime. One problem remained: the old bread lines.

For Fedya there was one unfailing consolation in this jostling: young women's sweet faces. No matter how busy observing the revolutionary ways, the eye always picked out those faces. Some seemed imprinted on his heart forever. Fedya had that quality.

Each dug in like a caressing splinter and whimpered for a moment. And each splinter was all the dearer to him since right now the time was swiftly approaching for him to put the kibosh on his forty-seven-year bachelorhood.

Clearly, it was time to marry, but when? Zina was coming to the Don soon.

Today, Saturday, cabs had come out for the first time on the streets, which had been swept by a nighttime blizzard—and because of this the first semblance of normality had begun to return to the city. The major newspapers weren't coming out yet, but the newsboys were running around with their bulletins, shaking them, and shouting:

Here's how Nikolai the Tsar
Came tumbling from the throne!

The work of destroying coats of arms had now spilled throughout the city. Where they could be knocked down, they were knocked down, but signs were smeared with paint or pasted over with paper. "Purveyor to His Majesty's Court" was painted out everywhere. In places, entire signs were burned. At Vindava Station, they wound rags around the bust of Nikolai I.

They dragged moldy books from cellars out on Nevsky to sell. They shouted:

"Banned books! Louis Blanc! Engels! Lafarge! Programs of revolutionary parties!"

He stopped in at the *Russian Notes* office, where they told him Peshekhonov had insisted Fyodor Dmitrich write a vivid revolutionary sketch about these days.

He'd been planning to anyway. But how to compose it? This meant writing carefully, obliquely. You couldn't say everything directly.

He wrote down others' words about what he himself hadn't seen. He came across a Cossack he knew who complained about a motor company next to their barracks. Every morning they heard the prayer of the Cossack hundred through the fence—and didn't respond at all. But today, after the prayer, they started clapping for the Cossacks and thanking them for the concert. The Cossacks frowned, and no one responded.

Kovynev walked on—and pondered the Cossack lot. After all, something on the Don was going to change now—but how? For the better, but how would it play out? Oh, all he wanted was to make it to Easter—and go to the Don!

As night fell, a chill, a clarity drew in. The bells started ringing for vespers. Something from his childhood years began to whimper.

But Fyodor had no love for priests.

[4 3 0]

This inner quiet distanced Vera from her surroundings.

Not that she attended church often, maybe once a month. No matter how much she concentrated when praying alone, she didn't soar the way one does with a choir, or by standing united with hundreds of people. During the church service, it seemed, a protective envelope constructed itself around you—and protected you later in all your ways, until it dissipates.

But today was one of her favorite services of the year: the veneration of the cross. Vera would go around to different churches, her nurse only to St. Simeon's, their parish church, she didn't like to change churches, but now she could go a short block down Karavannaya, by bridge across the Fontanka—and the dark blue cupola and spire were immediately on the left. Her nurse always went before the service, to take her usual place by the left pillar, by the icon of the Descent into Hell—and was pained if it was taken. She liked the church before the service, when she had room to greet the people she knew and go around to all her favorite icons, kissing them, lighting candles without having to pass them over shoulders. Today, too, she'd left earlier, so after the library Vera was already lagging behind.

She walked in—and it was already crowded. The veneration of the cross service is never poorly attended. But she found a way through, lit two candles in two candle stands, and made her way closer but not right next to her nurse. Lighting a candle has its own good magic. Taking the flame from another wax body, from another stranger's hand and soul, and then the candle foot gently melting, also with the help of a friendly flame, and the candle's planting in its separate holder—the beginning of its brief life, poetically compared so many times with a person's life, a profound comparison. You have lit a candle and moved away, but the bodiless threads between you and it remain. In its accelerated and flaming form it will offer up to Heaven its own (and your) life, its own and your prayer—and in a way foresee and foretell your, perhaps not yet brief, fate. Vera loved it if she stayed close and followed her own candle with her eyes, didn't lose it in the dozen similar ones crowded in—and she sighed when, burned down, it was extinguished in a plaintive wisp of gray smoke.

Vera entered after the initial censing, when it was fragrant and clouds of incense were still rising through the church's entire expanse. At the service leading into Sunday, the black Lenten vestments are exchanged for colorful ones—and today they were red. Not the brazen scarlet that spotted the city commotion, but a noble crimson, yet red. . . . As if it had made an incursion here, too.

But floating, too, in the censer streams was "Bless the, Lord, O my soul," and the outside world moved off and shrank. What was being sung here was only a small part of the magnificent psalm that stunned Derzhavin—only about the honor and majesty in which the Lord clothed Himself, and about the waters running among the hills, a panorama from peaks to canyons, but so much beyond remained in the psalm: how the Lord walks on the wings of the wind; touches the mountains, and they smoke; and the Earth shall never be shaken; and how the Lord gives drink to every beast of the field and causes the grass to grow for cattle and food for man; and made the Moon to mark the seasons, and the Sun, which knows its time for setting; and how dismayed are all living things when He hides His face; and how living things die when He takes away their breath.

Glory to Thee, O Lord, who hast created all.

Meanwhile, led by the deacon with his thick candle, the priest walked around the temple along the walls, censing all the principal icons as those praying stepped back, and also from the ambo swinging the censer like a fan—and closed the gates to luminous heaven, cutting us off on this earth, leaving us to ourselves.

However, a firmness has been communicated to us: The Earth shall never be shaken, pray with your whole self and assurance. Revolutions will flare up and revolutions will die out—but the world of the Creator stands.

In his thick deacon bass, as if not letting himself use full force, the Litany of Peace flowed along with its usual exclamations, rhythmically responding with a consoling "Lord, have mercy"—for the peace from above, and the peace of the whole world, and the Synod, and further, how thousands upon thousands of familiar times, surprising no one, there should flow "For our most pious, most Sovereign and Great Emperor" and his spouse, about his mother, the Heir, and the entire reigning house—those who had given themselves over to the service were not expecting a stumbling point here, but someone had managed to give thought over this day, and the resourceful Holy Synod must have given a rushed command (no more rushed, of course, than the way the Tsar himself had abdicated), and now the deacon bass was droning:

"For the great, God-protected Russian land, and for its pious and right-believing Provisional Government."

Right away Vera saw the sneers of her friends and acquaintances, and she felt ashamed for she couldn't bring herself to object. Of course, since the Tsar was gone, they should stop praying for him—but perhaps not with such haste? There was a comic obsequiousness in this "piety," so clumsily attached to the Provisional Government, whose members had forgotten how to cross themselves. The outside world, set aside and made small, had reached its hand in here nonetheless.

But Vera did not so much feel this jolt herself as she did for her nurse. What about her nurse? She glanced at her over several shoulders—and she turned her head toward Vera, as she never had since Vera had grown up from a child—and there was angry astonishment on her nurse's dry face.

Movement, glances, and whispers passed through the entire church crowd.

. . . Her nurse went to church to heal from the anger of the past few days. Right in front of their building, across the square, arrested people had been driven like cattle into the Mikhailovsky manège. It was said there were already nearly a thousand locked in there. And she had gone to the church past the circus, where a crowd was jamming in for a meeting, and a red scrap had been tacked onto them all. There was a meeting there a few times every day, even now during vespers, so they probably weren't going to go to church. When she walked into the church, a few soldier boys were standing around, but look—with red scraps. She went right up to them: "You devilsprites, have you lost your mind? Where do you think you are? Come on, off with them!" Two took them off, but the other two shifted from side to side—and left. She went to pray at the icons, but some slattern had tacked a big red silk bow under the icon of the Transfiguration. Vera's nurse removed it then and there, without hesitation, took it to the trash bin, and then thought—and put it in the candle box. She entrenched herself in her spot, the people gathered, the bells stopped ringing, the royal doors opened, the Father censed around the altar, and the service began—and her nurse now had hopes of a brightening after these accursed days. That was when the litany caught her unawares. She gasped, but silently. She couldn't believe such a thing. Let the city raise all the hell it likes—but how was it they switched things around **in here**? Do you mean they want to corrupt us here in the temple? Where was a soul to go if not straight out of the temple? What was this? Had the church fallen away, too? Now even the church wasn't going to be genuine? . . . The Tsar was alive, after all. How could they not pray for him? . . . Maybe they'd moved further along? No, the deacon read: "That He may help them to place at their feet every enemy and adversary." Place at whose feet, then? Under these very adversaries? . . .

Everything had been so brought down and confused! But the service continued its course, and now they were singing "Blessed is the man who walks not in the counsel of the wicked." This stood! We will not walk with the wicked, and the hallelujahs cascaded. Then there came "Let my prayer arise"—and her nurse calmed down.

"For He has established the world so that it shall never be moved. . . ." It wouldn't be moved by your mutinies, either.

But she held her breath in the Augmented Litany: if only now! No, they left the Emperor out again, instead of him again inserting the right-believing government.

Well, must be they know better. . . . And the whole service was the same, unfailing. Where were we to go? We would pray quietly.

And what about Yegor? Pray for him.

. . . While Vera was thinking that there really was no contradiction between city and temple. People were seeking brotherhood both there and here, only the form of expression was different, the level of understanding was different, and the level of success different. Here it had already been achieved; but there it was still a long and tangled path.

The incomparable evening prayer grew softer and softer: "Vouchsafe, O Lord, to keep us this evening without sin. . . ."

She heard "Lord, have mercy" and hummed along a little with these most capacious of all prayer words. They got to "for every Christian soul, afflicted and weary"—and she prayed then for her brother Georgi, not only now but in every prayer, both morning and evening—for his threatened life and his troubled soul.

But also, with despair—for herself. And for *him*. For this torment to be resolved somehow, resolved as the Lord saw fit, opening a path if possible, and if not, then closing it off visibly.

"Lord! All my longing is known to Thee; my sighing is not hidden from Thee."

And if not—then cast aside what is impossible, and if so, then make us understand what is possible.

She dared not asking for anything directly, for the path had clearly been blocked. But her soul did not want to cease hoping.

Meanwhile the lamps had dimmed, and vespers were moving into matins.

The priest in his black cassock in front of the closed gates, with grief-stricken head and shoulders, recited his secret prayers for them all.

And once again the Litany of Peace flowed—and inflicted the same nonpeaceful blow on her astonished nurse and probably many there.

But the choir was reassuring in its thoughtful, repetitive way: "Blessed is He who comes in the name of the Lord!"—as if taking all those here away from the disappointments of this world.

The lamps were lit brightly—and the troparion of today's holiday blared: "O Lord, save Thy people." The choir turned out to have been retrained already and now, not without a hitch from unfamiliarity, faltering, brought out not "grant victories to our faithful Emperor" but "victories to the Russian Land and its Christ-loving host over their adversaries."

For her nurse, this had to have been more acceptable: both the land was Russian and the host was Christ-loving. And no provisional government.

The enormous book of Gospels in its precious setting, with sparkling gemstones, was brought out solemnly. And in his powerful voice, the deacon:

". . . For as yet they did not know the Scripture, that He must rise from the dead . . ."

As yet they did not know. . .

But the world of the temple triumphed over the outside world. Nothing could extend its paws to halt this soaring holiday in the heated fragrance of burning wax, where everything bad that could happen in the outside world was being expiated beforehand.

In the royal doors, now flung open, the priest made a unique ancient gesture, welcoming the first morning ray, and spread his raised arms back:

"Glory to Thee who has shown us the Light."

The supreme moment of today's service was approaching: a drawn out "Holy God, Holy Mighty," and everyone knew, although not everyone could see through the open gates, that the priest was lifting the large, flower-entwined cross from the altar, a cross larger than his head, and placing it on his head.

Now he came out with it to the ambo, preceded by two altar boys with large, thick candles and the deacon, censing. Now he carefully descended the steps and, to the choir's "O Lord, save Thy people," moved toward the center of the temple and there lay the cross in flowers on the lectern. And censed it, walking all around it. And fell before it to the carpet in a bow to the ground. Followed by the second priest. Followed by the deacon.

And suddenly, following the choir, everyone in the temple, alertly, knowingly, by some miracle not breaking ahead, nor lagging behind, not adorning those better voices but supporting them with their might, raised up something full-throated that soared with an earthly power unlike everything delicate and beautiful sung so far:

"Before Thy cross we bow down in worship, O Master!"

It was like a wave washing over everyone here and so whole that it seemed to carry the Cross through the air without dropping it—to the lectern in the middle of the temple.

No, not a wave, a unifying force that truly nothing on Earth could break.

"Before Thy cross we bow down in worship, O Master!"

And the entire temple fell to the ground in a single bow—and got back up again. And once again, triumphantly:

"Before Thy cross . . ."

Then the choir sang alone, "Let us venerate the Life-Giving Tree"—and a jostling arose in the crowd, but a brotherly, mutually yielding jostling until it streamed toward the lectern, where space had been made to bow down and then kiss the large silver crucifix surrounded by thornless flowers.

By Thy Cross, the dominion of death shall be shattered.

[4 3 1]

If in all the State Duma Rodichev had a rival for eloquence, then it could only be Vasili Maklakov. But Maklakov adopted the tone of a confidential discussion, with lots of arguments (not disdaining their counterarguments), lenience (contrived or genuine), and even the beauty of his eyes and his sudden smile of seriousness—all devices calculated for a select and not very large audience. Rodichev's speeches were the gallop of a zealous, ironical intellect who began without even knowing himself where it was going to take him (as it had to his duel with Stolypin); only as he went did he come upon strength and sustenance inside him. He never prepared for his speeches, and even his best were those he hadn't thought through. He was moved by the strength of his emotion, and if a topic didn't engage him passionately then the speech didn't work. His speeches never lost the archness of his mind and frequently gave birth to unintended aphorisms that then took on a life of their own. All this, too, enjoyed a particular success in an elevated audience, but his force, conviction, vividness, and volume were so strong that not only in the Duma and not only in front of intellectuals, in front of zemstvo members—but in any audience Rodichev couldn't help but have success, and the Kadets considered him their sole orator for the masses. While he was speaking, he held all his listeners in thrall to his word.

True, the main day of the revolution, 12 March, found Rodichev in Moscow, where he had an appointment with a notary for the sale of a forest tract of his that had brought him more trouble than income—as had his other property, actually. While he was returning to Petrograd, the main soldier columns had already tramped through the Tauride Palace, so that Rodichev did not get to deliver speeches either from the front steps or in the Ekaterininsky Hall. Meanwhile, he was eager to deliver them. When yesterday he had learned of the alarming situation in Helsingfors, his colleagues had decided immediately that Fyodor Izmailovich was the one to go to calm things down because there he would have to give speeches before large crowds, and especially because Rodichev was known for his devotion to Finnish independence, understood the essence of the Finland question, and had many friends there. (He was, actually, even more closely tied to Polish independence; people said he liked defending Poland more than the Poles themselves did.) And so, on the evening of the 16th, quickly, without any special session of the government, he was appointed minister to Finland and he hurried to the Finland Station, where the first train since the revolution was supposed to leave that night.

But inasmuch as there was still a Soviet of Workers' Deputies, Rodichev had not been entrusted with representing Petrograd alone but had traveling with him the rather vulgar Skobelev, who came from a wealthy Molokan family in Baku, and traveling with Skobelev was also a sailor who had a St. George's cross and also a medic wearing a soldier's greatcoat. (During his long years anticipating the revolution to come, Rodichev never would have dreamed of ending up in this company, representing all Russia. But his saving irony never let Fyodor Izmailovich be too despondent.)

Rodichev was already sixty-two, while Skobelev was half his age but affected a certain gravity (to mask his lack of talent) that extended to his questioning:

"Mr. Minister! What are your authorities? We demanded that the government give you authority to arrest officers, should the need arise."

Rodichev could have given himself such authority, but had refused disdainfully. He was going there to calm and persuade.

The train wasn't ready right away. They were still preparing it in the middle of the night. They had to lie on the stationmaster's bare benches, which were not suited to Rodichev's bones or age.

But they were in for worse in the train car, which was not heated at all, the entire way. There was no lying in the compartment; he had to sit up, in his fur coat. Rodichev was not preparing for tomorrow's role in the best way.

In and of itself, an agitated sea of people did not frighten him. He thirsted to see those thousands of heads and change their minds loudly, resonantly, and vividly! That the first unsettled days of the revolution had vacillated toward anarchy he considered natural. Now the task of the honest orator was to help these people sober up, help consolidate their native pull to labor and order. As a military man, albeit quite cultured, Admiral Nepenin had not been able to grasp the social-revolutionary breadth, but Rodichev would help him with his dogged powers of persuasion. Under no circumstance would he indulge the crowd's base instincts—nor would he allow anyone to be arrested for the sake of show or demagoguery!

Rodichev was a figure of too long standing and merit in the Russian Liberation movement to allow it to be debased during the great days of revolution. It was he who was the author of the Tver zemstvo's 1894 petition for a constitution that had caused the novice tsar to stumble. At the end of the last century, Rodichev had been blocked from being chairman of the provincial zemstvo board over this. In the first year of this century, he had been banished from Petersburg for his protest against the dispersal of a student demonstration. A year later he had nearly become editor of *Liberation*. And then—four State Dumas and so many speeches. One might say that not a single important issue of Russian life in the previous twenty years had gotten by without an opinion and speech from Rodichev (most vividly, most unforgettably of all, were his speeches delivered against the death penalty). It was right that now, too, he had been called upon to clarify to the roused popular sphinx the true radiant meaning of the movement under way.

He could still stand tall and proud in front of soldiers, too, recalling how, after university, forty years before, he had volunteered to fight the Turks in Serbia.

Making a visit to the Helsingfors city hall and delivering a historic speech to the Finnish Sejm—no one could do that better.

It was already growing light when, wearing his fur coat and cap, deep in the corner of the compartment, Rodichev dozed off.

People along the line already knew about the deputies' train. Beginning with some morning station, they were met at every stop, sometimes with music, and welcomed as heralds of freedom. They would come out and answer questions, and Skobelev's companions would pass out to the crowd their provocative Petrograd leaflets, of which it turned out they'd brought handsome stacks. As if on the minister's behalf. But he had no authority to forbid it.

So they dragged along for quite a while, and it was well past noon when, one stop shy of Helsingfors, a delegation from the Finnish capital entered the train car—not a single officer but several brutish sailors and soldiers. In response to Skobelev's concern about the counterrevolutionary nature of some officers, a giant of a sailor said:

"The ones that need arresting—we've already arrested them."

"How could you take that upon yourselves?" Rodichev was incredulous. The sailor gave him an out-and-out brigandish look:

"Calm down, Mr. Deputy. You'll have plenty else to get worked up over today."

He didn't explain anything, but his prediction quickly came true.

On the Helsingfors platform they were met by army officers (with no swords), navy officers (with no daggers), and civil authorities, but at the head of the brass was not Vice Admiral Nepenin but Vice Admiral Maksimov, his face closed and darkened, who presented himself to Rodichev and invited him to go straight to the train station square, where many garrison units were lined up. They were awaiting explanations about what was happening in Petrograd. And then he would have to go around to the ships and barracks.

"But where is Admiral Nepenin?"

Maksimov's unrefined face shut even tighter, and he looked away:

"Admiral Nepenin was killed, an hour ago. I've assumed his command. At the sailors' request."

He said it in a very strange voice, as if he'd killed Nepenin himself.

"How's that?" Rodichev dropped his pince-nez, which flew off on its cord.

He could have said "how's that" a thousand times and no one undertook to answer him, and they were out of time. (He failed to understand that the rally hadn't started just now but was already under way, and without them, and they were shouting about bourgeois officers, officers who were the Tsar's accomplices feasting on free bread and drinking our blood, but now our turn had come. Admiral Maksimov vowed to the crowd to serve faithfully and honorably.) They were already leading the deputies out on the broad square in front of the train station, beloved since the 1905 revolution, where the left part of the infantry square was gray with soldiers and the right black with sailors. (And someone from this infantry square had killed the commander of the fleet an hour before? . . .) There was a red flag at the head of some rows; St. Andrew's at the head of others. They had already brought the arrivals up on the makeshift tribune and announced that a speech would be delivered by the State Duma deputy. . . .

But his head felt like it was splitting, and all this time one eye saw a black maw and the other a gray maw. The news had struck him like a club to his legs and knocked him down, but he hadn't fallen and had remained hanging as if by the cord of his pince-nez, and now he was swaying above the

crowd and everything was floating—but he had to proclaim a speech. Proclaim it—because the crowd was quite dispersed, such as Rodichev had
never had to project his voice. From his high swing he was supposed to talk
to them—about what? Not knowing anything about what was going on
here, he couldn't respond to that. He could only tell them about Petrograd.
(But did they need that?)

Habit won out, though, and Rodichev delivered his speech ringingly, not
even considering the order of his words, they fell smoothly in place themselves. How things began in Petrograd. How the rotten Tsarist government
had scattered. How the Duma Committee had been forced . . .

And then about the Tsar's abdication. And then about the Tsar's brother
who—only from the Constituent . . . But now the Provisional Government
was in power and it would be advancing the people's freedoms. . . . You, the
soldiers and sailors, must observe military order and discipline that we may
vanquish Russia's evilest enemy. Hurrah for the Russian army and the Russian navy!

No, he couldn't remember delivering so banal and pallid a speech—but
the black and gray halves both shouted a thousand-voice "hurrah!" on all sides.

Then Skobelev came up to speak, that total incompetent, and knit together something indistinguishable—but they shouted "hurrah" no less for
him. And for the accompanying sailor. And for the medic. Eloquence
proved to have been so unnecessary, Rodichev had no idea why he'd come.

While he stood nearby in silence, he would have liked to question Maksimov or someone, but this wasn't the place. He would have liked to search
the sailors' faces, but he couldn't see that far. And if he could have? Ordinary people's faces can be so favorably deceptive. You find yourself doubting if it was true that a foul deed had been committed here an hour before.

All the speeches had been given, and people rushed the tribune on all
sides—not to tear them to pieces but to respectfully carry them on the arms
of sailors to motorcars with red flags. The motorcars headed for the harbor.

Now Maksimov was sitting next to Rodichev. He never did explain about
Nepenin, but he did report that at dawn the arsenal in the city had been
looted, and in the afternoon officers had been killed on the streets and on
torpedo boats. He had a muddled way of speaking.

Today they were supposed to tour the battleships and tomorrow the torpedo boats. No work had been done on the battleships for a long time—
and political discussion had been under way for days on end.

What about the land regiments?

Maksimov avoided the question.

The cold was fairly stiff and the motorcar was open. On deck, the soldiers
would line up in a circle. Each time, Rodichev was the first speaker. But he
was starting to come around. Admiral Nepenin was gone, but the fleet was
here, Russia was here, and both had to be saved in the face of Germany. Once
again Rodichev regained his oratorical freedom and ardent confidence. His
noble and pure words could not help but affect the ignorant, agitated masses,

free them from evil feelings, help the lost younger brother pull his legs out of his anarchic folly.

Rodichev gained momentum and spoke better and better from ship to ship, stepping higher and higher.

Crews were lined up on all the decks, with a small number of officers or none at all, and when there were officers, Rodichev watched their more intelligent faces and saw more distinctly the effect of his speech. He now would speak about them first on each battleship: killing officers meant acting to the Germans' delight; the fleet couldn't fight without officers; and Russia couldn't fight without the fleet—and then the merciless enemy would trample Russia. So, loving Russia and saving Russia . . . Even if there were individual officers who were supporters of the Tsarist regime, they were not supporters of the Germans! There had been opponents of the Tsar before in the army—but they had fought as one, as Russians. And here all around were Finns. Everyone was looking at you—and they would judge the entire Russian people on your example! The Allies would turn away from Russia if . . . What a disgrace!

They shouted "hurrah!" marvelously, and the faces of the few officers were transported—and Rodichev regained his enthusiasm and confidence as a victor-orator.

And so it went, without a break, from a battleship under a red flag to shore, and from shore back to a battleship, wholly occupied with his speeches, Rodichev never got a chance to talk with the ships' officers (who did not approach the deputies themselves) or even with those accompanying him. The light was already fading, and he learned what had happened over the course of that day only from snatches that happened to reach him, from silences and chance phrases. (Maksimov was by his side the whole time but made no attempt to help him understand.)

That while they were on their way here, officers were being shot and slaughtered in infantry regiments.

That the commander of the *Inerrant* torpedo boat had been killed.

Only on the small flagship *Krechet* did the deputies stop by the officer cabin, where Nepenin's agitated staff told him that fifty or sixty officers had been killed. That this morning they had all been arrested here and led through Sveaborg, with Nepenin in front, but the sailors had gradually forced aside all the officers, except Nepenin . . .

Maksimov kept them from hearing the full story and said they needed to go somewhere else.

Right then, on the gangway, they ran into sailors leading arrested First Lieutenant Budkevich off the *Krechet*. Rodichev shook off Maksimov's wardship, feeling bellicose forces leap up inside him, and demanded to know why they'd arrested him. They replied that no one on the *Krechet* knew themselves, but for the second day the *Petropavlovsk* had been signaling them to arrest him or else they would shell the *Krechet*.

Now the deputies were on their way to the Naval Officers' Club, to a gathering of delegates from all ships and regiments. Rodichev shouted out clearly that he would assume all responsibility—and he ordered Budkevich brought with them to the Naval Officers' Club.

There the deputies from the *Petropavlovsk* were immediately found and asked—and no one knew Budkevich and no one had demanded him.

Thus an officer was saved.

Meanwhile, the Soviet of Sailors' and Soldiers' Deputies opened.

Maksimov announced that, having been chosen by the crews, he had already received telegraph confirmation from Minister of War Guchkov. Maksimov said he would consider the Soviet's Executive Committee attached to his own staff, that he would not take any important decisions without them, and he would transfer some actions of an internal nature to them.

Through hurrahs and a vote they welcomed their chosen admiral.

Once again, Rodichev gave a speech—about victory over Germany, but by now in despair. Immediately following him, a civilian Social Democrat spoke against imperialism.

After the debates, it was decided that all ships would lower their battle flags. (Rodichev hadn't realized they'd been raised. Did this mean the fleet considered itself at war with Petrograd?) And release detained officers. (How many of them were there, though? No one had said.) Right then men approached and reported to Maksimov next to him that Captain Rybkin and Lieutenant Lyubimov had been led off the *Diana* to shore—and both killed.

Rodichev roared at Maksimov (he kept gleaning more and more energy from somewhere) and took the fleet commander straight to the *Diana*.

Off they went. They went up the gangway.

The entire crew was lined up, now under electric lights. Rodichev nervously examined them, even walked along the ranks—and was horrified to see their bulging, dull, impenetrable eyes up close.

Had he really been delivering all his speeches today to such as these? . . .

Everyone standing here was one of us, the killers were our own men, not strangers—but no one would admit it. They even swore they hadn't killed anyone. That this was all the Sveaborg Executive Committee.

It turned out that the *St. Andrew* had not lowered its red battle lamp, which meant it had not released its officers.

[4 3 2]

Each had his own ministry, where he spent his time, and had already moved or was moving to his official apartment or had decided when or whether he would (Shingarev was not going to at all), but where were they supposed to gather for joint meetings? The Tauride Palace made no sense now. By accepting Lvov's offer to temporarily meet at the Ministry of the Interior near the Chernyshev Bridge, they had quit for good the shelter of the Duma that had promoted nearly all of them, leaving its filthy halls to the unattached Duma remnants and the growing numbers of the Soviet of Workers' Deputies.

Where did they now find they had moved? Back to Protopopov's again? An ill-starred connection! The chairs where he had presided with his accomplices were still warm.

The ministers' session started at noon—and went on nearly to midnight, with an hour's break at dusk. Some of the ministers—Guchkov, Milyukov, Kerensky—either didn't come at the beginning, or went off on business and returned, while the others sat as if shackled to those chairs, many with no idea at all of where they were to begin in their ministry: hoping to get some clarity here. Strangely, though, while accustomed to sessions and knowing the procedure, they were now going round and round on an unstoppable and confused carousel, and over the course of the whole day never did understand whether they had an agenda or what they wanted.

The well-known Kadet Nabokov, Milyukov's friend, took up the duties of the Provisional Government's executive secretary, set up a chancellery for them, and in this way created firm guidelines for government activity. But the chancellery clerks had showed up for the first time today, and the first minutes, still rough, were in progress, and they hadn't decided how to proceed: include dissenting opinions and the vote tally, or just the result?

They all realized they had to begin with major issues of principle and then everything else would come clear. But not in a single head, dusted with the fuss, patchiness, and jerkiness of these past few days, did a single issue become clear—not even how to formulate it. Besides, today was just the first night they'd slept, and they weren't over their exhaustion.

Surely there must have been something, though. Oh, there was.

They sat around the big table, stretching significance over their faces.

Yes, apparently there was a big question, much bigger? The Constituent Assembly!

Specifically: in which building would we convene it?

Although there were quite a few buildings of all kinds in the capital, what immediately came to mind was the Winter Palace.

The Winter Palace in and of itself was a major problem. What was to be done with it now? Declare it a national property—that was certain. But what did it contain? No one knew or had seen it from the inside. Deputies from the First Duma had been in the Throne Room once for a meeting with the Tsar.

"Me! Me!" Kerensky jumped up like a delighted schoolboy. "I'll inspect the palace and report to you."

Well, then, fine. Thus one big question was decided right away.

And now a second big question became clear: Shouldn't they address the entire country somehow? So far they'd spoken in the Ekaterininsky Hall and from the front steps of the Tauride Palace, and they'd sent a wireless telegram to the West "to everyone, everyone, everyone"—but shouldn't they present themselves to Russia, too, tell them what events had occurred in Petrograd, how the new government had arisen, and what its program was (other than the eight points the Soviet had compelled)? Officer delegations had already approached the prime minister and ministers, saying that it was essential to broadly inform the masses, that the soldiers and the people were both starting to listen on the streets to accusations that the Provisional Government were traitors, they wanted to betray the people to the old regime, and they were resisting a republican system! The Provisional Government had to distribute millions of leaflets dispelling these charges; otherwise it would be impossible for officers to serve it.

Writing a major appeal, though, is not that easy. You aren't going to write it at the table in a group of ten. It has to be assigned to some one person.

Milyukov had already written the wireless telegram. The overburdened Guchkov—it was awkward even to suggest it. All the more so to the prime minister. While Kerensky was too much in motion, coming and going impatiently, he had to be in so many places, and if there was something he was good at, they'd already noticed, it was talking, not writing. It would be quite befitting to assign the writing of the proclamation to the Minister of Education, the universally respected Aleksandr Apollonovich Manuilov, an undoubted luminary. When Manuilov was removed as rector from Moscow University by the raging reactionary asso, the entire liberal professorhood resigned in his wake, considering it impossible to work under anyone else, while Manuilov himself was immediately invited to *The Russian Gazette*. But as the years went by, people noted with disappointment that he hadn't quite shone at the *Gazette*, and had even turned out not to be of a bellicose nature, and this became especially clear during the present bellicose days. But who else could write it? Who else had a good pen? And here he sat wanly, tersely, and for some reason refused. He was now busy, perhaps, firing all the professors who had come in under Casso.

So now by process of elimination . . . the very good prime minister smiled charmingly: Shall we assign the proclamation's writing to Nikolai Vissarionovich Nekrasov?

As soon as his name was uttered (and not theirs), everyone liked it. Nekrasov frowned slightly, but importantly, too. Writing, composing—this wasn't his work, either, but he immediately decided to head it up and seat someone else at this business.

Approved.

Guchkov sat there sullen, propping his head up on the table by his elbows. They should have been talking about Order No. 1. About the Soviet of Deputies' effrontery. That neither a war minister nor an entire government could function this way. But even Guchkov himself had still not sorted out all the circumstances and figures, had not tested all his possible powers. What could he unload on these helpless civilians? They couldn't do anything anyway.

Of all the thoughts and plans he had had these past few days, only one could be expressed clearly while still in the spirit of the revolution pleasant to all: in promoting lower ranks to officer, eliminate ethnic, confessional, and political restrictions. That is, open admission to the cadet academies and officer ranks to Jews.

"Yes, yes!" the Minister of Education perked up, cheered up. "Also immediately eliminate the Jewish quota in educational institutions! And restore the right to continue their education to those removed for political unreliability."

Approved unanimously.

But no one had immediately identified any other major issues.

Now Kerensky (he was in a hurry) had a few questions concerning justice. First of all (he proposed it orally, there was no time to write up a document, that was for later), a Superior Court had to be instituted for top officials.

Fine, institute it. Assign someone to write it up.

And he said who exactly were to be appointed to that bench. (And then skipped off.)

Tereshchenko hastened to catch the session's attention. (He'd already come up with a ploy: everything he didn't understand he would pose as a question to the united government. And if it turned out to be wrong, then they would answer for it, not him.) To begin with, he encouraged his colleagues, saying that the creation of a government of popular trust had already had the most favorable effect on Russia's credit-worthiness. Not only England and America, which had so reluctantly given money to the Tsar and were now overjoyed at our democratic order, but even the Japanese currency market was now open to our state loans!

Marvelous.

For this must we confirm that our Provisional Government is inviolably responsible for all the financial obligations of the previous one? Yes, we'll have to.

But for now . . . Should we increase the State Bank's right to issue banknotes by, say . . . 2 billion rubles? According to Mikhail's text of abdication, the Provisional Government had that fullness of power. Well, then. They wrote this down. Simultaneously, the economy: cease the issuing of credits for any secret expenditures. Oh, no more secret expenditures, of course! Henceforth, everything would be open. Then: Can't we cut expenditures from the war fund? Hmm. Hmm. . . . (Guchkov wasn't there, he'd left.) This was for the ministers of finance and war to consider jointly. Subsidies for war victims? For now, for a week, continue as we have and then we'll discuss it. And all the state pensions allocated under the old regime? Gentlemen, for now we'll have to keep them. We cannot so abruptly . . . They've been doing the bureaucratic heavy lifting all their lives, they're burdened with families. Many, after all, would have to be removed from their posts. But what does that mean? Must we pay their pensions? We can't abandon them like crabs on a shoal.

What are we to do with the State Council? It has nothing to do now. But it has worthy members—and why should they be deprived of their salaries or pensions because of the revolution?

One would obviously like to pay additional rewards to all employees of government institutions. It's such a difficult time, after all. . . . Approved.

But then the normal influx of taxes, duties, and assessments takes on significance. In this stormy time, people might stop paying. Should we write an appeal to the populace about paying taxes?

No. No, let's wait a while. . . . This is an unpleasant appeal and could undermine our government's authority at its very first step.

So, transfer the property of the His Majesty's Personal Cabinet to the Ministry of Finance. . . .

Yes, gentlemen! But to whom shall we transfer all the property of the Ministry of the Court? And charge of the palaces? And administration of the Appanages?

Appoint a special Provisional Government commissar.

Gentlemen. Gentlemen! We are going to have to appoint a great many more commissars, and to all kinds of places. What about to the State Horse-Breeding Administration? And the management of the Philanthropic Society and the institutions of the Empress Maria?

We have to confirm all the commissars appointed so far under the Duma Committee if they are still in those posts.

Sitting among the ministers, as their equal, but next to Prince Lvov, was gray, colorless Shchepkin, administrator for the Ministry of the Interior, inasmuch as Prince Georgi Evgenich himself, given his busy schedule and responsibility . . . Now he slipped a register to the prince, and the prince (who was chairman of the Union of Zemstvos) graciously stated that the current expenditures of the Union of Zemstvos had to be approved, well, here was 175 million rubles . . .

No objections.

What should be done with the Chief Administration for the Press? Eliminate it! There can never be any censorship in Russia again! Maybe leave the foreign clippings bureau.

What should be done with the Chief Committee on Railway Security? Eliminate it, naturally.

And—whoever remembered what. They should dismiss the military hospitals inspector. Fine, there will be a resolution to that effect. We should eliminate, Rodichev requested as he was leaving, the general imperial legislation on Finland. They did. (No one yet had a single written note, all the requests were first passed and then drafts were assigned to be written up.)

Nekrasov, too, was anxious to advance his proposals, realizing the occasion could not be let slip. He was preparing an increase in wages for all rail transport workers. Yes, they'd earned it.

Shingarev barely participated, burdened by his own thoughts and looking at his own papers. What he saw and proposed was this: although the agriculture minister in the narrow sense should not deal with the Empire's food supply, right now, as long as there was no separate food ministry, there was no one other than him to which to assign this. And he would take it on. Well then, everyone agreed.

But he also proposed stopping the insane destruction of German landholdings, the best cultivated farms. Stop the eviction of Germans.

But wouldn't this look like an unpatriotic act? . . .

It was only the summaries that were easy to retell, but how many doubts, worries, and side considerations there were here! Five, seven, nine hours of the session of the first free public cabinet went by.

Weren't there any other problems from the Ministry of the Interior? Dear, pliant, clear-eyed Prince Georgi Evgenich understood that there were perhaps a few, which should also be touched upon. What about the Okhrana? Well, that disbanded of its own accord during the first few days. The separate Corps of Gendarmes? Unquestionably, we are getting rid of this stain and will decree so immediately. The railroad police? Well, inasmuch as they all belong formally to the gendarmerie, we are getting rid of them, too. (It would be excellent to send them all to the army.)

There remained another such detail: what about the provinces? Oh, obviously, we are getting rid of the police throughout the country by a single decree. As the Duma had always demanded, they can all be sent to the army.

But then, get rid of city governors everywhere?

Yes, of course, them, too.

And the governors. And the vice governors.

Yes! Yes! Dismiss everyone at once, throughout Russia, with a single telegram directive.

Someone piped up: Do we have that right? Are we authorized?

Our authority has no limits until the Constituent Assembly.

Does the Ministry of the Interior have candidates at the ready to administer each province?

No, there are no such candidates. But it would be undemocratic to appoint them from above or prepare them in advance. For simplicity's sake, appoint all the zemstvo board chairmen—for the eighty zemstvo provinces and eight hundred districts—commissars of the Provisional Government. There's your solution!

Thus it was decided. Remove the governors, city governors, and all the police. And this wholly in accord with our democratic program. The old police are utterly intolerable! And if someone needs it, let them create a local people's militia.

"But gentlemen!" Prince Lvov smiled radiantly. "Why do we need any police at all? Why does a free state need police at all? Does a conscious people really need that?"

As Lev Tolstoy taught, all misfortune stems from authority. We need no authority.

No one objected.

The rest of the administrative mechanism, well, within tolerable limits, can be kept. To maintain at least a normal course of life in the country.

Prince Lvov, if he experienced any awkwardness in his new position, consoled himself by saying he'd succeeded at every endeavor, ultimately. Gradually, he would at this one, too. Gradually, political figures' good sense would take the upper hand, as would the profound wisdom of the Russian people and the divine principle that lived in their soul.

*　　*　　*

"HEY, AKULINA, YOU'RE SEWING'S COCKEYED."
"DON'T WORRY, MA, I'LL DO IT OVER RIGHT."

*　　*　　*

18 March
Sunday

[433"]

. . . When a politics called the dictatorship of insanity put the country at the brink of an abyss, the people's instinct for self-preservation found itself a way forward.

. . . The old regime, surrounded by hatred and contempt, hid like a coward in its underground vaults.

. . . Khabalov's announcement about the shortage of flour in Petrograd was a provocation, as if to say, go storm the shops, it's the traders who aren't giving it to you. But the people realized what they were being lured into, treated Khabalov's trick with contempt, and did not start a pogrom.

. . . On the second day, 9 March, the police were already firing on the people, and many were killed and wounded.

. . . For three days, the police did not fire, counting on a provocation. The police needed popular excesses—at which point the cannons made ready in the Admiralty would start to rumble, the machine guns would crack from the roofs, and the city would drown in blood. However, the people and the troops divined exceedingly well Protopopov's program, and not only were there no excesses, there weren't even any individual rough patches observed.

. . . The government intentionally provoked the first shot so that they could cite the threat of revolution and demand the Allies' consent for a separate peace.

. . . The madman Protopopov studded the building roofs with machineguns. . . . By 27 February, building roofs and fire towers were armed with machine guns . . . as many as fifteen hundred machine guns that were supposed to fire on the people.

. . . The shooting of the first few days was, obviously intentionally, ineffectual.

. . . Preobrazhensky Regiment soldiers who had fired on the people approached, and were seized—and under their Preobrazhensky greatcoats there turned out to be knee-length police coats.

266

. . . Mounted policemen who had changed into soldiers' uniforms rushed at the crowd a few times, but the crowd was so dense that they couldn't do anything—so they galloped back and went away.

. . . As has been established, during the first few days of the revolution, police fired exploding bullets at the people. . . . And received 100 rubles a day per man.

. . . On the 11th of March, it wasn't Volynians and Lithuanians firing on the people but police agents who had put on those regiments' uniforms.

. . . Kirpichnikov is a university student and a professor's son.

. . . They didn't want to let the Wheeled Battalion men live, but at the public's request they were only arrested.

. . . At two o'clock in the morning, policemen behind the fence of the Aleksandrovsky Garden fired machine guns at the people along Nevsky. And to keep from being seen, they put on white overalls; later, these overalls were found during a search.

. . . Oh how they fawned over the police, what generous gifts they promised them for firing on the people!—800 rubles for the whole job, but then a police inspector announced it would be 200 rubles an hour.

. . . Now the reasons for the stubbornness the police officers showed in the revolution is becoming clear. It turns out, Protopopov promised each officer a thousand-ruble subsidy and another hundred-ruble raise in pay. For this purpose he received several million.

. . . They dragged the machine guns on roofs and, terrible to say, even onto churches.

. . . There were machine guns stashed all over. They tethered a machine-gun to the bell's clapper in the bell tower of the Cathedral of St. Andrew to make it easier to fire. They desecrated holy places and sneered at the Orthodox faith.

. . . 800 machine-guns were removed from the front for firing on the people! Protopopov installed them on towers. Along with food stores. All convenient places on the roofs of churches and buildings were used for ambush. But thanks to either their inability to deal with machine guns or to the impossibility of firing down, there were very few casualties.

. . . They prepared to fire on Petrograd by strewing 1300 machine guns over its roofs. The story of this unprecedented perfidy will, of course, be clarified in all its details.

. . . The greatest number of casualties was near Gurevich High School.

. . . The ministers who had hidden in the Admiralty got away.

. . . Punishment for General Stakelberg was quick. He conceived the idea of shooting off his gun, and he was shot on the embankment and thrown into the Neva.

. . . A draft of a separate peace with Germany was found in the Empress's possession.

. . . Only for some reason the clergy did not come to the Tauride Palace all those days, did not bless the people in its struggle against the old regime. By this action they undermined the people's trust, it is as if they have disbanded.

. . . Former dignitaries and bishops met in the same pavilion from which they looked out laughing on the agonies of a homeland gushing blood.

. . . Disturbances in the Baltic Fleet. Evidently, the fleet had yet to realize the essence of the great events. The crews did not have a clear understanding of the fact that the entire officer contingent had ecstatically taken the people's side.
A. F. Kerensky asked the sailors to immediately cease their attack on the Russian fleet, which Russian democracy needed. The sailor-deputy standing by the telegraph line explained that the disturbances had come about due to a misunderstanding. The number of killed and wounded officers is being clarified.

. . . Our great February Revolution passed quietly and bloodlessly, to our great good fortune.

[4 3 4]

Battery life proceeded undisturbed by anything: the Germans weren't shooting, we weren't shooting, all was quiet on the front line.

The day before yesterday, a strange rumor had leaked from the brigade, saying that there had been bloodshed in Petrograd, 20,000 killed and wounded. This didn't fit with anything, and they simply didn't believe it.

But yesterday word had come from the infantry that there had been changes in the government in Petrograd. Well, that meant there probably had been something and we'd find out. Then Chernega brought the rumor that Rodzyanko wanted to lock up the Tsaritsa in a convent, but she had taken refuge in the English embassy and had now left for England.

Something probably had happened after all. The officers had no love for the Tsaritsa herself. Even if she hadn't gotten mixed up with that swine Rasputin, the fact that she had allowed rumors to spread and corrode Russia's fate—they didn't mind one bit if she'd gone to England. But how could that be? And where, then, was the Emperor? This was poppycock.

The officers fell asleep, having failed to attach the proper significance to this, so that when very early the next morning Second Lieutenant Lazhenitsyn was summoned to the battery commander, he remembered nothing of this, and since the front was quiet, he thought it was for a dressing-down for some offense or that he was to go somewhere urgently.

Lieutenant Colonel Boyer's dugout was about a thousand feet behind the guns, on the way to brigade headquarters, in a small clump of trees. His batman knocked, reported, and disappeared. Lazhenitsyn walked onto the wooden floor and saluted. The dugout had been dug deep, the height of the lieutenant colonel, and had a decent window, facing east. A desk attached directly under the little window had papers on it, and sitting at it was the lieutenant colonel in his tunic and pince-nez.

He turned his head lethargically toward Sanya; he was more than gloomy. He pointed out the chair on the side for him. Sanya realized that this was bad, a scathing look. He sat down.

He had pointed to him to sit but didn't say anything. He looked indeterminately, and not at Sanya. Well, there had always been a sliver of ice in him.

Right then Sanya noticed that the paper on top on the desk was not the usual official kind, handwritten or typewritten, but a printed leaflet. However, it was impolite for him to squint and read the heading.

The lieutenant colonel did not begin either. Then he turned around. He was very close, without his cap, and there was sufficient light—and suddenly Sanya saw on the other side of the pince-nez not those icy, disgruntled, but terribly possessed eyes. These unexpected, unprecedented eyes showed him, for the first time, that the lieutenant colonel was lost—and he felt compassion for him, while still not understanding anything. Clearly, this ever firm man had suffered some misfortune and might have been dashing about had he had not had the habit of restraint.

But the lieutenant colonel could not find the words. He picked up the leaflet. And laid it in front of the second lieutenant. And said not even in a whisper but almost soundlessly:

"Read it."

And Sanya read the large letters:

ABDICATION OF EMPEROR NIKOLAI II

What???

Where had this come from? No thunder, no rumble—and abdication? . . .

He read quickly to himself. Yes, popular upheavals . . . that means they were right. . . . We have deemed it a duty of conscience to facilitate the people. . . . He read, not grasping every sentence. . . . Not wishing to be separated from Our beloved son . . . we bequest to our brother . . . And all faithful sons of the fatherland . . . in obeying the Tsar. . . .

That meant Mikhail.

"Turn it over," Boyer said.

Sanya turned the leaflet over, and printed there as well and just as large was this:

REFUSAL OF POWER BY
GRAND DUKE MIKHAIL ALEKSANDROVICH

My goodness!

And almost without reading—skipping to the end: so what, then? to whom?

And it turned out: to the Constituent Assembly, which would decide on a form of government.

Sanya had had occasion to hear those words, "Constituent Assembly," more than once, like the name of a heavenly phenomenon descended to earth. This wasn't Sanya's line of thinking, but this was how it had stuck in his mind—a holy cloud.

Elusive and unexpected—seemingly too big to grasp all at once. What, was this the end of the monarchy in general? A republic?

Boyer hovered motionlessly in front of Sanya: a high, stiff collar and in it a separate narrow head under a modest crewcut; on his face, a stiff old-fashioned twisted mustache that had not softened in the least, had not relaxed even today. And distraught eyes. Moist.

How long had he sat over this? He hadn't received it this early in the morning, had he? So, since yesterday?

Did Sanya have to be the first to say something to him?

Boyer—in an unvoiced voice, but confidingly, as he had never lowered himself with the second lieutenant:

"I'm afraid the Manifesto was not given voluntarily."

Even brows, like the marks left on his forehead by his cap:

"There are oddities in the language."

He squinted a little:

"And why in Pskov?"

His pained eyes sought to find confirmation of his guess:

"Perhaps they've forced him to sign? Perhaps the Emperor is not at liberty?"

It was true, why like this? What had changed? And why in Pskov?

Boyer confided:

"If I could avoid proclaiming this, I would wait twenty-four hours. Perhaps it will all be righted, clarified?"

Indeed. So he'd held it back? Perhaps not even since last night, perhaps since yesterday, waiting for clarification?

And maybe he was not alone in waiting? Perhaps in the corps, too, and the army? . . . But it was going to leak out anyway, inevitably. Telephone operators would always know everything first.

Boyer was overwhelmed.

"This is hard for you to understand, lieutenant. Our brigade has not existed without the Emperor for a single day. Ever."

Sanya didn't grasp what he was saying. Why the brigade? Russia hadn't so existed, either, right?

But this is the Grenadier Artillery Brigade of General Field Marshal Count Bruce!

"You were a little boy in 1905. But we've already been through this, in Moscow."

His full eyes made it painful for Boyer even to look.

"Lieutenant. I can't read this with my throat. To take this out to the battery . . . I can't. Please, dear man, line up the battery and . . . Try to read it."

"Yes, sir. I will."

Sanya waited. Any more instructions?

Yes, this: the grand duke's order, he's returning to the Supreme Command.

The second lieutenant stood up, all the documents in hand. And sympathetically rather than harshly, like over a sick man:

"May I go, colonel, sir?"

Boyer nodded slowly, in silence. Two times. Or three. Nodded as if not with just his head but his whole self invisibly tottering.

Or as if parting with the lieutenant for good.

A thought flashed in Sanya's mind. . . . But he didn't dare let the colonel see.

Nor even, after meeting the commander's batman outside, did he advise him to look in on the colonel.

The lieutenant colonel was left to himself and could not be helped. Sometimes people remain inevitably alone even while among people.

The second lieutenant hurried down the trampled snowy path to the battery, but before he had come out on the clearing, under the last birch foliage, he stopped.

He had hurried as if he knew everything. But he stopped as if he didn't.

He looked up and through the birch's bare, pale-mauve branches saw either a stretched or unstretchable cloud shroud—the sun had yet to rise so it was not yet clear how the day would go.

Sanya had accepted so easily the assignment to read this out, but only now, stopping under the solid morning sky, did he stop and think about what was going to have to pass through his throat. How did he understand it? And how should he read it?

Before lining up the battery, did he want to share this with someone? Ustimovich? No.

Chernega? For some reason he didn't feel like it, despite Chernega's quick mind; he might cut in from some unexpected angle.

And even: should he reread it to himself? Or immediately to the formation?

From Boyer he bore a feeling of tragedy—and this would be one kind of reading. But he pictured the ironical Barou standing in the first rank with a subtle grin on his lips—and he got flustered. For him, a different expression and feeling were dictated, not as Sanya would have read in front of Boyer himself. Yes, and for Chernega, too.

Thus, without rereading it, holding the folded papers in his lowered hand, Sanya headed uneasily for the battery. He hadn't found any kind of answer inside himself.

He sent the first soldier he encountered for the sergeant major.

And ordered Sergeant Major Zakovorodny, who was always ready to perform any service, to immediately line up the entire battery.

[4 3 5]

Arseni stood in the first rank, on the right flank of his third platoon, while the lieutenant, reading, stood about seven paces away on the diagonal, facing the middle second platoon. Close. Arseni could well see and hear that the lieutenant himself was reading rather shakily.

The sergeant major had lined up the battery with their backs to the breeze, but the breeze kept trying to whisk the paper out of the lieutenant's hands.

The very first words were some mischief about some upheavals among the people. Good gracious! Where was that? Not in our Tambov District, surely? How is it there? Not pressing on ours, are they?

But there were no further explanations about that, just that the war must be prosecuted to victory. Well, that was clear already.

Immediately after that this plopped out: he considered it desirable to abdicate the throne of the Russian state. And from that it became clear that all this had been written by the Tsar. At first the lieutenant hadn't said out loud whose name it was in, had he?

Good gracious! His mind couldn't keep up. Why was he so angry at us?

Not wishing to be separated from Our beloved son, we leave to Our brother.

But if there were upheavals among the people and the war needed winning—why was that all now on his brother? What about him? And us?

But there were no further explanations right then—just may the Lord God help Russia—and signed, Nikolai.

That was fast. The Tsar had been replaced, the way people switch hats when they've put on the wrong one going out the door.

For as long as Arseni could remember, there had always been the same Tsar. How could there be another? And if the Tsar died, then it would be the Heir, but where had the Heir gone? You pass any holding on to your son, that's the rule, whereas to your brother—that's pretty odd, that's only if all the menfolk in the family have died out.

But the paper didn't make it seem the Tsar had died.

Though the paper still wasn't finished. The second lieutenant's glance passed down the rows—either asking whether they understand or thinking his own thoughts—it would have been quite right to read it a second time and clarify why this had happened and where it was going. But he didn't read it a second time and said nothing on his own behalf but took a deep breath and continued.

A heavy task has been entrusted to me by my brother. (That meant it was from his brother.) Again about the war and domestic strife—guess things came to a head somewhere, off the rails. But what was it his brother had decided—it was kind of muddled—but he was invoking God's blessing and for everyone to obey the government until something *secret* and *equal* happened. And at the end—Mikhail. That was brief, and that was all.

Something ominous slipped by: secret. Equal—yes, that was about justice, but why secret, and secret from whom? A good cause was never secret, only a bad one.

The second lieutenant stopped, too, totally stumped. His face said it all. He lowered the paper and seemed to want to say something personally. Well, say it. Say it! Oh, how they needed that!

No, he didn't.

And quietly, quietly the battery stood there and no one spoke up. Not that you're supposed to from formation.

The second lieutenant was still passing his eyes over the first rank, thinking (and lingered on Arseni, too, straight into his eyes)—and then he said not in a reading voice but more softly:

"Have you understood this, boys? The Emperor has abdicated the throne in favor of his brother Mikhail. And Mikhail—in favor of a Constituent Assembly, which will establish the form of government—maybe a Tsar, maybe not."

He paused.

They hadn't understood, but Arseni held his tongue. It made no sense to speak up; it would clear up on its own.

But near him was Shutyakov, the second gun bombardier:

"So who's Tsar now, yr' honor? I don't get it."

That was the thing that no one got. They listened.

"The Tsar now," our second lieutenant said gently, as he always did, and he smiled with his lips as if it were his fault, "the Tsar now, there is no Tsar."

"How's that?" Arseni let out like a bellows. "No one at all? How can that be? No one?"

"So who's the Tsar?" is what came out of him.

And the second lieutenant said to him, as if himself amazed:

"No one."

They stood there.

In silence.

They wished he would explain some more.

They didn't get it. How could that be—no Tsar? If you remove a head, be so kind and replace it.

"Yes!" the second lieutenant remembered. And he started reading one more paper: Supreme Commander Grand Duke Nikolai Nikolaevich orders all superiors to encourage the lower ranks to stand firmly against the enemy and calmly await the people's decision on the election of a Tsar.

Ah, so they're going to elect one! That's good. Wait and stand firm—that we can do. Nikolai Nikolaich had popped up again from somewhere, but people knew him. Nikolai Nikolaich was order. He wouldn't betray the soldier.

Still they waited for something from the second lieutenant.

He looked over the ranks again and said:

"There you have it, brothers. Such is the will of the Tsar."

And he waved his leaflets for the sergeant major to release the formation. While he himself took the path that led to the commander's dugout.

They waited in case the sergeant major had something, but all he came up with was: "Dis-missed."

Some stepped slowly, reluctantly.

Some stayed.

While Beinarovich blurted out—not about the Tsar, but what about smoking, and where was breakfast?

They were silent.

The battery dispersed, each to his own. Dispersed—and the sergeant major didn't say what came now. Apparently it was a free day. Nothing came now. Actually, though, it was still early; breakfast hadn't even come around.

A few more steps—and Arseni and Shutyakov met.

Shutyakov was a little older than Arseni, a broad beard, although short, and he himself was thickset. Sound in service, Shutyakov was also master of his homestead, oh, it was true. He stood facing Arseni—the bombardiers had their own conversations, people didn't crowd in with them—and said softly:

"Well? How do you see it?"

"Yes, well"—Arseni smacked his lips—"you go figure it out."

"During wartime—how do you abdicate? How could he? Well?"

"Well" was all you could say.

Shutyakov continued:

"The Germans hold lots of the main posts. They did the toppling."

And more softly:

"What if the order's a fake? Could be, right?"

They stretched their legs, stepped aside, walked back and forth, utterly lost. And one to the other, and so together:

"So if the Tsar takes off his crown, does that mean he also gave up on the army?"

After all, they remembered him, the Tsar himself, in the Grenadier Brigade. Not this winter but last he had come to Uzmoshye, and had even gone around to the dugouts, though he didn't visit our battery. He wasn't just a thought, an exalted Tsar somewhere, he was right here, with us, on his own two feet.

"He's abandoned us?"

"But go look how it's turned out."

"We're up a creek without a Tsar."

"We can't without a Tsar!" Taciturn, skinny Zanigatdinov shook his head.

"How's it he turned bad so fast?" Sidorkin with the scar under his left eye asked.

"Up and slipped."

Zavikhlyaev, Arseni's gun layer, into his beard:

"Smooth going, to look at it, but they iced it over."

Shutyakov insisted, to everyone:

"No, brothers, they were right sayin' it: treason all 'round the Tsar. Now it's shown itself."

They'd have gone on hemming and hawing, stabbing at guesses, making noise—but they saw the kitchen. The cart had come from up ahead, sending smoke up its chimney.

They started hurrying, scurrying after the kettles.

Isakov the cook, small and quick, secured the reins, hopped down, and from his usual spot, behind the guns, banged his ladle against the pot's iron side. They'd have come even if he didn't bang.

They each got half a mess-tin of thick buckwheat groats, nice and greasy, and went to their dugouts, wherever they were used to going, the Tatars to their own. Those on their way to observation points sat down right there, on stumps, in their padded trousers, to scarf down their mess-tin first—and then to get more in it and take along to the others. When wet wasn't coming down, Arseni always sat on his gun's spade and ate there.

Caps removed, they crossed themselves—not all of them—and dug in. They spooned up the thick groats with drippings—straight into their mouth. Whether breakfast or dinner, this was sacred business, no time for chit-chat.

Carried it and dug in, some with a wooden, some with a steel spoon.

But you never do stop thinking over your groats.

And think what you will, one thing was clear to Arseni: they needed a new Tsar and fast. You couldn't put it off in war time.

They carried the food, dug in, and Sarafanov goes and asks:

"So what's gonna happen with the Heir now, brothers?"

Indeed, what about the child?

"Yeah," Arseni responded. "For some reason they don't want him."

"It's his own father who didn't," Zavikhlyaev's voice was thick through his beard.

"His very own father? Or maybe someone else is behind it?"

This was what was strange to Arseni, that his very own father didn't want to pass his heritage on to his own son. How could that be?

"Or maybe someone else is behind it?"

Senior bombardier Dubrovin, the reconnaissance chief, with his still whiskerless face, precocious but smart, perched close by:

"The Heir's not going to be ruling, men, that's over."

So who was, then?

"They'd better choose another and quick. In wartime—how can we be without a Tsar? They'd better be quick."

But Beinarovich, seemingly near to Sidorkin and nodding to them all, said cheerfully:

"We anointed him and we ditched him."

Shutyakov pounced on him:

"Shut up, fiend. It wasn't you that anointed him."

It was beyond all understanding. Where had this come piling in from? What was this?

A household without a head.

*   *   *

THAT LAND HASN'T LONG TO LIVE,
WHERE THEY START BREAKING RULES

*   *   *

A crowd of peasants born
Gets scared when their master's gone—
Who will sit on the throne?
Crush and grind the people to bone?

[436]

The week of the Veneration of the Precious Cross was beginning. The cross of Golgotha sufferings brought out to the middle of the temple becomes the center of the world. The cross had been brought out yesterday during the vigil, but Nikolai was in such anguish, he had actually simply forgotten. Yesterday evening, when the storm was in full swing, he had dinner with Mama on the train—and over and over again they spoke heart-rendingly about the same thing. He simply could not see a way to return the throne to Aleksei. Open military actions? He hadn't been able to cross that bridge from the very beginning. And now, what could be done when the entire army was in the revolutionaries' hands? (This was an excuse he gave Mama.)

And today, he'd awakened on this quieted, windless, snow-whitened morning—and suddenly remembered about the Precious Cross. And he'd thought: My God, how trivial all our cares are compared with Golgotha! What some provisional government permits or refuses, allows to go here or there, what gets written in revolutionary leaflets—all that shall pass. His abdication from the throne, too, even if it was a mistake, a clouding of the mind—that too shall pass. But Golgotha would remain eternally, as the principal sacrifice and principal mystery.

There has never been justice among men. In apathy and despondency, one must give oneself over to God's will alone. Prayer—no one can take that away from us. It holds all purity and all relief.

And with a joyous light in his soul, Nikolai arose to go to church for Mass. He had put nothing in his mouth.

Outside, the square was white and clean after the night's snow. Snow freshly covered the tops of the drifts, a luxurious layer on gratings and fences. The thermometer said it was below freezing, and the grating no longer had yesterday's irritating handful of gawking little boys directly opposite the governor's residence—now that no one could drive them away. But the cold did.

A policeman still stood at his post. Dressed not according to regulations, though, in an ordinary short coat.

And two red flags at the entrance to the city hall.

And perhaps because of the cold, few if anyone were reading the abdication Manifestos pasted to the city duma's wall. Or else everyone already knew.

Yesterday, when he and his dear mother had been riding through town in the motorcar, she had been stung by every red flag over a building and every red bow on someone's chest. Nikolai urged her to pay no attention. On the other hand, as they passed, some people turned to face them and saluted, some civilians removed their hats, and one old man on the street knelt. But no one shouted "hurrah," the way they used to. His mother retained sharp impressions from the first few days of the revolution in Kiev: passing by her palace, the demonstrations shouted "hurrah" so loudly, she thought they were about to burst through the gates. The garrison guard had been removed, and all there was left in the palace was fifty convoy guards.

But that was nothing compared to what happened in Kronstadt! And the same in Helsingfors! Outright murders, and a lot of them.

The time was approaching to go to church when suddenly the sounds of a military band rang out on the square. And came closer.

And it wasn't a march appropriate for a military band but was rather— the Marseillaise?

Enemy music played right by the GHQ building!

Actually, he was in a military alliance with the Marseillaise, wasn't he? . . .

He could see well from the bedroom window (where his son would now never appear). An army column was streaming onto the square, and its St. George banner in front and single orange epaulets with black stripes revealed who this was. Marching in its full complement and in formation, with its band and all its officers, with all its George crosses on its greatcoats, was the St. George Battalion! Brave souls selected from the entire army to protect GHQ and for parades.

When had they returned? After all, the Emperor had sent them to Petrograd.

He was no longer hearing reports, was not in the know.

They came out on the square from Dneprovsky Prospect—without great need, merely to display arms—and immediately turned onto Bolshaya Sadovaya, to leave.

But why the revolutionary music? Lord, what has it come to . . .

A nagging feeling from the music.

True, they were not wearing red scraps. Nothing was blocking their George crosses.

They had been marching—to express their delight? Delight at the elimination of their beloved Emperor? Delight at the inception of a republic? . . .

Their faces had been martial, cheerful, merry even, and they had swung their arms vigorously.

As if waving away, waving away the whole past. . .

And a crowd of joyous little boys had accompanied the formation.

Tears came to Nikolai's eyes. If these had already . . . if already—the flower of the army? . . .

Then he had done the right thing in abdicating.

But how, while he had reigned, had he failed to notice this? Had there been this even before?

And he had sent this battalion as the first force against the revolution! . . .

And on this square, could it be that on this very square, last spring, under the pouring rain, a very long service had been held in front of the Vladimir Mother of God? It had been brought there, and a prayerful soldier crowd of many thousands had stood, including this entire St. George Battalion—and everyone had patiently prayed and crossed themselves, including the Emperor and the Heir, and then they had gone on venerating it for a long time, under the torrents of rain?

All this on the same square. . . .

He let them all pass and leave—and only then went to the headquarters church.

As always he entered unnoticed from the left side entrance and stood in his usual lonely spot in the left choir stalls.

A week before, also at the Sunday liturgy, he had stood here, still crowned. And here he was again, as if nothing had happened . . .

The convoy Cossacks stood in straight rows, from pylons to pylons, opposite the royal doors, leaving room to pass in the middle.

There were quite a few staff officers and civilians praying, it was crowded. Three priests and a deacon were serving.

At first Nikolai felt the attention of many people praying behind him. Then—less and less, and he escaped into prayer. He knelt down with the same simplicity as a lonely pilgrim no one could see.

He prayed for the Lord to forgive him his mistakes, such as they were—both from years past and recently. They had never held any evil intention.

He prayed for God to bring Russia its deserved victory in this war—and for prosperity after the war.

For God to forgive even all those who brought catastrophe to Russia un-intentionally.

And fervently for his family.

And for all the faithful people, known and unknown.

The service passed as always, most worthily. The chorus was small but superb. (Nikolai did not like concert singing in church, in his presence they always sang what was most ordinary.) Suddenly the deacon's faltering bass uttered a phrase—a phrase made up of battered words that his ears couldn't take in. There was "most pious"—but not "Great Emperor."

There was an extra pause. Over the whole temple.

The temple fell still.

The whole church and choir was silent. As never happens.

Nikolai's breathing stopped: they were silent because of him! The divine service had faltered—because of him. . . .

But listen—the usual exclamation to "help them and place at their feet" . . .

The deacon's bass rumbled on confidently, for this city and country, for travelers by land and sea, for the sick and the suffering, for captives. And—for our deliverance from all affliction, wrath, danger and necessity.

He hadn't just removed himself from the throne . . . but from the Divine service, too. From the people's prayers.

Here it was, the Precious Cross. . . .

After the Gospel there was no prayer for the Emperor.

And when, at the end, Nikolai, as was his custom, approached first to kiss the cross, the protopresbyter silently presented the cross to him. And said not a word of parting.

[4 3 7]

Since the murder of Admiral Nepenin, since Order No. 1, General Ruzsky had gone numb. He literally felt like a wave-tossed scrap of wood. A torrent—and there was no holding it back, we'd been smashed by boulders from behind—and that was it. It was over. . . .

The finishing blows were coming from Vyborg: Vyborg, too, was seeth-ing; the fortress commandant General Petrov had been arrested. These communiqués reached beyond army group headquarters, they were distrib-uted generally, and everyone was learning of them. The arrow of rebellion had flown from Finland—into the back of this same Pskov.

The situation in the city had become increasingly alarming. The conta-gion had spread from the railway. At the very same Pskov train station where two days before the imperial trains stood in the desertedness of the platform, still under perfect order, and only the first red bows from Petrograd were handing out impudent leaflets—yesterday evening a crowd of a thousand had seethed, under no supervision whatsoever—neither by the civil authorities nor the military command. There wasn't the tiniest place on the tracks, or at the train station, or a room inside the train station, where people from the crowd and unknown arrivals could not have access or take charge. But most of all, they were disarming the officers—all of them at the station, and approaching the station, and in passing trains, streaming into the cars for this purpose. Some officers relinquished their weapons voluntarily (but even then, they had to hide quickly afterward), and those who resisted had theirs swords or revolvers taken away by force and were beaten, and even knocked down. Colonel Samsonov, head of the distribution point, resisted—and was killed.

Similarly, one of the reserve infantry battalions, after hearing the Manifestos about the Tsars' abdication, decided all was now permitted and went so far as to loot the food storehouses at the freight station.

Even imposing, decisive Quartermaster General Boldyrev felt uncomfortable. But yellow, skinny, short Ruzsky looked positively awful. Take up arms against the revolutionary crowd? Ruzsky would have considered this the biggest mistake. And Boldyrev liked that: for such an unusual moment, one's conduct ought to be unusual! Only unusual how? . . .

But if Northern Army Group headquarters thought to put down the disturbances in Pskov—then just what forces it would use was unknown, since there was no such reliable unit. What was raging at the train station could at any moment burst into army group headquarters itself, and the headquarters guard was insignificant, assuming it could even be relied upon not to join up with the violence. Even the headquarters clerks had met the previous evening and discussed whether to salute officers and wear red bows. All headquarters work, headquarters papers, and all the personnel of its command were under threat of a crowd suddenly bursting in, disarming them, and wreaking havoc.

But no directives whatsoever from pathetic GHQ. Alekseev was silent.

Boldyrev understood that there was no help coming from anywhere outside. So how would they extricate themselves?

Headquarters spent the night on the alert, if not trembling. But they got through it. No one broke in.

In the morning they learned that in the night the propaganda against officers had spread through the combat units along the entire front. The earth had begun to quake under the entire Northern Army Group. They began writing a circulating telegram to all the headquarters of the armies, a poultice on a corpse.

While they were writing, someone ran into headquarters to say that rebellious soldiers in town had arrested General Ushakov, head of the Pskov garrison, and however many officers were with him! Apparently, they had dragged General Ushakov away to drown him in the Velikaya River.

And they might burst in here the same way and arrest them all!

Danilov sagged. Ruzsky was dead, his arms were hanging. They had to rescue the garrison head, but he couldn't order action against the revolutionary crowd! Not that there was anyone to give the order to.

And they only had a few minutes to consider. More news was brought: the military units had taken it upon themselves to go on parade to the city square! And a crowd of civilians was thronging there.

All ancient Pskov was tottering! What could he do? By no means could such a thing be allowed, but what could he do?

While Boldyrev sensed a fervor, a decisiveness, and a solution. He didn't even ask his generals, or explain, he just gave a wave and rushed out. And rode in an open motorcar to the designated square.

Boldyrev had a mighty voice, a natural gift. A voice is no less important than muscles. There are situations when a voice can rescue someone better than anything else. Like in a revolution.

The square was droning, teeming. The garrison units had formed up spontaneously on either side of the idle streetcar line, in the sun and light frost. Of them, only the cadets, first-year cadets from the ensign school, and field gendarmes had the usual military look; all the rest were out of uniform, not in strict ranks and rows, an assemblage in greatcoats, a pottage joined on its edges by high school and modern school pupils.

There were thousands of red patches from ribbons and scraps. Here and there, red flags poked up in the air. Even bearded militiamen raised red rags on plain sticks. (Where had they taken and torn off all this red?)

All heads turned toward the motorcar, so opportunely had General Boldyrev shown up, as if he were reviewing the parade! It was unclear who else would. In his moving open motorcar, he rose to his full height and began greeting everyone loudly.

The troops responded fairly harmoniously, still not out of the habit. Making it up as he went, Boldyrev sent hearty, bell-like congratulations to the troops on overthrowing the autocracy, the coming of freedom, and the establishment of a new state system. In response he heard "hurrah" and "hurrah." He shouted out sure-fire slogans, like, "Long live Russia!" and "Long live the Russian army!"—and heard a roaring, unified response. Had he gone on shouting for attacking the Germans or looting the rear, the crowd apparently would have been ready for either. His voice was such, everyone all 'round could hear its sound. Then he shouted out a hope, rather pointless, that the populace would take on maintaining order during the parade—and he heard an utterly crazed "hurrah."

Then he stopped in the middle and risked wondering why some had come with weapons and some not. How could they be shown to the Army Group Commander?

The troops willingly began dispersing to their barracks and then coming back together with their rifles and lining up again. In this time and in this movement, in this mixing and jostling, their energy was defused to the good.

And Boldyrev managed to go see Ruzsky—to warn, convince, and summon him.

Then he began issuing formal commands to the well-ordered parade, while a frail Ruzsky reviewed it shakily.

In the ensuing silence, in a listless, weak voice that did not project, he began talking about the happy, free new system, about the necessity of calm, coordinated work, and even about the danger of drinking methylated spirits.

*　　*　　*

The thrill of holy insurrection
Again ignites the world.
A promise made—a triumphant feast—
For the people's flame of suffering.
(F. Sologub)

[4 3 8]

Only someone who has first learned how to obey can know how and dare to command. The wise hierarchy of the whole world is comprised this way: you are a link between older and younger, and you can only lead if you have been led. The more powerful a person's will, the more joyfully he gives himself to the world hierarchy of powers. Whereas weak characters require the illusion of independence.

The bigger an organism, the more it needs hierarchy and unified authority. The entire Universe above all. (You get a good sense of the laws of the universe in the Arctic Ocean, in a rowboat with Pomors, with a fresh wind between ice floes, north of the New Siberian Islands, where the mouth of the Lena seems like an unattainable springboard of civilization.) And surely, an organism like Russia.

And that is why Admiral Kolchak had so confidently suggested to Nikolai Nikolaevich a Russia-wide dictatorship. Russia could not dither in one or two hundred directions. If the throne toppled and floated away, other firm hands had to take hold of the country.

According to his calculations, Kolchak's messenger could only have reached the grand duke yesterday morning. And a telegram of consent could not have been received before noon yesterday.

But before that came Mikhail's abdication. It reached Sevastopol with the following mishap: Printed on the tape was this: "Right now we are transmitting to you the manifesto of Mikhail Aleksandrovich"—at which point, the line cut off. And cut off in a major way, not to be repaired in half an hour or an hour.

Doubt strained, as did hope. Might this be not a line cut off but a change at GHQ? Or with Mikhail himself? What could be conjectured about the untransmitted manifesto? Something very important and new!

Anything but a repeat of the abdication that came in when the line was repaired.

Now Russia was left without any Tsar at all, without any Supreme Power! Power had been conveyed to—no one. . . .

So Kolchak had been correct. He had guessed the situation and Mikhail's lack of firmness and readiness when he had dispatched the courier.

But all could still be saved even more so by declaring the dictatorship of the grand duke! A republic introduced in the flush of war—that would mean ruin.

However, the reply from Tiflis kept not coming.

Over the repaired line, by indirect means, via GHQ, orders were sent out from the very same grand duke, now as Supreme Commander.

. . . Inscrutably appointed, he crosses himself and calls on wondrous heroes. . . . He enjoins all troop leaders and army and navy ranks to calmly await the expression of the Russian people's will. . . .

That is, a Constituent Assembly.

That is, this was already a response to Kolchak.

It was nearly evening yesterday when a direct telegram came in from Tiflis, but not from the grand duke, oh no—from the Duke of Leuchtenberg. The lieutenant was reporting to his admiral that he could not return to Sevastopol because the Supreme Commander had ordered him to accompany him to GHQ.

This was the final and poignant reply.

Kolchak had had a presentiment of this in the grand duke: a weak soul under a knight's armor.

A missed step. We shall come to regret it . . .

The grand dukes . . . And how many of them there were.

But he did not regret having sent it. Any path of hope had to be tried. Any impasse had to be proved.

Was that all that remained, to submit to the new government? Both Manifestos inclined one to submit.

But what kind of government was it going to be? And where would it lead? A telegram arrived from some Prince Lvov. Yes, evidently the dynasty had ended its own existence and a new era was beginning. And whatever kind of government it was, we had a duty to the homeland.

As it was—the Tsar had abdicated at the very height of the war. But the war hadn't abdicated, no one had canceled the war. We were obligated to perform our military duty as before.

Just a few days ago, it was such a simple, precise objective, generally speaking: to be smarter, stronger, and braver than the German and the Turk and substantiate this superiority on the sea and on its shores. If the young admiral was talented (and he was), then he must seek out and find a path.

But a revolution had come crashing down from out of nowhere, like a boulder on the back of a crawling soldier. And still under fire, and still not daring to raise his head, the fighter could not crawl forward or creep back or move his limbs freely.

That was how Kolchak felt with his fleet.

What was immediately obvious was just issuing a decree saying that now a surprise strike by the enemy was especially possible. Our foe would want to take advantage of events in Petrograd and rely on the disturbances here—so vigilance and calm in the performance of one's duty was mandatory.

At first, though, nothing happened. There were no disturbances. Service proceeded calmly on the ships and calmly in shore crews, as if they hadn't learned anything especially new.

Now, though, you couldn't stop the avalanche of agency telegrams and stacks of newspapers brought from the capitals. And the newspapers were filled with appeals fomenting strife.

Here, on land and on ships, men began forming clusters. Small ones for now. They discussed, falling silent in front of their officers. Quietly for now.

It was the Black Sea Fleet that had known mutinies—in 1905 and even in 1912. And if *it starts* here, then it would be a terrible clap of thunder.

And suddenly, on the best ship of the line, *Empress Catherine II*, the sailors had presented their commander with a demand! That he remove officers with German surnames from the ship.

That's how it starts.

Tonight, Midshipman Fock, a marvelous young officer, was on duty on the ship's lower decks. When he was checking the men on duty at the artillery vaults, the sailors accused him of planning to blow up the ship.

Powerless to vindicate himself, in despair—the midshipman went to his cabin and shot himself.

In the morning, Admiral Kolchak pounced like a tiger on the *Catherine*, lined up the crew—and with fervor and anger upbraided it for stupidity. In Russia we have lots of people with German surnames, and they often serve better than we do. Just recently the glorious Admiral Essen died. . . .

This hit the crew hard, and they asked forgiveness.

But the first victim lay dead.

It was in Kolchak's character not only not to wait for danger to pass but always to rush toward it, to seek it out, so as to clash with it, having his own momentum.

For now he had sent the compulsory telegram to the new government saying that the Black Sea Fleet and Sevastopol fortress were wholly at the disposal of the people's government and they would apply all efforts to prosecuting the war to a victorious conclusion; and to Guchkov as Minister of the Navy separately (he, at least, had always wished the fleet good and maybe now would agree to the Bosphorus operation? . . .); for now that was all. The admiral ordered an assembly immediately on shore in the barracks of the half-crew on the Korabelnaya side, two representatives from each company—from the ships, the shore crews, and the garrison.

They sent telegrams and signals—and representatives of the companies assembled in less than two hours, bewildered: the fleet had never had this form of meeting or form of address from an admiral.

Gathered were about three hundred men, black and gray on the benches. The admiral stepped out on the platform in front of them and started speaking ringingly, almost joyously. (An encounter with disaster always gave rise in him to a feeling of joy, too.)

He explained to them how he understood things, without preparing for this, the sketch was too simple: the Tsar was gone but the war continued. There was a new government in Petrograd that was going to be thinking about necessary changes. They would flow in as necessary. But for now, the war continued and what remained to us was strict service, vigilance toward the enemy, and full discipline. We will maintain our strength against the Germans!

So unspoiled were the sailors by speeches, let alone admirals' speeches, that Kolchak's appearance went very well. They clapped. Their look, their faces—they promised to do everything!

A question rang out: Here we have Order No. 1. Should we carry it out? Kolchak had heard about this balderdash transmitted over the radio from Tsarskoye Selo, and he replied:

"Until it is confirmed by the government, it is not the law for us. Why should an order from a council of Petrograd deputies be binding in Sevastopol or Odessa?"

At the conclusion, Kolchak did not think to line them up outside but went out to his motorcar past the black throng.

Good-natured faces moved in emboldened smiles, and eyes stared to examine the wonder of seeing an admiral so close up. One tall, droopy-lipped sailor suddenly bellowed:

"I guess the time's finally come, Your Excellency, for you to pay attention to us! Why didn't you ever ask us like this before? Why don't we start gathering like this all the time!"

His own people shouted at him. How dare he? Had he lost his mind? But others joined in support. And their eyes—their eyes burned, probingly, at the admiral—in a correlation he hadn't remembered since his midshipman service.

"That's not done in military service"—was all Kolchak could think to reply, smiling.

On the streets of Sevastopol, the Tatar honeysuckle was green and fragrant already and the almond trees were just about to bloom. It was a sunny, bright blue day. The bay's high shores were covered in young grass. A motorboat, frothing the dark blue water with sun flecks, was taking the admiral to the *St. George*. But he was still under the impression of that simple movement toward the people, their trust, but also their insistent touch.

This wasn't done in military service, but here he had done it. Herein lay the daring of discovery, the opening of communication! But herein also lay a threat: that after this episode hundreds just like could easily be imagined.

He clambered up the gangway actually cheerful.

Barely had he stepped on deck when he saw the flag captain from the operations unit, who looked awful.

What now?

An encoded telegram.

In Helsingfors, Vice Admiral Nepenin had been killed by sailors!

It was like iron had been poured into his whole body and stopped him in his tracks.

He dragged his feet to his cabin and sank onto a chair.

Adrian!

Fellow admiral! . . .

How could he save the naval command?

How could he save the Black Sea Fleet? . . .

[4 3 9]

Spring always bursts out early in Rostov, with an uneasy spirit—as early as February. And now, coming down from the latitude of Minsk, Yaroslav was all the more struck by the blow of warmth and spring mixed with the smell of melting snow, horse manure, and the first buds. Despite the inner alarm he'd arrived with, this gentle blow came to him as the most desired, just what he'd been searching for!—and the most painful.

He had arrived on leave supposedly to see his mama, sister, and brother, but in fact he had come more to see Rostov itself than them. Because near its stones, in its alcoves and front doors, on its boulevards and in the low spot between Sadovaya and Pushkinskaya (and in every side street in its own way) something lingered, settled, like a light fog the morning sun hadn't dispersed: the insatiable secret of his youth. He had come to finally know this secret, to scoop it up with his hands, to whisper it over again. No matter where he had fought or passed through in this time, the secret—strangely— had remained specifically and only in this city. Nowhere else could his lonely meandering carry off and wrench his soul as here. Only from here, it turned out, could he trace it back and find it. Only here, from the pink of the sunrise, could it turn in blazing heat. That was how he was made.

He had no bride, no beloved waiting for him. But he carried a few tender and keen memories in his breast at once, and they swelled up in a rafter of hopes. None of them had been reinforced by fresh correspondence, but he imagined all these young girls in their former places and each ready to take up where they had left off with him.

So he took the streetcar past Krepostnoi Lane to Nakhichevan to see Lara—but it turned out she and her entire family had left. With great hope he sought out Toma on Turgenevskaya—and found her betrothed. One other tender old friendship—Nyusha Kocharmina—enticed him to take the early morning local to nearby Novocherkassk. But Nyusha was very much married, and Yarik naturally didn't go around to the new address. But he did meet her brother Vitali, who was graduating from high school and next year wanted to go to university in Rostov. A smart, fair-haired young man. Yarik invited him to stop by the Kharitonovs' when he was in Rostov.

He hadn't found anyone! But all the street corners, low spots, dead-ends, benches under acacias, now bare, shimmered in a way that told Yaroslav they remembered, they were still true, and they thanked him for returning.

On the streets small bouquets of violets and snowdrops were already being sold for someone. In this springtime awakening, the faces of young girls as marvelous as anywhere flashed by, so fresh and blooming.

It was inexplicable, but for some reason he had to search only in the footsteps of his youth.

One incident in the afternoon on Sadovaya struck Yarik. A soldier with a crutch and two George crosses and medals on his greatcoat, and the people parted before him. Suddenly he walked up to a lady exiting a store, saluted, and said something. The lady quickly took a banknote out of her handbag and gave it to him. Yarik stopped, stunned: a wounded St. George officer was asking for alms? Unheard of! But right then a civilian walked up to the soldier, took him by the arm, and began pulling him away, saying something. The soldier dug in his heels. Passersby began stopping and voices rang out: "Where are you taking him? . . . He's a hero! He shed his blood for us!" Another lady exclaimed that there was no living because of cops. The civilian, obviously a police agent, shouted that this wasn't a soldier at all but a swindler dressed as one. "We know him! He's not even a cripple!" A full-faced, clean-shaven gentleman in an expensive fur coat and cap: "Who is this 'we'?" And he demanded that the agent show identification. Standing at the sidewalk's edge with a wooden shovel was an old woman, who said to Yarik: "They killed my sonny boy, and this swine's horning in, making money by pulling at people's heartstrings." But the crowd was getting thicker, and several voices were shouting, and all at the agent. Yarik took a step to intervene, but right then the agent got out his whistle and gave a sharp blast. A husky policeman came running around the corner. The agent ripped the block of crosses off the swindler's greatcoat. The well-dressed crowd started dispersing and one could hear: "Oprichniks!"

The swindler's speculation was one thing, but this undisguised hatred for the police astonished Yarik.

Meanwhile, his mama, not admitting, not sensing that he was commander of a company, wholly wanted to take her foolish, stubborn little boy into the house, fearfully felt the scars from his shoulder and leg wounds, and imperiously demanded she have him by her side. The servants listened respectfully, as did Dmitri Ivanych, to his stories about the front, and even five-year-old Lyalka quieted down, though Yarik did not reveal the full picture to them so as not to frighten his mama. Did that world of his, those two and a half years, really fit into this unchanged apartment?

But his mama had a peacetime-style service jacket and bright blue officer's diagonal breeches sewn for him as a present, from his old measurements. Yarik turned out to have lost weight, so it was a little wide at the sides, but this wasn't the time for taking it in. He did want to show off a little around Rostov in his new jacket with the stitched braided epaulets, since he had just fabric ones for his active-service greatcoat and tunic. He took his greatcoat to have braids sewn on, too. And then his boots, lined with fur and smeared with grease, didn't go with the breeches—so he went (with Yurik) to buy fancy boots with stiff bootlegs.

Fourteen-year-old Yurik clung to his brother and asked him question after question. He was growing up not coddled but keen on everything military, a loyal sword-bearer. Right now he would be better off in the Cadet Corps instead of his modern high school; but this war wasn't going to last long enough for him.

But all his conversations with his brother and all the family ways were suddenly shaken up when the Petrograd revolution thundered and Rostov was strewn with flocks of news. And whatever was left that was his own, hidden, personal—all that spilled out, into the earth, curled up, while chests exploded to inhale and shout out, and throats shouted, faces shone, arms waved—and although the Rostov public was known for its extreme expression of both joy and abuse—right now even the accustomed Yarik was astonished.

Had this news reached him in his own regiment, he would have taken it sternly, perplexedly, and that was probably how it was there now. What was there to rejoice in here anyway? How could one do such a thing during time of war? It was impossible to imagine the officers of their battalion in their company dugouts, to say nothing of the soldiers, suddenly experiencing headspinning, maddened delight and hollering heart-rendingly that they had no more Tsar or Supreme Commander, but who knew what instead. Even when the regimental commander used to go on leave, fully in keeping with all regulations—even then the regiment constantly felt itself short. And now, this came right before the high point of the springtime battles . . .?

But his native Rostov was seething, no greater joy could have befallen this city, especially coinciding with spring—and Yarik had to experience this all here, and it turned out, this city had not for a moment stopped being dear to him. Just as joy involuntarily passes from a dear face to us, so it had begun to spin Yaroslav around, too.

And even more so because his family was around him! But his entire family—his mama, Zhenya, Dmitri Ivanych, and Yurik—were exulting around him in these very rooms.

Yarik swallowed his perplexity.

His mama had become so triumphant, her faded eyes seemed to recover some of their former blueness, and her rounded shoulders straightened up. She put her hand on Yarik's shoulder, looking up:

"It's a pity your papa isn't with us and can't rejoice. These are the happiest days of my life. I never thought I'd live to see the day! And you—here during these days! A special happiness!"

For two days, the Kharitonovs' high school was closed. Betraying her prim habit, Aglaida Fedoseevna had gone outside to celebrate—not onto her balcony, rather she had crossed Cathedral Square and gone as far as Moscow Street, and then all the way to Sadovaya, where she stood at the edge of the sidewalk, right up against the passing marches, and almost nodded, almost smiled—and there wasn't a person who didn't see and recognize her gray figure! Her former pupils came up to her from all sides and greeted and congratulated her.

And how Yurik and his fellow pupils were borne off in this exulting, and spun around and around! He ran to excited high school assemblies and joined in with choruses on the street and was intoxicated. A couple of times Yaroslav sullenly hinted that he didn't have to rejoice quite so much—but this didn't dampen his brother's soaring soul.

It was enough to make him start doubting his own notion and be amazed at how little effort, almost without blood, and how instantaneously the state system fell, a system that a week ago seemed eternal. Just a week ago the agent was dragging that swindler away, and now just try to take anyone away from the crowd! What was that system then worth, really worth? Had his mama truly always been right and Yaroslav been feeding on stardust?

Only when people got carried away and spoke rubbish— "Oh, all our military misfortunes were because of Tsarskoye Selo, and now things will go better"—would Yarik put them in their place, unembarrassed.

It wasn't just Yarik! In this city of 200,000, not a single malcontent, not a single opponent of the coup had come forward! There had once been "rightists" and they'd seemed strong—and suddenly they'd all vanished in a single day, as if blown away! Their newspaper and printing press was seized, and the Russian Club hurried to recognize the new government. There turned out not to be a single person in Rostov officialdom who was loyal to the Tsar! Never before would anyone have supposed such a thing. The entire police recognized the leadership of the Revolutionary Committee, and in the meantime two hundred criminals managed to escape prison and scatter throughout the city. And now, welcoming the revolution, the garrison marched in formation, the units led by officers, and bands played the Marseillaise—while First Lieutenant Kharitonov stood among the public along the sidewalk's edge and was bewildered as to how to understand it. Soldiers and university students were embracing. They were starting to tear down coats of arms and two-headed eagles. Nor was there any salvation from the Marseillaise in the theaters, where they played it before all the performances.

The Nakhichevan Armenians were behaving with much more propriety and restraint than the Rostovans; there was no such general embracing and kissing on the streets, and they are a passionate people. They displayed a circumspection the Rostovans had totally lost.

But even in Novocherkassk, in that most faithful of cities, opponents of the coup didn't so much as poke their heads out, and university students and intellectuals exulted just like the ones in Rostov.

No, something was wrong. He told his mama that he had to get to his regiment. It was time to be in place. His mama was imperious, but she wasn't one of those fussy mothers. She may have been hurt, but she didn't show it. Or try to talk him out of it. But another day or two with us?

It was time to get to his regiment, but Yarik's entire visit to Rostov, derailed by that sludgy revolution, had proved quite unsuccessful at its core. His native stones had deceived him, and he had begun to languish. He had to go some different way.

Now he thought, on the return journey, he'd stop off in Moscow. Moscow places were dear to him, too, three years of military school. He had memories there as well.

Because death always lay ahead, he still wanted to see all the old familiar things.

And Oksana was there, after all, the Pecheneg girl.

All of a sudden he pictured that white-toothed Pecheneg girl with the soft shoulders—and his heart started pounding.

Pounding in a new way. But he didn't let on.

[4 4 0]

It was enough for Sasha to show up just once at the Tauride Palace and ask who there had called for "Socialist officers"—and it all became clear. He was taken to see Lieutenant Filippovsky, a navy man, who immediately recognized him.

"Where on earth have you been? You went missing!"

Sasha was surprised to learn that he was far from a grain of sand lost in Petrograd but someone very much noticed by important people. Above all, he was an "officer of the 12 March revolution," such as could be counted on one's fingers, and Filippovsky had not forgotten that Lenartovich had taken the Mariinsky Palace. And then, as he himself now declared, he was a "Socialist officer," which was also a great rarity, there being just a handful of such. So he was badly needed here, and it was an error on his part to have left the Tauride Palace and not shown his face here for several days.

It was a mistake, him getting stuck in that Petersburg side commissariat and plunging there into sentry shifts, rescuing storehouses, breaking up fights, and catching robbers conducting searches without permission—and now he would have been clearing away overturned poles and streetlamps and helping the streetcar. His business was not there, of course (yesterday he realized it and promptly resigned), but right here.

Many many thousands of officers were showing off in Russia—arrogant, rude, foolish, menacing—but were there many socialists among them?

Right now, this proud mass (in which Sasha had been choking for several years) was shaken, churning like a herd, cringing, pretending in front of the mutinous people, signing degrading documents, but naturally the soldier mass didn't believe them—and they were right! Could this old officer class really exist without a Tsar?

The army couldn't get along without officers, though, and who should be chosen first to bring along this revolutionary officer class if not the socialists? Just as Socialist lawyers had been called to the new magistrate courts, so, too, Socialist officers had to rally a sincere revolutionary officer class. Career officers were going to be pushed out and even swept away, while even rank-and-file were going to soar up, as in any revolution, as common stablemen became generals in the Great French Revolution.

Filippovsky explained all this to him, and Sasha took it in joyfully, took it in and moved to act. There were neither enough "officers of the 12 March revolution" for notable actions, nor enough officer-socialists (which was how Ensign Znamensky, head of the captive former ministers' guard, ended up here). But here was the goal: to split the officer class and from its entire sinister, monarchical, secretly hostile mass separate out at least a few who were consciously in favor of a republic and prepared to say so out loud. Once they had said so out loud, they were already cut off from the rest, and those who remained would feel they were doomed behind a fateful line.

And so? They would launch a Union of Officer-Republicans, an open union. But if a sign-up is simply announced, all kinds of secret monarchist swine are going to push forward and adapt to the new circumstances.

Here's how to do it: founding members can only be officers of the 12 March revolution and no one else. For all others joining, it's not enough to approve the republican program. They also have to present a recommendation from two current Union members. And preferably also a reference from lower ranks in the unit where they serve.

And the wheels began to turn! It fell largely to Sasha to write a communiqué, submit it to the newspapers, make a couple of trips to the Hall of the Army and Navy, and finally to assemble—today—a general members' meeting and approve the Union's general provisions.

Unfortunately, just twenty or so gathered in the Tauride Palace. Oh well, for starters. Conditions for acceptance were tough. All the better.

An energetic Filippovsky presided. He would also be the Union's representative on the Soviet's Executive Committee. And he assured the officer-republicans of the good will toward them from the Soviet of Workers' Deputies, which would in turn delegate several soldiers and workers to the Union.

Soldiers and workers? Joining us? Some frowned, but Sasha fully understood. Exactly right! This is the time. If you're going to join ranks with the people, then join ranks!

And so, the Union's goal?

Sasha proposed "to continue and deepen the revolution!"

That scared some.

"But the victory over Tsarism is far from assured, isn't it?" he sought out understanding people.

They decided their goal was to establish a democratic republic. Propaganda in the army of republican views.

Many gave looks suggesting that's not enough. Sasha proposed:

"To organize the army on democratic principles. To assist in this."

That's where things were going. Anyone who didn't like it—the process couldn't be stemmed anyway.

You couldn't limit yourself to opinions alone. Revolution demanded action—swift action. What would the army's thorough democratization yield? The army would go from being Tsarist and class-based to a genuine people's army. (Eventually Sasha's idea passed, but in other words: to continue the revolution.)

They decided to put out their own newspaper. And call it *The People's Army*. As editor-in-chief they named Maslovsky. (He had sat there, in the presidium, as the most senior and most sophisticated, but for some reason was sour and morose.)

But then—did they need their own journalists?

Although he knew how to use a weapon, Sasha had been born able to wield a pen, too, and probably no worse than Matvei Ryss.

Whatever people whispered, we're going to prove that unity between the army and the laboring masses cannot weaken the army's military might.

Sasha didn't have his own company or subordinates, and he honestly couldn't imagine what was going on in the barracks.

[4 4 1]

Meanwhile, the monster kept growing! It was already well past fifteen hundred people! (And two out of three were soldiers, so that worker black was lost in greatcoat gray.) When they had been starting to throng in, the entire Tauride Palace trembled. And the White Hall was bursting. That hall had already collapsed once, so how to avoid a second time? The Executive Committee could work with this Soviet less and less and was beginning to fear it greatly, a completely unmanageable body. The imprudent norm of the first few days—one deputy per company—had to be rescinded so there wouldn't be this soldier advantage, but how? How could anyone bring himself to say it? They could simply be swept away along with the Executive Committee.

They had met yesterday from noon until late in the night, first the soldiers separately, then together with the workers, and over the entire day had managed to discuss almost nothing other than relations with officers, which was the one thing that bothered the soldiers—and they didn't even lead these relations to any result, it was just that Order No. 1 had become constraining for them, they couldn't decide whether to choose new officers for themselves by voting or keep those they had. All the rest of their ungainly agenda—if you could call it that—they tabled to today.

By now another dangerous question was coming to a head: about resumption of work in the plants. The Executive Committee had met about this today at noon and listened to Gvozdev's urgings, and listened, of course, to the Bolsheviks' objections. The thought of taking this question before the worker mass was frightening, but it could not be put off. So they came to a decision. Send as chairman to the Soviet the fearless Sokolov, who doesn't know better, and as speaker throw in the respected Chkheidze, whose name was known, after all, and every day he was heard from the front steps, he would be accepted, and then let it all come raining down on his old head.

The fact that yesterday's agenda remained was even better. Let all their zeal be spent on something else, and let the resumption of work be pushed toward the weary end.

The monster's stamping, shouting, howling, and applause could already be heard from the White Hall.

This hall! Which had seen all the ten years of Duma battles, revelations, inquiries, and passionate, and subtly caustic, and crudely breaching, and coldly boring speeches, and exchanges of curses, and obstructions, and expulsions for fifteen sessions, and Muromtsev's plump, swanlike figure, and the cast sculpture of Stolypin, and the weak-voiced Goremykin, the relaxed, ingratiating Stürmer, the puzzled Golitsyn (only not once the Emperor himself, just his portrait, immobile until the past few days, and now nothing but dangling shreds around the edges and the crown over the empty frame)—this hall, where for ten years intellectuals and gentlemen had shouted that Russia didn't hear, did hear, would hear them, this hall where the Social Democratic group had been so weak and insignificant—was now filled to bursting with a genuine, somber popular crowd, and on the rocky Rodzyanko rostrum made of carved oak it was all Social Democrats, and that tragicomic Chkheidze, who united the two halls, the former and the present, who had called for giving the street a channel—and who was now in a persistent state of happy exhaustion that he had lived to see these days.

What pressure from the street! All the amphitheater-style deputy seats, all the stepped aisles between them, all the columnar galleries for the public, all the railed loges—for the Council of Ministers, State Council, and journalists—and all the aisles leading to the tribune, and the final space near the eight flung-open doors, and in the doorways, and outside the doors—soldiers, soldiers, soldiers (rarely with rifles now), and workers sitting and standing. Everyone in caps, shaggy tall fur hats, fur caps with flaps, greatcoats, pea jackets, and tunics, and the cloud of cheap tobacco smoke filling the hall space, to the glass ceiling (and the butts thrown under the deputy desks). Even the most uneducated here understood that this grand, white stone hall filled by a light from the ceiling that he could never usually get to see—it had not been built for us bumpkins, after all—and now here he was assembling in this very place, smoking his tobacco importantly and listening to whatever was coming from up above.

They kept climbing up there, like for an assault—this one with a greeting to the Soviet of Deputies, that one with a greeting to the Soviet of Deputies, and that one from Moscow, to say how things were going there, and that one from a distant regiment, how things were going for them. You listen and can't get your fill. So an-teresting!

But they also remembered and climbed up with another concern, more important: a *funeral for the martyrs*! Stray bullets had flown around Petersburg, after all, and a certain number had struck, and killed a number on the spot. Where were we going to put them, our best heroes?

They climbed up and argued: on the very square by the royal palace, so the memory is eternal of how we overpowered the Tsar. There was no more prominent spot in Petersburg. But what about the pavement there? And the column? Excavate the pavement, leave the pillar to the side, and strew the square with precious holy graves.

". . . As a symbol of the downfall of the Romanov hydra!"

Hurrah! Hurrah! And the blackbearded man high up directed with gestures, content.

But others climbed up: No! Better we dig up the Field of Mars.

". . . On the Field of Mars, comrades, right next to the martyrs' graves we'll erect according to all the rules the hugest building for the Russian parliament. Columns will shine there, and a telegraph office, and it will be the center for Russia's administration!"

No! No! We want it by the palace!

And prepare the funeral this very week (or else the frosts will ease up and the bodies won't keep). Until that time, the factories and plants must remain idle, out of respect.

Right then, some woman, already getting on in years, was led, squeezed through the crowd—and up she went. And not one bit embarrassed or lowering her eyes, she looked in all directions. And the black beard announced that this was also a great moment because here before the workers and soldiers deputies was ". . . our holy revolutionary! A woman, a fighter, and a martyr! She's come from exile! Each of us has known and honored her name well since our youngest years! Vera! Ivanovna! Zasulich!"

This was so heartfelt, how could they not respond? The hall bellowed, clapped, stamped.

". . . our prowletarians have been patiently awaiting her return to us!"

A prowletarian—that's someone prowling around without a kopeck to his name.

In this way the pressed crowd gradually let off steam and then let off more. Picking up on the drop in strength in the hall and the weariness, Sokolov, with a dignity no less than Zasulich's, brought up to take his place on the rostrum the chairman of the Soviet of Workers' Deputies, a man beloved by the entire proletariat, Nikolai Semyonovich Chkheidze.

Nikolai Semyonovich may have been delivering his hundredth speech of the past few days, but each one was delivered with renewed emotion. Not because he had been put up to it by his Executive Committee comrades, or because it was the most burning question, or because he had to be diplomatic and couldn't stir up the masses' fury, but because no matter how many times you entered that hall, your heart hammered, your eyes glittered at the way Markov the 2nd abused the Social Democrats here; no matter how many times you went up on this tribune—and dancing before your eyes were morning coats, long ties, bow ties, and starched collars, and you were given only an hour to tell them the worker truth straight to their faces—but now our happy, unlimited time had come! And all this was churning, boiling over in his chest, and skipping out of his throat in some sound or other, but everyone understood. . . .

Comrades! Comrades. . . . And now what? We have vanquished the enemy! Have we vanquished the enemy? Have we toppled him for good and can we now go to work calmly, without fear of an attack? Oh no, we can't. Not for a long time! Because at the present time we are waging a *civil war*! And there can be no question of working calmly. But comrades, here we decided a day ago that we have to resume gas mask manufacture. After all, our comrades are sitting in the trenches and could die from gas despite the glorious revolution. And now the Executive Committee has come to the conclusion that other work should resume, too. But how? Naturally, while standing at the workbench, being on guard every moment and prepared every moment to go out on the street and show our strength. Nevertheless, we can also say that we've sufficiently put down our most evil enemy. We did this! Starting from the position we occupy outside the plants, we can now go back into the plants—but, I repeat, with the determination to come out on the street again at the first signal. This is what the political moment calls for us to do, comrades. Yesterday we couldn't have done this. But now the enemy is well enough disarmed, well enough prostrate, that there's no danger whatsoever in us going to work and standing at a workbench. This is what the military situation calls for. But most important for us, of course, is organization. In recent times, I must confess, we were working in the plants and factories without sufficient organization. This, comrades, was justified by our impulse for freedom under the unbearable Tsarist regime. But, comrades, at the present time this simply cannot be allowed. Therefore, you must not only engage in your trade at your workbench but—organize intensively! . . . On what terms, comrades, can we work again? It would be ridiculous if we went back to work on the old terms! And let this be known by the bourgeoisie, which found such support in the old government! No sooner will we get to work than, yes, then and there, we will begin to draw up the terms on which we work! But we must get to work, comrades, because there is also the matter that the former regime, which controlled Russia's destiny, brought the economy to a state of total disorganization.

Thus, in his raspy but sincere sing-song, Chkheidze vindicated the EC's hopes—and the assembly did not go wild or rise up, did not rumble with objections.

Right then they brought up to speak a typesetter, three soldiers, and one worker, who were all in favor, and from the Executive Committee Yermansky and Pumpyansky—and they all argued that the comrade workers must go back to work.

True, Bolsheviks and Interdistrict men got up there, too, and said that having suffered a defeat in the EC, they were now trying to turn the entire assembly around, and Sokolov wasn't the chairman to want or be able to stop them.

Their arguments were powerful: Nikolai II was still at liberty. And the revolution had been altogether suspiciously bloodless. The Provisional Government had been too easy on its enemies. And the distribution of land had yet to be decided. And the worker question had been skirted altogether, here no one was talking about the eight-hour day. And there were plants unwilling to go back to work!

But the Executive Committee had calculated correctly that the assembly from the very beginning had dissipated the bulk of its energy on funerals for martyrs and on Vera Zasulich. And now everyone was hungry; it was time for dinner. The point about the gas masks seemed clear enough. The soldier advantage in the hall decided the matter: they weren't the ones going back to their workbenches.

And the Bolshevik orators did not turn the hall around. When the resolution readied by the EC was taken up to the tribune and read aloud once, it was stipulated that those workers engaged in *direct organizational work* (all deputies sitting here, and those who had found work in the militia or some new position) would not go back—well, that suited them just fine! They voted, and however many they counted, more than a thousand, they were all in favor, with only thirty or so against.

Later, when dispersing, they asked each other what they'd decided and when were they to go back. Surely not tomorrow straightaway, as of Monday? How were we going to tell our people this? In the past ten days they'd gotten out of the habit, you weren't going to round them up. So if workers went back, then were the soldiers going to training?

Oh what clever fellows! They want us back to work tomorrow! Couldn't we have just a little more . . .

* * *

ONCE YOU'RE ON A SPREE—YOU DON'T COUNT THE DAYS

* * *

[4 4 2]

Late the previous day, Peshekhonov had been riding in a motorcar down Bolshoi Prospect when he came upon a huge crowd clamoring and shrieking as it moved from Kamennoostrovsky. Aleksei Vasilich stopped the motorcar and ran toward them. What was this?

The crowd was mainly female and terribly jubilant, waving their arms but not threatening anyone. This turned out to be domestic servants, cooks, maids, and laundresses, who had spilled out from a general rally and were tearing down the street, feeling unprecedentedly strong and in charge!

Could one do anything but rejoice at the awakening of such feelings? (The crowd had been joined by men, too, passersby—and at the tail-end Peshekhonov noticed that proud rider draped in ribbons from the first few days, who was now weaving behind the servants looking pathetic and tipsy.)

But Peshekhonov arrived at the commissariat to more news: all over the Petersburg side, someone's proclamations were being distributed inviting all the people to Nevsky on Sunday for a demonstration.

Why this now? Large crowds with an undisclosed aspiration raised the alarm in him because they could go on a rampage.

He got in touch with the Soviet of Workers' Deputies, who replied that this was a provocation. Ask citizens to refrain from the obviously counterrevolutionary demonstration.

That's how the rumors got started, that this was counterrevolutionaries intentionally inciting the people, but tomorrow they'd start getting plugged by hidden machine guns.

It was too late to print and paste up their own dissuading announcements on the streets, though, and besides, Peshekhonov didn't believe in any counterrevolution and attached no importance to the rumors and hoped the demonstration would not come to pass.

But today (Sunday or no, the commissariat was seething as always) at about eleven o'clock in the morning, it was reported that an enormous crowd was moving from Novaya Derevnya down Kamennoostrovsky, more than ten thousand, and it kept growing as it went—and it was obviously thronging to Nevsky.

So that's how it was! He had taken no precautionary measures—and now here they were thronging—and what could he do? There was no way to stop them! He wasn't going to let weapons be used, after all! Not that there was such a detachment, to bar their way.

The crowd kept coming closer, it was coming even right now, watch out—it would sweep away the commissariat.

They sat and waited in dread.

But for some reason it didn't come. Where had it gone? They sent out a scout—it turned out to have turned into the Sports Palace.

What should be done? He had to hurry there or else they'd smash the Sports Palace, too.

Peshekhonov headed off with two or three others. He somehow had never once been afraid for himself; he was only afraid of torpedoing the commissariat's work.

Whether ten thousand or not, it was a great many. And a rally. Now this was good. If there was a rally under way, they weren't going to smash the palace.

Some were applauding, others whistling.

The speakers were seated at a table. They jostled their way there, found a place for Aleksei Vasilievich, and he climbed up.

He was recognized from various places and met with applause. Peshekhonov honored them as a "popular assembly," welcomed them on behalf of the commissariat, congratulated them on their newly won freedom and that, with their freedom of assembly and speech, they were now putting it into practice. He stated that the revolutionary authority stood on guard for this freedom and would not let anyone violate it, that the commissariat was happy to protect this multitudinous assembly. He also asked the citizens for their part not to violate anyone else's freedom, to patiently hear out the speakers, and to give thought to each speech because the situation facing them could not be more difficult.

All went well, they applauded a little more, and Peshekhonov climbed down from the table.

But before they could get outside, they heard agitated shouts in the crowd. What was this? Someone had suspected the person next to him was a plain-clothes cop—and now several had latched onto this man and wanted to tear him apart, and the entire crowd was pushing that way.

His colleague whispered to Peshekhonov: "Arrest him." A fortuitous idea! They started shouting, parting the crowd, and pushing to the center of the scuffle.

Peshekhonov ominously arrested the suspected man and appointed the strongest loudmouths as convoy guards—to take the "plainclothesman" to the commissariat. And the person who identified him should come with them.

The assembly calmed down and the rally continued.

At the commissariat they questioned all the witnesses, and it turned out no one knew this man or could prove anything.

They let the witnesses go and half an hour later the "plainclothesman."

The rally went on all day until late in the evening, but now without any fisticuffs.

[4 4 3]

How pleasant to enjoy the confidential services of a count! One always eats deliciously, aristocratically (the count's kitchen, mobile, in an auxiliary room of the Ministry of Justice, and the count's wine cellar). And in gen-

eral, to push back the bounds of life and learn about layers heretofore unknown, merely dreamed of.

He is most amenable, the splendid Count Orlov-Davydov! And very rich
to boot. Aleksandr Fyodorich convinced him to give a generous sum to the
Soviet of Workers' Deputies. (They have to be given something to mollify
them, since they are clattering their teeth at Kerensky.)

There were many places in Petersburg previously in no way accessible to
Kerensky—and now they were flinging their doors open! One such place
was the Senate! Another, the Winter Palace!

Aleksandr Fyodorich decided to swoop past both today, Sunday. (He had
also had time early this morning to order Vyrubova arrested.) But he had
not gotten dressed up for that, so he went in his black, Austrian-style jacket,
sort of like a service jacket, somewhat worn, and with a fully buttoned,
standing collar (this, too, procured by the count). No one wore it that way,
he didn't look like anyone, a unique attire—both democratic and revolu-
tionarily expressive. And he didn't have to change starched collars three
times a day because the collar couldn't be seen.

Before, you had to be a respected and elderly lawyer to aspire to the right
to enter a session of a Senate department or section, but here he was, a
young lawyer, and he just scheduled this over the telephone, and despite it
being Sunday, all the senior members of the Senate had assembled in the
large hall and, upon Kerensky's impulsive, quivering entrance, they'd stood
up! (This morning the apprehensive count had asked, "But what if they
don't recognize you?" "Then we won't recognize them!")

One of the Senate's functions was to register and make public all the
laws issued by anyone, which became law only as of that publication. Thus,
the Tsars' abdication manifestos put out yesterday morning in fact still
meant nothing and were not laws at all until they passed the Senate. (So the
senators must surely have been astonished all day yesterday.)

But probably never, not since Peter created the Senate, had laws ever
been submitted to it by a minister personally. A courier brought it in an
envelope, then the secretary registered the law's title in the log-book, which
meant "Heard. Resolved to publish," and sent the envelope on to the
printers'. No, never had the Senate had occasion to see a minister riding
in with a law!

But, then, never had there been such a dazzling, charming, and legendary minister!

But never had there been such a fateful event in the Russian Empire as
an abdication from the throne—not only of the Tsar but of all his possible
heirs at once!

An event worth his coming!

And his coming was worth the entire First Department assembling in
the large hall around the table in a horseshoe. And in front of the table were
two thrones: an old chair dating from Paul I, and a small chair for the heir.

The Emperor himself was considered to be presiding in the First Department, and as a sign of this, every session opened standing.

But Kerensky did not know that; no one had explained it to him. He entered with his swift, springy step (followed by two ensigns armed to the teeth) and saw twenty senators in embroidery, galloons, and insignia respectfully greeting him in a horseshoe. Kerensky found it wholly natural that these elder statesmen were standing. But since they remained standing even when he came up to the thrones and surveyed them, then he finally coughed:

"Well, gentlemen. . . . Perhaps you would care to sit down?"

The elders sat down, reluctantly, it seemed. And Kerensky discovered near the throne a tall reading-stand, which he walked behind, and he delivered a brief but quite significant speech. (He now could give speeches at the drop of a hat.) He talked about the Manifestos' significance and the Senate's significance—and suggested they preserve it for all time, so now the responsibility for their preservation would lie permanently on the Senate.

He extended a light arm toward one of the ensigns, and the packet flew into his hand. With his other hand, the minister beckoned, invited a senator to . . . .

And one senior statesman accepted the packet, took out the precious Manifestos, unfolded them—and everyone again stood, so the minister in the black service coat could not sit either. And the historic texts were read out in a cracking voice. Tilting his smart, crewcut head to the side in approval, the minister assigned himself the job of patiently listening to it, too; he felt he was starting to know these texts by heart.

Then there was a question from the senior elder statesman: who was opposed to publication?

And all of a sudden Kerensky had a flash of inspiration:

"One moment, gentlemen, one moment! I'll go out so as not to constrain you."

And sliding over the parquet, with satisfaction, swinging his arms powerfully, he went out the door, his ensigns following.

But before five minutes had passed—four, more likely—he was invited back. Still standing in a horseshoe, they reported to him that the First Department had no objections.

And Kerensky was even more favorably disposed to these elders. Not wishing now to leave them in their timid state and aspiring for them to like him even more—he was in a mood and condition for everyone on earth to like him—he said:

"I thank you, senators, sirs! This is all I came for. I also want to tell you that I'm no Marat from the justice department, as urban rumors are going around about me, rather I want the Senate to be a genuine Senate. Please, work under me as well. Follow your conscience, freely, as you see fit, without second thoughts or paying any attention to what outsiders want."

He thought. So gloriously said. For some reason he liked it here very much. What else could he talk about?

"Yes!" He remembered. "You will also be receiving a decree soon. . . . I am instituting an Extraordinary Commission of Inquiry to investigate illegal actions by high-level officials—former ministers, top dignitaries, and per-haps"—for some reason he slipped, not checking himself, something that happened with him—"senators? . . . And on this point, gentlemen"—his voice sounded more ringing, even younger—"here I must warn you that I shall be merciless! That is"—he corrected himself—"there will be a fair trial against the accused."

And what a nightmarish scene would unfold before the investigators!

They may have shuddered, but they still stood just as nicely and listened (there was still no occasion for sitting) and even looked with ecstatic tears (when had they seen such a young, effective, ebullient minister?)—Keren-sky actually liked these old men and felt like saying something more to them. He looked around to see whether there was a portrait of the abdi-cated Emperor still hanging—but there wasn't, and they had obviously re-placed the thrones.

"These thrones, yes . . ." Kerensky determined, and himself caught regret in his own voice, for some reason—"the thrones will have to be removed."

In his own ministry, yesterday, instructions had been given to take to the attic all the direct and indirect portraits, while department officials were prohibited from wearing any insignia or ribbons earned under the old regime. It would be a pity to take away the old senators' toys, though; they looked so imposing on them. He left out the part about insignia.

He could also, of course, have told them that he was readying a politi-cal amnesty, and about how successfully the arrests of dignitaries were going, according to plan, starting with Shcheglovitov, and that he had closed the case on Rasputin's murder and ordered the exiled Prince Yusu-pov and Dmitri Pavlovich be informed that there were no obstacles to their return. . . .

But in the minute the minister took to think, the elders undertook their own action, which they had prepared in advance. Tall, imposing Senator Vratsky with his apoplectically red face stepped forward and began reading out in a new tremolo what was apparently a Senate resolution: The Senate offers its most profound gratitude to the Provisional Government for its al-most bloodless establishment of domestic peace and for its swift restoration of law and order in our precious fatherland.

So they had joined the whole people in rejoicing at the coup? Splendid!

Good, good, Kerensky directed tiny quick nods at them in different direc-tions, good, he accepted this for the entire Provisional Government. In the past few days he had already felt that he meant more than an individual min-ister and even than part of the government and even in individual instances was almost the entire government put together. (Which was why he no longer felt the need to go to all their meetings.) He exclaimed:

"Gentlemen! I consider it my duty to convey your statement to the Provisional Government. I am happy that it has been my lot to submit documents of utmost state importance—to this institution created by the genius of our great Peter!"

Taking off! Soaring! Flying! That was what Aleksandr Fyodorovich had been experiencing all these days and every hour. Here he was already riding-flying to the Winter Palace, having taken along a familiar liberal senator, Zavadsky, whom he had decided to include on the Extraordinary Commission.

The Winter Palace! For some reason he had always had a mad desire to go there! How it grated on his nerves, standing in the very center of the city, and you ride by it so many times—but what's inside?

In the back seat of the motorcar, he got to talking with the senator—and was greatly surprised to learn for the first time that the Winter Palace was not the Emperor's personal property, as were, for example, the Anichkov and Tsarskoye Selo palaces, but was merely presented to the reigning Emperor for his use. This only eased now the formal seizure of the palace under the authority of the Provisional Government! (The senator commented that the Emperor's abdication did not necessarily mean his rejection of his private property rights, so that, for example, the Anichkov . . .)

Right then, the motorcar stopped all of a sudden, and the soldier sitting next to the driver went off somewhere.

"What's this?" Aleksandr Fyodorovich was stunned.

The driver replied that the soldier had told him to wait while he bought a newspaper.

Aleksandr Fyodorovich felt his face flush with heat in front of the senator.

"What an outrage!" he exclaimed delicately. "Drive on immediately. Let him go on foot!"

The driver set off uncertainly. And Kerensky quickly regretted it. What if this soldier was from the Soviet of Deputies or had connections there? He might say something malicious, and that would reflect on the minister's reputation.

"Fine, then, we'll wait a minute"—and he stopped the driver.

And indeed, the soldier returned with a newspaper and started reading it in the front seat. Off they went.

The Winter Palace! What a special feeling—to enter it with absolute power, through its main entrance, of course, from the embankment! What an incredible marble staircase, two split flights meeting at the top, and with marble vases on the balustrade.

Hurrying toward him were the forewarned palace footmen (or major-domos, perhaps?), hurrying with great pomp, as if they themselves were the most junior ministers, knowing their own value and that of the palace being presented; however, to the newly arrived young man:

"Your Excellency!

"Oh, no! No!" Kerensky protested. "Simply 'minister.'"

How the space soared to the ceiling—like the sky! The height of fifteen men? Twenty? Decorative windows, lancet vaults, intertwined sculptures right below the ceiling, and below them, crowning the staircase, polished, dark granite columns beckoned the high-level visitor.

Here's what: the minister ordered the entire palace staff assembled—in the Throne Room! (He knew there was such a thing.) But for now—up! Deeper! Farther! An inspection! On wings!

Oh, what a pleasure to pass with authority through these deserted, luxurious halls with their gleaming floors, past walls hung with old paintings in ponderous frames, a gallery of historic generals, and in the corners, carved furniture, and overhead, figured chandeliers.

It would be positively bizarre to bring 600–700 badly raised members of the Constituent Assembly here. No!

"Tell me, where is the Malachite Room here?"

The pompous, formally dressed footmen led him on and on, and the senator kept apace, as did the minister's attendant.

Kerensky rushed forward, as if conquering these lacquered expanses. That was what this palace was for—to be lived in, inhabited! How suitable it was! And how historically and magnificently so!

"And where was Aleksandr III's bedroom?"

Aleksandr Fyodorovich thought that in the future he would definitely have to arrange to live here for a while. The royal family would not set foot here again.

He remembered Himmer's prediction to him yesterday: "In two months we will have a Kerensky government."

Only in two months?

They swept through—and popped into another suite of rooms completely taken up by an infirmary. Well, this was a familiar business—medicinal smells, bandages, patients, cots, spittoon bowls. But he was already there, so he told a handful of medical personnel nearby to gather and delivered a speech to them: No one need fear anything!

A prostrate wounded man called him over. Kerensky democratically approached. The man whispered in complaint that this week the soup hadn't tasted good.

Later, later! About face and back!

"To the Throne Room! . . . And where do you keep the crown and scepter?"

The numerous palace servants had already assembled in the grand, murky hall—clustered together, but at a distance from the throne.

Kerensky went up two steps of the throne (no higher) and from there announced:

"Gentlemen! From now on, this palace has become national property, and you are state employees. I've been told that you're worried about taunts and threats from the people. Have no fear! The Great Bloodless Revolution has come about for our universal good! . . ."

[4 4 4]

The madhouse began with Petrograd, but now all warring Russia was becoming a madhouse, too. No more Baltic Fleet! The Northern Army Group had begun to fall apart: Ruzsky was no longer master in Pskov itself, and for everything he had only telegrams to Alekseev. Now it had already started to reach Brusilov, who now sent a telegram asking to stop the printing of candid telegrams about how admirals, generals, and officers were being killed. Brusilov, like Evert, already had self-appointed armed "delegations" running the show in the rear, arresting military officials and inciting soldiers to choose new ones. In Mogilev itself, they had removed the governor, changed the administration, appointed provincial and district commissars, and taken down the old portraits of Paul I, Catherine II, and Aleksandr I in the city duma, and here and there through the city agitated gatherings popped up, especially of the Jewish populace. In Mogilev, the St. George Battalion returned with Ivanov, but his arrival made the town not calmer but more agitated. Early this morning, he had passed down Dneprovsky Prospect and through Governor's Square accompanied by music—and strode on through the town. Behind him came an electrician detachment with a red flag, and behind that a headquarters one—with red scraps! A crowd gathered and headed for the municipal prison "to free politicals"—but it turned out that only three had been held there and they had been released the day before yesterday. People congregated on Haymarket Square—"the revolution will be announced there." Did they really have to announce something?

General Alekseev had been vacillating since morning about whether to go to Mass at the headquarters church and then left off this intention—and saw no other solution than to order a general formation of the Mogilev garrison in two hours to give an explanation of events. The order was sent out. He scheduled it for Haymarket Square, so as not to offend the Emperor with the sight out his windows and set the routes of the marches so as not to cross Governor's Square. The decision was correct. This way Alekseev averted an illegal gathering, legitimized it. He went there by motorcar with staff officers. The military formation was quite proper. A crowd gathered around as well. Convoy guards as well as the soldiers of His Personal Railway Regiment were wearing the imperial monogram. The duty general read out both Manifestos and Nikolai Nikolaevich's order for the army. The soldiers shouted hurrah. From the balcony of the public building, straining his throat, Alekseev exhorted:

"Soldiers! Here we have an overthrow that has come about by Divine will. I'm calling on you to serve the new government honestly and loyally. Do not forget that we face a terrible enemy. Any army is strong if it is unified. We must prosecute the war to a victorious conclusion!"

Then there were speeches from the city duma—about the moment's significance and the need to maintain calm. So that it all went quite decently. No, GHQ was still a calm place. No one here had been disarmed yet, and there had been no attacks or intrusions.

After the parade, though, the head of His Majesty's convoy, Count Grabbe, appeared before Alekseev with a sensible request: to have the convoy remove its imperial monogram and be renamed the "Convoy of the Supreme Commander's Headquarters."

This was right. There was no reason to keep the monogram now.

Alekseev, too, would have to scrape it off his own adjutant general epaulets. . . .

The abdicated Emperor had absolutely no idea of how the situation had changed in these past few days. How it was changing every hour. He understood nothing if yesterday he could babble about taking back his abdication! . . .

His big, sad, reproachful eyes looked so trustingly, it was heartbreaking. While he was Emperor, his eyes had never looked like that, so defenseless. This had only now been revealed.

Even less did the Emperor understand how he was constraining GHQ by staying here. Yesterday, he had come to the quartermaster department twice, and everyone—the revolutionary elements in headquarters itself, especially the lower ranks—had seen. So to forestall the Emperor's possible arrival and not offend, Alekseev today had sent him a copy of the reports on the military situation. And in order to advance his departure, Alekseev repeatedly telegraphed Lvov and Rodzyanko asking them to speed up the review of the abdicated emperor's requests and to order government representatives to accompany his trains to their destination.

As Alekseev understood it, the former emperor could no longer travel on his own, without oversight.

General Alekseev, who had never served without a direct superior, now found himself during these ominous days both alone and most senior. The Emperor had silently fallen away. Although a new government had formed, it was so elusive and volatile, he didn't know how to get it to do things. And the new Supreme Commander was sitting three thousand versts away, beyond the Caucasus ridge, and could neither have any sense of the situation here nor have the proper influence on it. Meanwhile, the commanders had just sent ominous reports and demanded the gangrene creeping into the army be halted.

What did Alekseev have left? His hands were tied; he couldn't deal with the gangrene. All he had left was to complain to someone by telegraph.

And so he did. This afternoon he had submitted to Guchkov a very stern telegram, which said that the government had to at last speak up and point out to all military ranks, the population, and local civil authorities the criminality of actions such as the arrest of military officials and the election of new officers by soldiers! The Ministry of War in its own published program had allowed the most ill-defined, dangerous point about the fullness of social rights for active duty soldiers. This point had to be either immediately eliminated or else clarified by a delimitation of soldier rights and duties. Alekseev simply howled to the Minister of War that he had to energetically rescue military discipline in the briefest time possible and until the war's end maintain the customary structure of service and relations.

The telegram went off—and got bogged down: hours passed and no reply.

Did the government actually want to prosecute the war? For it had done nothing to preserve the army.

A response came from Tiflis, but it offered no assistance. The grand duke ordered General Alekseev to announce in the most categorical terms to Lvov and Rodzyanko that he, the grand duke, was demanding that they make a categorical statement to the troops, otherwise he, the grand duke, would on no account vouch for the maintenance of discipline, the consequence of which would be the inevitable loss of the war.

The Supreme Commander also ordered him in his high name to announce to the troops that no such "delegations" had been sent by the government; they had all been sent by Russia's enemies.

There, far away, he could have no sense of how this would convince no one here.

And now six silent, responseless hours had passed—and Alekseev dashed off a new telegram to Lvov-Guchkov-Rodzyanko. Saying that certain elusive elements were creating soldier organizations in the Northern Army Group, and what we were seeing was an attempt by them to become masters in Pskov. If they were to prevent Russia's disgrace, the new government must at last assert its power and authority and immediately, definitively, and firmly say that no one dare touch the army. And the Minister of War must proclaim that the army's basic duty was to fight the foreign enemy, and no delegations whatsoever had the right to make changes in troop life regulations. The troops had to be saved from collapse by every power and means!

They were all in their places there and ready to respond as long as they were talking about securing ministerial posts. But once they did, they became deaf and dumb. What was going on at the front, from Sveaborg all the way to Kiev, should have made the government of a country at war quake, they should have been answering telegrams every ten minutes and gone to the telegraph every half-hour. But clogged up, stupefied Petrograd had no desire to understand or respond.

And three hours later, in the evening now, Alekseev sent a new telegram to the same threesome about the same thing: the army was careening toward total battle-unreadiness and there was the threat of losing the war. Any delay in sending the text of the new oath would lead to fatal disaster. The ferment in the army could be explained exclusively by the fact that for the mass of common folk the government's true attitude toward military officials remained unknown.

It was like banging his head against a wall. The government was silent.

But after Guchkov's warnings, General Alekseev could not bring himself to act boldly on his own by military means.

[4 4 5]

Where was that multitude of paths that open up in a vast, talented country for a talented man who has finally come to power? Such a burdened, humiliating position as befell Guchkov during his first few days as War and Naval Minister he could never have imagined, it could not have been gathered from any experience. People said that they'd been killing the best officers in Kronstadt and Helsingfors according to some sort of prepared *lists*—and had beheaded the fleet in the total absence of chaos! But Guchkov couldn't arrest, execute, or even punish, or even chide those killers, not even Nepenin's killer, but he could write for the Ministry of the Navy an order that the revolutionary rabble would agree to carry out: ". . . restore order everywhere in Russia. Obey your superiors, who, just as you, have recognized the overthrow brought about by the people . . ."

Today was Sunday—but what did that matter for anyone now? All the ministers were going to their ministries, and after three o'clock the entire government was supposed to convene. (How could he stay home? For the three hundredth time a looming unexplainedness, his wife's serious looks—to waste his nerves on that at such a moment, too! He had the idea of moving alone to the ministerial apartment at his official residence. It looked like a natural step: he had to be near the direct line.) So early that morning, Guchkov went to the residence.

Telegrams awaited him there. From Evert and Brusilov—about the arrests of military officials and unauthorized elections. From Mozdok: the ataman of the Terek Cossack forces had been removed. From Chita: the ataman of the Trans-Baikal forces had been removed, not by Cossacks but by some general citizens' committee. And in the 171st Infantry Division the soldiers had arrested the entire headquarters. Right here, too, nearby, in Sestroretsk: soldiers had arrested all the officers!

What should he do?

He would have willingly broken off with the Soviet of Deputies now! And started an open conflict with them. That would have been in his nature. More din, please! It was even easier for him that way.

But the entire government would then recoil, he could just see those cowards, and there were even ministers eager to ingratiate themselves with the Soviet.

And then, since the Petrograd military units had been seized by the Soviet, what might this kind of conflict lead to if not civil war? How could he venture to raise it when there was a foreign war under way?

He didn't have enough support in the army as a whole. Guchkov thought to send inquiries to GHQ and all the army groups asking how they had taken Order No. 114, sent out yesterday, and what their thoughts were. (For consideration when taking further steps.)

Right then it was reported that Lieutenant General Kornilov had come straight from the train station to see his minister.

Excellent! Call him in.

Short, precise, and with a front-line freshness—he doused even Guchkov with fresh hope. Dry, nothing extra in his figure, only what was for war and reconnaissance. A general famous throughout Russia, he had spent a year in Austrian captivity and had escaped in the greatcoat of an Austrian soldier, and his portrait had gone all over Russia. A somewhat common face, especially under that short, unpretentious haircut—he could have passed for a common sergeant, you would never take him for a general, he had nothing in common with that aristocratic blue blood that was identically hateful to ordinary soldiers, the Soviet, and Guchkov. There was something Kalmyk or Buryat in his face, his light olive skin, and his narrow eyes, a testing mistrust with verve—oh, yes, he would be excellent now in talking with the unbridled masses!

When a question doesn't yield to theoretical solution, maybe it can be solved by one personality?

Of course, don't go expecting any overall development or overall grasp of events from him. Or even a strategic outlook. But those kinds of operations were not part of his job. And his personal courage was beyond doubt. A faithful executor. A marvelous choice!

As master of the Military Commission, Guchkov now had every right to say (although it hadn't been his idea):

"Lavr Georgievich! It was I who nominated you. I hope very much . . ."

One George cross on his chest, one around his neck, he wore no other decorations. A sergeant mustache, with a curve not fixed in any way. Glowering and serious, and seemingly not at all flattered by his appointment to the District, he listened as to an assignment for local reconnaissance.

And this authentic military quality of his, without any intellectual airs, decisively confirmed for Guchkov that this was the kind of military fiber now lacking in the capital.

He explained the situation to him: the mood of the units, the agitation, Order No. 1, the officers' situation, the Soviet of Deputies, the obligation not to bring out the garrison. He would see it all for himself. And now, a way had to be found to restore discipline. To create a buttress for the Provisional Government without any external means and using this seething material. As for personal appointments and removals—unlimited authority to dismiss those unsuitable and appoint others, from the front even.

They agreed to meet tomorrow or the day after. And at that, Kornilov, not having smiled once, or relaxed, left for the General Staff.

But before he could leave, Guchkov was brought a tape just pasted to paper: a new telegram from Alekseev. Alekseev was asking him not to take up any reforms and to leave the customary system of service and relations in place. He was so upset that this ruptured the tone of an official military telegram. He insisted on energetic governmental measures to eradicate the contagion of troop disintegration—before that contagion spread wholly from the rear to the army in the field. The governmental program itself, the promise of social rights for soldiers during time of war, threatened ruinous clashes. Alekseev had simply written that they had to *save* military discipline.

Guchkov sat over this telegram—but had nothing to reply.

Was he supposed to struggle from the very first minute? Even yesterday, to completely **cancel** Order No. 1? . . .

But this wouldn't have yielded, wouldn't have affected anything. Alekseev could not imagine how entangled things had become here, in Petrograd. Alekseev couldn't want civil war for the sake of saving discipline, could he?

And so? Quit as minister in a crash of thunder on his third day?

What, then, of all his reforms, all his dreams? If people like him were going to leave, who would be left to steer Russia?

Meanwhile, he had to go to the afternoon government session; he was late as it was. Today, when he had fewer matters to attend to, he should go; another day he might not be able to.

Thus, having accomplished nothing definite after several hours at the residence, Guchkov rode toward Chernyshev Bridge, downcast.

They had already begun.

He sat at the oval of the large polished table where there was a seat; he didn't feel that he was sitting among his own. It had seemed that they were all making the same assault on power—but it turned out they were separate.

They were discussing something boring, actions for Nekrasov: creating under the Ministry of Roads and Railways a 15-man commission, paid for by the treasury, of course. . . . And creating a unified transportation department under the Ministry of Roads and Railways, also paid for, in order to better distribute freight.

How had they been distributing it all these years? . . .

The deuce knows. A dozen of the people's favorites were sitting and pottering around like children in a sandbox when the whole country and army had been shaken and every minute was precious if the state wasn't going to fall to pieces.

Milyukov wasn't there, of course, he wasn't a fool to be sitting there.

Prince Lvov, with his idiotic, unctuous smile, was running the meeting as something terribly pleasant. He tossed two telegrams to Guchkov across the table. From Nikolai Nikolaevich, to Lvov. Sitting beyond the Caucasus ridge, he promised to establish discipline throughout the army. And hoped that the government would put the plants back to work.

Such was the tone and such his understanding of the situation! Well, he was sitting beyond the ridge now—so let him sit there.

A second one, from today. Saying that all governmental wishes must go through GHQ, while he himself had issued categorical instructions, the better to . . .

No, this kind of turkey-cock as Supreme Commander did not suit Guchkov at all.

Meanwhile, Nekrasov was reporting that they were demanding he forbid operation of the letter trains. (The flurry had come following the Dowager Empress's trip to GHQ.)

Then the discussion touched on Guchkov, too. Grand Duke Mikhail Aleksandrovich (who was now in favor with the government) was asking that measures be taken to guard members of the royal house. They must. A guard? That was a matter for the War Minister.

Apparently so. Another burden.

But the royal house was scattered all over, living in different places. What about Tsarskoye Selo?

Another concern.

Right then Kerensky appeared, like the rushed man of the moment without whom everything had been held up. And it was immediately essential to give him the floor. In his intoxicated voice he started reporting on the day's adventures, how he had arranged a formal session of the Senate and how he had visited the Winter Palace and what impressions he had from that.

Prince Lvov smiled foolishly and approvingly.

Guchkov was annoyed that he'd come to the meeting. When Kerensky finished, they announced a break.

Only in the break, and only because he stayed for the break, did he hear from corridor conversations a small piece of news that for some reason had not even been discussed at the meeting, that in the name of the Soviet of Deputies Chkheidze had presented Lvov with a resolution saying that the Tsar and the royal family must be arrested immediately!

Lvov hesitated. Even Kerensky did. The ministers whispered in twos and threes, and nothing was decided.

Well, I'll be darned! Having accepted the abdication, Guchkov had a moral responsibility to the former Tsar! Arrest him for what? He had surrendered easily and abdicated voluntarily. He'd made no attempt to prevent revolution. Nor had he broken any laws. Here he had sent points of inquiry— about going to Tsarskoye Selo and to England. Why not let him go? He would be harmless.

Concerned and decisive, Guchkov objected to Prince Lvov.

Nor did Lvov insist. It's not that he wanted the Tsar's arrest. But here they were demanding it so confidently! And they had the plants and the garrison.

To hell with them all! Wasn't the garrison under the Minister of War?

Oh, what kind of rock was the Soviet, trying to crush them!

If the arrest was to be made, then who would it fall to if not the War Minister again?

Guchkov was walking away in a funk when Prince Lvov was brought another telegram. He glanced at it and handed it over:

"This would naturally be for you Aleksandr Ivanych. An appeal, probably, you must . . .

The telegram had three addressees: Lvov, Rodzyanko, and Guchkov. Which meant the same telegram awaited him at the residence.

It was again from Alekseev! The old man was beside himself with alarm and insistence. Unauthorized soldier groups in the Northern Army Group. In Vyborg. Ruzsky's authority was barely holding on in Pskov, and a colonel had been killed. Finally, the government must demonstrate its authority and speak out decisively. Save the troops! A continuation of the collapse means the end of the war! And give overall explanations about the new state structure.

Prince Lvov felt the same. If they explained it well to everyone now, then it would all come clear and everyone would be kinder.

"Write a nice vibrant appeal, Aleksandr Ivanych."

"Hasn't it already been commissioned to someone? Nekrasov?"

"But you could do another, along your remit." The prince smiled.

Precious hours really were slipping away!

He was riding back to the residence, the motorcar's wheels churning and splashing the brown slush. He was riding with decisiveness and tensed will.

But what exactly should he do?

And on top of it all—this arrest of the Tsar? What about Tsarskoye Selo? And what if they were attacked there?

[446]

(THE PROVINCES ACCORDING TO
CONTEMPORARY NEWSPAPERS. FRAGMENTS)

*   *   *

All of provincial and district Russia learned of the coup first from the railroad telegraph, over the signature of some unknown Bublikov. Later, by ordinary telegraph, over Rodzyanko's signature. These telegrams were believed everywhere immediately, for Rodzyanko's name instilled confidence.

Before these telegrams, no events had taken place in a single town.

✳   ✳   ✳

Nowhere was the revolution greeted more docilely than in **Ekateri-noslav**. The governor published the resolution: "Any protests against the new government will be prosecuted to the full extent and punished with all severity." The city duma resolved to place in the duma hall a marble figure of our native son Rodzyanko; to put up in the city a monument to Liberation with the figure of Rodzyanko in the center; to name the main square after Rodzyanko; to expand the representation of Jews and workers in the duma.

✳   ✳   ✳

In **Kharkov** military censorship as late as 15 March still banned the printing of news from Petrograd, declaring that news false, but the news was conveyed by telephone through private persons. Crowds of people surrounded the editorial office, and telegrams were read out by employees from the balcony. The manifesto of abdication was received late on the evening of the 16th and, at the end of a performance at the dramatic theater, announced from the stage by the newspaper's editor. Even though it was night, the news spread quickly through the city. On 17 March, a public committee went to the city administration and the governor was arrested. Officers of the Kharkov police welcomed the election of the Provisional Government and expressed their firm belief that only those elected by the people could secure for the country a sure path to victory. It was decided to leave the police. Lawyers were sent to be in charge of police precincts. A student fighting squad arrested the garrison chief and several officers. Student medics halted their studies henceforth until professors appointed by the old government were removed.

✳   ✳   ✳

Reval. More than 800 prisoners were released from the local prison (two of them politicals, the rest criminals). Immediately upon release, they rushed to storm the district court and brought a crowd with them; others went to disarm the police. The courthouse was burned to the ground, and all criminal and civil files, notary documents, and the archive perished in the fire. Pogroms, robberies, and murders rained down on the entire city. Then the police and gendarmerie were again issued guns—and in a few hours calm ensued in the city.

✳   ✳   ✳

In **Tver,** Governor Bünting, known as an avid reactionary, seeing a menacing crowd heading for his house, reached the bishop by telephone and made confession. The crowd burst in and arrested him. He was bayonetted by soldiers on the way to the guardhouse. The ancient palace and its wine cellars were destroyed. There was disorderly shooting on the streets the entire day, and there were people killed.

* * *

Yaroslavl. On 15 March, a Committee of Public Safety was created. The governor, gendarmerie, and police officers were arrested. Policemen were removed from their posts. The sale of methylated spirits was halted, in order to contain drunkenness. When the Tsar's abdication was received, the Soviet of Workers' Deputies at first banned its printing, for fear that it was false.

* * *

Kostroma. In the homeland of the Romanov boyars, revolution triumphed without a single shot. The vice-governor fled, and the governor was led through the streets to bared swords. The entire administration was arrested, the police disarmed, and the gendarmerie's archive burned. The bishop performed a prayer service, and the Kostroma clergy decided not to pray for the Romanov family.

* * *

Nizhni Novgorod. Crowds of thousands at the Nizhni Novgorod kremlin. The mayor came out to the demonstrators and announced that the city was joining the new government. The garrison chief was the first from the administration to reject the old government. The governor stated that he was submitting, but he was arrested, and his wife followed him voluntarily. The commander of an infantry regiment lined up his regiment and said: "I am a Catholic, but I cross myself with the Orthodox sign." And he proclaimed the regiment's attachment to the new government. The prison guard raised a red flag and released the political prisoners. The crowd also obtained the release of the criminals (1300 men). There were no more police. Several shops were smashed. The crowd tore the imperial monogram off all the buildings. The entire police administration was arrested, as was the entire prosecutorial inspectorate, and arrests of police began district by district. Citizens asked for the removal of the un-Christian pastor Archbishop Joachim, who had given shelter to gendarme administration officials. A group of noblemen declared themselves in favor of joining the new government.

In honor of the revolution, the city duma decided to build a people's university and immediately collected 700,000 rubles from merchants.

*　*　*

Kazan. A university student meeting resolved that street demonstrations were impermissible. The governor and military district commander, General Sandetsky, telegraphed the Provisional Government about their submission. But Sandetsky was arrested.

*　*　*

In **Saratov,** on 14 March, reactionary leaflets about the events in Petrograd were greeted ecstatically. In the editorial offices, day and night, there were thousands of people demanding more news. Demonstrations came up to the duma, people lifted the mayor and duma members up in their arms, and like that, from their arms, they delivered their speeches. Bands played the "people's Marseillaise" nonstop—and the crowd carried freed politicals as it played. The Executive Committee has been meeting continuously. The garrison chief, General Zayats, has joined. The entire old regime has been arrested, from governor to constable, 250 members of the police, as well as the marshal of the nobility. Black Hundreds leaders have been arrested. Three bishops joined the new government, a group of clergy addressed a fervent appeal to pastors to clarify the significance of a Constituent Assembly. Wishing to serve the homeland, police officials are asking to be sent to the front.

*　*　*

Tsaritsyn. A stunning impression and unusual animation after agency telegrams. Investigations department officials and the prison warden offered resistance to arrest, firing from behind a barricade. The priest Gorokhov gave an incendiary speech in church with a call to come to the defense of the old order and rise up against the new. He was arrested on Executive Committee instruction. Files from all the police precincts were thrown outside and burned. The city's security was assigned to a university student battalion. A military band has been playing incessantly.

*　*　*

In **Morshansk,** high school boys gaily thronged behind the soldiers to a demonstration with their dark blue velvet and gold school banner, in which they had cut a hole where the two-headed eagle had been, and with a red banner that said "Long live free schools."

*　*　*

Orel. Everything ordinary has been forgotten. Life in the city has begun to seethe and the main street is overflowing with people. Regiments and a detachment of convalescents arrived to music and shouts: "Hurrah! Freedom!" When the prison was liberated, all the criminals were freed, too. They included General Grigoriev, the traitor of the Kovno fortress, who had already gotten into a cab but was noticed and not allowed to leave.

*   *   *

Tula. The soldiers were sleeping, and the crowd got them up in the night. All the authorities and the garrison chief were arrested (but he gave an oath of loyalty to the new order and was released). All police precincts were attacked and the entire police force arrested. A detachment of soldiers was sent to put down the resistance in Bogoroditsk. All the train stations from Tula to Moscow have red flags.

*   *   *

Voronezh was still in the hands of the old regime on 16 March. But in the evening, a train arrived with a military unit from Petrograd, and they installed a new order, disarming the station gendarmes and energetically removing the city police. The Petrograders' hunt for policemen continued all the next day. After that, there were rallies.

*   *   *

In **Kursk** the mood is ecstatic. The governor has fled to Crimea. The vice-governor has unquestioningly submitted to the committee. The police have been left their cold steel. The fellow fighters of Markov the 2nd have gone into hiding. *Kursk Stories* has been shut down for its harmful influence. Archbishop Tikhon has stated that he fully sympathizes with the coup that has come about and blesses the new government's actions.

*   *   *

In **Ryazan,** the governor took a signed statement from the newspaper's editor not to print anything about the events. But this did not save him, the vice-governor, the gendarme officers, or the garrison chief from arrest a few days later. Also arrested was a regimental commander who had prevented lower ranks from participating in the liberation movement. Many criminals have been let go.

In **Vladimir,** the governor, his wife, and several officials with German surnames have been arrested.

*   *   *

Vyatka. The Petrograd events came as a complete surprise. Crowds of exulting people in the streets, the police nowhere to be seen. Bishop Nikandr called on his flock to trust the State Duma. The *Diocesan Brotherhood* newspaper sold out with the headline: "Greetings to you, liberated nation!"

*   *   *

Suzdal. The chairman of the district zemstvo board took charge of the police and refused to recognize the new government.

Arzamas. The police captain armed the entire district police and does not want to recognize the Provisional Government's authority.

*   *   *

In **Ufa,** Bishop Andrei (Ukhtomsky) issued an epistle to his flock about submitting to the Provisional Government.

In the cathedral in **Ekaterinburg,** Bishop Serafim called the Duma Committee a gang of rebels.

*   *   *

Tashkent. The coup was announced with special solemnity. Governor General Kuropatkin, having received a telegram from Prince Lvov, assembled the military units, educational institutions, representatives of government institutions, and the Russian and Turkic populace—and personally announced what had happened, and then a service was held and a parade reviewed. Even before the Tsar's abdication, Kuropatkin had called for submission to the Duma Committee.

*   *   *

Astrakhan. The Cossack Assembly announced that the Astrakhan Cossack Army was putting itself at the full disposal of the Provisional Government. A new chief ataman was elected, and a Cossack chorus performed the Marseillaise. A public committee congratulated the Cossacks on their move to the side of the people.

In **Baku,** the heads of the Union of the Russian People and their archive were arrested.

*   *   *

Kherson. In the hard labor prison, 1700 inmates disarmed the guard, took over the prison, and freed another 200 inmates from another section. At this time, an agitated crowd gathered at the prison gates, smashed through the gates, and freed another 300 criminal inmates. More than 2000 released men scattered through the city. In the absence of sufficient forces for the administration, capturing the escapees has been complicated.

*   *   *

Odessa. On the streets, thousands of people holding leaflets exchanged impressions. A meeting of police officials in the presence of workers discussed the possibility of the police sincerely serving the new order. The political prisoners were released from prison lockup; there were seven. There were fears of Black Hundreds excesses. Meetings of the Union of the Russian People and the Union of Archangel Michael were banned. The reactionary *Russian Speech* has been transformed into the progressive *Free Russia*. The newspapers are full of articles about the dawn of a new life. Rumors have gone around the bazaars saying that now serfdom will be restored in Russia. The head of district headquarters, General Marks, offered a red rose to the "Odessa press from the free army."

*　*　*

Kiev. Men freed from Lukyanovskaya Prison were showered with flowers. The people freed included the famous female anarchist Taratuta, who had been sentenced to twenty years' hard labor and had already escaped from the Odessa prison once. Preliminary arrests are being made for the sake of expediency. The crowd is demanding the arrest of dissenters. A number of searches have been made throughout the city for Markov and Zamyslovsky, who, according to rumors, have arrived in Kiev. The city duma resolved to include five representatives of the Jewish population in its number. A combined council of Kiev's Jewish public organizations is being organized. The city's bazaars have everything in abundance, but dark rumors are being spread. Sinister forces are not sleeping.

[4 4 7]

Yet another grief: yesterday Aide-de-Camp Mordvinov was asked on behalf of certain unnamed headquarters officers to tell Voeikov that powerful agitation reigned in GHQ against him and Frederiks, and among the soldiers, too, because the two of them were felt to be to blame for everything that had happened—and their arrest was predetermined. Because of this, both were advised to leave Mogilev as quickly as possible.

Who these headquarters officers were, Mordvinov himself did not know; he had heard at second hand.

So was that it all of a sudden? Pick up and go? Go where at a time like this? What a delusion. What did Voeikov have to do with this? Or Frederiks?

Then Alekseev invited Voeikov to come see him and also confirmed this agitation, and he said such offensive words, that in a revolutionary period the people need victims, and if they were not to be those victims, the son-in-law and father-in-law had to leave as quickly as possible. If they left, nothing would happen, more than likely, but otherwise the garrison might rise up.

Then Alekseev appeared before the Emperor, with a report about the same thing, saying that if both remained in Mogilev, danger could arise even for the Emperor himself. Then came the unfortunate, dispirited Voeikov himself. What could he do? Where could he go?

He felt sorry for him and even sorrier for elderly and helpless Frederiks, with his many years of loyalty, and now with his home ravaged and his ailing wife in the hospital. Where else could he go?

But since the sensible Alekseev had said that they were irritating everyone, then of course it was safer for them to leave. It would be worse if they were arrested.

Go not to Petrograd, naturally. Maybe to Penza Province, to Voeikov's estate, make their way by a circuitous route so as not to be detained along the way.

Alekseev also advised traveling incognito for their safety—and separately. It was decided that Frederiks would head south, through Gomel, and Voeikov north, through Orsha. But how could they go incognito if Voeikov had a great deal of baggage, having furnished a fine apartment here?

The suite had begun to melt away. . . .

Even from hour to hour, the space around the Emperor was emptying out noticeably. Now there were no guests for lunches and dinners, whereas there had always been men from GHQ, unfailingly, or generals and colonels arrived from the front. GHQ was still next door—but what was it doing? It had fallen into a void. Nor were agency telegrams being delivered to the Emperor—so as not to upset him? Alekseev said they contained absolutely infuriating expressions. Perhaps that was true. But it felt very empty.

Previously, there had been daily, detailed letters from Alix—and now all correspondence with her had broken off. He felt deserted. What was happening to them there? What was she feeling and thinking? All that remained were telegrams—and these with great delays, by a roundabout route, doubtless through the Duma, through hostile—soiled—hands. It was unpleasant even to send simple kisses and inquiries about her health. Nikolai even encoded one such telegram in their family code.

And only like a bright flare did a telegram break through from the Southwestern Army Group, from Count Keller, commander of the 3rd Cavalry Corps, saying he did not recognize the revolution and was breaking his saber.

He sent a reply: "Deeply touched. Thank you."

Scarcely had he abdicated than all his might and all his entourage had quickly receded. There were only isolated noble voices.

How precious it was that his dear mother was here. Who else could he talk with these endless hours, who else could warm his heart! (He also summoned his sisters, Olga and Ksenia, from Kiev, but they couldn't come.) Mama decided not to go to Kiev but to stay here to the end, "as long as my son is at GHQ."

The day today was clear but very cold. After Mass, Mama came for lunch. Afterward, he sat quietly with her for a long time, talking unhurriedly. Hanbury-Williams had already sent his government a telegram about Nikolai's plan to go to England. (He was surprised that there had been not a word from George.) As soon as the family left for England, Mama, naturally, would immediately leave for Denmark, and once there they would see each other. Mama was trying to talk him into going to Denmark rather than England.

Right then a woman from the Kiev household arrived and told them that after Maria Fyodorovna's departure a commission from the revolutionary committee had come to the palace—to search for the wireless telegraph she was purportedly using to contact the Germans. They searched for a long time, and one especially zealous member fell from an attic beam and hurt himself. Now Mama was even fearful of returning there.

God, what impotence! Three days ago he had been Emperor of All Russia, King of Poland, and Grand Duke of Finland—and now he couldn't protect his own family from outrage!

Indeed, it was more sensible for Mama to go farther away, to Crimea.

State concerns fell away—and the importance of family concerns mounted. They agreed that every day she would come to the governor's residence for lunch, and her son would come to her in the train every evening for dinner.

After Mama's departure, he took a walk in the house garden. He felt like a drive in the country, but he couldn't bring himself to taunt people unnecessarily with the sight of him, with his outing. To see people he knew turn away?

But here was the person Nikolai had been expecting since the St. George Battalion had returned to Mogilev: dear old Ivanov! In the afternoon a report came from him saying he was waiting to be received. And now, after afternoon tea—the light was already fading—Nikolai received the general.

He entered, erect, despite his old age, and on his puffed out chest were all his 15 decorations. There was a steadiness in his gray beard, a vital core, a courageous, honest, and devoted look. Now, when everyone had turned away, these devoted servants had become three times, seven times dearer to his heart. Nikolai quickly walked toward him, embraced him, and even lingered for a moment in his beard.

He didn't have to say anything! Nikolai understood everything.

But the honest old man unfailingly wanted to explain step by step his tragic, failed campaign.

Above all—about the St. George Battalion's mood. Did the Emperor hear them marching by earlier today? And perhaps even see them? So you see, Ivanov had to rely on these rogues to establish order, how about that? And their General Pozharsky was just the same.

But most important, the assigned regiments hadn't arrived. Someone somewhere at headquarters had intentionally slowed them down, delayed their transit. General Ivanov did not want to accuse anyone personally, but there was intent here. And then the unfortunate incident in Luga with the Borodino Life Regiment! One of the very best and most reliable! Who could have anticipated such cunning from the scoundrels! Who could have anticipated such methods! A base rumor had gone around to the effect that the Borodino Regiment had joined the uprising!

And right when General Ivanov had finally made his way to Tsarskoye Selo and was about to go into action—he didn't have the forces! The whole town was packed with rebels, and they were making trouble, they held nothing sacred.

Of course, had there been a threat of danger to the royal palace, Ivanov would have scattered the entire St. George Battalion in the snow. Fortunately, though, no danger had threatened the palace. Both the Convoy and the Combined Regiment were in place, and the rebels respected and feared them.

The poor old man was upset, awaiting the Emperor's condemnation for making some blunder somewhere or retreating somewhere—but Nikolai reassured him and thanked him, one couldn't expect the superhuman from anyone.

Yes, but the main thing! The main thing was that he had gone to the palace and been able to personally convey to the unfortunate Empress support and aid from her royal spouse!

There were deeply moved, noble tears in the old man's black eyes.

My God! He should have begun with this! Nikolai Iudovich saw the Empress with his own eyes? He spoke with her?

Yes, of course! For two whole hours! It was the Empress who had told him to go back.

My God! In this entire terrible week, the sole person who had himself seen her and could now tell him about it! So tell me, tell me, dear man! And the sick children—did you see them, too?

No, it was the dead of night, and no matter how much Her Majesty wanted to show me the children, it wasn't worth waking them. But how courageous the Empress is! She has such self-possession and clear judgment about everything. In these ominous moments, left alone, and with sick children—how she commands the palace's numerous populace, the entire service, the servants and the guard.

Nothing more joyful and relieving for Nikolai could the general have said! To think! He had seen her with his own eyes! And how does she look? Thinner? Unwell? Is she very worried about him? Did she say whether she was receiving his letters? Had she thought to send a letter with the general?

Your Imperial Majesty, who could have presumed when your loyal servant might reach you? What if he first were laid out before then at some train station, a corpse sliced by the sword of a bandit-soldier? Indeed, literally immediately after he returned from the palace, he learned that a major attack on the station was being readied, including with artillery, and they had already surrounded the train. The station master was in cahoots with the rebels to keep the train from leaving. Only by foresight and roundabout measures was he able to take the battalion out from under the blow.

But still, even without a letter, through the old general's story, Nikolai felt the breath of something dear and encouraging—and he sensed his steadfast friend, his Alix, with pride.

The experienced old general clung to every rail stage—so as not to get too far away and gather his forces closer to Tsarskoye Selo and Petrograd. But that was when His Imperial Majesty had deigned to change his instructions, saying not to act until his own arrival—and bowing to his most august will, General Ivanov had been forced to wait. Ensconcing himself in Vyritsa, he proposed holding this line or even moving toward Gatchina. But there were no more orders for a full day, and all the troops en route had been halted without the general's knowledge. Then, on the 16th, instructions came from GHQ, but for some reason through Rodzyanko, to leave for Mogilev. He didn't believe it and inquired again with GHQ.

The general's eyes, overflowing with devotion, expressed this agonizing search for a decision. The poor, honest old man, how much had he put up with and what efforts he had undertaken, well beyond his years.

On the return journey he was told that at the Oredezh station he was awaited by a raucous performance by the soldiers and workers, who were going to demand the battalion join the revolution. He prepared to offer serious battle. But standing on the platform was a cluster of workers, maybe a hundred, who undertook no actions.

And so he rode until the evening of the 16th, still knowing nothing of the abdication. Only early on the morning of the 17th, at the Dno station, did the commandant tell him, and that was from passenger rumors.

The general burst into sobs. These rumors hit him harder than his own death. Could nothing really be saved? Why had GHQ, why had Grand Duke Mikhail Aleksandrovich surrendered to the villains from the State Duma?

Nikolai reassured him now, moved and proud of his devotion.

The general had not told the battalion at the time; he had still hoped! But in Orsha he got a Vitebsk newspaper with both abdications.

Even today he was sick over that. Returning to Mogilev, he said goodbye to his battalion and wished them good service under the new government—but where was he to go now? . . . What was he to do here, at GHQ, when his Emperor was no more and the old adjutant general had been orphaned? . . . (At the Mogilev station, too, there was rioting, and he moved from his train car to the town's hotel. Here, too, some crowd was making demands.) Evidently he would go to Kiev, where he was remembered, where he was valued for his former service.

Yes, but even Kiev wasn't without danger.

The Emperor was helpless to assist his loyal servants. . . .

In a firm hug and kiss, he said goodbye to Nikolai Iudovich, thanking him again and again.

He submitted his second tender telegram of the day to Alix, constantly thinking about and sensing her.

Right then it was reported that an unknown Life Uhlan officer was asking to be received on an important matter. He handed the Emperor a letter from General Gurko.

When Gurko had served as chief of staff, the Emperor had shuddered at his brusqueness and loud outbursts; he had found it much more pleasant to be with quiet, obliging Alekseev. Even now he took the letter with prejudice. But it turned out to be a fine letter, and he a fine general prepared to serve loyally. What a pity that all the generals like this had disappeared somewhere during the days of the abdication.

A few places in the letter touched him; tears even welled up. But what struck him especially was Gurko's idea that abdicating on behalf of the Heir may have been inspired by God. That right now the Heir could not have held the reins, but in later years, perhaps, he could return to the throne, called upon by right-thinking people.

This thought was dear to the Emperor's heart (he had to share it with his mother). Perhaps he hadn't made such a terrible mistake! The Lord's ways are providential.

It was already time to go to Mama's for dinner, to the station.

Right then the despondent old man and his son-in-law—the loyal Frederiks and Voeikov—came to say goodbye. Frederiks was completely bent over, completely lost. He was weeping—in his old age he was forced to abandon his beloved Emperor in misfortune, his home had burned down, his family had been devastated—and he had to wander off into the unknown.

The Emperor's heart sank, he felt so sorry for him. But this was better for him, he had to submit, it was not worth arguing.

He embraced them in tears.

[4 4 8]

The way to the ministry turned out to be blocked off by demonstration excesses as well. Yesterday, when Shingarev had gone to Mariinskaya Square to join the administration, the soldiers of the guard had wanted to greet him in an especially honorable way: they lined up according to rank in front of the building, presented arms, and barked out: "Your health, minister, sir!" Shingarev was embarrassed, he hadn't been expecting this at all, and he smiled gently: "I thank you"—and then they shouted again: "Willing to do our best!" "For the good of the Homeland"—Shingarev coaxed them, as if they were the ones now going to plunge into the ministerial thick.

Once he'd gone into the building, he discovered all the employees gathered for a general reception. What could he do? He thanked them, and then immediately:

"Gentlemen! Every minute is precious. For the good of the homeland! Go back to your places, please!"

This encounter could have been sincere, but it could also have been the old servility, and that grated.

He was horrified at how big his office was, with windows on Mariinskaya Square.

The ministers' table was also not cleared for work but heaped with artfully laid out telegrams of greeting—to him personally as incoming Minister of Agriculture. It was truly touching, but also truly impossible!

"All this—clear it away. Clear it away quickly!" Andrei Ivanovich ordered his secretary, although he couldn't miss a line here, there, and in yet a third.

He cleared it away—and got into his papers! The shipment summaries! The binders of instructions! Even the estimates, for finances moved everything.

Indeed, he felt prepared both by the old debates with Rittikh and by the recent days at the Food Supply Commission. He had always been able to get his bearings quickly even in the most unfamiliar matter.

Right now he could see increasingly that the matter wasn't in Petrograd, where all the debates, alarm, and revolution had arisen. Here there was no tightening bread noose at all; there was plenty of bread for a month to come. But that same "bread noose" threatened to draw around the front, where the alarm had yet to be revealed. The army groups did not have food reserves, especially the Southwestern, due to the three weeks of drifts. The situation was grave, but in a much broader, deeper, and more prolonged sense than Shingarev had imagined. Sixty billion pounds of grain—the surplus over Russia's consumption—were languishing in granaries and cribs in the country's interior—but how could it be tapped? The very mechanism of purchase and shipment had broken down, as had the psychology of the producer. Added to all these obstacles was also the impending long season of impassable roads after the very snowy winter.

The minister's difficulties had begun not only on Russia's expanses, in the impenetrability of the rural world; now there was this Food Supply Commission directed by the Soviet of Workers' Deputies, too? The minister could not allow himself to be a pawn of the Soviet of Deputies. Everything suggested that he forestall them and promote some other new organization controlled by the minister alone. In the provinces and districts they would have to create local food supply committees and also food commissar posts. They needed a system because the Ministry of Agriculture did not have one for food collection and supply. That had never been its job, dealing with food distribution; there'd been no need. Food had flowed of its own accord from producers to consumers through a network of trading agents. If the recent system of dispatching empowered representatives had been exceptionally clumsy and harmful and was now subject to cancelation, then it was becoming all the more apparent, in the guesswork and impulses of the chaotic revolutionary days, that a new system of end-to-end food supply committees was needed.

Also on his desk Shingarev discovered a terrible obligation of the former government: taking advantage of the Allies' empty tonnage in the opposite direction, to send to England in 1917 800 thousand tons of wheat and a certain large amount of alcohol. While experiencing a grain crisis—to also send grain to England? What could Shingarev decide? Well, not decide, but what could he propose the government should do? Of course: don't send any grain! But on no account would his colleagues ever agree to that. And even he himself—how would it look to the English M.P.s? (That vivid trip last year to England and France remained picturesque in his memory and soul. He had filled with such love for the Allies then.)

There was no time to work things out and delve deeply into the matter, though. Just as the ministry lacked order, so too did the entire Provisional

Government—and he was required to spend nearly half of his waking hours at its sessions. And shift the administrative work in the ministry to his deputies.

Constrained by all the proposals and plans, Shingarev went to Chernyshev Bridge for the government's evening session. He now faced six hours, in two stretches, until late at night.

Hour after hour, issues flowed by that could have been decided without him.

For all his good nature, though, Shingarev could not look at the young millionaire Tereshchenko, a sleek dandy and silly brat who for some reason—through some secret influences never explained?—had taken Finance instead of him. It was painful—being right here, meeting alongside him. And Tereshchenko did not demonstrate by a single comment any experience or notion of the matter at hand.

Finally they gave Shingarev the floor. The others were doubtless tired, too, and bored, and there was no need for others to listen to the affairs of agriculture and food—but Shingarev rejoiced at sharing the burden with his colleagues.

He met with no sympathy on the grain deliveries to England. Everyone felt that meeting this obligation was a duty of honor for the new government.

Shingarev complained that transport was not ensuring supplies for the front—and dark-faced Nekrasov jealously, touchily put forward that transport was sorting itself out. Shingarev had never considered Nekrasov a smart man, and he saw no boon to the government in the fact that he, young and inexperienced, had been assigned Russia's transport during these days.

In the sessions, Shingarev for some reason spoke worse than in his public appearance, where the audience inspired him, and his speech was worse, of course, than his work. He did notice that he spoke at too great length, he should be briefer. All those minor details should not be discussed here; the session was dragging everyone down. But so novel, so inexperienced was his position in agriculture that he wanted to learn the measure of his colleagues' sympathy and perhaps get advice from them. Here was a not insignificant question: since last autumn, since the upheavals in Semirechye, there were many destroyed public buildings left, and Russian families had suffered. Could they now allocate a million for their relief and restoration?

But boredom and impatience were expressed on all their faces. Semirechye was so far removed, so abstract—while right here the Petrograd revolution was seething, far from settling down. Issues like this—where money should be spent—everyone had plenty of those.

Here was Konovalov, straightening the pince-nez on his burly nose, hurrying to consult and gain assent. For the new government's prestige, it was very important now to pay all workers in government plants for all the days of their participation in the popular movement. This was many millions, but we could not do otherwise.

Tereshchenko was prepared to pay. But the other ministers looked drawn in the face. If they paid wages for revolutions and demonstrations—where might that lead in future?

Milyukov (who these past few days had cooled for some reason toward Shingarev, or else they had no common business in their faction), who had not once brought up for discussion a single major foreign affair, sat there with the expression of floating omniscience. But now he perked up, too. The governments of Great Britain and the United States were asking permission to export light hides from Russia.

Right then Kerensky, too, until now also plunged in thought, roused himself: here's the thing, we must offer the Soviet of Workers' Deputies the official printing press for their publications, free of charge.

They wanted to agree automatically, but still objecting voices rang out. There would be no end to the Soviet's demands, would there?

At that point, Prince Lvov began gently coaxing and drawing Kerensky himself into his plan: go to Moscow, where there was a broad, sweeping public movement, but not everything was correctly understood and it had to be authoritatively explained.

It looked as though they had an agreement already because without expressing surprise or asking any more questions, Kerensky with impulsive readiness immediately agreed to go.

There remained an even bigger, if not the most important, issue: the new government's address to the people, its first major address. Nekrasov presented a draft (actually, Nabokov had written it, not he), but Manuilov, who had refused to at the time, now began to object in a caustic professorial manner, to cavil against what was important and at trifles alike. Then they instructed him to finish it—with the help of Kokoshkin, and to ask Vinaver. Three professors. And this had to be not an ordinary appeal but a great and earthshaking one!

It was late already, the umpteenth sleepless night, and their minds weren't fully functional.

[4 4 9]

Lenin had studied a great deal in many previous revolutions and revolutionary attempts (he had been born and lived for revolution only; what better for him to know?) and had his favorite individuals, moments, methods, and ideas. But he had seen with his own eyes only one—not from the beginning, not entirely, and not in the main places—and in it he had taken no part whatsoever, against his will having only observed and drawn his conclusions and post-conclusions.

But there had been another—in another country and during his infancy—with which he had felt a sincere and fateful connection, the way your heart beats at your beloved's name, a kind of irresistible passion, pain and love: its mistakes are more painful than all others; its seventy-one days, like lofty, decisive days of your own life, have been probed thoroughly, one at a time; its name is always on your lips: the Paris Commune!

In the West, if they were awaiting explanations, if they deemed his opinion important, then it was on the Russian Revolution of 1905, and he regularly gave talks about it, most often on 22 January, the date most conspicuous for the Western understanding. But he was bored talking about a revolution which had been snatched away from him (and his jealous arguments against Parvus and Trotsky, that was better not to say out loud for now). But no one asked him about the Paris Commune. Many could speak more authentically about it. Yet he himself was drawn to nestle up to it— torment to torment, wound to wound, as if they could heal from each other. And when everyone—the revolution's participants and nonparticipants— were forced one by one, under cover, secretly to flee a Russia where all was lost in that moldering Geneva winter of 1908, he, dispirited, having quarreled with everyone of like mind, irritated beyond any nervous possibility, he nestled up, all alone, to write about the *lessons of the Paris Commune*.

Thus, this current nervous winter, bored by the Skittle Club's exchanged whisperings, feeling a physical timidity about appearing before a large, filled hall, before lots of people—having suddenly received an invitation arranged by Abramovich to go to La Chaux-de-Fonds to deliver a paper on the Paris Commune on the anniversary of the uprising, 5 March (many French refugees had lived around La Chaux-de-Fonds since Huguenot times, and the Communards had fled there as well, and all their descendants were there now), Lenin agreed with the greatest zeal.

And now there was this news about a new Russian revolution that was gathering steam with every passing day.

Three days had not passed from the first unverified news from Russia (three solid days because there had been no sleeping all three nights, but his headache was gone—that was amazing!—any morbid condition was gone, so abruptly had he gained strength!), and how much in these past 70 hours had raced, burned, droned through his chest and head, like through the flue of a large stove! Knowing so little, he scraped together from clippings, put together picture after picture. **How was it there?** And to each version he gave a solution. His solutions, given his experience now, were all irreproachably correct, but each time the picture was deceptive, and subsequent telegrams repudiated and changed the previous ones. But Lenin did not have his own reliable information from Russia, nor could he have any.

With the years you recognize yourself. Even without intellectual soul-searching, you can't fail to note some of your own characteristics. Inertia, for example. At age 47, casting about didn't come easily. Even when you've seen, guessed the correct political steps—you don't get going right away. And when you do, stopping is just as hard.

The thunderous news from Russia did not instantly shake him from his former movement, did not take possession of him in a single minute—but take possession it did, and more and more powerfully. The first night was spent in agony over his mistake. Why, oh why hadn't he moved to Sweden a year and a half ago, as Shlyapnikov had called him to, as even Parvus had proposed? Why had he stayed in this hopelessly dull and bourgeois Switzerland? It had seemed so clear all the years of war: don't leave Switzerland for anything! Sit it out here to the end. But now it was clear: Oh, he should have left in time! Be it for the schism in the Swedish party, or for the proximity to Russian events—but to Stockholm! One could summon someone there from Russia.

Even before, this could have been done perfectly imperceptibly—via Germany, naturally, the sole sensible route. But now that everyone has started stirring, seething, and discussing—you couldn't slip away without being noticed, damn it!

However, you couldn't remain idle for a minute, either. Whether it did or didn't succeed there, you had to start acting! On the morning of the 16th, having barely woken, he got busy sending out by a tested route a photograph for a travel passport—to Hanecki. (Poor Kuba had also gone through a lot. In January he was arrested for illegal trading and deported from Denmark.) Immediately following that he had sent a telegram, explaining openly (as if they themselves couldn't guess; he'd dropped his guard, out of impatience): send *Uncle's* (read: Lenin's) photograph immediately to Sklarz in Berlin, 9 Tiergartenstrasse.

He had to make peace with Parvus's whole company without delay; no one else could help get him out.

On the morning of the 16th, new telegrams brought news that the Tsar had apparently abdicated! (Was that possible so swiftly? Without putting up a fight at all? What could have compelled him? Oh, there's some kind of trap here. But who instead of him? If not Nikolai, then someone else, someone smarter.) And apparently a Provisional Government had been formed (but had the Tsarist ministers been reliably arrested?) with Guchkov, Milyukov, and even Kerensky (shades of contemptible Louis Blanc, so much did these pseudo-socialists like to stick their asses into bourgeois armchairs).

And what was this ecstasy among émigré loudmouths? Not a single mouth shut from evening to morning, rose-colored bleating. But think about it: for an entire week Petersburg had been flowing with workers' blood, and, as throughout European history, in 1830, in 1848, the masses' eternal credulity! They had surrendered clear power to those bourgeois swine, those Milyukovs and Shingarevs. The same old pattern!

Let them wag their tongues in the émigré reading room, but a true revolutionary—be on your guard! Strain! Watch him! **There** right now they were making such a mess, giving everything away in a spirit of charity, since there were no genuine tactical heads on anyone. What burned was that he himself wasn't there, he couldn't intervene, he couldn't direct.

He hadn't thought of Kollontai all winter, but in the past few days she had become one of his main correspondents; the center of events had shifted to her there. No sooner had he sent the photograph to Hanecki than he sat down to write a letter to Aleksandra Mikhailovna to explain how *we* were going to be now. Our slogans were still the same, of course: turn the imperialist war into a civil war! And the fact that the Kadets were in power was actually even good! Let them, let that dear company provide the people with the promised freedom, bread, and peace! And we shall watch. We are armed anticipation! Armed preparation for a higher stage of revolution. No trust whatsoever for the socialist-centrists, for Chkheidze! No joining up with them whatsoever! We must do this separately from them all! Only *separately*! We will not let ourselves get mixed up in unifying attempts. It would be a terrible misfortune if the Kadet government were to allow a legal workers party; that would weaken us greatly. We have to hope we remain illegal! But if they do foist legality on us, we must definitely retain our underground part: our strength is in the underground, and we cannot abandon the underground altogether! We are going to have to wrest *all* authority from those Kadet crooks. Only then will there be a "great and glorious" revolution! . . . I'm beside myself, beside myself that I cannot go to Scandinavia immediately!

But early on the morning of the 17th, all the information turned back the other way: the Kadet government hadn't won at all; the Tsar hadn't abdicated in the least but had fled, but no one knew where he was now, and based on the template for all European revolutions this was perfectly understandable: he was assembling a counterrevolutionary host, he was assembling his own Koblenz. Even if he didn't succeed, he could throw out this, yes, this: for instance, he could flee abroad and issue a manifesto about *a separate peace* with Germany! Yes, it was very simple! They were very crafty, those Romanovs. (In *his* place that was *exactly* the step to take, a brilliant one: the peasants' own Tsar-miracleworker!) And right away there is popular sympathy for him in Russia, the Kadet government staggers and flees, while Germany—Germany ceases to be an ally of our revolutionary party and they no longer need us. . . . (Oh, there is going to be even more of a wait to go to Russia, there's nothing to do there. Why had he sent Hanecki the telegram? What foolishness, he had left a trail.)

Aleksandra Mikhailovna, we're afraid we are not going to be able to leave this accursed Switzerland any time soon, it's a very complicated matter. We can help best of all if we send you advice from Switzerland.

And so, the comrades leaving Stockholm for Russia had to be given a precise tactical program. This could be presented in theses. . . . His hand was already writing the theses. . . . The main thing for the proletariat was to *arm themselves*. That would help under all circumstances: to crush the monarchy first and then the Kadet imperialist plunderers. . . . Ah, Grigori! Help me, sit down. So the new government isn't going to be able to give the people bread, and without bread no one needs their freedom. But bread can only be *taken by force* from landowners and capitalists. And only a

workers government (only *we*) can do that. . . . Yes! Finish writing to Kollontai: familiarize Pyatakov and Evgenia Bosch with these theses. (The
time had come; they couldn't neglect even the piglets. Right now, no one
could be neglected. Right now who would come in handy was Malinovsky!
Ah! They'd sullied the man so badly you couldn't rehabilitate him. But he
was doing very positive work in the prisoner of war camps. In January another plea had been made in his defense. He had to be saved, had to be returned.) Furthermore. . . . Here was an important thought: we couldn't fail
to arouse the benighted servants against their employers; this would be a big
help in establishing the Soviets' authority. What did genuine freedom mean
today? First of all, re-elections of officers by soldiers. General meetings and
elections, elections everywhere. And removing any and all oversight by officials over life, over school, over . . . Present-day freedom in Russia was extremely relative. But they had to know how to use it for the transition to a
higher stage of revolution. And neither Kerensky nor Gvozdev could provide a solution for the working class. . . . All right, the post is going to close
soon, I have to take it off to send.

But look, Grigori, are they promising an amnesty? An amnesty for everyone, meaning freedom for all the leftist parties? Have they really made up
their minds? That's bad. Bad. Now a legal Chkheidze and his Mensheviks
will flourish—and occupy all the positions, all the positions before we can.
And outdistance us again? . . .

No! No! We can't sit here with our hands folded. We must prepare something. And quickly! Whether we go or not, the revolution can still be rolled
back. How many times has that happened? You can't trust anything—but
we have to prepare a path in any event. Here's what. . . . Today is Saturday?
That's bad. No matter. Go back to Bern, yes, go back immediately, there's
no one else. Try to catch Tsivin at home, late tonight would be the best or
else he might go somewhere on Sunday. And have him go directly to the
German embassy. On Monday! This cursed circle must be broken. Why is
Romberg himself silent and not sending anyone? One has to wonder. They
ought to have more of an interest than we do. We can at least contemplate
a route via England, but they have no other solution without us. Teach
Tsivin this: under no circumstance refer to you and me specifically, that it
is we two who need to go, but say that many would like to, and we among
them. So as to sound them out. What are the possibilities? . . . What should
we ask? For instance, that Germany make a public statement saying it is
prepared to permit everyone to go to Russia who . . . who brings with him a
love of freedom. That's the way. For us, such a statement would be a perfectly acceptable basis.

And something else! All these diplomats—they're dolts. They don't distinguish anything or anyone in the revolutionary movement. Have Tsivin lend
us weight. Have him put it mysteriously like this: the revolutionary movement in Russia is being directed *entirely* from Switzerland. Every important
action must be decided first in Switzerland. Literally: in Russia they do not

take a single important step without receiving instructions from us. There-fore, in the present situation . . . Understand? Well, go on. I have to take a train early tomorrow morning, too, to La Chaux-de Fonds, to deliver a paper.

He'd been in such a mood about the Commune three days ago—but now he was torn.

This morning, out of haste and distraction, Lenin had put on a com-pletely worn cap, not the right one—and in La Chaux-de-Fonds they had taken him for a vagabond and didn't want to believe that this was their ex-pected speaker.

That afternoon (Sunday), at the watchmakers' club, lecturing in German—not from a written text, expatiating freely on brief theses—Lenin delivered his paper, "Will the Russian Revolution follow the path of the Paris Commune?" in front of an audience of two hundred. He did not have a good sense of his audience, of what interested them and what they ex-pected, as if he had lost his sensitivity. He didn't see the room, didn't feel the papers in his hand, and lost his sense of time. Even more, he had lost his affection for his long-beloved Commune, and was drawn, imperceptibly drawn, more and more, he had now merged the two experiences of the two revolutions, not so much in formulations as in his racing thoughts and emo-tions, the two experiences—the Commune and **this** one, suddenly blos-soming, perhaps deceptive, or perhaps unique, the one he had prepared for his entire life. We mustn't repeat the Commune's mistakes, its two main mistakes: it did not seize the banks and it was too magnanimous. Instead of cellar executions for the enemy classes, it safeguarded everyone's life and thought it could reeducate them. There it was, the most ruinous thing threatening the proletariat—this magnanimity in revolution. The prole-tariat had to be taught pitiless mass methods!

Whatever the watchmakers of La-Chaux-de-Fonds concluded, Lenin himself was gripped increasingly by alarm: time was slipping away! While he was delivering this paper, there, in Petersburg, something was slipping away irrevocably, someone pathetic and unworthy was latching on to power more and more.

Right then a French speaker came up to the lectern, and Abramovich as-sembled all the local Russians, and while there was time before the train, about twenty-five minutes, Lenin began to deliver something like a paper— on the same subject, only now without comparisons, directly, about what captivated both them and him, concluding with these direct words:

"If necessary, we will not be afraid to hang eight hundred bourgeois and landowners on lamp-posts!"

The train rolled in, but he was still thinking and thinking. There was no genuine force in Petersburg. Force was the Tsar and his apparatus, but they had been pushed out. Force was the army, but it was shackled to the front. And the Kadets were no force whatsoever. And the Soviet of Deputies—did that carry weight? How was it there? There was the great, almost certain, danger that it would be taken over now by Chkheidze's Mensheviks. There was a void in Petersburg, a void in the Soviet, that was suckingly waiting, calling for—*his* force. If he could take Petersburg—he could contend with both the army and the Tsar.

So, should he go? Make up his mind and go?

Rocked by the train's speed, in second class, Lenin sat by the window, reflected in its darkness along with the train car's bright interior, and looked and looked and didn't notice showing his ticket once and then again, didn't hear them coming through, announcing the stations. He was thinking.

Should he go? . . .

The condition when you neither see nor hear—whether others are sitting right there in the car. At the window, alone, in the train alone, and so Inessa was not in Clarens, Inessa was traveling by his side. It was wonderful, they hadn't talked like this in a long time.

You see, going is out of the question. And not going—that's also out of the question. . . . But how about this: couldn't you go on ahead for now? You aren't risking anything. You'll be let through everywhere. (This was perfectly innocent; it wasn't a contradiction. Whoever you love is who you send ahead, naturally, whoever you worry about most—when you take care of that person, you're taking care of the cause. That's how it always is. How else? And if she didn't refuse directly, that meant she agreed.)

Soon it would be a year since they'd seen each other. Things had fallen apart somehow. . . . But on this memorable day, this happy Commune anniversary spent chatting in a train side by side with Inessa, he had the warm and joyous feeling of her former closeness and an urgent necessity for her, felt it so much that he had to say two honest-to-goodness words to her; it was rekindled immediately, it could not be put off until tomorrow!

At one station he hopped off and bought a postcard. At another he dropped it in a mailbox.

. . . Dear friend! . . . I read about the amnesty. . . . We are all dreaming about traveling. . . .

Definitively so: dreaming. That's what's so distinct now: the dream!

. . . If you go—stop by. We can talk. . . .

You know it's true, we need to see each other. . . . What a moment! Come! . . .

. . . I would give you an assignment to find out on the quiet in England whether I could travel through. . . .

England, naturally, won't want to let him through. An enemy in war, an enemy of the Entente. But isn't there a way to trick the English?

Actually, going by way of France-England-Norway—that could take a month. And in that time the new regime will solidify, find its channel, and be off and running—and there'll be no toppling, no overthrowing it. He had to hurry before it consolidates.

The same goes for the war. Will people get used to the war continuing even given the revolution and not overthrow it either?

Then there are the German submarines. Having waited for such a moment—and now take this risk? Only fools could.

That night, back at his place on Spiegelgasse, he slept intermittently. And through his waking and sleeping the thought began to burn more and more insistently: should he go? Go? . . .

[4 5 0]

In the unswept lecture hall of the women's medical institute, cigarette butts on the floor, and three of five lamps gone, unscrewed, the assembled Vyborg District Soviet of Workers' and Soldiers' Deputies was meeting for the first time. Wearing workers' jackets, wearing greatcoats, so jammed onto the benches in front of the desks, they would have gladly ripped them out. Sixty or so people—not everyone knows, not all the delegates have been sent yet.

The Vyborg Soviet is very important for us; it has to be seized. Based on familiar faces, Kayurov and Shutko estimate that the Bolsheviks will probably have a majority. But the Mensheviks' leader, who goes by Maks, a pompous intellectual, still managed to get to the rostrum to make the first report.

But before he could say three sentences, the door swung open witlessly, like by the wind—the doorknob banging against the wall!—and in walked two sailors in black pea coats with big, Mauser holsters at their sides not according to regulations. The first was gangly, brutish, and badly unshaven; the second came to his shoulder and had a head like a round gourd.

And from the door, all four arms swinging hard, quickly up to where the chairman and speaker were. And from there, turning around, brutishly menacing:

"Comrades! We're just now straight from Kronstadt!" People clapped for them.

The chairman managed to interject:

"You have the floor."

And the gangly one was already rasping and droning:

"Comrades! Four days ago, the revolution freed me from the Schlüsselburg fortress. I did my time there, seven years of hard labor. And right away I went to have a look at my Kronstadt. And what did I see?"

There wasn't enough light, and you couldn't get a good look at his face, but he threw back his head, as if gasping:

"Counterrevolution reigns and rules in Kronstadt! They've bamboozled the Soviet of Deputies and sent in Pepelyaev, a commissar from the Duma. Sailors can't keep their hands in their pockets, the revolution is over, stop the anarchy, war to a victorious conclusion. They're holding services in the Naval Cathedral for their newly won freedom. Pepelyaev is presiding at the officers' club, vats of flowers, invited sailor deputies are being served little cups of tea and cookies at little round tables. A telegram from Guchkov: freedom has been won, lower your battle flags, the enemy is at the gates, and agents are tearing the nation asunder. Comrades! The bourgeoisie is in power, and we're taking a back seat?"

That's what the Bolsheviks had sent brainy Semyon Roshal there for—hadn't he managed it yet?

Shouts from the hall:

"You mean they've been letting the officers go?"

The gourd, solemnly:

"No, about two hundred are still under arrest. They're taking them out to sweep the streets and work as loaders."

And the gangly one:

"Comrades! Who's going to take up Kronstadt if not the Vyborg District? You have to send steadfast and reliable men to Kronstadt right away! We have to give them all a good shake there and pull the contagion out by the root! Otherwise we're going to be left with revolvers against forts and ships."

And his holster, turns out, was unbuckled—and he whipped out a huge Mauser over his big fat head:

"We have to drive out the hydra right away—and seize the fortress!"

Right then Maks got up the nerve to object politely:

"But none of that affects us, comrades. You should go to the Petrograd Soviet."

The brutish one turned toward Maks, gave his gun a shake—and looked like he was about to drill him right where he was:

"I know who it affects! I know where I've come! To hell with your toady Menshevik Petrograd Soviet! We'll be checking that Soviet, too, to see who's in charge there! We don't believe Chkheidze and we don't believe Skobelev. You bastards can all go to effing hell! The forts and ships are our blood! There's no lowering the battle flags! The revolution has only just begun! Whoever we aim our guns at is who we aim our guns at. We! Ourselves!"

And the gourd shouted to the assembly, his eyes rolling from side to side:

"Our-selves!"

And they clapped for him, and clapped.

The gangly one stowed his Mauser.

And the agenda went to hell, as did Maks' report—and they started choosing reliable comrades for Kronstadt.

Kayurov and Shutko had already wised up that this was that same Ulyantsev who'd been court-martialed in October. Shlyapnikov had defended them with a strike, and three days ago he'd sent Ulyantsev to Kronstadt.

Although Roshal was there, and not alone, either, but let them recruit more volunteers, our force will only be stronger!

[4 5 1]

General Ushakov, chief of the Pskov garrison, was rescued at the last minute—but by no means through the strength and will of the army group commander-in-chief. They'd already dragged him out—to shoot him, hack him, or drown him in the Velikaya River—when two young educated soldiers galloped up and shouted furiously, stopping them. The matter had now reached army group headquarters in its retellings like this. Ushakov had been dragged out because he had been strict and kept a tight rein on the garrison, raining down punishments. But the young soldiers held the crowd back with testimony that they themselves had obtained an amnesty from General Ushakov for an innocent soldier. The crowd was immediately appeased and let the general go, even asking his forgiveness.

They'd been able to save Ushakov—but no one had saved Nepenin.

And would they save Nikolai Vladimirovich Ruzsky if he was dragged out? . . .

He'd had a fierce migraine ever since reviewing the parade. And he couldn't calm down in any activity.

In his whole life, he had simply never experienced the kind of precariousness and uncertainty he was now.

And it was more Ruzsky's tendency to fall into gloom and even despair. But he forced himself not to show it.

Had today's parade perhaps calmed something? Nothing of the sort: by evening the riots and violence had flared back up. Admiral Kolomiytsev, a St. George officer, was grabbed on the street; enraged soldiers from an unknown unit insulted him and took him into custody. People came running to report to the commander-in-chief—but what could Ruzsky do? Who could he send? He held out no hope even for the garrison headquarters' company. And if they'd had no shame about dragging the admiral around, what could Ruzsky himself do about them with his three George crosses?

The entire situation—with respect to Petrograd and the revolution—was too delicate to allow himself to act hastily, crudely. Ruzsky had no orders from GHQ or the new government to carry out specifically repressive actions. Even if he did, he wouldn't have dared oppose the revolution's moral authority.

In the present catastrophic situation, Ruzsky discovered the most correct and tactical solution: he, the commander, could go straight to the Petrograd Soviet of Workers' Deputies in search of understanding—and support—from them. He just had to wait for Mikhail Bonch's return.

That's what he had thought, but suddenly, the most unpleasant dissonance: he was brought a letter from Petrograd practically by a soldier—a letter from Bonch!—only from that other Bonch, the revolutionary, Vladimir. Who inquired (addressing him directly by some unknown right), quite forwardly and with a superior tone, how sincerely the officers of the Northern Army Group had accepted the new state order.

The question was point-blank, and the question was, of course, primarily about Ruzsky himself. The general actually flushed at the insult. Such a thing asked, and about him, when it was he, you might say, who had created the new state order, toiling away for this more than Petrograd itself! (Actually, you had to understand the revolutionary, too. Why should he trust a Tsarist general?) The question put in doubt Ruzsky's revolutionary loyalty—and could not go unanswered!

But Mikhail Bonch still hadn't come, was delayed on his assignment!

At poorly defended headquarters, when a revolutionary element was sweeping through the streets of Pskov, one felt particularly the reality of the Petrograd Soviet's authority and the inevitability of having to justify oneself.

The charge was so serious and the entire moment so acute and unstable that Ruzsky decided to send Bonch an open telegram in reply. Still counting on family ties, though, he sent it not to the Soviet's Chairman but to Bonch specifically.

Saying that he himself, General Ruzsky, as well as the army and military officers under his command, had fully accepted the new existing government—from now until the decision of the Constituent Assembly. However, he was asking for assistance so that . . . what could he gently call them? . . . the Soviet's authorized *representatives* and other individuals coming within the boundaries of the Northern Army Group, before addressing the workers or troops, went first to see the commander in order to establish full contact. That Pskov, as the closest point to Petrograd, had enormous significance, and any unrest in it was absolutely impermissible. Meanwhile . . . hmm . . . *delegates* had been coming and directly addressing the populace and the troops. . . .

He could not put it any more gently while at the same defending the status of army group headquarters.

While on the streets of Pskov, people continued to seize more and more officers. What was going on?

Rolling over Pskov, the wave of violence and uncontrollability was on its way to Riga! And Dvinsk! In the Sumy Hussar Regiment, the regimental commander disappeared—evidently murdered in secret? But another colonel of the same regiment was killed openly. In Rezhitsa, a mutiny of hussars flared up. Telegrams came in from various places on the front-line disposition about the arrests or murders of military commandants, garrison chiefs, and commanders of individual units!

This could reach as far as the front lines tomorrow, to the combat units on the Western Dvina.

And wasn't Dvinsk practically the forward line? Things were blazing there, too. Soldiers had arrested General Bezladnov, and 5th Army Commander Dragomirov hadn't been able to prevent it.

The soldier crowd hadn't broken into army group headquarters itself (they weren't used to dealing with that place; nothing from there affected them directly); on the other hand, the despairing officers trickled in: how could they go on serving and commanding? Simply remaining in his official place now demanded from the officer better nerves than in an open attack.

Here the threat was not only death but also disgrace and humiliation—worse than death! And what could be done against a crowd of their own soldiers?

If mass paralysis ensued among the officer class, then what kind of army would it be?

Ruzsky lapsed into the deepest gloom. It fell on him to find a solution beyond anyone's strength—because his army group was the closest to Petrograd and the first to experience the onslaught—and had to be the first to find a defense. Wait for something decisive and saving from the current GHQ? But who was GHQ now? And it wasn't going to reach them in Mogilev right away; they were going to stagnate waiting.

But in Pskov they could wait no longer. They either had to withstand the blow of events or collapse. Another three days like this, and Ruzsky wouldn't be holding onto any high command whatsoever. Ruzsky's nervous organization itself would not let him linger in inaction. Bonch's reply from the Soviet had not come, however. He couldn't have firm hopes. Meanwhile, the main salvation was undoubtedly not in the government but in the Soviet.

Ruzsky had this thought: don't wait for a reply from Bonch. He had to appeal to the Soviet itself, energetically and directly. But through the soldiers' mouths—that was his discovery! Send a direct soldier-officer delegation to the Petrograd Soviet and explain it all to the Soviet orally, to say the things he could not write.

Put it together immediately. And send it without delay. They could make the round trip in a single day—and save everything. Explain to the Soviet informally how ruinous for the army in the field Order No. 1 was. The Soviet's deputies could not want the Russian army's collapse! In their understandable impulse toward freedom, they themselves simply hadn't understood what they were doing when they issued it. But now the Soviet would understand and call for calm—and everything would calm down.

And after this, after this—it wouldn't hurt for Ruzsky himself to appeal to the Provisional Government and the napping Alekseev. None of them could help separately, but maybe together they could? Send the identical telegram to all the powerful people in the government: Prince Lvov, Guchkov, and Kerensky, and a copy to Alekseev. This way, rank would be observed, and the voice of appeal would reach them by the shortest path. Remind them that the entire command structure had wholly recognized the new state order. (Most insulting was that the fact of this recognition, especially by Ruzsky's headquarters, had gone missing.) Now a danger had arisen of the army's collapse just before the spring offensive. This collapse was inevitable if an immediate and authoritative explanation did not follow from the central authority.

He prepared the delegation for the next day. And ordered the telegrams sent.

Ruzsky calculated this all out sensibly.

And all of a sudden, General Bonch showed up! He'd arrived! At last! Wholly self-possessed, and approving everything.

Immediately Ruzsky put him in charge of the Pskov garrison instead of Ushakov. If this one doesn't patch things up! . . .

[4 5 2]

Guchkov's thoughts developed as follows. If a guard did have to be arranged for Tsarskoye Selo, then it could not be put off, it needed to be now. Today. Before anything happened. And obviously through not just anyone, but none other than the new District commander Kornilov. He had to go take a look at the Tsarskoye Selo garrison in any case. And it would not be a bad idea for Kornilov to be accompanied by Guchkov himself. Not that it was so necessary for this matter, but he was languishing from the lack of progress on all other matters, from his powerlessness, and it was an empty Sunday evening, and he didn't feel like going home.

He telephoned Kornilov and invited him to come that evening for a trip to Tsarskoye Selo.

He remembered one other obligation: the Vyazemsky family. He telephoned Lidia, the dead man's sister. He could call on them today, but tomorrow, he learned, was the funeral service at the Aleksandr Nevsky Monastery. He promised to go.

How quickly death separates us. How quickly life distracts us from our duty to the dead. Four days ago? Was it really only four? Had a bullet not struck Dmitri, he would now be the Minister of War's adjutant, by his side at all times, essential at all times. But it had struck—and now purely out of obligation tomorrow he needed to carve out the time to go to the Monastery.

He waited with pleasure to see Kornilov again. This general gave him much hope, especially because he was so dissimilar to those conceited, exalted Tsarist generals who all had to be dispersed now. Indeed, remarkably discovered, democratic, simple. (Who was it—Polovtsov?—who first suggested him? Polovtsov himself, a smart man, would be a good person to task with the minister's personal correspondence, which required knowledge of the military milieu.)

Well, things would come right somehow.

He and Kornilov set out in a motorcar, down the highway, shining their headlamps. There was snow in the city, slush, and it was tough going, but outside the city it had been rolled smooth by sledges, firm and easy.

There was also something reassuring about a nighttime motorcar ride, perhaps due to the headlamps' whimsical light. The light sways and picks out objects. It began to seem that things weren't as bad as they'd been the previous day. Things would come right, we would overcome.

There was an imperturbability to Kornilov in his manner. Not in the least worked up, no matter what he was talking about. Or else Guchkov still had to get used to the nuances of his expression.

But he may perhaps have been gloomier than that afternoon. He hadn't managed to get much done that day. He'd gotten to know his staff, canceled the military parade scheduled before him in honor of the revolution, received the Izmailovsky battalion's commander newly chosen by the soldiers, and prepared his inaugural order.

An elected commander of the Izmailovsky battalion—how could he not receive him now, dismiss him?—fed General Kornilov vital information. The battalion was still safe, they'd only killed two officers and removed twenty or so. A lower rank, an educated type from Petersburg, set the tone for everyone, and officers' meetings did not take place without representatives from the committee. What had he had to say in his first order to the battalion? Gratitude for his election and happiness at the coup, that the mighty Russian spirit, which should make everything German choke, had been set free. . . .

"You mean there's some truth to this, Lavr Georgievich?" Guchkov chimed in hopefully.

After all, everything German and Baltic has been crushing us for two hundred years. A common language with the soldiers could be sought on this basis. Purge the army of Germans—even if, let us allow, they are all loyal.

The elected Izmailovsky officers came up with yet another idea: immediately begin creating "iron enlightened discipline." But the barracks, they said, is our sacred place. Don't let the workers go trying to teach us military conduct.

Guchkov liked this even more:

"Marvelously said! I must borrow that. Iron and enlightened!"

Beggars can't be choosers. The terrified officers had no choice but to come up with a way to adapt to the new circumstances—and they didn't do badly! Now that everything had been let slip, bungled, adaptation might be the only solution. But under the influence of the ongoing war this had to be unified somehow.

Guchkov had cheered up. Perhaps, somehow, it would all be welded together by the Russian spirit, by patriotism.

Kornilov hadn't been terribly responsive, hadn't been excited about agreeing.

"But why cancel the parade? It's a good way to unite people."

"It's a bad way," Kornilov responded. "Who would review it? You? Me? With the Soviet of Deputies by our side? Without the Soviet it can't be done. So better no parade whatsoever. I'll go around to the battalions."

He did get his bearings quickly, it's true. Quite the general. Albeit a little dim to look at.

They were sitting side by side in the back seat, and to the light of a handheld lamp, Guchkov read the draft of tomorrow's order for the District. It was brief, and the language considerably more restrained than the Izmailovsky one; Kornilov had not promised too much. The great Russian people have given their homeland freedom, and the Russian army must give it victory.

The people have given you much but are expecting much from you. Be a joyous bulwark for the new government. And may God come to your aid!

He was right. They couldn't bow to the soldier. He was right.

Yes, a manner was gradually being worked out, a form of address. Guchkov may even, in his Order No. 114, have been too hasty.

Kornilov had been taken captive because he had stayed with the rear guard and covered the retreat. Taken seriously wounded. In Austrian captivity he had studied their army and their manuals for soldiers—looking for weak spots. Then, somehow, he had feigned an illness and they'd transferred him to a hospital, and from there he escaped with a Czech, an Austrian soldier. They walked over mountains and through forests—to Romania. They fed on berries. They exhausted, lacerated themselves. His companion was caught—and shot. Kornilov managed to go over to the Romanians one night just before their declaration of war—otherwise he wouldn't have made it.

Everything about him was good, genuine, military.

Where was he from? He was born on the Irtysh and had known poverty in childhood, his father a Cossack, his mother a Buryat. Starting at age thirteen he'd been in the Siberian Military Corps, and then the Mikhailovsky Artillery School. He'd served for a long time in Turkestan and the Caucasus, done reconnaissance in Afghanistan, and studied all the local languages. He'd been a military spy in China.

A natural. And how old was he? Forty-six, younger than Guchkov. But if you were to start trying to choose new officials from the lists, you'd pass him up, not notice him.

Get to know the Tsarskoye Selo garrison? They could do that by visiting their barracks, the 1st, 2nd, 3rd, and 4th Guards Riflery Regiments, or they could go to the town hall, where, as they knew, a gathering of all the local agitators was meeting. (They went to the town hall.) Tsarskoye Selo had a large garrison because many barracks had been built here over the years.

As for being in Tsarskoye Selo—why had he come? . . . Why had he come? It all came clear to Guchkov why he himself had come: to see the Tsaritsa!

They, so omnipotent a week ago and having hated him so, were separated and could not see each other. But Guchkov had gone to see *him* and accepted his abdication and was now going to see *her*.

Make an appearance? Have a look at her?

He himself didn't know precisely why, but there was a passion, a morbid pleasure as when going over a painful but healing spot.

The tie of hatred is in a way similar to the tie of love. It preferentially connects two people acutely curious about each other.

He had seen the Empress one single time, in 1905, when he had returned from Manchuria—and she'd liked him. The suspicions and hatred blazed up later, entirely at a distance. Guchkov knew that—and never flinched, never stood down.

And she? What was she feeling now? What would she feel when he walked in? He needed to see her—how she was feeling the pain!

But they arrived at the town hall at a far from early hour, when the deputies' session was in full swing—this newly fledged session of the past few days, when people were thirsting just to talk and listen, it didn't matter to whom or about what. And all of a sudden, this gift: the Minister of War and District commander! Those assembled were ecstatic and prepared to listen. Kornilov, just a few hours from the train, was still entirely unused to this. Why should he speak if not in front of a formation? And what should he explain to his subordinates when it would all be in the order?

But his natural simplicity suggested to him how to speak, and he held himself in anything but a superior way—and in him they sensed one of their own and roared out ovations.

Guchkov did know how to speak! In the past few days, he had spoken in barracks, and he remembered his unfortunate experience at the depot. He already knew how to steer clear, and he knew how to be liked. No matter what he spoke about, it all went well: about the people's great victory, about the dawn of happiness, about the makeup of the new government, about the anticipated democratic transformations, some of which had already been started, about the new iron enlightened discipline, and about the victory over the fierce foreign enemy. It all went with equal success and kept being interrupted by joyous greetings. (Only Guchkov didn't know for himself why he was wasting his strength on this, why he was standing here and speaking as if in a dream.)

Afterward they sorted out the positions of units, who was carrying out what patrols where, who was close to the palace—and Kornilov read and corrected the sentry orders. Much time passed on all this, and when they approached the Aleksandr Palace, after passing the pickets, it was already after midnight. Not that many windows in the palace were lit, but many may have had their curtains drawn.

The new style of relations: without asking either the minister or the commander, members of the revolutionary Soviet tagged along in three motorcars; they, too, wanted to check on the palace. How quickly this boorishness had been aroused in the people—and here they'd let it be aroused. As with the military parade, it was simpler to cancel the visit altogether than to share it with the Soviet.

But Guchkov was already being led unswervingly to this meeting.

Although on the telephone half an hour before they'd warned of the visit—here the sentries were refusing to let them into the palace. They summoned the sentry chief. It was an ambivalent situation: the units guarding the palace, although they had recognized the new order, nonetheless obeyed only their commandant, General Resin.

He was summoned. They could not fail to let the Minister of War and District commander through—but at the same time the revolutionary Soviet had dug its heels in, a dozen and a half with their red bows. (Who wouldn't want to visit the palace, take a look, and then tell about it!)

Dry old Count Benckendorff, with his monocle, descended the staircase to them in the entrance hall, retaining his bearing but obviously terrified. He identified himself, high chamberlain, and asked what he could do for them.

Guchkov had warned beforehand that Kornilov had to initiate all conversations. It would have been too obvious and improper if he, Guchkov, were to do so himself.

But Kornilov spoke reluctantly, scowling more than usual.

He said they needed to see . . . the former Tsaritsa.

"But the hour is very late, gentlemen," Benckendorff objected pitifully. "Her Majesty is more than likely asleep. Or with the children. You know all the children are gravely ill."

Yes, this late hour had not worked out well; it hadn't been a part of his plans. But since they'd come, they couldn't leave without seeing her.

Guchkov held his firmly set head and brows steady, yielding in nothing. Kornilov cast a sideways glance, understood, and said:

"But it is essential that we see her."

"Fine, if you please, I will try," Benckendorff replied reluctantly, embarrassed. And he invited them to follow him.

Kornilov, suffering from the revolutionary deputation much more, evidently, than the inured Guchkov, not having yet smoothed out under Petrograd democracy, rapped out a sullen command—without any "gentlemen" or "comrades"—that they not follow them anymore.

This was uttered so confidently that the "delegates" obeyed and did not follow.

But they did pace around the entrance hall in such a way that the first floor could scarcely be defended from them.

Servants flitted by in braided caftans, stockings, and buckle shoes.

They waited in a small intermediate room without sitting down. Benckendorff was so distracted he forgot to ask the purpose of their visit, and Guchkov immediately thought how alarmed and frightened the Empress would have to be by the late hour, and the unexpectedness, and the fact that it was *he*. She must be dressing with shaking hands.

But so much anger had accumulated inside him over these years that he not only did not pity her but, feeling in his pocket for his dark green eyeglasses, which he wore in the daytime when he had to ride in a motorcar in the blinding snow—all of a sudden, for some reason, he removed his pince-nez and put on the eyeglasses.

Not for some reason—something inside him told him that this would be inexplicable and frightening to her. Now he was her master—if not of her life and freedom, then of her mood and day-to-day existence. Even more of a master than she from the throne had ever had power over him, an independent Russian figure.

He and Kornilov did not say a word all these minutes. People might hear them now, and this general was not from his usual circle and wasn't someone with whom you got to talking. He stood like a sullen Mongol, dry, as erect as in formation, having no need to shift his weight to one foot.

Benckendorff entered, quite pathetic, and stated that they would be received in the linden drawing room, which was a few rooms away. He led them.

When the Emperor had received Guchkov as Duma president, Guchkov had been in this palace, too, but had been led rather differently. Now he examined the milieu he was moving through not without interest; he too, just like the soldiers from the revolutionary deputation, wondered about this life, elevated above all that existed—what was it like?

In reality, it was not royal but like in a landowner's large wooden house, nothing more.

They entered the linden room. Here there was little upholstery, but there was delicate linden paneling on the walls, and the armrests were linden yellow.

They did not sit down here, either.

Benckendorff left through another door, opposite.

Soon after, he opened it, letting the Empress through—but she was dressed, as could not have been expected, in a nurse's plain gray dress, wearing a kerchief with a red cross on her head.

Behind her walked someone else—an elderly, graying, tall, handsome man in a formal black suit. From the Romanov type of his face, Guchkov realized this was one of the grand dukes, but he didn't understand immediately who it was or where he'd come from—and then he realized it was Pavel, who lived nearby.

Benckendorff closed the door, leaving.

The four of them, so different, stood in arbitrary places in the drawing room, forming neither a square nor a rhombus. They stood there as if meeting by chance and for a purpose unclear to all.

Even beside Pavel the Empress seemed tall—and taller than both the men who had come.

Still the same unvarying majesty as seen so much from photographs, a stern, cold majesty—but once beauty? But for true beauty there had never been enough of the play of life in her.

Majesty—but a woefully weary majesty. She would not let herself express this weariness, though—or express anything, for that matter—other than her incomparable endurance, her most august spouse's abdication notwithstanding. Her mournful look and thin, pursed lips created an impression of disdainful contempt and ill will.

She was quite pale—with spots of nervous redness on her cheeks.

Pavel stepped out farther, but she took just two steps from the door, leaving ten to her visitors. And not only did she have no thought of extending her hand, or even referring to the furniture, and in general proposing no ritual whatsoever, asked aloofly, with glittering eyes:

"What may I do for you, gentlemen?"

Pavel had adopted as imperious a look as he could. He was standing to the side and half-turned toward the Tsaritsa, like a higher class of courtier, like a strict observer of ceremony.

Suddenly Guchkov felt that this red cross on her nurse's kerchief was embarrassing him. His own life had often been entwined with just this red cross. He had marched up and down the Manchurian valleys with that insignia on his sleeve during the last war, and through small Galician towns in this one. This very red cross, aimed at him now from the Empress's brow, was sending him an embarrassing greeting. He had come to see this haughty woman as he would have come to see his eternal and worst enemy. But the red cross was strangely signaling to him that they were of the same brotherhood.

Embarrassed by this in part, in part he could not reveal that there was no purpose whatsoever to their visit.

But Kornilov stood erect and in an extremely respectful tone said:

"Your Imperial Majesty! The Minister of War and I have verified the reliability of the palace's defense and your safety from the direction of Tsarskoye Selo."

And immediately—a string relaxed in her! She shrank. And her head was no longer held back so firmly.

"Yes," she remarked with a metalated weariness. "These past few days there has been great unrest in Tsarskoye. There has been a lot of shooting and stealing and shouting. I beg of you, general, to give my ill children peace. And keep those people from attacking the palace guard."

To the general alone, as if not noticing Guchkov. Guchkov found himself on the sidelines altogether.

But this way the entire point of his visit was lost. So he joined in the conversation, too, noting that the Empress shuddered at his voice. He did not address her as "Your Majesty," did not refer to her in any way. He did not soften his voice—though perhaps he did? He himself was not master of the moment. The sense of his words was gentle, and this was automatically expressed in his voice:

"The Provisional Government has instructed me to find out whether you have everything necessary. What assistance do you need? Medicines for the children perhaps?"

How many years had he thought of her without a single ounce of good, first raging, then swearing he would bring her down. He had come here also not intending to say anything gentle but merely to check to see whether she had softened from her fall. Yet it had been spoken as if he had come to express magnanimity or even to be reconciled.

In surprise, she turned her elongated head with the tall hair hinted at under her kerchief. Her brows had parted out of stark arrogance: this horrible man had come during these horrible days not to gloat but to offer her children medicines?

Medicines for her children? There could be no mockery or dissimulation in this. Medicines for her children? Balm for a mother.

"I thank you," she replied completely differently now, but not addressing Guchkov by any name. "We have plenty of medicines. And doctors. The only thing we don't have is peace."

And with a new thought, she added (her voice was low, beautiful):

"My hospital is here, in Tsarskoye Selo, but I am now deprived access to it. If possible, take care that it wants for nothing."

And for a half a minute they looked each other in the eye, as if twelve years hadn't passed, and with surprise did not find the former force of hatred in themselves. Her eyes had lost their arrogant gleam and were simple and human, weary. His were covered by smoky green eyeglasses of some unknown sort. But who was there to hate? This baggy, unlikely Minister of War, unmenacingly offering medicines? This tormented, demeaned, forty-five-year-old woman with five sick children?

Suddenly for some reason he recalled and was stung with repentance that he had ascribed to her and disseminated through society letters which she turned out not to have written.

A phantom vision passed between them that the entire past may have been a mistake—and then savages with red scraps wouldn't be roaming through the palace right now.

Guchkov promised about the hospital.

And in the grip of this feeling of belonging to some shared stratum with established rules, he suddenly for himself, but while preserving his voice out of consideration, asked whether she didn't have any other wishes.

And the Empress immediately did:

"Yes! Give those innocently arrested back their freedom—General Groten, Putyatin, Tatishchev, and Gerardi."

Oho! Show the least softness and she immediately takes advantage?

Guchkov did not reply to that.

The conversation suddenly broke off, having no further topic or point.

And so, not having sat or addressed each other in any way, not having exchanged greetings at the beginning, and merely bowing slightly at the end, they had exhausted everything.

Having stood this whole time with immobile imperiousness, Grand Duke Pavel moved to escort them out. And in the next rooms, proceeding alongside them, he said:

"Her Majesty did not fully explain to you how extremely upset she is by the troops surrounding the palace. They shout and sing and now are opening doors and allowing themselves to peek inside. The devil knows what they are going to permit themselves. Could you not appeal to the soldiers' sense of decency?"

Guchkov replied that he would send his own officer.

Pavel inclined his head slightly and hung back, never having offered them his hand. Apparently there had been some movement toward doing so, but he feared being left with it extended.

Guchkov left quite dissatisfied. He had taken nothing away from this and had merely promised something, and the entire plan to visit now seemed idiotic.

If one looked at events to come — the groundwork needed to be laid for a possible arrest.

He therefore instructed Kornilov to find and appoint a reliable new chief for the Tsarskoye Selo garrison.

[4 5 3]

SCREEN

The Red Cross.
Known to all, straight and square,
    maximally simple geometrically, without any curved narrowings,
        like the St. George cross, and without a single extended tip.
    The cross of universal mercy.
=   Only placed not evenly as usual, but slightly tilted, as if moved,
        turned on its axis.
    More noticeable.
    Even more noticeable.
=   Why, it's slowly turning on its center. Its sides are already on the
        diagonal,
    already past the diagonal. It was just about to even out
    but kept going straight on.
=   Its revolving is now quite noticeable,
    for all to see.
    It is simply spinning, pinned at a central point.
=   Wound up not by its own force — it
    keeps spinning — faster and faster.
=   So fast now that we can't keep up with its positions —
    no longer a cross, no longer of mercy,
    does it have eight tips?
    twelve?
    sixteen?
    It's flickering — and blurring! —
    into a red wheel.

19 March
Monday

[454"]

(FROM THE FREE NEWSPAPERS, 18–20 MARCH)

THE NEW MINISTERS. Above all, these are honest men. Moreover, these are intelligent, strong, and steadfast men. Russia could not have made a better choice. Our duty is to give them our complete trust. . . . Not the pitiful figures of the pathetic, thoroughly rotten, operettic regime but outstanding representatives of Russian public circles, which rest on the country's undisputed respect and trust.

. . . Now we have nothing to fear. The new government, invested with the people's trust, will take all measures. How different is the Provisional Government's honest declaration compared with the hypocritical promises of the old regime! We have made a headspinning leap from absolutism to full democracy. . . .

. . . Counterrevolution may rear its head at any moment, be it in the rear or at the front. The authorities' sharp gazes must be aimed in both directions.

. . . Nor is it even worrisome to hear about disagreements between the coup's two main forces. There is a firm confidence that a middle line of conduct will be found; and Berlin will have no cause to rejoice at our discord. . . .

. . . Are there any reasons for alarm or concern? Three times no! With respect to the final aims of the war, all currents of Russian democracy will converge in the passionate affirmation of our immediate military objectives. Faith in Russia's victory has been reborn! . . . If the slogan "Everything for the war" ever had meaning, then it is now.

Helsingfors, 17 March . . . It's said that some officers who did not wish to recognize the new regime were killed in the night. Arriving delegates were quickly able to lift the tension. . . . Some of the officers immediately joined the exultant mass. The Executive Committee has energetically set about liquidating the old system's stooges who were completely forgotten during the general turmoil.

. . . There is no call to worry about the new relations in the army in some way reflecting harmfully on the military front. There is no trace of strife between soldiers and officers; German bullets there have cemented them into a unified monolith. . . . We cannot help but welcome the idea of the Soviet of Workers' Deputies and the formation of election committees.

(*Stock Exchange Gazette*)

. . . The organs of old police retribution have been burned down by the revolutionary people, but meanwhile, violations of the law have multiplied over the week of revolution.

What is to be done with the **RAILROAD GENDARMES** protecting the stations, bridges, and traffic? The Ministry of Roads and Railways proposes giving them over for inclusion in the troops.

Citizens! Do not spread false rumors! The Russian press is free and it will tell the people *everything*.

AMONG THE JEWS. On Saturday, a service was held in a Moscow synagogue with a huge convergence of people come to pray. Rabbi Mazeh, instead of the previous prayer given for the Tsar, uttered a new prayer for the new government. Then he delivered a speech, saying that the best aspirations of Russian Jews had come true because these aspirations had always fully coincided with the best aspirations of the best Russian people. And what has been accomplished fills Jewish hearts with unutterable joy.

THE SUICIDE OF S. V. ZUBATOV. One of the biggest zealots has shot himself. . . . The morbid soul of this reactionary lackey could not bear the bright light of freedom. In the past few days, the deceased had languished terribly, seeing the destruction of the monarchic order. . . . Recently he had promised Burtsev his memoirs. . . .

THE MOSCOW NOBILITY. An emergency assembly. Noblemen must do everything they can to assist the new regime and obey commissars' instructions. . . .

. . . Telegram addressed to Rodzyanko: "The Vologda nobility believes that the new government will lead Russia onto a bright new path."

. . . The internal enemy has been defeated but not destroyed! The bear has not yet been killed; he is merely stunned. . . .

Kshesinskaya's flight. There turned out to be machine guns on the roof of her palace. . . .

. . . The disagreements and arguments will come later. But now, there's no need to cast any gloom on the bright days of our transfiguration. Russia has recovered its former rule by the people!

. . . There are pessimists who are frightened by everything, especially the Soviet of Workers' Deputies.

. . . A group of Moscow deacons and sextons, having assembled during these historic days of the triumph of Gospel truths, is welcoming the dawn of the newly born righteous life. . . .

APPEAL FROM POLICEMEN. "Brothers, citizens! The hearts of the lower police ranks have always been with the people. If we have failed to please someone, then it was while carrying out the will of their higher-ups, while remaining unwilling slaves. At the first summons, we shall show up to fulfill our shared civic duty. We ask you not to embitter those close to you against us, since we have suffered so much physically and morally."

Arrested city policemen collected among themselves 215 rubles, signed over for the revolution's needs.

. . . Petrograd turned out to be supplied with enough sugar for the entire month of March. Enormous stores of frozen fish and fowl have been discovered.

The Fate of the _Moscow Gazette._ There is complete disarray in the editorial office. All employees, with the exception of comparatively few, have declared themselves to be supporters of the new regime and intend to put out a newspaper with articles that correspond to the spirit of the time. They sent a telegram to Lvov and Kerensky greeting the new government.

. . . Employees of the lowest pay grade in the prison department sent telegrams of welcome to Minister of Justice Kerensky and the Provisional Government.

. . . Don't celebrate! Let the joy burst from your heart but go to work . . .

. . . A general meeting of employees in the printing business. In his speech, a Committee member said: "Now that the old system has collapsed and a revived Russia is creating the forms of a new order, there is no place for timid, temporizing souls, and therefore department employees must show their political face and say convincingly that they see the new government as Russia's savior."

Censorship employees adopted a resolution welcoming freedom of the press.

. . . All citizens who love Russia stand behind the new system. And those who are not with us have to be considered felons and traitors.

(_Russian Will_)

ORDER to the troops of Moscow, 19 March. . . . The lower ranks have been engaged in the sale of uniforms, boots, and linen issued for military service. . . . Their manufacture costs the homeland large sums of money. It is the sacred duty of every soldier . . .

Military District Commander
Lieutenant Colonel Gruzinov

. . . Petrograd and Moscow have accomplished for Russia a great national deed—and the Russia of the towns, villages, and provincial cities have no choice but to stand under the new regime's banners. The main thing has been done; all will go well. A new order is being forged.

. . . The Central Committee for Food Supplies appeals to the honor and dignity of each and every citizen and asks them to limit themselves in their consumption of staple foods and to make purchases only out of true need, and not to put in reserve. . . . Your economical consumption will be the best assistance for the government in its work.

. . . The Petrograd City Duma is preparing to rename streets and bridges: everything "Aleksandrovsky," "Nikolaevsky," and so on will be named "Freedom," "12 March," and so on. A special commission has been created.

ARREST OF SASHKA THE SEMINARIAN. This beast of a man who holds nothing sacred. . . . After release from Butyrskaya Prison. . . . All criminals wishing to elicit trust have pinned on red ribbons. . . .

N I K O L A I   I I   M O V I N G   T O   E N G L A N D
In the next few days he is supposed to leave Mogilev for Tsarskoye Selo, and from there he and his family will move to England.

. . . The Social Democratic *Pravda*, which was routed by the old regime, has come out. Greetings to the voice of the proletariat, from now on a free voice!

(*Stock Exchange Gazette*)

For immediate sale, a **fashionable mansion**, aristocratic street,

Pure-blood **Siberian cat** for sale.

✻   ✻   ✻

NEVER TRUST A RED MORNING

✻   ✻   ✻

[4 5 5]

While constantly changing trains, moving farther from Petrograd and closer to his loyal regiment, Kutepov was prepared to consider both his own fight on Liteiny and the arrest of the Preobrazhensky officers, that mirror room and that disorder in the Tauride Palace, some kind of delirium. If he could only wake up—would it disappear? So that his regiment wouldn't even believe it when he told them? And if it wasn't a delirium, then they were already putting it down there, or firm troops were already on their way there, a matter of another two days?

Then suddenly, at one of the stations, he was struck by the news that the Emperor had abdicated the throne!

A fabrication? . . . No, a Manifesto. And the Emperor's brother had abdicated, too.

That was it. Like they had let the air out of your chest.

And from the enormous Front, no one had come to disperse the inexperienced, untrained, unbridled garrison crowd. And now it was the end of the Dynasty?

The end of Russia? . . .

And we, the immortal Preobrazhensky Regiment—whose guard were we now?

> Firm our bayonet three-sided
>> Honor's voice has yet to burst.
> Onward, onward, glorious regiment,
>> Russia brings its very first. . .?

When after the Japanese war Kutepov was transferred to the Guard, he'd felt tense and constrained: upper nobility, bluebloods, the upper classes' world alien to him. Himself a descendant of lower Novgorod nobility, he was wary among them at being lost or humiliated, and his heart did not accept their belated pretensions to overwhelming superiority. It seemed to him that he would nowhere feel as good and at home as in his own 85th Vyborg Regiment.

But there were strict rules of military service, and honing to them, Kutepov joined with dignity and was accepted with dignity in the Preobrazhensky. Soon after, he was put in charge of a training detachment—and during the years between wars he had educated and trained more than half of the present-day Preobrazhensky sergeants, who were the support net for the entire regiment. The mobilization schedule had left him in Petersburg—so Kutepov requested a war assignment, as he once had in the Japanese. For a long time he had not distinguished between himself and the Preobrazhensky Regiment in any way, and now, battle after battle, he had been tied to it by blood. In the very first battle, in August 1914, his leg was shattered. The regiment was moving away, and Kutepov couldn't raise himself, so he took out his revolver for a shootout to the death. But Preobrazhensky men, themselves wounded, dragged him out. After his injury he had barely returned to the regiment when he was wounded in his other leg by a grenade fragment. In the summer of 1915, seeing that the regiment was being flanked, he threw himself into a counterattack from the battalion reserve, suffered a groin laceration, and while lying on the stretcher would not let them carry him out of the battle but continued to command his company. After his third recuperation, he was given His Majesty's company to command.

Before him, the killed Captain Baranov had believed that, while commanding the Emperor's company and wearing the imperial monogram, he did not have the right to lie down during rushes. This was the Preobrazhensky spirit! Staff Captain Chernyavsky, in his dying delirium, had sung the words of the regimental march. The Guard does not hide, the Guard marches openly! (And how much we have been laid down, laid down for this!) Not because he had accepted the wisdom of this pride—never to lie down in battle—but last year's battles had shaken out in such a way that his 2d battalion could not attack the village of Raimesto any other way than through swamp and open approaches, up to their knees in water. In the famous battle of Svinyukhi-Korytnitsa (the "Pigs' Trough"), again from the reserve, this time the corps reserve, and again without an order, relying on his own understanding, Kutepov swiftly led his battalion and a half through a barrage of German fire, merely tacking between them as openings arose, and for speed's sake not hiding or firing—there was no point in hiding—so they ran as fast as they could across this fiery verst and joined battle with the attacking Germans (golden officer epaulets shining openly in the sun). The Germans surged back, leaving behind machine guns and prisoners. In the Svinyukhi forest, Kutepov took command of several companies of Izmailovsky men and Jaegers—and continued to advance toward the Bug, while the Germans were blowing up bridges across the Bug, leaving their guns and piles of ammunition on this bank.

Where had all those battles and all that blood gone now?

Under the trampling and spitting of the maddened capital?

To pigs at the trough indeed? . . .

Kutepov was standing at the train car window on the final stages to Lutsk—choking from bitterness. His entire life, his entire career, everything he had lived through had been shaken to the core. What about his whole life, he was only thirty-five, after all—how was he to go on?

The only hope was that, once he reached his regiment, he would find a fortress here.

But the Guard was in those ruinous places where Brusilov had positioned it in July 1916, on the Stokhod River, which was overgrown with sedge, amid swamps and small woods. They had moved only a little from the same Svinyukhi and Korytnitsa where so much of the Guard had been pulverized the previous September. They were in the same dampness, especially the observers in some places—up to their knees in dank mud, those resting in dugouts didn't sleep but bailed water, and even in regimental headquarters so much water flowed in that they chopped down more logs for the floor and walked on those. True, today, the day of Kutepov's return, it had frozen and snowed a little, at which everyone rejoiced.

The problem, though, was that as they had been called back on their way to Petrograd, the Preobrazhensky men on 16 March had returned to their thirty versts from Lutsk—but had not enjoyed being in reserve for long. For some reason they were once again put on the front lines, for another three weeks.

At first glance, Kutepov thought he was seeing what he'd expected. Nothing in the regiment had changed, the soldiers were performing their service beautifully, and there was perfect order and deference for rank. And of course not a single red scrap.

But the officers' mood was unrecognizable. Everyone was depressed and gloomy—no, killed, killed by fear for the future—of Russia, and the Emperor, and the Emperor's family—although they felt no love for the Empress here—and for the Guard's future and their own, and they spent all their time in harrowing conversations, attempts to understand, the construction of fantastic plans, and their immediate refutation. Events had come crashing down, bringing with it everything built in their minds, and now had only barely, just barely begun to be put back together.

How cleverly they had timed their coup! There were almost no old officers, and the young ones were non-gentry. The Provisional Government were English stooges, Russia's enemies. English money had overthrown the legitimate Emperor.

Yes, the Emperor was patriotic, selfless, had sacrificed himself. . . . But, but . . . Let him abdicate for himself—but why for Aleksei? How could he leave us without a monarch?

Kutepov arrived—the first live messenger to the regiment from Petersburg. He was taken in greedily, his every word and episode, in order to picture the unimaginable capital gone mad. Before him, perfectly absurd rumors had come into the regiment—and nothing could be believed or refuted. But when he told them, what offended everyone here most bitterly of all, what insulted them, was the conduct of their Preobrazhensky soldiers and officers there, in the reserve battalion. How could they have? We weren't summoned or allowed to go, but they were there! How could they have failed to try! What kind of Guard were they?

The regiment's commander, Major General Drenteln, asked his aide Kutepov in detail about each and every one of the officers. And responded like this:

"With regard to the young, what consoles me, at least, gentlemen, is that they had not yet sworn an oath to the regimental banner and had not yet had the honor to perform service in the Preobrazhensky's fighting ranks. Just one thing is clear: they all violated their oath, and I forbid them from coming here from the reserve battalion."

Kutepov saw them all in the flesh—and in part let it be understood how they could have lost their way like this in the Petrograd situation. Not that there was any forgiveness.

"The Petrograd garrison, gentlemen, as a whole, is a plague and must be amputated from the army!"

"Yes, but then so should all Petrograd! And we will learn nothing of our near and dear. . . ."

The Guard's heart-wrenching despair, which tormented not only the officers but the sergeants as well and the old-timer soldiers, too. They cursed the fact that they had not been loaded up that very night and taken there. It was the Emperor's will, and no one dared judge him, but still: what was the sense of us twiddling our thumbs here and not being in Petrograd? Wouldn't we have served Russia more loyally there than we are sitting here in flooded trenches?

The day before yesterday, when the two abdication manifestos arrived here at once, the officers went mad and the old men sobbed openly.

Meanwhile, company officers had to explain it to the lower ranks. But what could they say?

Not even the first, the Emperor's Manifesto, but the Manifesto of Mikhail Aleksandrovich mowed down any faith in the future.

And what of all the men we lost and buried? . . .

A Constituent Assembly? The army—the nobility and peasantry—was going to be sidelined from voting. On the other hand, everyone freed from the war would vote. One could imagine what they were going to vote for.

When had all this happened? When finally our weapons were superior and our ammunition abundant—nor was there any complaining about the food supply, the army was not fed badly at all. Was there anything being rationed in Russia? Was this really comparable to Germany or England?

Even now it wasn't too late, before this anarchy spread to the army. That would be a terrible beast nothing could withstand! Might they still manage to drive out this rabble? March on Petrograd and wipe out all those swine?

It had slipped, the moment had slipped.

But it would be good to fully understand what our lower ranks were actually thinking. Did they actually share our despair? Did they understand the meaning of it all? Would they themselves not be infected by the Petrograd example?

The Horse Guard frowned, glowered at the coup—not just down to the last cavalryman but even down to the last horse.

Nonetheless, it was impossible to live and not obey any state system whatsoever. But was it possible to obey the Duma's Provisional Committee or the Provisional Government—those empty words?

These past few days the ray of light and sole hope had been the appointment of Grand Duke Nikolai Nikolaevich. Here was someone on whom to rely! The grand duke would stand on guard of the Russian State's ancient principles! The Preobrazhensky had to say its piece to the grand duke. A telegram was sent from all the officers to Tiflis.

Meanwhile, they received an order from the Supreme Commander saying that he had submitted to and called on everyone to submit to the Provisional Government.

Well, if that was so, then it was so. It was an order, so there was nothing to discuss. That made it a little easier, though why should it?

Drenteln, limping badly, his leg doing worse, said to Kutepov:

"I went so far as to send a letter to the Emperor. With Lieutenant Travin. But he didn't come back, and I was very worried. Whose hands might it fall into? How will they interpret it? Travin had indeed been detained. But not searched, fortunately. And he, in despair, brought it back."

"Maybe send someone to GHQ? To say that the regiment remains loyal, is grieving over the abdication, and is prepared to do *everything we are ordered*?"

Drenteln squinted:

"To Alekseev? Something could be sent. If only I knew what would be useful to him."

"But by then the grand duke will be at GHQ."

"Correct. I'll send Colonel Oznobishin."

[4 5 6]

What could be seen from GHQ? From Naval General Staff, from the center of the capital, a certain Flag Captain Altfater was systematically reporting that there was perfect order in Petrograd, in Reval, too, and this calm was spreading more and more from Petrograd to the Baltic Fleet. Nepenin and many officers had been killed, but here naval headquarters reported that the officers were returning to their ships, bringing apologies and regrets, and the vessels' crews were swearing to uphold order. Seemingly, though, if the vessels' crews repented, then they should give up Nepenin's murderers and condemn them. Without that, how could stable discipline be restored? Alekseev had the feeling, though, that even a murmur about this now was impossible, and things had to be restored somehow, ignoring all the men murdered and everything routed.

And the politicians? The well-known Rodichev who was able to take in the situation in Helsingfors—but boldly proposed immediately restoring independent Finnish military units, which, he said, would replace in Finland the disorderly Russian units and bind the Finns to Russia in some unknown way. This was dangerous nonsense. Forgotten was the bitter experience of the past. Quite the opposite: then the Finns would join the Germans against Russia. Be that as it may, Rodichev was not embarrassed in the least to propose this kind of rubbish, and they had to hurry to submit this plan to Nikolai Nikolaevich while he was still in his last hours in Tiflis, after which the connection would be cut.

What he had seen and might resolve—he didn't dare, but he had to keep sending on inquiries to the Caucasus, even those from the Black Sea received from Kolchak. While Nikolai Nikolaevich's replies were always to wait. Well, finally today he had started out, and in three days he would be at GHQ.

The only remaining obstacle to the grand duke's return was the abdicated Emperor's delay at GHQ. Prince Lvov had tried to hurry him along, saying that Nikolai II's sojourn at GHQ was causing alarm among public circles, and it was advisable that his departure from Mogilev be hastened. Alekseev himself longed for that very thing! Suddenly the Emperor sent to Tsarskoye Selo an encoded telegram, and the Tauride Palace fell into turmoil. There was a persistent awkwardness from the ambiguity that the chief of staff and former Supreme Commander might have some kind of concealed relations. (And they did. Suddenly the Emperor sent Alekseev a confidential request: Couldn't he be allowed to read Order No. 1? The request was trivial, but the delicacy was in the contact itself, and who could be asked to print a copy on royal paper? He got the idea of asking the modest Tikhobrazov and privately sent it off to the Emperor.)

The awkwardness arose even from the Emperor's invisible eye, his imagined (for they no longer saw each other) gentle gaze, which held no reproach but only gratitude.

That gaze, completely distraught, without any reproach whatsoever for the refusal with which he had brought his impossible telegram about rescinding his abdication the day before yesterday. (Alekseev had hidden that telegram out of sight so as not to cloud anyone's mind ever.)

As long as the Emperor was here, it was awkward to remove his portraits at headquarters. But at the same time, keeping them up any longer was now reckless.

The Emperor, too, however, having been burned on his last journey, had no desire to go now without guarantees.

And now, this morning, fortunately, they had arrived. Prince Lvov approved all three of the Emperor's requests as conveyed by Alekseev: the government agreed to the abdicated Tsar's passage to Tsarskoye Selo, his stay there due to the children's illness, and then his passage to the port at Murman.

Alekseev was immediately relieved. And he swiftly reported this to the grand duke in the Caucasus.

[4 5 7]

One could wonder at (and learn from) the tact, good sense, and magnanimity with which Nikolai Nikolaevich managed revolutionary events in the Caucasus. If only they had guided the revolution as he had, there would have been no riots or false starts.

Nikolai Nikolaevich had spent the year and a half of his vice-regency and High Command in the Caucasus in harmony with his new location, had found himself here in full, and had not longed for Russia, which had not managed to stand up for him. However, in literally the past two or three days, he had felt himself steadily growing, indeed outgrowing this place;

and he felt the need to share his feelings with Russia even before returning to it himself.

This kind of objective is best served by newspaper correspondents. So yesterday he had been pleased to receive in his palace for an interview a correspondent from the progressive *Morning Russia*. And he had shown him much kindness and spoken with him most graciously. He had expressed his hope that the journalist would note that there was in Russia a region where events were proceeding quite calmly. The new government had been instantly recognized, and the Supreme Commander, in the fullness of his power, would not permit any reaction in any form anywhere.

"I think"—and the grand duke smiled—"with this communiqué you will give joy to many."

"Your Imperial Highness"—the flattered journalist was looking for more—"Russian readers would like to hear your authoritative word on how much the revolutionary events that have taken place have brought us closer to victory."

The grand duke could not deny him this authoritative word! He replied, illuminated by the awareness of his own destiny:

"The trust of Russian society has always supported my work. With divine assistance I will lead Russia to victory. But for this it is essential that everyone be conscious of their patriotic duty. If the new government finds itself without support and fails to ward off anarchy, it will be disastrous!"

A few ominous signs had nonetheless appeared at a few geographical points in Russia—and this disturbed the grand duke.

This, of course, should have been said not to the correspondent; he should warn the government itself, Prince Lvov. But Prince Lvov oddly had not responded to several telegrams already. There was nothing to be done, though, and yesterday Nikolai Nikolaevich had sent him another telegram. Complaints were coming in constantly from Alekseev about certain orders that were bypassing GHQ. And here the grand duke reminded him that unity of command was of the utmost necessity for victory. Since the government could not fail to hold Russia's well-being and ultimate victory dear, the Supreme Commander hoped that all the government's instructions or, more accurately, desires, concerning the army would be sent only to GHQ. While the Supreme Commander himself . . .

Was going to GHQ—yes. But why was the government being so indecently silent? Not only had there been no replies, but, the grand duke noted, the Provisional Government's confirmation of the Supreme Commander had not been published yet. This was, of course, a simple oversight. They weren't used to this and were in a spin, but the Senate knew its business. Why hadn't it published the appointment signed by the Emperor? As it was, everyone in Russia knew, everyone considered the grand duke to be Supreme Commander, but this had not been officially confirmed in any way. An odd situation.

And because of it the grand duke felt a need to shore up his position. It occurred to him to send out through Alekseev the following order:

"For the good of our homeland, I, the Supreme Commander, have recognized the authority of the new government, thereby demonstrating an example of our military duty. I enjoin all ranks as well to unswervingly obey the established government."

And for Alekseev to send copies to the government. This was an expressive step, a seemingly indirect but public letter to that same Lvov showing all the grand duke's loyalty, but also — make the appointment official. What are you waiting for!

They should know and appreciate the loyalty with which the grand duke had rejected Kolchak's mutinous proposal. After all, he might have, oh, he might have acted entirely otherwise! . . .

Alekseev was the one officer unquestionably subordinate to the grand duke: he sent everything out, reported on everything. But Alekseev was also a secretive figure. Under Nicky he had become accustomed to independence and was de facto Supreme Commander, and now he faced falling under the grand duke's powerful, fracturing will. Could he want that? Wouldn't he himself take aim at the Supreme Commander post?

This nagged at the grand duke a little, but he was obligated to hold himself proudly and cheerfully in front of everyone. The previous night he had submitted yet another telegram to Prince Lvov, saying that today he was leaving for GHQ and proposed being there on 23 March. He did not know how free his route would be and could not draw up a precise schedule. He would be telegraphing en route. He would be very glad if the prime minister would join him there for a private meeting of extreme importance.

Go? Yes, it was time. But the grand duke could not leave the Caucasus orphaned, either. Yesterday, Sunday, he had had to honor with his presence a large military rally on the square — about sixty thousand officers, soldiers, and populace, all ecstatic, exemplary order, the Caucasus Army's chief of staff spoke, calling for trust and order, followed by other officers. A rally and a parade — here were manifestations of a magnanimous revolution.

He also had to address a parting, fatherly word to the populace of the Caucasus. Aides who wielded the pen well had been writing this appeal for two days, and at last, satisfied with it, the grand duke signed it. Expressed here was the feeling he had experienced and wished to convey to the people. The State Duma, which represented the entire Russian people, had appointed a Provisional Government. Meanwhile, Germany was keenly following to see whether our marvelous but confused armies might be unable to offer it resistance. Meanwhile, riots were increasing, and this threatened the army, though not in the Caucasus, of course. The peoples of the Caucasus had regarded political events with the dignity of patriots and with wise calm. Thus they should remain after the Viceroy's departure: not listen to those who called for riots but heed only the instructions of the government, and then, with Divine assistance, our most valiant armies would carry out their sacred deed, and the Russian people, blessed by God, would say what kind of state system they considered best. In addressing you, the peoples of the Caucasus, I want you to know that I have ordered all officials to obey the new government, and any attempts at resistance will be prosecuted with the full severity of our laws.

The grand duke quit the Caucasus with a feeling of pride and warmth. A part of his heart remained here.

This morning he had gone over to his vice-regal chancellery and told the employees that, alas, he would not be able to arrange their affairs, but he hoped to do so upon his return to the Caucasus after the war, when he might settle here as an ordinary landowner, since he held his own piece of land in the Caucasus.

At that moment he believed it, too. Why not? Maybe he would settle here. Although he did have a plot of land and palace no worse in Crimea and an enormous, beloved estate, Bezzabotnoye, outside Tula, with a famous kennel.

Go—yes! His military duty was now calling insistently! But could you really leave promptly with these women? Stana and Militsa's packing had dragged out endlessly, and since early morning it had been clear that they would not manage it today. Perhaps by night.

And so there was now an extra day. For yet another extra day the standard of the royal family would wave over the palace. But the program of farewells had already been completed, and there was nothing to do. Once again he received the compliant Khatisov, to whom he had grown so close these past few months, and thanked him, thanked him for everything.

The extra day, though, also brought extra and gloomy news. A communiqué arrived from Bezzabotnoye saying that the estate had been ransacked by a mutinous crowd, primarily the wine cellar.

Oh ho! What turmoil! What were the authorities looking at? (True, after this, they had been embarrassed and had now posted a guard of 12 cadets.)

Who knew how it would go in different parts of Russia? Perhaps it wasn't a bad idea to have a reserve in the Caucasus, where they loved him so.

But here, in Tiflis itself, soldiers today had begun to disarm city policemen at their posts.

What outrage was this?

And a Soviet of Workers' Deputies had formed in Tiflis. This was good.

And the officers of one regiment, having arrested their superiors, had offered their services to the Soviet.

What on earth was this?

In Nakhalovka, a Soviet of Soldiers' Deputies had formed.

And Stana and Militsa still weren't ready and wouldn't be before tomorrow!

He and his brother Petya decided the wives would not go to GHQ anyway but to Kiev. Let them stay there and Petya would escort them. The Supreme Commander would take the reins and then summon them all.

To GHQ! The practical and familiar military situation at GHQ excited, called, and enticed him—the true place where Nikolai Nikolaevich should have been throughout the war without a break, had it not been for the envy of the now punished Nicky, an envy incited by Alix's eternal hatred for Stana.

[4 5 8]

(HOW IT WAS IN THE PROVINCES. FRAGMENTS)

*   *   *

A new station look spread from Petrograd over all the railroads: on the platforms were soldiers with red scraps, then also without belts, then also with straps undone, emphatically scruffy, with provocative shouts.

On the trains, ticketless soldiers began to fill all classes of train car. Only the International Sleeping-Car Company for some reason still inspired respect for a while.

*   *   *

In **Tver,** the crowd that stormed the governor's residence had many infantrymen from a reserve regiment. No sooner had they removed the governor from his apartment than the soldiers burst in to steal, drink brandy and wine, and take the sugar. Besides the governor, they killed several policemen on the streets. The soldier Ishin bayonetted Colonel Ivanov, commander of the 6th Reserve Battery, and immediately pulled off the dead man's patent leather boots (for the sake of which he'd killed him) and put them on in the snow. No one laid a finger on him.

The provincial prison was burned down and the jailbirds roamed through the town, freely stealing in the police's absence.

*   *   *

On the banks of the frozen Volga is little **Rovnensk**, Samara Province, abundant in unsent grain and tar-caulked barges. At two in the morning, a Samara duty officer warned everyone on the telegraph line to be prepared to receive an especially important state telegram. The young Rovnensk telegraph operator, Ivan Belous, full of regrets that he was not at the club that evening and hadn't danced the pas d'Espagne and pas de quatre with the sweet young girls, received the tape—and his eyes popped out of his head: the Tsar's abdication! He couldn't even fully understand, couldn't properly understand—and suddenly such a heavy feeling! He hurried to rouse the office chief in the same building. The chief read the handwritten form and with shaking hands checked it against the tape. Then he ran around to his superiors' homes—and in half an hour the small telegraph office could barely hold them all, roused from their beds, shocked, pale. In alarm they kept rereading it, sharing it, and asking questions—but there was no one to answer them. Their small town was still asleep, it knew nothing; they had found out a few hours earlier—but to what end? What could they do? The Emperor had rejected them. . . .

The next day a small crowd would appear on the street carrying a red cloth panel never seen before in Rovnensk. The institute director, a fat, sleek gentleman with a red bow and a red armband, read the Manifesto out loud, inveighing against the "old regime" and extolling the oncoming freedom.

Not one of those who had been at the telegraph the night before was to be seen. The town had been left without a government.

*   *   *

The most elegant public frequented **Odessa's** famous Café Fanconi, which was as chic as any in Paris. All of a sudden, a noise came from the street, the singing of "You Fell Victim," and a procession appeared carrying red flags, two hundred or so young people looking fairly untidy and unruly. The café's customers rose from their little tables and walked over to the mirror windows, young men and young ladies both. They stood and watched. The procession passed without looking this way particularly.

It felt alien, frightening. They returned to their coffee, chocolate, and pastries, but the mood was spoiled. And they soon went their separate ways.

*   *   *

In **Saratov,** the revolution began with the killing of city policemen. The morgues were filled with their bodies. Rallies on every corner. A crowd packed the square opposite the prison and carried on their shoulders someone holding the keys to the prison over his head.

A wounded soldier wept in the university hospital. "Why are you crying?" a nurse asked. "I feel sorry for the Tsar." She was from a landowner's family and educated, and she replied: "He'll be fine."

*   *   *

In **Vitebsk,** the governor's doorman Mikhail wept over the abdicated Emperor as he would over a dead man. But in the governor's dining room, no regrets were heard, rather they discussed how Nikolai Nikolaevich should come to power as quickly as possible. Then there would be no more grounds for gossip about the Tsaritsa. They reported on street events: one policeman had been beaten to death and a priest had been knocked off his feet. Vitebsk Mayor Litevsky tried to justify it: "You have to understand the people. After all, they've been oppressed for so many years!"

The police remained in place, awaiting the governor's instructions, while he laid all his hope on the grand duke—he would take matters in hand! For now, the governor himself was trying to be as democratic as possible. The officials peered around: was this serious or would things go back to the old way? In any case, they stepped back and turned away from the odious figures of the former regime. Vitebsk's liberals walked around with their heads high: we won! Crowds of Jewish youth exulted through the streets and had success at propaganda with everyone but the peasants making deliveries at the market.

*　　*　　*

All that happened to the **Tsaritsyn** priest Father Gorokhov was this. He didn't call for any kind of uprising, but at the end of the service, after removing his vestments, he addressed to the congregation a word about the governmental changes under way, saying that out of his sense of conscience as a clergymen he could not bring himself to betray the oath he had given the throne—and because of that he did not find it possible now to continue serving at the altar. Then a local lawyer spoke, saying that with the transfer of the throne, a vow made under oath fell away. Meanwhile, Father Gorokhov withdrew from the church. Soon after, a military patrol went to his apartment and arrested him.

*　　*　　*

In **Penza,** the old authorities were arrested, while their replacements (instead of the vice-governor, an assistant attorney Feoktistov, a revolutionary) stood sporting red bows on a plank tribune swathed in red bunting, while below that was the garrison chief, Major General Behm. From the tribune, crowding out the genteel public, certain revolutionaries were shouting about freedom, which would now fly across the barbed wire barriers of the fronts. A parade of troops who had "joined the people" went by. Excited intellectuals broke into the formation, shaking the hands of officers and soldiers. Three regiments passed by—and then a few soldiers suddenly ran out of a fourth, shouting: "Here's your leave warrant!" —and started beating up the general. (His strict order had been not to allow soldiers to roam the town without leave warrants.) They ripped to shreds everything the general was wearing, leaving his naked corpse at the base of the tribune. Other soldiers ran up and kicked the body.

Right then, the newspaper's editor was delivering a speech to the troops—and they chose a new garrison chief.

Meanwhile, the crowd liberated the prison—more than five hundred prisoners, many of them sentenced to hard labor. They were driven around town by cabbies for free, wearing robes and little felt caps, rattling their broken chains and shouting to the people.

In the evenings, Penza turned off the lights early and locked itself in from robberies. Drunken, unstrapped soldiers inundated the town.

*   *   *

In **Ekaterinburg,** unknown civilians and soldiers began gathering independently at the City Duma for a rally, crowding out the council members: "If you don't agree with us, the 126th Regiment will come to democracy's aid!"

The next rally was at the theater. Very few civilians and almost no women, but the hall was overflowing with soldiers, so ominously that disaster was about to strike. An actor standing on the parterre barrier called out loudly: "The governor . . . the bishop . . . the regimental commanders . . . the gendarmes . . ." and a drunken ensign waved his sword from the stage after each one: "Arrest them! . . . Arrest them! . . ." And the hall exulted. The actor shouted: "Occupy the telegraph! The telephone! The station!"

Meanwhile, in the theater's small buffet, railroader Tolstoukh was opening a secret session of the revolutionary democratic committee: "Anyone who doesn't agree instantly will be killed on the spot. We are immediately sending out details to arrest those in power and regimental commanders."

Present also were several radical members of the City Duma. After breaking away from that session, they discussed among themselves whether or not to warn the regimental commanders. Better not. It would be viewed as informing.

*   *   *

Irkutsk. At the first news about the coup in Petersburg, the Irkutsk administration came to a stand-still and gave no signs of life. The populace's gazes turned to the political exiles as their leaders now. Everyone saw authority in them, and wealthy circles, famous industrialists and lawyers, made no attempt to seize that authority, rather on their faces was a respectful expression toward the revolutionaries. The 40,000-man garrison did not resist submitting to the new revolutionary organs. In the name of the exiles, Irakli Tsereteli and Abram Gotz themselves set out at the head of a detachment to make the arrest. Governor General Pilz, a stooped old man, greeted them with frightened bows. They told him that he, a prisoner, would be held in this same building, and he dissolved into words of gratitude, saying he had always been confident of the "nobility of men of ideals."

*   *   *

In **Achinsk,** they spent three days honoring Breshko-Breshkovskaya, who had been freed from exile in Minusinsk. On her way to the station, a stream of troops presented arms, and people with religious banners thronged in front of her carriage.

* * *

In the small town of **Zeya,** beyond the Amur, soon after the Tsar's abdication, local intellectuals convened a large assembly of the inhabitants, mostly common folk, gold prospectors. They proposed selecting a committee and named Abramov, a native Siberian and successful prospector, one of the region's pioneers. He rose to his full gigantic height:

"I can serve the Tsar, but since he is gone, I refuse any public work."

His words were drowned out by hurrahs and applause.

The Tsar's portraits remained hanging in nearly every house.

* * *

Cadets from the **Khabarovsk** corps met the revolution with indignation. Forced to remove the Emperor's portraits from the company halls, they moved them to their classrooms. They began pasting images of the Emperor to the undersides of their desks and two-headed eagles and imperial crowns to their sword-belts. When a Provisional Government commissar scheduled a garrison parade for the square, which was fitted out in red, the cadet corps came out under the tricolor flag and without a single red bow.

* * *

In **Samarkand,** the high school pupils' exultation was so mandatory that even the prosecutor's son asked at home that they make him a red bow. The son of a local lawyer had held on the whole war as a rear officer and at the time had flattered the prosecutor—now he reprimanded him in public while the prosecutor smiled guiltily under hundreds of eyes. A chariot decorated in bunting moved with the demonstration, and those standing in it bowed to all sides. All the former rulers were forced to march with red bows; they pressed close and smiled ingratiatingly at every soldier they met. Spring was in full swing, but they were denied water for their gardens, so they would dry up.

* * *

In **Novocherkassk,** on the afternoon of 14 March, the traditional requiem was held for Aleksandr II with the usual ceremony at the Cossack army cathedral. But Bublikov's telegram was already being passed around the town, and an alarm went up. On 15 March, more rumors broke through, and great agitation arose among the intelligentsia and in the workers' district of Khotunka, where two reserve regiments were stationed. On the night of 15–16 March, an Executive Committee arose on the revolutionary spur of the moment; it consisted of forty people—members of the duma, the war industry committee, the Zemgor, university students, lawyers, and representatives of workers' sickness funds. The Executive Committee, with the addition of revolutionary officers like Captain Golubov and Lieutenant Arnautov, took into its own hands the telegraph, telephone, mail, and the Don *Gazette*, confiscated the archives of the gendarme administration and the ataman chancellery—and then went on to arrest the ataman for his "insincere and ambivalent attitude toward the coup d'état," forcing him to hand the Don atamanship over to a teacher at the Don preparatory boarding school, Lieutenant Colonel Voloshinov.

Demonstrations went past the bishop's house—and the old bishop made the sign of the cross over the people through the window. The less enlightened gathered in the army cathedral to pray. They wept.

Six versts away, in **Persianovka**, the director of the agricultural institute, Zubrilov, an actual state councilor and Don nobleman, assembled his pupils in the recreation hall and, seriously agitated, announced that the monarchy had fallen and delivered an ecstatic speech, saying that the monarchy had only held back the country's development and now Russia would take seven-league strides.

In the Cossack village of **Glazunovskaya**, they sounded the alarm. People came running with buckets and pitchforks—to fight a fire. And then two village constables and two former warders (the three had suffered convictions in the past, removal from their posts for extortion and bribes, and even prison), egged on by a resourceful commissary soldier and truly sozzled on moonshine—declared themselves to be the executive committee, and down with the village ataman and chairman. Later, in the village office, they started smashing shelves of papers and called on the people to make a search of the priests and teachers and divide up their food stores among themselves.

*   *   *

In the middle of the day, a teacher at the **Poltava** modern school—a puny, ginger man wearing the tabs of a collegiate secretary, walked into the two older seventh-year classes and invited them to come out quietly to the auditorium. (They had already heard something as it was.) Three portraits had always hung in the auditorium, Peter I, Aleksandr III, and Nikolai II, and now they had been draped with white sheets. But there wasn't a scrap of red anywhere either. The teachers and Inspector Rozov, the Russian teacher, were standing in a cluster in the corner. They also led in, just as quietly, a group of older seminarians, older commercial school pupils, and a covey of girls from the neighboring high school. Their negotiations were barely audible.

Inspector Rozov icily announced the Emperor's abdication.

Who wished to say something?

His well-known favorite, seventh-grader Surin, handsome and slender, with a flush on his cheeks, stepped up to the podium and with exalted movements declared:

"We are no longer pupils in a modern school, or any other! We are free from the oversight of swine like Inspector Rozov! We will carry the revolution through the town! The province! The whole country!"

The pupils took fright, as if snow had sprinkled down their collars.

The inspector was weeping in the corner.

A journalist from the local newspaper spoke and called on the pupils not to remove their caps when they met their teachers on the street. That was a symbol of slavery, and they were now free.

✻   ✻   ✻

In **Kiev**, on the night of 16–17 March, the first night after the abdication, bands formed and tore down signs with the two-headed eagle and destroyed national flags. The crowd watched sullenly. Threatening shouts rang out from it.

On the morning of 17 March on Kreshchatik—an exulting, shouting crowd and a great many red flags and posters. ("War on palaces.") A terrible, enormous, homogeneous crowd in a spirit of joy and rage. Soldiers wearing unbuttoned greatcoats stood out, Dnieper sailors, too. A worker heard two old men, pushing out of the crowd, complain to each other that they were scared—and he started cursing and punching them. An officer climbed onto a sidewalk post, unbuttoned his tunic, pounded his chest, and shouted that he was happy to throw off the hide of a tsarist dog.

The wife of wealthy Kiev jeweler Marshak (a merchant of the 1st Guild, possessing full rights, all sons with a higher education), when she learned about the revolution, went out on her balcony without a coat or hat and hung red fabric like a flag: we're free from slavery!

At a general assembly, the Kiev police expressed readiness to serve the new order before other institutions did.

✻   ✻   ✻

In **Temryuk**, at the mouth of the Kuban, there was a modern school whose graduates went on to study in the big cities and on vacation brought back the revolutionary spirit and songs to the local high school, the middle school, and the many youths who gathered from the Cossack villages. So that even here, in this remote backwater, high school girls understood that autocracy had outlived its era, and they sang "Hostile Whirlwinds" and "The Little Cudgel."

On one of those March days, the seventh-year students kept waiting for their mathematics teacher, who for some reason hadn't come. He had always been gloomy (he didn't like teaching mathematics; he liked music, a fine violinist)—and right then walked in joyous and, waving his arms, congratulated the pupils on the revolution! It was like a clap of thunder. They had supposed it would come in the future, but no one had expected to live to see it so quickly. The teacher began recalling in front of his pupils his student years in Moscow—and they stayed on during the break.

What kind of next lesson could there be? It was nothing but break now. They poured through the building. The teachers themselves couldn't explain anything, and they no longer were any different from their pupils in the general exultation.

Meanwhile, though, the school guard came and brought the news that everyone was being assembled in town on Alexander Nevsky Square. Many of the girls were burning to go and incited the others as well. It was so infectious: go to this unusual gathering and hear extraordinary words. None of the administration dared detain them, for fear of being called reactionary or Black Hundred; there could be nothing worse.

Vera went, too, but at the very first corner she heard a speaker saying nasty things about the Empress—and she ached with alarm and revulsion. She didn't go to the rally but turned off and wandered, deep in thought, coming out at their small train station, where the platform was deserted. An emptiness overtook Vera, just as it had when her papa had died a few years before.

Soon after, her classmate Lyuba, with whom she wasn't even friends, came up to her. She asked:

"You, *too*?"

She didn't say what "too" meant, but suddenly this brought them together. They clasped each other by the arm, as before an impending disaster, and practically without discussing it, wandered down Uporny Lane, also deserted, and looked from afar at the white columns of their high school and at the white Cathedral of St. Michael—and still couldn't part with each other, as if something special had been revealed in each of them—and had united them.

Meanwhile, the entire mass *pushed off* toward the rally.

[4 5 9]

Village winters are always rich in weddings. But this winter, Kamenka did not celebrate a single one.

Shrovetide, too, went by without festivities or horse races. Two or three die-hards came out—and stopped short, turned back.

Since the autumn sweeping up of men for soldiers, the village had emptied out noticeably. The war, the damnable war, went on and on, swallowing up men, and there was no end to it. They took more youngsters, their call-up year.

In December and January the frost held steady, but beginning in February blizzards started up such as rarely twist and wind like that—and they twisted and wound for two weeks in a row. So much snow swept in that for three or four days there was no path of any kind going anywhere. Then the blizzards died down, but in mid-March there was not even a whiff of spring. With the freezing temperatures, snow fell—sometimes every other day, sometimes every night. The livestock and horses stayed calmly in their sheds, not displaying their usual pre-spring uneasiness. The men finished up repairs on the harness, still not going out to their plows, undercarriages, and seeders. And the women finished up their weaving, completing their piles of winter work, and some tap-tap-tapped their Singers (there were about a dozen of them for the village, bought for a hundred rubles in a hundred monthly installments). Only the children didn't lose track that it was this Thursday they were supposed to bake lark-buns, enriching their boring Lenten fare. They nailed together birdhouses out of boards or hollow logs—the older ones by themselves; some badgering their grandpa.

Life fell off—and so did trade. Here and there throughout the district the invariable annual fairs were not held on the usual days, and it was clear that in Kamenka, too, the March fair would not take place. There was no one to buy and no one to sell—what was the point of that money anyway? At the Sunday village markets row after row was deserted, and even the birch brooms, which used to go three for a kopek, now you couldn't buy one for five.

Evpati Bruyakin wasn't buying new lots of any kinds of goods, and his shop got emptier by the month, although it still had plenty of many things—and there was no way to tell how the goods could be used up or what he could do with these heaps of goods. Had he made a mistake in his presentiment? Business was dead, yes, but there was the war. Would things pick up afterward? There was still no threat sticking out from anywhere. Had his heart deceived him?

He had plenty of other concerns, if only with his children, especially his older daughter Anfia. The two younger ones had already left home, but she hadn't. She'd just turned twenty-four and still a spinster. Since childhood she'd had a passion for her studies, and her father had sent her to high school in Tambov. She never did graduate. All that came of Tambov was her getting entangled by a university student, Yakov, the son of a Tambov merchant, who inveigled her to read seditious books, while he himself went to prison. Evpati had burned those books of his daughter's more than once, but she had gotten hold of them again, without Yakov now. She was an eye-catching girl of marriageable age, she stood out, and her dowry was large, but no matter how many tried to propose to her—she refused them all and wanted only Yakov. But his trail had gone cold. And she had sat too long, and had begun to dry out, to ail and ache—and what was to be done with her now?

True, she worked excellently at the shop. She sold more than all of them. His older son was on the land, had now married, and they were getting ready to set him up on his own; as breadwinner, he wasn't subject to the draft. But the younger one, Kolya, hadn't wanted to study and was drawn to debauchery beyond his years. Evpati ached as a father over him: if he hadn't raised his son to be practical, better he hadn't raised him at all. Our children are our sorrow.

And Kolya just couldn't settle down in that school! He was so much bigger than everyone there, even when they played at war, ours against the Germans, with snowballs or sticks (and the school guard, Fadeich, drew up military plans for them, so that the Russians would always win)—that didn't catch his fancy either, he was even embarrassed to play. He was already running with Mishka Rul (although that same Mishka had been drafted into the army recently). But most of all—what a ladies' man he'd grown up to be! All the girls had sensed this, and he was quite in demand with them; they sussed out, no doubt, what he was like now. He liked all of them, every one, as if they were peeled from the same egg, and he was prepared to love each of them equally. His romance with Marusya the soldier's wife broke off because her husband came back from captivity crippled. Marusya wept and wanted to keep on meeting with Kolya, especially since her husband had been sent for year-long courses for horticulturalists. But Kolya Satych didn't want that. Why should he get mixed up with a married woman when he had girls unbosoming themselves to him? Three such ones decided at Yuletide to keep watch over the hut of some old people who had gone visiting—and "so they wouldn't be afraid," invited three boys, the other two older than Kolya. Alyona with the white-blond braids below her waist was there, and that caught his eye after the dark Marusya. For half the night they read the cards and the coffee grounds, and poured a yolk out in water, and looked into the mirror, and threw a shoe over the gate. How this would end could not be foretold. But after midnight, the older girl stated: "Boys, it's time for you to go home and time for us to go to bed." She told one girl to sleep on the stove bench, took the bed for herself, and threw down a felt and a sheepskin coat on the floor for Alyona—and put out the lamp with a laugh. And they went their three ways. And when Alyona later whispered on the felt: "What have you done?" Kolya, with a new voice of undue forwardness and triumph: "I'm not the one who did it, we did it together, don't be shy!"

After that night a new joy stained his soul—and he thought of himself only with the expression of a hero, and all his plans were conceived only in his love for young women. But his father berated him and drove him to school over and over again—though even Anfia tried to talk him out of it, saying the teachers weren't teaching but trying to hide the truth, that the whole world was a struggle for existence and the survival of the fittest.

Today, too, Monday, they were sitting in class, fifteen or so of different ages, boys and girls. From the frosty day the sun shone in merrily—but Yulia Anikeevna, as slim as a blade of sedge, paced back and forth in front of the desks leading a dictation:

"Dew, heaven's messenger, glistened on the flowers and the fragrant grass."

Yulia Anikeevna had been teaching with them for more than a year and was herself from Tambov. But there was also a second teacher, frail, his face covered in blackheads, and he twitched and he was mean—unanimously disliked by all and called Twitcheye. They shared the classes this way and that, trading off.

It was quiet. Pens were scratching.

Do? Dew? Flowers? Flours? . . . Kolya's deskmate didn't have the foggiest either, but Kolya peeked at what the girl cater-corner had written—and she wrote her letters big and distinct and always knew how. D-e-w, that's how.

Such quiet—not a rustle, not a voice, not a knock, not a rumble—not anywhere in the school or outside. The kind of quiet that had hung over the Kamenka all that winter, and especially after these blizzards, when they hadn't yet beaten down the roads.

And Yulia Anikeevna, placing her feet over the strong, uncreaky floor, in this silence, quite noiselessly in her felt boots—and with the feeling she always had when she was dictating, entering into the words even too distinctly:

"And the forest's dark curly head would dress in the silvery fabric of fog."

All of a sudden, the heavy front door opened and banged. Down the corridor rang out loud, confident, frightening steps, such as there should not be in a school.

Yulia Anikeevna shuddered and stopped mid-word. Looking at her, all the pupils were disturbed, too.

Steps—this way.

And the door—yanked. Without asking permission, which Yulia Anikeevna had never allowed, there entered silently— completely silently, like into an empty rick-yard for a bundle of straw, not into a classroom full of pupils—blackbearded Pluzhnikov, wearing a shaggy sheepskin cap, a short black belted sheepskin coat, and glistening wide-top boots.

Coming up behind him was Twitcheye in his tattered little coat, without a cap. But not stop him from bursting in. And not paying any attention to Yulia Anikeevna either.

The teacher stood there dumbfounded, too startled to ask. They could only have entered like that with something terrible—so the pupils kept their heads down. It got even quieter than it had been.

Pluzhnikov walked up to the front wall, raised both arms, grabbed the black lacquer frame of the Tsar's portrait—and pulled it down!

The nail clattered to the floor.

The teacher pressed her book to her chest and turned white.

While Twitcheye walked up to the matching portrait of the Tsaritsa next to it, but couldn't reach. He turned around, took Yulia Anikeevna's chair without asking, climbed on it uncertainly—and pulled down the second portrait.

Without returning the chair or explaining anything, they picked up the portraits and carried them out, leaving the class stock-still.

"And Vladimir Mefodievich?" the teacher exclaimed. "Did he give you permission?"

Vladimir Mefodievich was trustee of the zemstvo school and zemstvo hospital next to it, having built both with his own money.

"We don't need Vladimir Mefodievich anymore!" Twitcheye responded in his harsh, mocking voice, the way he knew how.

And they went into the corridor.

Pluzhnikov hadn't wanted to offend the teacher; he hadn't done it this way on purpose but on impulse. This news had come crashing down on him, the first in Kamenka, just half an hour before. The township administration didn't know yet, nor did the village constable.

It had come crashing down—without warning, like a boulder out of a clear blue sky. But in that half-hour he had already digested it—and learned that he'd been ready for this his whole life.

Because he wasn't a Tsar, he was a tsarling.

Being the first to learn—he had to be the first to do something. And the first thing he thought of was taking down the portraits.

The plover-teacher was nattering something alongside him, but Pluzhnikov didn't hear him. He stood with his feet set wide in front of the school on the hill over the village—and took it all in, in the bright sun, all of it covered in snow, unshakably calm, knowing nothing—and wondered how the Tsar's abdication was going to rumble through the village now. What would happen to the constable? What would the men go rumbling on about?

He stood above his village, where he had always been number one, and right now he had to take primacy yet again.

Pluzhnikov understood it thus: the inert shackles were falling off, and our strength, very likely, was now going to be unleashed all the more. Now the men themselves had to take hold of their own lives.

Here was when the peasant would find justice!

The pupils, released, ran past him and down the paths.

[4 6 0]

For another two days, the intercessor for religious prisoners searched out Kerensky all over Petrograd, in vain. Again he went to the Tauride Palace. In the Ekaterininsky Hall lay soldiers, their legs raised, even more litter and cigarette butts on the floor, and a whole lot of felt boots—but no Kerensky, and someone said he was at the Mariinsky Palace now. The conscientious Tolstoyan headed for the Mariinsky Palace, but the doorman there assured him that not only was Kerensky not there now, but he had never once been there.

He was undoubtedly in Petrograd, and in many places. Somewhere he was rushing around in seething, diverse activity, he was being torn to pieces, but Bulgakov could not get to him. That was when Bulgakov decided to leave for Moscow but before doing so to visit Gippius and Merezhkovsky, where they knew him, one more time. There they invited him to have a cup of tea and didn't question him but explained to him the following. Gippius—that freedom had already become a soiled word, and that there could be carnage, because the Soviet of Workers Deputies wouldn't give the Provisional Government any breathing room; and Merezhkovsky—that before that the Germans would come and they would start the carnage. Bulgakov seized the moment and interjected about his failures with Kerensky. And Filosofov, who was sitting right there, suggested that Kerensky's wife, Olga Lvovna, a dear and educated woman, had always been her husband's right hand in all his public activity. He could go see her at home, tell her all about it, and ask her to speak to her husband.

"That's right!" Gippius exclaimed. She immediately went to the telephone and connected with the Kerenskys' apartment. But the maid answered that the lady wasn't home and the boys were at school.

Then the writers composed letters—to both Kerenskys—requesting that they receive and hear out Lev Tolstoy's secretary. And an encouraged Bulgakov put off his departure. That morning he headed straight to the Kerenskys' apartment.

He took a cab to quiet Tverskaya Street, past the Tauride garden; there were no carriages or pedestrians, no traces of revolution, either, on this street. The indicated address turned out to be an old three-story building with dirty gray paint peeling in many places. The entryway was rather soiled and unpretentious. There was no doorman.

But a young girl came out and pointed to a door on the first floor. Bulgakov was deeply touched by the plain tastes of this famous man whom the entire revolution lived by and admired.

A brass plaque on the door: "Aleksandr Fyodorovich Kerensky." Both the building and the staircase were so deserted, though, it seemed to Bulgakov when he rang the bell that no one would answer. However, the door was opened, and a clumsy, sleepy maid wearing a warm cardigan and a warm scarf on her head, as if the rooms behind her were freezing cold, confirmed that Olga Lvovna was at home. Bulgakov handed her a letter, his calling card, and his request that she see him briefly.

The maid went away, came back, and showed him into the small drawing room:

"The lady asks you to wait right here for a moment."

No, this wasn't a drawing room but a very modest lawyer's waiting room. Two embroidered Japanese pictures on the walls. Very simple furniture. Actually, another room could be seen through the door—larger and more comfortably furnished. And from somewhere far back a young woman's voice was heard, evidently from the telephone.

Soon after, Olga Lvovna came in, hurriedly. Her hair was parted to the sides and combed high, but also slanting to reveal her forehead. And this slant, which was conveyed to her large eyes, and then her slanted mouth, created the impression of a kind of constant surprise on her face.

"Forgive me!" she said immediately. "But I can't receive you now. I just had a call. My husband has suddenly taken ill, he's fainted, and I have to go to him at the Ministry of Justice."

Bulgakov realized they could not have his conversation. But:

"Mrs. Kerenskaya. Might I be of any use to you at this moment?"

She livened up at the support:

"Do you know a doctor? Over the telephone they said a doctor was needed."

Bulgakov was amazed. The hero of the revolution, the Minister of Justice, had taken ill, and in the ministry near him they couldn't come up with a doctor otherwise than through his wife?

Unfortunately, he was not a resident of Petrograd, but the ministry could not be lacking a doctor. They must have already found one!

"Do you have a cab?"

"Oh, I just let him go!"

"I don't know how I'll get there," Kerenskaya said uneasily, and her face looked even more surprised and distraught.

Olga Lvovna threw on a light, cheap coat with white fur at the collar and cuffs and they went outside. The street was deserted as before. They strode toward the Tauride Palace.

To deliver the wife of Russia's young, beloved hero to him—Bulgakov felt himself authorized to stop any motorcar or eject the riders from any sleigh—but there was neither one nor the other. There was no one!

They walked quickly over the snowy, trampled sidewalks, not terribly wide or cleared here, just enough for two, and at Tauride Street it widened.

"Aleksandr Fyodorovich must have become greatly overtired over these past few mad days. How much does he sleep? Can he sleep?"

Serious alarm flashed across Olga Lvovna's face, which was very pale; as could be seen in the light, she herself was exhausted:

"Oh, if only! This last week he hasn't once slept through an entire night. He's never even gone to bed." (She couldn't tell a stranger that he hadn't been at home at all! That she herself kept watch over him at the Duma, exhausted from insomnia. . . .) "Can you imagine his condition? And how much he's been through!"

"But you yourself are exhausted! Completely exhausted!" He now got a good look.

"Yes." Olga Lvovna tried to smile. "I'm necessarily torn in all directions. And how many telephone calls! Believe me, in the morning I simply can't get dressed, what with one call and another. I put on one stocking and run. I put on another—and another call, and again I run!"

They finally found a cabbie. He was standing, and his steaming horse's sides were heaving.

"Do you know where the Ministry of Justice is? On Ekaterininskaya. Please go, and quickly."

"I can't, sir, the horse's all played out."

"Well, just take us to another cab! We're rushing to a sick man!"

They got in. The cabbie dragged along little by little. Barely faster than on foot. As if to mock them!

They reached another cab and transferred. But that one's emaciated horse was no better.

A motorcar. A motorcar! Bulgakov wanted to see and stop one.

Finally they heard beeping behind them. It was coming with a red flag on its hood. Bulgakov jumped down and ran in front of the motorcar, where a university student was next to the driver.

Blocking the way and stretching out his arms, he stopped it.

"Comrades! Comrades! This is the wife of Minister of Justice Kerensky. She must be taken immediately to Ekaterininskaya Street. The minister has taken ill!"

The motorcar's passengers also panicked. The minister taken ill? The student hopped down and politely seated Olga Lvovna.

And off they raced.

Bulgakov paid the cabbie and now, not hurrying, wandered down the sidewalk pondering what fate it was that kept interfering in this matter of his?

With Kerensky, an even tragic outcome was now possible, but if he did recover, then obviously it wouldn't be soon or easy. So there was no point waiting to be seen by him, or even his wife.

And he knew of no one else to whom to turn. That meant he should leave Petrograd.

Hours remained, now entirely for himself, so Bulgakov went to the Academy of Sciences, on foot, economizing on a cab. There, in the manuscripts department, they promised to show him the authentic manuscript of Lermontov's "Demon."

[4 6 1]

At a certain point, the Duma President felt very slightly relieved.

He himself was so used to bearing the entire rockface of Russia that he didn't even notice this easing in his shoulders right away and remained tense and continued his tremendous work. The actual moment of this easing he noticed subsequently, when he'd already sent the smooth flow of events on its way. (He heard praise for himself, that he was "the old Kutuzov of our coup": when everything depended on his single word over the telephone, he never once erred in tone, pitch, or calculation.)

That day, Rodzyanko recommended that the two acts of abdication be proclaimed for the first time at a public session of the State Duma. In that way, the Duma would be manifesting itself as the bearer of Supreme Power to which the Provisional Government was responsible. But the Kadets and their lawyers sharply objected that this would only anger the leftist elements and rouse them against the Duma and that they would start demanding a democratic National Assembly.

How could the Duma be assembled if the left wing was opposed? Everyone would see the schism. Such a shame, but he would have to abandon the idea.

And so? Russia was not yet a republic but rather something amorphous, transitional, in anticipation of a Constituent Assembly. When it did assemble—there was no doubt that Rodzyanko would be chosen its chairman and the definition of Russia's future fate and its form of governance would depend largely on him. In the event of a republic, he could not fail to be Russia's first president.

But for now, a more ordinary, no longer revolutionary, life was beginning, with normal nights. The Provisional Government appointed by Mikhail Vladimirovich had begun its work and had left the Tauride Palace. Remaining there were the State Duma, its Provisional Committee, and also, in disagreeable proximity, the Soviet of Workers' Deputies. All the more disagreeable because it had occupied all the large rooms and many offices, so that the Duma was left with just three or four rooms and the library, which he had managed to retain.

They had gathered in the library the day before yesterday—not exactly a Duma session but a private conference of its members. With the question of what the Duma's members should do. Stay in Petrograd and take all measures to support the Provisional Government? Or disperse to their electoral districts and there explain to the populace the meaning of the events that had transpired, which was beyond the ken of anyone living outside Petrograd? And at the same time help with grain transport? They tended to prefer being here. However, they did form a bureau to record those wishing to go (some left of their own accord, without authorization). Whereas the extreme rightist members of the Duma had gone into hiding and not shown their faces in the Tauride Palace since 12 March. They could not be tracked down or controlled.

During those days, Rodzyanko himself had been incredibly busy. First he'd had to reply to GHQ's naïve protests against Order No. 1, to explain that they shouldn't worry because the Soviet's orders meant nothing because it wasn't part of the government. Then he had to receive a messenger from the peasantry, a wounded sergeant from Tver Province. Then he'd had to read the endless congratulations and good wishes, the entire rain of telegrams from all over Russia. All Russia trusted only the State Duma; so how could he refrain from responding sometimes?

Meanwhile, though less than before, all kinds of congratulatory delegations of civilians or military formations kept thronging to the Tauride Palace—and how could they be deprived of a vivifying word of response from the Duma? But there were no Duma members wishing to respond—and it was all left up to Rodzyanko, over and over. There were dangerous moments, too. One of the naval crews arrived, acting aggressively. The young midshipmen delivered incendiary speeches, and one of them, right there, in the President's presence, not beating around the bush, declared that Rodzyanko should be shot as a known "bourgeois." (You could just throw out a call to the sailors . . .)

It wasn't just the personal danger—the President was used to that by now—but he was painfully wounded by this senseless label "bourgeois," all that slander the leftists were allowing against the freedom-loving State Duma, labeling it "bourgeois," "reactionary," "franchised," "16 June" and saying it wanted to bring back the fallen regime.

What tact, restraint, and self-possession it took for the President, in the presence of the capital's raging passions, to maintain his equilibrium and not let bloody fighting break out! And this wasn't just about the capital! He was obligated to address all of Russia. Russia awaited mighty proclamations—and this may have been the President's main purpose. Whose voice was more authoritative than his? Over these past few days he had signed many proclamations. Saying that a great deed had been accomplished . . . That by a mighty upsurge of the people . . . But the enemy, shaken by the fall of the old regime, nourished a perfidious hope . . . Brother officers and soldiers, do not permit discord among you! . . .

Then he'd had to write a special proclamation to the shipbuilding docks in Nikolaev: . . . There are numerous secret concealed enemies among you. Do not stop building new vessels, for Germany wants to restore the old regime here. . . . In a moment of danger, the ship's commander calls on everyone to take up their positions! . . .

In all the proclamations, Rodzyanko called on Russian people to wait patiently for the imminent Constituent Assembly, which would decide each and every question. But if one thought about it, wouldn't the Constituent Assembly take the Duma's place? What about the Duma then, and how was it to go on existing?

By making rushed appointments of Duma members to every opening, the Provisional Government had weakened the Duma even more.

No! The Duma could not be allowed to weaken or lose its significance! Its parliamentary grandeur had to be given another jolt!

So Rodzyanko scheduled a general gathering of all the Duma members who had not yet dispersed for 19 March, in the afternoon. And he persuaded Shingarev and very much asked Kerensky to come and speak. The ministers' speeches would elevate the private conference of Duma members in the library to the significance of a general official session of the entire Duma.

In the cramped space, greeted by general harmonious applause, the President addressed to the deputies a short speech in which he indicated that that applause should be directed to the entire State Duma . . .

". . . while I am merely the expresser of the State Duma's moods and desires, which I have been able to divine and sense."

The President went on to inform the Duma members that the general situation in the country inspired peace of mind:

"Throughout Russia there has not been any sign of disturbances or events that might arouse concerns. True, we did receive a communiqué about unrest in Helsingfors, but I sent a telegram there with an appeal for calm—and in reply received a simply ecstatic telegram, from Admiral Maksimov, in which the Baltic Fleet, under new command, declared its full readiness."

A weary Shingarev was already sitting there with his untrimmed beard and worn, stuffed briefcase (on his way either from the ministry to the Council of Ministers or the opposite). He went up to the small table by the bookshelf—such a familiar speaker for them all, with his conversational manner, his pleasantly muffled, convincing voice and smile—and gave a report on the food supply situation in the country. Saying that in the villages there were no self-organized efforts, nor were there sufficient forces for all this work. He reported how he was involving the cooperative movement, how local food supply committees were forming, what proclamations had already been made—and proposed that the State Duma also address a proclamation to the rural population with an appeal to come to the homeland's aid.

The meeting liked that idea, and they assigned the writing of the proclamation text . . . to whom, if not the President?

Shingarev could not stay, unfortunately, and left right then, and the meeting moved on to other important matters.

What were they to do about the Provisional Committee of the State Duma? Of its thirteen members, five had joined the government—and now practically, physically, and legally could not be members of the Committee. One member, Chkheidze, comported himself as not belonging to the Committee, or to the Duma. What was to be done with a Committee that had lost half its members? Voices rang out saying they shouldn't insist on preserving it. But Rodzyanko rejected this solution, for how could one contemplate a Russia left without the Supreme Power? And the distribution of all incoming donations for the revolution lay wholly on the Committee. The President insisted on strengthening the Committee's activities and holding by-elections. And he carried the day. They filled empty seats but avoided the number thirteen this time in the membership count.

They were very much looking forward at the meeting to Bublikov, wishing to hear his report on his stormy actions during these revolutionary days. But Bublikov was still saying goodbye to the railroaders and couldn't be here.

Oh well, Rodzyanko began working indefatigably with his literary assistants on the proclamation with which he'd been charged. Citizens of Russia, inhabitants of the countryside! The old regime that misappropriated the people's patrimony is no more! In a mighty upsurge . . . It falls to you, the tillers of the earth, to help immediately—with grain, flour, groats, and other foods. Brothers! Do not let Russia perish! Take your grains to the train stations and storage depots immediately! Do not betray your homeland! Bring and sell your grain voluntarily, not waiting for special instructions. Bring your grain right now! With God's help—for the cause!

Signing, Mikhail Vladimirovich vaguely recalled that among the seething of these days' matters he had written almost the same proclamation, definitely about grain and almost in the same words, and apparently had already signed it? Shingarev had brought it.

But that one he had signed, most likely, as Chairman of the Duma Committee, or on his own behalf—while this he had signed on behalf of the State Duma, the sovereign of the Russian land.

[4 6 2]

With the revolution's onset, the rule about the universal shortage of practical men had apparently gained strength. Even among the military—Russia was swarming with military men—and there too a shortage? The revolution, for sure, didn't have enough. And so the civilian geologist Obodovsky was even signing orders about taking control of the capital. And he was trying to pacify a bloodthirsty soldier delegation that wished for officers' murders.

And Guchkov, having become Minister of War, drew Obodovsky as well into the commission on military regulations reform, on Saturday, to the Moika, to the ministerial residence, to the meeting of that commission chaired by General Polivanov. There, at a long table, Obodovsky sat among nothing but military men, at the colonels' end—but even from the generals' end no one mocked his presence. Podgy Guchkov, pensive and even depressed, proclaimed that he intended to bring the most progressive elements into the leadership of the army and navy, to heal and transform the army without destroying its military spirit and discipline. Many reforms responding to the army's urgent needs would be carried out in the most expeditious manner, but also without causing confusion in army ranks. The set of these reforms and the methods for their implementation Guchkov was entrusting to those gathered to work them out.

And he left immediately.

The idea, of course, was correct, marvelous even. There was so much that was unfit and even corrupt, decaying in the army, blocking all channels for advancement for those who understood the modern dynamic and were equal to it. Indeed, who could bring about an instantaneous cleansing of this stagnant rubbish if not the Revolution?

Though he had been preoccupied tenfold these past few days, Obodovsky was still happy over this marvelous, unanimous revolution! When it started out, he still hadn't believed it. He had feared anarchy and mass carnage. But the days passed, and blood did not spill in rivers. Apparently, things had begun to settle with the officers. And now they were to find new forms of relations in the army and reinforce a true fraternity of fighting men?

The commission's two wings—the cautious generals' and the revolutionary colonels'—began to feel each other out regarding which reforms they should be discussing. Some of them Guchkov had already announced in his Order No. 114, skirting just the one hot-potato issue: saluting. Even Obodovsky, a civilian outsider, could not imagine an army without saluting. Engelhardt, who had been elevated by the previous days, demanded that they begin by replacing certain high commanders. The generals objected venomously, saying that the invited colonels were not authorized to be some superior evaluation commission. At that they abandoned the general plan for reforms, opened the regulations on army service, and began examining its articles.

They were astoundingly fusty. The soldier was forbidden to smoke on streets, boulevards, and squares. He was not allowed to visit clubs, public dances, or even taverns and lunchrooms where they served alcohol, even just beer. So where was a soldier supposed to have a beer? He was forbidden to attend public lectures or participate in public ceremonies, and he could go to theaters only with permission from his company commander. Only noncommissioned officers were allowed to ride inside streetcars; of the soldiers, only the injured, while the rest on the platforms. On trains, only in third class; on ships, only on the lowest deck. They could even have books and newspapers only with the signature of their company commander, unless they were from the church library.

Now that the revolution had taken everything itself, all that remained was to write opposite these points: rescind, rescind, rescind. But up until now? But if the fatherland's defenders were considered its citizens, even only its subjects—how could they have been kept like this, like quasi-livestock in a harness? Obodovsky had always raged against this—and even now, right after, he was raging. Out of his characteristic of doing nothing superficially, taking any task up with fervor, he now went into all these points, and waxed indignant, and voted with the others.

However, Pyotr Akimovich could not put too much of himself into this. He had sat through and participated here honestly this long Saturday night, but what was thrashing at him were the plants! Although he had been pulled in here, he couldn't abandon them there. The revolutionary celebration had stretched on, and the streetcars were still idle (they hadn't managed to get them going today because on Sunday the workers didn't want to clear the tracks), and the military plants were idle, meanwhile the war was pressing. The revolution's main question right now, of course, was not smoking outside or using the familiar "you" with soldiers but how and when the plants would start back up.

This would be decided on Sunday in the Tauride Palace, and Obodovsky approached the doors of the Duma hall several times while the hundred-voice roll-call and voting was under way there—and when it had finally passed successfully, he and Gvozdev congratulated each other with a handshake.

It was odd here as well. An entire revolution had unfolded, Russia's entire state system had been replaced, but it was still he and Gvozdev who kept toiling with the organization of defense work, although during this time Kozma had even spent time in prison, due to Protopopov's insanity. Now Obodovsky, torn by his military obligations, had just about flown into the room where Gvozdev's little headquarters had set up.

Now the obstacle of the Soviet of Workers' Deputies was no longer im-
peding their work! Apparently, as of Monday they might be able to set the
plants to work? Somehow not the case. The unbridled brigandage of the
revolutionary week had not confined itself even at the Soviet's instruction.
The working class, which had roamed the streets with rifles, somehow had
no desire to return to their boring workbenches. Ten days before, industry
had been putting out copious arms continuously, at a driven pace. But once
the revolution shook, everything stopped.

Not managing to straighten his shoulders, with his thatch of hair hanging on his forehead, Gvozdev went back and forth between his two small
rooms in the Tauride Palace, from the telephone to the representatives sent
from the plants and to his own people who had been sent to the plants. And
was managing to keep up less and less with the explosion of events.

The principal battle of the revolution—here it was. It was beginning.
How were the victors now to climb back into their grubby skin? They were
right in a lot of ways—but also very wrong, if one remembered about the
German army on Russian soil.

[4 6 3]

And what had been ordered up in that Order No. 1? Everyone understood it differently. Each regiment proceeded in its own way, and queries
flowed in from everywhere about how exactly it was to be understood. The
Military Commission, still considered subordinate to both the government
and the Soviet, moaned under the strain.

Still, the members of the Executive Committee felt uneasy at having
overdone things with the Order. Many now muttered that they hadn't even
heard, it was done without them. But the blowhard Sokolov didn't regret it
in the least, you weren't going to dump it on him, anyway he had all kinds
of matters of his own to attend to, he barely stayed at the EC more than an
hour straight, he was spurred to race on. But today at their meeting they discussed what kind of clarification to give to the Order so that it would maintain its former direction but take a short step back. It could be called an
Order, too, Order No. 2.

From the thickets of the talk at cross purposes about whether the Soviet
of Deputies had abolished the army or the army remained, they now had to
come out in a dignified way, as if merely clarifying further. And so, this
would be an order again—to the troops of the Petrograd District—but also
for the information of Petrograd's workers. Clarify that, yes, soldiers' committees should be elected in all military units, but these committees were
by no means charged with electing officers (it was good they'd deleted that
then). These committees were to organize the soldiers for public needs and
for participation in general political life. The question of the election of
military leaders was handed over to a special commission for consideration.

(In fact, there was no such commission, but what else could they say? And what about the elections of officers that had already taken place in many regiments?) All the elections of officers already held? Those must remain in force. . . . In addition, the Soviet recognized the soldiers' committees' right to object to any given officer. But in public and political life, soldiers were required to obey their elected organ—the EC of the Soviet of Workers' Deputies—as indicated in Order No. 1. (So they didn't really have to make any special apology.) Soldiers were required to obey military authorities only with respect to their military service. In order to eliminate the danger of armed counterrevolution, the Petrograd garrison would not be removed from the city and Petrograd soldiers must not have their weapons taken away.

Naturally, the Bolsheviks made a fuss, saying that this was capitulation to the Provisional Government, that this would bring down the committees. But they fell far short of garnering a majority.

Who would sign? The Executive Committee, in general. They could force someone from the Military Commission to sign as well. What about the Minister of War's signature? That would be very desirable, of course, but as of now relations with him were unsettled.

But it would be even stronger to ignore him. Immediately send the readied Order No. 2 by courier to Tsarskoye Selo, to the transmission station, to go out as quickly as possible over the wireless and be sent to absolutely everyone—all military units, the entire army in the field, whoever could pick it up.

They sent the courier on his way.

As of today the excessively numerous Soviet had been divided up, with the soldiers separated from the workers, which made it easier to fit in the hall, and made for less nonsense, and they each were to assemble on alternate days. In the Duma's White Hall today the soldier section had assembled— and the soldiers that had been foisted on the Executive Committee, of no use in its work (after three days, they didn't want to be excluded, of course), now went there.

So the Executive Committee felt roomier; its numbers had risen to thirty and there'd been barely enough chairs. True, a few people never sat at the conference table but jostled by the snack table, with their backs to the meeting, and fortified themselves, for free, naturally. EC members had abandoned their usual occupations in order to meet here daily, and they had more than a right to this kind of sustenance. Today they'd even promised a hot meal.

But this flurry at the snack table irritated the chairman, Chkheidze; it took away from their devotion to the revolutionary cause. Chkheidze protested several times and called for order.

Still, the question did not fall away: how were they to influence Guchkov? His position was quite puzzling. After all, he hadn't taken part in the talks about wielding power and seemed to be holding himself above all the various obligations. He was openly and arrogantly violating the good-natured style of relations between the government and the Soviet that the other ministers were maintaining. For instance, Nekrasov himself had asked a representative of the Soviet be assigned to him at his ministry to participate in fundamental decisions. But Guchkov had declined direct relations of any kind. Compel him?

Hurt our own pride and send a delegation to him? Yes! And today, do not delay! Here, with Order No. 2. And send the strongest delegation possible, one that will be able to make demands. Above all, of course, Steklov. (He was now being proposed to go everywhere a Soviet battering ram was needed; people sensed the strength in him.) Then Skobelev. (He had become the Soviet's perpetual representative here, there, and everywhere.) And here was Sokolov! — he'd just rolled into the session — task him with it. He had written Order No. 1, so let him express his convictions to the minister. You're the expert, so finish the job!

Sokolov said he would, willingly! He ran to telephone the minister's chancellery.

But should someone also be sent to mollify him, diplomatically? Send Gvozdev — he and Guchkov had worked together, and Guchkov knew him well. (Gvozdev himself was in another room, at the labor commission.) Then one of the officers. Filippovsky — he was both one of us and was on the Military Commission, and was entirely in the know. Well, and one soldier.

Bring Guchkov Order No. 2 and make our demand? Sign it! Not enough! He should be the one, not the Soviet, to institute officers' universal appointment by election! And why not, comrades? We have to be consistent in our democratic principles. How can all those appointed by the old regime be recognized as officers? Meanwhile, Guchkov was even refusing to abolish saluting.

They decided.

Now Chkheidze had an important announcement. He had been ordered to hold talks with the government about arresting the entire House of Romanov. Alarming rumors were coming in saying that Nikolai now for some reason was at GHQ and at liberty there and, according to rumors, was getting ready to go to Kiev and perhaps even to the Crimea. Chkheidze told the government about the Soviet's decision and insisted it be implemented immediately! The government didn't exactly object, but it was sluggish, and not capable of anything. One of the favorable ministers (who? Nekrasov . . .) stated that the government was prepared to relieve the Executive Committee of this, should it want to arrest them itself.

Passing the buck? Didn't want to get their hands dirty?

No, make them do it themselves! This, comrades, was another bourgeois maneuver: foist the arrest on us. We can, of course, we always manage, but they are the government and they are obligated first. Nikolai Semyonovich, insist they do it themselves!

The latest news: Nikolai Romanov wished to arrive at Tsarskoye Selo.

That was good. It would be the simplest thing to arrest him there. But there could be difficulties at GHQ. The generals were there, a counter-revolutionary nest.

And the other Romanovs?

Wait a bit on the other Romanovs or else we'll scare them off. Not all at once.

But what was to be done with Nikolai Nikolaevch? After all, they had handed the Supreme Command over to him on the sly!

The Soviet of Deputies was not being sent over the mandatory copies of military orders, but they should be. Nikolai Nikolaevch's order had been roaming through the army for three days, yet it was only now here. And what did he write? That he had been appointed by the Emperor's will! And the prime minister, Lvov, also by the Emperor's will! And then he lists the ministers, so it came out that they were by the Emperor's will, too. Here was how they wove their sinister rings. And we were letting it all happen.

Force the government to cancel this order immediately! And tell Guchkov to charge the delegation to cancel it!

Nikolai Nikolaevich himself should be canceled. How could the army be entrusted to him? He was going to return us to the old regime in no time!

It was intrigue by the enfranchised class—entrusting the army to the not yet wiped out dynasty!

Don't let Nikolai Nikolaevich get to GHQ. Intercept him!

But not before Nikolai himself.

This was why they had to hurry with the Tsar's arrest.

Steklov-Nakhamkes, a large man as it was, was standing at full height behind those seated—and he thundered out particularly impressively:

"So what sort of orders are they writing? Have you read Alekseev's?— 'purely unbridled revolutionary gangs'!—this is him about the delegations from Petrograd that are disarming police! '. . . To have at all stations garrisons made up of reliable units under the leadership of firm officers'! Do you understand what 'reliable' and 'firm' mean? Not only that: take them alive and immediately appoint a field court martial and put it into effect immediately! Eh? A substantial document! A courageous general! The very kind we shall force to knuckle under immediately!"

There's no way, they objected, there's just no way we can get to them all immediately. If we remove Nikolai Nikolaevich, we can't remove Alekseev right then, too. We would be calling down chaos on our own head.

"No, make him submit to the revolution!" Nakhamkes blazed. "Fine, I'll bring him in myself!"

And he would! All the comrades were amazed at where his orderliness and modesty of the past few years had gone—such was now his dynamic revolutionary fervor.

Was this really just a matter of Alekseev? The generals' entire body corporate had to be reeducated and reborn. Of course it was outrageous that the Provisional Government had not even begun to disarm reactionary generals!

Let the delegation demand that of Guchkov!

Meanwhile, Chkheidze had absented himself to have a bite. Now, he wiped his mustache and returned to the chairman's end, and the next issue was about allowing the press.

Three journalists from bourgeois newspapers had long been waiting outside the door. They were let in but not invited to sit. (They are just like us and, at the same time, not at all like us.)

The society of journalists and editors was concerned that the Soviet allow absolutely all publications to come out without restrictions. The society considered any censorship after the revolution to be impermissible in principle.

But the issue did not concern all publications, actually. No one could bring themselves to make a fuss for the Black Hundreds' publications—but it did affect *Kopeika*, whose press *Izvestia* had confiscated, leaving nowhere to be put out. It also affected *New Times*, which, as a rightist newspaper, had also been forbidden to publish, though it had come out without permission yesterday. But as of today—it had been banned. So you see . . .

The threads again all led back to Nakhamkes. He had acted as sponsor of *Izvestia*. Fine, he would see whether *Kopeika* could be allowed to use the press. But *New Times* and everything rightist—yes, he banned them, as chairman of the Soviet's publishing commission.

But with its first issue, *New Times* had demonstrated that it had made an about-face toward the revolution and approved of it—so why ban it?

Well, if it had made an about-face, then let it come out.

However, the editors started speaking out against censorship in general. And sympathetic voices were found among the right wing of the Executive Committee—Zeitlin, Bogdanov, Bramson. We can! Let's abolish it and be done with it. And if we were to think it through, freedom of speech is actually the most sensible policy. Under the present circumstances, rightist publications will have neither material nor moral grounds, and they will wither away ingloriously in a few days. On the contrary, if we drive the Black Hundreds underground, we will just be removing our enemies from our own field of vision.

The EC center, though, inclined toward the Bolsheviks, said ban them unconditionally.

Nakhamkes did not have to respond, though. Chkheidze looked distraught and somber. Indeed, in the Duma he had always defended full freedom of speech—but could a true revolutionary give free speech to those foul creatures? Now, all of a sudden, he exploded (his pen flew out of his hand to the floor, describing an arc and lodging there). He jumped up, rolled his eyes, gesticulated, and shouted:

"No! We won't allow it! When there's a war under way, we aren't going to give the enemy a weapon! When I've got a rifle, I'm not going to give it to the enemy! I'm not going to tell him, Here's a rifle for you. Go ahead, shoot me! No! I'm going to say, How about you go and . . .?"

They laughed.

[4 6 4]

This astonished General Ruzsky! An army was perishing during time of war—without any war!—and as if it was no one's problem. Overnight, some news had trickled into Northern Army Group headquarters—again about violence against officers and arrests—and the appearance of soldiers' committees. These soldiers' committees had taken hold wherever the leaflets had arrived. Let them have their committees, but if they were mixed, with officers included, then they might help deal with circumstances and make the soldier mass see reason. However, according to that idiotic Order No. 1, they were purely for soldiers—and were deepening the gap of hostility.

While GHQ was silent.

And the government was silent. There had been no response to the army group commander's very eloquent telegram.

Was that self-confidence of some kind? Dismay? Blindness, deafness? Right then they brought to headquarters an outrageous document. Clerks in his own quartermaster administration had written a collective letter to the Minister of War and sent it with a delegation to Petrograd. They asked for no more or less than the removal of the chief of provisions, General Savich, and several other officers from the headquarters administration— "for the salvation of our dear homeland, remove them immediately and keep them in isolation"—and even indicated to the minister who should be appointed head of the army group's medical unit.

All this was a bad joke (yet he would now have to refute the telegram to the minister with a telegram of his own), but Ruzasky was wounded by the ignorant ingratitude. Savich was called an "ardent Black Hundred" (apparently, only because he had curtailed leave and trips to Petrograd for lower staff ranks), while having no idea that Savich was among the Emperor's three advisors who, on 15 March, had persuaded him to abdicate.

Such is the fate of popular ignorance. It could not be ruled out that Ruzsky, too, would have to experience this ingratitude.

Ruzsky's delegation to the Petrograd Soviet had left. At its head he had put smart officers who knew how to speak convincingly and with them had sent several sensible soldiers.

He'd sent them—and been satisfied for some two hours. Pskov itself seemed to have quieted down.

Meanwhile, though, an ordinary mail train had arrived from Petrograd bringing the reply to Ruzsky from the Soviet of Deputies in the most unexpected form: the smudgy print of *Izvestia* of the Soviet of Workers' Deputies.

General Ruzsky would not have picked up and soiled his hands on this newspaper, but headquarters men noticed and brought it to Boldyrev, who brought it to the commander.

His name was honored in a small headline, and his yesterday's response to Bonch the revolutionary's inquiry quoted in full. But right then the editorial response followed—and the response was like a stick over the head.

It was a language in which it is impossible to explain oneself or object or defend one's point of view, a language that drags everything down like high water and turns everything upside down. From the very first words, an unexpected rude and haughty tone:

"Obviously, Ruzsky has yet to master the proletariat's tactic, something new to him."

A turnabout of concepts: there existed an ancient, primeval tactic of the proletariat, and the commander was a midge on the periphery.

"Being firmly organized and of iron discipline, we"—who was this "we"? rather frightening—"not only are not afraid of freedom of action, speech, and organization anywhere in Russia, including at the front"—they weren't afraid!—"on the contrary, we think this is what will quickly bring a tremendous cohesion between our comrade soldiers and workers."

Quite the thought, "on the contrary." Cohesion among *you*—possibly, but the Army meanwhile was losing all cohesion.

"We stand for complete democratization of the army and so it is not like us to be afraid of freedom for citizen-soldiers."

They should come take a look at this freedom.

"It is essential that generals—*including Ruzsky*—who wish to truly join the rebelling people and army firmly remember that the Great Russian Revolution . . ."

Ruzsky had always been sensitive about not falling into a demeaning position. He tensed completely, anticipating this moment and averting it—even by employing some involuntary disrespectfulness—even when received by the Emperor or a grand duke, just so he could defend and emphasize his own independence.

And here he was burning right now—from humiliation, disgrace, and his own impotence. He had written a humane, amicable letter—and received a newspaper article in reply! He'd always feared humiliation at the hands of arrogant aristocrats—and here it had come in shaggy and tattered, in the dirt of smudgy letters—from the Ochlos!

"It obviously has never occurred to General Ruzsky that his own authority, derived from the power of the old order, still has to be confirmed by the new regime."

And so he lost heart. Was he supposed to understand this to mean that the Soviet of Deputies intended to remove him?

Oh well, not many did, but the Soviet apparently did have enough power to do that.

A week ago, Ruzsky had been a fully empowered commander-in-chief, bestrewn with medals, one of the few trusted adjutant generals—and here some unknown soldier riffraff was getting ready to vote on whether to remove him.

Two fingers crept into his chest pocket and pulled out a yellow glass cigarette holder, and his other fingers, trembling, started inserting a cigarette—but he couldn't get around to lighting it. He couldn't tear himself away without finishing this very small, dirty, smudged, crushing column.

"Holding a more correct point of view is his closest aide, General M.D. Bonch-Bruevich, who in his telegram to the same address reports that he is prepared to serve the homeland but any new work of his must be approved by a representative of the new government. . . ."

Now that was a doublet! Reliable and close (and friendly through their wives), Bonch the general, whom Ruzsky had awaited as a deliverer and had appointed garrison chief (actually, he wanted to be the army group's chief of staff again), had managed to contact the Soviet apart from Ruzsky? And now, praising him, contrasting him to Ruzsky was—the Soviet? Or was it his brother, Bonch the revolutionary?

It was signed: "Ed. note."

You could tell—but not prove—it was Bonch.

And what a clumsy, illiterate contrast. What was the accusation? That Bonch the general recognized the new government? Didn't Ruzsky? Ruzsky had done a thousand times more. He had obtained the abdication!

It wasn't so much the brothers' separate mutual aid that offended (did Bonch want to be commander-in-chief under the new regime?) as this clumsy ignorance, the unsubstantiated nature of the accusation impossible in a respectable newspaper to which you could send a refutation, but here—what could he do? The smudged letters in the lines nearly ran together—and were impenetrable.

Meanwhile, the thousands of soldiers in his army group were reading this now and would read it—and suspect him of something sinister with that very ignorance that is available only to the crowd.

The most absurd state of impotence and injury.

What could be hoped for now with the delegation he'd sent? How would they be received at the Soviet?

From his stable standing in the solid-bone military hierarchy, Ruzsky suddenly felt like a helpless nubbin in a general's uniform. At any moment his army group, his own garrison company, and his headquarters might refuse to obey him—and then what could he order or do? What **could** he do in general? All his capabilities were based on a customary convention of army subordination.

Which had suddenly collapsed.

But even in this state the Soviet of Workers' Deputies had not let him step back from the blow. Ruzsky went to headquarters, where there was a new telegram, from the Soviet, with the undue familiarity of the past few days, saying that anyone who wanted to could address the army group commander. The telegram stated that the Soviet of Deputies was now sending out Order No. 2 as a supplement to Order No. 1.

Why an *order* anyway? An order from and to whom?

In the heading it said that this order was for the Petrograd garrison. Yet it had been sent to the entire Northern Army Group.

The "order" was so incoherent that it was hard to read closely and grasp. The unauthorized election of officers had been halted apparently? But even here all the results of elections already held were confirmed. Also confirmed was the right of soldiers' committees to object to the election of any officer!

So was this better than the previous "order"—or worse? From the frying pan into the fire.

The army!—the most stable of society's organizations, which had nearly achieved a state of complete firmness—was now melting and spilling away. All the commanders and headquarters, all the superiors and officers had sagged and were slipping.

The only thing that remained for headquarters was this: as long as the telegraph line was intact, they could send each other the latest telegrams.

And Ruzsky sent another to Alekseev. Asking him to inform him at last what had happened with the string of previous telegrams.

It was strange that Guchkov had done nothing to support him. Seemingly they had only just obtained the abdication as one—but he had left and was no longer responding.

[4 6 5]

One thing seemed right: avoid recognizing the Soviet of Deputies. Without stating so openly, but—avoid it. Don't fawn over them, the way Nekrasov, Lvov, and even Milyukov had.

Besides Petrograd there was also all of Russia. And a stream of telegrams was pouring in from there that the war minister's large desk couldn't even hold. Telegrams of congratulation, utmost congratulation, affirmation of loyalty (they all drew him into inaction, took up his time)—but also telegrams about the removal of old authorities—garrison chiefs, commandants, military officials. And petitions from all kinds of newly born committees to approve their new appointees, replacing those removed. But the day had passed, and the same committee, disappointed by its first candidate, reported that it had removed him and asked approval for the next. Also, there were many anonymous letters and denunciations against officials for being counterrevolutionary, and against the committees themselves. Could he really even attempt to sort all this out from Petrograd—and in a single day? A single hour? Even if he could, in some unfathomable way, he still couldn't correct or change anything. By trying to change something he could be setting himself up as a counterrevolutionary. All this was at a distance, all this was out of sight, all this was quick—so the simplest thing for Guchkov was to confirm all local decisions indiscriminately. And confirm all the changed personnel once again.

Thus, overwhelmed, Guchkov involuntarily had become colleague and ally to all the committees, which he didn't know, scattered across Russia.

So then why had he dug in his heels so against the first and main committee, in Petrograd? . . .

He lived and slept at the ministerial residence. He took a look at what had been scheduled for today—no getting out of it, and why had he promised?—to go to the Academy of the General Staff and attend the Special Conference on defense, at least for a while. And an early hour had been scheduled. It was already time to go.

The minister was met by the head of the Academy, mustachioed General Kamenev, and lined up were a half-squadron, a Preobrazhensky detachment, and, of course, a party of the requisite clerks. (But the most revolutionary of them all, the librarian, was still sitting, not dislodged, at the Military Commission.) It was to them that he had to deliver the first speech, according to the new era's customs: to thank them for their service, only with their assistance could the war be brought to a victorious conclusion. ("Hurrah!" "We'll try, minister!"—"Willing to do our best" had been taken out.) Then, to the staff-officer room, where he cast about from one alarmed, uncomprehending instructor to another, not that there was much time to talk, and he couldn't call things by their names. There were disloyal people, unwanted ears, everywhere, and by evening the Soviet would find out. (The staff officers themselves were looking at him mistrustfully. What kind of dubious civilian had come to direct them?) After that, to the Dragomirovsky Hall, where both professors and audience had gathered. Another speech. A kind of speech automation had worked itself out, and if he was sick of the bright future, he couldn't go wrong talking about the gloomy past, how little ammunition there had been under Sukhomlinov, two shells a gun per day, to welcome the rising and setting of the sun. He sketched out Russia's situation now—not bad at all. He asked them to apply every effort for the homeland—and the officers shouted "hurrah" and carried him out to his motorcar.

He returned to the ministerial residence. He appointed his general to the Chief Administration of the General Staff, replacing Zankevich, whom he demoted to quartermaster general. (A complaint had already come in from General Staff clerks saying that Zankevich was "insincere about the revolution," was Khabalov's right hand, and with him had tried to put down the popular movement. Zankevich hadn't tried to put down anything anywhere. He had apparently delivered one speech near the Winter Palace—but there was a complaint, and not the last, of course, and the wind of complaints is such that it cannot be ignored.)

Then, people were waiting for the government to address the army in the field. The men of letters at the residence had already composed a draft, which Guchkov and Lvov had to sign. . . . An indestructible bulwark, the heroic Russian army . . . Russia's bright future on the principles of freedom, equality, and justice . . . Soldiers' obedience to officers is the foundation of the country's security . . . Otherwise—an abyss of ruin . . . your happiness and your children's . . .

The ideas were correct and the pens skillful, but could this scrap of paper overpower the entire deluge?

He signed and sent it to Lvov.

The time had come to go speak to the Special Conference.

Very recently these Special Conferences had seemed so important—without them the war could not be won. However, there had been a revolution—and from government offices it was immediately evident how unnecessary these cumbersome conferences were, and that tsarist ministers were justly reluctant to attend them.

A new assembly—and a new form of speech was required. Here—in the public spirit rather than the army spirit. But this had become increasingly familiar. They greeted him with a storm of applause and rose to their feet. At last—a people's minister of war, and defense was in loyal hands! This kind of meeting left Guchkov feeling inspired, and he delivered what seemed like a vivid speech. Here he presented information from all ends of Russia: the people everywhere were confidently seizing power. Doing so perfectly peacefully everywhere. How strong the people were when they were masters of their own fate, having shaken off the decrepit tokens of the past! Today, all doubts about the new regime's stability had fallen away. The army, too, was greeting the new government ecstatically. Now victory was in our hands. Now no one at the top could betray us.

Another din of applause, everyone was touched, and Guchkov, sitting down, realized he didn't even have to give a speech, it was all superfluous. And he felt miserable, so miserable. For decency's sake he still had to sit here for a while. The empty yet truly difficult day dragged on.

Right then he was called to the telephone. They'd found him. Adjutant Kapnist reported that the Executive Committee of the Soviet of Workers' Deputies had a serious conversation for the Minister of War and was inviting the minister to come to the Tauride Palace or else was prepared to send a delegation to him at his residence.

Himself? Of course he wouldn't go. Not a step toward those swine. But there was no basis to refuse them an appointment. He set it for day's end.

But now it was time to go to the funeral for Dmitri Vyazemsky.

The motorcar left him at the Monastery entrance. While he was passing through, he asked which church it was in—they'd already begun.

The service was held in the right side-chapel. He saw about twenty bowed heads from behind. Holding candles. And the unattractive widowed Asya, her eyebrows frozen upward, standing at the head of the long, flower-bedecked coffin. (Flowers from Guchkov had been brought earlier.)

Four candleholders burned at the coffin's corners.

He picked up a candle. He passed down the middle slightly toward the front. (Not without the thought that people should see he was here.)

How difficult this transition was, from the cares of a ministry and hundreds of telegrams from every city, from conferences and applause—while here, among just a few, in the gloom and candle illumination—the lonely reckoning of a human life that had had its own scale, its own path, its own end, through revolutions or without.

After losing his Old Believer faith in his youth, Guchkov had not joined the ruling faith. Generally speaking he didn't believe in God anyway, but he considered it useful and necessary and observed some of the rules, and Easter and Christmas, like everyone in Russia. And a year ago, dying—he had taken communion, yes.

At first he had entered with jostling thoughts—about the army, about how Nikolai Nikolaevich could not be allowed to take Supreme Command, how he couldn't yield to the Soviet, and the best way to conduct his meeting with them. Thus he stood with the candle, praying by the looks of it, but inside plucked far away.

Gradually, though, the reading of the cantor, the exclamations of the priest, and the heavenly chant, "Give rest, O Lord . . ." entered into him as it died away. Dropping awkwardly to his knees, as not by his own will, he felt on everyone's shoulders, and in part on his own, the touch of that powerful, all-extended hand under which we can all rise up or fall flat, the way he himself had fallen flat a year ago. He looked closely ahead at the candle of life, whose full length no one knows. Dmitri had raced alongside it, gay, agile, and valiant, not knowing he was already a cinder.

All these past few days, Guchkov had been fighting the thought, but now it flung open in him for certain. After all, he had played this young man, drawn him into a conspiracy, taken him into the revolution—and here had led him up to death.

And another suppressed memory: Myasoedov? . . . Accusing him once of espionage, Guchkov had sincerely believed it. Unable to prove it, he had washed it away with a duel. But what a find it was when the accusation surfaced again of its own, without Guchkov—and he was glad to use it to bring down Sukhomlinov. We fall into that kind of certainty during a struggle. But when he was dying last January, suddenly the hanged man wove together and took shape before him—invisibly, somewhere there: Myasoedov.

What if he hadn't been guilty after all? . . .

He crossed himself when everyone else did.

The funeral was over, and they said farewell to the dead man. Guchkov joined the line, reached the spot—and saw up close the slightly surprised expression preserved on that long face. An athlete. A fine man. He kissed his smooth brow, near the crown.

Asya remained at the head of the deceased. While the family stood to the side. Guchkov walked over to them. There was no crying. The dead man's stately, imposing mother stood erect, unmoving and unseeing. They helped her sit.

The little ones still didn't understand what had happened.

All these past few days and hours they'd been waiting for and even now were hoping to see their older brother, Boris Vyazemsky, and his wife Lili arrive from Lotaryovo, in Usman District. On the basis of his telegram, they had delayed the funeral, but his train was still late.

The coffin was zinc and soldered. It had been decided to bury Dmitri not here, at the Monastery, but, according to his dying wish, to take him in the spring to his patrimonial Lotaryovo and there lay him in the vault alongside his father.

Guchkov went out on the parvis with the sister, Lidia, to see whether Boris was coming.

Right then, in the full light, the revolution returned to his consciousness. And Lidia, with her rather gruff and decisive face and low voice, rather than shrink at it had found a bitter sweetness:

"Ever since childhood, for some reason, the French Revolution had always excited me, as if it had some direct relation to me. I thought that in that era, in another incarnation, I had lived in France. I may even have had my head chopped off there. . . . It seemed that if I were hypnotized, then I could show doors and passages at Versailles that even the guides didn't know. . . ."

No, Boris wasn't coming. She invited Guchkov to come on the ninth day, for the mass for the repose of the dead.

Today's funeral was on the fifth day, not the usual third.

Lidia also said that today Count Orlov-Davydov, Kerensky's voluntary underling, had tactlessly come to see them on the Fontanka—and tried to get Mama to give them Aspen Grove (her grandmother's estate, on the Finland side of the border from Petersburg) for keeping the arrested royal family. Her mama had been indignant. She was no wardress, and she decisively refused. But had it really been decided to arrest them? . . .

Guchkov was enraged. What kind of impudent joker was Kerensky to have been readying all this? Guchkov himself had begun to realize that detaining and guarding the royal family were inevitable. He himself had given Kornilov instructions yesterday—but why was Kerensky doing this?

The devil only knew what kind of government we had. Everything followed on whisperings and private meetings, in twos and threes.

[466]

Guchkov, whom she had called a brute just the night before because he had gone to compel the Emperor's abdication, a filthy man who could release gossip or false letters to the public—this Guchkov, in coming to power, why might he have shown up at the palace at half past midnight, trampling all traces of etiquette with regard to a woman, let alone the Empress?

The Empress understood this as meaning he'd come to arrest her!

At that moment, she'd needed a defender, a witness, someone to place by her side, even if he had no way to defend her—and her immediate happy thought was to summon Pavel (there was no one else)! She'd instructed her valet Volkov to immediately telephone the grand duke and ask him to come at once!

Pavel had already gone to bed, but he understood, got up, collected himself quickly—and with his stepson reached the palace three minutes before Guchkov's arrival. The Empress now felt more confident.

For all her revulsion and indignation, how could she fail to receive those who had come? In her bedroom, in front of the icon, she recited a prayer to the Virgin, perhaps her last in a state of freedom, and went out with Pavel, leaving Lili Dehn and Marie on the sofa in the back room dying of fear.

Kornilov's first sentence lifted her fear and clarified the situation. She gazed with sympathy at the withered, Kalmyk-looking military general famous for his escape. He had an embarrassed look.

The Empress even found that Guchkov, despite his repulsive dark glasses—why was he wearing them in the middle of the night?—had an embarrassed look as well.

His sentences, too, seemed gentle. Although later she tried to recall and couldn't how he had expressed himself, something like: "We have come to see how you are bearing up to your situation." Not that, but she thought his meaning was worse than she had perceived at the time.

He had come, then, not out of malicious curiosity but out of a desire to relieve her? . . .

She later regretted having forgotten to complain to him about the restrictions on the telephone contact with Petrograd.

Returning, she calmed her people and sent them to bed (Lili was now sleeping in the pink boudoir, next to the Empress's bedroom, not letting her stay alone on the first floor), while she herself for a long time, all night, could not calm down after this visit.

She had many icons in her bedroom, on all the walls, and several icon lamps burning.

She sought assuagement in their midst.

Her lady's maid also ran in to tell her that during the visit revolutionary deputies with red rags on their chests had been wandering through the palace and taunting the servants as "slaves" and laughing at their court liveries.

So little did she feel like sleep that she went to her study and, under the overhead light, in the night's deep silence, stopped before the portrait of Marie Antoinette above her desk. Throwing her head back onto her entwined hands, she joined gazes with her and stood there perfectly still.

From the very first moment, she had felt a magical connection with this portrait, which had been given her in France seven years before, when she and the Emperor had visited the apartments of Antoinette and Louis XVI. Since her childhood, the fate of this queen had stood out from the fates of other queens. The entire French Revolution, taught to her since she was a child as a concentration of inhuman brutality, still had not had anything to do with Russia—but Aleksandra had perceived Antoinette as her secret sister. Of what was she not slandered? Even debauchery and theft—all the hypocrisy, all the hatred, all the revenge fell so thickly on that proud woman's head—what noble heart would not start beating at being power-less to ease her fate?

This portrait had hung here permanently ever since. But in just the past few days, Aleksandra had seen clearly that their connection was even more fateful, that their situations were similar.

And now, her head tilted back, she was searching for something for her-self from these large eyes with the enigmatic expression—eyes that had not yet suffered as they would but that seemed to have a presentiment. An elon-gated but also full, calm face, without any trivial feminine coquetry. Severity and intelligence.

As in Aleksandra Fyodorovna.

"Not understood by her people . . ."

She placed her beloved Virgin icon under her pillow for the night.

She finally drifted off at dawn.

Late in the morning she went to see Lili, who already knew Botkin's morning rounds and said that Olga had symptoms threatening inflamma-tion of the brain.

My God!

And there was more: dear, devoted Lili did not try to hide her own vital concern. She, too, had slept badly that night and had got to thinking that given these kinds of visits and in this situation one could not continue to keep diaries blithely. The Empress had not only her own but also the diary bequeathed to her by her departed lady in waiting Princess Orbeliani, and both diaries contained many intimate details about various people who had come into contact with the court.

"I'm agonizing," Lili said. "I'm advising you to commit terrible vandal-ism—but I do so out of a sense of devotion. All you can do with these di-aries, Your Majesty, is burn them."

The Empress became very agitated. Her thoughts had not run in that di-rection. She was not used to anyone having oversight over her—but right now Lili's advice pushed her like an ocean wave.

Something struck her immediately and convinced her: she could not imagine these diaries in the hands of the revolutionaries! Or of Guchkov? . . .

My God, burning the diaries was like burning herself. Twenty years of daily minutes of candor, her main feelings of each day, the real, unbroken thread of her life—into the fire? By her own hands!

Yet there was no other choice.

She and Lili went to the red drawing room (Marie Antoinette and her children were there as well—a tapestry, a gift from the French president), sat down by the brightly blazing fireplace, and began burning Orbeliani's diary, setting the Empress's aside.

But the diary was in nine volumes, all in leather bindings, and it was a difficult task—tearing them up.

Even more difficult was what felt like a betrayal of the deceased.

It would be more forgivable to burn her own.

The Empress's were all in leather bindings as well, every last volume (the English lavender, the French green, the Russian red, the German sky blue), as well as all her notebooks, and her daughters', too. Now this leather had to be slit with a knife and torn at her chest, the way the ancients rended their clothing at their chest. Like rending your own soul.

The fire took its own, took it devastatingly, irrevocably, her hands couldn't keep up with it. But her thought raced ahead: what about her correspondence?

Her correspondence? Letters from the then heir to the throne and suitor, letters of their first love, their first spring?. . . And the husband's letters to his wife—of twenty-two years?

What was now beginning to frighten her was not that she would have to burn these but whether it could all be burned in time, before *their* next visit.

There were also her letters to Anya—six boxes at Anya's.

And her letters from Anya.

Would they be able to determine everything that needed burning?

She instructed the valet Volkov to carry in and place on the table the oaken chest with the Emperors' letters.

She opened them, turned them over, read them—and couldn't bear to toss them into the fire.

Her heart was torn.

[4 6 7]

Before: if you didn't do it yourself, no one would. Since the revolution, though, everyone had suddenly come flocking as knowers and doers. Every speaker on any front step. Here was freedom for you, so this was probably right: like spilling from a sack—and everyone free in all directions who hadn't dared say a word before. This had cheered Shlyapnikov, but also dismayed him. It turned out he swam well only in the depths, like an unseen fish. On the surface, he gasped for air but couldn't take any in. All public life had entered such a fluid, mobile state that Sanya Shlyapnikov's mind couldn't keep up. But right now the party needed a unified opinion. Oh my, how it did! Without a unified opinion, what kind of party would it be? They wouldn't be Bolsheviks!

Before the revolution, issues hadn't come up so acutely and swiftly. But now there were a dozen of them, one more complex than the next, and the correct tactic had to be determined for each. What was eating at him most was whether or not to overthrow the Provisional Government. Three days before, the Petrograd Committee had resolved not to overthrow it. But his tortured insides kept saying this was a mistake. How could they not overthrow it? What had Bolsheviks grown up on if not the need to overthrow the landowners and capitalists—and all of a sudden that was gone? They couldn't let this franchised band get entrenched. They had to be constantly burned down, driven out or else they would take their seats at our head as the new tsars.

Once again, he gathered his people, Zalutsky and Molotov, and hammered away at them for an hour, quoting Lenin, and finally shook out of them a new resolution of the Bureau of the Central Committee: our objective is a democratic government, that is, the dictatorship of the proletariat and peasantry.

And with this resolution he had made the Petrograd Committee debate yesterday and vote again. And once again they failed. The party no longer obeyed Shlyapnikov! . . .

Well, you're not going to agree to an uprising—we're still going to create a Bolshevik armed force. Right then, the city's franchised authorities were swarming to create, in place of the disbanded police, a unified militia subordinate to the city duma. Have a taste of that: unified! But we're going to create our own separate—workers'—guard. Since the first day of the revolution we'd been collecting as many weapons as they could. (Shlyapnikov himself had once taken a rifle away from a gendarme.) We had called on soldiers not to surrender their weapons at their unit but to surrender them to us—and many soldiers had done so willingly. And during the Arsenal's plundering we'd acquired more. Those rifles would come in handy! And as the Executive Committee had put Shlyapnikov in charge of arming the workers (he had outwitted the conciliators, who didn't understand what this smacked of), he now went, as if from the Soviet, to argue against the city duma. He well knew what he wanted. Were we to join up with the city militia and put on that idiotic white armband? That was a betrayal of the workers' guard. We weren't going to be directing street traffic. Our work was being the armed bulwark of the revolution. (We shall yet march in iron ranks!)

But 7000 volunteers had already signed up for the city militia, mostly university students and cadets, but also workers, who didn't have a good understanding. Many of those squeaky clean boys from bourgeois families were at the meeting, and in Shlyapnikov they immediately sensed an enemy and lobbed questions at him: Why pass out so many weapons to the militia if there aren't enough to fight the Germans? The militia doesn't need to be armed at all, they said, the white armbands are enough. (He could only laugh. Then why any militia at all?) And, they said, why arm the police when there are soldiers right here?

The soldiers are here now, Shlyapnikov replied, but later they'll go to the front or to their homes. And in the event of the revolutionary moment's need, who was going to defend it? Both he and those on his side present would not yield. Basta! Strength was behind the workers. It was resolved that the little students with their white armbands would not take a step into our factory districts; we had our own armed force.

One proletariat force is the rifle; the other, the press. Among all his concerns these past few days, one was restoring the Bolshevik *Pravda*. And yesterday, they had put out the first, free Sunday issue, 100,000 copies had fluttered around the capital!

The newspaper was even stronger than the party itself. You open the newspaper all the way, and you'd never guess the strength that stood behind it, but its lines slashed correctly! The bourgeois press fluttered from flower to flower: go die, soldiers, while we rake in our profits, as usual. But there was a sense of uncertainty in all their voices. Only *Pravda* alone, from its first issue, spoke raspily, like a worker. Everything about it was plain and honest from the outset: down with what, give us what. This would now be the sole place in Russia where one could speak out openly about the Provisional Government, too. What could still not be implemented, what couldn't even be done in their own party—we would print all of it in *Pravda*, we would gather up everything not yet taken, as understood by steadfast Bolsheviks and fervent fellows from the Vyborg side. No matter what *Pravda* wrote about— it would be the decisive essence of the matter. Even Demian Bedny put his soul into it, right-minded poems! We'll be publishing more *resolutions* (even where there had been none): when it went not like a journalist's article but like a soldier's resolution—it would ring ominously for all bourgeois nerves!

The press was a menacing force.

And also how to strengthen our Bolshevik ranks. The party charter had added requirements for those joining. Abolish them. Right now we had to draw everyone who might want to come into the party, at any price. Abolish membership dues even.

We also can't let the opportunists from the Soviet put a stop to the plant strike. The Soviet is laying down its weapons before the capitalists! After such a successful revolution, how can people just go back to the plants without firm gains? The worker heart in Shlyapnikov was indignant. None of the Executive Committee leadership had ever stood at a workbench for an hour, and they didn't understand what it meant for a worker to do it for eight hours instead of eleven. Nonetheless, he couldn't bring himself to do battle over this. Right now any divisiveness in the working class would be considered a sign of weakness by the revolution's enemies. Fine, we'll stop the strike for now, to save our strength for another fight. Return to the plants—but temporarily, keeping a keen eye on the government so that, at any minute, at the first signal, we can abandon our workbenches again and—the revolution continues!

———————————

Because of all these conundrums, Shlyapnikov had no desire to sit through the Executive Committee's daily sessions, especially in the middle of the day. Only those who had nothing to do could sit there and natter.

If you come, they'll saddle you with something unpleasant:

"Aleksan Gavrilych! Look, Kshesinskaya the ballerina is waiting with regard to the return of her mansion. That's for you. Clear this up with her yourself."

Oh, he'd landed in it! Those scoundrel-conciliators, they didn't dare give orders to the Bolsheviks themselves, so now they'd sicced the woman on Shlyapnikov. Embarrassed, he went out to see her. He was prepared to create an iron Red Guard—but here was a harder task, to go clear things up with an aging ballerina.

Many new needs and organizations had popped up in Petersburg with the revolution, but the number of buildings hadn't increased, and there was a great need for buildings. The Bolsheviks had learned that Kshesinskaya had fled her mansion with her diamonds, her son, and his tutor. Her garages and outbuildings had been occupied by an armored division, but her house stood empty, not even badly looted—so they decided to quickly shift the Petersburg Committee there from its attic in the Labor Exchange nearby. Of course, the house had been built for love and relaxation, not party work. The Bolsheviks had never dreamed of being set up so luxuriously. True, there were rustlings of some kind in the walls—maybe secret passageways?

Here is how he knew bourgeois power and vulgarity had triumphed. Kshesinskaya had made bold to return from her flight and had even showed up here at the Tauride Palace to demand her rights! Too bad she hadn't been caught on 13 March! . . .

Actually, Shlyapnikov went in part out of curiosity, to take a gander at the Tsar's former mistress—not something you see every day.

Standing in the corridor was a short woman dressed all in black but with a special flair, attractively. Though not young, she couldn't help but try to please (quite inappropriately, but women of all classes can't do without that), and her still not erased features and movements let it be known that she had been extremely pretty in her youth, as anyone who knew about these things understood.

With her was a lawyer, dressed like a gentleman, who just introduced her—"Matilda Feliksovna"—but she spoke herself. She addressed him without any sign of eccentricity or awkwardness. Two weeks before she would have ridden in a motorcar past this ordinary man, would not have looked at his typical face and primitive mustache—but now she spoke with respect and conviction, as before one of the leading grandees of the new state, on whom everything depended.

She dared only to ask and ask. First and foremost she asked that he not believe all the bad things people wrote and said about her. She lived by her labor. It was untrue that she had speculated; she had all of 900,000 rubles in the bank, and that could be verified. And she had a document, here, signed by Kerensky, saying that she was perfectly free and not subject to arrest of any kind.

Now she was asking him to help her move back into her own home. There was an overwhelming crowd there, and the building was being looted.

Shlyapnikov knew how to look quite impenetrable, the way he sat on the Executive Committee against the conciliators. But answering this woman was hard. He even felt like saying something reassuring to her—but what could he do? The Bolsheviks couldn't give up the house now. Where would they go? Where were you going to find such a fine building?

But she was ready to burst into tears and was barely holding them back.

He politely replied that of course he would try to help. But this was a difficult matter and did not depend on him. The problem was (right then, on the spot, he came up with a plan), the problem was that there was also an armored car detachment there, and they had nowhere to move.

But Kshesinskaya had foreseen it and was a step ahead of him! It turned out, she had already been at Military District headquarters and at the Military Commission and arranged everything; they did not object in the least to the armored cars leaving there. She told everywhere that her home had been seized by the Bolsheviks, not the military authority.

Shlyapnikov suddenly felt himself turning red. That was the case, after all, so what could you say?

Oh no, he insisted, it was the armored cars, not the Bolsheviks.

But then! But at least! The woman implored him for permission to at least let her look at her own house! Just to know that everything there was in place! And as a last resort, to gather all her possessions into some of the rooms and set off a space for her to live. The armored cars could stay in the courtyard.

Pfah! Even harder to wiggle out of.

"So who is preventing you? Please, it's all open there," Shlyapnikov lied. She bent over, and with an old grace:

"I admit to you that I'm afraid simply to go there. I beg your protection and assistance!"

Now he was trapped. Shlyapnikov murmured that yes, he would assist.

And no sooner had he disengaged than he went to the telephone to call the mansion immediately and warn the armored detachment that they must take it all on themselves and not agree to leave for anything, and let no one call for them to do otherwise. And they were not to allow the lady to see the house.

[468]

Something was keeping Tolstoy's secretary from surrendering and conceding like that, however. After all, people had suffered in prison for nothing, people of like mind! Why does it always have to be Kerensky? He decided to search for Maklakov again—he had been to see Lev Nikolaevich and had himself conducted a brilliant defense in the "Tolstoyans' trial," so they knew each other. The newspapers had written that he'd been appointed commissar for the Ministry of Justice. It might well be that he was now replacing the ailing Kerensky. Stop by the Ministry of Justice? Maybe he was still there?

Bulgakov walked into the ministry on Ekaterininskaya and was going to ask the doorman about Maklakov but for some reason first asked:

"Well, brother, the minister's not here now, is he?"

"Just so, he is."

"Who? Aleksandr Fyodorovich Kerensky?"

"Who else? Just so, the very same."

"But didn't he faint this morning?"

"He fainted, it passed, and now he's seeing people."

"Seeing people?"

"Just so, you're welcome to go up!" The bewhiskered doorman was already taking his coat.

A stunned Bulgakov raced upstairs.

The reception room was very large, and many were milling around, all men in frock coats and jackets, not a single ministerial uniform with medals to be seen. What had become of them?

Only the courier by the closed doors to the next room stood stiffly in uniform. Bulgakov stepped up to him, showed him the letters from famous writers, and asked that he inform Kerensky. The courier went through the door.

A short while passed. Suddenly, the minister's door swung open hard and wide. It was the courier who had opened it, and he rolled out of there as if flung—and immediately came to attention, sideways to the door.

His agitation passed through the reception room, everyone jumped to the sides, blown back—and an aisle formed.

There was an odd, frequent rapping, like wood on wood. It was the stick of someone walking rapping on the floor—no, the stick of someone flying madly, trying to catch up with someone, although he was holding the stick in his left hand while his right arm was in a black shoulder-belt.

Dashing adjutant officers, holding onto their swords, sped behind the minister on two sides.

The minister with the stick disappeared, rushing past, and the adjutants disappeared—and those waiting just stood there along the aisle, fallen respectfully still.

They whispered:

"To the telephone. . . . He went to talk on the telephone. . . ."

And so they stood, not disturbing the aisle. Until an oncoming breeze started blowing—and the exit door was opened by an oncoming whirlwind—and the revolutionary minister with a face so pale it was blue, with his black shoulder-belt and rapping his stick, raced back to his office, hurrying so frenziedly that he led with his narrow head—onward, faster!

And his little adjutants, holding onto their swords, wheeled after him.

But when he came to the door, suddenly—stop! The minister came to a halt. He was halted by an irascible lady wearing a black velvet mantle, for even a second of his passage grabbing the minister's attention.

She spoke quickly—and the minister stood with the back of his closely cropped head facing and no taller than Bulgakov. He shrugged, told the lady something, and was already about to rush into his office when Bulgakov, almost surprising himself, exclaimed:

"Minister, sir!"

Kerensky, gripped, amazed, turned his pale bluish face abruptly toward Bulgakov—and fixed his eyes on him, as if asking for one second, Isn't this an impudent one?

"Aleksandr Fyodorovich!" Bulgakov hurried now, worked up and not swallowing: "I am the former secretary of Lev Nikolaevich Tolstoy. I have letters to you from Zinaida Nikolaevna Gippius and Dmitri Sergeevich Merezhkovsky. They sincerely request that you receive me and give me a minute or two to discuss an urgent matter!"

At the list of brilliant names, a smile of pride could not be concealed on Kerensky's mustacheless and beardless face. With scarcely a moment's thought, he turned to the first adjutant he came across and, with two fingers pointing out from his shoulder-belt describing two incomparably free loops that seemed as if he'd used them his whole life, in the direction of the lady and the direction of Bulgakov, fired out on the exhale nearly without consonants:

"These two."

And he was gone. And the door closed. And once again the courier stood tall, a barrier.

The aisle was commingled. People started talking excitedly, envying the lucky ones.

And right then, the door opened. And a narrow little adjutant officer, beaming from the duties assigned to him, but also with an expression of desperate superiority, announced:

"Gentlemen! The minister has only half an hour at his disposal. And only for the lady and Bulgakov," and supremely politely: "Please."

They went in. This turned out to be not the office but merely a waiting room with secretaries wearing ordinary jackets, without any signs of a service uniform.

The lady was let into the office. Bulgakov waited his turn—but right then an extremely self-confident, strikingly elegant old gentleman with a shaved face and a luxuriantly lionish head, also in civilian dress, entered from the reception area. He put his briefcase on the desk there and made it clear by his entire demeanor that he was his own man here and it was he who would go now. Indeed, the adjutant jumped up when he saw him and immediately invited the minister to follow the lady, while to Bulgakov he explained:

"The minister will see Mr. Karabchevsky first."

Ah, Karabchevsky! The famous lawyer and even, apparently, the dean of the profession?

The stately lady came out in tears. The secretaries brought her a chair, and one of them began trying to give her encouragement, but she sobbed and sobbed.

Bulgakov thought that this was probably the wife of some prominent dignitary who had been arrested asking for clemency and the minister had refused. He had probably argued to her that thousands of Russia's "best people" had experienced the same thing—and he was right in part. When Bulgakov spent a brief time in the Tula prison, his sister wept over him, too. Thus everything in life can be turned into a lesson.

The half hour passed, and more, and finally Karabchevsky emerged solemnly with his briefcase—and Bulgakov was invited to go in.

He did—and saw Kerensky sitting, the fingers of his healthy and unhealthy hands joined, leaning on the armrests of the tall and deep ministerial armchair, but in the middle of the office rather than behind his desk. Apparently he was inviting Bulgakov to take the same kind of armchair half-turned toward him.

But right then he was told that he had been called to the telephone—to yet another telephone—from the Tauride Palace. With a sudden, almost desperate movement, Kerensky struck the armrests and jumped up, a narrow man, from the broad chair—and rushed for the door, without his stick, managing however to shout:

"You wait here!"

Fate had hindered everything, impeded everything, but apparently there was hope.

Bulgakov looked around and studied the office. It was comfortable but plain. Old armchairs, but with a cheerful aspect nonetheless. Many had sat here, including Shcheglovitov—and now here was Kerensky. Brighter rectangles stood out rather blatantly on the walls—where there had doubtless been portraits, royal portraits, now taken down.

The minister returned, plunked down in his chair with satisfaction, and picked up the writers' letters. He took them out of their envelopes with quick light movements, crackling them as he unfolded them, and then either read them or just looked at the famous signatures, but Bulgakov looked at his tall, agile neck, the imperious fold of his lips, his small eyes, and his symmetrical crewcut.

When Kerensky began reading the letter, however, which was not at all long—due to the full frenzy of his current pace, he seemed incapable of penetrating its simple meaning and, as if it were in an unfamiliar language or illegible, he asked quickly, nervously:

"What's it about? What's it about?"

Bulgakov began laying out his heartfelt plea: they had refused military service, the purest of people—could they really remain in prison? The amnesty must not bypass them! But they were counted as criminals, not as religious offenders, and . . .

Kerensky slapped himself on the forehead quick and hard, as if slapping a mosquito:

"How could that have not occurred to me!" And he immediately jumped up, as if the chair's seat had propelled him with a powerful spring, and ran to the door and immediately summoned someone who proved to be not simply a secretary but the deputy minister.

They were introduced.

The deputy minister assured him that they would be part of the amnesty, they would, and these people had already been included, the document had already been written.

"How's that? It's ready?" Kerensky exclaimed. "Then give it to me for signature right away! I want to sign it!"

Bulgakov became agitated, anticipating becoming a witness to a great moment in Russian history.

But no, the document was not quite ink-ready, as it turned out.

"Then hurry. Hurry!" Kerensky nervously pressed, as if he were being bitten or were himself languishing in prison. "Hurry up and finish and send it to me at any time, day or night, no matter where I am—at the Council of Ministers or the Soviet of Deputies, or the train station, or . . ."

The only place he didn't name was home.

Documents – 15

Telegram from Zurich to Stockholm, 19 March 1917

Our tactic is total mistrust and no support whatsoever for the provisional government. Kerensky is especially suspect. Arming the proletariat is the sole guarantee. . . . No rapprochement with other parties.

Ulyanov

[4 6 9]

The Executive Committee session dragged on for many hours, to the point of an exhaustion fought only by sweet tea, sandwiches, and, later, buttered rice porridge. The Executive Committee members apparently had lost hope that the session might go more quickly somehow and apparently were no longer even striving toward that. They sat listlessly, spoke listlessly, and the items kept coming, probably twenty of them on the agenda. They got distracted, exchanged comments, came and went. During the voting they didn't check to see whether they still had a quorum. The new room had turned out to be less than convenient: directly across from the drone and roar of the White Hall, lacking an anteroom, so that as soon as anyone found it they were right there, and delegations and messengers with complaints kept breaking in.

They had got a delegation from the Northern Army Group from General Ruzsky. But they were told to wait, the Executive Committee was not going to let military issues take up the whole agenda.

Skobelev gave a long and rather joyous report about his trip to Helsingfors and Sveaborg. (He talked about himself the whole time, and it was very hard to tell that Rodichev had figured there as well.)

The session was interrupted on an emergency basis twice—with regard to streetcar traffic, which was supposed to open tomorrow. Once: how to avoid a crush, since everyone was going to rush to them, maybe somehow institute a line for boarding? The other time there was a call from the city duma saying that there were still uncleared tracks, they wouldn't get them done today, and couldn't they do it early tomorrow morning? But can you order workers to go to work early in the morning? What if they don't obey? No one but the Executive Committee could issue such an instruction.

Then they discussed General Kornilov's appointment to the Military District, and that they had to take him in hand from the very start and appoint their own permanent representative to him—and just let him try to object.

Also, remove the head of Petrograd's telephone network, a dubious individual.

Although all these items might have been considered political, they didn't touch upon anyone's party interests, did not raise arguments between factions, and were decided peacefully.

The delegation from General Ruzsky insisted it be heard.

Oh, all right, they'd already taught the general a lesson. Let them come in.

They entered: a captain, a lieutenant, one sergeant, and two soldiers. They entered not in cadence but rapping their boots distinctly. They didn't look for a place to sit but stood there in a closely knit group. By seniority, the captain began speaking—loudly, convincingly, and fluently. Occasionally the lieutenant would interject with his own examples. The lower ranks only offered a slight rumbling and brief exclamations, but they gave their officers their full support. Also, they stood very close together and united, military fashion, as if this were the first reconnaissance group and after this the entire Northern Army Group might come pouring in.

And the stories they told! What was happening in their army group and in the near and far rear as a result of Order No. 1. Soldiers were disarming officers. Removing them from their command. Arresting them. Plundering military chancelleries. They tore a colonel to pieces. Tried to drown a general in a river.

Like an injured leg with gangrene—it was no longer an army, it was about to be dismembered.

From this entrance by the delegates, from their tough military speeches—the stunned members of the Executive Committee sat wherever they'd been caught, unable to dispute the events, so accurately had they been called out.

Wouldn't anarchy like this lead to restoration of the old system? And wouldn't this come crashing down on the Soviet? Only one thing saved them:

"We clarified Order No. 1 today. We issued Order No. 2."

"And what was it, if you'll permit us to know?" the captain now demanded. Chkheidze nodded, and Kapelinsky read it out loud in his unmilitary voice.

And the officers took a step back in astonishment.

"What, wrong again?" The Executive Committee members felt something wasn't right. They scrambled:

"Comrades! Hold back and study Order No. 2!"

"How can we hold it back when it's already been transmitted?"

"And why was it transmitted? It only refers to Petrograd!"

Well, they let it through . . . They didn't realize . . .

"So, comrades, we have to send a new telegram right away explaining both orders!"

"But that still has to be written . . .!"

"But now our delegation is on its way to see Guchkov. Let them . . ."

Something's wrong indeed. . . . Yes, coordinate somehow with the war minister. . . .

And hold back Order No. 2 for now!

And send one man to Pskov with clarifications!

Why just to Pskov? . . .

The discussion churned for a long time. They announced a recess and released the delegation. But when they assembled again they couldn't get away from military issues so easily.

What about Kronstadt? There seemed to be a continuous uprising going on there. They were undermining not only the Provisional Government's commissar but the Soviet's authority as well.

Who is it stirring things up there? (They pointed at the Bolsheviks.)

Send someone there, too!

Yes, they had to gradually send their own commissars to all the military units and all the military authorities so that the Executive Committee had an eye and grip everywhere.

How can we work when our Military Commission isn't one of us, isn't trusted? We have to change its composition. Take out the reactionary officers and bring in republican officers we already have. Ordinary soldiers, too.

But waiting in the wings was the question of representation on the Executive Committee for several socialist groups. This question was controversial, fraught with insult, and had to be sorted out delicately. Every tiny grouping that had arisen or been roused wanted to have its own representatives on the Executive Committee. But the committee couldn't expand anymore, could not consent to all and sundry. But in some instances it was impolitic to refuse. They heard out the claims and debated. The Bolsheviks were pressing to give one seat each to Latvian and Polish-Lithuanian social democrats. (And their representatives, Stuchka and Kozlovsky, both were Bolsheviks.) The maneuver was sussed out and held up: that was Petrograd, what did the Polish-Lithuanian party have to do with anything? They did add one more seat for the populist socialists, though. And one advisory vote apiece to the Zionist Socialists and Zionist Territorialists. After long debate, the Jewish Sejmists were refused even an advisory vote. No defenders were to be found for the anarchists and anarcho-communists—and those groups, too, were refused.

Nervous Himmer, his Adam's apple trembling, demanded they discuss the preliminary draft of an appeal to the international proletariat. But that promised to drag on, and it was complicated, and there were no takers, they were yawning. Tomorrow.

There were also financial issues, and plaintive Bramson reported about those. But they took a lively interest in what he said.

First of all, it was known that Vera Figner's committee was collecting money very successfully to aid returned political prisoners, many rich men were donating, and half a million rubles had been collected. It would be strange for such a tremendous sum to be in the hands of a private committee and not under the Executive Committee's supervision.

They had to take steps. They issued instructions.

Second: Comrades, thought must be given to the members of the Executive Committee. After all, many of us have abandoned all activities, our main employment, and have been sitting here for days on end. Probably, they—all of us—should be on staff and receiving a salary. That is natural and legitimate. Moreover, the Executive Committee already has considerable support staff—secretaries, typists, expeditors, and for commissions—and somehow we have to feed everyone?

A slight difference of opinion arose. Some felt that the Provisional Government should accept the Soviet of Deputies as permanent state staff. Others objected that, according to savage bourgeois notions, the Soviet of Workers' Deputies was a private institution and could not be supported by the state.

"But in that case, can appropriations be demanded from them in the form of loans?"

"Loans?" short, mercurial Krotovsky chuckled squeakily. "Do we really have to repay them? We have them in our hands. We are dictating terms to them—and we're supposed to take a loan from them? What nonsense is that? Only without repayment!"

He was supported. A loan was bad. It would introduce an element of subordination into our relations with the government.

They resolved to demand from the Provisional Government nonreimbursable salaries for the Soviet of Workers' Deputies. How much?

Someone suggested 200,000—and they only laughed at him.

500,000, then?

Kapelinsky subtly suggested no less than a million.

What's a million? A million can be enough for how many?

Shekhter proposed two million.

They thought and exchanged glances—didn't that still seem too little?

They came up with five million!

But Nakhamkes, not sitting down at all, having developed the habit, with his healthy height, of also standing behind someone's back, like a mountain, weighed out calmly, richly:

"Ten million."

Everyone was staggered by that figure. They couldn't even understand why so much.

"You can't imagine the scope of our future work." Nakhamkes gestured largely with one arm.

And . . . well . . . perhaps? To what end—that would come clear in time. But for now the Provisional Government was behaving very graciously.

Fine: ten million!

They wrote that down.

There was another favorable circumstance, namely, there was a report that in Oranienbaum our people had taken a great deal of gold, silver, and other valuables into safekeeping. Now that was excellent. Bring it to the Provisional Government's knowledge that we can hand over this gold to them, but only upon receipt of the allocations demanded.

[4 7 0]

Now they came to supper as if from battle—still fired up, still with much to say. But after battle men are always especially hungry. And how many more of them piled in every day! Based now on her previous days' experience, Susanna ordered the cook to prepare three times as much, and the maid, who wore starched lace in her hair, could barely contend with serving the table.

These past few days, Susanna herself had spent time in the city, and at home she had the telephone invariably close to hand—but she could only learn and rejoice in the very latest news when her husband came home in the evening. Her son Mark had started imbibing the vividness and acuity of the moment, so that he did not disappear until late at his student parties and was instead drawn here to listen, and was very receptive.

Usually they came in a throng, on foot (during these unsettled days, David had kept the motorcar in the garage), noisily conversing on the staircase, and in the doorway, and in the front hall—besides her husband, there was Mandelstam, a few other lawyers, and a few other journalists; the journalists went to these dinners to hone the day's night articles in conversation. Even Ardov, the pride of *Morning Russia*, a well-known wit and paradoxicalist, finished up on a high note:

"Yes, gentlemen, we are now *doomed* to be victorious this war! We absolutely do not dare lose this war—that would mean falling back under reaction. Defeatism and passive defensism are unthinkable now. By carrying out a revolution, we have signed our own fate!"

"We signed our own fate," David objected, "back in 1914, when we accepted war, and that means we're obliged to wage it as honest men. And what, *what* has the government given us in return?"

Susanna pulled a long ribbon hanging from the ceiling that rang for the kitchen, immediately seating her guests at the table, and firmly demanded the full logical story, not the tail end of their argument, that wouldn't do. That feeling that wouldn't leave her of a Miracle, how everything they'd anticipated for years had suddenly come to pass, in three days' time—don't rush through it, take it, pluck through it feather by feather, don't leave anything out.

After covering the gold chains attached to their vest pockets with snow-white napkins, a few loud ones turned their attention to the aspic, but the fish had a lot of bones—allowing others to gradually tell their stories.

We're settling into the English Club! This old home now hears other speeches and sees new people. The plenary session of the Committee of Social Organizations has just ended. Gruzinov had shown up there and made himself the center of attention, of course: "I accomplished," "I take pride," "I'm endlessly happy"—it was becoming hilarious the way he projected himself as the Moscow Bonaparte. After the parade on Saturday, which he had received with a bouquet of tulips, looking simply like a clown, having completely lost his head, he wrote in an order: "my troops."

Laughter from the plates.

Meanwhile, though, it was all very funny, but he had rather deftly entrenched himself. He had contrived a delegation from his own staff, which was now imploring the government to appoint Gruzinov permanent commander, otherwise the Moscow District troops would not overcome Wilhelm. This kind of fluid revolutionary situation, like now, was very conducive to sudden, nimble nominations.

Actually, all this scoffing wouldn't get into the newspapers tomorrow: the shared slogan was unity and good will, and all the vituperation was against the old regime.

Yes, but can we be serious, gentlemen?

What was serious was the formidable debate over what to do about the royal family. After all, Nikolai had gone off to GHQ, as had his Mama, and apparently Aleksandra was on her way there, too, while Nikolai Nikolaevich had been appointed Supreme Commander—and was going there, too? So the entire counterrevolution was gathering at GHQ? A stop had to be put to that!

And this was immediately conveyed to everyone. The coup had come too easily! There are no such miracles! Certainly, there were intrigues being

woven. This was so clear, though, what was there to debate? Safeguard ourselves from Nikolai, certainly!

Well, the Russian tradition of magnanimity! They were prepared to forgive, forget, and reconcile. Objectors were found, and they prepared their
own resolution in a separate room. But people were overwhelmingly on our
side, and they approved the following: make it known to the government
that it is essential to subject the Tsar and the members of his family to personal detention and not to appoint any individuals from the royal family to
any important posts!

Sensible. It suggested itself.

But it wasn't so easy to talk about this in one's own apartment. A few
times, when Sasha the maid entered with a tray, Susanna had made a warning sign to the guests and the conversation had broken off. Sasha stupidly
worshipped the royal couple. Her little room was hung all around with
icons and royal portraits. The Korzners had always laughed that in the
event of a pogrom they could put up Sasha herself at the window or opposite the doors. Since the abdication, she had sobbed for three solid days, the
cook not one bit, and Sasha could see that her employers were rejoicing,
and there was a feeling of heavy menace in the home, but this was not the
time to argue with their housemaid. She would gradually reconcile herself.

"Gentlemen. Gentlemen!" Erik Pechersky, from *Early Morning*, was looking to make a toast, wiggling his electrified fingers, and in front of the maid,
allegorically: "We mustn't repeat literally everything the French Revolution
had, or all history as a whole, but rather repeat everything wonderful in it!"

They drank to that. Sasha went out.

"Gentlemen!" Derzhanovsky, from *Morning Russia*, sought their attention. "Let us ask this. Among the grand dukes and grand duchesses, are
there any innocents? With their whole affected opposition to Rasputin—
weren't they deceiving the country with their silence? They should all be
meted punishment!"

"Even Yusupov—even he has revealed himself now in his telegram!"

"What telegram? What telegram, gentlemen?"

"*Morning Russia* asked him to comment from his place of exile on the
overthrow. And what did he reply?" Ardov was simply seething: "'Being of
lower rank, I do not believe I have the right to express my political opinions
for the press.' What cheek was that? And this was Rasputin's murderer?"

"Spitting in the press's face!"

"I find this sweet, gentlemen! And witty"—Susanna did not agree.

What were the courtiers like? Well, it was a waxworks. They started running through them. Nilov was a staunch Black Hundred. Benckendorff, a
tenacious Black Hundred. Frederiks, an inveterate Black Hundred. Voeikov,
the inspirer of all Black Hundred initiatives. Apraksin, an open member of
the Union of the Russian People, the nucleus of the Black Hundreds' party
at court.

Oh, so many needed purging!

But was that only in the court circle? How many have changed their spots in the revolutionary crowd? How many recent friends of the police precinct are wearing red bows in their lapels? All these poisonous roots have to be found and torn out!

Even today at the session it was made clear that the former city governor, supposedly arrested, was being held in the Kremlin, but in luxurious rooms, where he had communication with the palace steward and wanted for nothing.

And the telephones? An instruction had now been issued to remove several suspicious telephones. And to subject conversations with locations outside Moscow to censorship. Because figures in the old regime . . .

David mentioned a telegram from the Moscow lower middle class begging the Almighty that the freedom won by the people not be lost. Oh, their habit of fear! Timid thoughts of yesterday's twilight.

"Careful, gentlemen! What about in the provinces? Do you know them, the provinces? How are they behaving? Will they be ours?"

"Gen-tle-men!" insisted young, blond Fialkovsky, David's protégé. "The provinces will be ours, too. It will all be ours. Just don't run out of breath from the headspinning race we've run. After all, we've made the leap from absolutism straight to full democracy! Who could withstand that? The coup was lightning quick—but the restructuring of domestic life will be even more so! The new Minister of Justice (by the way, he will be in Moscow tomorrow, good news!) is decisively driving the "dark injustice" from Russian courts. The administration is moving on from the talentless minions of the old regime to people with public experience."

Able even more than all of them to fly into a passion was Mandelstam, but at Kadet congresses, when he was trying to undermine Milyukov. But here, among his own, where he was senior and esteemed in all respects, he spoke with convincing restraint:

"We who have been accustomed our whole life to being in the opposition and in revolution—we, gentlemen, also find it difficult to realize that we have become a material force, we have become the government. And a government stronger than the former regime could ever have dreamed of being. At hand is that strength of power, supplied by the people, for which there are no obstacles of any kind. All the parties understand identically the foundations of freedom—and therefore there will be no disagreements in the popular cabinet but only intense, constructive work. The entire state mechanism is now in our hands! Now no one can rip freedom from our firm hands!"

"If only, if only . . . the people's ignorance doesn't get in the way. You see, the people despise everyone who wears German clothing, collars, and ties."

"But won't there be conflicts with the Soviet of Deputies?" Mark asked worriedly.

None whatsoever. Everything that caused episodes of conflict has been cleared up as a misunderstanding.

"Act more through the press!" exclaimed Erik Pechersky. He'd had a drop too much and always got quickly muddled. "Its voice is loud and now it's all come together. People can't help but listen to it, and it will lead society! The Russian press! At what an unattainable height it has always stood! We all used to speak with an iron hand clamped around our throat. We all have memories of directives, fines, and prohibitions. We have all been reared on great deeds. Our era must be glorified in hexameters!"

But Derzhanovsky, incapable of hexameters, jokingly complained:

"I've been writing about the Black Hundreds all my life. Who am I going to fight now, gentlemen? Give me a topic! There's no one left to fight!"

They had made good progress on their meal, which brought them solidity. Susanna surveyed the table with satisfaction, most content of all. She was pleased to be in this place of strength, among the strong and the conquerors. Previously, she had agonized most painfully when she observed the cowardly weakness of her milieu.

Apparently, the news was already coming to an end. They also talked about the hero journalist Liskovich. As people said (the other, official version notwithstanding), he and a handful of soldiers had taken Butyrskaya Prison (the prison warden's bullet had flown past his head)—and then the Prechistensky police station.

But their thoughts were racing ahead. Mandelstam again developed the idea that, having become the state, we more than anything had no need of the strikes and riots that had brought down the former government power. Now all this has to stop and all the people's forces thrown into work. To fortify the newly won freedom by establishing order.

Once again Ardov, regretting having let slip his brilliantly found and so well received phrase, sent this rolling across the table:

"We are now—*doomed to be victorious*! I remind you, gentlemen, there is a war under way! And if recently we could think about a 'conditional peace' if nothing else, then now we are compelled to fight and secure our freedom! Forgotten is the weariness, the excruciating split in the Russian soul—and once again our hearts have begun to burn! Only now will Russia be able to fight—without schism, without treachery, without despondency. The real war is only now beginning, together with the revolution! Friends! We have experienced no greater happiness in life. Our faith has been vindicated, and Russia is truly a great country, and this the whole world sees! This air is intoxicating us. Our heads are spinning, the way Camille Desmoulins's head spun when he pinned a chestnut leaf to his hat and exclaimed: 'To the Bastille!' Gentlemen, we are seeing too much of the similarity between our two revolutions. . . ."

And Susanna saw it! She had seen and felt it and could even have expressed it further, more deeply and acutely, than the intoxicated men here at the table—but she had no need of coming forward to speak her piece.

She was content with the fact that she had sensed this beauty, and even more vividly than the vision of Camille Desmoulins. She had sensed all the combined beauty of the Moment, in which one truly could die of happiness, as in love.

It was worth living to see this day!

Right then she was called away to the telephone.

Although the speaker gave her name and one could guess her voice, Susanna had a hard time tearing her soul away and switching her thoughts over and simply couldn't understand who it was.

Alina Vladimirovna had returned from Borisoglebsk and was now asking in a plaintive, fearful voice how her husband was.

Susanna was still having trouble switching gears and concentrating. Naturally, she hadn't forgotten that, whatever revolutions there were, people's main joys, their main sufferings, were still from the heart. And now she felt pity for Alina, especially given the negligible possibility of assistance. Yes, he had called once. But hadn't found her home. And then he hadn't come.

She agreed to meet her the next day and tell her the full story in detail.

But she herself, after this red whirlwind, now found it strange to remember why she had toured with those patriotic concerts. What guilt had she been expiating, and toward whom?

[4 7 1]

Through the long, quiet winter evenings, without shooting, without rockets, in their dugouts, the artillerymen sang songs, laughed and poked fun at each other.

But these past few days something had happened that put an end to the songs and laughter. They lay in their dugouts—and languished. Thinking.

They had a makeshift earthen platform for a bed, earth that hadn't been dug out, long enough for the tallest of them, Blagodarev, with boots on, and wide enough for seven. So they lay side by side on the straw, from pole wall to pole wall—heads in first and legs this way, toward the entrance. When it got warmer, they took their boots off; colder, felt boots or regular boots. They had enough space to lay their felt boots and firewood around the stove. Under the window was a tiny table, for whoever was writing a letter, or for bread during meals, and for the tin teapot—but they ate meals in their laps.

It felt homey, like a hut. But if anyone smoked a cigarette, then, by agreement—he was to lean down toward the stove, to draw the smoke away.

The favorite soldier thing was sipping tea—they had bricks of tea—but they would wind up their sipping before dark. They only lit the lamp when absolutely necessary, so as not to spoil the air, and to save on kerosene, and they lay in their bunks, even if not dozing, and fed the stove, whose glow came and went. Right now it was very small, dying out. It was warm.

Just yesterday they'd spent the entire day going over it and trying to make sense of it all. How could the Tsar have made such a blunder all at once?

And how will things be managed without him?

"Our Tsar wasn't so bad, boys."

And what about the boy Heir. Were they going to go 'round him altogether? They argued like this:

" 'Sthere gonna be someone instead, how'll it be without a Tsar?"

"What kind will the new one be, though! . . ."

In the evenings, yesterday and today, too—as they lay on their backs in the dugout—it felt like they'd had a load of hay dumped on to cover them. Dumped but not tamped down. The pile was a living thing you could rummage in, pull apart. Put your hand to it if you like.

They pulled it apart.

Each thought about his own lot, mostly: everyone has his own little hut, his own little family, and the way all this is here—you couldn't explain it to someone else.

Which is why it was like a load of hay: it muffled but didn't crush you. And drew you in with the meadow smell of home.

It was such a pity without a Tsar, but the artillerymen got to thinking that this, brothers, wasn't something you got through easily. No. If there wasn't any Tsar at all, then who was going to run the war now? Did that mean no one? It couldn't go on by itself.

Must be—peace is coming?

Yesterday, later in the day, they started catching hints of that, and today it came over them more and more. Like now, they were lying in the warm darkness, their usual sides on the lumpy bed, then on their backs again, yes, looking into the darkness, imagining their own pictures. And from time to time someone would go and say:

"No, brothers, it won't just pass. Seems there's going to be peace."

True, in the daytime the officers explained that there'd been another new order from Nikolai Nikolaich saying all was to be done for the war's good.

No matter what he said, though, Nikolai Nikolaich wasn't a tsar, just a grand duke. And whatever they tell him to do was what would be, he wasn't in charge.

Yasenkov, impatient, torn away from his young wife, himself still a pink-cheeked boy, was as if begging the seniors:

"Men, isn't peace coming after all?"

And not immediately, after a pause, Zavikhlyaev let loose like from his barrel-beard:

"It will. Now it will."

The more Arseni thought about it, the more fragrant he found the meadow smell and the more alive his hometown Kamenka, and the more often it came to mind. The way it was playing in the dark in front of his wide open eyes—it was as if he were home already. You see, he'd put Katya in a family way with their third, and she'd shyly reminded him she was due mid-summer, a month or so after St. Peter's Day, so closer to St. Panteleimon's.

Smack mid-harvest—what a time to have the baby!

But Arseni had no thought or even dreamt of seeing her before that time, and hardly knew when he would. And now, if there is peace, would they let them go home? He'd catch her big-bellied. What sweetness—to lay his hands on her belly and feel a little foot tapping at the wall.

The other two were born without him. This one could be with him there!

A homey feel came to life, oh, it came to life and burst—almost close enough for him to put his arms around Katya, and Sevastyan, and Proska, and his father's work.

Senka tried to imagine what the order of jobs was for his father right now on the farm. What did he have to do first now?

If only he could go back—and get to living on his own land. And gather up some more pieces of land—from the Vysheslavtsevs or else Davydov. Room!

Listen! Someone's coming. Arseni was so befuddled that at first he didn't remember he was in the dugout. But someone coming down the earthen steps.

The door was pushed—and a creaky voice, Sidorkin's:

"Now, brothers, you won't believe this."

"Well, what?"

Sidorkin had already sat between their feet.

"Close the door, will you?"

"Here's what I heard, brothers. Vasyatka's come from the infirmary—a nurse there told him. Listen, they found a secret direct cable to Berlin coming from the Tsaritsa's room in the royal palace. She'd been telling Wilhelm all our secrets over it."

Ay yay yay! Ay yay yay!

About our Grenadier brigade, too? And we're lying here and don't know anything.

Well, how do you like that.

"You know she's a German. Her heart reaches out to her own."

"Yeah," Arseni drawled. "Yeah, brothers. Now there's sure to be peace. There's no getting around it."

[4 7 2]

So they'd shown up.

No matter how much Guchkov wished he could fail to recognize them, disaffirm them, sweep them out of reality—they existed and had shown up. And had taken seats in his office.

Gvozdev alone here was a born worker and had the right to come from the Soviet of Workers' Deputies. Well, and this very stupid soldier with the dashing mustache and incomprehensible singsong, well, at least he came from the soldiers. But who else had they slipped in here instead of the people? A naval lieutenant sitting in his Military Commission—now he'd come from that side. (Drive him out of the commission.)

Guchkov was feeling a repetition of the tightness he'd felt in his chest at the Luzhsk station when he'd had to meet with overly familiar, halfwit motorists who'd been playing at being the People.

Skobelev was here, too—he didn't really know but also didn't *not* know him, a generalized silhouette, a State Duma member after all, an inexpressive loudmouth from the far left bench. But this lawyer Sokolov here, with the black brush of his stiff beard, roly-poly, and for some reason very merry, quite out of place—to what end and why was he here, come to discuss the military question? Why even more was this robust Steklov-Nakhamkes here, judging by his figure the leader of the delegation, and sprawling in his chair as the leader, also the European cut of his suit. That meant he'd sat out the war like a fine-looking, proper gentleman and suddenly been tossed up by the revolution. Now he took his seat commandingly to talk with the Minister of War about the army's fate, and with the aplomb of military judgments, as if he were an old regular officer, while seeming to take the minister for some kind of fool, and also in the spirit of propaganda, saying that tsarism's army had been armed and organized only to suppress the worker-peasant movement and the soldiers were groaning under the yoke of inhuman and anti-popular discipline, whereas they perceived Order No. 1 as liberation from the infamous aspects of the militarist yoke.

This *façon de parler* was, apparently, already so accepted among them that it did not seem ridiculous and could not be interrupted as improper. Through the barbs of this spewing of propaganda a practical conversation had to be conducted—perhaps the most important conversation of this entire revolution.

And Guchkov could not seat such a direct, sharply hewn general as Kornilov by his side because he would spoil everything.

But Skobelev? After all, he was a Duma member and had sat in the same hall with people, hadn't he? Not only that, he'd just returned from Helsingfors, seen the killings there, seen them but his empty pupils did not mirror the bodies of the dead. He was going on about how the sailors and soldiers later showed their consciousness. And he twirled his twisted mustache.

Skobelev's was the stupidity of a man who had been beaten and stunned, while a windbag's stupidity came out of Sokolov, who kept trying to speak, interrupting everyone, even Nakhamkes. He was holding a piece of paper and reading from it. At first excerpts from some new Order No. 2, of which they in the Soviet were very proud and which they had already sent out today to the entire army.

"What do you mean to the entire army?" Guchkov was stung. "In what manner?"

The military radio station in Tsarskoye Selo.

And the radio station didn't take the time to ask the minister's permission but immediately obeyed the Soviet?

Caught off guard, Guchkov did not grasp the essence of this new order from hearing it. Apparently somehow, thank God, they'd retreated from Order No. 1? But Sokolov wouldn't let him take it in or catch his breath and from the same piece of paper read the Soviet's demands to the Minister of War, saying the minister must issue his own order confirming . . . And not just a small part, as he had with Order No. 114 . . . And especially to abolish any kind of saluting whatsoever. And . . .

What's that? So Guchkov hadn't done enough yet? He'd squeezed so much out of himself in support of that thuggish, cursed No. 1—and that wasn't enough? They weren't letting him ignore their civilian idiocy in the form of an "order"—no, now he had to sign and publish this idiocy *in his own name*! They wouldn't even allow a draw, neutrality. No, the Minister of War had to wreck the entire army with his very first order—and then go on to wage war.

Actually, Nakhamkes had a slogan at the ready about the war:

"The vilest of all wars history has ever known."

And with a brazen smile on his puffy face, he squinted at the war minister as at someone caught on a clothes-pin and examined him with curiosity, while lovingly stroking his beard. He was the one person of them all who did not attempt to hide his sense of triumph from holding power. Even in his part-velvet armchair he did not simply sit but bore down with his large back and rear end.

". . . and," Sokolov continued from his piece of paper, "create courts of arbitration to hear disputes between soldiers and officers. . . ."

Disputes between soldiers and officers?

". . . and establish the electoral principle for officers throughout the army!"

This was what they had come for!

Guchkov glanced at Gvozdev. But he said nothing out loud; men like that always keep quiet. He was cowed among them and couldn't serve here as an ally.

Guchkov had no allies. The Soviet of Workers' Deputies had his back to the wall.

But his frenzied indomitability blazed up in him, of life's best actions, he loved in himself the fury that bore him along in his loftiest speeches, threw him into duels, and from the Duma president's rostrum—straight to Mongolia! He stood up—and slammed the half-open door of his desk. The door struck—and his clutch of keys jangled to the floor. Guchkov himself scowled at Nakhamkis and shouted imperatively:

"Take my seat! Command!" To Sokolov: "Or perhaps you will? And go hold talks among yourselves!"

And he kicked the second door shut.

He started toward the back door and slammed it shut.

No one had a chance to say anything in reply. They fell silent.

Guchkov's adjutant was in his office. He picked up the keys and followed Guchkov into the back room.

"No, you go lock the cabinet and center drawer right in front of them. That's the kind of group it is. Don't be shy!"

No, he himself should have picked up the keys and thrown them in their faces. Because none of them were fit to be challenged to a duel.

All his burdens seemed to abate immediately after that slamming. What had so held him back that he got so stuck among them? They could all go to hell! The only truly worthy gesture was to fling everything and . . . Drive them all out of the front door onto the Moika and . . .

And what?

He paced around the small room in anger.

Due to his pride, due to his old duelist's refusal to forgive, he would never say another word to them!

However. He recalled what a swamp the whole Provisional Government was. There had been no strong, brave men, after all, and if he were to break with the Soviet now, none of them would back him.

Nor did Guchkov feel the support of the whole great Army, either. He still hadn't learned how to feel the Army as a part of himself. That would take time. That would take a trip to the front.

Here is how you get caught off guard by revolution. . .

Here is what you get for being late with the coup. . .

No forces, no allies. His entire support was the stream of ecstatic liberal and tabloid press from the two capitals. And that was it.

He had nothing to stand on, and he was in *their* power.

They knocked on the door from his office.

"Yes, come in!"

In walked Gvozdev. Looking very guilty, as if he were the main offender.

"Come on, Aleksan Ivanych," he mumbled. "Don't be angry. They're getting their feet. The situation's new, you know that, not everything's in its place, everyone's up on their hind legs. . . ."

Oh, that practical Kozma—give him freedom to command! But the Social Democrats spun him in the Workers Group and now here, too. Why don't good men have real strength?

Guchkov looked straight into his guilty flaxen eyes.

"Come now, Kozma Antonovich, you do understand that the army can't exist like that, don't you?"

"That's all right, Aleksan Ivanych, there's no sea without waves. Just wait, it will all fall into place. Stormy freedom, it pulls at everyone. . . . In the plants, too. . . . It will fall into place."

His warm eyes promised that. Maybe it was true? Stormy freedom, swinging arms. And then things fall into place. People come to their senses. Our people aren't insane.

Kuzma persuaded Guchkov to return to his office. He had no other choice. But did he return in a stronger position than when he left? Or a weaker one?

Sokolov had lost all his good cheer and was sulking. And Nakhamkes was sitting straighter, not sprawling so much.

He looked at these delegates and was amazed. Had they really spent all these years in the same homeland with him? Guchkov had lived fifty-five years, he'd had rivals and enemies, but they were always names, and together with him constituted Russia, so it seemed. And now, having reached the height of a ministerial chair, he had to deal not with all of them but with these newly appeared mugs. This was what revolution was: having to deal with people unequal to, beneath you.

No, he could not give way to his contempt. Guchkov could not break them, could not by his authority rescind the already distributed Order No. 1. That would yield nothing and would just make himself ridiculous. What remained was to persuade them and insist that they be the ones to rescind it.

He started persuading. His arguments were simple and correct, but on what soil had they fallen? What he warranted was that the officer class could not become the weapon of a reactionary coup. The officer class served the homeland. But it could not serve if the ground was knocked out from under it. If every officer instruction required the sanction of an elected soldiers' committee, or even the Soviet of Workers' Deputies.

Nakhamkes interrupted. You're talking about the sole authority that has emerged from the depths of the revolutionary people!

From the depths or not, the army ceases to exist if officers are not in charge of their unit's weaponry. The army becomes dangerous not for the enemy but for its own population. Order No. 1 must be rescinded immediately as senseless. Or, alternatively, a declaration made that the army is being sent home. That would in any event be less dangerous for the country. Order No. 2? Let's take another look. I didn't quite grasp it.

They read and looked over the Sokolov paper again. Not elect officers? But anyone elected can remain? And whose commission is this deciding the appointment of officers by election? We haven't lost our minds yet, to accept that. Committees can object to appointed officers? No, that's a circus, not an army. Those corrections are worse than the first "order," which said nothing about the election of officers, whereas this one does. No!

The stupid, mustached soldier Kudryavtsev sat with his lips spread wide.

The far from foolish Lieutenant Filippovsky was silent. Go on, talk! You understand! What breed of men these are.

In a chill, Guchkov felt that he wasn't going to be able to move this heap of debris.

Because disbanding the army was no threat for them. They would be happy to stop the war.

Resign? That was no solution. Turmoil would have a heyday throughout the army. But this was the ploy that worried them. They couldn't imagine a "bourgeois" minister not holding onto his post. And they neither knew who to put there or how to do it.

So the threat of resignation put them off a little. He insisted with new energy: rescind both orders, No. 1 and No. 2.

And what real reforms would the Minister of War bring about in exchange? Let him bring about all soldiers' rights by his order.

You're asking a lot! Look, General Polivanov's commission has been created and is meeting this minute. We can go there right now if you wish. There will be a purge of reactionary generals. The commission was gradually studying and arranging everything it could.

"That is, so as to set everything up in a new way while leaving everything the old way?" Sokolov grinned again.

Gvozdev began speaking out in favor of order in the army.

While Nakhamkes, so as not to lose the initiative, tacked on here Alekseev's instruction to disarm bands at train stations and try them by field court-martial. These weren't bands, though, but revolutionary cells, and their cause was the progressive cause of revolution. So, had Alekseev's order already been rescinded? And would Nikolai Nikolaevich's order be rescinded?

(Which order? In three days, that impetuous grand duke had dashed off several. Which one of them? Nikolai Nikolaevich himself had already been rejected and doomed, but it was humiliating to say so here, to these men.)

If they had their way, they would rescind all army orders, and all of us.

Agreeing to a compromise with them now would mean opening up for good to the Soviet the right to interfere in the affairs of the Ministry of War.

In a new version of his exit from the room, Guchkov stood up with a resigned face, as indifferent as possible, and declared that he had already said all he could and he was leaving them alone to consider his . . . propositions. (He could not bring himself to call them demands or conditions, however.)

After leaving the delegates, he left for the same back room, but now without any slamming.

Guchkov realized he hadn't overpowered them, hadn't had sufficient force and had gotten stuck. He'd diddled himself away in argument and was bereft of hope.

The weakness of his side astonished him. Never before had he imagined that from the very first days he would find himself in such a helpless overreach.

Where in Russia were the men this great country deserved? A great country, fine, but just try to call men to any cause — and no one came. The enigma of the Russian character!

The adjutant came and summoned Guchkov. He said that everyone had agreed to rescind both Order No. 1 and No. 2 even more so, if only in a way that didn't embarrass the Soviet — but Nakhamkes was implacable and had blocked it.

Still. Still, they had some more negotiating to do — and something to take.

All right, your "orders" can stand, but only for the Petrograd garrison. (All was lost here, no stopping it.) State clearly that they do not apply to the front!

(As if one could draw a precise line today between the rear and the front. . . .)

We can agree, presuming the Minister of War brings about new relations between officers and soldiers as quickly as possible.

Retreat was inevitable. The question was how far. Reforming the army — Guchkov himself had already planned to do that. Disband the committees — no one in the country had the heart. Now the task was whether they could be reined in.

Yes. Such an order would be written. Yes, it would be presented to the Executive Committee for approval. But you must limit Orders No. 1 and No. 2 as well.

A slight spirit of reconciliation ensued. Even Nakhamkes expressed the thought that they actually had come to establish normal relations, not to quarrel. A discussion began. Couldn't all this be disentangled by a single general proclamation, to be signed by both sides?

Depending on what was written.

The Soviet needed to be able to declare a victory over the old regime. That there would be no going back to the old regime.

That was so. That was possible, fine.

Then let it say: strife between officers and soldiers could impede the consolidation of freedom.

That was very good.

Let the officers who had recognized Russia's new order (others could not be contemplated or suffered!), let them show their respect for the soldier-citizen as an individual. If officers heed this appeal, then we *invite* soldiers to carry out their military duties in formation and in service. At the same time, the Executive Committee announces that Orders No. 1 and No. 2 do not refer to the armies of the front. For them, the Minister of War promises to quickly issue rules for relations between soldiers and officers. (Issue them, naturally, in accord with the Executive Committee.)

He did not resign. Or drive them out. And now, imperceptibly, he was conceding to them.

But maybe it wasn't all that bad? Something had been won, after all.

Only *signing with* the Soviet — Guchkov could not do that! It was too loathsome.

They would sign for the Military Commission. And it could indicate that the proclamation had been composed in agreement with the Minister of War.

Order No. 3, then? . . .

Guchkov felt exhaustion. Prostration. Despondency.

✳   ✳   ✳

LIKE WOOD STRIKING IRON!

✳   ✳   ✳

[4 7 3]

Probably nothing can compare with the state of a person who has pined his entire life for the activity he was born to do, while that activity has languished without him from the lack of talent that has beset it—and now, at last, they were joined!

That is how Milyukov felt in the post of Minister of Foreign Affairs—that he had not occupied it by accident. The revolution owed its victory not to spontaneity, by any means, but to the State Duma and the Progressive Bloc, which had prepared the atmosphere for a coup and given it its sanction. The angry popular movement had long been led and brought out by the Duma and the Bloc, and they had been led by Milyukov—so he had legitimately emerged in his new position.

Somehow you're immediately ten years younger. How much more vigorous and confident everything looked!

At last, after so many years, perhaps for the first time ever in its history, Russia did not have to be ashamed of its highest diplomatic representative in front of enlightened Europe, for this one was on the European level. At last there was someone fit and equal to explaining to Europe everything that was happening in Russia and Russia's prospects. With a heart open to their allies, devoted and sincere, but also with a deep understanding for explaining to them this seemingly puzzling, seemingly unexpected outburst: the country was worn out by the incompetent, foolish conduct of the war and had leapt up against that conduct. The loftiest feeling of the people and the army was to prosecute this war to victory together with its loyal allies!

The first European newspapers arrived with responses to the revolution— and Pavel Nikolaevich read with great satisfaction the long columns of raptures: at last Russia had progressive minds in power!

Pavel Nikolaevich felt pleasure at the entire smooth and respectable internal procedure of the Ministry of Foreign Affairs—an excellent system that the new minister had no intention of changing. Change individuals? But the majority here were appropriate. Naturally, there were also Stürmer stooges, whom he would gradually have to sort out and purge. (Only Pavel Nikolaevich could not deny himself the satisfaction of immediately dismissing our envoy in Switzerland, Bibikov, who the previous summer had treated the Progressive Bloc leader discourteously when he was visiting in Switzerland.)

Milyukov experienced great pleasure from interacting with the envoys, especially the English and French, his sincere friends of long standing. By conviction and sympathy, Sir George Buchanan was simply like a member of the Progressive Bloc and shared their indignation at the way affairs were conducted in Russia as well as their desires for reform. The previous year, Milyukov and other Duma leaders had frequently visited the English Embassy and felt perfectly at home there.

These past few days, although official recognition for the new Russia by the powers had been held up a little, for diplomatic inertia was inevitable, the meetings with envoys could not have been more pleasant. French Ambassador Paléologue had even come to the Tauride Palace—to demand a declaration of loyalty to the Allies. A separate declaration? On this point, the Allies had shown understandable concern and perhaps even a slight nervous lack of tact, forestalling and insisting with somewhat excessive energy, saying that it would be too little to express *hope* for the continuation of military efforts, they needed a *guarantee* and a public repetition of the point about Prussian militarism and the commonality of Allied goals, as had been done under the old government.

"But you cannot imagine," Milyukov tried to object, "how hard it is for us with our Socialists. We cannot allow a breach with them, after all, otherwise there would be civil war."

The Frenchman neither imagined nor understood, for their own Socialists all supported the war.

These past few days Sir Buchanan hadn't left his home, due to a cold, and given their firmly established friendly personal relations, Milyukov felt it was perfectly permissible yesterday to visit the envoy himself. Buchanan said candidly that there were considerations delaying Allied recognition of the Provisional Government. Before taking this step, the British government had to receive assurances that the new Russian government was prepared to prosecute the war to its conclusion and restore discipline in the army.

Ah, some things could not be seen from the European heights. Discipline in the army could not have helped but totter if by that means alone the coup was accomplished. This was an epiphenomenon of the revolution. But this disturbance was temporary, and the shocking behavior of the soldier mass was already petering out. With respect to the goals of prosecuting the war, here the Minister of Foreign Affairs firmly and responsibly assured the English ambassador that the war would be prosecuted *in optima forma*. However, he asked Sir George to bear in mind that in public statements about the war the government had to observe exceptional caution—in view of the radical leftists.

Sir George himself was deeply confident of the Russian revolution's favorable outcome for the Allied cause; inasmuch as the revolution had begun at the top, anarchy should not arise. Inspired by civil liberty, the Russian soldier would be able to stand for the democratic principles of the whole world. The autocratic reactionary regime had never inspired sympathies in the English government. Nonetheless, diplomatic caution demanded they wait for absolutely unambiguous statements from the new government about the war's continuation.

Unofficially, they discussed Russia's future state system. Milyukov thought that the monarchy was not yet lost altogether. "But why these extremes? Why are they destroying imperial emblems here?" "Well, because we must give the popular consciousness satisfaction, which is why they are also arresting ministers. But a monarchy of the English type is the best thing that could be offered for Russia." Milyukov hoped that Mikhail, with his noble refusal, had acquired greater chances of being chosen once more to be sovereign.

Even less officially about the departed Tsar. The problem was . . . what to do with him. He was now a burden hanging on the Provisional Government. Obviously, he would be requesting asylum from the English king. This could be discerned from his pleadings, which General Alekseev had conveyed from GHQ: to remain in Tsarskoye Selo until the family recuperated, and then the right to leave via Murman. Candidly speaking, this would be the best solution for the Provisional Government: not to protect or defend them from the leftists. Absolutely not needed by anyone and absolutely harmless, if he did indeed go to England, many problems would go away immediately, and the Provisional Government could move more freely. And in England, under the shelter of a mighty democracy, he would be a silent private person. We would be extremely grateful if the English government . . . What did Sir George think?

Sir George, thin, graying, and red-faced, very English and very energetic, had already thought about this, naturally. Yes, he did think King George would invite his cousin. Sir Buchanan judged partly because here, in his hands, was a telegram from King George to the overthrown Nikolai. The ambassador had a physical opportunity to send it to GHQ through the English military representative there. However, Sir George . . . had begun to experience doubts. Was it proper to bypass the new government to convey such a telegram to an overthrown monarch?

He believed it more correct, here, to suggest its conveyance to the Minister of Foreign Affairs.

W-well, perhaps it was more correct, but it wasn't all that joyous for Pavel Nikolaevich. An awkward circumstance.

What did it say?

". . . Events of the last week have deeply distressed me. My thoughts are constantly with you and I shall always remain your true and devoted friend, as you know I have been in the past. . . ."

Just so, and this was remarkable. Fortunately, it was politically vague. And it gave hope for an invitation—although, we must note, there was no invitation per se. . . .

Just so, and remarkable, but Pavel Nikolaevich would have preferred not seeing this telegram. Not knowing. Not taking it. Eliminating it as if it had never existed. Because if delivery of this telegram became known—and it would—to the Soviet of Workers' Deputies . . . King George's words of sympathy might be falsely interpreted in revolutionary Russia. . . .

All this was clear between the two diplomats and old friends, though.

That the telegram contained no invitation, Sir George, naturally, could see perfectly well. Due to the reality of the English situation this . . . this was a highly risky undertaking. There was the mood of leftist Members of Parliament . . . And there was the not inconsequential question of who would support him in England.

Well, that was not a problem. The former emperor, more than likely, possessed sufficient personal means. In any event, the official request was that Sir George sound out London regarding a British safe haven for the former Tsar.

Fine. An encoded inquiry would be sent immediately.

In fact, circumstances had come together with even more compulsion and haste than Milyukov could express to the ambassador, for fear of creating an unfavorable impression in him of his government. The former emperor's departure for England, if it was to be brought about, had to happen within hours, not weeks. Milyukov already knew that the Soviet was already putting tacit pressure through Chkheidze on Lvov to arrest the entire Romanov dynasty or else the Soviet of Deputies would make the arrests itself!

A most difficult matter. It hadn't been long since they'd reached an amicable agreement with the Soviet that did not envision ultimatums such as this. But here the Soviet had put its heavy hand outside all agreements—and the government did not have the firmness to remain insensitive.

A most difficult matter. It had not been brought up yet to an open government session, or even a closed one, when they were left alone at night—but it had been discussed in a confidential way, above all, of course, between Prince Lvov and Milyukov.

And today, before the government's evening session, alone with the prince in his office, he had complained bitterly that the Soviet's pressure was ongoing, they were irreconcilable, and the prince saw no way to withstand them. Even hinting at sending them off to England was impossible; he could not bring himself to say such a thing to them. But a discussion was under way as to why the Emperor hadn't been arrested yet. He'd even been allowed to go to GHQ, where he could abuse his freedom.

Oh my. . . . They had also held back the Tsar's telegram to the Tsaritsa, although he may only have encoded endearments. So it was now even more tactless and dangerous to send on George's telegram to the Tsar. Yes, the Tsar could be kept here by our side, at Tsarskoye Selo, with his family—and from here, as soon as the consent of the English government arrived, they could quickly be put on a ship or sent through Sweden.

But the Soviet insisted on an answer, and they could not go on not giving it, and the prince could not drag this out any longer.

Pavel Nikolaevich was not the least bit bloodthirsty and did not wish a turn such as this for the revolution, which had already taken an ominous tilt toward its French analog. Nonetheless . . . nonetheless . . . what was to be done? They couldn't get into a conflict with the Soviet on this most disadvantageous, losing matter, for which you could never garner anyone's sympathies.

"Come, Georgi Evgenievich. . . . Come. . . . We're going to have to . . . I guess arrest him. And convey him to Tsarskoye Selo. And there we shall see. All right, give the order."

"But look here, Pavel Nikolaevich. Kerensky is going to go to Moscow now. Won't he be sounding out the Whitestone City's mood and which way the scales are tipping?

Is that fidget really going to sound out anything?

Pavel Nikolaevich tried to attend government sessions daily—not because he had any questions that could only be resolved here—his questions were all resolved within the confines of his ministry—but for the government itself, for its authority, to give it weight, for Milyukov was its most important figure, and without him it would look desolate here. They also might be badly mistaken about something.

However, while in attendance, he was silent nearly the whole time, as if he weren't even in his seat but hovering over this conference table, all overflowing with how well matters were going in his own ministry, how worthily and intelligently he was representing Russia, and how wonderful Russia's future was in the now victorious war, and even in his reverie drew himself pictures of the future peace conference.

The issues at the sessions could be amazingly trivial, especially Nekrasov's, who vexatiously turned himself inside out in order to wrest more in favor of his ministry and his people. Just today he had pestered them to appoint to him, besides the two deputy ministers he already had on salary, another two Duma commissars with the rights of deputy ministers, and since there were no more salaries, then on daily allowances. (No sooner had they allowed him this than the question arose as to why other ministers could not do the same, so others began making their requests.) Three days before, he had been the first to solemnly announce that he was dismissing any and all guards at railroad installations—and now he had discovered that the sites themselves were not being guarded and asked the government to give some employees rights to perform protective services. But it would look reactionary to introduce new security rules at the present moment.

With regret, Milyukov had long seen that this leftist Kadet leader of his was actually simply foolish (to say nothing of an insincere intriguer). But as he had already been promoted to a prominent place in the party and was now in the government—Pavel Nikolaevich was doomed to support him rather than rein him in. The Kadet party's interests could not be forgotten. It remained the sole nonsocialist party in Russia (everything further to the right of the Kadets had been swept away in the first revolutionary days and had disappeared). And five Kadet party members were in the government. But Milyukov did not foresee rejoicing at his collaboration with them.

The very tedious Konovalov rolled out his entire program at the government session, how broadly and comprehensively he was planning to concede to the workers—on the length of the workday (although in a war they might work a little more), on insurance, and on the legalization of strikes—

but even before that to announce all concessions publicly, in order to reassure the masses.

Shingarev either simply couldn't (or never would be able to) overcome his own limitations as a provincial intellectual and now was mired in the minutiae of the food supply, as he had been before in finance, and had suggested an utterly impossible measure insulting to the Allies: refusing to supply the wheat promised to England. So that Milyukov had to intervene and point out the utter impermissibility of this.

Manuilov? What was there to say about Manuilov? He had been given the education post merely because at one time he had suffered from the authorities. And now all he could do was ask to have appointed to him a strong deputy—and subsidies.

There was only one other smart Kadet in the room—that was Nabokov. He hadn't managed yet to make him a minister, but he had managed to make him the government's executive secretary, in fact a very important position. He directed the staff of secretaries, himself kept the main minutes, and was always present at all sessions (and remained for secret ones). He was truly of like mind, a European who grasped all problems—and Milyukov, not understood by anyone among the ministers, would cast satisfied glances in Nabokov's direction, at that narrow, mustached, always guarded face, the keen, intelligent eyes, or the trace of a caustic smile.

Here were smiles with regard to the proclamation Vinaver had written, while Manuilov proudly read it to the ministers:

"A great deed has been accomplished! In a mighty upsurge . . . The moral decay of the state, which had wallowed in the disgrace of sin . . . The Provisional Government deems it its sacred duty to realize the people's aspirations . . . And believes that the spirit of lofty patriotism will inspire our valiant soldiers. . . . Only in united, nationwide cooperation . . ."

Milyukov and Nabokov exchanged ironic looks. The Nabokov version was drier, more practical, and briefer. Vinaver was both wordy and lagging behind events, living in the past, again quite a lot and off topic about 1905 and, of course, the First Duma, of which he had been a member. So be it. This wasn't something to argue over or to split the Kadets' front.

They approved it.

Prince Lvov's protégé, the rather tiresome, colorless Shchepkin, had temporarily halted any censorship of the post or telegraph. And had asked earnestly for credits, credits for the committees and the local commissars. They decided to give them.

One other inexpressive and pallid visage, State Inspector Godnev, reported that the Soviet of Workers' Deputies was insisting on sending its own representatives to the state inspectorate and keeping them there to keep track of outlays of state funds.

The ministers did not just approve this, they actually rejoiced: magnificent. This could allieviate the distressing situation with the Soviet. No financial concealments in the government were envisioned.

There were also church affairs, which in this country fell into the governmental sphere. Well, that called for patience. Gloomily ardent Vladimir Lvov, with desperate decisiveness (and very much resembling a barking guard dog) began reporting on efforts essential for the church's recuperation and asked that he be entrusted to present (he hadn't had them yet!) ideas about the transformation of the parish, the restructuring of the diocesan administration on public principles, and the restoration of the Pre-Council preparatory activities . . .

Yes, some kind of bone had to be thrown to Orthodoxy, too.

This was not the first time they had encountered the need to make tactical use of popular faiths to fortify military service. That is, in other words, compose a new text for the military oath or, if you like, solemn promise to replace the old imperial one. Instruct Guchkov . . . No, he still wasn't there.

They'd been sitting for two hours, and Guchkov still wasn't there! Fairly rude neglect of his colleagues, although one could imagine he had gotten bogged down in affairs.

Pavel Nikolaevich and Guchkov still had a difficult relationship. Milyukov understood rationally that Guchkov was his sole real and worthy ally here. But so many old offenses stood between them, so many acts of ill will, that thinking well of him was difficult.

Instead of Guchkov, in flew the also very tardy Kerensky. They had already assumed he wasn't coming at all. The previous evening the government had resolved that no one but Kerensky, due to his expeditiousness, should go to Moscow—to defuse the mood there, which was somewhat alarming and competitive with Petrograd. He was supposed to take the night train in a few hours. And here he had burst in!

Burst in, in an almost insane rush, as if everyone had been sitting here on pins and needles waiting for him and he had burst in to reassure them, gladden them, dashing from door to chair. And taking little measure of the fact that some other issue might be under discussion here, that someone might have the floor, said half-gasping and freely:

"I've brought it, gentlemen!"

And he collapsed on a chair to rest a minute.

It was actually puzzling: what might he have brought? Yet another abdication? But everyone who could abdicate had already done so.

Here, in the government, he might leave off with his histrionics and behave sensibly. In addition to his clownish behavior, all that unconcealed conceit and egotism had begun to seriously irritate Milyukov. Kerensky irritated him especially with his tempo, his jerkiness; before, when fighting for power, Pavel Nikolaevich had himself been highly strung at times. But now, having gained the helm, the decent thing was to behave respectably, as befit his high position in enormous Russia.

But Kerensky took the floor out of turn and, gasping for air, continuing to gladden his colleagues with his presence, his person, and his accomplish-

ments, quickly reported—and shook the pages in front of him: a draft decree on amnesty! (The very same shining, desired Amnesty they had demanded in all four Dumas as the main popular good—and here it had
come in a buffoonish moment complete with grimaces.) Mostly for political prisoners, but with a seductive bonus for criminals: those criminals the
people themselves had spontaneously released from their places of incarceration, if they showed up voluntarily, would now have half their remaining sentences thrown out. Sentences would also be shortened for those
criminals who themselves had not been released—so that no dissatisfaction
or outburst arose in the prisons.

And when all the ministers could do was nod in agreement for the decree on amnesty to be brought to the governing Senate for publication,
and Kerensky had only to fly up like a lark—and to the train—at that very
moment the door opened and slowly, with heavy feet, in walked a morose
Guchkov.

He walked in so preoccupied or so ill that he didn't even try to look apologetic before those present. He dragged in—quite in contrast to Kerensky—
so slowly, and with such difficulty, that it seemed he might not even get to
a chair.

He did and he sat down. And sadly ran his hand over his heavy head.

They were bewildered and kept their eyes on him.

But the air was filled with Kerensky's trills. He was speaking ringingly
about his trip and how he would do everything well. Then for some reason
he announced a greeting to the Provisional Government from the officials
in his ministry. And suddenly, without asking permission, or perhaps his
glances at Prince Lvov had become that quick and mutual—with the same
new, chestnut brown briefcase, now relieved of the amnesty pages—he
darted out—and off he went. To the train!

But now Guchkov was present—and they took advantage of that. Here,
Aleksandr Ivanych, regarding the adoption of a new oath. Here, Aleksandr
Ivanych, a separate appeal for the soldiers and officers of the Russian army
is essential. Here, Aleksandr Ivanych . . .

While Guchkov sat with the same morose distaste or incomprehen-
sion—or continued absence? (Compared with Kerensky, this was another
extreme of rudeness, which Pavel Nikolaevich also condemned.)

"And so?" he asked in a muffled voice. "Kerensky—will he be back soon?"
He uttered the very name with disdain.

"Aleksandr Fyodorovich has gone to Moscow," Prince Lvov told him
gently, invitingly, especially gently toward Kerensky. "He'll be back the day
after tomorrow, in the morning."

"Only? How is that?" Guchkov looked at him crazily. "But issues don't
wait."

"You yourself were late, Aleksandr Ivanych," his excellency the good
prince said regretfully.

"I've been meeting with the Soviet," Guchkov said morosely.

"The Soviet?" Everyone was astonished and perked up. "And so?"

"Very little that's good," Guchkov replied in a muffled, almost indifferent voice. "But I believe that the situation we have with the Ministry of Justice is even more alarming than regarding the Ministry of War. I don't understand it. How can he go to Moscow? For two days? Has the Minister of Justice really resolved all matters? So I have to report in his place? If you please."

He crossed his legs, sat more firmly, and surveyed several ministers over his pince-nez, but stopped at Milyukov and began to speak as if to him alone, not even to the prime minister:

"A revolution has been brought about in the name of individual freedom, but true individual freedom has by no means ensued. The press does not have freedom to act, and several organs have been banned. Citizens have no guarantees of any kind of inviolability. If we do not have the physical force to implement this, then we must, at least, issue an appeal to the population asking them to refrain from arbitrary arrests, confiscations, and searches. I have received complaints from many places. You doubtless have as well, am I right? We still have to send a directive to local authorities saying that arrests cannot be made without judicial authorities, and the legality of the detention must be verified each time by prosecutorial oversight. Gentlemen, all this functioned under Imperial authority. How could this have become so difficult since the victory of freedom?"

Having lifted his suspicions from Milyukov, who, of course, was least responsible of all for this, Guchkov began looking . . . but who could he look at here?

Many averted their eyes.

"I'm even thinking," Guchkov said raspily, "why don't we create some kind of agency in charge of the population's general safety?"

He couldn't mean a *new Okhrana*—could he? But maybe . . . a new police?

"We have removed all the governors, disbanded all the police, and lifted security on the railroads. . . . But meanwhile, gentlemen"—he nonetheless searched for whose eyes would meet his, but none did, and he couldn't catch the radiant eyes of Prince Lvov—"but meanwhile . . . isn't there a war going on?"

He—was asking. He did not seem entirely confident; the shooting didn't reach here.

[4 7 4]

Monday morning brought telegrams all as one, without contradictions: The Tsar has **abdicated**! Abdicated without a doubt! Both he, and Mikhail, the entire dynasty, the entire gang—**abdicated**!!

There will be no restoration!

The only question burning now was **how** to return. By what path? By what means? Quickly! There mustn't be an hour's delay—come right away! Don't be late! Seize the helm! Correct and direct, and quickly!

Today Tsivin was at Romberg's. Fine. But for now that's just. . . soundings, inquiries, replies. . . . The "deaf-mute Swede" idea had been thrown out three days ago, and also at Hanecki, blithely. More serious was his passport photo (it was good he'd sent it). Could it have reached Sklarz today? Of course not. The day after tomorrow. And then it would be examined at the ministry and General Staff. *They* ought not to wait. They themselves ought to realize and hurry—to send him, to propose his trip. They were silent. The blockheads. The bureaucratic ladder.

Or had they been asking too high a price so as to get more? Then they were worthless politicians. Up ahead, on the broader path, lay a real alliance, a separate peace. But there, there . . . Prussian junker minds of course were not capable of tracing the spirals of the dialectic. Could they really see past today's trenches? What did they know about the world proletarian revolution? Of course we'll go on to outplay them; we're much the smarter. But for now all they get is a separate peace, and taking the Baltic provinces, Poland, Ukraine, and the Caucasus—that's something we'd give up ourselves, as we've long said.

Siefeldt hasn't come. And Moor isn't responding.

But Parvus? That proven, clever man! What about him? Izrail Lazarevich! I'm sitting in this Switzerland like in a stoppered bottle! You do understand, *you* do know how I have to be there for the revolution. Why haven't I received proposals to go? Is anything being done?

The room on Spiegelgasse was like a burrow; the sun never came into the window.

So . . . So, there's no time to collect yourself, you're definitely missing something. What is Shlyapnikov doing there in Petersburg? He's incompetent. The *theses* filtered through to them, but that was when . . . And now there's this. I have to repeat myself briefly by telegram. A telegram to Stockholm; it won't break the party till. Nadya, who will go to turn in the telegram? Our tactic is no trust in the new government! No rapprochement with any party! Only arms! Arms! . . . Wrap up well in your scarf. Bronchitis! . . .

But in general, just in case, if we end up not waiting for the Germans, we must prepare a route through England, too. Karpinsky can prepare it, for example. He can get travel papers in his own name and we'll insert my photograph. Mine, but in a wig, otherwise they'll recognize me by my bald head. Write him immediately! To Geneva immediately! Who will take it to the post? All right, I'll run down myself.

A strong, chill wind was blowing down the narrow side-streets, and when the gust got stronger, and was oncoming—it actually stopped him. But it was fine going cross-wise, counter! I've gotten so used to this my whole life, I've always gone that way—and I don't repent. I wouldn't want a different life!

The same wind swooped him up his side-street and home—and just in time: they were calling him to the telephone on the other floor. Who could that be? Almost no one knew that telephone number, which was for extraordinary instances.

Up the dark staircase.

Inessa! Directly from Clarens! Her sweet voice was like the piano's modulations when she played. . . .

"Inessa, it's been so long since I've heard you! . . . Dearest! . . . I sent you a postcard yesterday from my journey. . . . I have to go immediately. We all have to go! I'm preparing various options here, and one is bound to work! In general, though, we have to explore the English route. And it might be most convenient for you to . . . What? . . . Not convenient? . . . Well, I would never insist, you know that. . . . You're not sure you're going at all? At all? You're hesitating? . . . (Some kind of malfunction, their thoughts weren't meshing. When you haven't seen each other for a long time—there's always a malfunction, your moods don't match up, and here it's over the telephone as well.) . . . Why not? How can you bear not going? . . . And I was absolutely certain! It never occurred to me . . . Yes, nerves, certainly. . . . Yes, nerves . . . (You don't go on at length about nerves over the telephone, a franc a minute.) Well, all right . . . Well, I'll try somehow, yes . . . ."

Better she hadn't called. It just spoiled his mood. . . . She cut his mood and his plan short. . . .

No way of knowing how their relationship had spoiled. For what reason? Don't things get spoiled for a reason? How he'd paved the way for her, how he'd yielded—to whom, when? . . .

He was amazed that it was a *threesome*—yet it held. But here it hadn't. . . .

He ached, throbbed from that conversation. He couldn't make himself do anything. He sat down by the window, where there was more light, to write an action program for Petersburgers, on his lap. They themselves would never do anything, after all. . . . Outside, the wind was simply roaring, and blowing through cracks he'd not noticed before. It was March, but maybe stoke the stove? His landlords would say he was wasting coal. He threw on his coat.

He had to start from an analysis of the situation. He didn't know the exact situation and couldn't reconstruct it based on his meager newspaper excerpts, but he had a good understanding based on general theory, and nothing else could have happened in Petersburg. . . . Had there been a miracle in Russia? But there are no miracles in nature or in history, it just seems like that to the Philistine mind. . . . The depravity of the Tsar's gang, the full bestiality of the Romanov family, those pogromists, who had spilled the blood of Jews and workers on Russia. . . . An eight-day revolution. . . . But there had been a dress rehearsal in 1905. . . . The cart of the Romanov monarchy had overturned, spilling blood and dirt. . . . In essence, this was the beginning of the universal civil war for which we had been calling. . . .

What had been left unsaid with Inessa was keeping him from working. He'd gotten riled up because of the call—and hadn't calmed back down. Mutual misunderstanding, obstinacy . . . It stung . . .

Naturally, the revolution had broken out in Russia first. That should have been expected. That was what we expected. Our proletariat is the most revolutionary. . . . Moreover, the entire course of events clearly shows that the English and French embassies and their agents have been directly involved in organizing the plot together with the Octobrists and the Kadets. . . .

So are we going to leave while she stays behind? Stays behind for good? After all, events might scatter us, separate us for good. . . .

In the new government, Milyukov is only for saccharine professorial speeches. It's hangman Stolypin's henchmen who make the decisions. . . . The Soviet of Workers' Deputies has to find an alliance—not so much with the peasants but first and foremost with agricultural workers and the poorest peasants, separately from the prosperous ones. What's important now is to split the peasantry and set the poorest against the prosperous. There's the clincher.

It was quite a storm! As if the snow were wrecking everything. No more light from the window, the lamp again . . .

No, there was no calming down until he wrote to Inessa again. Do it right now.

. . . I can't conceal from you how seriously disappointed I am. Now I must race off, for people there are "expecting" something . . . Via England under my own name—I'll simply be arrested. . . . But I was certain you would race off, too! . . . Perhaps your health won't allow it? . . . But it would be important at least to make an attempt, to find out how visas are issued, what the procedure is.

Now the heartache had eased up, died down, and a new idea had taken hold and drawn him, to use this letter:

. . . Right now just think about this: near you there live so many social-patriots and various unaffiliated Russian patriots, and rich people! Why couldn't the simple idea of going via Germany occur to *them*? *They* could request a train car to Copenhagen. I can't do that. I'm a "defeatist." But they can. Oh, if only I could teach those swine, those simpletons, to be a little smarter! . . . Would you suggest this to them? . . . Do you think the Germans won't give them a train car? I'll bet they *will*! I'm sure of it! Of course, if this were to come from me or you—that would spoil everything right away. . . . But aren't there fools in Geneva for this purpose? . . .

This is what the whole problem has come down to now. No sense reconnoitering France and England, no, go only through Germany, of course! However, how to do this so that it doesn't come from us, so that it originates with someone else? . . .

If anyone has doubts, you can convince them well by saying, Your worries are utterly laughable! Are Russian workers really going to believe that old, tested revolutionaries are acting to please German imperialism? Are they going to say we "sold out to the Germans"? That's what people have been saying about us, the internationalists, for a long time, because we don't support the war. But we will prove by our deeds that we are *not* German agents. For now, we have to go, if it means going through the devil himself.

But who is going to take the initiative? Without this, there will be opportunity, but we can't go. We alone, we above all, can't do it *ourselves*; that would cause us difficulties in Russia.

Thus another day flashed by without yielding a decision or a solution. . . .

And in that one day so much might have happened there in Russia!

Go there, through the howling darkness, leaning against the dark glass — a flash, and a flash, and slant bullets flying! **That** was what there was in Petersburg now. The chimney was wailing madly, there was a knocking somewhere on the roof, where there had never been knocking before, something had torn off. Well, things had begun to turn!

As if we were letting slip the last few hours, the last few hours. Write to them, write more:

. . . Milyukov and Guchkov are marionettes in the Entente's hands. . . . It's not the workers who should be supporting the new government, but this government "supporting" the workers. . . . Help arm the workers—and freedom in Russia will be invincible! . . . Teach the people *not to believe words*! . . . The people have no desire to go hungry and will soon learn that there is bread in Russia and it can be taken away. . . . And so we will fight for a democratic republic, and after that socialism. . . .

His insides were twisted up, and the veins in his hands and feet were swollen from inactivity. He needed to go out in this storm, and walk himself out! Otherwise there would be no falling asleep anyway. Let the wind push and blow right through him.

Down the stairs—he lapped his coat closed and jammed his cap down tighter. (The chairman of the Chaux-de-Fonds trade union had asked: "Who's this pilot?")

Immediately he was pushed, carried along—a genuine hurricane! But dry underfoot, very little snow. All the streetlamps could be seen, but the sky was dark. Smash! A streetlamp globe broke. Tile clattered, nearly landing on his head.

The old town's narrow, narrow, narrow little streets, no matter which direction you went, it was a labyrinth. If you got lost here, like a mouse, you'd never break out onto Petersburg's broad squares.

Russia was run by 40,000 landowners—could we really not come up with just as many and run it better? . . .

On Niederhofstrasse, a street of nighttime merrymaking, there were almost no passersby; everyone was crammed behind bright windows. And floundering in that wind, helpless, a stooped, listless, frail, familiar figure: Grigori!

From the station? He'd come again?

"Vladimir Ilyich, there is a great deal of importance, I decided to come."

"And what about Tsivin? Have you been to see Romberg?"

"I did today. I'll tell you right away. He was so glad!"

One was swaying that way, one this, beating off the wind with their arms, holding onto their caps. They wended their way back. It was hard to talk, but they were impatient.

In Bern, the émigré committee on homeland return had met all day, and Zinoviev was there representing us. Well, and what happened, how was it?

Shop talk, shop talk, they went through all the options—both through the Allies and through Scandinavia. Then Martov suggested going through Germany!

"Martov?"

"Through Germany!"

"Martov??"

He didn't have the breath to shout.

"Yes! In exchange for German prisoners of war in Russia!"

"Mar-tov??"

"To get the Provisional Government's consent . . . And with Grimm's help negotiate with the Swiss authorities . . ."

What luck! What a stroke of luck! Yuli suggested it, not us! That's what we'll call it: **the Martov plan**! We're just joining it.

The first word has been spoken!

[4 7 5]

And yet again he hadn't called.

Well and good. The soul and mind needed time to take in everything and let it find its place. And then it would be ready to keep growing.

That is why Likonya was so crumpled, because everything was moving too quickly.

Now she couldn't lose her confidence with him. What did he need with a lost woman?

She shied from saying what was on her mind. But she should have. No matter how much movement and air there was in his world, the special narrow space Likonya offered him was not extraneous.

Otherwise he wouldn't have gone to the theaters.

Likonya wasn't an artist, but truly, she had collected the best fragrance. Drink me! Drink all of me! I have it.

A day passed, though. And one more. And one more. And he didn't call.

He must be busy! In the hours Likonya had been with him, he'd gone to the telephone twice. And then there were all those struggles—on the streets, with the government—and they concerned him. She herself had even been dragged to some ridiculous feeding of soldiers.

But he had not left the city! (She'd checked at his hotel.)
Had he forgotten? . . .
But he'd been so tender. This could not end just like that!

In the daytime, reason soothes and heals.
In the evening—no.

What then? Might something have happened to him? Because of these
events? Oh, just so he's not hurt! Just so nothing has happened to him!
Go herself? Telephone? Forgive me my boldness?
A second time! Impossible!
Let this all get cleared up soon.
His mustache and beard have something sunny to them, not just the
color even. He himself is like a shard of sun. Rolling over Russia. (How she
wished she could sit in his lap again! Lose the ground under her feet. Sit per-
fectly still and say nothing. When she is in his lap, he is completely hers.)
But what if she doesn't have another day with him?
Life can't be appreciated by avoiding the pains of life.

. . . Let the hurricane
Rip me apart!

[4 7 6]

Guchkov sat through to the end of the government session without saying anything out loud on the plans for Aspen Grove—and no one mentioned it! The slippery Kerensky had disappeared.
Now that the session was over and the clerks had left, shouldn't a secret
session be starting? But no. Supposedly everything had been resolved exceptionally favorably and calmly. The most serene Prince Lvov, with his
dear, good smile, stood up, nodded to some, shook hands with others—and
headed for his ministerial office, and then Milyukov caught up with him
and they went together.
No, he turned around, with the look of having forgotten something:
"Aleksandr Ivanych! Will you come with me?"
There was nothing else left for Guchkov to do. He followed them.
And here they were, the three of them, and the prince invited them both
to sit down and ordered tea served.
What Milyukov wanted to talk about—he didn't say. He sat in silence,
his neck stiff, and held his self-confident head with the stony look through
his eyeglasses (he switched between eyeglasses and pince-nez; looked sim-
pler with eyeglasses).
On the other hand, the prince was kind and obliging, inviting them to
discuss with a smile, rather seeming to have lost his nerve.
But Guchkov did not like softening his sharp edges:

"Georgi Evgenich! What's going on? It's rather odd. This afternoon, completely by accident, I learned from private individuals that Kerensky's messengers were galloping through the capital searching for a suitable place to incarcerate the royal family. Was such a decision really approved? When? By whom? Yesterday you and I spoke about this—and there had been none of this. There wasn't a session about this, was there? Or did I miss it?"

With readiness and understanding, the prince smiled gently:

"Aleksandr Ivanych, believe me, I myself had no inkling of this even this morning. But in the middle of the day, Aleksandr Fyodorovich had to take several precautionary measures. . . . Just think how it would look if the Soviet of Deputies arrested the Tsar without us. What kind of government would we be then? And the Soviet is very insistent on this point. The Moscow Committee of Social Organizations is also demanding the Tsar's arrest."

The door opened wide immediately after a light knock, and without waiting to be asked, in walked the swarthy Nekrasov with an amazingly light step. If the prime minister was talking with the ministers of foreign and military affairs, the minister in charge of transport might have held off a little.

However, he—perhaps had he become accustomed to his status as Rodzyanko's second?—proceeded as entirely his own man here and also sat without asking.

The prince was apparently pleased by the timeliness of this entrance:

"Here Nikolai Vissarionovich will attest to you that today in the Soviet for a second time it was resolved to arrest the Emperor, and the Military Commission was even instructed to do so. So that we . . . What choice do we have, Aleksandr Ivanych?"

Guchkov might have heard about the Military Commission before, but he hadn't either.

"Nonetheless, Georgi Evgenich, I'm in the government and not incidental to it, and you might have found me and discussed it with me . . . and with Pavel Nikolaevich here . . ." He looked questioningly in his direction; so Milyukov hadn't known either? But right now he was very still, as if unconcerned—". . . before the Minister of Justice starts giving orders? I cannot put myself in such a foolish position."

But was the prince disputing any of this? Why, all he sought with his eyes was for a way to accommodate—his blue, sinless eyes and with his gentle voice:

"Aleksandr Ivanych, my dear good man, but this is even better for the Emperor himself, you see. This will protect him from possible excesses, from an attack by any savage masses. This is even the best way to protect him, better than any other we might have devised!" He made a smacking sound with his lips. "Not only that . . . not only that . . ." the prince himself found it painful to say this—"not only that, you know . . . an investigation has been opened. . . . And if anything is uncovered . . . then it's even natural. . . . But how do you understand it?"

Indeed, how did Guchkov understand it? He was right in his indignation that they had gone around him but wrong in essence. What else could they have devised? After all, he himself had already failed to see any other solution, and in his own plot he had envisioned the Tsar's arrest.

But Milyukov sat there like an indifferent lump, as if the question of the former Emperor's arrest were too trivial for the Minister of Foreign Affairs.

"But doesn't the government need to approve the decision?" Guchkov grumbled. "Why was this left out at the session?"

"Caution required it," Nekrasov interjected promptly in a muffled voice. "So that it doesn't get out. And here we need preparation."

Yes, yes, the prince agreed with the practical Minister of Roads and Railways. That was exactly what he had thought. He even looked like a nanny singing a lullaby: do not disturb.

Also correct.

But after all, this was Guchkov's own mistake. He himself for some reason had let the Tsar go to GHQ, he'd simply been flustered. And that trip to GHQ was what had caused the greatest public irritation. And maybe no arrest would have been required. (And for what offense? And how untoward for Guchkov . . .)

But now there might be no way out, yes . . .

The ministers exchanged looks. Exchanged looks in silence.

And maybe Milyukov was right. In comparison with the general issues of the revolution achieved, was this separate private matter really so important?

What also smarted for Guchkov was the exhausting argument with the delegation from the Soviet, he still hadn't managed to recount this to the ministers—and did he need to? When he pictured the whole huge muddle and bewilderment in the armed forces—did they want to be arguing about the Tsar's arrest, and not even on principle but more out of vanity, why this boy, this impudent Kerensky, had acted so high-handedly, without asking?

But here's what—it was all clear to them now—. . . what the hell was Nikolai Nikolaevich doing taking the Supreme Command now? The Soviet wouldn't allow it, and public opinion wouldn't allow it, and even for them it was awkward. What did they need him for? Why hold onto him?

In the military domain, Guchkov hadn't the slightest need of Nikolai Nikolaevich. Let Alekseev command for now. (If he doesn't oppose a purge of the army.)

Even more so, the rest of the government had no need of the grand duke. But he had probably already left Tiflis.

So detain him en route! There was no point letting him get to GHQ.

But this was exactly what Alekseev had to be warned about. And the simplest was right now, tonight, by telegraph.

Prince Lvov wanted to go with Guchkov and inform Alekseev himself that he would for now hold the responsibilities of Supreme Commander.

Well, then.

The prince's eyes shone with an angelic light:

"But we aren't going to tell Alekseev about the Emperor. On the contrary, all is as before."

[4 7 7]

In the evening, Alekseev was summoned to the telegraph for a conversation with Petrograd.

It was the heretofore elusive Prince Lvov. He began by saying that the capitals had calmed down, order had been enshrined throughout, and reassuring news was coming in from other cities as well—all thanks to timely measures. (Was this by way of thanks to Alekseev for his help during the days of the abdication?) Regarding the penetration of revolutionary tendencies into the army, measures had also been taken. Yesterday, a notice was printed for the populace and today a notice to the troops was being printed. In response to Alekseev's alarming telegrams, Duma deputies with official authority were departing tonight for all the army groups.

Apparently, though, machine guns, not notices, were necessary at this point. . . .

The printed line stretched out evenly, but then something seemed to jerk it and something started coming through, from someone else:

"I beg you to bear in mind that it is impossible to keep up with the stormy development. *Events are carrying us along, and we do not control them.*"

Even Alekseev's permanently beetled brows seemed to creep up. It was this skipping around by Petrograd that he had been unable to understand all week. As if the people talking with him were deranged.

After that everything was smooth again: representatives would be sent today to escort the Imperial train. The journey would be wholly secure, but now it was desirable to know how the Emperor was going to proceed from Murman. Today Prince Lvov had received a telegram from the Supreme Commander saying he proposed arriving at GHQ on the 23d. He telegraphed him back about the general state of affairs and about his welcome at GHQ.

The fact that the head of government and Supreme Commander had immediately come to terms pleased Alekseev greatly; it would be easy to work.

And all of a sudden—again as if the tape had jerked—the words flowed pell-mell on the even strip. Prince Lvov had been applying all his efforts for more than a week to turning the trend in favor of the grand duke. But his vice-regency had lost all relevance, and . . .

"The issue of the Supreme Command has become just as risky as Mikhail Aleksandrovich's former position. We have arrived at the shared desire that Nikolai Nikolaevich, in view of the ominous situation, take the attitude toward the House of Romanov into account and himself refuse the

Supreme Command. Suspicion on this issue toward the new government is so great that no assurances are being accepted. . . ."

That was a shock! Alekseev took a firmer seat, pressing back.

". . . I believe this outcome is inevitable, but I haven't told the grand duke, not having discussed it with you. Up until today I had dealt with him as Supreme Commander."

But why? It was beyond Alekseev's comprehension. Why not tell the grand duke first? While he was still in Tiflis, they didn't decide in a single hour. They could have consulted with him. It would have been more convenient for him to stay in Tiflis.

"The general desire," Lvov concluded, "is that *you* accept the Supreme Command—and thereby cut off any possibility of new upheavals."

Alekseev was shaken yet again. But the old man did not rejoice in the least, and if his heart had started to pound, it wasn't out of ambition. He replied:

"The grand duke's character is such that if he has said he recognizes and stands on the side of the new regime, then he will not swerve and will carry out what he has undertaken. The army already knows about his appointment and is receiving his orders and proclamations. There is great trust in him among the middle and lower strata of the army. They have believed in him. For the new government he will be a desirable helper and reliable executor. You can have full confidence in . . ."

Why were they suddenly in such a hurry? Why didn't they want to wait for the grand duke's arrival at GHQ?

No change of mind was forthcoming, however. Alekseev tried again:

"Removing him will cause offense. And if such a change is for some reason considered essential inside the government, then better to wait for the grand duke's arrival here so that you can speak to him personally here. Only when and if the decision is settled can the question of his replacement be discussed. . . . In a way so that there are no clashes with the Army Group commanders. That question is also delicate . . ."

Lvov did not hurry to reply. For some reason he had been thinking about this the wrong way, his thoughts were crooked. Alekseev summoned up all his powers of persuasion:

"God will provide. With every passing day the government's status will become firmer and more authoritative. Then, if the need arises, a replacement in the future will be painless. Plausible pretexts can always be found. But at this moment the army needs life to flow calmly. In the past few days it has already grown used to the appointment, it knows the man, and will greet him with confidence. All of us will be at the ready to do everything we can to help the government gain stability in the army's consciousness. But you have to help us survive the somewhat painful process now under way in the army's organism: keep the Supreme Command with the grand duke. Support us morally and give us a proclamation saying that what Russia needs is a disciplined army. Support the authority of our officials by saying they have been put in place by the Provisional Government."

If everything has already been consolidated in Petrograd, then why be in such a hurry to change? If, on the contrary, everything there is teetering, then how can you risk such a change now? Obviously, we must clarify the matter orally.

"Shall I detach my general to you? Or will it be possible to elaborate on our conversation during a personal meeting?"

Finally something came in from Lvov:

"Dear Mikhail Vasilievich. You must reply to the point immediately. All your thoughts are fully shared by all members of the government. The point here lies not in our personal trust or mistrust in Nikolai Nikolaevich but entirely elsewhere. If only this had been a month ago! But now it's a different matter. . . . The fate of our great mission is being decided more by the rear than the army. But after the very great coup that has been brought about, the scale of which no one anticipated, the rear decides everything! Events are born by the psychology of the masses, not the desire of the government. And we believe that removing the grand duke will not bring the collapse of our cause, but his appointment could yield phenomena in the rear that . . . You see, the noble decision of Grand Duke Mikhail Aleksandrovich saved him and us from a new storm. We don't dare risk it! The best outcome would be the same kind of magnanimous act on the part of Nikolai Nikolaevich. If he with his highly authoritative voice were to call on the army to obey the new Supreme Commander, that would increase his popularity even more. And considerations of personal insult? In Nikolai Nikolaevich's noble heart? I'm certain those cannot arise. . . . Now Aleksandr Ivanych Guchkov is going to talk to you."

He was there, too! Alekseev's fateful man. Either you can't reach anyone or they're all there.

A message came in from Guchkov, but not in response to GHQ's desperate inquiries.

"Previously I found the combination of the grand duke and the Supreme Command desirable and possible. However, events are moving with such speed that now this appointment would reinforce the dangerous suspicion of counterrevolutionary attempts and would dangerously compel the popular masses to maintain their battle position. Personally, I am convinced of the grand duke's unconditional loyalty with regard to the new order, but it's impossible to convince the popular masses of this."

This was what Alekseev didn't understand! Who were the popular masses if not the soldiers, who loved and were waiting for the grand duke?

". . . Therefore I am expressing my firm conviction as to the absolute necessity of rejecting the grand duke—in your favor. Let his noble patriotism dictate this decision to him—and it will help us instill calm in people's minds here, in the center."

Well, if they're so firm, should he go on fighting them on this? They hadn't suggested inviting someone new, and Alekseev faced no leap of any kind; he remained right where he was.

"If that is so, then come to Mogilev yourself by 23 March for a verbal conversation with the grand duke on the whole delicate aspect . . . But in choosing a replacement you must discuss the question . . ."

Alekseev wasn't chasing after this post, but he could, of course, accept it. However, he imagined Ruzsky's open indignation and Brusilov's stinging malice hidden behind his smile.

". . . whether to choose one of the army group commanders? One whom the popular masses could regard with greater trust than someone who had worked as chief of staff under the Emperor? The new appointment ought to be approved by all the commanders without discontent."

There would also be a complication with the Romanian king. How could he be under simply a general?

Guchkov replied decisively:

"The situation is so grave that all questions of delicacy have to be discarded permanently. The grand duke will understand the full necessity of the step. We see no one else but you. If we let the time slip now, in a few days the situation might change again. You can increase the government's trust in you and your popularity among the people tenfold if you take several decisions. For example, if you were able to immediately remove General Evert, whose total incompetence . . . And if in a further signal, broad measures for eliminating generals known to be incompetent, then your situation would strengthen swiftly and firmly. But these measures have to be taken without delay. Never was I so certain that I was right as in giving you this advice."

The civilian Guchkov had quickly got the hang of his post as Minister of War! Drive out generals? Alekseev was flustered by that kind of pressure:

"All such measures at the given moment . . . As chief of staff I do not have the right to take them, for the law does not permit me. . . . The grand duke has already announced that he assumed his position on 17 March. . . . First we must change his official status and only then . . . various decisions. . . . And bear in mind our dearth of outstanding generals. *Broad measures* will encounter a shortage of suitable men. Replacing one weak one with another just as weak is of little use. . . ."

But Guchkov would not waver; he, too, was tearing ahead:

"I fully understand that you can't carry out these measures right away, but we need your internal decision. Can we rely on you supporting the advice to the grand duke about rejecting the Supreme Command? I absolutely cannot agree regarding the difficulties of finding gifted generals to replace the many dullards. New appointments like this made in one sweep would give rise to the greatest enthusiasm and would win tremendous trust!"

A big step! A big one! . . .

"However, Prince Lvov's arrival and mine at GHQ in the coming days is out of the question. We will be in a condition to discuss with the grand duke only by telegraph. I understand just how straitened your personal position is, but I beg you to give your consent. If you and I can't take these decisions freely and voluntarily, then they will be foisted upon us."

This was how they had turned around! Not just to agree with them but to do everything with his own hands. But also to take on the full weight of an explanation with the grand duke?—and in the idiotic position of deputy on top of everything . . .

"It is with profound distress that I have to speak with the grand duke. . . . I propose you send him a letter and then finish with a telegraph conversation. . . . I personally would like very much to remain in my present position. I am prepared to collaborate honestly with anyone the government might select for the office of Supreme Commander. . . . Naturally, duty above all, and I will have to accept the inevitable. . . . Although since my illness there have remained in my health several . . ."

"In the name of Prince Lvov and my own, I repeat that other than you we have no one in mind. The letter to the grand duke will be sent. Show him this tape. . . ."

Was the conversation over then? And he had so much for both of them. Alekseev had been trying to get a hold of them for days. . . . But through the whole avalanche of the unexpected he remembered only one thing:

"I would disturb you with an inappropriate extraneous matter. Count Frederiks has ordered his train car uncoupled in Gomel and asks for permission to go to Petrograd. If possible, allow the old man to do this. He has completely lost his memory and his ability to cope even with himself."

Guchkov:

"We advise Count Frederiks not to return to Petrograd just yet. There are no guarantees of his safety. Tell the count that everything is fine with his family. Details to follow."

As if there wasn't trouble enough, now this Count Frederiks was adding himself to it: a communiqué came right after from Gomel saying that the count, poor man, had been arrested there.

One felt sorry for the demented old man, and Alekseev could not put aside his own guilt for having sent him there. He had been overly anxious, no one at GHQ would have touched Frederiks probably, and nothing would have happened.

So that night he had to send Prince Lvov another telegram saying not to hold the unfortunate Frederiks under arrest.

20 March
Tuesday

[4 7 8]

No sooner had he stepped away from the telegraph than Alekseev felt he hadn't refused brusquely enough. He should have been brusquer.

His proposed appointment as Supreme Commander did not please him in the least. Throughout these days of revolution, in all the steps and decisions he'd taken, not for a moment had he had his own personal promotion in mind. He felt guilty before the grand duke. One might easily think that this intrigue was Alekseev's doing.

A person should occupy a height and space appropriate to him; only then does he feel his best. Why should he advance further? It was as dismal as sitting in a draft.

The grand duke enjoyed eminent authority. He had boldly instructed Alekseev to collect information from various places about how his appointment as Supreme Commmander was being received, and the response from everywhere was—with pleasure, joy, and faith in his success, ecstatically even. Even the seething Baltic fleet understood this to mean a strong, firm authority was being restored and order would ensue. Fourteen cities, including ones like Odessa, Kiev, and Minsk, had already sent congratulatory telegrams addressed to the Supreme Commander expressing their confidence in victory. In the universal upheaval of recent days, the grand duke had been the sole rock and buttress, the sole hope!—and here the hands of the government itself were recklessly, hastily, and secretly pushing him out! This was awkward in the extreme. As if it wasn't the government that was in greatest need of order!

And for ordinary soldiers used to the sound of his name?—this would be utterly inexplicable.

What did Guchkov want from him anyway? The wholesale replacement of generals, at one fell swoop? . . .

Late that night, Alekseev made his final decision: refuse. He had slipped up at the telegraph. It was too late to summon them again, but tomorrow morning . . .

He had been caught so flat-footed that he hadn't said the most important thing: What was this Order No. 2, let alone No. 1? And again from the Soviet of Workers' Deputies, and again bypassing GHQ! As if this were some kind of puppet show, not an army.

All this could rob you of sleep for ten nights, let alone one! Oh, he hadn't said it! Now, tonight, he should have sent a telegram. To all of them again, he saw no difference among them—Rodzyanko, Lvov, Guchkov (although for some reason he'd heard nothing from Rodzyanko, the chief tempter).

Telegraph them saying he was compelled to address them, so that no instructions of a general nature be sent directly to the army groups. Instructions from a Soviet of Workers' Deputies—which no one knew and was not part of governmental authority—could not be binding on the army and would not be announced to the troops.

Hadn't he sent them quite a few complaints, though? And all useless.

. . . It is with sorrow that I must add that many of my representations to the government . . . These kinds of "orders" threaten to destroy the army's moral stability and battle readiness, putting officers in an inexpressively difficult position . . . without the means to fight . . .

Not only that: . . . Either you need to give us your confidence—or replace us with others . . .

Instead of appointing us to the Supreme Command . . .

Alekseev got angrier than he'd ever been.

And what are the orders of the Minister of War himself? After all, this isn't some Soviet of Deputies—but he, too, was ruining everything: no using titles; smoking, cards, clubs, and political societies for soldiers. He even intended to abolish saluting! It was some sort of madness . . . And he also had to respond to his No. 114, which had been published already, the harm was done, yet now for some reason was being sent late to GHQ for review. They were splitting the army at the very root—and asking how the commanders-in-chief would view this! All the GHQ officers who had read it were unanimously indignant. And along with Lukomsky, Alekseev had already begun to compose a response—which they were continuing deep into the night. A comprehensive response.

. . . That completely abolishing saluting was inadmissible because the army would become a militia of low quality. The majority of senior officers would leave military service, and there would be nowhere from which to assemble a decent corps of officers. Saluting could be abolished when standing at attention, but the most junior must be the first to greet. Ease up on titles, allow smoking, streetcars, and clubs? Oh well . . . But the idea of soldiers participating in meetings with a political purpose was absolutely inadmissible because extreme leftist ideas would come to predominate in the army. The army had taken no part whatsoever in current events, but once drawn into politics it might also be drawn into state coups, and it was difficult to predict in which direction. For the sake of victory, we had to strive to keep the army calm and not let its thoughts be taken up with political issues . . .

Another night lost. Lying in bed, he kept coming up with arguments and even rather caustic phrases, and then he would throw his greatcoat over his undergarments and sit down at his desk—and add his even, precise, close-set loops, which got bigger the angrier he got.

. . . If the army gets drawn into politics, then Petrograd could be in the Germans' hands by June.

And here, apparently, was something clever Alekseev came up with: send Guchkov's question about saluting to all the commanders-in-chief, and so that they can send it on to the regimental commanders. And let all the regimental commanders respond! Not to Alekseev, to whom everything was clear as is—but to Guchkov himself! Let the torrent of those letters— negative, of course—crash over Guchkov's head!

This was good what he'd come up with, and he smiled for the first time.

Everything that had been raked up was spinning in his head and keeping him from sleep—both Order No. 114 and Order No. 2—so in the middle of the night he stopped in at the telegraph room—and there lay yet another wild new telegram from Kvetsinsky saying that Evert had received a telegram from Purishkevich alleging that "Order No. 1" was a fake, a malicious provocation, and that this had been certified by Minister of Justice Kerensky and Chkheidze himself from the Soviet of Deputies, and Evert was asking whether he could tell the troops.

That would be a delight, such a delight! However, given the disarray of recent days and his own soberness, Alekseev now did not believe it. Purishkevich was a psychopath and could well have confused things.

He felt besieged beyond bearing and absolutely could not sleep.

The following idea occurred to him: as long as he was only chief of staff at GHQ, he wasn't stirring up a storm of ill will. But if in the present insane situation he was promoted to Supreme Commander, then everyone would be beside themselves, especially *society* circles. They would bring up what they weren't bringing up now—for instance, his secret directive of the previous fall saying that many Zemstvo Union institutions were waging revolutionary propaganda, and it was essential to establish the strictest surveillance over them and, if the facts were borne out, then shut them down. If someone were to drag out that directive now, what might rear its head?

Another point was offending Nikolai Nikolaevich. And another—enraging the commanders-in-chief. No! No! On no account did Alekseev want to accept the post.

He dozed off briefly just before dawn. But in the morning, without waiting for further events, he sent by way of continuation of their conversation a new telegram to Lvov and Guchkov asking them to keep Nikolai Nikolaevich's appointment in force! Reports that had come in from the troops showed that he had been accepted with delight . . . (And about the two fleets and the 14 cities. . . .) A cry from the burning soul of all officials who loved their homeland and the army . . . In moments like these, subjecting the army's fragile organism to a new trial, a change little understood by the simple mass of soldiers . . .

This is what he wrote: I trust . . . no, I *believe* that you will take everything said here into consideration. This was not the time to sacrifice the army's order and cohesion!

He sent it—and waited all morning. The government had been pestering GHQ over all kinds of nonsense but had said nothing in response to the most important questions; this was their way.

Meanwhile, the workday was under way and bringing things of its own from unexpected directions. Hanbury-Williams, the English military representative, who was senior among the Allied representatives, had requested an appointment with Alekseev. Alekseev was anticipating anxious questions about the army—and had steeled himself.

But that wasn't why the English general had come. He brought a long letter to the chief of staff in the name of all his colleagues and orally explained that they were all offering their services for the protection of the Emperor should he return to Tsarskoye Selo and on his further journey. So that no revolutionaries put up obstacles to him en route.

Williams stood in an official pose and with chilly English restraint—but was offering an anything but ordinary, extra-official step, moved by his undoubted loyalty to the overthrown sovereign, who had always been extremely kind to all the Allied representatives.

However, this step looked extraordinary from the Russian side as well. It might look like a gesture of distrust for the Provisional Government, Alekseev thought.

He replied that such a measure would constrain the former Emperor himself in his new position as a private individual and would help nothing, for there was nothing to protect the Emperor from. There was nothing threatening him.

After the Englishman's departure, closely reading his letter, Alekseev learned that yesterday he had held talks with the Dowager Empress, whose train was still at the Mogilev train station. Had this idea been somehow inspired by her? Her son might not even have known about those talks.

She should leave, the sooner the better; GHQ was no place for her.

So should the Emperor . . .

The document also contained another proposal from the Allied generals: publish a joint memorandum of support for the Provisional Government.

This might well have major significance. It was a good idea.

What other choice did Russia have other than to do all it could to support and strengthen the current moderate government? No matter how bad it was or by what means it had ensconced itself in power, if not this government, then they would see the most extreme, unbridled forces and out-and-out ruin.

Even if he didn't like it, even if he didn't want to, Alekseev now had to serve this government faithfully and honorably.

If the Allies were now offering to publish something about their support, then there first had to be a telegram from GHQ so that they could run it in the newspapers.

This was essential, yes, he now understood that.

He sat down and wrote. Quick work.

. . . All headquarters detachments and all Mogilev garrison units are maintaining calm and discipline, filled with the desire to prosecute the war to a victorious conclusion . . . And they proclaim their loud "hurrah" for their precious Russia and its Provisional Government . . .

[479″]

(FROM THE SOCIALIST NEWSPAPERS, 18–20 MARCH)

WE AWAIT AN ANSWER. By what right is he, in whose name all the violence against the Russian people was committed, at liberty? Why is he roaming freely through Russia and allowed to the front? . . . The breast of yesterday's lords cannot help but seethe with fierce hatred for the people who shook off their yoke . . . The fragments of the old authority have in their possession colossal riches that will be thrown with a generous hand into the fight against freedom. In their possession are all the military secrets and knowledge of Russia's weak spots. They have much to tell the Hohenzollerns! Didn't the Bourbons plunge the poisoned knife of betrayal into the French Revolution's back? . . . We await an answer!

. . . Why didn't the Provisional Government publicly state that the Tsar's "appointment" of Lvov as prime minister is null and void? The blot of being "legitimately Tsarist" must be removed from the prime minister. Otherwise the government is openly acknowledging its monarchist sympathies.

The greatest danger for the revolution is that its forces will disunite before autocracy is broken . . . In order for all attempts by the people's former oppressors . . . If in the place of one severed head another grows . . . In a half-whisper, half-blushing, they exclaim: "poor Nikolai" . . .

. . . On the streets, active agitation is under way in favor of Mikhail. But for the people, a return to monarchy is out of the question. A monarch always expresses the interests of those groups which would be defeated in elections . . . Render the dynasty and its secret allies harmless! . . .

TO ACCOUNT! . . . The tyrant is still at liberty! . . . Nikolai and all his black forces could bring about a plot of counterrevolution. We know from the history of popular revolutions . . . Nikolai and his lackeys must be immediately brought before the people's court.

. . . in this way, are Petrograd workers going to have to leave the street, where they have been working over the course of a week to create popular freedom, and return to their workbenches? But how can anyone think about productive work if workers once again are faced with a solid wall of despotism on the part of their employers? . . . Above all, demand the immediate issuance of money for the days they have spent outside the factories and plants fighting for freedom for the entire people. Anyone who dares dispute this will cover himself in disgrace forever.

STRIKE HALTED—REVOLUTION CONTINUES!

Prohibition of Black Hundreds publications. The Executive Committee of the Soviet of Workers' Deputies has resolved to ban all Black Hundreds publications: *The Land, Voice of Rus', The Bell, The Russian Banner*. Because it came out without prior permission from the Executive Committee, the newspaper *New Times* is closed from now until there is a special instruction.

From the railroad gendarmes to the President of the State . . . to the Council of Ministers . . . to the Soviet of Workers' . . .

The Committee has not accepted our delegates and has refused to guarantee our safety and life . . . We request that we be deemed Russian citizens . . . The majority of us out of gratitude to the government would join active service at front-line positions.

. . . Revival of pogrom propaganda in Poltava and Kiev provinces . . . They blame the disenfranchised Jews for the army's defeats and absolutism's fall.

Comrade Uritsky telegraphs from Copenhagen . . . They are not giving visas to other revolutionary emigrés either. Isn't it time for citizen Milyukov to show a little more energy?

. . . On the Okhta and at the Gunpowder district, the people's militia has set about paralyzing local authority. The militia has been infiltrated by rabble that are using their weapons for requisitions.

. . . All the cadets have delegates in the Soviet of Workers' Deputies except for those from the Nikolaevsky Military School. How is such a phenomenon to be explained? By the cadets' backwardness in the political respect? Or do their leaders rule them with an iron rod? At such a time, it is shameful, cadets, not to take part in building the people's happiness!

A mysterious motorcar . . . It changes registration plates daily . . . It races at mad speed, at night with extinguished headlights, and shoots systematically at the people . . .

. . . a meeting will be held of tailors, dressmakers, furriers, hatters . . . In view of the exceptional importance of the moment in the country's life, all comrade tailors and dressmakers will consider it their duty to appear . . .

PREPARE BANNERS!—for participation in the funeral ceremonies for martyrs of the revolution! . . . The victims' bodies should not be committed to the ground before a public funeral.

Comrade hairdressers, masters and apprentices! During the days of the great creation of popular might on the ruins of the old order—hurry to organize a union!

Radiologists of Petrograd are invited . . .

In the Liteiny Theater, a general meeting of the Bund . . .

Comrade pharmacists, men and women! A storm has struck! The moment for building a new state has come. Let us gather and discuss the current situation . . . We are opposed to a constitutional monarchy . . .

HOOLIGANISM. "An appeal. Comrade thieves, wheeler-dealers, robbers, picklocks, swindlers, blackmailers, double-dealers, sots, marauders, pickpockets, cat burglars, vagrants, and other brethren. We did a lot of work in the first days of the revolution, and we have to meet in order to choose representatives to the Soviet of Workers' and Soldiers' Deputies for the sessions. Unite, comrades, for in unity is strength! There will be a meeting to elect a deputation on Wednesday at 12 midnight on the Obvodny Canal under the American Bridge. *Group of conscientious businessmen."*

Distributed throughout the city, this proclamation shows that the Black Hundreds are organizing to fight the revolution. It is no secret to anyone who these conspirators are: Markov the 2nd and Zamyslovsky are at liberty . . .

. . . It is proposed that everyone who voluntarily absented himself from the 175th Infantry Regiment return to their regiment in the next few days. Otherwise they will be considered supporters of the old regime.

COMRADES! READ *PRAVDA* OUT LOUD ON THE STREETS
AND AT RALLIES AND PASS IT ON TO OTHERS!

. . . Don't recognize any agreements of any kind with the bourgeoisie! We deem the provisionally approved government a failure and hope that this will be corrected. *(Pravda)*

. . . We are going to fight for the immediate elimination of war through mass actions by workers of all countries. We will stand for the creation of a Third International to replace the Second destroyed by war . . .

Contributions to PRAVDA'S IRON FUND . . .

[480]

Moscow, the Whitestone city, was at last coming to its senses after those intoxicating days. The Committee of Social Organizations published an appeal to high school pupils saying that it fully understood their fervent impulse, but they should not introduce discord into the life of the state—and as of Monday they should return to their lessons. Its other appeal was this: Anyone who has more than 700 pounds of flour should submit a report on their supplies. Actually, it was discovered that even without any flour incoming, there was enough in Moscow to last two weeks, and flour was pouring in to all the train stations, while Tambov and Saratov provinces, out of respect for the ancient capital, had each given Moscow a gift of 11 million pounds of rye flour. Meanwhile, all the first-class restaurants were back open (the chefs and waiters had stopped their revolutionary strike). The streetcars had started up, all decorated with red flags and slogans. Commander Gruzinov appealed for the necessity of confiscating military weapons from those to whom they could not possibly belong. The stock exchange resumed activity. At Ryabushinsky's apartment, a decision was made to assemble an Industry and Trade congress in Moscow. Permission was given to open the races, although without a betting shop. All the churches held services, and the priests delivered sermons on recent events. Theatrical life resumed to the extent that it could overcome the theatrical public's voluntary self-restraint: not offering performances during the week of the Veneration of the Precious Cross, but where performances were given, the orchestra played the Marseillaise and arranged a rally for both artists and audience. Cinematographers kept working, and a sensational film appeared on the screens, *The Dark Force*, about Grigori Rasputin, which had been shot for America with no thought that the fatherland would ever see it. In Likhov Lane, the apartment of the Union of Monarchy was searched, and the apartment of Okhrana chief Martynov was ransacked and plundered. It was decided not to release arrested city policemen, ward inspectors, and police officers. The historian Melgunov began to sort through police archives, and at 16 Petrovka a commission was created on extrajudicial arrests, in order to regularize arrests. On the contrary, Governor Count Tatishchev and Deputy Governor Count Kleinmichel, who had signed loyalty statements to the new government, were freed. The "black room" at the Moscow post office was abolished for good, but temporary censorship was established over telephone conversations from certain suspicious telephones and lifted from others altogether. The Committee of Social Organizations finally left the city duma, the heart of these revolutionary days, for Leontievsky Lane, as did the Soviet of Workers' Deputies for Skobolev Square—and the emptied, damaged city duma building was swept and scraped, its walls and windows washed, and the floor-polishers crawled through it.

Right during these days of recuperation, a rumor went around that a famous revolutionary figure was on his way to Moscow, Minister of Justice Kerensky himself!

And this turned out to be the truth! Up until then, only secondary members of the State Duma had come to clarify events, and Moscow's own figures had traveled to Petrograd to look and learn. Wounded by not being primary, Moscow jealously followed how everything most important was going on the banks of the Neva—and made designs about how to draw the Constituent Assembly to Moscow, at least. And now, the most vivid, most popular, most leftist of the ministers was on his way here! On his way to show himself and enlighten them! In particular, as the press warned, to familiarize himself with local judicial institutions. And also, in particular, to enter into direct relations with the Moscow working class and to familiarize himself with their views on the current political moment.

At the Nikolaevsky Train Station, which was decorated with red flags, as were all the stations, by midday there had gathered to greet him representatives of the Committee of Social Organizations, representatives of the Soviet of Workers' Deputies, representatives of the Moscow Municipal Board, Moscow Commissar of Justice Muravyov, and, of course, members of the Moscow bar, from the council of lawyers, from the High Court, and from the district court—and an honor guard was formed made up of cadets from the Aleksandrovsky School.

Now, approaching the cupolaed train platform, which had seen so many glorious arrivals from Petersburg and Petrograd, was an express train consisting of a locomotive and two train cars—and standing on the platform of the second car was Russia's first citizen-minister! (How young he was, how slender, how his light, fur-collared coat and soft hat suited him!) By removing his glove, he had demonstrated his accessibility, without any arrogance, and he waved his hand at the welcoming crowd. Right then the captain's command to the platoon of cadets rang out:

"For the welcome on the left, at my command, present arms!"

The cadets presented arms. The drummer drummed a welcome. Aleksandr Fyodorovich bowed prettily, touching his hat.

Not only he: farther back on the platform stood—and also touched their hats—two Moscow favorites, Chelnokov and Kishkin, who had also arrived from Petrograd and who had a few days before set an example of civic conduct. Chelnokov, appointed commissar of Moscow by Rodzyanko, had not felt it possible to take the post by appointment given the new era of freedom—and had voluntarily ceded the commissarship to the elected Kishkin. But even the two of them were barely noticed at the welcome.

Scarcely had he stepped off the train with a slipping movement of the foot than the citizen-minister exchanged kisses with tall, skinny Prince Dmitri Shakhovskoy (both had tears in their eyes) and with the railroad workers' representative, whom Kerensky called comrade. He accepted from an ensign a large bouquet of red tulips tied with a wide, moire ribbon.

Prince Shakhovskoy, with large, clear eyes, a renowned Kadet, secretary of the 1906 Vyborg session, trembling from the emotion that had gripped him, couldn't get even a word out for a long time. Finally he began:

"In these momentous days, which the Russian people will never forget, you have proven that the most zealous radicalism, the most fervent spirit can be invested in a vital cause and take on real forms! You have proven this with your ardent personal example! In the name of Moscow and in the name of . . . I offer you the most ardent . . . It is thanks to you that we have safeguarded our city from bloody excesses. In Moscow, all is calm, all is in exemplary order, as you yourself will be convinced."

And once again they exchanged fervent kisses.

After this, Kerensky was greeted by the city hall. And after this, from the Soviet of Workers' Deputies—

". . . as the Minister of Justice, but our dear comrade as well . . ."

They handed him a letter from Soviet Chairman Khinchuk. Freeing himself of the bouquet, the minister immediately read the letter, and his intelligent face lit up with determination:

"I will go directly from here to see you!"

This changed the proposed schedule and upset the representatives of the judicial authorities, prosecutors, and commissar of justice who had greeted the minister in the name of, in the name of, and also in the name of . . .

Adopting a highly official look, though, Kerensky stated:

"I would ask you not to wait for me! I will be at the court, too."

And then, responding to all the welcomes with an abrupt voice heard far away:

"Comrades! . . . Gentlemen! . . . I don't have the words to express what I am feeling! But I personally—I am only doing my duty. I know that the Russian people are a great people, and Russian democracy is a great democracy. For them, nothing is impossible, and I . . . I am merely their instrument. Yes, for me it is the greatest happiness that for the past few days I have been able to act with certainty. I followed a straight road, for I knew well the peasantry, and the working class, and the entire Russian people in general . . . Now I have come in the name of the Provisional Government, which enjoys all the fullness of power, I have come to convey to you our greeting, the ministers' greeting, and to state that we are putting ourselves at the nation's disposal and will carry out its will to the end! And now, I have come to ask you: Shall we go to the end?"

"To the end! To the end!" the crowd roared, having by this time grown to enormous size. Crowding here were respectable, well-fed public figures, a few officers, and many soldiers out of formation, workers, petty bourgeois, university students, and high school boys.

Throwing his head back in a fateful movement, accepting these shouts as the voice of the people, Kerensky took another step and addressed the honor guard:

"Gentlemen officers, cadets, and soldiers! In the name of the Provisional Government, I greet the Russian army, which has freed Russia from tyrannical authority for good! Henceforth we have but one people—the armed people!"

There was a thrum of admiration.

"The old strife between officers and soldiers, between the army and the people—is a thing of the past. Now we are all citizens!" He threw one hand in a rabbitskin glove and one without a glove over his head. "Now we are all sons of a great and free people." And he headed off, headed off lightly, freely, not stopping in at the station's main rooms but going immediately to the street, where a motorcar was waiting.

Taking seats next to him as his adjutants were two officers assigned from the commander of troops.

To a shout of hurrah and clapping, the motorcar left the station for the Soviet of Workers' Deputies and a friendly and private discussion among revolutionaries.

Meanwhile, the newspaper correspondents rushed to their editorial offices.

[4 8 1]

After Fergen's murder, that same evening, the limping Captain Nelidov was led under large convoy, so that he wouldn't be torn to pieces en route, to his 2nd Company and advised or told that he now must not leave the company building, not even to go to his quarters in the officers' wing, but must stay and live in the company chancery.

Actually, the 4th Company soldiers did later have their regrets over Fergen's body and some wept, even—and after they tidied up the battered body, they placed it in a coffin, took it to the regimental church, and held a funeral. But the staff captain's mother came—and for some reason they wouldn't release the body to her, and then once again they treated it outrageously.

Nelidov had already gone over in his mind everything that could be understood and not understood, and he lived now as if it weren't he, and it didn't matter. And perhaps it was safer in the company office, though he was never alone there, but like any soldier in the barracks, and there was a droning in his head, a constant droning.

Right away it came down to him to rescue the company sergeant major, who had been badly beaten. There was a drawer in the company where they kept the soldiers' own money, which was logged in a notebook, and when the soldier needed to, he took it. The sergeant major had safeguarded this drawer and kept this notebook; all this had been instituted to prevent theft. Once the disturbances began, the sergeant major stopped issuing money, which was why he was beaten. Now Nelidov ordered all the money be recounted and handed over.

Although seemingly no one was after the soldiers, everyone in the company was extremely agitated and even frightened—afraid of those same workers. They told Nelidov frankly: it's the *civilians* who aren't letting us salute or agree to go to our positions—but we don't have anything against going to our positions, and saluting doesn't bother us. The soldiers now explained to him something he hadn't supposed before, that all these past few months the Vyborg side had been riddled with deserters, who used fake passports obtained underground, occasionally Finnish passports, which released them from mobilization—and now these deserters among the workers were loudest and cockiest of all.

All the workers had gotten hold of rifles and even vehicles, whereas the company had almost no rifles. Overnight they set up a table opposite the front doors for the duty officer and the orderlies and on it put two loaded rifles, barrels facing the entrance.

Nelidov sent men to the clinic to get the disassembled rifles from there and was also able to obtain some from the arsenal storeroom—and then the company calmed down.

Now he was summoned as company commander to sit in on the sessions of the battalion committee—an idiotic, tedious, and endless sitting. Two or three soldier bosses, who had risen to the top by virtue of their insolence rather than any education or intelligence, gave almost continuous speeches, spelling each other—and now were spewing all sorts of nonsense. But the committee was unable to resolve a single vital issue, and the discussion of the most trivial issues went on for hours. Occasionally it felt as though they were getting close, that it was almost decided—and then one of the three would speak, saying something else was missing and had to be added, and it would stretch on for hours again.

Only one issue was decided unanimously and quickly: the battalion had an order about sending the next reinforcement company to the front. They decided not to send their own company but to put together arrested policemen and send them instead. They sent delegates to the Soviet of Workers' Deputies about this. And even to Moscow and Kazan, for them to round up their arrested policemen and send them here, to get credit for them.

Meanwhile, all companies were instructed that there were to be only two hours of military training a day. Then all the bread bakers, shoemakers, harness makers, and the transport started working just two hours, too. Everything in the battalion came to a halt. Clerks stopped writing out warrants, and the garrison storehouses stopped issuing flour and food. No one wanted to clean the latrines, which backed up with sewage and stank. Platoon and squad leaders went to see Nelidov and asked him to relieve them of their positions. Not only could they not force anyone to do anything, but they'd turned into manual laborers for their own subordinates, and if anything needed bringing or doing, they had to do it themselves.

That's when the battalion committee decided to bring back all the officers they could find. They started going around to all the city apartments of the scattered ensigns and tried to talk them into returning to the battalion. Captain Nelidov was put in charge of managing the battalion. He accepted, on condition that he would make all the appointments himself and that his instructions were not subject to discussion by the committee.

The committee approved.

Now they gave Nelidov permission to move to his own quarters. Everyone was especially pleased that he was able to give the soldiers their next month's pay.

It may have been only due to this popularity of his that he was able yesterday to save Captain Dubrova, when soldiers from the training crew, who all hated him, somehow sussed out that he was lying in the Nikolaevsky Military Hospital. They headed there in a truck and dragged Dubrova out of the ward and the hospital, and none of the doctors dared intervene, and they took him to their barracks in the truck, beating him up on the way and beating him up there in the guard-house. They were just about to execute him right there, by the woodpile—and Nelidov barely got there in time, with his walking stick, and stopped them and convinced them that they needed to send him to the State Duma, that such was the law. (Dubrova had already been saved there once.) Given his crippled arms and legs, the captain's bloodied face was a terrible sight.

And so yesterday, utterly exhausted, all his senses deadened, Nelidov went to spend the night in his own quarters for the first time—the first time since that terrible night when Sasha Fergen was taken away and ten minutes later Luka ran in yelling that the captain had been hoisted on bayonets.

The place where Nelidov had kissed Fergen's icy lips for the last time still seemed alive.

Nelidov was by now totally indifferent to his own person. Let them shoot him—but until they did, he would go to bed and fall asleep.

Before he could remove his boots, though, the bell rang, albeit a normal bell and without a menacing knocking. Luka opened the door—and in walked Captain Stepanov, straight from the train, just back from the Caucasus! He still had the unbroken freshness of a soldier on leave.

Did he know what had been going on here?

He did. . . . That is, he knew about Petrograd events in general but nothing properly about the battalion.

"Did the annex porter see you?"

"Yes."

"Well then, brother, make yourself scarce. Your company sentenced you to death by firing squad and now they're going to arrest you. That's how they killed Sasha Fergen, don't you know?"

He turned pale. He hadn't known anything, he was straight from the station.

Nelidov hurried to tell him but also to send him on his way, to save him. They decided he would stay with acquaintances on the Petersburg side— and he disappeared. It was later that Nelidov realized he should have taken away his sword, for safekeeping. They themselves just weren't used to this, it was unthinkable.

Before Stepanov could leave, a dozen soldiers descended:

"Where's Stepanov? . . ."

"I don't know. He left."

Nelidov sat there and twitched: at any moment he would hear shooting or they would run in and say they'd torn him to pieces, like Fergen.

But they didn't, thank God, they didn't, and Nelidov, broken by all the scrapes—this had been going for ten days, after all—fell into a dead sleep.

Early this morning he was awakened by his sergeant major begging him to save Captain Stepanov (who had led their own 2nd company). It turned out he'd managed to get away from his own men the previous evening but was stopped by grenadiers on Grenadier Bridge. They took away his sword, questioned him, identified his regiment, and took him back in the night, to the barracks. And a handful of scoundrels from the 2nd company fell on him and started spitting on him and beating him, and wanted to shoot him.

It just so happened, though, that for those twenty-four hours their company had been doing guard duty at the battalion guardhouse—and the sergeant-major (whom Nelidov himself had recently rescued) was able to convince the assailants that it was better to shoot him the next morning, took Captain Stepanov away from them to the guardhouse, and locked him up there— but under reliable guards who wouldn't give him up.

The full extent of Captain Nelidov's power was to send a reliable ser-geant quickly to the State Duma and get them to send a vehicle there with its own convoy—and take Stepanov to the Tauride Palace, under arrest.

The vehicle arrived in the nick of time.

[4 8 2]

Today Agnessa and Adalia went arm in arm to watch the streetcars let out for the first time.

The spectacle was worth it! First, a few service cars appeared swathed in red cotton cloth, and one had two open platforms attached to it, and on them sat a military band that played the Marseillaise the whole time! This streetcar train passed through the city to nonstop ovations. All the passersby stopped and admired it. On Nevsky and the major streets, the populace greeted the streetcar parade with bared heads.

Then came the ordinary passenger streetcars, but all with posters: "Land and Freedom"—"In struggle we gain our rights!"—"Long live the demo-cratic republic!" And the Marseillaise wafted from inside a few cars, as well.

Agnessa and Adalia made no attempt to hide their tears. To hear, openly, down Nevsky, to general exultation: "In struggle we gain our rights!" . . . How could this be described?

And those who had not been lucky enough to live this long! Holy heroes! They had given up what was most precious so that we now could live.

A beautiful dream! All the martyrs for freedom now redeemed!

At a few stops, rallies gathered around the streetcars, and then the streetcars were held up. As the streetcar pulled away, the rally would scatter. The general mood of good will and solidarity was touching, the collective joy, when everyone loved one another—the spirit of revolution!—and that was why it was so good, such as could not have been achieved under the old regime no matter what the coercion. Universal brotherhood was now coming!

The day was snowy white, following the snowstorm on Monday, frosty, sunny, a blue sky to gladden hearts. The sisters strode along, occasionally to music. Had it really *come to pass*? . . .

That phrase—"come to pass!"—in all the appeals, all the newspapers, the air was filled with it—a thunderous phrase—but what other could express this? The revolution was victorious! Understand, brothers: victorious! The barracks based on class had collapsed! Anyone who had oppressed the individual!—tribe, clan, caste, class, church, family, state, or nationality—it had all been cast off! The individual would rise from this rubbish, from these chains!

On Nevsky, in the sun, by a building wall, some old guy had spread a tarp over the trampled snow and set out stacks and was selling—banned books. Hawking them, offering them. Look, Adalia, look! Kropotkin, *Words of a Rebel*! Lavrov! Karabchevsky—*The Sazonov Affair*! Tolstoy against the church! Nietzsche's *Anti-Christ*! . . . The sisters leaned toward him and sorted through with trembling hands, happy fingers. Look at this! Look! If they'd told us ten years ago that this would be sold just like this, openly, on Nevsky, on a tarp? . . .—and a policeman wouldn't swoop in?

But it was an ungrateful public. They weren't swooping in either, now everyone wanted something newer . . .

An entire era was concentrated in this book stand!

The happy women moved on.

And all those smashed, smeared coats of arms?

Or: The Mariinsky Theater wants to establish its autonomy from the state! Isn't that a symbol?

What had many of us been so afraid of? That we wouldn't live to see the revolution or that its bloodiness wouldn't vindicate our hopes? And here it was—all different!

Down Sadovaya and on to Mikhailovsky Square, where there was also a major streetcar crossing. There they met and stopped in the sun (the cold did penetrate, after all) with acquaintances of Adalia's—an intellectual couple, actually just liberals, a penguin and a loon, but perfectly honest individuals. (Adalia knew people like this; Agnessa never had.)

They: *Who* were we afraid of? *Who* was it who clutched us so tightly in the double-headed eagle's claws? How easily we've won this incredible victory!

Agnessa cut them short: No! Not at all that easily. We were brought freedom by those who fell during the dark years. A high price.

The penguin-husband was contrite: Yes, we are ungrateful to forget . . . But where was the ordinary person to gain political practice? Up until now, only heroes could engage in politics. But here—the people shrugged their shoulders and . . .

The people? All around, everyone in unison praised the "people," everything was done by the people—and somehow they'd forgotten about the intelligentsia! Meanwhile, the 150 years of sacrificial struggle, from Radishchev to Spiridonova, was whose? And the people? What had the people done? They could have been more grateful to the intelligentsia, after all.

The loon grumbled at the criminals being released, at which point Adalia advised:

"Are they really to blame that social conditions threw them into a whirlpool of crimes? Are they supposed to bathe our freedom with tears in prison?"

The sisters set out for home, and Agnessa said in a fit of temper:

"What infuriates me is that today every small-minded person is 'shaking off the old world' and implying that only by happy coincidence was he not executed under the old regime!"

Oh, so be it. But how caught up the young people were! How proud that they had accomplished all this. Veronika was finally saved, she was in a life-giving stream. The Society for Aid to Released Politicals—there could be nothing better for her! A direct tie to their tradition!

And now might Sasha break with that awful slip of a merchant girl?

[4 8 3]

How the Executive Committee members wore him down, those dodgers: they wouldn't take power themselves and wouldn't let anyone else either. Nor could Shlyapnikov treat these conciliators with candor. He was reticent with them and suspected a trick at every step, which was in fact the case. The Bolshevik faction could not hold out against the Executive Committee's bloc of opportunists. But Shlyapnikov did know that he was distasteful to them, an obstacle—and an obstacle he was happy to be and so sat there, arms crossed his favorite way at his chest, saying nothing.

Today it was essential that Shlyapnikov be there because on the agenda was the issue of the workers' militia, on which he was considered the principal authorized representative. Also to be discussed was the question of the 1st Machine-gun Regiment's return to Oranienbaum.

But right now everyone was discussing animatedly and excitedly the rumor that gendarmes out of uniform were transporting stacks of pogrom literature along certain railways—and what highly energetic measures to take to prevent this. Shlyapnikov said nothing. He didn't believe this panicked story for a moment. All the gendarmes were scared to death and looking to save their necks, not to transport anything dangerous. And on exactly which railways? Who had seen those stacks? Why hadn't he taken them away? And why hadn't they been brought a single brochure as an example? How did they know this was pogrom literature? But all the top leaders here were very nervous.

Then they started discussing *Izvestia*, based on Nakhamkes's report. Three days before, Shlyapnikov would have had to be on the alert, and interject, and seize influence; now, though, he had his *Pravda*, so they could beat it . . . Their being so upset was understandable: all their power depended on the newspaper. The Executive Committee had now given Steklov dis-cre-tion-ary power over the newspaper, which meant he could act as he wished, however the spirit moved him. For the editorial staff he picked his good friend Tsiperovich, Bazarov, Goldenberg, and some other Mensheviks. There was also Bonch, coward and traitor though he was, but we'd make him carry water for us.

Bonch also had a personal issue being sorted out now. He had done a number on General Ruzsky in the newspaper, and Ruzsky had hysterically complained to the Executive Committee—but the Mensheviks couldn't take the general's side, and they were too timid to do anything with Bonch.

Now there was another major question: the funeral for the revolution's martyrs, already postponed ten days and now for another week. Not on Palace Square, they'd said! Gorky had intervened along with some artists and architects.

Shlyapnikov had taken offense at Gorky. All these years he had seemingly been at one with the Bolsheviks. Who else? But whether his head had been spinning these past few days with everyone claiming him as his own and praising him, or his head wasn't screwed on quite tight, he had joined up with the silver tongues of class harmony, the lovers of unity—and refused to collaborate on *Pravda*, which was so lacking in literary strength. Gorky's name would have meant so much to it! Shlyapnikov telephoned to exhort him—only to hear Gorky reply: "You're helping the revolution's enemies!" Us—helping the revolution's enemies? This—about our honest, proletarian *Pravda*? The bourgeois narcotic had eclipsed his own mind. Now he was planning some sort of separate radical-republican party of his own.

Well, finally, about the machine-gun regiments. The 2nd Machine-gun had been satisfied with the barracks on the Okhta and wasn't making trouble for anyone, but here the 1st Machine-gun had ravaged the House of the People and, most important, its latrines, and the soldiers had begun relieving themselves on the boulevard around the House of the People—so that by the time spring came this threatened to turn into a contagion in the middle of the city.

Apparently this was all so, there was no way to fix the latrines, and given the snow, it was impossible right now for the first revolutionary construction to start tearing up the boulevard and building new sewers. And it was natural for the regiment to live where it had fully equipped barracks, in Oranienbaum. All this was apparently so, however the 1st Machine-gun, stationed on Kronverksky cater-corner from the Petrograd Committee, was already inclining heavily toward us, our people had done some work there—and it was promising to be the Bolshevik's military force—and it was armed with machine guns! Was this the time to let it be removed from the city? Not on your life! Shlyapnikov was prepared to fight for this, but not too loudly or broadly, so that it wouldn't reach the front-line soldiers, who, for their part, were offended that these men weren't being taken to the front, while they had to fight the whole time. Nor could he overcome the majority here by a vote. Instead, he started frightening the Executive Committee with the machine gunners, saying they weren't going to stand for it! You never knew, might they turn their machine guns on the Soviet?

They were afraid.

He also mocked them with their own arguments. It had been their idea, they had worked to keep the revolutionary garrison from being removed, and now they were removing it? Who was going to trust them? Would other units rebel? Any battalion could sweep away everyone here.

But these dodgers were the kind who you could drive into a corner but never once lay a stick on. On the spot they devised and resolved the idea of sending a demand to the Minister of War that Oranienbaum also be declared a district of Petrograd, so that the minister would have no right to send anyone to the front from there without the Soviet's permission. In that way, this removal of the regiment wouldn't be a removal at all but actually an expansion of the revolution's gains. And also that the machine-gun regiment, in leaving for Oranienbaum, have its own permanent representatives here, in the Petrograd Soviet.

Most important, Chkheidze stated—and this is why he was so fearless—there was a statement from Comrade Peshekhonov saying that the machine-gunners' regimental committee itself wished to take the regiment to Oranienbaum, but they needed an order from the Soviet.

Shlyapnikov started fidgeting in his chair. This was a bad business; they'd try to cheat our boys there. But here—there was nothing he could do. The resolution was written: ask the 1st Machine-gun Regiment as of this day to set out for Oranienbaum and (the main point!) henceforth not to allow itself to be sent anywhere without the Executive Committee's permission. Skobelev was instructed to head for the House of the People immediately and make the announcement there. The scariest thing—this they understood—was making the announcement.

Shlyapnikov left quietly and quickly sent a courier to Kronverksky, where at that moment activists from the 1st Machine-gun were assembling at the Labor Exchange under the Petrograd Committee. The machine-gunners? We will not give them up!

[4 8 4 "]

STATEMENT BY PRINCE LVOV . . . I received representatives of the press . . .

"Naturally, this is no time for interviews or frivolous words. The Provisional Government is working day and night . . . Do not congratulate me, gentlemen. Congratulate the great Russian people, whose grandeur has been made manifest in the Great Russian Revolution. The events are so grand, so stunningly grandiose, that no words of any kind are needed. The incredible intensity and speed of the coup . . . the popular genius has accomplished miracles, has stunned the entire world with its grandeur and its magnanimity toward the past. The sun now shines over Russia. We are all in the rays of this sun . . . In Petrograd, the path has been cleared for new ideas. But Russia is great, and people everywhere have not been able to grasp the meaning of the stunning coup. Minor excesses have occurred here and there on the periphery. Grave misunderstandings have broken out only in the Baltic fleet. Our objective is to create faith in Russia's bright future in each citizen—and gradually reeducate the many millions of our population in the same spirit.

. . . For the first time, Russia stands even with the leading countries of Europe, for the first time a Western European order is being ushered in here . . .

. . . The Central Committee for Food Supplies has completed its inventory of all our current flour reserves. Petrograd is fully provided with bread for the near future.

. . . Under the influence of the coup that has taken place, the peasants' mood has changed radically. The peasantry, filled with trust for the new government, in a lofty patriotic surge, will start bringing grain . . .

AMNESTY. DECREE OF THE PROVISIONAL GOVERNMENT . . .
. . . The gleam of the reborn country's celebration must shine, too, on the life of ordinary criminals . . .

LONG LIVE THE REPUBLIC!

END OF THE RUSSIAN BASTILLE . . . The Schlüsselburg fortress has burned down. The bell has tolled for the Russian Bastille! Given the difficulty of determining who was a political, ordinary criminals and recidivist thieves were released. The old convict Orlov, who thought nothing of slitting a man's throat for a ruble, was now sobbing like a child.

REMOVAL OF ROYAL PORTRAITS . . . Make the royal vault in the Peter and Paul Fortress a Pantheon of Fallen Revolutionaries. Throw out the tsars and bring the sacred remains of our dear heroes there.

General Ruzsky's account. . . . It was a surprise to me that the Tsar's letter train had headed for Pskov. I ordered that the Tsar's arrival go unremarked . . . It is striking the sang-froid and inattention with which the populace and troops treated the Tsar's arrival . . . I personally stayed away from the Tsar, avoiding meetings and conversations with him . . . I could not express my opinion to the Tsar, having no directives whatsoever from the Executive Committee . . .

RASPUTIN AND THE COURT. Extraordinarily interesting details have come to light . . .

AMONG THE JEWS. A telegram from the joint committee of Jewish public organizations of Moscow . . .

In the coming week, a conference will be convened of Bund representatives throughout Russia.

A rally of Jewish students from all institutions of higher education in Moscow . . .

. . . The clergy, warden, and parishioners of the Church of the Annunciation are distressed about the gullibility toward the rumors that there was shooting from their bell tower and that a gun had been removed. . . . They ask that the religious population be left in peace to take prayerful part in current events.

. . . The northern capital seems to be following a magnificent instinct for governance.

. . . The editorial office has been overwhelmed with letters regarding a new anthem . . .

MATRIMONIAL CHAINS. Yet another type of chains must be sundered immediately, the **chains of matrimony**, under whose weight thousands of people have languished and are languishing, people who misjudged each other.

A regrettable typo found its way into a previous order from Lieutenant Colonel Gruzinov for the troops of Moscow. What was printed: "Then my troops marched past me in even ranks." What it should have said: "Then the people's troops marched past me."

. . . A meeting of savings bank employees sends its deep regards to the working class . . .

. . . To the State Duma President. The general meeting of Moscow cabbies greets Russia's new government. The old regime took many victims . . .

LOST LUGGAGE. On 12 March, at the Nikolaevsky Train Station, I handed my luggage over to a stranger who . . .

TWO PAIRS OF ELEGANT BLACK trotters for sale . . .

[4 8 5]

What was discussed in the Moscow Soviet of Workers' Deputies behind closed doors the press did not find out, the natural secrecy of revolutionary figures. But at three o'clock in the afternoon, Aleksandr Fyodorovich Kerensky rode into the Kremlin in a motorcar. (He was accompanied by the lawyer Muravyov, instantly appointed chairman of the Extraordinary Commission of Inquiry.)

As many representatives of the legal department and legal profession as Moscow could muster and fit into this hall had gathered in the enormous Oval Hall of Judicial Determinations, with its magnificent molded ceiling and chandeliers, and been waiting more than a full hour. Actually, during these rarest of events, no hours of waiting are hard, and the confluence of the best minds is intellectually stimulating in and of itself. People already knew that the new minister could not abide all the medals of the old regime, which he saw as illegitimate medals, and all departmental uniforms as offensively tyrannical. And so, although none of the officials of the judiciary had been dismissed, they all had appeared strictly in civilian dress, without their titles and medals, and differed from the colorful jackets of the independent legal profession only by the strict uniform blackness of their suits.

In the vestibule, Kerensky had been greeted by these designated representatives of the departments of the appellate court and prosecutor's office. On the other side of the runner the full complement of the Moscow Bar had gathered, the city's best minds and tongues.

Graciously and with great courtesy, the slender young minister (in an Austrian jacket, but this time with a white collar showing) nodded to one side, nodded to the other, shook a few random hands, and shot like an arrow into the hall, all the others behind him.

Whether the Oval Hall could recall such an overflow and such stormy and prolonged applause is for historians to debate in the future. The applause simply would not subside.

"On the table! The table!" enthusiastic voices rang out.

And Kerensky, like a pale angel in black, flew up onto the table. His speech resonated laconically, but how clearly it shone a light forward, like a projector, on his entire, highly promising program! And what modulations of the sacred anticipation of freedom crowded in the stream of this voice despite his somewhat staccato diction.

"Gentlemen judges! Gentlemen attorneys!" (He moved them forward.) "Gentlemen prosecutors! A free Russia has been born, and born with it is the reign of law and free judicial conscience. The old order has been brought down once and for all. I hope that those judges who served the old regime will now find an answer in their own conscience as to whether they will be able to offer their services to the cause of true justice or whether they will honor their professional duty and leave! I would hope that the onset of the reign of truth does not compel me to resort to extreme measures and thereby darken our shared joy."

Having warned the die-hards, in this polite form, of how the problem of judges' irremovability might be resolved, the minister turned toward where the lawyers crowded most:

"And you, gentlemen attorneys, I warmly greet the one estate that has heroically and fully guarded the lamp of justice in Russia!"

The one estate of Russia! How truthful this was! And how deservedly the lawyers' faces shone!

The minister did not address the prosecutors separately, but continued on:

"And you, gentlemen of the chanceries, and you, gentlemen couriers, I give you my word that henceforth you will enjoy all the rights that all free citizens of a free Russia must enjoy. Organize for the defense of your interests!"

And he flew down from the table.

After this the judges and prosecutors were sidelined, and only lawyers gathered in the room for the Bar, all their own kind, and the atmosphere warmed up considerably.

"Comrades!" the minister said, and there was love in his voice. "The law for us in Russia remains solely in your . . . our one corporation. Actually, superfluous words are scarcely needed. Simply put . . . allow me simply to relax with you . . ."

This sincere appeal touched the lawyers. The greatest unconstraint ensued. The minister sat at the meeting table, wiggling his tight collar, while the lawyers crowded on all sides and eloquently brought up burning questions they had raised in the past. One of them was about women lawyers.

"Oh yes! Oh yes!" the weary minister livened up. And he turned decisively to the council chairman. "I would ask you to begin immediately accepting women into the profession." He looked at his watch. "If possible—today even. Try."

The lawyers took a lively interest in the kind of punishment for the Tsar.

"Gentlemen," the minister objected. "At this moment let there be no unnerving conversations. The dynasty's representatives are in the government's hands, in my hands. We shall permit no compromises. However! There must be no place for the instincts of vengeance, either."

They touched upon how to organize a ceremony to greet those returning from Siberia. The minister was very encouraging and pointed particularly to the need to greet the "grandmother" of the Russian revolution, Breshko-Breshkovskaya:

"She is my teacher in SRism and my friend. When she passes through Moscow, let me know, and I will meet her in Petrograd myself."

Right then it turned out that among those present was a lawyer who had spent time in exile in Siberia. The minister impulsively exchanged kisses with him. All in all, the minister was kind and charming and instilled delight in the lawyers. He asked them henceforth not to be shy and to feel free to give him instructions on essential reforms or issues.

Unfortunately, however, business called him on; all Moscow needed him. To stormy ovations, the minister kept trying to leave and finally got into a motorcar on the Kremlin grounds and with his officer-adjutants left for the congress of justices of the peace.

They had all been waiting for him for a long time and not in uniform, as they'd been warned, but rather in black frock coats. Everyone was standing, and the congress chairman greeted Kerensky with a speech about how justices of the peace had been functioning for more than 50 years . . .

". . . and brilliantly!" the minister interjected (although he had already instructed that they be circumvented by temporary courts made up of workers and soldiers).

And all of a sudden he leaned forward swiftly, touched the floor, and people thought he'd dropped something—but no, this was him bowing low to the justices of the peace, who had always followed the truth and their conscience and thus had carried the torch forward to our day.

Apparently, he wanted to say many things here, but he looked at his watch and hurried up. He had to race to the Ars movie theater on Tverskaya, where he was awaited by more than a thousand delegates from the Moscow garrison. En route, the accompanying officers finished telling him how the movement was developing in the garrison, how officers and soldiers were meeting here together not for the first time, and the day before yesterday, after their session, they had left the Ars and gone down Tverskaya, to the Marseillaise, arm in arm—and in this way, drawing the delight of the populace, to the monument to Skobelev, where there were speeches, and then on to the university, to inform students of their decision to fight the war to a victorious conclusion.

Everyone in the enormous theater rose—khaki, mostly soldiers, and many, military-style, not removing their caps, and they greeted the minister with dense clapping, and he walked onto the stage and stood there—thin, modest, and infinitely important. When at last the applause died down, he roused himself to his speech, and his ringing voice reached the amphitheater's last rows.

"I, Minister of Justice Kerensky, member of the Provisional Government, am more than your comrade, for I am not only a convinced democrat, I am a convinced socialist, and I think I understand the people's needs. Tell me, may I inform the Provisional Government that the Moscow army is ours, that it trusts us and will do everything we tell it to do?"

And the entire audience started shouting: "We trust you! We're yours!" And there was more loud clapping.

Then Kerensky talked about how the time had come for the newly awakening army to demonstrate not the façade of strict discipline but the true iron discipline of duty to the homeland. It would take tremendous self-control. Now the fiery desire had come true: the command and the soldiers had coalesced into a unified whole!

Then either the speech was winding down or there was a delay for
thought, but in the ministerial tenor's pause a bass voice rang out from
the hall:

"Why was Nikolai II allowed passage to headquarters?"

"I assure you," Kerensky responded authoritatively, "Nikolai II is wholly
in the hands of the Provisional Government. He has no significance whatsoever at headquarters."

"But is it true Nikolai Nikolaich has been appointed Supreme Commander?"

"The question of Nikolai Nikolaich," Kerensky replied, "has also been
discussed by the Provisional Government. And I can assure you that if the
government reveals hesitations in this regard, I will quit it without a second
thought!"

Before they could figure out what kind of hesitations, in which direction,
all of a sudden the minister swayed like a reed—and officers from his suite
rushed over to him, caught him by the arms, barely kept him from falling
down—and lowered him into the armchair on the stage, his face ashen, his
eyelids lowered, in a faint.

The hall started buzzing. What had they done to their beloved people's
minister? He wasn't dying, was he? . . .

They rushed to bring him a glass, helped him drink, and sprinkled a little on him.

Someone started explaining over the collapsed, lifeless man that the
minister hadn't slept for a week or rested . . .

Oh! What intensity of revolutionary energy! He's not sleeping, is he?

Yes, apparently, he had just fallen asleep.

But! He was already stirring! He sipped some water. He even seemed to
be smiling wearily.

And now he was standing up!

Standing up already?

Yes! He was speaking again, and his voice took on its former resonance:

"Gentlemen! Where do these various rumors come from? Attach no significance to them! I assure you, no danger threatens us from the part of the
dynasty. They are all under the Provisional Government's unwavering supervision, and rest assured that as long as I'm in the ministry"—his voice was
menacing now, this instantaneous transformation was amazing—"there can
be no agreement with the old dynasty! The dynasty will be put into such conditions that it will vanish from Russia once and for all! Create a new nation—
and everything left behind give to me, the Minister of Justice!"

Once again, this was the commanding, strident minister from whom
nothing in the country could be hidden now.

Right then, District Commander Gruzinov appeared on the theater stage.
He was also greeted with an ovation, but he informed the audience that the
Moscow garrison troops wished with increasing insistence to see him,

Gruzinov, as permanent rather than temporary commander. What should be done?

The minister responded readily:

"This is magnificent! I promise to speak in the government for precisely this to happen!"

[4 8 6]

Lieutenant Colonel Boyer had not come out to his battery for two full days, something that had never happened before. Had he shut himself in his dugout? Had he gone somewhere? Not only had his soldiers not seen him, neither had his officers. The lowliest batteryman could guess that the lieutenant colonel was furious over the abdication.

But his black despair did not convey to Sanya in any way. Fine, no monarchy, then a *res publica*, the "people's cause," a sacred term, people living even more freely? When Sanya and Kotya were studying in Odessa—a forty-year-old senior cadet, an educated surveyor, would sit down at the piano, and there were cadets there who would sing along:

Let's drink to the man who wrote,
What Is To Be Done?
Let's drink to his heroes,
And the bright light he shone.

What had more of an effect on Sanya were the soldiers' stern faces when the manifestos were being read and how afterward they had split up into taciturn clusters without the usual flitting about and joking.

Chernega seemed not to attach any significance to it and casually cracked jokes about different things. But Ustimovich came up to see him, like a soldier would—with a question and a gleam under his thick rolled eyebrows:

"The soldiers are talking—there's going to be peace, right? They'll call off the offensive?"

And seeing how this fire had been lit in him, Sanya couldn't bring himself to put it out.

There weren't any newspapers; instead they had rumors rolling in. First: revolution in Austro-Hungary, Hungary splitting off. Then: the Tsar in hiding, the new government looking for him everywhere, and 12,000 killed in Petrograd. The horror!

Then one Moscow newspaper got through with faded photographs of the new ministers—perfectly ordinary faces, no kind of supermen.

Then an order came for the Western Army Group: reduce the daily bread ration.

But there were no military stirrings, let alone actions. After our events, the foe had stopped firing altogether—not just rifles but even machine-gun rounds, and no work whatsoever.

It occurred to Sanya that he might remove the lateral observation post for now, leaving one forward post opposite Torchitsy, to ease up on duty. But the battery commander was still nowhere to be seen. For now he'd have to go take a look himself.

The day was shrouded in gloom; it may have been snowing somewhere nearby. Not very cold, but Sanya put on his Caucasus felt cloak, which for him was like a soul mate from his Caucasus: soft, warm fur, good for sleeping at the observation point. Sanya was not after that martial look the cloak lent, but it did convey a certain strength. Although it did stand out, and in ordinary times he was careful about stepping out in it.

At the lateral observation post he found Dubrovin, the senior bombardier, on duty. Sanya liked him: he understood gunnery and took an interest in topography. He'd been awarded a silver watch "for excellent reconnaissance," which he would check demonstratively. On duty he wasn't idle, was constantly gathering useful information. His swarthy, always serious, even gloomy face did not seem boyish, though nothing was growing on it yet.

He handed the second lieutenant his observation journal. Basically, the front lines were asleep.

The lieutenant got out his favorite Zeiss and took a slow turn around the familiar location. The invariably snow-covered gratings and stone crosses at the Orthodox cemetery made it look deserted (though longstanding emplacements had been dug in well and camouflaged there). Those well-studied Skarchevo trenches emitted barely any smoke. You could hear a cart being driven down a slope hidden from view—which meant toward the bridge on the Shchara.

Sitting by the telephone deep in the bunker was Ulezko, a local. It must have felt odd to be near your own home. Dubrovin was standing by the sighting-slit, his chest pressed to the earthen jamb, beside the lieutenant. He asked quietly:

"Your honor. Would you like me to bring you a curious object now?"

"What kind? All right, bring it."

"I have to go to the infantry."

He left. Ulezko was dozing on a billet of wood with a pipe. About ten minutes later, Dubrovin returned. And on a board in front of the sighting-slit, well lit, he placed—a proclamation? A small sheet of rough paper, which said in large letters: "Order No. 1."

Whose? Sanya ran his eyes down: The Petrograd Soviet of Workers' and Soldiers' Deputies. What kind of outfit is that? He started reading.

". . . In all battalions, batteries must immediately elect committees from the lower ranks . . . Rifles and machine guns must be under the control of the committees and under no circumstance can be issued to officers even at their demand. . . ."

"What are they saying? Do they have a screw loose?" the lieutenant said out loud, and he couldn't help from covering the leaflet with an interdicting hand. He looked back at Ulezko.

Dubrovin, with imperturbable cheeks:

"Oh, they know already. Everybody knows already."

"How's that? While we know nothing."

"From the infantry. There's more than one going around the Pernov Regiment. The Pernov is buzzing. The Rostov men have it, too, I think."

"But where did it come from?"

Dubrovin sniffed gloomily.

"The devil knows. Brought from the rear. Maybe from men on leave."

"That's just foolish! Where do we come in? This is Petrograd, it has nothing to do with us."

He removed his hand and started reading further.

". . . Outside service and formation, in their general civil and private life, soldiers . . . Mandatory saluting outside of service has been abolished . . ."

"But what do we have that isn't service?" Lieutenant Dubrovina asked, as if the other man had written the order. "Everything with us is service."

Sanya, too, had once had a hard time getting used to saluting, but now, as he understood it, without saluting there was no army.

". . . Addressing by titles is abolished—your excellency, your honor . . ."

"Well, that's a different matter."

Those 'yrhonors' were worn-out rags.

". . . Rude treatment of soldiers is forbidden."

Quite correct.

". . . Using the familiar 'you' with them is forbidden . . ."

He grinned:

"There was this dictionarist, Dahl, who wrote that the teacher who was proud of using the formal 'you' with his students would do better to teach them to use the informal 'you' with him, and then he would know the Russian language. The formal 'you' isn't the Russian way. It's perfectly awkward for us. In the old days, people said, 'You'—informal—'Great Sovereign, are wrong!'"

However, the leaflet lay at his fingertips. Report it to his superiors? But this isn't in our battery. Dubrovin brought it—Dubrovin would take it away.

He looked around at Ulezko. And in the half-dark made out below him the no longer sleepy but rather curious, good-natured but tempted face lit by light from the slit.

[4 8 7]

And so, what lay ahead was no more and no less than addressing the peoples of the entire world, all at once! Although the signature under this appeal would be the entire two-thousand-strong Soviet of Workers' Deputies—Himmer felt as if his own thin and weak voice should resound throughout Europe and beyond. When he had set out to draft it, in competition with

Milyukov, who had distorted the meaning of our revolution, he had yet to sense the full difficulty.

If only he could enlist Gorky! Here was whose mighty word, the word of a lofty artist, might excite and grip the peoples! Himmer called Aleksei Maksimovich and asked him to write such an appeal. Gorky agreed.

But before he did—Himmer felt the urge to reach for the pen. There was nothing else for him to do now in the Executive Committee since this great task had loomed up to torment him. And once Chkheidze had suggested a quite good phrase—let the peoples take the matter of war and peace in their own hands—Himmer had written it down and so had begun to construct an appeal. He had no doubt that Gorky would write supremely artistically. But would he really be able to foresee all the hidden hazards of expressions, the clashes among the various socialist factions and wings of the Executive Committee itself, in order to carry out this project successfully, avoiding all those rocks? No, only Himmer could see and bypass all those reefs.

The main difficulty was restraining honest internationalism and Zimmerwaldism and under no circumstance nurturing and supporting defensism—but to be able to take this appeal through the Executive Committee, where defensists comprised the majority, and that meant tossing them a few crumbs. But while tossing those crumbs, under no circumstance could he allow the Executive Committee's left wing to accuse the author of even a shadow of chauvinism, recognized as an infection by any honest revolutionary public. Each expression of his had to be examined under a microscope. But there was also this: it must not be forgotten that besides the peoples of the whole world, this appeal would be read by Russian soldiers, too, and they thought about the German in the old way, only as an enemy.

In general, the "soldier question" and all soldier questions and affairs aroused in Himmer a nightmarish revulsion, a langour of the spirit, as soon as anyone raised them at the Executive Committee, and they raised them every day. He actively and aggressively recognized that the soldier mass was the greatest obstacle, an extremely harmful and highly reactionary element of our revolution, although it was the army's participation that had ensured its initial success. Its general harmfulness lay in the fact that it was a form of the peasantry's interference, its illegitimate, deeply harmful penetration into the depths of the revolutionary process, which ought to have belonged to the proletariat alone. Although the peasantry did represent the majority of the population, unfortunately, but greedy for land alone, directing all its thoughts to boosting only its own trough, the peasantry had every opportunity to sleep through the revolution's main drama and not get in anyone's way. After making a little noise in its remoteness, setting fire to a certain number of neighboring estates, and ransacking landowner property—the peasantry would get its desired scraps of land and would settle down to its idiotism of rural life. But because there was a war going on and the peasantry was wearing gray greatcoats—it was standing right here, over the very cradle of the revolution, close by, a distressing mass, and all with rifles! It was easier to talk to them about an offensive than about a peace. Even here, in Petrograd, the soldier mass simply would not allow talk of peace, prepared simply to hoist anyone on their bayonets as a "traitor" or "capitulator" for such talk.

There was good reason to despise this soldiery as he watched gloomily while these ignorant men in gray greatcoats filled the Duma halls—drowning out the progressive proletarians!

And here the appeal had to be written so as not to frighten or repel all this soldiery.

This is how things went yesterday afternoon. Himmer was agonizing over his text when he was sent a prepared text from Gorky, and there was absolutely not a single quiet corner in the entire Tauride Palace where he could perch and work. A paradoxical thought occurred to him: there's noise everywhere anyhow, so why not head for the session of the soldier section in the White Hall and there, in those alien surroundings, maybe thoughts would come even better as to how to adapt to this gray mass.

But the session, scheduled for two o'clock, was late as always, they hadn't come to order, although the chairs were all filled, some dozing, some walking around, some smoking, some rallying in groups—a slumbering mass, it was easy to imagine what foolish words were being spoken among them and how bewildered they were by the situation!

Himmer had not come to converse with them, however, but went up to the railed-off secretary's platform, quickly drove out a timid soldier, sat down, took Gorky's rolled-up text and his own raggedy folded one out of his pocket—and set to work, occasionally snorting to clear the tobacco smoke from his nose. In a way, his elevated position over the assembly symbolized his role as this sea's guide.

He started reading—and Gorky's magnificent, eloquent words simply rolled like ocean waves! But it was evident, evident right away that this superlative appeal wouldn't do, that it was entirely on the plane of world cultural perspectives. Insertions? Emendations? No, there was no way to save this. So he had to continue preparing this major maneuver on his own scraps of paper.

Meanwhile, the soldier section assembly had begun, but for a long time Himmer didn't hear it, not even the gavel of the chairman, Ensign Uthof, above him, or the report by Skobelev about his trip to Helsingfors and what was there. (Nothing special; hadn't much more blood been shed in the French Revolution?) Then they spent a long time choosing their Executive Commission—already more than eighty people, the asses!—including lots of ensigns, sergeants, and even clerks. When the debates began and Himmer started listening, he was amazed yet again at the soldiers' idiocy. They couldn't rise to a single major political question and kept going on about their civil rights (why did they need them? The beast had woken indeed!), and in hysterics painted the hardships of the soldier's life, and all in turn saying the same thing, while the chairman-ensign kept spurring them on, and they got so worked up that they demanded abolishing every kind of officer there was. Right then even Himmer, though disinterested, understood that this was foolishness, and out of loyalty to the government the Executive Committee could not agree.

All this sitting around here yesterday had only convinced Himmer just how hopeless it was to try to find not just a common language with the soldiers but even a few expressions their minds could grasp.

He kept working patiently on his appeal—both yesterday before day's end and since first thing this morning. The other comrades also admitted that Gorky's appeal, however eloquent, wouldn't do. Himmer sweated over and bore down on his composition, squirming at the presentiment of how it would go in the Executive Committee: if they supported it on the right or the left, the opposite side would break out in an indignant drone. A razor's edge, a razor's edge—but you could dance on it, you just had to know how.

Today, though, Aleksei Maksimovich himself came to the Executive Committee, somber, Himmer got worried that Aleksei Maksimovich had taken such an interest in his own appeal and now would take umbrage if he were told that . . . But no, he hadn't come about the appeal. He was tasked by the artists' committee, which said that the decision of the Soviet of Deputies to bury the martyrs of the revolution on Palace Square was nonsense. You could not dig it up, there was no room there, and the architectural complex would be ruined. The only appropriate place was the Field of Mars.

He rubbed his mustache upward in concern and looked around at one figure, then another.

The Executive Committee couldn't care less where they were buried. Right then, though, Chkheidze was on his way to the White Hall to preside over the workers' section, today being the workers' turn there. He took Gorky along. Let him address the masses himself.

Gorky was confident of the strength of his conviction. They set out, pushing through the people standing—and up the stairs.

It cannot be said that the writer's entrance was noticed by the hall, although they did give him the secretary's high seat.

The session had yet to begin, but the hall was already fogged with smoke. Nothing but workers' black clothing.

Chkheidze couldn't begin as he wanted, though, because people immediately started chiming in and bawling their out-of-turn statements. The first, Bleikhman, in the name of the Petrograd communist-anarchists: immediately kill all the arrested former ministers. And abolish everything that curtails our freedom; and issue people guns and bullets, since the revolution isn't over; and material support. The next deputy, saying he wanted over the signature of a hundred comrades present to immediately announce Nikolai

II's fate, and not just his but the whole ruling house, this was an urgent matter! The broad masses of workers and soldiers who had fought for Russia's freedom were indignant that the overthrown Nikolai the Bloody, his wife, his little son, and his mother were at liberty and riding around Russia. Why do we have to find out that Nikolai is on his way to tend his flowers in Livadia? Immediately demand that the Provisional Government imprison all members of the House of Romanov under the appropriate guard!

After this, Chkheidze began speaking formally, making up for the respect not paid Gorky:

"Comrades! Before you stands a man who emerged from your milieu and showed the world the might and creative powers the proletariat possesses."

They clapped lightly, as for anyone, but they didn't realize who this was.

"This is Aleksei Maksimovich Gorky!" Chkheidze scrambled to cover his omission in a loud voice.

Gorky began arguing forcefully about the burial location. People listened well, and no one shouted out against. Gorky said his piece, satisfied he'd convinced them.

But when they voted—they turned him down. That wasn't what they wanted.

Documents – 16

CERTIFICATE

Issued to the clergy of the Church of the Annunciation saying that the searches of the church on 14, 16, 17, and 19 March found nothing suspicious. Rumors of underground passageways and weapons in the church proved to be unfounded.

Vasilievsky Island People's Militia

| Chairman | *Solomon* |
| Secretary | *Kaplun* |

[488]

The Committee of Social Organizations was like a provisional government of its own in Moscow—that is, respected public figures beloved and promoted by all the people (and unpleasantly put down only by the Soviet of Workers' Deputies). True, they could only govern Moscow, but they could have opinions about all affairs of state, and so, for example, yesterday at a plenary session they discussed, at the suggestion of one professor, why Tsar Nikolai II was at GHQ and why Nikolai Nikolaevich had been appointed Supreme Commander. And they passed a resolution saying that the Committee found it essential to subject the royal family to individual detention.—Or about the Moscow Military District, which comprised ten provinces, they also composed an opinion: petition to keep dear Gruzinov as commander.

The past few days, they'd grown accustomed to holding their plenary sessions at the old English Club, long since the center of Moscow freethinking and in addition very convenient with respect to its offices, halls, and fine restaurant. Today, toward the end of the day, they had all gathered there and met when news rustled through those in attendance:

"He's come! He's come!"

The presiding Prokopovich immediately cut off the person who happened to be speaking and formally announced:

"Comrades! (They were already using this sweet word instead of "gentlemen.") We now will have the honor of greeting . . ." And the doors flung open, and in them, as an artist beloved by the public stops for a moment upon his appearance to allow the applause to break out, stood Kerensky (and behind him was the same Gruzinov). Oh God, the response! What stormy applause, what shouts of "hurrah," "bravo," and "long live Kerensky!" For several minutes the assembly simply could not calm down. The minister, touched, kept bowing and bowing, in thanks.

When everyone had taken their seats and silence reigned, first to speak was Moscow's newly elected commissar, Nikolai Kishkin, with his messy beard, very energetic, once a doctor but for a very long time a prominent public figure.

"I've just returned from Petrograd, on the same train as the minister, and I can testify—fervently—that were it not for Kerensky, we would not have all we have, here and throughout Russia! His name should be recorded on history's tablets in gold letters!"

And an ovation arose for another five minutes.

Then Kishkin attempted briefly to convey what was happening in Petrograd.

"When I was on my way there, I was concerned with whether this was how people felt and thought in Petrograd, whether their hearts were beating as ours were. So when I met with Prince Lvov, I asked him my first question: Did he realize that we could no longer follow the old paths? He replied: 'Yes, of course'—and said that now all laws had to come out of the popular mass, that the people themselves had to legislate."

Then Kishkin colorfully described the first days of events in Petrograd and what was going on there now. Moscow had borne it more easily, organized itself with more solidarity, and immediately after the coup all the arteries of its municipal life were pulsing again.

"It's different in Petrograd. It has yet to be welded together, it still has the spirit of confusion. On Moscow rests the duty of igniting Petrograd! Of injecting life into it! We must strike it from here with a slogan of freedom. And we Muscovites will do this, and the results will be reflected not only on Russia but all over the globe. The Russian revolution will move the whole world. We have to believe in that!"

As soon as he uttered the word "globe," the image of this magnificent march of revolutions all over the Earth began turning and turning in peoples' minds—and the assembly broke into applause.

While the man of the hour—not forgotten, no, but in anticipation of his moment—was sitting in full view on the presidium, wearing his strange worn jacket, encouragingly nodding his intelligent head with its short crew-cut and the bare face of an artist.

"I'm not finished, gentlemen," Kishkin insisted through the applause. "In parting, the prime minister handed me a document, and when I'd read it I said: 'It's come to pass!' This was a document from General Alekseev in which in the name of the deposed Tsar he asked Prince Lvov to allow the Tsar to take his family to England. You see? The revolution has triumphed!"

Oh, barely had he uttered this! Oh, what rose up in the hall!

And bore Kerensky up above the assembly as on spumous waves. It had seemed nothing could be stronger, but this had been anticipated even more strongly!

And what a silence fell! In it, though, unfortunately, the minister asked in a weary, weak voice for permission to speak sitting.

Even sitting, though—he was silent for a moment, even sitting he couldn't speak—such was the popular hero's exhaustion. The far rows stood up to get a better view of the people's citizen minister, even climbing onto arm-chairs, something the English Club had never known. The silence got tenser and tenser until it was simply unbearable, only the creaking of chairs. All eyes were on the minister—a scrawny young man with a tormented, pale face and eyes inflamed but full of energy, yes, full of energy. And now, at last, he began to speak in a weak voice:

"Citizens of Moscow . . . As soon as the opportunity arose, the Provisional Government sent me here. We—and I—wanted to see as soon as possible, with our own eyes, what was happening here, in the heart of Russia. I must say, Moscow has stunned me. And when I return to Petrograd I will convey to the Provisional Government my admiration for everything I've seen here."

He was gradually regaining his energy.

"Allow me not to deliver a speech. Is this any time, right now, for delivering speeches? I will simply tell you what is happening in Russia. Reports are coming in to us from everywhere about how Russia has been gripped by the sole desire of liberating itself from the old order. We think there is no longer any danger of counterrevolution."

A sigh of relief in the hall.

"People say we should pay the most serious attention to the royal family. These worries are laughable. We ourselves have had to render assistance to the former monarch's children, abandoned by all, having sent them a nurse and a doctor. I can definitely say that the entire old regime has put itself in our hands. I've already organized an Extraordinary Commission to investigate the old regime's actions and reveal to the country the full picture of the corrupt regime, which we will castigate. The picture all over is exclusively gratifying. I will admit that in the past few days we have known one horror: upheavals blazing up in the Baltic fleet. We immediately sent Duma members, and I personally spoke with sailors on a direct line, and as a result everything has quieted down and been taken care of. Yesterday the Minister of Agriculture told me that the food supply question is no longer acute. Our finances are stronger, for abroad they are promising us any and all financial support. The organization of transport is in the confident hands of people like Nekrasov, and this is enough for us to look to the future with confidence."

Did this mean there had been no disturbances whatsoever? No, there had.

"The one thing that worries me somewhat now is Petrograd. If I can put it this way, then after leaving Petrograd for Moscow, it felt as though I'd gone from a dark and stuffy casemate to a spacious hall filled with air and light. Naturally, everything in Petrograd is gradually easing, but the many police department institutions that permeated the capital have not been napping. For example, every night armored vehicles appear in the city, fire on our militia, and vanish without a trace. Provocateurs are trying to develop their activities as well. We also know that certain measures are being taken against some members of the Provisional Government."

Some members? Him above all, of course! Terror against a revolutionary? Raising a hand against the people's chosen ones—oh, what perfidy! That was also why this voice, now dear to us all, was so weary and disenchanted:

"I propose that Moscow's social organizations arrange several trips through the provinces and to Petrograd. They must be infused with the will and spirit of the nation."

Apparently this struck a chord, and it ran through the rows: Why not? Let's go! Let's infuse.

Finally about himself:

"I joined the government against the unanimous resolution of the Executive Committee of the Soviet of Workers' Deputies—joined it because I knew exactly what the country needed: to move toward a Constituent Assembly. In the government, I am the sole representative of democracy, but I must say we are acting in solidarity. Any proposal from the socialist platform is passed without objection. We have all decided to forget partisanship. I say this openly, in keeping with my personal impressions."

He never did find the strength to stand and so spoke sitting. Heads were already craning and turning so as not to miss his movement.

"About myself I must say that the serious lot has befallen me of guiding the Ministry of Justice down the necessary path. But I will not betray my principles. My principles are my belief in man, my belief in man's conscience. And you know, when we hadn't slept for six full days, when we didn't know whether it was day or night—that was when we saw what man and man's conscience were."

(Listen! Listen! This is astonishing!)

"And if, gentlemen, matters continue in this way, then we will create such glory for our country that our heads will spin!"

Through the applause, Prokopovich, straining his voice:

"Does anyone have any questions?"

"Our request is—down with the death penalty!" they shouted. While Doctor Zhbankov, standing on an armchair spoke at greater length:

"Abolition of the death penalty is the dream of democratic opinion!— which is amazed that eight days of revolution have passed—and why hasn't the death penalty been abolished yet?"

The minister held out his arm in a gesture of goodwill, and the hall quieted and heard:

"The act on the abolition of the death penalty has already been written, and I will sign it upon my return to Petrograd. The entire country will learn of it in three days."

Oh, the omnipresent man! He had even managed that! New shouts of joy bellowed, so that not everyone heard the representative of the League for Women's Equality try to get women's participation in the elections for the Constituent Assembly, while the exhausted minister replied to her that he personally, of course, was a supporter of women's equality, but bringing the principle to life might require significant technical preparation.

Prokopovich finally implored them to let the minister go—after all, he had several more meetings today!

They let him go. But then, before he left the club, journalists waylaid him to ask what was going to happen to the State Duma. (It was functioning. He himself had spoken there yesterday.) "Will a Constituent Assembly gather before the end of the war?" (Much earlier.) "How did Mikhail's abdication come about?" (He sat down on a sofa and found the strength to tell the story in detail.) "What about provocateurs?" (He had valuable leads.) "The nationalities question?"

The minister could not help but grin, yet said joyously:

"Gentlemen! Right now there is so much work that one needs to be a genius to complete it all in a short length of time. But we will remember absolutely everything, including the Polish, Jewish, Latvian, and Georgian questions. Everything will be decided very soon!"

At the English Club entrance, Aleksandr Fyodorovich was awaited by an enormous crowd. When he appeared, staggering, this entire thousand bared their heads and let out a thunderous "hurrah."

*　　*　　*

A SPARROW FLAPPING ITS WINGS DOESN'T BREW THE BEER

*　　*　　*

[4 8 9]

In out-of-the-way Mogilev, even before, there hadn't been any window dressing; they'd just maintained Governor's Square. And now it was inundated with a noxious red that was burying even that. Clerks, drivers, tradesmen, headquarters menials, and St. George medalists walked, roamed around with red scraps on their chests and service caps, or red scarfs under leather jackets, in ones and in groups, or fashionable *meetings* would form here and there, rallies where insolent young locals would shout: "the most free soldier there is" and "a curse on the overthrown regime" and would bellow for "deepening the revolution." Red flags hung over the city duma and official institutions, although not yet over GHQ buildings. Men were still saluting, but sometimes with a delay, it seemed, as if waiting for the officer to salute first. And in one peeling building the Soviet of Soldiers' Deputies met. Alekseev had allowed a Soviet of Officers' Deputies to convene, too, and to seek discussion with soldiers.

And what was the solution? Svechin didn't have a solution, Alekseev did: drive this entire gang all the way back to Petrograd before the revolution could find sure footing. Although the regiments sent had been brought back, they could just as easily be sent again. For now, all the front-line units, hundreds of regiments, were still untouched by the contagion, while Petrograd was a dough trough, totally lacking in strength. The task these past few days had been eased by the fact that the Emperor was at GHQ and the Manifesto could be taken back just as easily as it had been given. The supreme leader was once again with his army and was sending it where he liked. What were the obstacles? The Germans? Svechin was confident that they wouldn't stir now, even if you removed half an army group. And there was no reason to expect anything useful from the new regime. It was insulting to have to sit under that new mire.

Svechin himself had never been a leader of troops, though, but rather a headquarters thinker. He understood, but someone else had to implement. The commanders above him were all the same—Klembovsky, utterly superfluous at GHQ, and the general-bureaucrat Lukomsky, and Alekseev was basically the same, as were Ruzsky, Evert, and Ivanov. They were all uninspired snoops from Kuropatkin's school, all having amazingly circumvented Skobelev's!

For a year and a half, GHQ had sat tight in Mogilev, with its four plodding one-horse streetcars, two cinemas, and many Jewish stalls around the Brotherhood monastery walls, while cabbies watered their horses at the water tower. Actually, at the governor's residence where the Emperor was now, a female revolutionary had once fired on the governor. The GHQ officers were staying in the requisitioned Bristol Hotel, using a redecorated café chantant as their club. For the calm year just past, staffs had been more than sufficient. The general quartermaster unit alone had, not counting

Lukomsky, two generals, 14 staff officers, and several more senior officers. In the months past, hands had not been terribly strained at their work, and now they had let go altogether, due to the entire situation. Only the zealous were coming in in the evening to work until eleven. Others even during the day talked about appointments, about promotions and medals, about extraneous things, read newspapers, told jokes. (And in the diplomatic chancery and naval headquarters they even assembled jigsaw puzzles.) Alekseev himself worked tirelessly but did not admonish others. Nor did those lower in rank, such was the way things were going. Gurko had been the only one who spurred everyone on.

Some GHQ officers, especially those who had not served under Nikolai Nikolaevich, but had only heard about him, were now very much waiting for his arrival, relying on his severe, impatient manner, as he had promised to hang Rasputin. Would he really submit to an enfeebled Petrograd? He wasn't a ditherer, like Alekseev. Some hung portraits of the grand duke in their offices.

But not Svechin. He well knew that the grand duke was simply decoration.

Meanwhile, the abdicated Emperor remained at GHQ, to no end—and was already beginning to hamper his former subordinates. One might encounter him in the courtyard, on the square, on the street—and the awkward tension had mounted. It had spread through the air that it was now reprehensible, if not dangerous, to evince zealous loyalty or obeisance—and look ridiculous? old-fashioned? anti-revolution? This feeling had come on quickly, covering over the loyalty to the throne imbibed over the ages.

This manifested itself first in the serving staff. The rumor had gone around GHQ that the court barber had refused to shave the abdicated Emperor—and they had called in a different one, from town. They didn't tell the Emperor himself, naturally.

But although all interest in strategy had weakened, it continued to loom and live, and someone had to deal with its calculations, and this was General Svechin and a group with him, partly out of duty, partly out of interest.

Generally speaking, Russia was entering the 1917 campaign unusually well equipped and confident. But disarray lay in wait on all sides.

That winter, the war had seemed to die down, but not altogether. On the unfortunate Romanian front, a disastrous extension of the Russian front, given the general Romanian muddle, especially on the railways, where we had nothing like enough approach routes, the Germans kept advancing for a good half of the winter. One would have liked to amputate this Romanian front, like a maimed organ from a healthy body, to be free of it. On the contrary, though, in November, a conference of Allies at Chantilly (our representatives hadn't anticipated this and had blundered) approved an utterly idiotic plan for the 1917 campaign: drive all the Russian forces right there, into that bottleneck, into Bulgaria, in order to take it specifically out of action.

Had the roads been good, this might possibly even have been advantageous for Russia, a path to Constantinople, but with the roads as they were . . .

Once he had assumed his duties, Gurko immediately thought better of it and actively fought this foolish plan, this violence by the Allies against us, as always—but he only managed to get it canceled and to gain equal rights to advance on the main German fronts only at the Petrograd conference in February—and only from that moment could battles be planned on the principal fields. Before that, they had been obligated to carry out preparations for Bulgaria.

Once their attention shifted to the German front, disagreements emerged among the army group commanders as to whether to inflict a single powerful blow and then on which front? Or on several? It never was decided, and each army group commander drew up one applicable to his own front. Since last year, though, they had liked the success of the Southwestern Army Group against the weak Austrians, and this inclined them (and the ailing Alekseev had sent such a note from Crimea) to assign the main strike once again to Brusilov and auxiliary strikes to others.

As of February, this plan, too, had gotten under way, as always not so much coming down to the eye-catching fat arrows piercing the front lines, as to the number of men, horses, bayonets, sabers, guns, ammunition of various calibers and types, train cars, locomotives, fuel, metal for repairs, and manpower, which was already in short supply in Russia's own provinces due to excessive mobilization (here Nikolai Nikolaevich, Alekseev, and the Emperor were all to blame), and that meant bringing in non-Russians from Turkestan, Chinese, and Persians, and then feeding them all near the front lines, which again meant transport, food supply, unharvested grain, and stocking firewood.

But blizzards had raged all February, interrupting supplies to the Southwestern Army Group specifically. The army group had been reduced to a state not seen since the war began, with enough flour left for ten days, hay and straw for two, and fodder for even less than a day, and if transport was interrupted even a little more, horses might start dropping. (If Brusilov's reports were to be believed, of course, since each army group was underplaying its reserves.)

And now the Petrograd revolution had begun. All the main military plants had been at a standstill for two weeks, and the flow of equipment had stopped. Dragging the front through this disarray as well meant dragging out preparations significantly.

Svechin continued to work on the offensive, but was there even going to be one?

They tried to guess German intentions. Would they take advantage of our turmoil? Although the Germans had brought ammunition closer to the Northern front, here and there aeroplanes had noted road works—but nothing like the boom the newspapers had been shouting about, frightening the public, saying the German was on his way to Petrograd. Our revolution suited them no end.

The danger, though, was coming not from the Germans but from our dear Allies. The French and British command, in concert, set the day for the common offensive on the Western front—8 April—and the Russian armies' offensive was supposed to begin, if not that same day, then just a few days after, so as not to allow the enemy to deploy reserves.

Svechin could only whistle in disbelief. That left less than three weeks! If there hadn't been a revolution, this would have been acceptable, even with the storms, interruptions, and all the difficulties of the long, drawn-out winter. But now? . . . If the revolutionary collapse kept on like this, it would become doubtful not only *when* but *whether* our army would be capable of going on the offensive.

However, the Allies had them by the throat, so what was Alekseev— today so haggard and ill, a frown on his face—to reply now? How would the old man wiggle out of this?

Today Svechin had left for dinner with no intention of coming in that evening. Private life lets us escape from all hopeless situations.

Since October, he had not answered a single one of his wife's supplicating letters but had taken up with a marvelous lover. And he had now gone to see her.

She was a Pole. Such as only Polish women are in the whole world. For anyone who doesn't know—it can't be described.

[4 9 0]

Yesterday, at last, a dear breath flew to him from his clever, beloved Alix!—everything, how she dashed about, how she suffered—on folded sheets of paper the captain's wife pulled out of her coat lining—devoted, she had not been afraid to bring it. A letter from Alix, and notes from Maria, the only healthy one. Retiring, he kissed them. Three and two days separated the writing from the reading—but this gap was an entire ill-fated eternity. Pavel had brought her the cruel news of the abdication, but even that had not broken her courageous heart and in particular had not impaired her usual lofty understanding of life: "The Lord Himself shall have mercy upon them and save them." Despite events, she believed that everything would be fine again and that he would even be on the throne again.

And so? It might be. All was in God's hands.

The main thing, as Alix correctly noted, was that he had not inflicted damage on the crown itself. He may have felt this, but she was the first to say it.

Even the next day, when the news that came to Tsarskoye Selo was even worse, officers had been arrested very near the palace and been replaced by elected ones, Alix believed the troops would come to their senses.

What she did not believe was something else: that they would ever be allowed to go anywhere. For the past few days it had seemed strange even to Nikolai. He was a private individual, after all, so why not let him go? But here they had. Permission had come from the government regarding Tsarskoye Selo and their departure for England. There had still been no reply from George himself—but what kind of reply could come other than the most cordial? Hanbury-Williams, too, was confident that the English government would not oppose the Russian royal couple's arrival.

Soon, orphaned, they would be mourning quietly somewhere, on a wide-view balcony at Windsor perhaps.

God, how much freshness and strength these precious letters added! His heart felt embraced. He could live again. Enriched, agitated, Nikolai strolled in the garden once, then twice, walked himself out.

Alix's letters had absolved him from the past—she had understood and forgiven, without his explanations.

Overwhelmed—how could he thank her?—he came up with the following telegram (these latter days will teach you cunning!): "Tenderest thanks for many details"—and she would guess that her secret letters had reached him! Witty. And then, what he could say: "Here quite quiet"—which meant there had been no impudent attacks or insults—and there was no revolution per se. "Old Man and Son in Law left for country place"—let her be happy for old Frederiks and her heart eased at least for those two.

Although, in fact, no, we would not get to the point of reassurance so easily. Today Alekseev had informed him that Frederiks had been arrested in Gomel. Poor man. Poor, decrepit man! How could anyone have the heart to arrest someone like that? Where did such hatred come from? What was he guilty of? . . .

It was calm in Mogilev, yes—only very sad. The suite's impassive faces did not encourage any sort of candor. Not that Nikolai was used to laying out his sufferings and insults to anyone—other than his wife and mother. What he had acquired from his father was precisely these qualities of a monarch: self-possession and calm dignity.

How Mama had eased these days with her arrival! How cozy to have lunch and dinner and to spend the evenings with her. In recent years, he had imagined a tension between Mama and Alix. Mama disapproved of a great deal (while Alix had never judged her)—but now everything was good again, forgiven and understood.

Early this morning, two quite young little officers had shown up at the governor's residence—one from the Convoy, the other from the Moscow Life Guards Regiment—each with another hidden letter, folded many times, from Alix! It had taken them five days to get here! It was harder for them than a woman. One could not travel freely wearing an officer's uniform, so they had had to change clothes. First they'd gone to Pskov, got Ruzsky to receive them, and admitted to him (imprudently) that they were carrying letters from the Empress to the Emperor. Vile Ruzsky only grinned: "A little too late, gentlemen." At last they acquired soldier greatcoats and traveled as "revolutionary hooligans."

These letters turned out to be a day earlier—on the very day of abdication, still in great heat and confusion, but in faithful presentiment—so unerring was Alix's heart!—that they wanted to lure the Emperor somewhere and give him some abomination to sign. She wrote about Pavel's distress and Kirill's villainies.

Recalling his own feeble, powerless position that time with Ruzsky—truly trapped—was agonizing and shameful. However, in the past few days, Nikolai had also separated himself from his former authority and risen to such a pure state—like a dead man, he had lost his ability to take offense at anyone. What was all this power to him? Had it ever been a source of joy? Ever only a burden. How much just those dismissals and removals from positions had cost him—each time it had felt like killing a man. As for himself, Nikolai lost nothing by giving up power.

Freed from power, he could no longer rejoice at his former enemies' failure. In the maddened whirlwind of 15 March, Alix had expressed the hope that the Duma and the revolutionaries would chew off each other's heads, so let them try to put out the fire now. Whereas Nikolai did not now wish failure on the new government. On the contrary, he wished them success, and let them ascribe it to his incompetence and to their talent. Herein lay the full meaning of his abdication: so that calm might come to Russian hearts and over the face of Russia as soon as possible. If peace was not restored, that meant he will have abdicated in vain.

During these isolated days—first into a calming blizzard, like yesterday, then under softly falling snow, like today, during these quiet headquarters days, when nothing reached his residence from what was seething in headquarters next door, nor did Petrograd agent telegrams, and he himself did not want to read them, but only impersonal, calm reports addressed to no one about how the fronts were dozing—during these days, Nikolai became fonder and fonder of this lofty, forgiving point of view, when one could not see the details of the rocky paths of the present, but beyond mountain chains and more mountain chains there opened up the blue haze of the magnificent future. The fact that he had ceded power in the state did not hurt in the least. Most important, he had not reconciled himself to anything his conscience opposed.

We are all as nothing before God—and powerless in the face of world events.

Let these confident, educated men lead Russia. Let them. Perhaps they have the right to that.

In this lofty new mood, Nikolai found in himself the decisiveness to meet not only with Hanbury-Williams but also with the six other Allied military representatives. He had conquered his pain about the past and his embarrassment over the fall he'd experienced, his shame had dropped away, and he felt no distress whatsoever. All the representatives were sympathetic and showed a deep understanding. The Serb even wept.

The only thing to cause him pain was the handover of the Supreme Command, a special, exclusive seat which Nikolai considered himself born to and longed for so. He envied Nikolasha. As in 1914, and in 1915, fate kept knocking them together in this one place—who was to lead Russia's armed forces—and it simply did not work for the two of them. One had to push the other aside. Right now, even the governor's residence could not be shared. Nikolasha had obviously delayed his arrival in order to give Nikolai time to leave. Nikolai simply could not tarry here any longer. He had no wish to meet.

Nikolai tried to overcome even this last jealousy—toward Nikolasha—in himself.

Yes, that sad time had come—the time to leave. Late in the day, good Alekseev came to say that his train would be ready tomorrow—and it was convenient to go, there being no more obstacles.

Thus an end comes to everything, everything in the world. Today, after tea, Nikolai had a wrenching feeling as he started packing his things and his son's—who would never come here, never play here. Though he so loved to. . . .

Here and there they had begun packing the palace property in the residence—services in crates, antique tea silver, rugs rolled up.

Always this sadness of demolishing a nest.

Nikolai collected himself mournfully, but inside something else was mounting in him—the supreme farewell—not with the governor's residence, not with headquarters, not with Mogilev—but with the entire 12 million-man army—those sitting in trenches, those at the front close by, those marching in reinforcement companies, those lying in hospitals and riding on hospital trains, and those only just training in reserve regiments— this entire, united, powerful, brave being, heretofore so loyal to him, like a big, good animal.

His soul would not let him avoid this most important farewell.

And it could take no other form than as an order from the former Emperor to his troops.

This had not just come up today but had been maturing in Nikolai for several days.

And seeing that the air, the very terminology could change in a few days' time, and not wishing to grate on anyone's ear unintentionally, Nikolai asked Alekseev whether he might not send him the very recent Order No. 1 and Order No. 2.

And today they were sent from Alekseev—painstakingly typed on the best "royal" paper, which was kept at GHQ only for documents meant for the Emperor's examination.

However, both "orders" turned out to make no sense and to be decidedly unmilitary in form, and their absurdity was especially striking because they were typed on royal paper.

Nikolai did not delve further, not wishing to encumber or stain his soul.

No, he needed no one to help him find words for the present moment. In his new state these words were amazingly understandable and flowed of their own accord. He wrote them down sentence by sentence and then went over them on a walk in his garden.

". . . For the last time I address you, my fervently beloved troops!" (Tears clouded his vision—it was unbearable.) "For the last time . . . I address you . . . May God help the new government lead Russia down the path to glory and prosperity . . . And may God help you, our valorous troops, defend our Homeland from our evil foe . . . The hour is nigh when Russia and its valorous Allies . . . This unprecedented war must be prosecuted to full victory . . . Anyone now thinking of peace is a traitor to the fatherland, its betrayer . . . Submit to the Provisional government . . . obey your superiors . . . And may the holy martyr St. George lead you to victories . . ."

[491]

Grand Duke Andrei Vladimirovich had not participated directly in Rasputin's murder, but he had discussed various plots with his brothers, Kirill and Boris, and with other grand dukes, and in January, at the Emperor's behest, was forced to leave Petrograd to rest in the Caucasus, where his Mama was already undergoing treatment in Kislovodsk for all that winter's grand ducal troubles. And this was where he learned the stunning news from Petrograd, and the one bright spot: Uncle Nikolasha's appointment as Supreme Commander. This one thing gave hope for an improvement in the situation. In addition, Andrei Vladimirovich had served this war at headquarters and considered himself a military man. He very much wanted to see his Uncle Nikolasha before he left for GHQ. So he had rushed off by train to Tiflis. But the only reason he found him still there was that Aunt Stana and Aunt Militsa's packing had dragged out, although his uncle ended up not waiting for them. They met today right at the Tiflis train station. Prince Andrei's car was attached to his uncle's train. Also there was Seryozha—Sergei of Leuchtenberg—newly arrived from Sevastopol.

The grand duke, sensing everyone admiring his martial, commanding look, his astonishing size and build of a knight, stepped out of his open white Rolls-Royce, which had gone past the lines of troops training with red flags, and the policemen with red bows, went onto the station square, and continued onto the platform. Awaiting him there was the group seeing him off—from the city council, the Vice-Regency, and the military. Cadets were maintaining order.

He chatted with an anxious French colonel. He exchanged greetings with the exarch of the Georgian church. He exchanged greetings with General Yudenich (whom he did not particularly like). Exchanged greetings with the familiar Yanushkevich. From the steps, he thanked everyone for seeing him off so warmly and for trusting him to bring the war to a victorious conclusion and entered his train car, which was already full of flowers.

He gave a slight wave from the window, a slight wave with four fingers, conveying by nods of his proud head that he knew everything, understood everything, and would do everything.

And off it went, off went the train of the most picturesque railway under the sun—first through the green paradise of the Trans-Caucasus, then along the rocky narrow shore, with the Caspian Sea through his windows on the right and the outcroppings of the Caucasus range they were skirting on the left.

Soon after the train's departure, Uncle Nikolasha summoned Prince Andrei. He was sitting at a table in his half-darkened salon—in his characteristic manner, even while sitting retaining his full bellicosity and readiness to leap up—and drinking cold, refreshing pomegranate juice. He indicated that Andrei sit down, and immediately:

"I'm glad to see you. And glad you are with Mama in Kislovodsk. I am commanding you to stay there. Do not go to the front without my instruction." The uncle already felt a responsibility and a need to manage the entire royal house. "The entire family must correctly remain where they are. Of course, I cannot vouch for your safety." And his large, expressive eyes, so bright both in command and in anger, had the touch of the madman: "I myself could be arrested at any moment."

"What?" Andrei leapt up in front of the Supreme Commander.

Uncle Nikolasha's lively face knew how to express many nuances, here, the head-on blows of fate—but the sharp tips of his mustache had always expressed tension.

"Yes," he said gravely. "Know this. Anything could happen to me personally. I'm still not certain they're going to let my train through and I'll reach GHQ."

"But what is this? Uncle!" Andrei was now extremely frightened.

"That's how it is," the Supreme Commander spoke gloomily, as if having suffered a defeat, and whipping up even more gloominess. "What's going on in Petrograd, I don't know, but everything is changing there, and very quickly. Morning, afternoon, evening—everything's different and always worse. Always worse. Always worse!" He said with pauses and stresses. And looked gloomier and gloomier.

Grand Duke Andrei stiffened: he had been expecting from his uncle deliverance for all Russia, as well as the royal house. But if everything had become so much worse so quickly in a single day?

In this state of nerves, sipping pomegranate juice with ice, they began recalling the recent days.

"I'll tell you something in strictest secret. That unbearable Kolchak proposed uniting the army groups and opposing the new government. That cannot be! I rejected it!"

He sat, his face etched, and looked out the window.

"And at Alekseev's invitation I advised Nicky to abdicate. But he didn't even reply. His manner, you know. . . . Yet I had been telling him! I told him everything!"—Uncle Nikolasha reasoned, first sitting, then pacing. His deft, long arms would bend, first at the elbows, then at the wrists, and freeze for a second, expressing the twists and turns of his sentences. "The last time, on 20 November, at GHQ, I talked to him harshly on purpose, hoping to provoke him to be bold! But you know him: he said nothing and shrugged. I told him directly: 'It would be better for me if you scolded me, struck me, drove me out—better than your silence. Come to your senses before it's too late! Give them their responsible ministry while there's still time because later there won't!' . . ."

He stood at full height and squinted like an eagle:

"But you see Alix went and told him I wanted to seize his throne! That's why he sent me to the Caucasus. I asked him, aren't you ashamed you believed that? You know how devoted I am to you. I have this from my fathers and forefathers! . . . And still he said nothing. That was when I realized it was all over. In November I lost hope for his salvation. It became clear to me that sooner or later he would lose the crown.

"And ever since . . . Well, I was right! . . . He's gone against all Russian public opinion—in his blindness to prove his regime's stability. He's not to blame really. He has a marvelous heart and a beautiful soul. But people can't stand *her*! It's she who destroyed him. And now the newspapers have spread the notion that she was found to have a plan for a separate peace. That's nonsense, of course, but they can tear her to pieces. Popular hatred has come to a boil."

Uncle Nikolasha, menacing, paced around his salon; the popular hatred had infected him as well.

Gradually he calmed down and admitted to feeling great relief. He had received a telegram from Alekseev saying that Nicky was just about to leave GHQ. Good. He had no desire whatsoever to run into him.

After all, he had seized the post of Supreme Commander unfairly—and been punished. Lost everything. God's will.

That's all right, everything could be made right again. Russia loved Uncle Nikolasha. The Army worshipped him. Public opinion was always behind him, as it had been in 1915. Everyone believed that he would lead them to victory. And he would!

"Just now, a day before departure, I had two Georgian socialists come see me. Some of the most radical leftists, of course. And what do you think?

They walked in and apologized for their suits. They addressed me as none other than 'Your Imperial Highness.' They spoke frankly, saying they'd dreamed of a complete social reordering . But their dream had been a constitutional monarchy, not the anarchy now. They wanted no part of that! And they wouldn't go as far as a republican order because Russia had not matured to that point. Don't you know? One can deal with socialists quite well, too."

They looked out the windows. The landscapes kept changing, semi-mountainous, green. The train was moving, life was moving, taking them into the future. It was good thinking in a train, at the train's speed.

"I will gradually set all to rights! I'll have them toeing the mark!" Uncle Nikolasha's voice was harsher. "Your brothers. . . . I'm going to be frank, as always. Kirill's appearance at the Duma outraged everyone. It was a filthy trick. If it had been after the abdication, well, all right. But *before*? The duty of honor and oath! What kind of officer is he? To go over to the side of the Emperor's enemies? Where is the blood of our ancestors? Where is the awareness of dignity? And Boris?" His uncle's eyes flashed lightning bolts. "Seemingly a likeable boy, but in fact scum. What kind of field ataman is he? His name has become an obscenity, a curse, among all of Cossackdom. Wherever he went, he left behind a stench. I was presented with a bill from the steamer for his passage from Anzali to Baku. The entire passage was twelve hours, and the bill was for 10,000 rubles. Masses of wine and . . . If I see confirmation of all this at GHQ, I'll demote him from field ataman. Enough of the disgrace! The profligate! I cannot abide that kind of notoriety. Nor can the dynasty. Of course, we'll arrange a delicate departure. He'll submit his resignation—on the grounds of his health. And I will *command* it be so! Do you hear?" His uncle rolled his big oval eyes, and the movement of one of his hands was as if he were halting a regiment on parade. "Neither Boris nor Kirill must ever show themselves in Kislovodsk to see Mama. You must settle it, you'll find an inoffensive form. Now we all must be very cautious. Very!"

Andrei listened with respect and admiration. He was used to respecting military rank, and here combined with his uncle's integrity and imperiousness. He believed his uncle would save everyone and everything. Nonetheless, when it came to their large clan, there was a lot his uncle did not know. Here, in his Caucasian separation, he had not lived through the harrowing winter business after Rasputin's murder—whereas Kirill as well as Dmitri consulted with Andrei nearly every day.

Time stretched out, and Andrei began recounting everything to his uncle. Everything.

There was an irritant. Various rumors had incited the Emperor against the family. And Alix, naturally, would not let slip a chance to stir the pot. She was quite willing to raise a fuss over the murder of that filthy scoundrel! At a meeting with Uncle Pavel, they decided to demand that Nicky close the matter, not lay a finger on anyone, and leave Dmitri in Usovo—otherwise the most incredible complications might ensue! Sandro, too, headed for Tsarskoye Selo but could not win the release of Dmitri or Feliks. Then the entire family gathered at Mama's to sign a collective letter to Nicky, affixing sixteen signatures—but this had no effect on Nicky, who replied with stunning logic: "No one has the right to engage in murder. I know that many people's conscience give them no peace, and I'm astonished at your appeal!" Here he was implying the entire grand ducal family, that others were involved as well! While they themselves had arranged a scandalous night funeral service for Rasputin at the Chesmenskaya almshouse—and Alix, dressed as a nurse, went to attend. More scandalous still, they had come up with the idea of burying his body in the Cathedral of Our Lady of St. Theodore! Guards officers swore they would throw the body out that night! So they decided to bury it in the chapel on Vyrubova's land. While poor Dmitri was packed off to Persia.

What a coincidence! It was on this very railroad, only going the opposite way, that Dmitri had ridden quite recently, bathed in tears. What cruelty to exile him, so gentle and weak, to Persia. And innocent Nikolai Mikhailovich for a slip of his weak tongue—to be driven to the countryside so suddenly! All Petersburg gathered at his home for the New Year, saying their farewells. No, Uncle Nikolasha, we must forget family disputes and all unite in the present dangerous moment!

Alas, my boy, alas. It was the late Emperor Aleksandr who broke up the family, and now we will never unite. (Uncle Sasha had been quite unfair to him personally, excluding him from the suite, taking away his monograms, knocking him down a peg as a general.)

Crowds gathered at the major stops to welcome the grand duke passing through, and Uncle Nikolasha came out on the landing with his incomparable military bearing, threw out a few words—and everyone responded "hurrah!" Such was his impressive breeding; in every movement, every stillness— a soldier! How expressively he embodied the dynasty! Seeing him, the crowd could not, the soldiers could not fail to believe in the victory! In 1915, his entire army had retreated without shells, disgracefully pursued—and all kinds of people were upbraided, but not him. It was impossible to think ill of him, he was only praised! Legends were told about him. In one place he managed to uncover treachery; in another, he dealt with a general for his laziness and poor treatment of his soldiers. The people craved a leader and hero!

Uncle Nikolasha was very much moved by the triumphal train station welcomes. He became firmer, more cheerful.

Grand Duke Andrei left his Uncle Nikolasha's train car, came back again, and they dined together, along with corpulent Prince Orlov, with his grandee habits—Vladi, as all the grand dukes called him. For many years he had been extremely close to the Emperor, head of his traveling chancery, his closest advisor, but then he became estranged, disgraced even, and was ejected from the suite at the same time Uncle Nikolasha was from GHQ and traveled with him to the Caucasus as the Viceroy's deputy. They grew so accustomed to one another that now Uncle Nikolasha was taking him back to GHQ with him.

Night was falling. In the twilight and then the darkness the train trumpeted between the Caspian and the Caucasus, and just before dawn Grand Duke Andrei had to uncouple his car at Mineralnye Vody. He said goodbye to Uncle Nikolasha but couldn't sleep and talked with Vladi for a long time in his car, to the even knocking of the train.

Orlov recalled the 30 October Manifesto and how Frederiks—and everyone, really—had agreed with Witte and tried to talk the Emperor into signing it, but Vladi had implored him not to: if he was going to concede, then not now, not when he was being compelled. However, they convinced the coward Trepov—and the act was signed. That evening everyone dispersed, but the Emperor asked Vladi not to leave him. He sat in his study with his head leaning back, and large tears fell on his desk: "I feel as though I've lost the crown and it's all over now." But Vladi encouraged him: "No! All is not yet lost! We have only to rally all sensible men and the cause can still be saved!" But they weren't rallied.

As far as Grand Duke Andrei could recall, Uncle Nikolasha was there, too, during those days and also tried to talk him into signing. But now Vladi did not mention that. He only wanted to express the fact that the loss of the crown was long in the making.

They spoke French. Grand Duke Andrei asked:

"Tell me, do you think all is lost for him now? Is there no way he can return to the throne?"

Orlov adopted an enigmatic look:

"Perhaps. . . . But only without *her*."

The train kept knocking and knocking in the darkness—prophetically.

"More than likely, I think—the grand duke."

"You think so?" Grand Duke Andrei roused himself.

"Yes. He let the Tiflis mayor know that he was agreeable to leading Russia. . . . Even before all the events."

"Even before?"

Andrei Vladimirovich had a strain of the historian-chronicler in him, and he began questioning Vladi: how much earlier? Under what circumstances might he have spoken about this to the Tiflis mayor?

Under oath of eternal secrecy Vladi revealed that before the new year the mayor had come on an errand from Prince Lvov: if there were a coup, would the grand duke agree to lead Russia afterward?

And seeing how hopelessly Russian affairs were going, the grand duke only barely managed to keep himself from agreeing.

In Rostov-on-Don, the grand duke's train was greeted by a Novocherkassk delegation, a savage Cossack captain by the name of Golubov. The grand duke shook his hand. They talked about the coup in Novocherkassk and about how they had brought with them now the arrested ataman, Grabbe, who had not immediately recognized their Executive Committee. The grand duke agreed to take the ataman away with him on the train—and did.

[4 9 2]

To say that Kolchak loved the Russian navy more than he did himself would be an understatement—he was welded to the navy. The Arctic no less than the military fleet. All Russian marine vessels plowing the sea. The navy was a unified, multi-part, swift-moving, living being. The land army fell into regiments, companies, and men—one could hardly love it with the same integral love as one could the navy. During the war, Kolchak revived whenever the Baltic fleet recovered.

And having been given the excellent, shipshape Black Sea fleet—and not to be able to save it now? That could not be. He must not trail after events but stand at their head.

The improvised gathering the day before yesterday of crew representatives turned out fairly well. The report from one, another, and a third ship: the mood was improving. The crews had stated that they should fight and obey their officers.

The mood could be called charged yet peaceful.

So far, for some reason, the Baltic events had not spread through Sevastopol, as if they had gone unnoticed. Nor had details come in, saved by the fact that we were far away.

The police were gone, but there were military patrols throughout the city. Men saluted everywhere, impeccably.

Kerch, too, remained calm. It was calm as well on the Danube.

However, the gain achieved could melt away quickly. It had to be renewed now.

Newspapers were brought from Petrograd with crazed appeals from the workers' and soldiers' deputies—about civil rights for the lower ranks. The first spark hadn't started the fire, so they were throwing more.

What would this mean for the navy, with its highly complex structure, where everything was mathematically calculated for unsinkability, impenetrable compartments, stability, hull lines, sailing and speed characteristics, laws of navigation, angles of deviation? Was a crowd of barbarians and revolutionary ignoramuses going to swarm over all this?

The government needed to act in a matter of hours, not days, to make sure existing laws remained in place before new rules were drawn up. But the government was listless, and Kolchak accurately espied in it a hopeless slack. There was slack at GHQ, too. And the grand duke, having rejected a dictatorship, was now somewhere on his way—and he, too, would do nothing, as one could tell from the pompous verbiage of his first orders.

While the Soviet of Workers' Deputies was going to put fire to tinder.

But Kolchak's will, Kolchak's strength, Kolchak's mind was up to one task: saving the Black Sea fleet. So that it didn't blow up or sink, like the *Empress Maria*. Preserve unfurled, at full height, its flag with St. George in the center of a St. Andrew's Cross. Improvise, make shift for a few weeks, maybe—and take the fleet out to sea for operations as soon as possible. Even if it meant inventing an operation. (It was even essential to make a demonstration of force at the Bosphorus, so the foe wouldn't consider us in collapse.)

While the landing at the Bosphorus—that would pull us through entirely!

The threat to the fleet was unusual and so, too, must the decision be unusual, unforeseen by any tactics. How was he to espy it?

The peaceful South had not managed to stand against the rebellious North—and now found itself in new conditions. The South was far away. The South was isolated and would find its own path.

Kolchak recalled that strapping, droopy-lipped sailor who had enjoyed talking with the admiral so much. Might he have spoken the truth?

It truly was an ominous truth of many years' standing: the gap between commoner and blueblood, sailor and officer. In all our heat of reviving and building the fleet, this remained a known and unbridgeable gap.

And now, circumstances themselves had led to this. The darkest hour comes before the dawn.

A risk to be taken!

As in the movement of a ship, though, so too in the movement of human life, strict bearings had to be set beyond which you could not diverge.

What did it mean to command a fleet if at any moment it might stop obeying? If you didn't define strict limits for yourself, you turned into a monkey in the Commander's chair. He had to concede something, yes, but something secondary. And maintain his hold on substance.

Kolchak contemplated and formulated three conditions under which he would lower the admiral's flag.

If any single ship refused to put to sea or to carry out a single battle order.

If a single ship commander or head of a unit were removed, except with the Commander's consent.

If any single officer were arrested by his subordinates.

For no matter how much respect is accorded to "the People," the brains and nerves of the fleet are the officers, and without them there is paralysis. The Tsar had abdicated, yet the officers still had the Fatherland. But if the officers were to start to leave the service, the ships would become lifeless boxes and would not save the fatherland.

Kolchak informed the government and the navy minister (who, unfortunately, had already approved part of Order No. 1) of his three conditions.

But for now not one of these conditions had been violated, and inside these strict lines, inside this triangle, he had to try to overcome the infectious Petrograd breath.

But that breath had spread quickly. It was clear now that if any officer imposed a disciplinary measure on a sailor, he did not have the power to enforce it. No one could be forced to do anything now.

Attract, though? Convince, though? Summon up arguments daily in order to convince people over and over?

The task was not impossible. After all, officers surpass the lower ranks in their special knowledge of military matters, and in their devotion to them, and in overall development. Even if compulsory discipline were to collapse, they could still summon up all this and lead.

But how could he have predicted that he would be dealing not with trusting lower ranks but with those who even in peacetime were robbing banks, blowing up palaces, and firing at ministers and generals—with SRs? More than likely with them. Who else? And what a nasty word, full of sulfur and filth.

So! The admiral ordered all officers of the fleet, port, and fortress, sea- and land-based, to assemble at the naval officers' club on Ekaterininskaya. And told the officers clearly and directly that their disciplinary authority was lost and they should not count on it anymore. But the war had to be prosecuted—and there remained the patriotic spirit, which could not help but unite the officers and sailors. Might the revolution strengthen patriotism and the desire to reinforce the coup with a victory? That meant they had to seek out new ways to influence their command, apply new, unprecedented efforts to unite morally with the sailors, explain to them the correct meaning of all events, such as had never been done, to guide their understanding— and in this way keep them from irresponsible politics.

After Kolchak, an army general stepped up to speak. He did not seek out the difficult arguments Kolchak had distilled these two days since Nepenin's death. But he stood firmly in his own way: imperial authority was no more, and a patriot was obligated to carry out the instructions of the new regime, but that regime had to be one, not splintered. For the good of the homeland they could not allow any other regime in proximity and unsubordinated. For this reason, if the Soviet of Workers' Deputies was going to claim authority, they had to disperse the Soviet!

This was too frank. Another danger from which Kolchak now would have to restrain his generals.

Kolchak's demands were so unusual, though, and the general's marching step, on the contrary, so understandable, that many regular officers clapped hard for the general.

Next to speak was the chief of staff of the landing division, a young lieutenant colonel from the General Staff, Verkhovsky. He was a typical intellectual who had wandered into the army, put on the uniform of a staff officer, his entire figure with a gentle curve, and a similar voice with an ingratiating charm, and an intellectual's spectacles, and thoughts, but set forth resourcefully. Picking up on the current tone, he took a turn at kicking the "old order": there weren't any shells, and now a great miracle had occurred—the union of all classes of the population, and now in the Provisional Government the worker Kerensky and the landowner Lvov were standing side by side for the fatherland's salvation. Meeting in the Petrograd Soviet of Workers' Deputies were Russian patriots just like all of us here. Officers did not have the right to stand aside and let events develop on their own, otherwise we would lose the soldiers' trust. We had the same homeland, and we must build the homeland that has come out of the revolution.

Verkhovsky was applauded not by the regular officers but by the younger, wartime officers, intellectuals like the speaker. But as it turned out, his conclusions—about brotherhood and cooperation with the soldiers—meshed with Kolchak's conclusions. All the better. With his focused power and matter-of-fact figure leaning slightly forward, Kolchak stepped over all traditions and perhaps—perhaps? —seized the moment like a struggling fish.

In the harmonized spirit of these two speeches, representatives were chosen from the officers to meet with the representatives from the sailors and soldiers. There could be no delay. All the crews were tense with suspicion at a separate meeting of officers alone. Was it a plot against them?

So this evening, in that same mirror-parquet naval officers' club, in that same white hall, there, they met. It was wild to see common sailors sitting alongside officers.

It was a live, powerful, slippery fish that was struggling in the admiral's hands. Could he hold on to it?

So far, so good. Sailors went up to the podium and delivered unusual speeches to the officers—and stated freely that they felt obligated to obey and to prosecute the war with all their strength.

Meanwhile, outside, they could hear a band (the Marseillaise, of course). They were coming this way! What on earth was this?

It turned out to be a mixed crowd of two thousand—sailors black, soldiers gray, and civilians—on their way to the train station to meet a State Duma deputy (some socialist who was going to talk more rubbish). But the train was late—so they had staggered over here.

Armed men among them. Sinister, for they were not on watch or patrol.

Then officers, sailors, and soldiers, a few of each, stepped out on the club's wide balcony, above the columned entrance. Admiral Kolchak among them.

It was already dusk on a warm spring day, with the fragrance of flowers, a promising southern evening. The monument to Nakhimov rose up darkly to one side. A gentle breeze wafted in from the bay. The crowd dammed up the entire street in a disorderly way, facing the balcony.

Suddenly the band started playing a funeral march. And someone shouted: "To Lieutenant Schmidt." They had their own tradition.

And everyone on the balcony, including Admiral Kolchak, his jaws clenched, stood solemnly through the funeral march.

Then they started making speeches from the balcony: the admiral himself; that Lieutenant Colonel Verkhovsky, whose words came out quite convincing; and also a captain 1st rank, a lieutenant, a soldier, and a sailor. Saying that we were now all one family.

This pressing idea was conveyed to the crowd. That there were no enemies here. That left as we were without a fearsome regime, yet facing a cruel enemy, how could we not unite?

It was conveyed to the band, too. Which wanted to play something unifying. But the national anthem and Zhukovsky's words—"our powerful, sovereign, Orthodox Tsar"—were now out of the question.

They started playing "How Glorious," no one having any idea that this was in fact a Swedish Lutheran chorale.

Such was the power of innate trust, however, and on the balcony they stood at attention, and in the bellicose crowd others started dropping to their knees—on the sidewalk, on the thoroughfare.

The first stars came out in the quickly darkening sky.

On the city's hill, the Sevastopol lights, an outline unique in the world, its triangle of main streets, was lit.

High on the hill, the naval beacon blinked.

Dinghy lights slipped by along the harbor.

[493]

The deputies had worn Guchkov out: that night, his heart played tricks. First stopping, then rushing to catch up.

He arose late, and the gloom stayed with him all day. Everything now was perceived in succession in a bad light, and even if some garrisons had reported that things were fine, Guchkov knew they weren't, they were lying, and everything was going to continue to fall apart.

Indeed, Bryansk had reported that the garrison chief, who had recognized the Provisional Government, had been arrested, apparently in order to save him. The Totskoye POW camp demanded that in the name of saving the people's freedom, the posts of several generals and officers be eliminated. In Kars, a mutiny had flared up—because the fortress commandant had been slow to recognize the Provisional Government. From Riga, a Latvian Duma member had insisted on the removal of no less than the 12th Army's chief of staff—or else there might be a popular disturbance.

Desperate telegrams lay there from Ruzsky, too.

How was he supposed to keep up with this? How was he to forestall it all? What could Guchkov see and evaluate from Petrograd? All he could do was agree to everything. He had sent a telegram over Ruzsky's head to

Riga, to Radko-Dmitriev, his friend, telling him to temporarily remove his chief of staff.

What could he do! . . .

Although yesterday he and Alekseev had had that energetic discussion over the telegraph, later that night another telegram had arrived from him—it was a tone of complaint and weariness. Not only was Alekseev not cheered up by his announced appointment as Supreme Commander, but a few hours later he wrote: "or replace us with others, who will be capable . . ." Another blow! That meant not only did he have to remove Nikolai Nikolaevich tactfully and swiftly, but he also turned out to have no one to put in his place? Must he remove Alekseev as well?

Guchkov could not muster that kind of maneuverability. All this just added a layer to his gloomy mood. The government was a nonentity. His hands were tied in his ministerial duties.

How brief all human possibilities seemed to him . . .

That day even the easy things were turning out gloomily for Guchkov. If he was studying the minutes from yesterday's session of the Polivanov Commission on forming company committees in the army, and their oversight of the company's management, quartermaster, forage master, cook, and platoon distributors, he was brought to despair at the immensity of the reform that was to be undertaken during the war. When he was signing the pleasant appointment of Professor Burdenko, who had pulled him back a year ago from a fatal illness, as chief health inspector of the armed forces, he was still struck by the paucity of his capabilities, and again thought about his heart.

Also this: yesterday the government had instructed the Minister of War to write a new oath to replace the expired oath to the Tsar, an oath to the Provisional Government. Guchkov realized that for the common, God-fearing people, an oath was important and ominous. The Polivanov committee members had just brought him their draft, and he made a few corrections.

The Octobrists' central committee sent Guchkov their party appeal for approval (all the parties had printed one, and the Octobrists had been compelled to as well), and he was beset by bitterness. He had invested so much energy in these Octobrists, but no party had come of it, while for other parties things came together for some reason.

Irretrievable hours had ticked away, an irretrievable day. The army entrusted to him had shuddered from the blows of destructive propaganda—but not only had Guchkov not been able to interdict this stream of idiotic "orders," but together with the civilian revolutionaries he had "clarified" them. The days had slipped away, and he hadn't done anything important and couldn't even grasp what he should do.

Meanwhile the day was leading to just one thing, to going to the long evening session of the Provisional Government.

A total of five days in this government, and Guchkov had begun to despise it: an assemblage of smiling, polite cripples incapable of pounding their fist. An impulsive figure his whole life, never before had Guchkov been a member of a more helpless association.

As of today, they had moved from the Chernyshev Bridge to the Mariinsky Palace, which Guchkov knew well. It wasn't filled with trash or covered in spit, like the Tauride Palace, and its formal halls, colorful marble, bronze, expensive parquet floors and carpets, and footmen had not suffered in the revolution. He ascended the formal staircase, bypassed the luxurious two-tiered rotunda with the light from above, and then lowered himself into a sesquialteral armchair at a formal table covered with a deep blue velvet cloth. If one didn't know better, one might imagine they were truly members of a great power's authoritative government.

Guchkov did not even try to drive the gripping gloom from his face and pretend to have faith in their activities. He sat down with a stooped back and sagging shoulders and looked at them.

A very important question was being discussed: the appeal. Guchkov did not understand: another new appeal? Or was this yesterday's again? To both the populace and the army at once, and so that all the members of the government sign it for authoritativeness. And what else should be expressed in such an appeal.

The gentle Minister of Finance, surprised to feel himself not in a celebratory post but in a cruel world, asked whether they might in the appeal begin to prepare the populace for a tax increase.

No, that would not suit the appeal, the goal of which was to unite the government and the people. They set that notion aside.

Now, at last, a question was posed at the session that could be shocking, extremely intense for the government: the arrest of the Tsar and his family. However, so well prepared had this been in the corridors, now through the efforts of the obliging Prince Lvov, it went quite quickly, even as secondary: it had already been discussed privately with those who mattered, and those who didn't could not offer any opposition.

Even before the cabinet's decision, Prince Lvov had already issued an instruction that four Duma members should go to get the Tsar. (In this ticklish matter, it was convenient to shield oneself with Duma members.) They were already at the train station.

For the Minister of War this led to the conclusion that tomorrow morning, it would seem, he should organize the arrest of the Empress and her children in Tsarskoye Selo.

Why, actually, had Guchkov agreed to this? The good thing, the right thing, was for the Ministry of the Interior to deal with this. That is, this very same smiling prince.

They were also waiting for a new oath from the Minister of War. Here it was.

They barely argued about the text. Anything, just so it happened as soon as possible.

They also hastened to instruct the Ministry of Justice to speed up the legal proceedings against Sukhomlinov on the charge of state treason. And the investigation into Shcheglovitov, Protopopov . . .

Guchkov sat there, drooping, amazed that he had ever been so worked up about bringing down this Sukhomlinov.

He barked that the army was badly off. And they were cut off from GHQ here.

Prince Lvov rejoined with quick-witted civility that Guchkov had yet to join Alekseev in a single document, a single appeal. And now, especially given the new oath, united voices like that might . . .

The deuce knows what it might. Guchkov did not think that the half-literate Russian masses could be distracted by appeals, and his tongue was not moved to compose such a thing, but since no other measure was in the offing, then perhaps an appeal?

It was quite late when he returned to the ministerial residence, wrote Kornilov instructions to arrest the royal family early tomorrow morning, and sent it off by courier (this could not be done by telephone). And once again he called Alekseev to the direct line.

No matter what the discussion with GHQ, it was always difficult. Was he still hanging on there, he hadn't fallen apart? And how could he convey to him by telegraph just how ticklish the situation here was? How could he enter into his ticklishness?

An encoded telegram had been sent about tomorrow's arrest of the Tsar. That was not something for the telegraph.

About Nikolai Nikolaevich. That the decision absolutely could not be changed. That was no longer in the government's power.

About the appeal? . . . The sober Alekseev suddenly proved sympathetic to this. He even had a leading thought for the appeal: based on the danger posed by the enemy. That Germany was preparing a terrible blow—possibly directly against Petrograd!

Yes, that was a powerful means. Given the government's current helplessness, what else could you use to move the public?

You there, Mikhail Vasilievich, you can see better, and you have GHQ staff that have not been replaced, you have competent pens. Let your side compose this appeal. You can say the hardships of military life are identical for soldier and officer, that bullets and bad weather slash them identically.

Alekseev agreed. He would compose it tomorrow. And would also not fail to express the fact that anyone who called for insubordination was a traitor to the fatherland and was working for the Germans.

The old man was angry, he'd been driven to that.

Yes, yes. And maybe that the fatherland, the homeland, would not forgive us. And our descendants would brand us with disgrace.

Might a harsh word bring back our soldiers after all? . . .

What else was there?

[4 9 4]

Not giving weapons to officers—did that mean a war was beginning against the officers rather than the Germans?

No, something more had happened than what Sanya sensed when Boyer put the abdication manifesto in front of him. Something bigger had shifted— and he didn't understand what.

This was the third year Sanya and everyone else had lived in the same state: that war filled the world and any escape to the future lay only through the war's end. Any event that shaped the future could take place only right here, in front of them: either we go forward or we go back. But here they hadn't budged, not a shot had rung out, they hadn't even had time to think, while somewhere far away, behind and at an angle, something had suddenly turned around—and everything here had been displaced.

Right away, the main idea in their actions was lost, as if a stereotelescope had blurred, or a compass had conked out, or ammunition had gotten damp.

Today, if he was to decide about the lateral observation post, it would be good to repeat the survey once an hour and stay here until nightfall. Sanya did repeat it hourly, but observed nothing worthwhile anywhere; the foe had frozen still like never before, and genuinely. Toward the end of the day, the whiteness was stretching thin, the sky was clearing, it was cooling off, and beyond the shaft-like poplars a sunset glow was revealed—not the sun, but a horizontal stripe of bright yellow. However, even with the clearing, the Germans had not sent up observation balloons anywhere. As if directly indicating a ceasefire.

Envisioning that he would be sitting here idle for a long time, Sanya had brought in his pocket a tiny volume of Pushkin from the Pavlenkov ten-volume edition—of which he had three separate volumes, which he read often.

And he always gained new strength for himself in Pushkin.

The whole present revolution couldn't have any affect on that.

So he sat on a billet of wood in his felt cloak, and in the weak light from the observation slit he read his small volume. Then he stood up and observed through the binoculars and the stereotelescope.

As the sunset progressed, the stripe behind the poplars on the hill went from pink to purple to gray.

He told Ulezko to keep watch and left, first passing through the communication trench, then jumping up and out.

It was not yet dusk. Frost was setting in. The icy snow crunched loudly under his boots.

All of a sudden, something gave his heart a tug, nudging him to turn around. It was as if he felt an inaudible presence, observation: someone was behind him and watching.

He turned around (good that it was over his right shoulder): the new moon! The slenderest of crescents, barely bright enough to see, only visible in this kind of heavenly purity.

Close by and to one side was big, bright Venus.

There is something mysterious in moonlight! Why do you feel the presence of a new moon as a living being even with your back? Why can you tell the sky isn't empty? After all, it wasn't its light that had made him turn around, because there was no light from it yet. But there was something from it that radiated, nudged him.

Sanya was superstitiously pleased that he had seen the moon over his right shoulder, and kept looking back at it. At the front, every month is a long time and also decisive: will this be your moon or not?

There was a blanket of pure and freezing cold. Though it wasn't dark yet, stars were coming out in the sky, even the weaker ones. And in the southwest, frozen solid and precise, a blueish-green new moon and Venus.

This peaceful heavenly light made him feel better—cleaner, too. Somehow all would become clear and settled, it would be over. One day life as such would begin.

War, no matter how used to it you became, was not life.

At the battery he immediately went to see Sokhatsky, who sent the clerk out of the dugout, and then very mysteriously, looking quite nervous, took out a folder, opened it—and there lay a single typewritten page, retyped, evidently, at brigade headquarters: that same Order no. 1!

Now, by secret means, brigade headquarters was bringing it to the knowledge of only officers.

Understanding that it would be unpleasant for the captain, Sanya told him carefully that the soldiers were already reading it.

The captain was devastated. This order clearly was burning his hands.

What about the battery commander? He was gone, absent.

Sanya returned to his own dugout to learn that Chernega and Ustimovich had also been given it to read. (Of course, Chernega had read it even earlier.) Ustimovich was drinking tea with a little sugar, his big feet in soft-soled boots stretched out—and was thrilled by the one hope that peace would soon ensue, and with this kind of new order, even sooner. But Chernega was away seeing his woman in the village, no longer Gustava but another one, Beata—and he was cheerful, not a bit burdened by the order or all the news. Sanya would have been glad to talk with him, but he was like a ball that kept rolling away, a roly-poly always moving.

What he wanted was to talk to someone, to understand what other minds thought and to express his own. It was something so big that it didn't fit in one man's chest. Go to another battery? To brigade headquarters?

But right then Tsyzh brought a stack of newspapers! Moscow newspapers, several issues at once. Usually indifferent toward newspapers, now Sanya pounced on them. (Ustimovich hauled some to his spot, too.)

These weren't newspapers in the ordinary sense! These were voices never before heard, words never before combined. His eyes shot up to his forehead. This was a grandiose wind, a whirlwind inside which the members of the dynasty, dignitaries, public figures, old revolutionaries, and new ministers were tumbling as if made of paper. Everything had given way, was in motion, promising. Nothing could be properly understood or predicted—and you couldn't tear yourself away. Sanya didn't notice the people coming and going, some bringing newspapers, others taking them away. You couldn't read your fill, swallow your fill, accommodate it all. No longer his usual contemplative and aloof self, he sat doubled up over the table and then on his cot.

In their Grenadier brigade what especially struck everyone, of course, was that their former commander, General Mrozovsky (whom everyone here feared and disliked), promoted by the Tsar to District commander, not only had not opposed the revolution for one minute but had easily submitted to arrest and, once arrested, had immediately joined the Provisional Government! And how menacing he had been here, how unapproachable!

One could join the Provisional Government—why not?—but not if you are a prominent servant of the Tsar! If he had showed only a little dignity.

Sanya read and read—and suddenly:

"In late February, Lieutenant General Nikolai Aleksandrovich Zabudsky, distinguished professor of ballistics, member of the Artillery Committee, honorary member of the Mikhailovsky Artillery Academy conference, and outstanding artillery specialist, fell victim to the revolution. Moscow University had bestowed upon him the degree of doctor of applied mechanics. The Paris Academy had elected him a corresponding member."

That name, heard before in passing, now came to mind: Zabudsky! The professor-general with the furrowed brow who had inspected their battery cannons! The way he, against regulations, wiped his sweaty bald spot with his handkerchief, the way he stooped, the intelligent way he explained—and his hand was so gentle and weak . . .

Why on earth him? What did he have to do with anything? How on earth could he have *fallen*?

How was Sanya supposed to imagine this death?

These past few days, Sanya had perceived events through a shroud of incomprehensibility. But now, suddenly, that shroud was removed: he saw that bright, intelligent old man with a shattered, bleeding head—on some street? Or stairs?

And Sanya staggered back.

Was **this** the way freedom came?

[4 9 5]

The news that the Minister of Justice was in Moscow raced through the entire city, reaching even those deprived of their freedom. General Mrozovsky, arrested in his apartment, requested a meeting with the minister. The royal satrap Voeikov, who had been arrested on the railway and brought to a cell at the Kremlin commandant's, also asked the minister for a meeting. Somewhere during his movements, these requests were reported to the minister, but not only did he have no desire to see them, he could not afford to stain himself and merely ordered Voeikov transported to the Peter and Paul Fortress. Here was an idea: latch the car to the minister's train today, that way was surer.

Despite physical exhaustion, the minister rushed to complete the day's program. He was already being driven down Tverskaya and across Okhotny Ryad to the City Duma, which had been thoroughly scraped and cleaned after the revolutionary days.

Meeting there was not the old elected duma, partly reactionary, but a duma of a new makeup—corrected for all those who should have been elected earlier but weren't. The tall starched collars gleamed. All public Moscow was eager to attend this session! For the first time in fifty years, the public was admitted with tickets, although there were twice as many seats and the duma galleries were open. And still there were a thousand people who hadn't been able to get in, crowding in front of the building. On the other hand, those who did get in were rewarded.

Thanks to the formal occasion, the resolution of the former reactionary regime on economizing electricity had been forgotten—and the duma hall had received full celebratory lighting. Entering into this shining at almost nine o'clock, to a storm of applause, were Aleksandr Fyodorovich Kerensky, the rather stout Gruzinov with his military staff, and Moscow Commissar Kishkin.

They took seats alongside members of the Municipal Board, while Mayor Chelnokov, rather lame and saggy, but on the ball, gleamed with his pince-nez from the dais and drawled in his slow, Moscow accent:

"You realize that at the present moment I could not convene the old duma. At my own risk I decided to publish the lists of the new duma members and convene them specifically today. In this regard I did not want to disturb Prince Lvov and took responsibility for altering the duma's makeup, in hopes of receiving your approval."

The applause confirmed that only decisiveness like this would do in revolutionary times . . .

"We are obliged to honor the memory of those who perished in Moscow for freedom." (Those three soldiers killed by accident on the Bolshoi Kamenny Bridge.) "Please stand."

The duma members stood, the minister stood, and the audience stood.

"Then I must turn your attention to *the person*"—the first impatient applause broke out, they thought he meant Kerensky—"without whom Moscow could not have passed through the maelstrom of events without bloodshed. I am speaking, naturally, of Lieutenant Colonel Aleksei Evgrafovich Gruzinov!" (passionate applause) ". . . who with great simplicity and decisiveness came to the City Duma . . . And what he said was the highest civic accomplishment! He proposed organizing Moscow troops, that is, he offered his head for Russia's freedom! And we are filled with wonder and respect . . .

Aleksei Evgrafovich's deed has gone down in history! I would ask the duma to choose a special commission for the worthy commemoration of Lieutenant Colonel Gruzinov's name!"

And a storm burst, a storm of applause! Yes, carry it down through the ages! Yes! The entire hall was standing—and, naturally, standing facing Gruzinov himself, who did not stand all that erect (he had not been in military service in a long time), but what a handsome man, with burning eyes and a small fuzzy mustache created, one imagines, to tickle the ladies' imagination.

They stood, clapped, stood, clapped—and finally Board member Astrov, a Kadet, took the floor. With a rather dull face and a weak chin, he read out a resolution:

"We are living in great historic . . . Moscow will never forget that standing at the head of Moscow's troops at this critical moment without any thought for himself . . . carrying along in a great, unified upsurge . . . Moscow's eternal gratitude . . ."

And once again the hall shuddered from an outburst of applause.

Gruzinov rose to respond. There was a velvety quality to both his voice and his manner:

" . . . That which I am now experiencing is enough that I might die peacefully . . . If I was able to grab hold of this upsurge and direct it into a channel . . . I will apply all my efforts to ensuring that the cause of freedom flourishes bloodlessly. Let me conclude with a soldier's words . . ."

A powerful "hurrah" shook the Duma building.

Finally, through shouts and cries, the long-awaited Kerensky stood up. (After the English Club he had napped for a couple of hours in an apartment and had some strong tea, and although he was still pale and underslept, he held himself like quite the fine fellow.)

The ovation—truly grandiose—drew to a close. Kerensky stood through it buoyantly, with a slightly enigmatic smile—and at last was able to state:

"Mr. Mayor! The Provisional Government, which holds full power, has enjoined me to appear here and present its deepest regards to Moscow"— and with a quasi-knightly movement he gave the mayor a deep bow—"and in its person to the entire Russian people, and to state that we shall give all our powers and all our life to carrying the authority invested in us by the people's trust all the way to a Constituent Assembly."

He found it especially pleasant to express within the four walls of the Moscow city administration . . .

"which since Moscow first appeared" (that is, evidently, since 1147) "has created two such mighty organizations as the Unions of Zemstvos and Towns and now will help create an invincible Russia."

A storm of applause.

After this they awaited a major, brilliant speech, but the minister expressed nothing more, unfortunately, but rather gave a sign that he wished to leave.

The duma got busy with reading out the telegram from Ambassador Buchanan, an honorary citizen of Moscow, and with the telegram responses to England and France, and honored in turn Kishkin, Chelnokov, and Astrov, and instructed Chelnokov to work out the question of immortalizing Resurrection Square as the center of the popular movement: to widen it at the expense of properties on Okhotny Ryad; to raze all the buildings between Theater Square, the Manège, and the City Duma; and to construct a grandiose new building for the Moscow duma—the Palace of Revolution.

Meanwhile, they informed Kerensky that a case of hand grenades had been discovered in the City Duma building, placed there by persons unknown. What perfidy! Was this not that very same sinister attempt at assassination? The minister ordered the strictest investigation.

And sped onward through Moscow.

Despite the late evening hour (though a special train awaited him no matter the hour), he also hurried to the Polish democratic club, where, to more applause, he explained that he was not surprised that the Poles treated Russia with mistrust. The problem was that even Russians had yet to trust themselves.

Finally, concluding his magical, inspiring turn around Moscow on motorcar wheels, he rushed back to the Soviet of Workers' Deputies, where he had begun that morning. The greater Soviet was meeting at the Polytechnic Museum, and the applause and shouts of "hurrah" for their loyal socialist comrade-in-arms lasted several minutes.

No heart could withstand so much glory in half a day. Kerensky stood on the podium holding a bouquet of scarlet flowers against his black jacket, his eyes closed, his head lowered, twitching.

The Soviet's chairman, Comrade Khinchuk, greeted him as deputy chairman of the Petrograd Soviet:

"Generally, workmen do not let their own figures join ministries. But as long as you occupy the ministry, Comrade Kerensky, we know there will be no betrayal. We trust you!"

And again and again, a noisy ovation!

Kerensky handed someone the flowers, stepped firmly, and even more firmly—and now stood up straight and spoke with his previous resonance. Once again he explained to his dear comrade workers (and intellectuals) how it came to pass that he had decided to join the ministry, and who was in favor of it and who was against it—and with increasing pride:

"If you trust me, undertake nothing without consulting with me. Telegraph me at any time, if required, and I will come to tell you the whole truth. Remember"—he pressed his hands to his chest dramatically—"that I am yours! Wholly yours! Here I am not a minister but your comrade. I am your *comrade*! And the proletariat must become the country's master!"

The hall was very pleased, although there were shouts:

"But why is Nikolai the Second allowed to travel around Russia?"

"Isn't it time to crack down on the children?"

"Who's going to be Supreme Commander?"

And even:

"Death to the Tsar!"

Ah, that nettlesome question! Here, too. All the places he'd heard it. Russian subjects could not enjoy their freedom as long as the Tsar enjoyed his.

But not only did this not fluster Kerensky, he seemed to rejoice at the question! It was as if he were walking into a refreshing wind. Something akin to a smile played on his big lips.

"Nikolai Nikolaevich **will not be** Supreme Commander!"

Silence. That was that.

"As for Nikolai the Second, the former Tsar himself has come to the new government with a request for . . " Some instinct, an instinct Kerensky had, let him know that he could not mention England directly, the way he could at the English Club. "With a request for protection. And the Provisional Government took upon itself responsibility for the Tsar's personal safety." And now very ominously and mercilessly: "Nikolai the Second is now in my hands! In the hands of the Prosecutor-General! The entire Romanov dynasty is in my hands!" This shook the hall. Was he about to announce the execution of them all? "And I will tell you, comrades"—his face was terrible, and one could not envision mercy—"The Russian revolution has passed bloodlessly—and I don't want . . . ! I won't allow . . . !" (the Tsar is done for) "it to be sullied! We will not allow freedom's bright triumph to be sullied! And a *Marat* of the Russian revolution . . ." he thundered, practically choking, "I will never be! Very shortly, however, Nikolai the Second, under my personal observation, will be taken to a harbor and . . ." (and drowned?) ". . . and from there will board a ship for England. Give me the power and authority to do this!"

This was so remarkably prepared and expressed by his voice that the audience had already softened and agreed: Indeed! Let him go! They actually clapped, they actually shouted "hurrah." We give you the authority!

Pale, Kerensky closed his eyes and stood there for half a minute. (He had sensed the moment well! He had understood the crowd! And now he had averted blood.)

But his companions were hurrying him along, his adjutant officers were bustling, Kerensky said goodbye, shook hands with the Soviet's leaders— and was leaving—had left—and in the vestibule there was a final burst of applause for him.

They made a dash for the Nikolaevsky Train Station.

The special train was already under steam, and Voeikov's car had been attached.

The fearsome Extraordinary Investigator Muravyov was already on the train.

With his last bit of strength, Kerensky said goodbye, said goodbye to the lawyers, to the Soviet's representatives, to Chelnokov, to Kishkin—and now he was standing on the train car landing, and now he was waving. The train started to move. It was eleven-thirty.

Staggering on his feet, Kerensky got as far as his compartment.

But he did not collapse. For a fascinating interrogation of the palace commandant now awaited him.

Right now he intended to have some tea with Voeikov, stunning him with his graciousness and eliciting the facts about the treason at court.

[4 9 6]

He had already put her in a cab and she was pulling away from the hotel when she suddenly felt—a squeeze, a doubt: was everything **all right**? Might she have misunderstood? . . . Might everything be bad? . . .

And immediately, ignoring the cabbie's displeasure, she turned him back to the entrance, wait here, and ignoring the doorman—up the staircase again—and knocked at his door again!

He opened, surprised.

She was out of breath:

"I just thought . . . Is everything between us—**all right**? Is everything fine? . . . Well, that's all I came for. I'm going . . ."

But again, again she hung in his arms. And again he went to see her out.

No one saw them on the dark street, but she was as if at a crowded celebration: Look, everyone, look!

She got home, and her eyes were so happy.

How good it is to feel like this!

How extraordinary it was with him—this was impossible to convey! He was all around her. How had she deserved this?

Oh, if only tomorrow were like today!

And after that, again.

No matter where he summoned her.

But even if there wasn't another time, she had it all inside her. For her whole life.

Likonya had so much now, you could take and take from her and never take it all.

[4 9 7]

The Tsar's stay at GHQ dragged on unbearably. But this was not the only reason Alekseev felt constrained in the former Emperor's presence. No.

Alekseev found himself averting his eyes from the Emperor, as he had never done before. Their relations had always been simple.

Ever busy with work, Alekseev did not have the habit of rummaging around in his feelings. Now, though, something lay unusually heavily on his chest, like an extraneous object.

Alekseev realized what it was: it was as if he felt guilty. Guilty? But what had he been guilty of before the Tsar in recent days? He had acted precisely, strictly by the rules, and had not issued a single order on his own initiative other than halting the regiments: from the Southwestern, those he had called up himself; from the Western, he had received the Emperor's confirmation afterward. He had not violated a single order. He had done everything honestly. It was the Emperor who had gotten it wrong with his departure; the guilt was rather his.

Mostly, though, all the events had bypassed them both.

Yes, so it was. Nonetheless the guilt weighed inexplicably. Weighed, and what's worse, might it not even linger after the Emperor's departure?

When word had come from Petrograd today saying that the former Tsar was scheduled to depart tomorrow—so to prepare his train, and that several State Duma deputies would be coming to escort him, finally—Alekseev felt uncomfortable conveying this important news to the Emperor in a note. He went himself.

In these past few days of even-paced GHQ life and frequent conversations with his mother, the Emperor had begun to look much calmer, the terrible incised quality his features had had upon his arrival had smoothed out. A certain brightness even appeared on his face, as if he were actually pleased, as if he had not been through a disaster. A bright gaze—and without the slightest reproach for Alekseev. But precisely for this reason, Alekseev did not have the heart to refuse the Emperor's last request, an almost childish pleasure: to issue a farewell order to the Army. Formally, he had not been Supreme Commander for five days, he was no one, and he could not issue an order like that, but one had to have a heart of stone to refuse him. Alekseev had already refused his mad plan to rescind his abdication, but might he as well satisfy this request? The Emperor was like a child in wanting to say goodbye.

The general gnashed his teeth and agreed.

Before nightfall, the Emperor had sent him his text.

The order was indeed quite useful overall. It called for fighting to victory and for loyalty to the new government, saying any weakening of the order or service only played into the enemy's hands. During these days of confusion, having the former Tsar add his voice in this way could only help the cause and serve unification, just like the appeals Alekseev intended to write with Guchkov. This was a dangerous moment. Use all forces right now to collect all the loyalty there was. And the kind the Emperor would collect for them would also be useful, even the most useful of all.

Formally, though, the order could not be issued over the former Emperor's signature.

Alekseev decided to print it as a statement, as part of his own order, signed by the chief of staff.

He passed it along for retyping.

Agreement was also reached with the Emperor about his morning farewell tomorrow with the personnel at GHQ.

Late that evening, the duty officer reported that General Kislyakov was asking to be received.

Alekseev rolled his weary eyes—what was so urgent on the rail lines? Kislyakov had not made a peep since the day, a week ago, when he'd come to report on the impossibility of taking all the railways under his charge. But what was the urgency now? He hadn't telephoned ahead but was already waiting in the reception room.

Fine, then, let him come in.

Again this unhealthy impression of friability despite his youth, nothing military about him, a bureaucrat. There was no directness in his eyes, his gaze was constantly twisting. This time, though, it was understandable. He was agitated, flushed:

"Your Excellency. I do not have the right to report to you . . . However, I feel it is impossible not to report . . . But I am counting on you . . . That no one else? . . . It is a secret."

And he looked tensely.

Now that was a subordinate! Doesn't have the right to report. Although it's true, he did have his own superiors, the Ministry of Roads and Railways.

He all but demanded a vow from Alekseev. But he kept looking at him in a frightened way and had broken out in red spots. Unstable, shifty.

"Your Excellency! I have received an encoded telegram from Minister Nekrasov. He . . ."

And he did not go on. Instead, he placed in front of Alekseev the telegram itself in printed figures and fair decoding in his own hand, in ink.

Alekseev began to read—and felt himself turning red as well, although that never happened to him.

Nekrasov had informed Kislyakov that he had to prepare not two letter trains, as usual, but one—but with special care and with a reserve locomotive, since the former Tsar's departure from GHQ would bear the character of **an arrest**, which was the assignment that the State Duma delegation was to carry out.

So that was it? Like that? Alekseev had not guessed this at all!

An *arrest*? A delegation?

He himself had asked that representatives be sent for an escort.

But who could have thought this? . . .

So that's what . . .

Pursing his lips, Alekseev reread it. He looked at Kislyakov. Who must have had his own correspondence with Nekrasov, and maybe Bublikov as well? Better keep a close eye.

There was nothing more to discuss with him. He thanked him.

"Go on, get it ready."

"But what about you, Your Excellency . . . ? I thought I had to report to you, correct? . . ."

"Yes, correct. Thank you."

He let him go.

Would he have been better off not thanking him? Yet another burden heaped on him.

The Emperor had abdicated voluntarily, he hadn't fought it—so what ever for? . . .

But if one stood in the Provisional Government's place, one could understand this measure, too. The first few days of the government's existence—and here the former Tsar was traveling around freely?

One measure or another was inevitable.

Now what? Did he have to do everything?

Not that they had asked anything of Alekseev; they'd demanded it of Kislyakov.

Although it was strange—and insulting—that the Provisional Government had not gotten around to informing him personally.

Or did they not trust him?

Meanwhile, who was going to do the escorting, make arrangements?

A new, burning jolt of reproach to his heart: What about *telling* him? Telling the Emperor.

How could he not be told?

But he seemingly had given his word. To avoid excesses.

But at a certain moment, saying *this* was unavoidable, wasn't it? . . .

Or say nothing at all? Just let him go?

No, decency demanded that he at least be told. They had worked together so long.

Go over there now and tell him? He wasn't asleep yet.

But then he would get worked up.

Tomorrow would be the farewell ritual—and what if the Emperor said something harsh or excessive in front of everyone?

If he learned ahead of time, the Emperor might rethink something. Change his mind, the way he'd wanted to change it over the abdication. What if he refuses to go? Refuses to submit? Or decides to go somewhere else?

What could Alekseev do then?

It was a terrible pity, but however much of a pity, the Tsar has to bear his own destiny and all the consequences of his actions.

Yes, it was more sensible to conceal this until the last moment.

If only they would take him away quickly! How weary Alekseev was from this duplicity, these concealments.

Tonight he was not dragged to the telegraph. Alekseev locked his door, lit the icon lamp, and knelt in prayer for a long time.

Asking the Lord to forgive him.

There was something running through all this that required forgiveness.

[498]

The farther Vorotyntsev drove into remote Romania, the more grueling the feeling that his entire journey was a disgraceful disease you wouldn't tell anyone about, or a lapse into imbecility. He would have liked to forget it altogether! He hadn't guessed, had missed his chance, had trailed like a useless appendage right through the centers of events. With the passage of days, this had become increasingly clear. He might not have been able to do anything, but in battle you can take impossible steps. He hadn't moved a muscle, though. On 14 March, at the very least—couldn't an officer go to Petrograd? But he had stayed home. Change into civilian dress and go? But go where? Seek out whom? For what?

It was no relief to learn that Vorotyntsev was not alone in losing his head. *Everyone* had. The entire Imperial Army. And GHQ. The Tsar himself. And his brother. All Russia.

Why stop at Vorotyntsev, when the entire Baltic fleet "had joined the revolution to avoid ruin." The ruin of *what*? Itself? Or the revolution?

Here at Ninth headquarters, Vorotyntsev had found everyone distraught, and no one could say about the past what should have been done. With his abdication, the Emperor had pulled the ground out from under everyone. The Supreme Commander—suddenly, first, had left his post and had not turned to any of us for help. Those who would have wanted to defend him, though, hardly knew **how**.

General Lechitsky had paced around headquarters with a somber look (still not having removed the imperial monogram from his epaulets). He was silent. He did not assemble anyone, did not call on anyone to do anything.

How one wanted to get something from him. A decision? A clear order? He was silent.

Fragments of events reached the 9th Army, the far flank, with a delay, and Guchkov's Order No. 114 trickled in—and brought no cheer. Apparently, even the Minister of War was now confirming for the lower ranks that the rules of military discipline were a symbol of servile relations . . .

The same feeling of impotence that had discouraged Vorotyntsev in Moscow and Kiev had now crushed everyone. With every passing day, the situation was increasingly destructive and irrevocable—but what could be done? No one could say.

But if we didn't intervene in the course of events, what were we worth? There were still reserves of will and movement—but where should they be applied?

For the past few days, Vorotyntsev had been rising very early, when it was still dark, much earlier than required. Both because sleeplessness clawed at him. And because this was a reliable means of recuperation. The early morning hours, the earliest morning hours, when everyone else is still asleep, have a special force and capacity; all the aspects of one's duty show through especially distinctly, and all aspects of weakness fall away more easily. Even without a specific goal, just to begin wakefulness before everyone else, to get ahead of the common life, to find yourself on your feet with a healthy mind—this is bound to bring you some discovery, success, or idea. God provides for those who rise early—the saying is a proven fact. Making the rounds of one's positions at that hour always reveals something you wouldn't spot in a year during ordinary daytime hours. This goes for headquarters life as well—to come to work when no one else is there yet, the duty officers are fighting early morning sleep, and the night's news has piled up—is always good for contemplation and decision.

So, too, today he arrived at the headquarters building and took his room key off its nail, and the telegraph duty officer handed him a typed document received that night, now being transmitted to the corps.

An order to all the armed forces.

In Alekseev's framing and with his signature—but an order from the Emperor himself.

This was unexpected.

He took it to his room.

He felt like smoking. But in the morning he avoided that on an empty stomach, it was noxious.

A farewell order?

A brief one. The eyes could take in its entirety in one glance.

But here's the thing: it wasn't formal and bombastic as they used to be. There was no doubt he wrote it himself, one could almost hear the Emperor's voice, soft and passive.

"For the last time I address you." He called his troops "fervently beloved," while Allies were left with the stiff "valorous."

Actually no, his tongue was tied up by forms like weights, and here our troops also show up as "valorous."

For the government that had removed the Emperor, there was this: "May God help it lead Russia," and "Submit to the Provisional Government."

How his ill-wishers had abused and scorned him! The gentlest of their nicknames had been "the colonel." And no matter how angry, how maddened Vorotyntsev himself had been at him—now he was touched. Touched not for the Provisional Government but by the Emperor himself. This mildness, this humility had always been a weakness of the Russian

Tsar, perhaps, but right now . . . After all, no one had compelled him to bless the new government or call for obedience to it, and here . . .

What could you do . . . A Christian . . .

Too much a Christian to occupy the throne.

He left the same as he had been.

That meant not only did he adjure a thousand times his love for Russia—but he himself had readily removed himself for Russia.

What could you do. Such he was. Such he was given us.

Perhaps there was something to this elusive thought.

Here . . . Himself . . . Easily. Without a struggle.

And how was he doing now? To fall from that height—and in just two days? . . .

It was illogical, unprovable, but Vorotyntsev's pain was such as if he himself had put his hand to this vile revolution.

Although he had **not done** anything. Nor had he done anything against his conscience. His thoughts had merely tottered.

Now that the republic was being handed out in sheafs on every street corner, Vorotyntsev found it sickening to feel himself in this howling stream. Right now it even seemed implausible. How could he have raised a hand? How could he have wanted the Emperor to renounce his throne? . . .

The Emperor concluded touchingly, as had never been the custom: with St. George, Bringer of Victory. He had remembered him—and attached him to his abandoned army: he will lead you to victory!

Vorotyntsev honored his patron saint, George.

But there was a short phrase in the order that singed him. The first time his eyes skipped it; the second time they rested—and Vorotyntsev felt himself turning red:

"Anyone now thinking of peace is a traitor to the fatherland, its betrayer."

Possibly because there was such a profound silence and solitude, no one else knew or had read this order, or had sought it, and it lay in front of Vorotyntsev alone—it was as if the Emperor had spoken to him directly, knowing everything about him, that he, Vorotyntsev, was a traitor, had betrayed Russia.

Knowing *everything*? The fact that he wanted peace and *what* he had conceived that fall?

Vorotyntsev became feverish.

He snapped two matches before he could light a cigarette.

This is what had tormented him all last week, starting in Moscow, and had then festered en route, and then he had checked it with Krymov, who had not hesitated—here is what had tormented him: that with his autumn idea he had sullied himself in this revolution.

Had he betrayed his oath then? His duty?

But Emperor! Now you, too, have betrayed your oath! Your duty!

To whom should he cry out? To a man prostrate? . . . That was easiest of all.

But it wasn't all Vorotyntsev's fault. No, not all of it! Yes. He had thought this since last year and thought so now: Russia needed peace. Peace alone! Peace above all! Peace first of all! Why was this betrayal?

He was even certain that we should neither have entered this war for anything nor even signalled our willingness to do so. This was our fatal error. Only if Germany itself had advanced on us. Then it would have been a Patriotic War and without question for every last man.

But now that we were mired in war, choking on it, and we had to have the intelligence and courage to get out of it.

This is what there was in the farewell order: "The hour is nigh when Russia and the Allies will break the enemy's final effort." . . . The Emperor was sure of this.

Oh, how sure you all are!

No matter how victorious our column might be, someone mowed down by case shot falls in battle, and the victory is no longer his. Even if there was a victory for us and the Allies, what would be left of us?

How many Russian heads we had laid down pointlessly in our history, how many heads, not sparing them! Wherever you point. The present war—what made it any better than Anna Ioannovna's wars? First we tried to seat the Elector of Saxony as the King of Poland. Then came Münnich's bungling marches on Ochakov and Crimea, 100,000 Russians laid low in the South merely for the right to gain Azov and its leveled fortifications? Under Elizabeth, we drove the Russian infantry to help England and the Netherlands on the Rhine. And the absurd Seven Years' War—was that any better? Why did we take on this European housecleaning—besieging Frederick the Great while in no way even benefiting from the fruits of those sacrifices and victories?

His cheeks were burning, his brow was burning. Yes, I've faltered, but I refuse to admit to betraying the Fatherland!

Because this war is not higher than all of Russia's objectives!

Of course, if one is referring only to valor, to valor alone . . . But Russia has something besides valor to preserve.

All of us, the gentry and the educated class alike—how carefree we were sailing through Russia, and how much about it we let slip, partly in those valorous wars of ours.

Me a traitor? All of us betrayed our people—and long ago, and in so many ways! We gave them up to this war, too—betrayed them.

Along with you, Sire . . .

The telegraph duty officer knocked at the door, agitated:

"Colonel, sir! I must warn you that an instruction has just now come in from GHQ to halt the distribution of this order!"

Vorotyntsev didn't understand immediately: an order to halt it? . . . (And the part about *him*? . . .)

He started to understand:

"How dare they! Halt his farewell order? The scoundrels! The miserable brutes!"

[4 9 9]

In unfamiliar waters, even the most experienced swimmer is off his stride, swallowing water, and lucky not to drown. The waves at the rear proved to be such that General Evert got utterly lost in them, merely held on to his important look, but had lost his grip on the situation. He had recognized the new government, but that turned out to be not nearly enough for stability. He was still commander-in-chief of the Western Army Group, and was in charge of those three armies and fifteen corps—but in fact nothing remained of his absolute rule. He had not foreseen that a new authority would take shape a few buildings away from him, in Minsk itself. No sooner had he let them assemble in those first hours than they began spilling out quite independently. No sooner had he allowed the Committee of Public Safety to convene than it appointed some unheard-of "civilian commandant" for the city—who ordered the arrest of city policemen—and violence immediately spread to all the District's railways, and railway gendarmes were disarmed at all the stations. Immediately, Minsk formed its own Soviet of Workers' Deputies—and put out its own newspaper, outrageous in its content—and Evert simply could not impose political censorship, not having those kinds of instructions or rights.

The entire city painted itself red, people gathered, and there was a lot of street movement—and Evert had no rights, instructions, or even methods, let alone forces. How could he stop all this? Meanwhile, GHQ itself had been beheaded for a few days, until the grand duke's arrival. The grand duke was remembered for his tested leadership of the troops—now much awaited, but so far missing. General Evert not only lacked the decisiveness to put down this irregular turmoil, but he himself was drawn irrepressibly to be a participant in this turmoil, as if drawn in by eddying water.

On 19 March, the new regime, without asking General Evert, scheduled a citywide demonstration in conjunction with the garrison, and so unavoidable was this, due to the current cheekiness, that Evert not only did not try to find a way to prevent it but felt he himself should participate in order to lend the demonstration legitimate decorum.

People thronged to Cathedral Square from every direction, out of desire and curiosity. There were no police left anywhere, and self-appointed civilians wearing red armbands pretended to direct traffic. Nearly all the inhabitants, and especially all the student youth, were here. Many were carrying red flags and red pieces with inscriptions, and many walls were covered in red rigging—while the black silhouettes of spectators could be seen on the roofs, balconies, and bell tower. All the garrison troops present had to be lined up on the square—and Evert sent Kvetsinsky to make their rounds, congratulating them on "the new government order and people's government." The troops shouted "hurrah," but municipal figures on the same balcony with Evert pointed out that he should make the rounds of the troops himself. Fine. Stately, almost heroic, erect, bearded—Evert walked the full length of the formation, and all the troops shouted "hurrah." Apparently, his personal participation had been the right decision for keeping the movement within the bounds of good sense.

After this, clergy from the cathedral led a public prayer (far from the entire square removed caps, and besides there were many Jews, and red flags kept poking up all over). Afterward, a speech had to be delivered from the newly built wooden rostrum. Who first? Evert again. Swallowing with his dry throat, he said: "I believe that with God's help the new government, which is made up of individuals chosen by the people, will lead the homeland to new happiness." After that it went more easily—about the war, about the enemy, about championing Holy Russia and the Supreme Commander. Evert managed to deliver his speech well, and a "hurrah" thundered across the square. Evert held his heavy arm in a salute.

Someone started slamming a crowbar against the imperial coat of arms above the pharmacy.

His heart felt scalded.

But what were you going to do? You'd already come here and delivered a speech. What were you going to do?

Elsewhere where coats of arms hung, people started smashing them.

Then the ceremonial march began, and the Minsk population came thronging. Evert still held his arm in a salute—and felt a tremor pulse through it.

The generals had left the square, and the soldiers were leaving it—but more and more civilians started climbing up to the tribune and shouting out their own speeches.

Evert couldn't tell where he had made his mistake or whether he could have done something different, but he felt foul. Here he had handed over to these red flags and speakers not only his entire Western Army Group but also, behind its broad back, the vast Moscow Military District, for which he also answered, and also given them telegrams to announce the manifestos that left Russia tsarless instantly and all round.

For a few hours, an unexpected telegram from Purishkevich in Petrograd had gladdened him: a permanent confederate of the Western Army Group with his hospital train, he now hastened to tell Evert the wonderful news that the criminal, disruptive "Order No. 1" was a fake!

Was that so? Thank God! What kind of no-goods had written it and telegraphed it everywhere?

Evert wanted to announce this joyous news then and there in an order to his army group, but he'd grown used to vacillations these past few days.

What if something else was wrong? He didn't want to make a mistake! He contacted GHQ—and what did he learn? Order No. 1 was not a fake. Purishkevich had falsely informed him, even though he was a member of the State Duma and a reputable person.

This municipal demonstration on Monday was not the end of the red flood, as General Evert had hoped, but only its beginning. Now it had spilled through the small towns and garrisons, too—not love for the homeland or a passion for victory over the Germans—but even greater degradation, insubordination, and the arrests of individual officials, especially those with German surnames.

Those German names were an easy target! As for Evert, Minsk was abuzz about his German name—and they didn't want that! He had to debase himself and provide a rebuttal to the newspapers, saying that his name was Swedish, not German. Whether they believed him or not, he no longer had freedom of command. How could Evert command against anarchy when he himself had been at the *meeting*? (Where had they come up with these words, the likes of which had never been in Russia and which no one understood.)

O Lord! If only the grand duke would arrive soon and take the army into his experienced hands!

Every evening, going to bed late, Evert didn't know what new disaster the morning would bring.

Today's was an article in the *Minsk Voice*, which said that the arrested palace commandant Voeikov had intended to open the Western front to the Germans in order to crush the revolution.

Evert's face became red hot. After all, the palace commandant did not command the Western Army Group! If he could make that promise or have that intention, that meant the readers might now think that Voeikov either had an agreement with Evert or could count on him. Readers might think that General Evert himself was prepared to open the front to the Germans!

And those readers, the Minsk readers, too, had now become all-powerful even over generals.

There was no solution now for the commander-in-chief of the Western Army Group other than to sit down and write a rebuttal to that mangy *Minsk Voice*. Saying that Voeikov had defiled the Western Army Group with his assumption that it could possibly let in his homeland's enemy. But no one here was capable of such a foul crime. And even if this order had been given, even from the *very* top, neither General Evert nor a single military leader would ever . . .

O Lord! No! He couldn't stay on at his command if he had to justify himself to every last news rag! Evert decided to telegraph Guchkov and request that he be appointed to a different post, preferably, the Council of War (for a rest).

The telegram reply from Guchkov was swift in coming:

"I consider your sojourn at the front dangerous and harmful. I propose you immediately resign your post."

Without a replacement. His service was over.

"I propose" . . .

Nonetheless, didn't the grand duke have to give this order? So let's wait and see.

[5 0 0]

Svechin arrived at headquarters in the morning—and was given the Emperor's farewell order to the army.

Unexpected.

But also natural.

Had it been sent out? They'd started sending it out in the early morning hours, but Guchkov had found out and forbidden it.

Svechin's kneaded his large eyebrows and lips. This was simply base, nothing but political calculation, not a soldier's soul. There was good reason he had never liked Guchkov as a man. No matter how he dressed up as a soldier. A soldier has to respond to the chord of nobility.

And what was in this order? "Submit to the Provisional Government, obey your superiors." What were they afraid of?

He read the brief text carefully. Headquarters types had eyes trained to evaluate an order. Nikolai had never been any kind of Supreme Commander, of course. He had never directed anything. But he was devoted to the army heart and soul, that was true.

That was here, too. He used familiar, resounding expressions, but the order was like a howl. He was in pain.

They hadn't sent it out, the swinish souls.

And Alekseev? . . .

It was known, it had been conveyed, that at ten-thirty, in the Duty Hall, GHQ officers who so wished would say goodbye to the Emperor.

We would go, naturally. Who would show such baseness as not to go?

The Operations Section went in full. As did others.

The Duty general's office occupied the district court building across the square. In the present rectangular Duty Hall there remained a low balustrade perpendicular to its long sides, which separated the public's former seats from the court's, but with an opening in the middle. Because of this balustrade, those now gathered into several closely packed rows along all the walls formed a kind of figure eight, narrowing where it went around the balustrade, now hidden behind their backs; and leaving a small empty space in the middle, at its narrowest.

Those who had forgotten that a large portrait of the Emperor had hung right there now saw an empty rectangle a brighter shade of the wall paint.

People started lining up. The entrance was at the corner of the figure eight. From it, the right flank stretched along the long wall. At its head were the three grand dukes, then Lukomsky and Klembovsky, and then by department and section, the senior generals at the head of their own men and in the first row. Then came the Convoy officers and the officers of the St. George Battalion. So went the entire figure eight, while at the end of the other long wall, on the left flank, about fifty men lined up, lower ranks, delegates from the sections and units of the Convoy, St. George's, clerks.

A low drone of quiet conversation hung in the air.

Then Alekseev walked in, modestly as always, not seeking notoriety, and quietly exchanged words with Lukomsky.

He stood facing Svechin, and close up he seemed more like a cat than ever to him, with his whiskers, little eyes, and small head—an educated masked cat in a commander's tunic.

And where were the commanders?

Then an adjutant ran up and informed Alekseev that the Emperor had left his residence and was on his way.

At exactly ten-thirty, a loud staccato was heard from the stairs, through the closed doors:

"Good-morning-Your-Imperial-Majesty!"

They'd barked that well, just as before.

For the entire procedure, the soldier shout would be all that remained "as before."

The silence of the grave fell in the Duty Hall.

When the door opened, General Alekseev commanded quietly, in a squeaky voice:

"Gentlemen officers!"

The Emperor walked in. Not at all dashingly, his face a yellowish gray. Bags hung under his eyes.

He was wearing the gray Circassian coat of the Kuban Foot Scout Battalion, a sword across his shoulder on a narrow strap—and since everyone was standing there with bared heads, he removed his tall brown fur hat with his left hand and held it tight at his sword hilt. He was not wearing any Allied medals, only his white St. George's Cross.

He shook hands with Alekseev and the grand dukes.

Then made a general bow in the officers' direction.

He turned to his right, toward the soldiers, and greeted them softly, as one does in small rooms.

And they barked out here, too, not as many voices, but with a fullness and zeal:

"Good-morning-Your-Imperial-Majesty!"

And although they came from different detachments, their voices did not falter at the jerky tempo.

Then the Emperor took a few steps toward the middle, closer to the figure-eight intercept—and stood there, still with his hat squeezed at his sword hilt, the sword strap cutting into his chest.

He stood there—directly facing the spot of his removed portrait.

His free right hand was shaking hard, noticeably. He took it and lifted the shoulder-strap from his chest, as if seeking room for his chest, breathing room.

He had never been good at speaking in front of multitudes, and so it was in this last speech of his life.

The silence was absolute. But nervous.

This was the officer milieu, though, the most familiar and dear to the Emperor! But today . . .

Nonetheless, he began speaking in a voice loud and clear, but he was badly agitated and paused in the wrong places.

"Gentlemen . . . Today I see you . . . for the last time. Such is God's will. And the consequence of my decision. What has happened—has happened. . . ." His speech had not been at all rehearsed, he only right there thought and wondered: "God's will sees afar. It is hard for us to read. In the name of the good of our dear Homeland . . . to avert the horrors of internecine strife . . . I have deemed . . . I have abdicated the throne. . . ." He himself seemed to shudder at the horrific sound of these words. ". . . My decision is final . . . irrevocable . . . my only hope is that our Homeland remains standing. And our fierce enemy is broken. Our dear army . . . our Russia . . . its prosperity. . . ."

His voice was near to breaking:

". . . you all for your collective service . . . for your loyal and excellent service. In this year and a half I have seen your selfless work, and I know how much effort you have invested. And you will serve your homeland just as honestly under the new government . . . to total victory over the enemy. . . ."

Everyone looked without blinking or stirring.

Whether or not he had finished—he could not go on. His right hand was no longer trembling but twitching. He was holding onto his sword knot and fingering it. A few more words and the Emperor would break into sobs.

He raised his trembling hand to his throat and bowed his head.

Svechin wanted to object, if only inwardly: "Oh, you did your fair share." But in that moment he was undone and couldn't.

The silence got tenser, and thinner and thinner—and someone behind the Emperor sobbed convulsively.

And it was as if this push was just what the silence had been waiting for—and sobs broke out in several places at once.

Men simply wept, openly wiping their eyes. And:

"Quiet, quiet! You're upsetting the Emperor!"

The Emperor turned to the right and left, toward these sounds, and tried to smile—but no smile came, rather a tense grimace, which bared his teeth and twisted his face.

Right then he took a quick step toward the right flank, toward Lukomsky, where he put his hand out—and now he was continuing, shaking hands, slowly, going down the first row. He couldn't shake everyone's hands in the crowded back, but he tried to shake everyone's in front.

This was all before Svechin, in the first arc of the figure eight, before the balustrade. The Emperor was moving along the generals and staff officers, leaning forward toward each man, nearly eye to eye—and could barely keep back his trembling tears. He and Svechin grasped fingers rather awkwardly, and there was no correcting the handshake or holding onto his hand longer.

But his hand was warm and dry.

And Svechin, who had never been at all inclined toward emotion, was torn apart.

The Emperor, nearby, was already shaking the hand of Lieutenant General Tikhmenev, chief of army communications.

And all of a sudden he stopped in his passage, looked hard at the general, and, still holding his hand, said:

"Tikhmenev! Do you remember how I asked you? You must definitely manage to transport everything the army needs. Do you remember?"

His voice softened to the point of pleading.

Tikhmenev, touched, gave a trembling reply:

"Your Majesty! I do remember—and General Yegoriev here remembers, too."

He dragged up a tall, thin, nervous Lieutenant General Yegoriev, his chief field quartermaster, who looked like he hoped to drop back to the second row and hide his face.

The Emperor gladly took the hand of Yegoriev, who was a head taller than himself, and shook it.

"So, Yegoriev, you will definitely supply everything! This is more necessary now than ever. I'm telling you, I can't sleep at night thinking the army is going hungry."

Those standing far away, not close by, couldn't hear these words, of course, but it was as if in response someone from the other side, from the soldiers' side, let out a cry to the entire hall, in the way of common folk, as if mourning that the army was going hungry. Or all those here, abandoned. Or the Emperor who was abandoning them.

The way people wail over someone who has died.

At the other end of the figure eight, a Convoy captain of enormous size collapsed to the floor.

After finishing the rounds of the staff sections, the Emperor did not proceed toward the Convoy, perhaps assuming he would say goodbye to them separately—but instead began most gratefully shaking hands with the officers of the St. George Battalion, which had made the futile trip to Vyritsa. Among them were many who had been wounded several times. The sobs and shouts through the hall quickened. A giant cavalry sergeant-cuirassier exclaimed:

"Do not abandon us, father!!!"

Sobbing came from a cluster of soldiers.

It was as if a blow had broken off the Emperor's rounds—and he stopped.

He wanted to speak to the soldiers—and couldn't.

He threw his head back, perhaps to return his tears to their source.

He made a low, abrupt bow to those remaining.

And with lowered head quickly made for the exit.

Right then, though, Alekseev blocked the Emperor's path with his cautious, off-kilter walk—and began saying something, modulating his cracked squeaking into human speech—and people started shuffling in the hall so that even Svechin could not hear everything from there.

This was what: His Majesty need not have so appreciated the labors of GHQ, they had done what they could. But he wished the Emperor a safe journey and a happy, new life.

Happy? . . .

The Emperor, ignoring protocol, put his arms around Alekseev, who had also begun to weep, and kissed him firmly three times.

With each long kiss thanking him for his loyalty.

[5 0 1]

Maria had held out for so long—and had now succumbed, like the others. Olga was often delirious when her temperature was high. Was it true her father had come? And what crowds had come to kill everyone? The children's health took another turn for the worse in the exhausting measles cycle—and it would be God's mercy if no one went deaf or suffered other consequences. For them all to be sick at once—nothing like this had happened for many years, if ever. God had sent this trial during the crown's most terrible days!

Thank God, Aleksei's illness was the lightest of all this time. On the other hand, a precise understanding of events reached him by the hour.

"So does this mean I'll never go to GHQ with Papa again?" he wondered.

"No, my dear, never."

And after a short while:

"I won't see my regiments? My soldiers?"

"No, my dear little boy. I fear you won't."

And a little later:

"And the yacht? And my friends there? Are we never to go on the yacht again?"

Of his "friends on the yacht," changed unrecognizably was the old boatswain Derevenko, who had been assigned to the Heir: he was embittered, he snarled. And Sablin, his favorite Sablin, his companion on all his yacht outings, now captain of the *Standard*—had not shown his face at the palace!

The children's illness called for and required Aleksandra Fyodorovna— but also shielded her from the baseness and humiliations that now blanketed the palace. From the drunken soldier songs outside, nearby. From the curious stares through the park fence. From the fact that the watches of the Combined Guards Regiment, instead of the former handsome procedure of the change, now congratulated each other on their newborn freedom.

None of the palace officials arrested in the preceding days had been released, but General Resin had been arrested in addition.

A few telegrams had come from Nicky these past few days—laconic as always, hiding all his emotions and thoughts from outside eyes. No matter how closely she read them, these telegrams did not reveal the main secret or even hint at what was going on there, at GHQ, around him and in the Army itself. Was anyone *rising* in defense? Were Russian people coming to their senses about what they were losing in the crown, in the throne?

Not with Alekseev, a damaged man, of course, but with someone else. Evert?

No military leader arose in the Empress's mind's eye who could take charge of everything.

The Empress began every morning with the hope and prayer that a movement would rise up in the army in the Emperor's favor. But neither the newspapers (which lied in any case) nor the rumors she heard brought her any encouragement.

There remained a noble force—the Allies, especially the English monarchy and Georgie himself. What a horror for the Allies! The Allies would not stand for such a disgrace and failure in time of war! How unfailingly loyal the Russian Tsar had been to them, flouting all of Russia's private, special interests—so too would they be loyal to him in turn! The English and French governments—they could not act in just a few days, but they would find a way to influence the rebels and make them see sense! The Empress was waiting.

Though these days since the nighttime visit of Guchkov and Kornilov she had been burning her diaries and letters—nonetheless she had calmed down somewhat. She especially liked the fact that Kornilov was so chivalrous, and as long as he was in charge of the Petrograd garrison, she could rest assured for the children, herself, and the palace.

This morning, however, early, just after nine, the telephone rang in the palace, and Benckendorff was told it was General Kornilov speaking to him from here, from the Tsarskoye Selo Train Station! Kornilov asked him to find out from Her Majesty the time soonest she could receive him.

Aleksandra Fyodorovna was caught off-guard, having barely risen. After that night-time but successful visit—he was back? And so early and suddenly? Did this mean he had left Petrograd at dawn?

This could not be for any joyous reason. Some misfortune. Her heart sank. But misfortune coming from what direction? There was no guessing, it could come from anywhere.

Benckendorff thought quickly while on the telephone and asked agitatedly what had brought the general. But Kornilov refused to explain over the telephone and merely insisted on being received.

Nothing remained but to set a time. However long she needed to dress and get ready. In an hour. At ten-thirty.

At exactly ten-thirty, a short, rather sullen, swarthy General Kornilov entered the Aleksandr Palace accompanied by a colonel and staff captain. Benckendorff met them on the first floor and invited them to the second. The captain remained downstairs and the two senior officers went up.

The Empress—together with High Chamberlain Benckendorff—came out in a black, buttoned-up dress. She knew she looked quite awful, as always in the morning, and no longer tried to conceal the aging of her face, just the helplessness of her eyes. She felt bursts of agitation and put all her efforts into hiding this agitation, although it was undoubtedly expressed on her face by occasional red spots. Exhausted by all the alarms and the children's illnesses, she felt as if she were in a haze.

She was somewhat reassured by her first experience that Kornilov had a chivalry to him and he should not bring her anything bad.

Kornilov presented the man who had come with him, Colonel Kobylinsky, the new chief of the Tsarskoye Selo garrison.

Kobylinsky did not have a brigand's face and manner either.

Not extending her hand, the Empress suggested they all sit.

They sat down in the nearest chairs.

Two St. George Crosses flashed white on Kornilov—one at his heart, the other around his neck. For some reason he wasn't beginning. Was he politely awaiting the Empress's question?

How many generals had she had occasion during this war to honor with her supreme attention, to congratulate or thank, and they had watched ecstatically, loyally, gratefully—but she had never seen a general so aloof. On his last visit he had seemed more respectful.

His hair was cropped quite short and had a gray streak but no forelock, which emphasized his soldierly appearance. Ears protruding, face pockmarked, eyes as if squinting, peering out.

Boldly meeting his gaze, which held power and mystery, the Empress asked, keeping her voice from failing her and trying to speak precisely, without an accent, which made her speech sound wooden:

"What can I do for you, general? To what do I owe your visit?"

Kornilov rose sternly. And said very quietly:

"Your Imperial Majesty. A heavy task has fallen to me. I am here at the behest of the Council of Ministers. Whose decision I am obliged to convey to you. And carry out."

Something bad. Something so serious in these muffled sentences—the Empress had no necessity whatsoever to rise—that she stood up.

And the other two rose immediately.

She did not calculate her voice and said, louder than necessary:

"Speak. I'm listening."

Kornilov took a document out of his field map-case. And unfolded it on the case, like on a portable table.

Her heart started pounding: his reading a prepared document was worse than she could have expected.

He read it—not very smoothly.

". . . deem the abdicated emperor Nikolai II and his spouse to be deprived of their freedom . . ."

So it had come! The irrevocable. Like Antoinette. But as much as she had been expecting this in the night—she had not expected it today for some reason.

She clenched her teeth. Just so she didn't show it, didn't admit the force of the blow. She bowed her head.

". . . and deliver the abdicated emperor . . ."

Either the writers or Kornilov seemed to like repeating that formula.

". . . to Tsarskoye Selo."

Oh, Lord, if only he would come here! Just to be together at last!

". . . Instruct General Mikhail Vasilievich Alekseev to put a detail for the abdicated emperor's protection at the disposal of the State Duma members sent on assignment to Mogilev. Aleksandr Aleksandrovich Bublikov, Vasili Mikhailovich . . . Semyon Fyodorovich . . ."

Next to "the abdicated emperor"—oh, what extensive titles they gave themselves, clinging to the great moment! And for whom, for what were all these details on the heels of the thunderbolt: that Holy Russia had arrested her own tsar?

She bowed her head lower—she could not support it, could not look: "Do not go on."

But Kornilov did go on, at full tilt, to the end: these four deputies must then present a written report, which would be promulgated. That . . .

For three nights the Empress had been so afraid of learning of this arrest—she had trembled inside. But now, for some reason—no, she wasn't afraid. Now, for some reason, her own fate and that of her children—seemed not to exist. Now just one thing tolled like a heavy bell: Russia had raised her hand to arrest her tsar!

Kornilov folded the document and put it back in the map-case, which he let drop to his side. He stood at attention.

And with the same quiet, muffled voice explained what all this meant in practical terms. That garrison troops were taking over the palace guard from the Combined Regiment and Convoy. That use of the telephone was forbidden. All correspondence would be subject to inspection.

That is, they frankly declared that they would be reading other people's letters.

That was as it was, but Kornilov's own appearance was ingenuous, dull-witted, unintelligent, unsophisticated, more like a sergeant's, not at all meant for a historic moment in the Russian dynasty. . . And then what did this unknown colonel have to do with anything?

". . . Those individuals from the suite who do not wish to recognize the state of arrest must leave the palace today before four o'clock in the afternoon."

The Empress imperiously lifted her head and looked down at the general:

"All my people are ill. Today my last daughter fell ill. What about medical assistance for my children?"

Doctors would be admitted unimpeded, but accompanied by a guard.

Could she keep the palace servants?

For now, yes—those who themselves wished to stay. Gradually, however, those servants would be replaced by others.

"But we're all used to each other . . . And the children? . . ."

Kornilov stood at attention—in the same place, at the same distance, without visible softening, his thick black continuous mustache curved over his lips. A sergeant.

If there was anything else to be learned or obtained (the Empress herself poorly understood what), then it would only be if they were alone.

She asked whether she might be left alone with the general.

Benckendorff immediately glided to the door.

The colonel faltered and looked at the perfectly still general—apparently he, too, must go.

Another second, and another—and it would be just the two of them. What should she ask? Why had she requested they be left alone?

She didn't have time to think, didn't have time to find a question.

The doors closed—the general looked back at them. He took two steps toward her. And suddenly she saw, in this heartless attacking cavalryman's narrow eyes, sparks of life. His mustache stirred when he spoke, more quietly than before:

"Your Majesty, do not be upset. Nothing bad threatens you. All this is a formality, a measure of precaution against the raging of mutinous troops. You're tied to where you are anyway, as long as your children are ill. And when they recover . . . I've heard that a British cruiser will be waiting for you at Murman."

[5 0 2]

Kornilov had known military intelligence for years, along all our eastern borders, from the Caspian to the Sea of Japan, and on the other side of them as well—along with half a dozen Oriental languages, and the tireless life on the move of an inconspicuous soldier with a Buryat appearance. During the Japanese war he had commanded a brigade, in this one a division, and he was known among officers as a fatalist, for the fact that he behaved at the front as if there were no such thing as death. His observation post never left the forward trenches, so he did get captured. For any general, captivity usually means the end of the war: sit out the rest of the war in privileged conditions, contemplating your mistakes. But Kornilov escaped— over mountains, through forests, moving at night, feeding only on berries, and this way for three weeks—and his escape, which thundered across Russia, stood among the valorous events of this war.

After he was given an army corps in Gurko's Guards army, he became his favorite, quick-witted aide and readily picked up the advancements in military practice he'd missed out on during his year of captivity. Up until the last few days, Kornilov could not have guessed that his entire military life would suddenly take on this distorted continuation. When Gurko had enthusiastically seen him off—to use for the good of Russia his exclusive appointment to the thick of the revolutionary turmoil—Kornilov did not have so much as an inkling of the turns that awaited him.

But in Petrograd, before Kornilov could blink, the very first evening, Guchkov took him to Tsarskoye Selo, to the palace, and ordered him to prepare reliable officers for assignment here. Now it was clear what this was inclining toward, and it left a bitter taste.

The role of jail-keeper is repugnant to any soldier, but especially if you yourself were recently a prisoner for fifteen months and you know what the loss of freedom means.

Late the previous evening, Guchkov had sent Kornilov instructions. Early today he was to go to Tsarskoye Selo to arrest the Empress and set conditions for a military guard on the assumption that the arrested Tsar would be going there as well. Added to this were detailed written instructions for detention that had evidently been drawn up at the Ministry of Justice. In reading the instructions, one could only wonder at what refined minds these prison keepers had, their precaution, and their winding ways in forestalling any and all impulses of the prisoner.

Justice itself hid in the shadows, though, and sent a combat general to do its bidding, as if to mock the army. However, the order had come from the government, so how could he not carry it out? Service does not ask for consent.

Actually, Guchkov explained, and Kornilov was relieved to hear, this arrest was a temporary measure and primarily to protect the royal family from ruffians and rebels.

It had been readied in secret. Colonel Kobylinsky learned everything from Kornilov only on the train that morning. At the Tsarskoye Selo Train Station, they had summoned the Tsarskoye Selo commandant and, in anticipation of a time set by the Empress, discussed the location of the palace and park. Naturally, a topographical map is apolitical and a military guard can be posted purely as a combat assignment.

But military superiority was being applied to a solitary woman.

Although this woman, too . . . When after his escape Kornilov was presented at Court, he brought up the inhuman situation of our military prisoners in Austria and Germany, saying that they needed to be protected, at least through stricter treatment of the Germans and Austrians we had taken prisoner. But he had met with no agreement. The Empress said strangely:

"Oh, let Russia set an example of magnanimity!" A cooling ruffle ran over Kornilov's head. Fine for her to be magnanimous, sitting in her palace! . . .

Now it had fallen to Kornilov, and no one else, to announce the incredible news to the Empress. This legendary, carefree, high-class family, which had sailed high in the clouds over Kornilov's entire life to date, had suddenly plummeted to the earth, painfully—and now her cordon and watch was assigned to a combat general who had given his oath to the Emperor.

Not only that, all the children were ill, and the Empress was agonizing over that, and quite helpless, although she was trying to hold onto her pride—and all this clouded Kornilov and tied his tongue.

There was only the relief, which he was able to convey to her when they were alone, that this was temporary and for their sake.

With all her arrogant bearing, as imprinted on so many portraits, here she was barely holding on, tottering—and she looked at him gratefully. Her eyes were helpless, her smile forced.

Lavr Georgievich left the Empress even darker and sterner than when he had entered.

Now he had many small actions to carry out.

First, he ordered the telegraph and all the telephones in the palace turned off, leaving only two at the gates and two with the officers in the watch buildings.

Then he ordered all the individuals in the suite and the servants who were in the palace, a total of as many as 150 people, to gather in the hall. He told them that anyone who wished to leave had to leave immediately, and those wishing to remain with the royal family would henceforth have to submit to a prisoner regime.

Then he gave orders about replacing His Majesty's Personal Convoy and the Combined Regiment.

Then, of the many external palace doors, he made three of them operational and guarded by a sentry from now on. The rest he ordered locked and the keys given to the watch.

Through the new palace commandant, Staff Captain Kotzebue, whom he had brought with him from Petrograd at Guchkov's choice, he indicated the placement of guards inside and around the palace.

He drew up a list of assignments for watches from the Tsarskoye Selo garrison's Guards Riflery regiments and the order for sending out patrols. Twice a day, the guard would be checked by someone from District headquarters.

Preparatory instructions now had to be given to all those remaining who had dealings with the palace. All produce and rations had to be supplied only through the kitchen entrance, received and issued only in the duty officer's presence, and while this was happening, no conversations could be permitted about the individuals inside the palace. All incoming and outgoing letters, notes, and telegrams had to be reviewed by Staff Captain Kotzebue personally; only those of a domestic and medical nature could go through; the rest had to be passed on to Military District headquarters. Entrance to the palace was permitted only for summoned laborers and medics—and then accompanied by a sentry or duty officer. No meetings with individuals held in the Aleksandr Palace were allowed without permission from the District commander. Outings by the abdicated Emperor and former Empress were allowed during daylight hours of their own choosing, on the palace's great balcony and in the adjoining section of the park—but accompanied by the duty officer and with a reinforced outside guard.

All this came out as a wonderfully precise, almost military instruction. The Provisional Government could not have found a better executor.

He was finished, apparently, and was getting ready to leave, to go see Prime Minister Lvov and report on the implementation—when something new was reported to the general: in the forest past the park, a chapel had been discovered that was under guard, and in that chapel was Rasputin's body in a metal casket.

Yet another concern. He couldn't leave the body there, it would get violated. Dig him up? Move him to Petrograd?

[5 0 3 "]

(FEBRUARY'S FIGURES OF SPEECH)

. . . Newspaper bells are singing! . . . The great deed has come to pass that makes the head spin and the tongue fall mute. Russia is resurrected!

. . . One day, decades, maybe centuries from now, historical plays from the era of the Great Revolution will be staged in the people's theater.

. . . History will say that this was the greatest and best of revolutions, grandiose in its inner essence. . . . The Great Bloodless . . .

. . . Our Revolution is the eighth wonder of the world!

. . . The Great Revolution has splashed billions of sparks of happiness and hope into the hearts of the long-suffering Russian people.

Free Russia began its genesis seven days ago. Writing about it now would mean writing the Book of Genesis. It requires Biblical language. . . . Out of chaos came life. . . . The February Revolution came about with an unforeseenness that likens it to the creation of the world. . . . I am filled with joy and awe. I have seen the freedom and light I've been waiting for for a thousand years.

. . . Henceforth, 12 March shall be a great day for eternity. . . . The revolution struck with Cyclopean force. . . .

. . . From the greatest despotism in the world—to the greatest democracy! In a few days' time, the Russian revolution achieved what took other revolutions years. Russia immediately reached the heights of modern political culture.

THE RED SWAN. The fairytale swan with red feathers, the flamingo of the North, Petrograd, Petrograd, where are the words to glorify you? Let us be just as steely as Peter and, if necessary, just as merciless.

(Tan-Bogoraz)

. . . The banners' bloody color speaks to the people's will of steel.

. . .The violent whirlwind of revolution has cast down all the old gods from their pedestals and into the mud. . . . The funeral's final word has been said to a millennium of Russian life.

. . . The all-Russian prison called the Russian Empire is no more.

. . . the dynasty of Holstein-Gottorp, who called themselves Romanovs . . .

. . . Nikolai the Last, the overthrown despot . . . Murderer of the people, red with the blood of his countless victims . . .

. . . Entire generations of Russian liberation's passion bearers. We remember them with prayerful veneration.

. . . You will understand the happiness of our new existence later, when you wake up and see that you are not at the Okhrana, that there are no gendarmes dragging you out of bed. . . . We bend our knee to those who have made this miracle: the People! They are a storm in a red cloud.

. . . In truth, only a great people could prove capable of such great achievements . . .

. . . In the Duma, the work of giants has begun. . . . A brilliant pleiad of names known to all the people . . . Can you imagine a Russian parliament without Milyukov?

. . . Reorganizing state governance with one hand, prosecuting the war against the German hordes with the other.

. . . Exult, citizens! You are teaching the Germans to make freedom! Russian freedom offers an ominous warning to the Prussian cannibals. The victory of the Russian people has turned all the Germans' calculations on their head.

. . .When all Russia as one man lays on the altar of war . . . This is not the first time our heroes have endured deprivation. They have broken more than one campaign with only rusks in their knapsacks.

. . . Timid hearts say, How can this not harm the war? Be not disturbed! Now the war is being waged by a liberated Russian people.

. . . How wonderfully Kerensky put it: a people who in three days over-threw a dynasty that had ruled for three hundred years has nothing to fear!

. . . Russian democracy has revealed not only titanic energy but unimaginable moral discipline.

. . .The political coup deeply affected the popular psyche, so that not everyone could maintain their emotional equilibrium. . . .

. . . Our future, lit by freedom's bright sun, can be considered assured. Our present, though, is not easy.

. . . We are tracing designs on a magnificent pediment that our descendants will admire for thousands of years. But how are we to keep from spilling the nectar of the gods! . . .

. . .We have picked up the burning torch. We will use it to light candles in the temple of Russian freedom! But God save us from setting fire to the temple itself. . . .

. . . Our duty is to transform the rabble into a democracy.

. . . Happiness is close and possible in a way it has never been in the history of nations. The freedoms other peoples have been acquiring step by step fell to us here in one fell swoop . . .

. . . The Russian people will carry their sacred precepts to other peoples.

. . . What days! The revolution has unfolded as calm and beautiful as a blue river. The moment passed—and we rose up, great, mighty, and beautiful! Trumpets, be loud and cast the sounds of freedom into the air!

. . . We ascribe tremendous significance to this zeal. The people are living through the greatest holiday of the national soul, the likes of which have never been seen and never will again. . . . Don't lead the people away so quickly from the holiday of revolution to everyday life!

(Stock Exchange Gazette)

. . . The foam of revolution has covered our life with a vivid pattern of extraordinary beauty. . . .

. . . Why did we fear the red banner when Christ wiped away his sweat in the Garden of Gethsemene? This is the banner of the Russian revolution, too.

. . . A liturgical mood! . . . An act fanned by the spirit of certain sanctity! The inspiration of the Holy Spirit! The sluggish flesh of our daily life has plunged into the sweetest joy of being.

(F. Sologub)

. . . The stamp of God's presence is on every face. Never have people been so much together.

(Z. *Gippius*)

. . .We pinch ourselves in blissful and trying perplexity: is this a dream or waking? The lightning pace of our revolution is incalculable. . . . The rapid-fire tread of the Russian state—whom will it not grip?

. . . We have shown we can do anything. Nothing is out of our grasp, nothing is prohibited. . . .

Russia, one Swiss journalist says, has taken its place at civilization's head. Yes, we know that! We accept all the praise and enthusiasm with pride because they are deserved.

. . . A wonderful temple of freedom, equality, and brotherhood will send its peak into the infinite azure of the sky without burdening anyone's shoulders. . . .

. . . Like a red sun, a resurrected justice must shine on the Russian land, creating the holy cause of truth.

. . . Like a spring whirlwind, the revolution is ripping out the thistle of evil, refreshing the shoots of good, and sparkling with lightning bolts of great deeds. It knows no baseness, not an atom of cruelty. . . .

. . . pull out the last poisonous roots of what has passed into history!

. . . clear away the old bureaucratic mold. Rip out the weeds, rip them out mercilessly! No need to worry that there may be healthy plants among them: better to weed with sacrifices.

(*Stock Exchange Gazette*)

. . . The Star of the Orient has become the guiding star for the new manger of liberty and equality. . . .

*   *   *

THE CRICKETS WILL COME, BUT WILL THE HUT BE NEW?

*   *   *

[5 0 4]

Newspapers, newspapers, newspapers . . . Now that the Immensity had collapsed, irretrievably, beyond all saving, evidently, all that remained was getting to know the new life. There still were no classes at the women's courses, and Olda Orestovna, who had dressed early, as she would have for lectures, sat down not in her study but at her empty dining table and chafed herself with reading all those unfolded newspapers one after the other.

Until the newspapers started coming out, only the savage side of revolution could be seen, its teeth bared: on the fenders of fancy motorcars and inside them were ugly faces, and rifle barrels pointing at everyone they met, aiming at an invisible enemy. But now something new crept from the papers: vulgarity.

Every Petersburger had seen the revolution with his own eyes. But with the first newspaper page they were told about something quite different. There were vague mentions of "excesses" and "anarchy"—but no one was explaining exactly what that meant. Everyone knew soldiers were going from apartment to apartment and stealing, but the newspapers wrote: "thieves and hooligans dressed as soldiers"—as if "hooligans" were some known social class, or it was so easy for lots of people to dress as soldiers. Regarding the murder of Admiral Viren and the officers at Kronstadt, the press, having found its long-awaited freedom, wrote essentially approvingly ("he stood for the old regime") and did not see murders but rather the fact that in this way Kronstadt had joined the revolution. Inasmuch as the revolution had been immediately declared great, bloodless, sunny, and smiling, then, in the name of freedom's idols, they had to hush up officers' bodies and the policemen torn to shreds. All the red everywhere obscured the blood of those killed. The *New Times* even referred to the executed Valuyev as "deceased" rather than killed. And no newspaper besides *New Times* could bring itself to print an obituary of the murdered Admiral Nepenin. A dismal picture took shape: yesterday he was good, our hero and pride, and he had even *joined* us, but today he'd been killed—oh well, be done with you. Everyone in the city knew about the attack on and ransacking of the Astoria—but the newspapers reported that the Astoria had fired machine guns on the people. The most bald-faced lie was woven—but was also successful and caught on—about supposed police machine guns in attics and on roofs. First to spread it was Propper's *Stock Exchange Gazette*—the vulgarest of the vulgar—and it was picked up by everyone and repeated so many times, later even orally, that everyone believed it, although no one had ever found a single such police machine gun and the police had never even had them. Another separate lie: that machine guns had been fired from churches and bell towers. Only a stock exchange rag could tell a lie like that. But everyone believed it. You might as well put it in the history books.

The lie became the principle of newspapers starting from the very first days of this unchecked freedom. Actually, they hadn't been afraid of a lie before the revolution, either. And famous writers flocked to be printed in that *Stock Exchange Gazette*.

Newspaper liars had already seized the English press, too. A pushy *Stock Exchange Gazette* reporter made his way onto the pages of the *Observer* and advised the English to refrain from criticizing the new Russian government at the moment when the Russian people (he was speaking for the people, naturally) were in such need of a sympathetic attitude.

Olda Orestovna went to see the incinerated District Court—the unfortunate creation of the unlucky Bazhenov, his only building in all Petersburg, and it was this one that had burned down. These were grandiose ruins. The interiors had burned up, the staircases had collapsed, and the statue of Justice had been smashed. All the newspapers had mentioned this fire and all, apparently, with pride, as an achievement. No one wrote the word "barbarity."

On the other hand, they adopted a pitiless and mocking tone with regard to the arrested dignitaries and maliciously described the impotence and complaints of these seventy- and eighty-year-old men, how one of them was so weak he could barely raise his eyelids to see who approached and another was afraid to drink raw milk. A *Stock Exchange Gazette* correspondent explained to the arrested General Putyatin, who did not see the reasons for his detention: "Possibly you were taken as a hostage"—and the newspaper published this without blushing. As if about a favor, they wrote that the administration had magnanimously *allowed* the arrested gendarmes to accept a bed and food from home. What this meant was that at the Tsarskoye Selo high school and in the Horse Guards barracks, the arrested men were not being fed and had not been given a place to sleep, treatment no one before had ever dared when holding revolutionaries. And of course they wrote all sorts of vile stuff about the overthrown dynasty. Some newspapers called the Empress "Sashka" and made up nonsense about how she had organized an assassination attempt against the Tsar and how she had arranged for chandeliers in the palace to fall—in order to glorify Rasputin's prediction. They chewed voluptuously over Rasputin's murder. *Russian Will*, yet another stock exchange shark, where Leonid Andreev had sparkled, wrote that in 1914 military intelligence had supposedly got wind of a spy radio station at Tsarskoye Selo, but they had had to stop their investigation. Newspaper poets published vulgar verse broadsides about the reign of Nikolai II that included depictions and caricatures of the abdicated Tsar.

Basest of all, though, was the report, savored through all the newspapers, that during the Revolution the Emperor had intended to open the front to the Germans and supposedly had given Voeikov his consent to do this. Even if anyone in the suite could have come up with such an idea—out of frustration, blurted something out, not as a real plan—they would never have dared say such a thing to the Emperor! (It never occurred to any newspaper man that the Germans simply *would not have entered* those gates. What more could they wish for than our revolution?)

Olda was exhausted, both by this lie and by how clearly she saw it and because she could never convince the reader herd.

For so many years the liberal press had dreamed of freedom (while actually having plenty of it) and had promised that the moment freedom came . . . But now what had come was this unexpected, unbroken baseness, this thoroughgoing, vilest ignobleness. And not a single protesting voice! Nastiest of all was the rightist *New Times*, which had changed its tune overnight. Its readers were astonished to learn now that it had always hated the monarchy (even ascribing executions to Elisabeth's reign!), had wished for only revolution, and they were even prepared to throw out Orthodoxy, keeping bald-faced nationality without all things holy, under the headline of a "Free Russia," as if up until now there had been no life of any kind in Russia but only unending servitude and a police inspector in charge of everything. Newspapers unwilling to change their tune were simply shut down tight now. A nasty sycophantic tone came over that long dreamed-of free press.

The newspapers were disgusting, yes, but that was because they spewed society's vile epidemic: the fear of standing out from everyone else that had erupted during the days of freedom. Now that the "police inspector was gone" and "we can breathe," people's greatest fear was standing out from everyone else, of being less enraptured than their neighbors with the revolution. The disease arose of not seeming sufficiently joyous. In a few days, a wave had risen up to which no one dared run counter, no one dared object out loud no matter what nonsense was being touted, what absurdity committed. The dictatorship of the current. Everyone all over Russia had been seized by the truckling of congratulatory telegrams to the government, which they sent to Petrograd in incalculable numbers. The Russian People's Union of Monarchy in Moscow "perforce was able to see the light along with the entire country." The Mariinsky Theater choir organized a service-performance in Kazan Cathedral—which was fashionable to attend. Motor-cars with red flags pulled up to the church porch, the choir sang the Cherubic Hymn and Credo marvelously, an actor read the Epistle, and Archpriest Ornatsky proclaimed that, thanks to the dawn of Russian freedom, the Orthodox Church had finally rid itself of caesaropapism. In Rogachev they tried to create an authority counter to the Soviet of Deputies—and were immediately proclaimed "pogrom-makers." Some engineer on the Voronezh Railway had the nerve to hold up a telegram from Bublikov, whom he'd never heard of—and now that engineer had been hounded and let go.

There was a highly characteristic instance with Pokhvisnev, head of the Administration of Posts and Telegraphs. A meeting of employees demanded he explain how he dared hide Stürmer in his apartment during the days of revolution. Pokhvisnev stood in front of the meeting of his subordinates, pale and terrified, and tried to justify himself: first Stürmer had ordered him over the phone to send him a coachman and a horse. What right did he have to refuse? And all of a sudden Stürmer himself arrived unexpectedly in this carriage at the Post Office and asked for refuge. Out of considerations of, well, simple courtesy, Pokhvisnev couldn't drive him out right away, but he did ask Stürmer to leave as soon as he could. If the crowd noticed, they would attack the apartment. Supposedly Pokhvisnev and his wife had tried to talk Stürmer into surrendering, and he stayed all of, oh, thirty minutes in their apartment. The assembly was hotly indignant. He should not have hidden a state criminal for even thirty minutes but should have telephoned the State Duma and asked them to send a guard to arrest him! Now the downed Pokhvisnev had a different explanation. It wasn't even thirty minutes! No more than seven or ten! I didn't even let him into the apartment from the vestibule! I didn't even let him speak over my telephone. I didn't even let him rest. That's what I told him: there is no room for you here! On your way and be in public! I pushed him out of the vestibule. I've never had anything to do with politics, gentlemen! My activities have all been open for all to see! . . . But the meeting was indignant and voted 213 to 93, expressing no confidence in Pokhvisnev, and to publish this in the press, so that the provincial post offices could express their opinion of their chief's immoral action. All Pokhvisnev could do was state that he would immediately resign his post.

Those who objected out loud during the first few days of the revolution were simply arrested.

It was vile breathing this atmosphere of defamation—and Shnitnikov's tune rang out boldly, gratingly, about why he was refusing to serve as deputy minister to Kerensky:

"I am a supporter of a democratic republic, but I respect sincere monarchists"—and this was in the city duma, publicly! Incredible!

Yes, but where was the throne's support? Our state order did not show it had either implementers or friends. Stunningly, not an official was to be found who would say out loud that due to his convictions he could not remain in service. On the contrary, everyone tried to assure everyone else that their fondest wish had always been overthrowing the old order. Those who had recently extolled the Tsar were now flinging mud at him. There wasn't a single donkey hoof that didn't hasten to kick at something it had recently cringed before.

But even more: where was that glorious aristocracy that had triumphed over Russia's expanse for three centuries? The aristocracy, whose face had expressed the face of Russia for three centuries—had been swept away in a single day, as if it had never been. In this fateful week, not one of those great names—Gagarin, Dolgoruky, Obolensky, Lopukhin—had flashed by in a noble sense—not a single person from the entire class, a class so cosseted, so well rewarded! They were dreaming of a "magical deliverance," but none of them was trying to do anything. Many of the aristocrats and senior Guards officers had put on red bows!

And where were the bishops? The Church?

Even worse than many, though, were the members of the dynasty itself, who had shamefully hastened to tell reporters things learned in intimate conversations, especially Kirill Vladimirovich and his Viktoria. And that busybody Nikolai Mikhailovich. And that overblown knight Nikolai Nikolaevich, who had no idea he was copying another uncle of another king—Philippe-Égalité, who had voted for his nephew's execution, but by doing so was not saved from the guillotine.

In those days, the French Revolution had gripped the minds of society on a mythical plane. Nonetheless, the French monarchy resisted for three years, while ours—all of three days. How on earth could everything have fallen apart so very quickly? When the old order was dying in France, there were people who openly went to the scaffold for it. They had their own legends, their own knights—Lavoisier, André Chenier.

Even the Emperor himself! He was one of the first to set an example of total and instantaneous retreat. How could he—how **dare** he—reject his anointment? (This brought to mind Georgi's sour grin. Had he been right in a way? . . .) The Emperor was the first to recognize this present government.

And following this—how could the air be scorched so instantly and massively?—and now it was dangerous not to admire the revolution, not to demand the Tsar's arrest. Arrest for what? After all, he had abdicated voluntarily, had not started a war for the throne, had not summoned a foreign power, as Louis XVI had—so why arrest him? . . .

Vilest of all was that even Olda now was turning coward in this scorched air. She disgusted herself. The professors at the Bestuzhev courses—some out of sincere conviction, others out of this new truckling—agreed to sign a humiliating appeal to our "dear students": instead of a direct order to show up to class at last, the council of professors felt it desirable as much as possible to establish a proper academic life and *ask* the students to help in this.

And although Andozerskaya disagreed completely with this tone, she could not let herself stand out and so signed as well.

But there was even worse. Two of these "dear students," Lenartovich and Sheinis, showed up at Olda Orestovna's home without a warning telephone call, ringing directly at the door, and requested—though this did not resemble a request, this was an insistence, in sure tones—that she donate to the freed political prisoners.

Olda Orestovna considered these political prisoners wreckers of life. She did not sympathize with them in the least and did not want to help, and she knew from the newspapers that the stock exchange committees had already donated half a million rubles to them—but the professor, at home, facing these two feverish students, not only could not express a single one of her objections, she could not come up with a handy phrase to dodge their demands. She didn't even look them straight in their demanding eyes but cast her own cold eyes downward.

She brought them fifty rubles, despising herself.

She had been shaken even in her own home by the change in, if not the betrayal of her maid Nyura. Always so loyal and agreeable, at the start of the revolution she had rushed to rescue Olda Orestovna's watch from the soldiers, which she did, but in this past week Nyura had started running off to meetings, returning distracted and gloomy, responding brusquely—such that Olda Orestovna expected some insult or outburst at any moment.

There it was—everything was falling apart. The streets were full of mer-rymakers—and Russia was deserted.

And not a letter from Georgi since his departure. Though it was true mail delivery was very bad. She wrote two letters to him at his address at the front, not knowing where else.

How had he survived all this? This whole collapse? What had he done, attempted?

But this was madness! Something could be done! Something important, major could be done, to somehow act decisively, to rally someone! . . .

They were all there at the front, a monolith, officers of their emperor—so why not bellow, why not thunder terribly, why not blow in a spirit that would sweep away the entire revolution as if it were cardboard?

The puzzle was, what were they doing there? What a representative giant General Evert had seemed in the photographs. Here was a servant of the Tsar! What about him? Yet he, too, had already hastened to retreat.

Write Georgi another letter? A very long one. Describe all this base new air, when it had become dangerous to think differently from everyone else. (Could one still write candidly in a letter? Would they intercept it?)

Ask him what was going on? How did he understand it? How did he un-derstand it *now*? What was he seeing? Doing?

The lady had found her knight and hero. Why wasn't he fighting for her colors?

[505]

The previous night—how was it Alekseev had decided so easily that the Tsar's order for the army would be beneficial? He was weighed down with guilt before the Tsar—but before dawn he awoke in alarm with a sense of the opposite guilt: was this even loyal with respect to the government? The Tsar was subject to arrest—and Alekseev was distributing his order to the army? This was turning out to be a major, politically important step and could not be viewed as a personal favor. In the overheated Petrograd situ-ation, how might this look there?

Alekseev agonized until morning came. He very much, very much did not want to turn to Petrograd after everything he had written to them in the past few days. The new regime had treated GHQ more insultingly than the old one had, as if they were subordinates whose opinion was not even interesting.

But fear for his action was gnawing at him, and he had to go to them. Al-though formally GHQ was not subordinate to the War Ministry, for the past few days it had come about that it was. He sent a telegram request to Guchkov and sent him the text of the Tsar's order.

Very soon after he received a prohibition on any kind of dissemination or printing!

Ah, he had predicted correctly! He gave instructions to immediately halt the order's transmission. It had already slipped out: they'd transmitted it to the army groups and were now trying to have it halted, so that it wouldn't be sent to the armies and corps.

Halted—just like the abdication Manifesto. Such was the fate of the Emperor's documents.

After that, he had to go to the Emperor's farewell with the staff officers. Once again Alekseev felt awkward, a feeling outweighed, however, by an awareness of his duty. Both stopping the order and concealing from the Tsar his imminent arrest—this was Alekseev's duty as chief of staff. His duty to the army, which remained higher than his duty to his former, now removed boss.

Alekseev feared only that the Emperor might overhear something and ask him outright whether they were arresting him or not. In any case, Alekseev did not have the right to reveal to him the secret of an encoded telegram, but it would hurt him to lie to the Emperor's trusting eyes. He was utterly guileless, after all, the Emperor, and for a man this might not be so bad. But for a monarch, it was impossible.

No, everything went smoothly in the Duty Hall. This was no place for personal explanations and questions, and the Emperor was unusually emotional.

While he was delivering his faltering speech, and later paused in tears, Alekseev felt even more sympathy for him as for someone weak and small. Precisely because he knew about the imminent arrest and about the difficult trials that might now await the Emperor, he did sincerely wish him happiness in his upcoming life. He truly did wish him well.

The Emperor embraced Alekseev and kissed him—earnestly, not formally.

And then he left—so for a few more distressing hours the possibility of conversation or explanation was ruled out. After all the farewells, the Emperor went to see his mother at the train station in order to wait there for the envoys, no longer to return to GHQ.

All the easier. Now he was no longer in the way.

And at the station he would have no ability to resist arrest.

Given all the awkwardness and difficult waiting of the final hours, though, Alekseev could do nothing during this time other than work. The staff officers and even Lukomsky and Klembovsky could understand a day or two as a break between the two Supreme Commanders—and now Nikolai Nikolaevich would declare himself with a firm hand!—but Alekseev alone knew that it would be yet another new abdicator and pariah arriving—and meanwhile the army's helm was wobbling without a firm hand.

He had nothing more urgent to do, though, than draw up the appeals he had promised Guchkov. And this matter, like every other matter, Alekseev could not assign to anyone else's pen either—so he himself strung it out in his tiny, even hand:

"Soldiers and citizens of free Russia! A terrible danger is advancing from the enemy's direction. According to our information, the Germans are building up. . . . The seizure of Petrograd would mean the rout of Russia and would enthrone the old regime with the addition of the German yoke. At the dawn of freedom, we are threatened by the danger of becoming German laborers. . . ."

In fact, Alekseev saw no danger of a German offensive, but he actually would have liked it to arise and for the army to tighten up in the face of it.

Right then Brusilov telegraphed that due to the political situation he would have to remove the royal monogram from his epaulets.

Alekseev responded, albeit after the fact: the abdicated emperor himself, understanding the situation, had given permission to remove adjutant general monograms and aiguillettes.

Documents – 17

French military mission in Russia, 21 March
FROM GENERAL JANIN TO GENERAL ALEKSEEV

Commander-in-Chief General Nivelle asks you be informed that, in agreement with the British High Command, he has set the date for the beginning of joint offensives on the Western Front for 8 April. This date cannot be postponed. We need to begin the offensive as soon as possible.

In accordance with the decision made at the conference of Allies, I request that you begin the offensive by Russian forces by early April. It is essential that your operations and ours begin simultaneously, within a few days of each other. The French High Command hopes that the offensive by the Russian armies will pursue the goal of achieving decisive results and will be calculated for prolonged conduct.

Gen. Nivelle is insisting to Your Excellency on full satisfaction of this request.

[506]

Today, after breakfast, the battery commander made his presence known by summoning the gentlemen officers to his dugout.

All four went.

In the gray light of the dugout, Boyer was sitting at a table by a little window, tired. His face was ashen, the bags under his eyes distinct, his look shell-shocked.

Chairs and stools had been readied for the officers. They sat in a semicircle. Staff papers lay in front of the lieutenant colonel.

He was silent a little longer, his eyes half-shut even. Then he began, and his voice trailed as over sharp rocks:

"Gentlemen, yesterday you read the outrageous, self-styled 'order.' One might hope that this was drunken raving and had nothing to do with the Russian army. But just now we have received an order from the new War

Minister. And I must tell you . . . I must ask you . . . Captain, be so kind as to read it out loud."

Sokhatsky began reading from the printed page.

Addressing by titles was abolished, and the formal "you" for soldiers was now mandatory. All restrictions on soldiers were abolished, including on membership in political societies.

This really wasn't the same "order" from yesterday, was it? In fact, though, streets, streetcars, clubs, and political societies—there was none of that anywhere near the front. Sanya was waiting for the decisive point. Was the minister really going to confirm that officers were barred access to weapons? No, he didn't hear that. Well, then this was still a perfectly tolerable order.

But Boyer's eye—or his pince-nez—glittered with bafflement. Incredible! Impossible!

Chernega's wide head was firmly set.

Ustimovich sat with his same mute, submissive hope.

And the lieutenant colonel noted that his officers were not shocked.

"But gentlemen, what kind of citizens can our soldiers be? What political clubs? How far can we go with these absurdities?"

Inwardly, Sanya was in lively disagreement. If they weren't citizens, then it was our fault. Someday they would have to be made citizens. Not that war was the best moment for that. But after the war, nothing could force this— and again nothing would happen. We have to begin sometime. Not to begin would be disgraceful.

He pitied the lieutenant colonel, though, and made no objection, even with his gaze.

It was gray in the dugout and seemed to smell of medicines, like a sick-room.

It was gray—and they said nothing.

They said nothing—but he didn't let them go.

Not letting rank put any distance between them, the lieutenant colonel slowly brought out his final conviction, as if he were pulling on his own sinews:

"Gentlemen! Russia has perished! . . ."

And all of a sudden—as if from a merry barrel—Chernega started muttering, quite forwardly:

"No, colonel, sir, she is not lost! There are hordes of people. If need be, we will always save her."

The lieutenant colonel leaned back in bitter recognition.

"Who exactly is going to save her? Not you, Ensign Chernega?"

Catching nothing contradictory, Chernega droned even more vigorously:

"Exactly so, colonel, sir! If necessary, I too will save her!"

Boyer shook his head ever so slightly, in bitter approval of his nerve.

No, in Sanya's view, the minister's order was not all that dreadful. It could even have been cause for relief, had not old man Zabudsky been lying on a Petrograd staircase with a smashed head. As were others, maybe hundreds.

(Sanya told Chernega about the professor's death, and Chernega said, practically as an afterthought: "Well, God rest his soul.")

The lieutenant colonel propped up his head with both hands on the table, to keep it steady. Never before had he known that pose. His head had always stood up on its collar and sailed through the air. He asked the captain to read as well the other orders, while they were gathered anyway.

After all, no arrow of an order could pass through the army pyramid without picking up additional feathers at every stage.

Sokhatsky began reading the typewritten pages. Western Army Group Commander Evert's order followed:

". . . Now, when events in the interior provinces of our Fatherland might trouble your hearts . . . I address to you an official order and a fatherly injunction."

This "fatherly" was an outdated tone. Evert hadn't found a new one.

". . . The first main demand of our new government and my first demand is to maintain strict military . . . The second demand is not to waste time and nerves on pointless discussion . . . but to look the enemy in the eye and think about how to crush him. . . ."

Go explain to the soldiers that they should think only about the German, not about the Tsar's abdication.

Now, an order for the 2nd Army from General-of-the-Infantry Smirnov:

". . . To you, brave officers! More than ever you must be the soldier's mentors. Associate more closely. Explain what he doesn't understand. Treat him with complete confidence, and he will respond in kind."

Oh, how true! What a pure voice Smirnov turned out to have! But—if only one understood everything well oneself!

Now there was also the order for the Grenadier Corps:

". . . In the theater of military actions, saluting while standing at attention is replaced by a simple mandatory touching of the headgear, the symbol of the armed forces' unity. . . ."

And for the 1st Grenadier Division: set three Lenten days a week in all units, and four in infirmaries.

They were thrown for a loop. All the fragments of the Immensity had yet to be fitted together—but the small things in life, in actual fact, should flow along even in time of revolution.

And also an order for the 1st Grenadier Artillery Brigade. A commission had investigated the 1st division and found that in the 1st and 3rd batteries, horse maintenance was excellent and the horses were in very good condition. . . . (A smile spread across Chernega's face.) "There were skinny ones in the 2nd battery. The soldiers' dugouts were found in good order, the soldiers neatly dressed, looking like fine fellows, for which we thank them. . . . Where garlic has come out—acquire it, no matter the cost.

And once again, an order from the Western Army Group commander, dated 19 March: all companies and batteries are to start putting in vegetable gardens.

And an order for the brigade: start transporting manure for the brigade's gardens.

Life went on! You could turn all Petrograd on its head, but the brigade had to live, and maintain its men and horses, and hold the front.

This was understandable and certain for every last man.

The lieutenant colonel asked sadly:

"Lieutenant Lazhenitsyn. Line up the battery and read all this out."

[5 0 7]

Peshekhonov was dashing about taking care of things—but the city was so snowy white, not sprinkled with ash from factory smokestacks, and sunny, and the sky was blue and pure, just the first bit of factory smoke, and everything covered in red flags. The revolution had won. Think of it! But except for the first evening, he hadn't had a day to rejoice, so much was crowded into his head, and some of it still had not reached his consciousness or had been immediately knocked out by something else.

The machine-gun regiment in the House of the People, its machine-gun barrels still aimed on Kronverksky Prospect, had become Peshekhonov's nightmare. Added to all the unpleasantness with latrines, streams of urine had already drenched the snow to the sidewalk, there were also several illnesses, the doctors suspected typhus, and meanwhile idle gunners were sitting in the taverns and teahouses and could spread typhus through the city. But they clung to their awkward theater building. In the daytime, Peshekhonov kept thinking about them, and at night he dreamed that a general epidemic had broken out or that the soldiers had gone out on the streets with machine guns and were cutting down everyone in succession.

He continued to be in touch with the regimental committee. Might they have been convinced after all that there was no room on the Petersburg side and would agree to return to Oranienbaum? He wasn't getting his hopes up. But suddenly, yesterday morning, this reply came: the regiment had agreed to return to Oranienbaum, but only if there was an order from the Soviet.

What luck! Peshekhonov immediately went to the Executive Committee, got there before the session began, and asked Chkheidze and others to issue this order as quickly as possible, right now, within the hour. The comrades from the Soviet went on their guard. Remove troops from Petrograd? Was there some counterrevolutionary scheme in this?

He kept trying to persuade them. If the gunners themselves had agreed, that meant they had had enough. Later they informed him that the Executive Committee had approved this decision and sent Skobelev to the People's House. Well, he'd accomplished at least one major task!

Today he was waiting for the machine-gun regiment to head home. But all of a sudden this came in: the soldiers had changed their minds and weren't going to go. But why? Peshekhonov himself rushed to the House of the People. The sergeants from the regimental committee explained:

"This isn't an order. It says, 'The Soviet *requests.*' That means we can stay."

"No, we're not going."

Something here had changed in the past few hours. Apparently some university students and young ladies had talked the gunners out of it. Peshekhonov guessed this had come from the Bolsheviks, whose headquarters were cater-corner across Kronverksky. Them!

He raced back to the Tauride Palace and implored Chkheidze to come himself, if necessary, but Chkheidze was sapped. If they hadn't listened to Skobelev, after all. . . .

Nothing shifted. They were staying!

And the latrines were just as before.

Peshekhonov had another frustrating concern on these trips to the Tauride Palace: motorcars.

Motorcars had become this revolution's demons. Nothing of the kind had been seen in 1905. They were racing around the city for no reason even now. The militia had started stopping them assiduously and checking their documents. There was also the "black motorcar"! No one had actually seen it, but everyone had heard that it was shooting militiamen, though not one had fallen. It was a favorite Petrograd legend, and every morning everyone rushed to the papers to see whether the "black motorcar" had been caught.

The problem was that everyone now wanted to have motorcars. During the first few days, they were requisitioned in the name of the revolution, during the next they were simply stolen, driven out of garages, but now the owners dared complain—and to whom if not the commissariat? Sort it out! Some demanded a search; others were prepared to pay generously that minute just to get back their motorcar. But the commissariat's motorcar department, Peshekhonov had begun to suspect, was both taking money from owners and returning motorcars to owners and then getting money from somewhere else again. There was shady business going on under his nose, and he had no time to catch them out. It reached him that somewhere someone was altering the license plates and changing their outer features, and that some motorcars might even have been driven off to other towns. Then Peshekhonov moved some people from his motorcar department to other departments and chose replacements—but then misunderstandings began with the Soviet's central motorcar department in the Tauride Palace. Before this they'd had no complaints for the Petersburg side, but now they'd started confiscating their motorcars. He brought the former suspects back to the department—and all was well again.

Indeed, Peshekhonov found a scoundrel not just in the motorcar department but also in the head of his food supply department, on whom he relied, who had joined him on the very first day in the Tauride Palace and now was revealed by chance to be pilfering and selling.

There was another worry. Yet another militia besides the commissariat's had appeared on his Petersburg side, so that it could even come to a clash on the streets between the two militias. Peshekhonov's was not that wonderful—it was undisciplined and inexperienced—but there couldn't be two militias next door to each other! Some third militia had appeared in the plants as well.

But this wasn't all. The commissariat, was that an authority at all? That pressing moment when he'd been appointed had been lost, and now it was impossible to tell to whom he was subordinate. In a few parts of the city there were no commissariats whatsoever, and on the Vyborg side there was the powerful Bolshevik one. Peshekhonov's body of active functionaries—lawyers, university students, male and female, and minor officials—had always been the most progressively democratic, but without any practical experience.

Peshekhonov craved authority over himself, wanted to support it, and also for himself to rest on instructions, laws, directives. But there was no connection with any superior authority. The Provisional Government had not decreed any local self-governance for Petrograd or the country. In the central institutions, Peshekhonov was met by bafflement. They didn't see what kind of authority he represented. He was never sent any instructions or inquiries.

And so, the central authority was left without a buttress, and the local authorities couldn't counter the harrowing willfulness. Here, nearby, the Bolsheviks had seized Kshesinskaya's mansion, and Peshekhonov could not summon up the decisiveness even to hint at evicting them. If it was so easy for the crowd to sweep away a regime that had lasted for 300 years, then how hard would it be for it to sweep away this week-old commissariat?

[508]

Today, in the large Duma hall, the Soviet's soldier section was again in noisy session—while across the corridor, in an uncomfortable room that they were in any case vacating tomorrow, here for the last day, met the Executive Committee. Presiding, as always, was Chkheidze.

Chkheidze understood his chairmanship in the Soviet and Executive Committee as a service of the greatest importance to the revolution—and he understood this not ambitiously, as his own mounting significance (he had unhesitatingly refused to be a minister), but as an opportunity to serve that to which his entire political life had led. He was suffering because far from the entire membership viewed the EC in that way. They would step out, not come to sessions at all, or come late without even apologizing, or disrupt the sessions, pass notes back and forth, and even simply chat. As he opened a session and looked at the agenda, Chkheidze could never be certain he would have a quorum, or that it wouldn't scatter. Indeed, the very concept of a quorum had ceased to exist in the EC. However many were there, however many voted. You couldn't even count exactly how many EC members there were altogether; they were constantly getting added from various sources. Ask Nikolai Semyonovich—he could never give an exact figure, but with the added soldiers it was already over thrity-five. That made it hard to work. Today the esteemed, gray-haired Chaikovsky, with his big beard, had come and sat down, and there was no way he could refuse membership to such a senior, distinguished revolutionary. And there was no getting around approving one member from the officers—so they approved Lieutenant Stankevich, who was in any case a revolutionary democrat, only in military uniform. He, at least, sat and listened very attentively.

Also, the agenda was fraught with surprises. Sometimes it went unfinished to such an extent that Chkheidze would take the previous day's page and continue on it for that day's session. But even the remainder couldn't be finished the next day. New questions were constantly popping up—from life itself, from telephone calls, from importunate outsiders—and from their own members, each of whom considered his question more important than all the others. There was a lot of shouting and many misunderstandings and clashes, and everyone was exhausted.

So it was today. The agenda included an appeal to the international proletariat. Relations with the government (they'd been rewriting this for two days already). Reviving work at the plants. The situation in Kronstadt. A funeral for martyrs of the revolution.

Rather than start in on any of this, they were immediately interrupted by a messenger from the 1st Machine-Gun Regiment. Yesterday it had expressed a desire to leave Petrograd, and today the regiment had changed its mind and wanted to have a final order from the EC. This changed the picture completely. It was one thing for a regiment to go voluntarily. No one could reproach the EC. It was another if it went under EC pressure. The entire soldier mass might be outraged at this and the Executive Committee itself might crack. (Across the corridor, in the Duma hall, soldiers were in fact noisily discussing whether removing even a single military unit from Petrograd could be allowed.) So the agenda began with the machine-gun regiment, and people expressed different, confused opinions, and they decided to send Skobelev back there now for talks.

Right then, quite irrelevantly, someone put in that the Petrograd clergy had had the impudence to ask to be allowed to participate in the victims' funeral. This outraged everyone on the EC. A funeral with clergy would lose all its revolutionary pathos and stray into religious superstition. Chkheidze himself loathed priests as he did cockroaches and frogs, and he twitched all over at the thought of that repulsive scene, which he didn't even want to imagine. They refused.

Right then Chaikovsky took the floor, with his enormous bald spot and still firm eyes, saying that they must arrest the priest at the head of the navy's clergy, who had still not been arrested. They so resolved.

They were going on about arrests when Shekhter jumped up and said he had information that some arrested policemen were being released. Impossible! What on earth was going on in our revolutionary capital, comrades? Kerensky, that's who was responsible for this! As Chkheidze's deputy in the Soviet he was supposed to be sitting right by his side, but he had not showed up for a single session. He found the time to dash off to Moscow and sit in on the government, but not with us. Chkheidze took great offense at Kerensky. They recorded: instruct Shekhter to personally inform Kerensky that it was impermissible to release policemen.

Then, as it had for several days, the *Petrograd Gazette* was asking for permission to publish. A reactionary newspaper. Refuse again.

The SR Zenzinov, ecstatic and foolish, interrupted: Breshko-Breshkovskaya, the "grandmother of the revolution," had left Minusinsk exile five days ago, and we still were not preparing a worthy welcome for her!

Rafes, due to the unimportance of the questions, took it that matters were wrapping up and so added his: congratulations had come to the Soviet of Deputies from the Left Social Democrats of the Swedish parliament, as well as from the entire Kirghiz populace.

Stop this! Chkheidze was beside himself. He started shouting at the top of his weak lungs: Don't interfere with the agenda! Don't keep coming in and going out! Don't have loud conversations! Quieter there, by the food table.

And seeing little Himmer with the feltish hair pacing nervously, beside himself, from corner to corner, stretching up on tip-toe, rubbing his broad hands, he rasped:

"We are discussing the draft appeal to the international proletariat!"

Himmer lit up, grabbed his prepared page from the windowsill, and began reading his draft in a thin, shaky voice. Chkheidze considered this appeal the most correct and important business. But it was met by incessant noise: the Bolsheviks making a racket with Krotovsky and Aleksandrovich, then the rightist Mensheviks and the Bund. And as everyone tore away at the points they opposed, very little remained of the draft. Chkheidze banged his palm on the table many times, calling them to order. But it was evident that they couldn't sort out or approve the appeal at this session. Right then a confident Steklov walked in and it was immediately agreed that he and Himmer would do more work on this draft.

Steklov had brought his Bonch-Bruevich from *Izvestia*—to provide explanations with regard to the insults against Ruzsky. Paunchy, humorously dressed army-fashion, Bonch-Bruevich explained that there were no insults there, that the top generals were all insincere, GHQ was a counterrevolutionary nest, and deserved a much rougher talking-to.

Rightly so, perhaps. Although yesterday Ruzsky's delegation had impressed the Executive Committee here, perhaps getting overly emotional in front of Ruzsky was harmful. They left it without follow-up.

Right then Bogdanov walked in and said that the soldier section was storming against Order no. 2 and demanding that it be declared only a draft order, not an actual order.

What the hell was this! Everything was tangled up. The order had already been limited by a clarifying telegram. But to say that such an order had never been issued at all—the EC still could not spit in its own face. But it couldn't ignore the soldier section, either.

The solution was to issue yet another clarification in *Izvestia*.

Then, on the subject of protests—there came a protest by the Kadet EC against Order no. 1. What, a discussion with those people—they can go to . . . No, the same thing, but written politely.

Comrades. Comrades! On resumption of work at the plants. Kuzma Antonovich, what is the situation?

Gvozdev had also arrived recently—worried, morose, he sat at the corner of the table and examined all the documents through spectacles. Not everyone stood up to report, but he did. What was going on at the plants! Total lack of coordination. At the Putilov, they'd started the shrapnel plant up and the laboratory, and the rest had demanded that the Romanovs be arrested and the banks confiscated first. The Russo-Baltic had already got the eight-hour day, and the Langensiepen had announced it for itself, but the Tube Factory had gotten rid of the entire administration and appointed a new one itself. Sestroretsk, Izhora, the printers, and the Old Parviainen were about to start but were demanding an eight-hour day. The Neva shipbuilders had agreed to overtime pay, the railroaders were demanding democratization, and the bakers were demanding confiscation of flour from the owners. But the entire Moscow district was wholly opposed and cursed them roundly, no one there was going back to work.

What could the Executive Committee decide? Not all the members even knew the plants' names. Here, the working mass was not listening. That meant issuing yet another confirmation of the resolution, energetically repeating that it was time to go to work. Calling on our comrade workers, saying that there is still hope for agreement with the factory owners. But also to warn the factory owners that retaliatory closings of enterprises were disgraceful in the days we were living through, and the Soviet of Deputies would not allow that kind of tyranny over those fighting for liberation. The Soviet would pose this issue of handing over such plants to worker collectives.

Actually, what the whole dispute had been about, and what business owners had to give, was an eight-hour workday at the same salary. But right then Bogdanov, who was constantly scurrying about, brought something from the soldier section: They're dissatisfied! They're making noises over the workers demanding an eight-hour day. While we soldiers have an unmeasured day! And at the front, in the trenches, we're round the clock. So does that mean they're smarter than us? Either no one gets an eight-hour day or everyone does!

Chkheidze clutched his poor, bald, aching head: No, this is a madhouse! Fighting a war eight hours a day? No, there was no way to please everyone. What was to be done, comrades?

No one knew.

Popular waves beat mercilessly against the Executive Committee's chest, and anger mounted at the government, which knew nothing of this, had retreated into the quiet and luxury of the Mariinsky Palace—and was dozing away there peacefully. What were they doing there? And what were they preparing in secret from us and the people?

People became heatedly agitated from different directions. The moment they gave this any thought, suspicions began tearing away at them. How did we let them slip from proletarian oversight? They're going to deceive us! They'd like nothing better than to restore the Tsar, anything reactionary! We have to know their intentions in advance—and whatever they do, not approve it!

The imposing Steklov—his significance on the Executive Committee had been increasing and he was already being promoted as deputy chairman—proposed, standing, that they immediately choose a permanent five-man commission and instruct it to constantly liaise with the government. Let it convey everything of ours to them and ask it everything necessary.

The Bolsheviks immediately: Don't! There can't be any understandings with the Provisional Government by definition. That is self-deception, we'll only get bogged down in negotiations.

But the majority liked the proposal, and three people were chosen, without so much as a discussion, so well did everyone recognize them, the Executive Committee's top three: Chkheidze, Skobelev, and Steklov.

And after them?

There had to be one military man, so they don't outsmart us. They agreed on taciturn, practical Filippovsky.

And the fifth?

It was felt they should add someone reasonable and prudent, and the rightists proposed Gvozdev (who had not yet left).

But Chkheidze and others saw little Himmer getting upset, writhing, twisting, even turning on one foot out of impossible impatience, sending looks to one, whispering to another. How could the most important discussions take place without him? After all, he was their main theoretician, and it was he who had proposed the bourgeois government!

They began arguing. The Mensheviks had seen through Himmer's pretense of not being part of a faction, but in fact he was playing a dirty trick on them, being the most leftist of leftists. Himmer had already pulled together quite a few supporters, though, and all the Bolsheviks were voting for him. They voted and swore at the tallier to be sure he tallied properly. They seemed to be neck and neck. But Himmer garnered one hand more than Gvozdev.

No sooner had they finished voting than the troublesome Sokolov rolled in with flapping coattails: What's this? You chose without me? Wait! I'd like to be there, too!

But they weren't going to choose a sixth, although this was Sokolov's favorite work: to take part in negotiations.

With respect to Nikolai II, we're specifically going to verify the Provisional Government's sincerity. Indeed, popular indignation could no longer be restrained, and petitions were coming in, like these (Erlich read them out): Chernomorsky, Ivanov, Sheff, ninety-five signatures total, members of the Soviet of Workers' and Soldiers' Deputies, extreme indignation and alarm that Nikolai the Bloody and his wife, who have been exposed for treason against Russia, and his son, and his mother, are at liberty. . . . Urgent measures must be taken to concentrate them at a specific point.

Yes! Yes! And although they had resolved this twice at the EC, under this kind of pressure to pin down one more time and cut short all the Provisional Government's ruses, it was **resolved**: arrest the entire family! Immediately confiscate all their property! And strip them of citizenship. And so that a representative from the Soviet is present at their arrest!

And what happened with the machine-gun regiment? They had refused Skobelev straightaway. They'd changed their mind and weren't going.

Chkheidze rubbed and rubbed his weary bald head and suggested they write this: cancel the order for removal to Oranienbaum.

The people's will.

And now, at last, it was time to listen to our delegates who had gone to Kronstadt.

They were not happy to hear that report. The rampage was ongoing. Any officers who hadn't been arrested were continuing to be killed. And many arrested officers were in jail. There were almost none of them left at headquarters. Some sailors had even been chosen to command ships, but they didn't know their business, of course. Lots of rallies, but no service. The German could take Kronstadt with his bare hands.

✳   ✳   ✳

WHEREVER YOU PEEK, IT'S SURE TO REEK

✳   ✳   ✳

[509]

Don't forget, remind yourself that you came to the Soviet to forestall the revolution itself and its invisible mad course. To forestall anarchy in anarchy's very nest and allow a new order to be formed. To remind yourself because, sitting in the seething Duma hall, in the thick of a thousand soldier deputies, Stankevich felt not like a rational guide but like a chip splashed up where everyone else had been, and no one could predict five minutes beforehand where one sharp-tongued speaker was going to turn this colossus.

What agenda! No matter what agenda was announced, it was never going to be followed, interrupted by a stream of speakers of unexpected inclination who were not used to sessions. Today, as always, people kept coming out with congratulations—from various garrisons and reserve regiments. . . . But they were supposed to be discussing "the rights of the soldier," and a couple of lawyers had prepared an entire declaration on circumventing and disbanding military discipline—but it was all turned around by a clerk who climbed up to the tribune and said that the Soviet of Deputies should send agitators all through Russia to *fight the zemstvo,* and those agitators had to be paid, he didn't forget that. "The countryside is poor in spirit!" he exclaimed. "It has to be made ready for the Constituent Assembly."

Right then, upon closer examination, they were "soldiers" in name only, very few common soldiers reached this hall, nearly half those sitting here were clerks and recently promoted sergeants with rudimentary training. Unfortunately, they already knew a thing or two—yet they knew too little.

Here one was trying to argue that we needed a republic, for there would never be any good under a tsar.

Another corrected him, saying that we didn't need just any republic but a democratic republic. Over there in France, the bourgeoisie was the oppressor.

And a third, again, saying no one left in the countryside could figure out what was going on and we had to go there and explain. Programs had to be pasted up everywhere so that they hung right in front of them.

Some naif also climbed up, removed his tall fur hat, and swore to the assembly that his father had been a serf and now he was ready to go explain things using his last funds, for free.

Others rejoined that the countryside had teachers, men and women both, who would explain everything to the peasants. We just had to send them the newspapers.

Someone shouted from his seat:

"I demand that all Petrograd's troops send letters home demanding a republic!"

And from the tribune:

"The most important propaganda is explaining who the land belongs to and how to divide it up. If the Tsar stays, then the land won't go to the peasants. If there's a republic, then all that precious land will be ours! The Romanovs' lands should belong to the populace."

Shouts back:

"We already have the people's will as it is. And that means all the land is ours."

"No!" they shouted at him. "If Wilhelm wins, he'll take away all the land! We have to beat Wilhelm first."

Others shouted: Choose the best cadres for the administration and put the money from the capitalists into peasant banks.

"No," people shouted, "let's tell the Provisional Government to sow all the land!"

A multitudinous revolutionary assembly might as well be a revolutionary street crowd. The crowd seems omnipotent, whereas in fact it follows the leader and even wants to be governed. In order to convince it, one has to assert very very confidently, or repeat the same thing over and over, or throw an outburst into it, like a torch. But today's chairman, Ensign Uthof, could do none of this. All he could do was try, in vain, from Rodzyanko's dais, to call them to order:

"Comrades! Comrades! We have to discuss the question about the army, and what are we doing?"

He immediately gave the floor to the French military delegation that had arrived.

A major exclaimed:

"Vive la Russe!"

But from a seat:

"No Frenchman is gonna bust a gut!"

After that, a dashing second lieutenant from the Republican Union stepped up:

"Comrades! A democratic republic—the people have to understand, too. If agitators are sent straight to the populace, provocateurs will slip in among them. Order in the military units has to come first. Here two soldiers left their post to sleep. That is improper. There are many examples. . . ."

But there were few interested in these many examples. There was a loud droning, people weren't listening.

Yes, that's what was needed first and foremost: order in the military units. That is precisely what Stankevich wanted to achieve, not in the disorderly droning of this hall but in the Executive Committee, to which he'd already been elected. He was training himself not to get lost in these waves anymore.

But they were lashing.

A strapping sailor with a machine-gun belt across his shoulder, crosswise, in the new fashion, stepped up. He gloomily rested his elbows on the tribune shelf and in a bass voice let out:

"Everything's fine on our end. The sailor's heart can feel the democratic republic. If necessary, we'll fire a volley at our enemies from Kronstadt."

And a nervous sergeant:

"First of all, the revolutionaries have to send agitators to the troops themselves! I'll go to the front myself! And I'll tell them that if someone forces you to go against Petrograd, kill that commander! After the war we're not going to lay down our weapons right away, oh no!"

So many of these brash, individual wills flared up now—and aimed in all directions. Who could ever guide them all?

One speaker mentioned the State Duma—and drew an immediate response:

"Somehow I don't remember our village voting for the Duma. Who chose them? No, let's have us another one!"

Now a strapping, bearded cavalryman, a private:

"Listen here. Every cause starts with a blessing from God." (They were already getting noisy.) "I'm an old soldier, I served without a blemish for seven years. . . ."

From a seat:

"And did you make seven spears?"

Laughter. They weren't listening.

"Hey," the cavalryman got angry. "It's just stripes sitting here, no real soldiers!"

He snatched his saber in the air and swung it—and people got scared and quieted down.

"Ho-oh!" He put the saber back, spat at someone somewhere, and went down the steps.

The chairman announced the deputation from Sveaborg. A ruddy-faced, solid, joyful colonel stepped up:

"Comrades! We are delighted with the new order and hope to work together with you! Long live the free people!"

His words might have sounded forced, but from his look—he was the revolution's lickspittle. Was he a combatant?

After him, a Sveaporg naval captain. But this one spoke muffledly, sorrowfully (Nepenin had been killed):

"We are working to reinforce the freedom won. Everyone here is united—the soldiers, the sailors, the workers, and the officers. Long live a free Russia . . ."

And again machine-gun belts, from the 2nd Machine-gun Regiment. Dashingly:

"Our regards to you, comrades, for your deeds of liberation! All the enemies of freedom have to be isolated and have everything taken away. Resolve and arrest them within twenty-four hours or else they'll sell off their property. And as a matter of urgency, the immediate arrest of the entire Romanov house!"

They clapped: very strongly put, confident and savvy.

But maybe because of the machine-gun regiments that had put pressure on Petrograd—the chairman was inclined to consider removing unneeded units from Petrograd.

Shouts at him:

"How can we remove them if the revolution isn't over?"

"And by whose order? Not the Minister of War. We have to judge this ourselves!"

"Even if you take them away, their representatives should meet here and be always on Petrograd's guard."

"Even if you take them out, keep in contact!"

And, from the most interested party, the 1st Machine-gun Regiment, a sergeant on the tribune:

"We recognize the Soviet of Soldiers' Deputies and no one else. Not even God! And we're not leaving Petrograd until we get land! Yesterday we disobeyed the minister's order to go to our position, even though our soldiers are very much needed there, and nowhere else in Russia are there special forces like our machine-gun regiments."

For all his love of freedom and all the breadth of his views, Stankevich was frightened. Where and when did such a thing come about without us noticing? Could it really have been in this one week?

They argued. What about transporting artillery shells to the front?

The chairman was replaced by the clever Boris Bogdanov from the Executive Committee, who convinced them to hand over all these questions to the Executive Committee. And here and now discuss the Declaration of the Rights of the Soldier. The draft was already in his hands. Here it was.

It was like a balm to soldiers' hearts. Henceforth, all soldiers are citizens. . . . The salute is abolished. . . .

Yes, there had been no need for all that pomp over the salute: six paces from the officer, turn your head, throw your turned-out hand up, and look the officer in the eye. This should have been simpler a long time ago: that this was simply a mutual greeting.

. . . No disciplinary punishments by anyone. . . . Mobilization and demotion hereby discontinued. Facilitate leave from the barracks. Permit the wearing of civilian attire and joining any organization. . . . Smoke anywhere. . . . All jobs discontinued. . . . Evening inspection discontinued. . . . Mandatory prayer discontinued. . . . Orderlies discontinued.

A doctor interrupted:

"Orderlies can't be discontinued in the army in the field. An officer is sitting hungry in a trench. How can he get along without an orderly?"

"Then pay the orderlies!"

"No, not for pay! Everyone's in the trenches, and the orderlies are sitting in the rear!"

"So what, take in women instead? What's going to come of that?"

"In the name of the Cossacks, I ask that you keep the orderlies! Orderlies are recognized in France. Without an orderly an officer gets mangy. If an officer is going to look after his horse himself, then what kind of an officer can he be? . . ."

＊　　＊　　＊

Liberty shines brightly,
A lamp o'er our home.
Happiness for our people
Rests in liberty alone.

("The New Marseillaise")

[5 1 0 "]

(FROM THE WESTERN PRESS)

ENGLAND

The Russian revolution will be a far less bloody and terrible affair than its great French prototype.

(Reynolds's Newspaper)

GERMANISM OVERTHROWN . . . We hope that these events are the end of what has been most tragic in Russia's tragic history. To Germany, this revolution is the greatest disaster since the Battle of the Marne. This blow kills German hopes for a separate peace. No eviler blow could have been inflicted on Germany! The Russian army will become even more terrible for Germany than it ever was before.

(Morning Post, 16 March)

Lloyd George in the House of Commons: ". . . One of the landmarks in the history of the world . . . Soldiers refused to obey orders (cheers). . . . It is satisfactory to know that the new Government has been formed for the express purpose of carrying on the war with increased vigour (cheers). . . . These events are a first-rate triumph for the principles for which we entered the war. . . ."

. . . The great danger was that the Tsar might fail to realize the position with sufficient promptitude, and that he might either resist the Revolution or defer his decision. He has had enough of wisdom and of unselfish patriotism not to take either of these courses. By laying down the supreme authority of his own free will, he has saved his people, we may trust, from civil war and social anarchy.

(Times, 16 March)

AMERICAN SATISFACTION . . . The Russian revolution has been cause for joy. . . . The commentaries from Jewish leaders, whose hostility to the former Russian government was a tremendous obstacle for the Allies, are filled with sympathetic hope. . . . In certain circles in Washington it is privately regarded "with undiluted satisfaction" as a long step towards the coming of universal liberal ideals lately advocated.

(Times, 17 March)

In financial and business circles in the City the news of the Russian revolution was very well received yesterday. In the market for roubles, the exchange improved. Among Jewish bankers and merchants in the City particular satisfaction was expressed yesterday at the news from Russia. Their view is that, under a regime of effective constitutional government, improved conditions for the Jews in Russia are sure to be forthcoming. Both at the outbreak of war, and during its course, there has been, let us say, an "imperfect sympathy" on the part of the Jews with the fortunes of our Ally. A notable shift in this direction . . .

(Times, 17 March)

JEWS AND THE REVOLUTION. It was with something far greater than keen interest that the Jewish community in London heard the momentous news from Petrograd, for it opens up the prospect of brighter days for millions of their brethren. . . . The joys and sorrows of the millions of Jews in Russia find a sympathetic echo in the hearts of their coreligionists more happily placed than they, and future events will be eagerly followed in the earnest hope that out of the present movement may emerge a brighter era for Russian Jewry.

(Daily Telegraph, 17 March)

. . . The events in Russia will come as a greater surprise to the millions there than to us in England; for the ground has been carefully prepared in this country by numerous articles on the "Dark Forces" and Rasputin and the so-called Germans ruling Russia. Indeed, British public opinion has helped a very great deal to bring about the success of the movement. . . . On the whole, there is less pro-Germanism in Russia than anywhere else in Europe.

If the Tsar has, indeed, abdicated, he has acted nobly. He undoubtedly could have found forces greater than those at the disposal of the Duma and fought a civil war, shedding the blood of thousands and devastating his own country. He has been consistently a monarch of ideals, and has reigned in the midst of a hurly-burly of intrigue and impropriety which obscured and often nullified his words. But most outsiders have felt that the Tsardom kept Russia together, and that if once that unity were withdrawn Russia would go to pieces.

(Times, 17 March)

The police's sinister role. . . . From the very first days of the revolution, we have learned that the police were offered fantastic sums to put down the national uprising. . . .

Russia's strength for war will be enormously increased. For that reason we must pray for the Miracle to proceed.

(Weekly Dispatch)

London, 22 March. In the House of Commons, Mr. Bonar Law stated: "It is not too soon for the Mother of Parliaments to send a friendly greeting and a message of goodwill to a government which has been formed with the declared intention of carrying this war to a successful conclusion." (Cheers.) "However, I hope I may be permitted to express a feeling of compassion for the last Tsar, who was for nearly three years our loyal Ally (hear, hear) and who had laid upon him by his birth a burden which has proved too heavy for him . . ."

The House of Commons unanimously passed a resolution with fraternal greetings to the Russian people ". . . in full confidence that they will lead not only to rapid and happy progress of the Russian nation, but to the prosecution, with renewed steadfastness and vigour, of the war. . . .

. . . From the Russian people they now wait only for it to collect all its energy for final military efforts. . . . Our Petrograd Correspondent points out . . . a Republican form of Government would be most unsuitable for Russia.

(Morning Post, 22 March)

Russia will not countenance either Anarchy or a Socialist Republic; but in all revolutions the disadvantages of a vacancy in the supreme power are manifest. Our correspondent compares the tactics of the Government to those of cowboys "heading off" stampeding cattle. . . .

(Times)

FRANCE

Paris. On the evening of 17 March, the newspapers finally reported on the change of government in Russia. The impression was indescribable. The public on the streets tore newspapers from newsboys' hands, and everyone stopped to read the historic reports. Now Russia is free to organize a mighty defense.

A revolution has been made, and it will bring disaster on the Germans.

(Echo de Paris)

. . . The revolution is preparing the Russian nation's military revenge, since the army is filled with an unbending will to victory. . .

(Petit Parisien)

. . . The energy with which the war has been waged will mount even more. . . .

(Excelsior)

Paris, 22 March. Before the start of its session, the Chamber of Deputies greeted the change in the Russian state order with a prolonged and touching ovation. . . . The place where the prime minister said that the New Russia's institutions would develop according to the principles of the Great French Revolution were met with stormy applause.

French Socialist members of parliament: "With ecstatic joy we welcome the great coup! Like our fathers in 1793 . . . In your revolution lies the entire future of international democracy, and you can bring about the world's greatest democracy. Ensure a peaceful republic and the brotherhood of peoples. We shall crush German imperialism, the last foothold of autocracy! . . ."

. . . The Petrograd government is made up of individuals whose intentions coincide with those of France.

. . . A swift rise in Russian securities on the French financial market.

THE CENTRAL POWERS

It remains a fact that in the course of the revolution, power has been seized by the pro-English party. . . .

(Neue Freie Presse)

The Allies' delight is insincere. Revolution is a heavy blow for the Quadruple Entente and in reality will end the war on the Eastern Front. The causes behind the old regime's collapse remain fateful for the new regime as well.

(Berliner Tageblatt)

. . . Revolution will lead to a weakening of the Russian front both physically and morally.

. . . The news of revolution in Russia was met joyfully in the German army. Everyone is certain that Russia will agree to a separate peace any day now.

. . . It is still unknown where the fomenting of passions among the people will lead, a people who stand only at the beginning of their political development and in whom emotions and mystical notions predominate over clear political reason.

. . . It is incompatible with history's lessons to assume that the revolution will stop where its leaders want it to and not lead to disintegration . . .

(Austria's former Minister of the Interior)

OTHER COUNTRIES OF EUROPE

Rome. The Foreign Minister stated that the new revolutionary movement in Russia not only will not slow the war's continuation but will make it more persistent and energetic. . . . All deputies rose from their seats. . . . The magnificent demonstration lasted . . . There can be no thought of the revolution causing a slowdown in military operations.

The Vatican. The Secretary of State of the Holy See has expressed his admiration with respect to the bloodless overthrow in Russia, unexampled in history. . . . Pope Benedict XV learned with the liveliest joy . . . He is certain that relations between the Holy See and Russia will now take on a quality unclouded by anything.

Amsterdam. The stock exchange responded to the news of the Russian state overthrow by raising the ruble's rate of exchange.

For half a century, Europe has been waiting impatiently for a Russian revolution. Now that we had lost all hope, the dam was swept away and the great rebirth of nations has begun! . . .

(Sozialdemokraten, Denmark)

In Switzerland, Russian events have called forth an outburst of universal enthusiasm, as if Switzerland's close interests were concerned. Geneva admires the greatness of the deed accomplished by the Russian people and the State Duma. For once, Russian citizens do not need to be ashamed of their state order and government.

(Vorwärts, Switzerland)

The new government includes the brightest minds in Russia.

(Neue Zürcher Zeitung)

The charter of freedom proposed by the Duma places Russia in a rank with the cultured nations. . . . The influence and commercial intelligence of 6 million Russian Jews will be given to assist free Russia.

(Prof. Masaryk)

REFLECTION IN THE RUSSIAN PRESS

The press notes the triumph of freedom-loving England, for which the alliance with old autocratic Russia was a heavy burden. In the House of Commons, the news of Nikolai II's abdication was met with a noisy and welcoming demonstration. Now Russian democracy will wield the death blow against Germany. . . .

. . . The Sunday newspapers reflect the general delight. . . . "At last the Russian people have found their soul". . . "A blinding program of political reforms". . . "The Russian revolution has brought a breath of fresh air to the world atmosphere". . . "Liberalism has won the greatest victory". . .

. . . At the crucial moment, the old imperial government did not find itself a defender in the Allied countries. One can say with confidence that the Allied nations and governments breathed a sigh of relief when the news reached them of the old regime's fall. Even the war could not smooth over the gulf between free England and France and enslaved Russia. Republican France had been forced for many years to maintain relations with the Russian autocratic government.

The enthusiasm of the French press cannot be conveyed.

(Stock Exchange Gazette)

According to news from the United States, there has been a complete turnabout in American public opinion with regard to Russia. Up until now, Americans did not trust Russia. It was somewhat strange to see the liberal and democratic nations of the West shoulder to shoulder with an autocratic empire. The United States did not try to hide their amazement at that alliance-making. Now the opportunity has been created for an open alliance of all free peoples against monarchical Germany . . .

(Stock Exchange Gazette)

. . . Americans, especially American Jews, are expressing enthusiasm. The well-known banker Jacob Schiff, who up until now has always opposed extending credit to Russia, is now inviting Russia to join in broad credit operations in America.

(Speech, 23 March)

As a result of the revolution, the ruble's rate of exchange has risen on foreign markets.

. . . The insinuations of the German press . . . It slanders the revolution, saying it was cooked up by a handful of liberals. . . .

All over Europe, people were expecting the fire that had seized Russia to turn into chaos. In the eyes of the whole world, when this did not happen, Russia took its place in the front rows of cultured humanity. Minister Milyukov's noble program has been received with sympathy in all the Allied countries.

[5 1 1]

The Russian revolution stubbornly refused to add Bublikov to its crown, but he knew he was its best adornment, that there was no one in the Provisional Government or the Soviet of Deputies with the same explosive energy and the same breadth of civic understanding—neither the inflated Milyukov nor the jester Kerensky. It was wildly unfair, plain and simple, that the revolution had not taken in Bublikov. He was scrambling as best he could to insinuate himself into it. In the course of any revolution there are changeable situations when the first rank falls in defeat—and the second rank steps up to lead events.

Having heard in Rodzyanko's circles that a Duma deputation was preparing to escort the Tsar from GHQ, Bublikov immediately made sure he headed the deputation. This brief operation did not promise him anything in particular other than to be on view and in all the newspapers—and he was curious to see the dethroned Tsar with his own eyes.

But how could he have failed to guess right away? This wasn't an escort, this was an arrest! Prince Lvov told them so when they came for the documents. All the more wonderful! The monarch's arrest was a dramatic point in any revolution, a crimson moment! And to be inscribed on the tablet as a participant in it!

The four Duma deputies—"commissars," in the new terminology—had left Petrograd late the previous night and slept through the night calmly, but in the daytime, at the large stations, especially in Orsha, their train was met by crowds—not massive ones, exactly, but decent little throngs—of railroaders and idlers who had heard that Duma members were on their way, though no one knew where, of course, or why. Deprived of the chance to speak in public until now, Bublikov now eagerly leapt up to meet them—

and was angry when he miscalculated and lost his voice. By three o'clock in the afternoon, when they reached Mogilev, he could barely speak.

There was a handful shouting "hurrah" at the Mogilev train station — but Bublikov could no longer respond and someone else spoke for him.

General Alekseev could have met them at the station perfectly well. However, he had not seen fit to do so. (He wasn't sincerely loyal to the revolution, Bublikov noted; he'd fall at the next wave.) They were met only by the informed General Kislyakov, a podgy, red-haired man with his military-railway ranks. He informed the commissars confidentially that the Tsar's train had been readied, and he himself was here, actually, in the train with his mother. But that he knew nothing.

Indeed, near the other platform two blue imperial letter trains were standing across from each other.

They could simply have taken him. And left.

But he couldn't be taken without military authorities — otherwise it wouldn't be official, and besides it was unclear how to arrest him. The commissars had no armed force. Alekseev had behaved tactlessly by not coming to the station.

Oh well, all four commissars got into a motorcar and headed for GHQ, through the outskirts and then down Mogilev's main street.

At headquarters, Alekseev did receive them immediately. He had a rather plagued, gloomy, underslept look. The chief of staff of all the armed forces might have been imagined looking more vigorous. Evidently, the revolution truly had grated on him.

On the other hand, Bublikov, despite his raspy voice, felt military, tensed, agile, swift. He presented the general with the Provisional Government's order over the signature of Prince Lvov about the former Emperor's confinement. And he insisted that this action be accomplished as swiftly as possible, before the Emperor could prepare for it.

The general asked, timidly it seemed, whether there was any point in announcing the arrest to the former Tsar right now. He had agreed to go, and he knew that Duma deputies were coming to escort him and the train was readied. Why not just let him go?

But the Revolution had no need to hide and bow its head in shame! Bublikov had no intention of taking the Tsar away by deception! No, the former Tsar had to be told sternly and solemnly that he was under arrest!

Then perhaps the deputies themselves would tell him? Alekseev looked imploringly. Utterly lost, not a combat general.

No, this was a matter for the military, for the chief of staff. It would be easier for the former Emperor to hear this from Alekseev.

(The only reason Bublikov refused was that he had lost his voice. That would have ruined any effect of the arrest; the Tsar might have grinned.)

Bublikov also wanted a separate train car attached to the imperial train for the commissars.

This met with no difficulties.

Bublikov also wanted a complete list of names of everyone who was going to accompany the former Tsar—from suite to servants, each and every one. (He considered them all potential prisoners.)

Now this demand, he thought, would cause difficulties and delay. As it turned out, though, this was extremely easy for Alekseev to do. He had kept any and every kind of list, obviously, and after combining different ones he immediately appended a list of forty-seven individuals.

Bublikov read it. What was the Emperor's suite? Like his entire circle, an entire array of nonentities. But here there was—Admiral Nilov? A military man, after all, he could give some military advice, undertake some decisive action en route. He had to be separated, not taken along.

That was all.

The commissars headed off in the motorcar for the station—and Alekseev followed immediately after.

On the platform between the two letter trains, the four civilian commissars stood at the tail waiting for their train car to be attached. With them was a detail made up of ten guards of the Railroad Battalion.

Alekseev shuffled ahead past them gloomily. They said the Tsar was still with his mother, so Alekseev went in there, into the Empress's train car.

Bublikov followed what was happening. There was no reason to expect it from Nikolai, but what if there were some kind of resistance or protest?

A group was drawn to the same platform, both those with reason to be there and extraneous people. The public had already heard or sensed something, and they gathered more and more densely, so that from a distance the commissars no longer had a good view.

Mostly there was silence.

The weather wasn't cold.

No one had come out of the Empress's train car yet. Meanwhile, Nilov was informed that he was to remain in Mogilev. Standing at attention, he asked whether he'd been arrested. They told him they had no such instructions.

This man—utterly useless in the state respect, for years had shared all the Emperor's movements, his meals and his leisure, always drunk or half-drunk but today sober, actually, simply the Emperor's weakness, simply a warm-blood creature of the court—now went to the imperial train to get his things.

The crowd was getting thicker and thicker—and was unusually silent, as rarely happens on platforms when seeing people off. Everyone was standing stock-still, their eyes turned toward the former Emperor.

About 150 people had gathered.

Suddenly, Alekseev emerged from the Empress's train car and walked this way, toward the commissars.

His expression was frowning and bitter, his mustache was climbing to his spectacles, his eyes were practically shut.

"All declared," he told Bublikov quietly. "The Emperor invites you to dine with him today."

Whatever Bublikov had been anticipating, it wasn't this. Whatever he had envisaged in his revolutionary mission, it wasn't this.

The arrested Tsar had given thought to where they were to dine.

It would be interesting to sit at the royal table once and look at him up close, and talk—after all, he hadn't seen him even after arresting him!

But the revolutionary pose was lost in this, and it could be a poor show for history.

Bublikov declined—for himself and all the commissars.

Alekseev shook hands in farewell—and set off ahead again.

Suddenly the whole crowd shuddered—and then in openings, and from the train car platform and over their heads, they could see that the Tsar had jumped rather than stepped out of the old Empress's train car wearing a Kuban Cossack uniform, a tall black fur hat, and a purple-lined hood and carrying a Cossack weapon, in aiguillettes, and nearly ran across the sloping path to his own train car, raising his hand for a salute as he went—and not lowering it, holding it there the whole time, at his tossed-back head.

Someone ran up and kissed his free left hand.

The whole crowd stood facing that way—in silence. Not a shout.

And then he was gone in his own train car.

Alekseev went in after him.

And then came out.

The individuals of the suite had all boarded the train already.

So had the commissars.

The three bells of departure struck. The stationmaster waved his flag for the engineer.

The crowd was silent. But had turned as a body toward the imperial train. Alekseev saluted as the royal train car pulled away.

The commissars' train car dragged along last—and saw the heads, the heads from the station platform. All facing this way.

But there was no approval on them. No wave of a hand.

Only Alekseev, when the commissars' train car came even with him, removed his cap and bowed.

And the thin, elegant old Empress stood in the wide window of her train car, across the platform—in despair.

[5 1 2]

Vladimir Dmitrievich Nabokov was one of those incomparable fortunate men whom fate had bestowed with everything possible without stint: wealth, gentility, rank, blooming health, an outstanding subtle mind, the gift of eloquence, the ability to show himself to best advantage, and unflaggingly high self-confidence. In part because of this confidence and the constancy of his successes, he did not try to hold onto the title of chamberlain and gave it up for one public revolutionary speech. A man of his intellect and education could not fail to sympathize with the Liberation Movement in Russia—and in his mansion on Bolshaya Morskaya he had hosted the very important Zemstvo Congress in 1904. Naturally, he was elected to the First State Duma and was, amid its gray-jacketed complement, an incomparable gentleman, each session wearing a new suit and tie. However, the demise of the First Duma meant the demise of his public career. Not only did he go to Vyborg, he was the session secretary there—and this was his last visible act. Because of Vyborg, all subsequent Dumas were closed to him. He himself had no wish to return to state service, even if they would have taken him. Being simply a prominent member of the Kadet Central Committee meant reducing himself to party activity—and that would have shown insufficient taste. But he could lead a life full of taste given his own means, his beautiful wife and excellent children, in the capital milieu, without doing much of anything. Thus the entire pre-war period had passed for him quite happily and vividly. During the war he became regimental adjutant for a militia squad operating in the rear, left Petersburg, and detached himself all the more from the Kadet milieu. When he did return to serve as a clerk secretary at the General Staff, he no longer joined with the Kadet Central Committee: in part he did not have the right as an officer, although he could have overlooked it, but there also wasn't much point. During these war years he had not restored vital ties with the Kadet Central Committee. Thus he was not current on their life, and they also perceived him as an outsider.

Then, all of a sudden, there were these unexpected Petrograd perturbations. 12 March found Nabokov at the General Staff, and he later made his way home, in considerable danger, through the bullet-riddled streets. On 13 and 14 March, while shooting continued on the streets, he didn't go to work at all, nor did he let any of his householders leave, and he learned the news from friends over the telephone and street news from the servants.

And now, instantly and easily, everything he had once been striving for, fifteen and ten years ago, had come to pass, something that obviously could be characterized by no other word than "revolution." (Although blood had not been spilled and there had been no fighting on the barricades, strangely.)

Inasmuch as it had happened, quite an interesting new situation had come about in society. Serving at the General Staff had nearly lost its meaning, and Nabokov began going to the Tauride Palace to see his old Kadet acquaintances and get a closer look. Previously, in the best, strongest years of the Kadet party, Nabokov had been considered one its three or four leaders. Now the provincial Shingarev and the dull-witted Professor Manuilov had been taken into the government. Of the genuine Kadet forces only Milyukov had joined it, and there was no place for Nabokov by reason of his break so long ago.

However, he watched the trifling makeup of this first free government of Russia with regret and alarm. There were only two figures of stature, Milyukov and Guchkov. There were also two who were hardworking, if not brilliant: Shingarev and Konovalov. The rest didn't even know how to work, to compose a document, to follow its progress, much less to run a ministry. Although Nabokov had no love for Maklakov, he now had to recognize it as a capital disgrace that they had chosen as Minister of Justice not Maklakov but that jack-in-the-box Kerensky. That was utterly frivolous. Himself a deep and subtle lawyer, Nabokov could not help but understand that Kerensky's legal knowledge wouldn't fill a pound sack. The rest was newspaper demagoguery, and he could be Minister of Justice with nearly the same success as he could a clerk in a clothing shop. He could only imagine with horror how this formless clump of ministers would start rolling.

No one had been capable of drawing up Mikhail's abdication on 16 March, so they called in Nabokov and Baron Nolde. But who after this was going to shape them and their thoughts, the documents, the decrees, and the resolutions? To let them go without a guiding hand was simply letting them go to their ruin.

Forming was the easiest thing for him to do. He himself was form.

Nabokov did not mind offering himself to Milyukov as the government's executive secretary. This was not a ministerial post and was not part of the disputed distribution of portfolios, but it had always existed and been filled by an official of the highest class: under ministers of strict preparation it was rather irreplaceable, but under the ministers they had now, he would be the sole saving guide. Milyukov understood how badly this figure was needed and was happy to see his own Kadet, a smart man and a well-wisher, in this seat.

After getting Guchkov to sign his discharge from military service as ensign, Nabokov went to work. The ministers came to government sessions to talk, be informed, and get some kind of indication for themselves, but they had no idea how to operate, how to translate thoughts and votes into legislation. Given the faltering State Duma and the disbanded State Council, the government found itself in a position of power that no Tsarist government had ever had: it could and was obligated to create and issue laws for the huge state without oversight. However, due to their want of skill and the flurry of events, for the first few days laws were issued on the basis of an oral statement by one minister and the oral consent of the rest. A decision was approved before it had any text, unaccompanied by any figures or budget. Shingarev alone submitted written proposals. All this muddle-headedness had rolled along chaotically, so that for the first few days Nabokov could barely cope. He had to organize rooms, secretaries, protocols, and recordkeeping in the Mariinsky Palace—and he was also swamped with writing an appeal to the populace—and unwittingly, for the first few days, it wasn't laws themselves, not reforms themselves that were pouring out of the government, but merely promises of them. They were in such a hurry that the most fundamental act—establishing their authority in the obedient provinces—was a frivolous improvisation by Prince Lvov: simply replace the governors with the chairmen of the provincial zemstvo boards. (Lvov explained, following Tolstoy, that no regime of any kind was needed.)

A few more days like this and the regime would have ended before it began. The Provisional Government would have fallen apart on its own from its inability to work with documents and conduct business.

Finally, though, Nabokov had everything prepared for today and was himself prepared. From the beginning of today's session he had kept it commandingly in hand. He started first and dictated conditions to the ministers.

From now on, no questions could be brought to the government without a written draft resolution. Disagreements in discussions and the opinions of the majority and minority would not be entered into the transcript of proceedings so that the government's will could be presented as unified. (In part, Nabokov did not want his secretariat to take on the tension of these debates.) Government sessions were divided into a few types: open ones, involving several secretaries and department representatives and the minutes published; closed ones, involving one secretary and minutes taken but not published; and top secret ones, attended only by the executive secretary and no minutes. Under the government, a Judicial Conference (Maklakov again, Kokoshkin, Nolde, and Adzhemov) would operate right here, in the Mariinsky Palace, to do preparatory work on fundamental issues and reforms. Its first assignment was to work out rules on elections for a Constituent Assembly. And the question of limits to the application of military censorship. (Going without censorship, as they themselves had demanded previously, turned out to be utterly impossible.)

It seemed they were seeing the very first framework for their work. The ministers apparently did not mind. They themselves had been worried that they were starting to drift.

Then it was reported that the train carrying the arrested Tsar was already en route without incident.

Milyukov came up with and proposed a smart idea: documents of special state importance from the former Tsar at Tsarskoye Selo must be safeguarded, so that he doesn't destroy them. Seal his study and post a sentry.

They agreed. (But for some reason didn't do it.)

Guchkov wasn't there. They were already used to his absences.

Kerensky, who had traveled so triumphantly yesterday to Moscow, had not shown up to report on his trip: either he was sleeping in, or he was putting on airs, or he had too much to do. His deputy, Zarudny, also a former lawyer known from the Beilis case, reported instead on the urgency of creating an Extraordinary Commission of Inquiry and beginning to sort through the tangle of crimes and betrayals by former ruling individuals. Disclosure of these crimes would stun the country. It was proposed that they create a major investigatory unit, then a numerous oversight unit made up of lawyers over the investigators, in order to avert favoritism. Then—a presidium of authoritative individuals. A tremendous amount of paperwork. This would be a major institution, lasting several months. They needed to set aside a large Petersburg building (preferably the Winter Palace). And allocate significant funds, the figure to be determined.

They agreed.

Alongside this another question could not fail to arise: what was to be done about the excessive arrests made the first few days of the revolution. If no evidence was discovered against someone within ten days, shouldn't he be released? This might cast a political shadow on the government, though. If that looked quite impossible politically, then could we at least differentiate among those arrested, saying that they were intended not for trial and prison but for, say, exile? Or deportation?

And could we somehow use some forces to put a stop to the self-appointed searches and arrests such as were continuing in Petrograd even today? How could we make the arrests stop, except pursuant to a judicial warrant?

An even more urgent question, though, was *funds*—and a lively chaos arose in the session. As it turned out, each ministry, in order to start functioning, needed money even more acutely. For what purposes could the special 10-million fund be spent? For example, travel allowances for people on assignment? What about the secret 4-million fund of the Interior? Could that be spent on the return of exiles from Siberia?

Hiring new officials and employees took money. But so did dismissing inappropriate judges, senators, and dignitaries, they now realized. Who was going to pay their pensions or ordinary support? Behind each dismissal loomed the payment of a pension—but out of what funds?

Tereshchenko had already done what he could. He had delivered a vivid speech at the Dispatch of State Securities and had called on employees to increase their output of banknotes. Now what else could be done? An appeal to the populace?

An appeal for the population to demonstrate thrift?

And promising the Provisional Government's thrift?

No, what Tereshchenko meant . . . After all, there was still the pressure of interest on Allied loans and the next payments to the Allies. It would dishonor the Provisional Government to default on its debts to the Allies. Doing so was out of the question!

Of course! No! Out of the question!

No matter which way you turned, the government had to pay. And the populace now understood the onset of freedom as meaning they now scarcely had to pay their duties and taxes, didn't they? In any event, during the revolution, payments had ceased everywhere.

Yes, gentlemen . . . yes, this was an ominous danger.

What could be undertaken? Obviously—an appeal. An appeal to the population's conscientiousness: revive payments.

But this would sound overly harsh. We want to take our time with this. During the very first, early days? Would this offend the ordinary citizen?

Wouldn't they reproach us with the Vyborg appeal? In 1906 we called on them not to pay taxes.

But this is unavoidable, gentlemen. All that's needed is the correct explanation of our motives. During time of ominous danger, all citizens of a henceforth Free Russia will bear their obligations readily.

Right then Kerensky flew into the session, and there was something angelic to that flight, so weightless and nicely fresh was he. And he wasn't carrying anything.

Everyone was ready to listen good-naturedly to his tale of the Provisional Government's successes in Moscow.

Angelic—but demonic as well. By right of his return from Moscow, or because he was the Soviet of Workers' Deputies' representative, Kerensky, not yet sitting down and with a sharp, slanting, angry crease on his forehead under his youthful crewcut, asked:

"Does or does not the Ministry of Foreign Affairs intend to energetically facilitate the return of our revolutionary émigrés from Europe and America? Telegrams have been flying in from everywhere, complaints about delays! What kind of revolutionary face do we have? How can we bear this disgrace?"

He could have said all this calmly and addressed Milyukov directly, "Pavel Nikolaevich." But combined, the impudent pressure of his angry tone and his speaking about the ministry in the third person threw Milyukov, himself an assertive man, off his stride. He was not used to encountering such a tone and did not rein in Kerensky but actually blushed and began justifying himself. Open, wholesale return to Russia for everyone was inauspicious, too, since there was also a criminal element there. But the old regime's investigatory agencies had collapsed, and now there was no one to help sort out the individual cases. As it was, the ministry had already allocated 430,000 gold rubles for émigrés' loans, travel, and expenses.

"You're not hearing what you're saying!" Kerensky yelling got even reedier. "These are heroes! These are sufferers! These are martyrs! Our revolution owes an unpayable debt to them! How can such mockery of them be allowed? How can the Fatherland not greet them with open arms?"

[5 1 3]

The farewell to his dear Convoy and his Combined Regiment tore him up even more than had the one in the Duty Hall. He wept quite openly.

Here it was, the day of farewells! His heart had yet to recover from the previous ones, and now came his parting with his dear Mama. This, at least, was not forever.

But Mama could not conceal her forebodings. For some reason, she thought they might never see each other again. How could that be, Mama?

The children will recover, we will go to England, and you can go to Denmark at any time. . . .

With the gentle, not yet old smile she had retained, his Mama nodded her narrow face and wiped away tiny tears.

The hour of departure was approaching, and on the platform, between the trains, an audience had collected.

Nikolai peeked around the curtain and saw a sweet group of five older school girls wearing black caps with brown ribbons at the side and golden cockades. The girls were standing directly across from their train car and kept looking with searching faces at the covered windows.

He couldn't help himself: he pulled back the curtain and showed himself to them. He smiled.

They noticed instantly, livened up, and ran up—not all the way—and began showing with lively movements and expressions how they sympathized. And they cried. And showed touchingly through gestures that the Emperor should write them something and pass it to them.

Nikolai was warmed by these girls' sympathy.

He took a piece of paper—but his heart ached so, and really, what could he write? He wrote in large letters: "Nikolai." And sent it with a messenger.

They received it—and showed their ecstatic gratitude. They kissed the piece of paper. One folded and hid it away.

Poor children.

Then the grand dukes came to say goodbye—Sandro, Sergei, and Boris. He spoke with them for a while. They had now become exposed, too—their status tenuous, unclear.

Standing on the platform was the Prince of Oldenburg, a large old man in a short fur coat, leaning on a cane, hunched over.

They kept bringing more and more baggage onto the imperial train.

Then they reported Alekseev's arrival. Nikolai walked over to receive him in the adjoining train car.

In the hours since the farewell in the Duty Hall, kind Alekseev had become unrecognizable: his eyes cast down, barely open at all, traces of suffering etched on his face. Quite the old man. What new thing had happened?

It turned out the Duma deputies had brought an order: the Emperor would proceed . . . *as if* under arrest.

What nonsense was that? Under arrest? What for? Wasn't he going himself, voluntarily?

And what did "as if" mean? . . .

Well, it was just that the deputies' train car was going to be attached to the imperial train and only they would be in communication with railway authorities en route.

"All right, let them. That is simply a formality. No need to get so upset, Mikhail Vasilich!" the Emperor reassured the general and finally calmed him down somewhat.

And he had the idea of inviting the deputies to dinner.

And one other unpleasant detail: they were forbidding Nilov from travel-ing with the Emperor. Now this was insulting. Did this mean the Emperor was not free in his own suite?

But he would not cause a scandal, it was indecent. Nothing so terrible, in the end. They would travel separately.

Alekseev left.

Nikolai conveyed the news to Mama—and her eyes widened, and there was fear on her thin face. This brought home to him that, indeed, it was rather strange and indecent. Why say "arrest" if this was only for appearances?

Very unpleasant, in essence. And there was this: everyone else probably knew already, right?

On the military platform between the two imperial trains an even larger crowd had gathered, rather sullen and still. Did this mean everyone already knew?

And just as the recently abdicated Emperor had been embarrassed to show himself to the Allied representatives, now his embarrassment was even greater. How could he show himself to all these people—ordinary and not—being "as if" arrested? What would they think? This was exceptionally uncomfortable.

He embraced his narrow-shouldered, aged, little Mama very firmly. And kissed her more than once. But we will see each other soon.

He did not have far to go—obliquely, through a train car and a half, but he was burning. How could this be? They were now going to see their ever-exalted Emperor as if he'd been arrested? Fallen?

Almost as if undressed.

These thirty steps burned him. All the gazes aimed at him burned him, including from those girls. He saw none of them directly but sensed them with his peripheral vision. Everyone had seen his fall—and this was an in-tolerable disgrace.

Out of courtesy, though, he had to respond somehow to the crowd—so he saluted for all thirty steps (partly shielding himself in this way).

Not a sound reached him from the crowd.

The loyal Nilov leapt up—his back bent, and fussed at his left hand, to kiss it, with a doglike movement.

But the scorched Emperor was hurrying and could not stop for him.

Once again, Alekseev went to say goodbye, now in the Emperor's train car.

Yes, he may have been saying goodbye to Alekseev forever. In any case—they would never work together so well as they had at the head of the Army. He felt sorry for the old man; it would be different for him with Nikolasha. He embraced the despondent Alekseev firmly and kissed him three times, running into his mustache.

Soon after, the train started—and Nikolai stood at the window openly. The crowd could barely see him anymore, at an angle, but from window to window, when they came even, his little Mama made the sign of the cross over him.

And all of a sudden, an inexplicable pressure squeezed his chest. Yes, yes, he would never see his mother again! There was just this final sliding gaze, after their windows had separated.

And that was all. Mogilev receded, receded. The train followed its usual route, such as it had taken the Emperor so many times.

He often used to look out the window—and he did so now, recognizing several notable places, though leveled by a snowy shroud.

But it was windy, melancholy.

Everything was as usual, the train car was the usual, and so were his compartment and icons.

He prayed.

How much ground he'd covered, how many miles he'd lain, how much he'd read in this train car. During the Japanese war, all his trips to bless the troops. During this war—either to GHQ or to the army groups. His final anxious spurt to Tsarskoye Selo, his unsuccessful breakthrough. And the terrible night of the abdication. . . .

This train had been his true home, the train cars' walls were like an extension of his own skin. He was home again. The present journey was not the worst of his journeys. He did not have to rack his brains over any problems, not even his route (this was the deputies' concern now), and he was going for certain to his Tsarskoye Selo, it was open to him, to join his beloved Alix and his precious children.

They would get well and go to England for now. He would impose on no one and not let himself get too bitter.

For twenty-two years he had borne responsibility for Russia—let it not be for his whole life, let others bear it now.

But what was the point of this rude arrest? . . .

Hadn't he abdicated voluntarily?

Had he resisted?

He had called for Heaven's blessing on this government and called on everyone to help and support it and for the soldiers to obey.

Of course, this was all just a formality and obviously just for the journey. Nonetheless, it was offensive and embarrassing.

But now the disorders had subsided, the disgrace passed. A quiet private life now lay before him.

Not the worst of his journeys.

His soul was calming down.

After the war, return to his beloved Livadia—and live quietly in those tranquil, blessed mountains.

The final sunset sometimes broke through the windows. But the west was covered over; clouds had appeared.

No. It was hard. Painful. Mournful.

Meanwhile the usual royal routine flowed along, unchanged on the train. He went to have tea with the suite.

My God! How it had thinned out! No Frederiks or Voeikov. They hadn't let the loyal Nilov come. And where was Grabbe? And Dubensky? And Zabel? Back at GHQ. But why? And why hadn't they reported? . . .

Mordvinov and Naryshkin were very nervous, and Mordvinov had already managed to explain to the Emperor that the members of the suite who had not reached their pension had been ordered by the new war ministry to remain in military service rather than the suite.

What minister was that? Was this Guchkov?

Of his closest suite there remained only the five men at the table—and also Aleksandr of Leuchtenberg, Dr. Fyodorov, and Prince Dolgorukov, now fulfilling the roles of minister of the court and palace commandant simultaneously.

Today there was still no reason to violate the abstractness of the table conversation, which was wholly separate from events, but it was mostly up to the Emperor and Dolgorukov to keep the conversation going.

Only at the end of their tea, when they were already standing up, the Emperor suddenly, surprising himself, spoke with the attempt of a smile:

"You know, gentlemen . . . I . . . I am, you see, as if under arrest."

[5 1 4]

Lili Dehn's seven-year-old son Titi, the Empress's godson, had fallen ill. Lili learned this over the telephone before it was disconnected, in the thick of the confusion. The maid had spoken and brought her son to the telephone in his fever, and he had murmured: "Mama, when are you coming?"

Lili was heartbroken, but it was impossible, it was a betrayal to abandon the palace during these horrible hours! She decided not even to tell the Empress.

The Empress herself, though, courageous, her eyes quite red, though, summoned her:

"Lili, you must leave. Do you understand this order? No one who remains will be allowed to leave the palace. Think of Titi. How could you not only be without him but without even news of him?"

She said this—but of course she dreamed of keeping at least one living, close soul by her side.

"Your Majesty! It is my greatest wish to remain with you."

The Empress's mournful face lit up—not with a smile, which had never suited her face, but with light from an unseen source:

"I knew it! But I'm afraid this will be a terrible trial for you."

"Do not think of me, Your Majesty. We will pass through the danger together."

"God, my sweet, dear girl, how grateful I am to you for your devotion."

"It is I who should be grateful to you, Your Majesty, for allowing me to remain with you."

These two days of burning papers together had brought them very close. The Empress kept turning over letters and photographs—reading silently but not hiding her face and not afraid to reveal anything to Lili, who was like family. What they lost together brought them closer than anything they might have gained together.

The previous evening, a loyal servant had warned that they should not burn anymore. The stove cleaners had noticed the excessive quantity of ash in the fireplaces—and everything could be reported at any time. One could not trust anyone.

Was that so! The Empress had even been deprived of the freedom to burn her own intimate papers in the fireplace!

True, they had already burned most of it.

The entire atmosphere around the palace was poisoned by betrayal, and this affected some of the servants. The Empress herself did not see the stream of mud the newspapers were spewing at her, the malicious articles and caricatures—but all this did flow into the palace and poison the servants.

There were also letters coming to the Empress. Lili read them, even today they were anonymous, cowardly suggestions offering to help bring about peace with the Germans.

The Empress's face naturally had been lent an expression of mournful grandeur. Or, when her eyes were still, a fiery, magnetic gaze:

"Oh, Lili, through our sufferings we are purifying ourselves for heaven. We who have been given to see all from the *other* side as well—we must perceive everything as the hand of God. We pray, and yet it is not enough. Afterward, from the *other* world, we will see all this quite differently. The Emperor's abdication means the end of everything for Russia. Nonetheless, we must not blame the Russian people or the soldiers. It is not their fault."

She was amazed that the morning's newspapers had already printed in large type word for word what Kornilov had read to her today. And so, all Petrograd had known about everything since early morning—and not one sympathetic soul had broken through to warn the Empress. The Benckendorffs, naturally, had remained. Anastasia Hendrikova had arrived from Kislovodsk—today, in fact, straight into a trap. Dear Botkin had remained with the children. Dear Gilliard, the French tutor, had declared he would not go anywhere now. Mr. Gibbs, the English tutor, was in Petrograd and was not being allowed back into the palace. Count Apraksin could not simply drop his obligations, but he let it be known that he could not stay under these conditions.

How long had it been since he had tried to teach the Empress what she was to do?

The palace's new commandant, Staff Captain Kotzebue, a former officer in Her Majesty's Uhlan Regiment—not that she remembered him—would appear, pass through here and there. But Lili—she knew him well!—he was her distant relative.

She lay in wait for him in a passage and asked what this meant.

He replied with great embarrassment.

"I cannot imagine why I was appointed to this post. No one warned me or explained anything. Last night they woke me up and ordered me to go to Tsarskoye Selo. Assure Their Majesties that I will attempt to do everything possible for them. If I can be useful to them, that would be a happy moment in my life."

Scarcely had Lili brought this secret joy to the Empress than a subsequent one was brought: the Combined Guards Regiment had refused to surrender the watch to the newly arrived riflemen!

How about that! There was news! Might a whole great turnabout of troops begin with this??

Although they would not surrender the watches until the night, there were no more internal posts left, and overly free, impudent soldiers had infiltrated the palace corridors from somewhere, wearing their torn red scraps—and peeked into the rooms curiously, and asked the servants for explanations.

While shots rang out in the park. The revolutionary soldiers had started hunting the tame fawns.

[515]

Back during the Third Duma, Guchkov had been the first to give a public slap in the face to the tightly knit pack of grand dukes. No surprise that now they had scattered: Nikolai Nikolaevich's resignation was decided; those grand dukes who still held inspector general seats were under Guchkov's control and had quieted down, awaiting their certain removal; the garrulous Nikolai Mikhailovich, returned from his brief exile in the countryside, now did his best to revile the dynasty; while Kirill Vladimirovich had already figured out that strutting on down the revolutionary road was not for him, but came to report, embarrassed, to the minister that he was resigning his command of the Guards Crew. His far from smart face had shown a good deal less smugness since that recent day when he had showed up at the Duma wearing a luxurious red bow and presumed, apparently, to play the part of the dynasty's chief representative in the new situation.

Enemies were falling away on the right, but enemies pressed ominously on the left: the Soviet of Workers' Deputies. He had to be able to contrive clever moves to maneuver the army out from under them, away from their degeneracy. For this, Guchkov had his hopes set on the Polivanov commission. It had been meeting every day, and Guchkov had stopped by to attend. At one end of the table, for weight, sat the generals; at the other, the young, energetic, sarcastic General Staffers, whose pressure, inventiveness, and revolutionary energy, which knew no sacred authorities above it, could not have pleased Guchkov more. The commission's work had been moving forward swiftly. They had already approved a change in the regulations in favor of the soldier's personal and civil liberties. They had approved a resolution on army company committees and the transfer to them of a sufficient share of economic life.

Yesterday, Guchkov had been discouraged by the Soviet deputies, but today he had taken heart. We will stand our ground! His chief hope was to make the army's command younger! How dear this idea was to him! Clear the army group, army, corps, and division commands of all the rubbish and junk, the protectionism and stupidity, and put in talented, young, and energetic men, and each would know that henceforth his career would depend not on his connections and chance—and as soon as the whole army was transformed and energized it would rush to victory! What an aggressive spirit would arise! Guchkov had been born for this task, and there was nothing higher he could do as minister. As yet, the pathways weren't entirely clear: how exactly to discover, unerringly and quickly, all the right candidates? He was counting very much on the General Staffers' help (he relied on Polovtsov especially, asking him to take charge of especially important correspondence).

All the rest Guchkov had to deal with was amazingly unpromising tedium. Here was a stack of congratulatory telegrams to the War Minister from garrison chiefs and municipal commandants. Here were garrison delegations assuring him that all was in order there now (but it wasn't). Here were greetings to him personally, from the French *Temps* and the English *Daily Chronicle*—they hoped and were certain, the sheep, that now Russia would begin a major offensive (and he had to reply to them in the same vein). But here, too, were reports on military supplies and the recruitment of reserves for the front. Military production remained at a stand-still (in Moscow, the Soviet's mood—"down with the war"—wasn't even letting the gas mask plant reopen), transport was seeing stoppages, and units at the rear were so agitated and turned inside out that they'd lost any battle-readiness, and there could be no thought of sending them to forward positions. The last place the War Minister might go now was a reserve regiments' barracks. There was no knowing whether they'd get up from their cots when he entered, and they were certain to shout out some Soviet filth. All there was left . . . was the one practical matter in the war minister's hands: writing and signing appeals. First to the populace, then to the army, then to the populace and army together. To the officers separately. And to the officers and soldiers together. Signing them personally. Or with all the ministers. Or with Lvov. Or with Alekseev together. Some of these appeals had been published a few days ago. Others proposed were ready for signing. Still others were being composed.

Finally, simply an order for the Army and Navy. All about the same thing: you must close ranks with and trust the officers. Free Russia must be stronger than the Tsarist order.

Guchkov discussed conjuring formulas with Polovtsov and his other aides, formulas that migrated this way and that from document to document—and he himself had already ceased to believe in them; however, there was nothing else to believe in.

And it took up a lot of time. There was a certain daze.

He was glad for a good pretext today to break away from his joyless time at the official residence—not to go to the extremely boring daily session of the government, for no, he had nothing to report or listen to there—but there was another excellent pretext. He was still entrusted with the War Industry Committee and all its activities, and today an expanded session of the committee had been scheduled in the Petrograd City Duma but, in a general way, to attract the public's attention to issues of industry and military provisioning.

A thousand people had assembled in the Duma's Aleksandrovsky Hall, a select society, the business world, military uniforms, many ladies, everyone wishing to take part in the capital's public life, which had been so rudely interrupted by the revolution, was now happy at this exceptional reason for assembling. Troops guarded the building at the entrance. Inside, the forgotten gleam of medals and stars, white starch, and ladies' outfits was blinding—an exciting, joyous atmosphere.

Guchkov was (unintentionally) late. Everyone was waiting for him and a shout rang out in the spacious hall: "He's here!" Russia's favorite and most famous son! Everyone rose and, with stormy applause of forgotten strength, greeted his entrance and then his passage to the presidium together with Konovalov and Tereshchenko.

Guchkov felt replenished, as indeed he had needed this lashing stroke, to find himself in the atmosphere of an intense, sympathetic, cultured audience—and garner confidence from his own confident voice, and feel the halo of his glorious past.

Guchkov sat at the podium gazing at the hall's accumulation in a happy, rejuvenated state, his former sense of being a famous man restored to him.

Meanwhile, speakers kept coming up, and how gaily their speeches sounded, in their newly won freedom.

In this hall, the laws of revolutionary turmoil that had frayed at the city seemed to be abolished, and the former, pleasant stability of life returned, albeit with full freedom.

And from the Council of Stock Exchange Congresses ("with the emotional feeling of an old Sixties man"). And the Committee of Commercial Banks. And the Moscow Stock Exchange Committee: at last, the eternal barrier to popular independence and lofty ideals had been swept away! Moscow folk were bowing to the ground to the first assembly of an all-powerful people! Money for the war would always be found among the people! ("Bravo!")

And especially—greetings to the ministers who had selflessly taken on the burden of governance in this terrible moment. Thus, gradually, the time came for the chief among the ministers to respond.

Aleksandr Ivanovich rose—happy, having forgotten all his ministerial troubles and gloom, excited by the joy of this assembly and the waves of new, unabating applause. In response—he could hardly project onto them all his alarm. An alarm that seemed much exaggerated even to him.

"Kind sirs! Dear colleagues of our recent difficult years! You and I are used to understanding each other at just a hint and under censorship. However, through your hearts I am addressing vast Russia, for whose sakes we are prepared both to live working and to die suffering!" (Applause.)

He truly did think this. He was fanned by a familiar feeling, his old right to speak directly to all Russia.

"Everyone was convinced that Russia's victory under the old regime was impossible, so it had to be overthrown. Only then would there be a chance of victory." (Applause.) "And when our comrades, members of the Workers' Group, were arrested, my friend and closest colleague Aleksandr Ivanovich Konovalov and I went to representatives of the old regime and said: 'We aren't playing hide-and-seek with you! We were not a revolutionary organization when we were created. It was you who made us a revolutionary organization, and we came to the conclusion that victory awaits Russia only without you!'" (Stormy applause.) "And then we, a peaceful, practical organization, included in our program an overthrow—armed, if necessary!" (Stormy applause.)

Guchkov stood before the exultant hall, his head thrown back. The time had come! Now he could speak openly, from the tribune, about the plans for the coup. It hadn't all gone exactly that way, but right now everything had coalesced and corrected itself slightly in his memory to be more elegant, and he took his revenge for the coup not made. At that moment Guchkov especially loved the combination of his intention and his triumph. (And how many sweet ladies' faces there were! Human desire never ages.)

"However, gentlemen! This coup was brought about not by those who made it but by those against whom it was directed. The conspirators were not me, Russian society, or the Russian people, but the representatives of authority themselves. We might proclaim Protopopov an honorary member of our revolution." (Laughter.) "This was not a sophisticated plot by a masked group, Young Turks or Young Portuguese, but the result of spontaneous forces and historical necessity—and herein lies the guarantee of its unshakable stability." ("Bravo! Bravo!") "Before us lies great creative work that will demand all the brilliant forces that lie in the Russian people's soul. We must now conquer ourselves and return to a tranquil life."

By "ourselves" he meant the mutinous soldiers.

"I believe that Russia will emerge from this incredibly difficult position to which it was led by its old regime. I'm seeing, on all sides, slumbering, oppressed popular forces awakening."

Even awakening too much . . .

"Never before has there been such enthusiasm for our work. The government is confident that the fall of the old regime will make our work even more intensive. With belief in the bright future of the Russian people . . ."

The entire hall rose and applauded long and hard—and from this stiff wind Guchkov summoned enough strength to lead two war ministries. Why, in fact, had he lost heart?

[5 1 6]

The arrival of the commissars and all the Emperor's farewells had been agony for General Alekseev. And why "commissars" when they were simply State Duma deputies? Then the most senior of them, Bublikov—Alekseev could not remember encountering such sharp, dangerous men in his lifetime. Decisive, eyes racing, intense but also discomposed, constantly turning around as if expecting to see someone standing behind him. You could tell he suspected everyone here—starting with Alekseev—of some scheme, conspiracy, or sham. There was also his bearing, his way of putting on airs, his head tossed back—this from a stranger, a guest in GHQ! It was shocking. For the first time in all these ten days, Alekseev sensed revolutionary Petrograd not over the telegraph but through this Bublikov—and it made his hair stand on end! Was this really how it was going to be. Was everyone coming from Petrograd going to be like this?

To think, it was to this Bublikov, as someone devoted to the rails, that Alekseev had personally handed all authority, not picturing his face and conduct, over all the country's railways, which meant the entire course of events.

Had he seen him, he might not have ceded them.

Now there was nothing left but to cede further. To remain polite and obliging with him for two hours. Why spoil relations for nothing?

How the Petrograders had arranged things! Everything difficult for some reason continued to fall on Alekseev, including the bitterness of telling the Emperor about the arrest. For all his audacity, Bublikov did not take that on.

More and more, Alekseev now understood that over these past few days they had done a great deal by his hands.

He dragged his feet into the Dowager Empress's salon car, with the step not of a general but of a woebegone old man.

Standing in the middle of the salon, already awaiting him, without his tall fur hat, was not the Emperor, not the colonel, not a Kuban foot scout, but a forty-eight-year-old, rather plain, weary man, downtrodden an additional dozen years, who opened his eyes wide at Alekseev, not concealing his alarm.

He had been expecting departure, but he sensed something and looked: how else would they strike at him! Cancel his departure? Not let him go to Tsarskoye Selo?

Ailing Alekseev's old heart beat cumbersomely, his tongue stiffened, so hard was it for him to tell him. Why had he agreed to this? . . .

He wasn't strong enough to look into the Tsar's large, trusting, good eyes.

Looking for a gentler, more roundabout way, Alekseev mumbled softly, embarrassedly, that as of this moment, the Provisional Government . . . as if . . . simply as a temporary, precautionary measure . . . basically, in order to ward off revolutionary excesses. . . .

Taking the blow head on, the Emperor's eyelids fluttered even wider and he himself began reassuring Alekseev, telling him not to be upset.

They stood facing each other, alone—for the last of the many times that their everyday service had brought them together. Now the most terrible part had been said—and it was all right. Now perhaps something gentler? Reminisce a little? . . .

No one was stopping them, overseeing them if they now said any words of respect or devotion. But the words didn't come. Something inside was blocked off, fenced off, and Alekseev could not utter anything of the kind.

Relieved that this had gone smoothly, Alekseev then walked down the military platform. To see the deputies. And back to the imperial train car.

It was unavoidable. He had to stop by one more time to say goodbye. Again it was very hard. He stopped in. In the green salon car the Emperor opened his arms wide and embraced Alekseev firmly.

And thanked him, thanked him for everything.

And did not just peck at his cheeks but kissed the general properly three times.

And then, from the platform, saluting, Alekseev honored the Emperor's departure.

The blue train cars with the eagles were off. The ordinary yellow second-class train car with the deputies-commissars followed directly. And Alekseev thought that he dare not fail to say farewell. Saluting them military-fashion would be inappropriate. Here the train car was coming close and he had to do something. Simply wave? Also not appropriate for a general.

He got flustered. And in front of the commissars' train car he removed his cap. And bowed his head.

And immediately regretted it.

He returned to headquarters feeling troubled. Insulted and humiliated. Used.

And again the feeling as if he were guilty before the Emperor gnawed at him. But there was no fault whatsoever. What fault could one name? If anything, the fact that last night he hadn't warned him about the arrest.

Not that that would have helped the Emperor, though. It would only have spoiled his mood sooner.

A troubled, vile state. There was only one true remedy for this condition: work.

Work always awaited, no need to make it up. The endless calculations for transport, food, and fuel. And added to them now was the Allies' intransigent demand that the offensive begin on 8 April!

Ah, easy enough for you to write that.

On top of all the other insults, there was also this one, from the Allies. It was amazing the extent to which they had never made anything easier for the Russians, never lifted any burden! And they did not remember our sacrifices—Samsonov's rescue, the two others in East Prussia, the Brusilov one. And they were constantly meddling in Russian strategy. And they didn't share munitions. They never helped properly in anything and sent help only when they had more than enough. And they kept demanding Russian troops join them at the front. They saddled us with the Romanians. And insisted on appointing a Frenchman as a joint Supreme Commander. And now there was this 8 April.

Both the English and the French manifested themselves only in the fact that they were constantly seeing their interests alone.

Alekseev did not have the right to get irritated and go out of bounds— but he would have liked to tell them!

Our own new government and our newly fledged War Minister, though—did either really understand the state we were in, undermined by ten days of revolution? Only Alekseev, by virtue of his position, could grasp the full extent. But all the more reason for him not to keep this to himself. All his interactions with the government in recent days had been brief twitches on extremely urgent but ephemeral issues. Why couldn't the top government officials themselves come here and try to understand?

That's all right. Alekseev had enough patience to write extensive explanatory telegrams to Guchkov and Lvov both.

It even gave him the possibility of exacting compensation from them for his humiliation. To shake them by saying they knew nothing about anything.

And the tiny loops of his lines ran on and on.

It began back with the Romanian entry into the war, which threw us off-balance, tilted us toward the left flank, destroyed the main operations transport, and exposed our north. Now even the Baltic fleet was not battle-ready, and they could not count on its restoration. Simultaneously, this disintegration was rolling from Petrograd to the Northern Army Group—agitators, insubordination, officers' arrests—and had almost reached the trenches. In this vise we should have recognized the capable clandestine work of our *enemy* taking advantage of irresponsible, backward people. All the hounding had led to a drop in spirit for the officers. What would be left of the army's strength? Given our poorly educated soldiers, everything rested on the officer. Entire military units would soon be unfit for battle. Under these conditions, the Germans could easily force us to roll back. We had to figure out where all the disintegration was coming from. From the factory class and a small share of reserve units in the rear. The farmers and the 10-million-man army at the front had yet to speak up—and they were not going to forgive the coup if it brings a defeat in war. Terrible internecine strife might begin in Russia.

Let it sink in with them that they were not yet rulers of any kind over Russia.

The one salvation was to calm the army and restore the soldier's trust in the officer. For this, the government had to stop indulging the Soviet of Workers' Deputies. Put an end to the endless stream of corrupting appeals! We are awaiting and requesting the arrival of the leading ministers at GHQ for a meeting with the commanders-in-chief. To discuss our demands. Our possibilities. And voluntary restrictions.

When Alekseev had written out his urgent documents in even lines and appropriate language, it was as if he had overcome all the mounting threats, all the distances and misunderstandings due to distance. Finding relief in his arguments, he felt as if he had surmounted the dangers and, as always, he felt better.

By the end of his two long, somber letters, he had calmed down greatly, evened out, begun to hope for good mutual understanding with the government and for that government to curb the Soviet of Deputies and stop the gangrene.

The frustration and awkwardness he'd brought back from the train station dissipated. Alekseev had coped well with the exhaustingly onerous, complicated day and could count on sleeping at least today without emotional anguish.

Tomorrow he would find a way to respond to the Allies, too. At the winter conference, Gurko had not promised them such an early date.

But right then Lukomsky came in with a worried face—and placed before him a copy of *Izvestia of the Soviet of Workers' Deputies*, today's, which had come with the evening mail.

On its soiled page with the smudgy print and many large headlines a small article had been singled out in headquarters red pencil.

And for some reason, Mikhail Vasilievich's heart skipped a beat.

What now? It was . . . It was the newspaper's comments on General Alekseev's order from back on 16 March, when Alekseev had learned only about the first band riding the railway and had telegraphed to Western Army Group headquarters saying not even to disperse these bands but to detain them and immediately appoint a field court martial—and carry out sentences immediately.

At the time, this had been composed so naturally, the simple measure of a military leader, Alekseev had written the telegram text without thinking twice.

Today he might have thought that he had expressed himself too harshly.

But here he was reading the Soviet's newspaper—and his throat and face filled with heat.

. . . Many naïve people consider General Alekseev a man of liberal views and a supporter of the new order. . . .

Yes, he did consider himself such now! Now, of course, he had no other choice than to be a supporter.

. . . In his eyes, disarming railroad gendarmes is a serious crime that merits the death penalty. . . .

Yes, he still did think that. But now he saw he'd overstepped. Based on what had followed . . .

. . . And this was after the new order was established specifically by a seizure of power. . . .

No doubt about that. Mikhail Vasilievich, apparently, had been confused: in fact—had *all* power been seized? . . . And then—why grieve for the gendarmes?

The heat of fear poured through him more and more, simple, crude fear, as he read the fateful, faded lines.

. . . But especially remarkable are the means the general intends to use. . . . General Alekseev is worthy of his overthrown master Nikolai II. The bloody tsar's spirit is alive in the chief of staff. . . .

Oh, that's not good! Linked so crudely.

. . . With this directive, Alekseev signed his own sentence in the eyes of the new order's supporters. . . .

My God, what was this going on? How were they talking? Even more harshly than Bublikov . . . A *sentence*?? . . . The Soviet of Workers' Deputies struck hard . . .

. . . But General Alekseev is not going to find those "reliable units" and "loyal officers."

Apparently that was true.

In the middle of GHQ, in his protected headquarters, over his soundless outpourings to the silent government—against the harsh voice of the Soviet of Deputies, Alekseev felt defenseless, seen through, threatened.

And on his own.

No! He had distanced himself enough from the abdicated Tsar and would not allow himself to be linked with him in any way!

However, the Tsar's removal was why he was now caught on his own.

Sometimes he got angry at the Tsar and forgot how good it had been to enjoy his protection. Without it, you were no force at all.

Never had he heard a single harsh word, or anything of the kind, from the Emperor.

The newspaper concluded: . . . Based on information in our possession, War Minister Guchkov has instructed not to apply the repressive measures General Alekseev had been demanding . . .

How about that! This was how they would abandon him, the brainless government.

Meanwhile here he was writing them not to indulge the Soviet of Deputies! . . . Everything was the wrong way around.

Suddenly he had a thought. The order about the bands was five days ago already, but the response was only today?

He realized: they'd **deceived** him! They'd been aiming at him for a long time but waited for him to arrest the Tsar and see him off!

He had even stopped the Tsar's farewell order. . . .

He'd been *used.* . . .

And now, how was he to defend himself? There was no one to lean on. No one.

He had to quickly vindicate himself.

Express his loyalty somehow.

Here: have GHQ approve a new oath right away.

22 March
Thursday

[517"]

(FROM THE FREE NEWSPAPERS, 21–22 MARCH)

ORDER ON THE ARREST OF NIKOLAI II

WITH PRINCE LVOV. Your correspondent sat for a few minutes in the office of Prince Lvov. An almost eerie, unforgettable scene. As electricity from the entire shaken country flies here, to the universal center . . . He quickly chooses papers, quickly reads, and at the same time picks up the telephone receiver and answers quickly. This magnificent speed of the state's helmsman is salutary and precious. . . .

. . . And this pace adopted by the new government naturally is not compatible with prolonged discussion of legislation in the State Duma. That is now impossible.

. . . The concerns about dual power have been exaggerated, fortunately. The Soviet of Workers' Deputies does not by any means consider itself a "second government.". . .

. . . The Society for Rapprochement with England believes that from now on, under your talented and patriotic leadership, deeply respected Pavel Nikolaevich . . .

. . .The old regime thought to destroy great Russia, but the free people sense with their entire being that right now their duty is to—*bring grain*!

Grain crisis in Germany. Danger of exacerbation. . .

. . . Admiral Nepenin's death was completely random. In port, he ran into a worker, who shot him.
Admiral Nebolsin was killed in analogous circumstances.

WITH GENERAL RUZSKY. Hero of the Great War Gen. Ruzsky joined the people immediately after receiving the first news of the dawn of freedom that had splashed over the capital. The Tsar headed to Pskov in hopes that Gen. Ruzsky would help him pacify the rebels. But from the general's first words, the tyrant realized that his hopes were absurd. . . . The general's horizons are so broad that he freely accommodates all currents of

582

political life up to and including socialist teachings. The *Russian Will* correspondent was pleasantly surprised when he was convinced that Gen. Ruzsky has easily gained his bearings with the subtleties of the Social Democratic majority and minority.

(Russian Will, 21 March)

WITH KIRILL VLADIMIROVICH. The first of the grand dukes to recognize the new government. A red flag flies over his palace. Admiral Romanov graciously met me at his office door. . . . He makes no attempt to hide his satisfaction at the coup: "My yardman and I—we saw identically that Russia would lose everything with its old government. . . . But there was no point telling the Tsar. What was he doing that he had no time to listen? There's no hiding it: Aleksandra Fyodorovna ruled Russia. Viktoria Fyodorovna spoke with her, shed light on the country's situation, and named the individuals worthy of being important ministers. The Tsaritsa was outraged."

(Russian Will, 21 March)

DISLOYAL LACKEYS. Future generations will be stunned. How did it happen that autocracy was abandoned at the first shot? . . . The caste that lived and fed at the table of autocracy then hid in its burrows, not moving a finger . . . while the Tsar they abandoned waited all alone in his train car for the Russian people's magnanimity. The English Carlists and French royalists offered acts of self-sacrifice, whereas these . . . In all Russia, there turned out to be one person with sufficient courage not to survive the regime's fall and shoot himself: *Zubatov*!

. . .On 21 March, the first legal assembly of the Petrograd Jewish Zionist Party. Take every measure to support the Provisional Government in its liberation work . . . in the interests of the flourishing of the Jewish people's life in Russia and the national-political resurrection of the Jewish nation in Palestine.

. . . A meeting of the Petrograd section of the Bund.

FALSE RUMORS. Over the course of 18 and 19 March, in Petrograd, ill-intentioned individuals stepped up their efforts to spread rumors about Jewish pogroms that had supposedly taken place in certain towns in Russia. They named Vitebsk, Kovel, and others. Upon careful verification of these rumors by State Duma Deputy Friedman, it turned out that they lacked any and all foundation. On the contrary, the news of the lifting of national restrictions was met sympathetically by all strata of Russia's population.

Statement by Procurator V. Lvov. . . . I have always fought procurators' autocratic directives, but in this instance I have entered the church department with a sturdy broom. This broom will touch everything unfit and harmful—for the good of the Orthodox church and the state. . . . All the trash will be swept out in the very near future. . . .

THE PALACES TO THE PEOPLE! One cannot fail to note with outrage the voices calling for the cautious treatment of the palaces, saying that there are art treasures there. We know the "enlightened" taste of despots. Their collecting has borne a repugnant character. There are almost no "art treasures.". . .

. . .There is a plan to raise on Palace Square a column of Liberty even more magnificent than the present column of Victory—and on it in gold letters will be written the names of all the revolution's heroes. It has been proposed renaming it February Square.

Two influential foreign diplomats have laid out in detail to Frederiks the demands and hopes of the Russian people. However, so that he would report this to the Emperor as if it were from him, for one cannot tell the Tsar that foreign diplomats are interfering in Russian domestic life. But he forgot everything, took out his sheet of paper in front of the Tsar, and the Tsar asked . . .

Pyotr Kropotkin on the revolution. Today your correspondent visited Kropotkin in Brighton. The great revolutionary said that since first receiving the news from Russia he hasn't been able to work at anything. His joy is indescribable. He deeply believes that despotism has collapsed in Russia for good. Now it is absolutely impossible to remain abroad.

THEY SUCCUMBED. Over the past week, 96 people have suffered psychic disturbances and entered the municipal hospital of St. Nicholas on the Pryazhka. Primarily men. On 20 March alone, 27 were admitted.

THE UNITED STATES RECOGNIZES THE NEW RUSSIAN GOVERNMENT

ON THE WESTERN FRONT. THE GERMANS' RETREAT.

CONVOCATION OF A CONSTITUENT ASSEMBLY IN MOSCOW. . . . There can be no other decision about the convocation's location. Moscow is Russia's heart and cradle. Moscow played an important role in the popular movement. The organizations that readied the revolution arose in Moscow. On the same basis, the central government should be moved to Moscow in order to make a final break with the Petrograd era of Russian history.

STREETCAR LEVERS. Anyone who **returns** streetcar levers to the Administration **will be given a reward**: 5 rubles for a large lever; 3 for a small one; for a lever with a brake cock, 5.

Servants' rallies. On 21 March, rallies were held at many markets for domestic servants demanding their emancipation.

Meeting of waiters and other employees of the tavern and restaurant business. On the question of the current moment, the meeting resolved that if the Provisional Government attempts to decline to implement the program, the Soviet of Workers' Deputies must immediately declare itself the provisional revolutionary government.

Do not refuse, dear people, to help a poor parish restore the church of St. Nicholas to replace the one that burned down.

A room is needed in a Jewish family for a young lady, a free artist.

For sale: a raccoon coat, a nobleman's uniform with a triangle . . .

ARREST OF ALEKSANDRA FYODOROVNA

ARREST OF NIKOLAI II

SEIZURE OF DOCUMENTS. At Tsarskoye Selo and, evidently, at GHQ and Livadia, a seizure has been carried out of documents of state importance. These documents will be examined by a special commission of inquiry.

. . . One can rest easy for the life of the crowned nonentity: it would never occur to anyone to confer on him the martyr's crown.

(Stock Exchange Gazette)

DO NOT BELIEVE THE ROMANOVS! . . . Make sure the emperor's dear mama shares the prisoners' fate as well!

CITIZENS OF RUSSIA! INHABITANTS OF THE COUNTRYSIDE! . . . It falls to you, the tillers of the earth, to help immediately with provisions. . . . Brothers, do not let Russia perish! Do not betray your homeland! Bring and sell your grain voluntarily, not waiting for special instructions.

Rodzyanko

. . . Minister of Finance Tereshchenko went to the banks' representatives in hopes that the country's financial and economic life would now richly prosper.

For the revolution's needs, about half a million rubles has been collected in the Petrograd stock exchange's wings.

SAFEGUARD THE ARMY! Alarming rumors have come in. Some people have infiltrated the army, for now there is full freedom of movement and speech, and they are preaching a speedy and inglorious end to the war. They're telling the regiments: refuse to fight and the war will end. One doesn't want to believe that any Russian citizens would be capable of this!

. . . Everyone who has absented himself without permission from the 175th Infantry Reserve Regiment must return to the regiment in the next few days. Otherwise they will be considered to be supporters of the old regime.

ABOLITION OF THE DEATH PENALTY BEING PREPARED. . . . Let the grandeur and beauty of the people's aspirations take full effect! Let us see the dawn of our free life without the death penalty! The weak and spineless regime could hold fast only by intimidation, the gallows, and the whip. The Russian revolution celebrates its victory differently! Powerful and mighty, it has boldly abolished the death penalty! And at this critical moment, as passions burn.

. . . Strange though it seems, the grandest revolution of all has not brought us a free press. Without special permission from the Executive Committee of the Soviet of Workers' Deputies, the issuing of publications is forbidden.

(Speech)

. . . Anarchy, excesses, robberies, burglaries of private apartments, property damage, and pointless seizures of institutions continue to this day. . . .

INTERVIEW WITH KIRILL VLADIMIROVICH. "What can I add to what the broad masses know? My credo? Who does not know it? It has come to pass. The coup is the former Emperor's fault. Only madmen could suppose that there were 1300 machine guns on roofs and churches. . . .
. . . Did I, a grand duke, not experience the old regime's knout?
. . . Did I conceal my deep beliefs to the people? Did I go against the people during the days of the great liberation? My beloved Guards Crew and I went to the State Duma, that temple of the people. . . . I say all this not to vindicate myself; I have committed no particular sins. Now, however, the old ships have been burned and ahead I see only the shining stars of the people's happiness. The Russian people will take a deep breath and set about forging happiness for themselves. . . ."

(Stock Exchange Gazette)

Tardy repentance. "We, the undersigned officers and civilian ranks of the surveillance police, mourn the fact that, being by the nature of our service scattered all over the territory of Moscow and left to the tyranny of fate, we have been deprived against our will of the opportunity to share in the national joy on the occasion of Russia's liberation. We dare hope that our belated sympathy will be accepted as a pledge of our loyalty."

(More than 200 signatures)

Odessa. Enrolled as lawyers have been 60 assistants, Jews. The local rightist newspaper, *Russian Speech*, has been discontinued. As of tomorrow, the same publisher will begin publishing progressively oriented newspapers.

Voronezh. Organizers of the local office of the Union of the Russian People have been arrested.

NORTH AMERICAN UNITED STATES ON THE EVE OF DECLARATION OF WAR AGAINST GERMANY. . . . The entire population of the United States thirsts for war. . . . A loan to the Allies of 1 billion dollars is expected.

. . . The capital's population is perplexed. Why does streetcar service cease daily at seven o'clock in the evening? This is explained by the fact that the streetcar employees must discuss a number of professional and political issues. This discussion will take only a few evenings.

On 23 March, a meeting of domestic servants will be held at the European Theater.

GRANDIOSE FIRE IN VLADIVOSTOK. In the fire, 2 million pounds of American cotton burned up.

Elizavetgrad. A military unit passing through released 40 deserters being held for crimes. Then the crowd attacked the criminal investigations department.

Chita. Spiridonova and others arrived from hard labor in Nerchinsk. The people have greeted the hero-sufferers with enthusiasm, bearing them on their arms.

WILL BUY AN ESTATE, district and price unimportant.

Grand mansion for sale on the Bolshaya Nevka embankment.

WILL PAY MORE THAN ANYONE ELSE for precious stones, gold. . . .

[5 1 8]

He had the misfortune to know what the pain in the center of his chest was: he had already had a heart attack. And that immediate helplessness of being unable to find a comfortable position lying down, let alone standing. You're instantly pinned down by this splitting pain, like a blade driven in, and you're no minister of great Russia and the Russian army but a doomed scarecrow who has overstayed his welcome.

And you call out—"Masha! Masha!"—for help, for a compress. Then you remember you were the one who left her and migrated to the official residence. It's strange, though, after a while she does appear instead of the adjutant—and strokes, massages your chest. Maybe it will ease up. Yes, it seems to be easing up.

The scale of our helplessness is conveyed to us, a signal reminding us of our limits—and all at once our righteousness is shaken, as is our power to blame other people, like Masha. Just yesterday he could not forgive her that during the unrepeatable days of revolution she had dared bedevil him with her petty scenes, her played-up, incessant conceit. She couldn't see events through his eyes but looked at everything her own way, insatiably.

And now, gratefully feeling her concern and touch on his sick chest, he thought: this is her misery, after all. Women's miserable, lifelong imbalance, first a prolonged maidenhood, then a frigid sexuality, but her heart, like everyone else's, required happiness, required it—even if it takes outbursts, insults, and tears.

Her misery was greater than his. But after all, three children had been born. And though one son was killed due to her negligence and one was a Mongoloid—that wasn't her fault, and then there was Verochka, his favorite—whose was she?

When you're together so many years, no matter how methodically you cut yourself off, any five-minute period, any event or look, can make the worst attitude suddenly turn warm and render you powerless to go on being cold. After so many years together, how could warmth not build?

And when you're already fifty years old and you're lying there helpless, and you don't know whether it will let you go, you can't help but reconcile with her and immediately forgive her for all the years of hysterical incoherency, reconcile yourself to her as she is. Suddenly you discover that despite everything, she has burrowed deep into your heart.

We are all going to die, even soon perhaps—so what is it we're always fighting over?

But whether his heart had grown battle-weary or just stale—even lying in death's shadow, he felt no urge to pray, for some reason. Nothing remained inside him from his Old Believer childhood.

He seemed to be getting better, anyhow.

He and Masha were now talking softly, amiably.

There was no explanation for why this happened today. He wouldn't have been surprised the day before yesterday, in the morning, after his harrowing conversation with the Soviet the night before. But nothing happened yesterday. On the contrary, he had given a speech in the City Duma, an evening of celebration, and had once again felt young, once again a hero. But here . . .

What was he to do now about his trip, though? After all, last evening he had been thinking about going to Riga.

The decision to travel had been born of the accumulated hopelessness of the past few days. For nearly a full week, the minister responsible for the army of a warring country had sat helplessly in his office and received soul-scorching denunciations: insubordinations, arrests of major officials, turmoil in the garrisons. Yesterday quite nearby, in Vyborg, the fortress commandant had been arrested—and nothing could be done. And now there were the tedious sessions of the Provisional Government, where, Guchkov would have said without error, there was not a single man besides him.

A war going on? That meant all the chief events should be happening on the fronts. But that was exactly where they weren't. All of battle-ready and

armor-clad Russia had stood stock-still along the fronts, stock-still as if perplexed: it had not responded to the revolution in any kind of full voice.

These past few days, Guchkov had begun to think that if he stopped ossi-
fying in Petersburg offices and broke away to the front he could solve this
riddle, and maybe even favorably. His true place was there, in the army's
midst. That was where correct ideas and actions would find him.

Touring Petrograd barracks, as he had done at the beginning, had disappointed him. This wasn't an army at all, not soldiers at all, but some viscous,
foolish mass not in the least drawn by what their minister had to say, spoiled
by agitators.

He felt like uniting with strength, movement, and success. That could
only happen at the front.

But he couldn't go too far away now either: Petrograd might need him at
any moment. The simplest trip was to the 12th Army, to Riga, to his good
friend, the Bulgarian Radko-Dmitriev. They had their old Balkan friendship, and Guchkov had defended him from attacks which said that he was
to blame for Mackensen's breakthrough outside Gorlitsa.

But how could he go now?

And Masha, inspired by their restored intimacy, in a sweep of her invigo-
rated energy:

"Sasha! It's fine! We'll go! I'll be with you. I'll look after you in the train
car, and you can lie down."

Maybe yes, then? He so did not want to cancel it, he had made up his
mind.

So, take Masha along? Just yesterday that would have seemed wild, but
now it actually seemed natural.

"Just lie there the whole day and don't do anything. We'll go this
evening!"

The Polivanov Commission is meeting today . . . He would like to.

"Well, you may be right. You are right. Let's go."

With his gratitude to her. And with her even greater gratitude to him.

[5 1 9]

Nikolai was riding in his imperial train—filled with lofty sorrow, regret,
contemplation, farewell, and dreams. He hadn't read anything on this trip,
no news had been reported to him, and mostly he had looked out the window. All he saw were snowdrifts and snowy fields (yesterday, between Orsha
and Vitebsk, a blizzard had even delayed the train).

Suddenly he remembered: today was the day lark buns were baked
among the people.

The cheerful return of the larks.

At stops, looking through a slit in the curtain, he saw strangely idle groups of railroaders and simply inhabitants. They stood in silence, saluted the train in silence, and removed their caps in silence—as if the train were carrying a dead man.

At the smaller stations, Nikolai did not see a single red scrap on anyone's chest; there were some at the larger ones, but even they gawked at the train silently. At the Dno station, however (how recently he had passed through here on the way to Pskov!), many soldiers crowded on the platform, quite peaceloving. Their eyes ran over the curtained windows, evidently searching for their Emperor, of course! They walked up to the conductors and asked, but it was all muffled, and sounded like whispers.

The entire progress of the train, his last, was accompanied like this, by snow, silence, and whispers.

The Emperor was shy and couldn't bring himself to appear to the people, did not see the point of letting them look at him or telling them anything. He was shy—and hid behind the curtains.

He was riding in the imperial train, but the train was less and less under his control, slipping out from under what was left of his influence, but Nikolai noticed none of this. Now there was no all-confident, all-knowing Voeikov, who would cheerfully come to report to the Emperor on the train's progress and ask for instructions. He had been replaced in the position by young Dolgorukov, but it was not he running the train now, he had been removed from the details, and it felt as if the trip were deaf and dumb. Now it was the deputies from the last train car who were in contact with the railroaders. And when at the 149th verst they stopped in a field—no one came to explain. Much later it was learned that the rails had heaved and the track guard had stopped them.

Nor did Nikolai know anything about what his half-dissolved suite was thinking and doing.

He did not know that Life Surgeon Fyodorov, in his own compartment, had scratched the Emperor's monogram off his greatcoat epaulets—so that he could disembark at Tsarskoye Selo without them. (But he left the monogram on his tunic, so that he could attend the Tsar's table.)

He did not know that dear Count Mordvinov had managed to find out before everyone else that the train from Vyritsa would not go directly to Tsarskoye Selo but would make a detour through Gatchina. What luck! He arranged with one and another train official for a stop to be made in Gatchina, where his family lived—and he would get off with his baggage (already packed).

He did not know that Aide-de-camp Naryshkin, who had recently written a transcript of the entire abdication scene, had now explained to one person and another that he could not be detained in Tsarskoye Selo for he had urgent personal business in Petrograd. He also seriously advised everyone to obey the Provisional Government's directives because that was the one right thing to do.

He didn't know that the rest of the suite, except for Dolgorukov, were petrified that they all faced arrest when they stepped onto the platform at Tsarskoye Selo—and were only calmed by the thought that they should be let go, nothing bad had been ascribed to them.

The rail officials were worried, too, recalling Valuyev's recent murder— also for no reason, after all.

Nikolai did not know that delegations from the imperial servants had crossed the train car platform and gone into the commissars' last train car— to recommend themselves, both with gifts of money and with royal dinners for the Duma deputies.

But they had their own concerns: sending telegrams to Petrograd from the major stations, being startled at every unexpected stop for fear an attack on the train was being readied—to free the Tsar?

No one had brought Nikolai all this news, not that it was the way of members of the suite to report on one another. They gathered for the next meal and talked about the train's speed, the weather, even military move-ments at the fronts, where there were no movements right now. Before, in good times, the Emperor had attempted to make jokes at the table—but somehow the suite failed to understand them.

At one of the stations someone got a newspaper and read about Voeikov's arrest in Vyazma.

The suite took this ominously, as a sign for themselves.

And Nikolai said, about Voeikov and Frederiks:

"I feel sorry for them. What are they guilty of?"

They passed through Susanino.

There was also a stir between Semrino and Gatchina, on the transfer line, a sharp whistle, a stop, and people walked uneasily from the commissars' train car.

They were stopping at Gatchina when Nikolai saw things being un-loaded off to the side, only he didn't understand whose.

At the Aleksandrovskaya station he was able to read the inscription on the arch on red cotton cloth: "Down with the vile autocracy."

His shoulders twitched like from the lash of a whip.

The closer they got to Tsarskoye Selo, all the journey's moderate, rolling gloom turned into alarm in the Emperor. He was suddenly troubled that all was not well: he wasn't traveling of his own accord but being taken—and where else? Would they even let him join Alix?

For the first time he felt powerless over his own fate.

For the final half-hour he had to say goodbye at last with all the train staff (Nikolai went to their train car) and with the train's upper-level personnel.

Then to his own salon car, where he had abdicated a week before.

And to his official study.

And to his sleeping compartment, full of icons.

He wiped away tears.

Here the train had pulled up to the royal pavilion—the small royal train station in the cheerful style of a traditional Russian tent, off to the side from the regular station and on a separate branch.

The sun was hazy but not obscured.

No one had been summoned to await this spectacle: the Tsar's arrival. Outsiders had not been allowed here before. Now a small silent crowd had gathered, but very few—a few in civilian dress, some curious soldiers without weapons but with red headgear and poorly belted, twenty or so. No one had come from the palace to meet him, though they always used to. The most senior greeters were two colonels and the railroad officials.

The royal car, deliberately as always, stopped directly opposite the tent— but no one invited him to get off right away, and Nikolai himself hesitated.

First, the commissars from the last train car walked up to the individuals in charge and discussed with them on the platform.

Meanwhile, people kept coming off the train, without lingering, and dispersing.

The aides-de-camp disappeared.

The sole person remaining from the entire suite of twelve men was young Prince Vasili Dolgorukov. He was waiting to accompany the Emperor to the palace and making arrangements for his things.

Finally, a colonel from the platform said he could come out. The Emperor was told.

Already prepared, dressed, wearing the same Kuban batallion Circassian coat with the purple-lined hood, his tall black fur hat, and his Cossack dagger at his waist, Nikolai stepped off the train car—no, he hopped off abruptly. And again to general silence, as in Mogilev, he ran across into the tent, his head lowered—as quickly as he could past another new disgrace!—through it—and into a closed motorcar, with Dolgorukov.

The garrison colonels got into their own. And so both motorcars headed off to the palace.

Dear Tsarskoye Selo lay in its cozy snowdrifts, but scattered on the clean snow were shreds of newspapers, papers, and empty cigarette packs, and the few soldiers they came across were so incredibly dissolute in their uniforms, it hurt the military eye.

Someone recognized the Tsar's motorcar, and someone even shook his fist at it.

At the Aleksandr Palace's lattice gate stood a reinforced guard—not his, but Guards riflemen.

They had always rushed to open the gate for the Emperor's motorcar— but now, as if not understanding, someone shouted sharply from behind the gate:

"Who's here?"

There was no one to answer from the motorcar.

And the unfamiliar ensign on duty at the gate was in no hurry to give the order to open it.

Meanwhile someone else, who was coming down the palace stairs, asked: "Who's here?"

And the same sharp voice from the gate, the first who asked, replied defiantly, clearly:

"Nikolai Romanov!"

A lieutenant appeared—a burning cigarette in his fingers, a red bow on his chest—and shouted:

"Open the gate for the former Tsar!"

They did. The motorcar drove in.

Standing on the porch were other riflery officers, and in a row below, the riflemen, all with red scraps pinned on.

He had to walk through quickly once again. Not looking. Not seeing. As quickly as he could.

Nikolai darted across and climbed to the porch—and no one saluted, no one stood at attention.

But he had to salute them. His hand rose to his hat all by itself.

How else could a military man walk past a soldier?

[5 2 0]

From the windows of Northern Army Group headquarters, one can see, across the snow-covered Velikaya River, the Spaso-Mirozhsky monastery.

Apparently, no one in the press has yet to notice this.

But we will. A call from one century to another. Which one? The twelfth probably? The thirteenth? And the twentieth. There—fantastical little domes, and silence. Here, in front of headquarters—motorcars snorting.

No, even better: after all, this was the old republic of Pskov. And so, across the Velikaya River (*nota bene*!), the old republic was reaching out to the new one formed right here, in Pskov. A marvelous beginning!

In front of Ruzsky's rooms, by the cloakroom, was a Cossack orderly. (We shall also write this down. The reader lives for details, and the *Stock Exchange Gazette* is nothing if not vivid.) A reception room. A worn desk with an inkwell. Worn, old-fashioned chairs.

Here comes the general. A fluffy gray mustache. A subtle, dimmed smile. Weary blue eyes. A shining white rectangular haircut. (Sprinkle the text with these details, in order to maintain the visual impression.)

"Is it true, general, sir, that today your headquarters has taken an oath to the Provisional Government?"

"Yes, these are solemn moments for us, and I have already sent a telegram about this to Prince Lvov and Rodzyanko. We have sworn our full obedience to the government until the Constituent Assembly, which will establish a model . . ."

A narrow, sunken chest. Cigarette-stained teeth, probably from constant tobacco. (Don't write that.) Sucking on a yellow glass cigarette holder.

"That means your army group is to be congratulated. After your oath, your spirit of confidence will mount. Tell me, what is the troops' spirit in general?"

"The troops' spirit is wonderful, despite some distraction." (A muffled monotone, but we won't mention that.) "It is the natural movement of joy for their liberated homeland. But the army will quickly suppress it and focus on the everyday work of war. We will hold on under all circumstances!" the commander-in-chief said with steely decisiveness.

He had a mole on his chin, and on the mole, a whorl of gray hairs. (Put that in? Don't put it in? It's valuable for a correspondent's acuity, but not helpful for the general tone.)

"True, sinister people have latched on to the great cause. A great many pretenders have appeared, and they are endlessly dangerous for the popular cause. In one township they burned down the zemstvo's food storehouses. But this is all temporary, transitional. . . . All this will die down and we will come to stand on firm ground."

"What do we know about the enemy's intention? Is he preparing a decisive offensive on Petrograd?"

"Very possibly. We are holding back the Germans only by force of arms. The Dvina is frozen solid, there are hard frosts at night, and if there isn't a sudden quick thaw, military actions are perfectly possible."

A completely ungeneral-like, but rather pleasant intellectual manner of speaking and interacting. His profession aside, the correspondent simply enjoys talking to him. And touching on subtler questions.

"And what can you say about the former Tsar, general?"

The general looked at him with intelligent, weary, piercing eyes:

"What is there to say! A spineless man. That's about all one can say about him."

This, for example: "The elderly general with the crimson bow on his strong, square old chest, shows a young man's white teeth when laughing gaily, raspily, through bitter tobacco smoke."

"By the way, the Emperor did not like newspapers. Although people are wrong in saying he didn't read them at all."

"But was he at least intelligent?"

"Whether or not he was intelligent, I don't know. I knew him so little."

"Really?"

"Rarely did I have occasion to speak with him. I was busy doing what I was doing. And he was always taciturn, and his silence was not without cunning. I don't know whom he trusted, but not me. He was always listening only to his daily advisors, who surrounded him tightly. Anyone who saw him once a month or less often, like, say, Mikhail Vladimirovich Rodzyanko—he couldn't have any effect."

"Frederiks? Voeikov?"

"Frederiks, you know, I feel sorry for him. How can he be blamed for his advanced age or for his devotion to the Emperor? But Voeikov—I don't feel the least bit sorry for him."

"Protopopov?"

"There were no two more opposite figures than Protopopov and myself."

"And what was the Empress's influence on him?"

"Well, it wasn't a good influence. Relations between her and the Tsar's mother were not good, either."

We'll write this: "With chivalrous restraint, lowering his soft voice, Ruzsky speaks about the Tsaritsa's role in intimate affairs of state."

"It's terrible, terrible . . . The Tsaritsa had a definite influence on the Tsar. This explains a great deal about his character. He was always influenced by whoever spoke to him last."

Possibly: "The general has a simply unconsciously good, absent-minded smile. It is as if he were hinting at the abdicated Tsar's lack of character and mental shakiness."

"He was . . . he was a cautious, secretly reflective man."

. . . Not long ago the absolute but liberal master of the Petrograd press (when he was District commander), Ruzsky enjoyed great sympathy in newspaper circles—and he valued that. He knew that relations with the press were a delicate point and an effective instrument. In order to win public opinion, the commander-in-chief of the army group closest to the capital could not disdain the press but should rather make friends with it. The press was Petrograd basically; and *Russian Will* was made strong by its support from banking circles; and he needed to be friendly especially with the *Stock Exchange Gazette*, a newspaper that was a power unto itself. Not only that, but any time he spoke about the Tsar or especially about the Tsaritsa, he was filled with the unforgettable, ineradicable offense of having been removed from the Northern Army Group, undoubtedly at the Tsaritsa's insistence, forced to rest even after his treatment, and then humiliatingly was not reappointed and had had to seek out roundabout influence. He had always had to suppress this deep down and discuss it only with his wife, who suffered from the humiliations—and now this pressure had shifted, let up, and for the first time he could speak openly, in front of society. However, it was precisely in the events of recent days that the general had lost his support to such an extent, his sense of balance, that he involuntarily looked for it, even in this interview. It was as if he had already gone too far.

"But you must remember that Aleksandra Fyodorovna was quite ill. A bad heart."

"Isn't she a hysteric, though?"

"No, you can't say that. She is a restrained woman, you can sense her character. Now the girls—I like them a lot. She has fine, amiable children. The boy, too."

"Tell me, though, did her relationship with Rasputin . . . mmm . . . were there any grounds . . .?"

"No, no," Ruzsky protested. "To speak of an erotic relationship is out of the question. There was nothing of the kind."

The correspondent, with a disappointed face, wrote his loops in his notepad in pencil.

"Tell me, though, at least, was Nikolai Romanov patriotic? Or was he indifferent to our country?"

Ruzsky tried not to show any rancor:

"To judge from his words, he was a Russian. Do you remember his statement about war to the end, until the last German soldier was driven from Russia's borders?"

"Well, that was a clever paraphrase of Aleksandr I."

Ruzsky searched for something good he might say about the fallen Tsar.

"Yes, he should have listened to society's voice, shown flexibility—and he would have survived."

He sucked on his cigarette holder. No arguments came to mind.

"Yes, certainly, he himself is to blame that everything came about for him as it did."

But then—he smiled an appealing smile, knowing it was attractive and this would be written down:

"Who am I to judge, though? I myself have so many shortcomings. . . ."

[5 2 1]

(ARMY FRAGMENTS)

*   *   *

On 17 March, Lieutenant Colonel Burya was walking past a guard in the Dvinsk Fortress—the guard was carrying his rifle like a cane and did not salute.

"Why aren't you giving me honor?"

"I didn't borrow it from you!"

*   *   *

When at the train station near Shtoksmanhof, in Livonia, a reserve infantry battalion on its way to the front learned of the Tsar's abdication, it rushed to ransack the station's food stores. The authorities called in the 5th Uhlan Regiment to suppress—but returned it to its positions out of timidity.

*   *   *

In some places the Germans are having bands and firework displays. They're throwing proclamations at us from aeroplanes or attaching them to the propellers of incoming mortars.

*   *   *

In Simferopol, the garrison chief, General Radovsky, read out the abdication manifestos to the lined-up troops. He announced that he supported the new regime and called on them all to sing together, "God Save the Tsar." The troops did.

For this the general was given a week's arrest.

*   *   *

Volunteer B., in a tall white fur hat, with an oriental face, wearing spectacles, shouted to the battalion commander who had stood on a chair to read the delayed telegrams:

"What are you reading there? Nikolai's gone now! Kindly step down. . . ."

The soldiers ripped off the commander's shoulder straps and his revolver and put them on B. He climbed on the chair:

"I am taking temporary command of the battalion into my own hands. We will arrest the gentlemen officers for now. We need to clarify whether they are with or against the people."

The soldier Alperovich thought, not too smart for him, being a Jew, to poke his nose in like that. Hope he doesn't spoil everything. If things don't pan out, we Jews will be the first to answer. (He himself was ashamed of this slavish thought.)

But B.'s intelligent face was full of resolve.

The officers were led to the guardhouse. The soldier crowd shouted: "Give him what for!" "Stick him with a bayonet!" "Let him eat lentils!" "They should be shot, the villains!"

When they'd been led away, someone shouted:

"Now arrest the sergeant majors and platoon commanders!"

"Arrest them!" came the echo.

Anyone who had a grudge against anyone said his name, and the crowd rushed to find the offender.

A soldier, a former surveyor, Zyornov, started to protest:

"What kind of freedom is this, brothers? This is chaos."

They pointed at him:

"This one . . . take him. . . . He's for the old government."

(*From Stock Exchange Gazette, 26 April 1917*)

*   *   *

General Count Keller, commander of the 3rd Cavalry Corps, was an indefatigable horseman who could cover one hundred versts in a day. When, showing off his smart seat, he appeared before the regiments wearing his tall wolf fur hat and the knee-length coat of the Orenburg Cossacks, his cavalrymen were ready to follow him anywhere, at the wave of his hand. Now, near Kishinev, he ordered a combined formation assembled out of all the squadrons and announced loudly from his horse:

"I have received a dispatch about the Emperor's abdication and some provisional government. I, your old commander, having shared your deprivations, and battles, and victory, I do not believe that at such a moment His Majesty the Emperor could willingly abandon the army and Russia to their death. I have sent a telegram: 'The 3rd Cavalry Corps does not believe that You, the Emperor, have voluntarily abdicated the throne. Give your order, Sire, and we will come and defend You!'"

"Hurrah! Hurrah!" cried the dragoons, Cossacks, and hussars. "Lead us!"

But a few hours later the irrevocable was confirmed—and Keller broke his sword in front of the formation.

*   *   *

In Kazan, in a reserve regiment, a rogue soldier proposed (so he wouldn't have to go to training exercises): "Let's go to prayers today to mark our new freedom." And everyone started shouting: "Let's go to prayers, we don't want to go to training!"

But the Tatar soldiers, about forty of them, lined up and approached their officer: "Lead us to training, your honor!"

First the company commander, then the battalion commander, then the regimental commander tried to persuade the rest. It didn't help. Then the colonel asked loudly: "And who is it wants to go to prayers? Who?"

"I do!" the instigator came forward.

"Here's a ruble. Go to the priest and have him say a prayer service for you. We'll all go when we get an order to go."

They settled down.

*   *   *

Colonel Oberuchev, a member of People's Will in his youth, then an SR, became Kiev's first war commissar and hurried to the military guardhouse to cheer up whoever was languishing there for avoiding service, escaping, and disciplinary infringements to say their release would soon be approved. There was no end to their raptures. And suddenly he was amazed to learn that the first "political prisoner of the new regime" was already there—a youthful officer, a Pole. The commander of their first Polish regiment, formed in Kiev, had demanded from his officers written explanation of how they regarded the coup. This ensign submitted a report saying that he regarded the coup negatively and stood for Nikolai II. The regiment's commander arrested him. Oberuchev, who had despised this Tsar his entire life, asked:

"And you, a Pole, you love Nikolai II that much?"

"Yes, I want to see him on the throne."

"And you will try to restore him?"

"Without fail."

"How are you thinking of doing that?"

"If I just find out that a plot is maturing somewhere in his favor, I'll definitely join it," he replied without hesitation.

"And if there isn't anywhere?"

The youth thought about that:

"I'll put one together myself . . ."

A few days later, though, after reading the newspapers, he admitted:

"It's hopeless."

✻   ✻   ✻

When Order No. 1 reached the reserve regiment stationed at Borisoglebsk, the reinforcement company's commander, a warrant-ensign from the sergeant-majors, a St. George medalist, attempted to hide it. But it was found by another officer, an ensign from the students, who assembled a company assembly and read the "order" out loud. After this the company demanded their commander be replaced before they were sent to the front. And they chose a new commander: the ensign-student.

✻   ✻   ✻

Reports came in from the heavy artillery regiment stationed at Tsarskoye Selo about a counterrevolutionary mood. Then the speakers bureau of the Petrograd Soviet of Workers' Deputies sent an agitator to the regiment. He clarified that these artillerists were dissatisfied with Orders Nos. 1 and 2 and were demanding another, sensible one. They believed that we had no free press and the Soviet of Workers' and Soldiers' Deputies was concealing its attitude toward the war—so let it make itself clear. And reports that not everyone in the Soviet had a proper mandate, and there were hooligans meeting there, and why weren't there any officer delegates there? And what was this instruction not to go to the front? The regiment was getting ready to go. And what about land? The soldiers were worried they weren't going to get anything.

*   *   *

In some rear units, the soldiers were worried that the old government might return. They regarded their officers suspiciously. In one unit they called a rally, and the regiment's commander ordered that they go without rifles. This aroused great suspicion, and everyone took rifles.

Here and there soldiers started posting their own guards in addition to the regulation ones—at weapons stores, and in excessive numbers. They suspected officer betrayal.

"Now let them give us ten a month pay. If they don't, we'll go make trouble!"

*   *   *

Outside Derpt, the 282nd Reinforcement Battalion arrested some of its officers and arrested neighboring landowners and their stewards—and started selling the produce and inventory from those estates.

*   *   *

Under the new oath, the soldier was troubled that each had to sign: "I may not lay a hand" (an old Russian concept). The delegates explained: "Because you are citizens now, and each man must sign consciously."

*   *   *

In the 80th Siberian Regiment, the first chairman of the soldiers' committee was a priest.

The Jäger Reserve Battalion in Petrograd chose a joint soldier-officer committee. An ensign chaired, the secretary was a volunteer with a university lapel pin, and the soldier deputies included university students, actors, and journalists.

*   *   *

Just yesterday the soldiers had been carrying Lieutenant Timokhin on their shoulders, saying they trusted him not to do anything bad. But today he came to the company and they shouted "Get out!" and announced they'd elected themselves a new company commander.

[5 2 2]

It was starting today that the Executive Committee thought to convene its sessions later, and in a new room: the larger no. 15, which was also in a calm corridor, from which it was also separated by an anteroom, conveniently.

The move began early in the morning. The Executive Committee members were far from all there, but hovering among them was the very excited Sokolov, who was trying to convince everyone he caught that they could not put it off, the Soviet had to approve a greeting to the Polish people and state that the entire democracy of Russia stood for recognition of Poland's independence. But they listened to him distractedly and waved him off. Some were busy with the move, others couldn't understand why Poland's independence exactly was the very first and most critical question today. Even Himmer the internationalist wouldn't agree with Sokolov. This was the influence of Polish bourgeois-patriotic circles, and the proletariat's global class unity forbade us from facilitating any national independence, as it did from preventing it, for that matter.

In the new room the furniture was scattered about (they had probably been dragging it around other rooms for the past few days). First of all, there was no table big enough for the whole sprawling Executive Committee. The chairs were all different and some wobbled. There were wicker armchairs, some with broken seats. And there was a luxurious Turkish sofa. And a magnificent gilt pier-glass that the eyes of even EC members couldn't help but give a sideways glance.

However, before they could set things up properly or bring in a conference table (in addition, the food table was still in the old room), a storm broke out: the Executive Committee's railways commissar reported by telephone that he had received an alarming communication from the railroaders saying that two royal letter trains were moving along the railway at the present moment—and they were both moving toward the border, evidently toward Tornio, and their goal was evacuating the former Tsar to England!

Stunning! Staggering!

Like any outsize and unexpected news, it wiped memory clean, took away the ability to correlate and consider. Everyone had completely lost the memory that just yesterday, seemingly, both the Tsar and Tsaritsa and their children had been arrested, separately, in different places, so it was unknown when they could have united. It never occurred to anyone to ask another question: on exactly which section were the letter trains moving? Directly to Tornio, bypassing Petrograd? They were moving ominously, and that was enough, and the pounding of their wheels, intensified by fear, was thundering in the Tauride Palace! And finally: how did the railroad employees come to know all these details, including the destination station? That must make it true!

None of the Executive Committee members, who were hastily called together now in the new room, had had the wit to verify this—so full of truth was the accursed news, so strikingly true to class distinctions, so inevitable. This was exactly how all crownbearers always fled, craftily and despicably! This was exactly how the bourgeois class government was supposed to act, craftily and despicably! This was exactly how their treacherous core was supposed to operate! And we proletarians should be ashamed! We should not have dozed off and trusted them! After all, we resolved yesterday! Resolved that our deputy be present at the arrest—and again the Provisional Government secretly sent its own people!

The incoming news quickly accumulated details that clung to it from out of nowhere, but were also beyond question: yesterday the government had held a secret late-night meeting about this. Up until now, the journey had been put off only due to the children's illness. The entire order about the Tsar's arrest was pure deception! They hadn't decided definitely whether to send the train through Tornio or Arkhangelsk, but they had instructed Kerensky to accompany the Romanovs all the way to England! No, only to the port of embarkation!

The traitorous Provisional Government—but Kerensky, too, was a traitor to revolutionary democracy! See how he was hiding, the snake, and never at the EC!

In the unfurnished room with the gaping middle, approximately a dozen Executive Committee members had gathered, standing—whoever they could find in the Tauride Palace. Everyone was gripped by disturbing alarm, no one was smoking, and no one was eating. Their faces were gloomy, their poses tense. The entire atmosphere of this unarranged room was reminiscent of the first Tauride days, when the revolution had reared up and the regime was tottering.

Skobelev's first instruction was to post a military guard at the anteroom door—so that no one could attack the Executive Committee suddenly, for it was unknown how far the black ink of treason had seeped.

No one attempted to sit down, even Chkheidze with his weak spine. So they all stood in a large circle around an empty middle, picking up concern from others' faces or staring, lost, at the empty floor.

An intense debate ensued. They didn't take the floor from Chkheidze but said whatever burst from their chest. They said everything, several at once even, and even Sokolov backed off the Polish theme and let his beard drop to his vest, defeated by the betrayal of the franchised set, while Chkheidze's Georgian accent became more pronounced, to the point of a sinister screech.

This was the continuation of that same villainous plan for Guchkov's trip! They wanted to do it without us, in a secret pact with the Romanovs. To decide the form of governance!

And decide it in favor of a monarchy!

Yes, it was clear! They wanted to preserve the monarchy!

This was a step toward a restoration!

And this would be very easy for them to do. Had there even been a genuine act of abdication, according to all the rules?

The counterrevolution wanted to preserve the monarch for its own sinister game!

Then imperialist Great Britain would interfere—and restoration would be inevitable!

There was also this: the Tsar knew our military secrets! He would transmit them to Germany and reveal all!

How could Nikolai II be allowed to go abroad? Possessed of tremendous means stashed away in foreign banks for a rainy day, he could easily organize conspiracies against the new order!

He was going to feed Black Hundred schemes!

And send out hired killers!

"Indeed, there is not a monarch on earth," Himmer, pale yellow, exclaimed, "who would hesitate to avenge himself against his native land using foreign bayonets, to crush his 'dear people' in order to assert his own 'legitimate rights'—and would see it not even as betrayal, but as his natural function!"

The greatest of tyrants, executioners, and where was he fleeing? To the "great democracy"!

Which had sheltered Marx! Herzen! Kropotkin!

Oh no, there can be no question of letting him go abroad!

Even leaving him at liberty in Russia would be fatal for the revolution's cause.

What could they do?

Ideas failed.

What to do was the hardest question. Arrest him—yes. But how? And where?

Their thoughts wandered. One person leapt to the danger of the grand dukes and, comparatively, who was more dangerous and in what order.

All this put together was even *more dangerous* than for the French during Louis's flight! At that time, only the king fled. Now, the government itself was doing the betraying!

The shadow of the Varennes flight, the king's nighttime carriage—grand shadows waved transparently over the staggered circle of EC members, a short quorum instead of three dozen.

They felt like the Convention, and even greater and more important than that Convention of old!

And whoever's sight fell upon the tall pier-glass—that pier-glass, framed in bronze, for some reason became especially sinister.

Arrest him, yes. But where and by whose forces?

The ever ponderous and decisive Nakhamkes could propose nothing concrete, either.

Right then, though, the spotless Filippovsky, in his naval uniform (which always looked strange among professional revolutionaries) offered a simple idea. No matter where the royal trains were right now or where they were headed, through Tornio or Arkhangelsk—they had to go through Petrograd. That meant, first of all, that reinforced military units had to occupy all the Petrograd train stations. And in order to ensure their loyalty to the Soviet, attach to them commissars from among the republican officers, from the new alliance organized by this same Filippovsky. Moreover, commissars with extraordinary powers could be sent ahead, down the three lines—to the Tosno, Zvanka, and Tsarskoye Selo stations—to organize pickets there.

This was approved immediately—and Filippovsky executed a navy-style turn and went off to carry it out.

After him they also had the good idea of arming workers' fighting squads! Throughout the capital!

But they had to ask the Bolsheviks about this—and right now neither Shlyapnikov nor the entire Bolshevik leadership were there. Only the spry, pudgy Kozlovsky. They asked him to go call his people and ask them.

These simple measures eased minds, making it easier to think.

Shouldn't they also send a telegram to all the stations, all of them, and all the railroaders, to detain the imperial trains wherever they were noticed?

Send it.

And what about the Provisional Government? Overthrow it? Arrest it? Disperse it?

Or clarify the situation? Send a delegation to find out what they had in mind? Give them an ultimatum to detain the Tsar under strict arrest!

And under the Soviet's observation! Any move of the royal family—only with the Soviet's permission? . . . And no thought of England!

But the thought of the main thing, the main thing, would not go away: what about the Tsar? For now, obviously, we'll arrest him—but what do we do with him after that?

Aleksandrovich's burning, contemptuous look showed that he was not expecting these pathetic Mensheviks to utter the main words: off with his head! All these Social Democrat types still were hushed at the throne's spell.

Now, in a few hours, the Tsar would be caught—and in our hands, not the Provisional Government's. So what then?

The Peter and Paul Fortress! The Trubetskoy bastion! Even if that threatened a complete break with the Provisional Government!

And replace the Peter and Paul Fortress's entire command—so that there would be no bribery or escape. We don't trust the old officer class!

That's all fine, but . . . someone must first—arrest the Tsar. That would be one of us. Who?

And when this question rang out, each began searching around the circle. Who of those present should be tasked with the Tsar's arrest?

They looked at Chkheidze—but how could he? Decrepit. Skobelev? Another blunderer. Sokolov? A loudmouth. Zeitlin, Shekhter . . . (They didn't even look at Himmer.) Aleksandrovich and Nakhamkes—here they had two suitable people.

But someone said:

"No, comrades, the Tsar's arrest is a historic act. This should be done, if possible, by a Russian, best of all, a pure-blood worker."

Again they started looking around. There wasn't a single worker among them, and you could count the Russians on your fingers.

"What about Gvozdev?" the thought came to them. "Where is Gvozdev?"

Gvozdev, it turned out, was not in the circle. They'd forgotten to summon him. He was busy in another room, of course, with his factories and plants.

They decided to task Gvozdev!

Everyone agreed. Only Aleksandrovich grumbled.

Documents – 18

22 March 1917

URGENT GENERAL COMMUNIQUÉ

From the Executive Committee of Workers' and Soldiers' Deputies. To commissars, local committees, and military units along all railways and other means of transport.

This is to inform all of you that Nikolai II is presumed to be fleeing abroad. Let your agents and committees along the entire railway know that the Executive Committee has ordered that they arrest of the former Tsar and immediately inform Petrograd, the Tauride Palace.

Chkheidze, Skobelev

[5 2 3]

Gvozdev was sitting at the Resumption of Work Commission and was pulling like an ox, starting in the dark and ending in the dark, and this was without attending Executive Commission sessions, so as not to lose time. But before there had at least been the War Industry Committee to help the Workers' Group, and now it was gone (except for a gathering yesterday in the City Duma, but only to celebrate). All the efforts at convincing the working class to return to work lay wholly on Gvozdev and his labor commission. The telephone in their room was never quiet, and messengers kept leaving for the plants and returning from them with distressing news.

Although four days before, the Soviet had voted to resume work, it had come with a proviso, "at the first signal abandon it once again," and for now "to work out your economic demands." As they were called, so they heard, and so the workers did return—not to their workbenches but mostly to make trouble. Rare was the place where work began in earnest, and even there they held rallies and demanded they be paid in full for the days of revolution and their wages be raised in general. Where they slacked off, did not stand at their workbenches, where they pretended to work, on the other hand, every plant came up with its own new demands, and worst of all they did not obey the foremen, insulted them, and even wheeled them out in wheelbarrows. Or demanded the director be fired. They said wild things: that now people should be foremen not based on their knowledge but chosen by the workers themselves, even one of the workers. But that was the end of any plant.

What was Kozma to do? He called on the workers to be reasonable and not demand everything at once, but just try to convince those strong wills! After all, the revolution had won! The least little pandering, and people always go wild from the easing up; only work restrains any man.

And then the plant owners were losing their patience, too, and threatening lockouts. Everything was teetering on collapse again.

But the Bolsheviks put the squeeze on the Soviet, which threatened the plant owners, saying at the slightest attempt at a lockout they would seize those businesses and put them under the administration of worker collectives.

The plant owners recoiled even more from that. And Kozma had to go hold talks with them, try to convince them.

Up until today, Gvozdev had been greatly helped with advice and adjustments from Pyotr Akimovich Obodovsky, who would often stop by the labor commission. But as of today they had appointed him also, instead of some general, to the commission on supplying metal to the plants—so probably now he would switch over to metal and his support for Kozma would drop off.

If only he had just this to do! But Gvozdev was also a member of the Soviet's finance commission, and motor vehicle commission, each of which had their own myriad matters, and he had to dig into those, too.

Yesterday at the Executive Committee they had nearly chosen Gvozdev for the Liaison Commission as well, for permanent talks with the government. That blew over, thank God.

Just what hadn't the Executive Committee dreamed up? Three days ago, for some reason, they had suddenly assigned Kozma, for some reason, to go and shut down *New Times*. Why him exactly, when besides him there were big talkers there both on the publications commission and the propaganda one? It was a nasty business. No one wanted to get dirty, so they offered up someone meek instead. This passed, too, though. They changed their minds about shutting down *New Times*, which had somehow patched things up with the Soviet.

Then all of a sudden, after dark, care-filled days, today brought Kozma a completely unexpected, immense joy: a telephone call from the Petersburg Society of Factory and Plant Owners, who had then sent people for talks—and they were so conciliatory! This same society of factory owners had never been willing to hear about an eight-hour day or a minimum wage. They hadn't wanted to hear about anything sensible. And then all of a sudden, something it made no sense even to dream of—in one fell swoop they agreed to an eight-hour day for all Petersburg and without any reduction in salary—and to sign this tomorrow, if necessary. There's the wonder! The workers had been repeating their slogans for thirty years, without ever believing it—and now, there you had it, the capitalists had caved!!

Did this mean, then, that all that mischief, insolence, and ruffianism—it had actually helped? Go figure! Did this mean you never got anywhere by being nice, only by force? Now they'd consented both to factory-plant committees and to arbitration offices—just so these arbitrators didn't fire foremen and administrators without review or permission.

That was what Kozma thought, too. Of course! Could it be that everything would work out in peace and harmony?

Kozma was just getting ready to go to the Executive Committee to report on this victory when they came running for him: Go, and quickly! Kozma went as fast as he could.

They were all standing in the new room, in a circle, agitated. Did they already know?

No, all their faces were somber, even frightened. Everyone turned to him as if it were his fault.

What on earth had happened? Where had Kozma misstepped? He opened his mouth to vindicate himself, to announce his delight to them—no. Chkheidze spoke for them all:

"Comrade Gvozdev! The Executive Committee tasks you with arresting the former Tsar, Nikolai the Second!"

What was this? Kozma felt all his color strike him in the face, all at once, such as he had forgotten it had ever done.

Everyone saw this color on his face and large forehead—and looked at him as if it were even more his fault.

"What's this?" Kozma mumbled, distraught. "As if I didn't have anything else to do? You have no one else? What's this?"

Indeed, he wasn't aware of any particular accomplishments, of having stood out to all Russia, that suddenly it would be him specifically to go arrest the Tsar. Nor was he any good for that. Nor was he . . .

Nakhamkes's bass was encouraging:

"Comrade Gvozdev! This is a great honor! You should be proud!"

Himmer hopped up, too, like a sparrow on one leg:

"First he arrested you—and now you will arrest him! It's just!"

Kozma, God forgive him, could not stand this Himmer: such a tiresome, boring man in the Soviet—and the most useless. He had never done anything, just squeaked out his speeches.

"But why me?" Kozma spread his arms. Even the victory he had come to tell them about had lapsed from his mind.

But no one explained why, why him, and why they themselves weren't going. They were silent.

But they said a warrant for the Tsar would now be written out for him. Unfortunately, no one knew exactly where the Tsar was or exactly where he was to be arrested, but it would soon become clear, and they would say where and when he was to go.

Right now, though, to help in the arrest, a company of Semyonovsky Guards and a company of gunners would be assembled.

Each and every member of the dynasty had to be arrested as well. And their property confiscated by the people.

Kozma raised his arms, to object—not about the dynasty, about himself, as if to say, for pity's sake, release me. No, they had closed ranks, in an ominous circle: only he!

Thus, with raised arms, as if lifting a burden, Kozma headed back to his labor commission. He had never gotten to tell them about the eight-hour day.

For some reason, he felt as if he'd been struck hard in the head. First of all, it was vexing to tear himself away from his work, he shouldn't. And secondly, it was unbearably hard.

Himmer had chirped this incorrectly: he arrested you, and you will arrest him. He was the Tsar, there was no way around that. If it weren't Nikolai II ruling Russia, it would be someone else.

And also in Russia there lived quietly one Kozma Gvozdev, machinist assistant and lathe operator. That man had reigned; this man had operated a lathe. Never would the idea have occurred that their paths would cross, especially at this irregular moment. And with such a warrant.

They brought the warrant. Bold flourishes. Boldface print.

Kozma looked at it incoherently.

Arresting the Tsar—somehow he was not up to it.

[5 2 4]

Sergei Maslovsky was a man of dramatically unutilized capabilities, such as the best talents are always to perish in Russia in its nightmarishly unfavorable history. An individualist par excellence, a romantic and a fighter with the soul of a conquistador. What he could do if he only had the scope! The failed revolution had nearly slammed the prison door on him, though. And now, in the successful revolution, he had been in the prime spot, in the eye of the hurricane—yet he had again not achieved anything, and here he was dragging along in the Military Commission as some clerk in an officer's post. In these first days he had also missed out on being coopted for the Executive Committee, an unforgivable miscalculation. The Revolution had taken giant steps, and other names had been inscribed in its blazing chronicle. Everyone took their seats, but Maslovsky was late everywhere and was only just putting together for himself how he might express himself venomously about these upstart ministers: that they had replaced the collar napkins of public dinners for the portfolios of the public cabinet. Oh, he knew how to express himself so very wittily and venomously, he had a bite like no one else, but no new journalist jobs had come up other than at that filthy *Izvestia*, and all the respectable newspapers' jobs were filled by their own writers.

All that remained . . . was again to give himself over to his literary hopes (his pseudonym Mstislavsky was good and even frightening in a way), and to visit the apartment of Gippius and Merezhkovsky at the corner of Potemkin Street, very nearby. They had always been attentive to him and were possible future patrons on his literary path. To them he poured out all his dissatisfaction with the Soviet of Workers' Deputies. If you thought hard, even the new Revolution hadn't been that successful.

And all of a sudden, the Revolution had summoned Maslovsky again, in its fiery, fleeting language. From the second floor of the Tauride Palace he was called to the first, to the Executive Committee, and there, in disorder, at the end of a random table, sat Chkheidze, Sokolov, Kapelinsky, seriously disconcerted, and Sokolov with twisted coattails, the always tidy Kapelinsky with his tie askew, and Chkheidze tragically rolling his eyes.

Here is what they explained to him. That morning, there had been definite news that the Provisional Government had misled the Soviet and was secretly taking the royal train to some port in order to send the royal family abroad. The Executive Committee had taken all measures to stop them on the railway! The latest news had just been received: the Tsar had arrived in Tsarskoye Selo and been taken to the palace as a prisoner. The need to intercept and arrest him had thus fallen away. However, their trust in the Provisional Government was shaken. Where was the guarantee they wouldn't take such a step, in fact? The palace's entire guard was in Kornilov's hands, but ultimately, what did we know about General Kornilov? He had a democratic reputation—but was he devoted to the people? We had to safeguard ourselves against any return of the Romanovs to the historical stage. It was unclear what needed doing—but something surely did! Many measures had already been put in motion: the train stations occupied, certain troops assembled. But some demonstration still needed to be made so that the Provisional Government would learn its lesson and be on its guard, and it was a shame to abandon the preparations begun. So here's what they proposed. To task Maslovsky, as a decisive man (Maslovsky could not help but respond with a grateful nod)—to task him with doing something effective, devised on the spot: intercept the Tsar and put him in the hands of the Soviet and the Peter and Paul Fortress? Or at least verify the conditions of his detention in Tsarskoye Selo? Establish the reality of the guard? Something like that, something the Provisional Government could feel, something to crush all the Romanovs' inclinations!

So! It had come. His great hour had come. The moment he had lived for, of course—and here he'd thought he'd missed out. For him—the descendant of a withered, sidelined noble family—for him to walk in on the Tsar with a stamping, merciless step! Our background obliges us to great deeds. For too long he had been helplessly squeezed in the aisles between library shelves. (And for a writer's biography—what a chance this was! What food for the keen, caustic eye!)

So! The revolution had come to its fateful, inevitable turning point—the king's escape! A fleeting moment! (Nota bene: don't stumble, though, this was a direct confrontation with the government.)

What was to be done? Above all—what was not to be done. The Soviet must not hand over power to the Provisional Government and put itself in some accessory position. Now—what was to be done?

Oh, it was all too clear! Why the half-hints, half-confessions, and half-oaths? Maslovsky's entire revolutionary core began to throb as it came to the direct answer: *regicide*! Here was the fiery language of revolution, here was the question's cardinal solution, and no restoration ever!

Of those present, however, daring Sokolov alone could approve this, could contemplate extremes. But those other two, like nearly the entire EC ruling group, were timid Menshevik rabbits whose eardrums would burst upon hearing this solution out loud!

Promising them only to strengthen the palace guard would be a contemptible compromise.

Before he had said his first words, Maslovsky grew so much inwardly, tensed so—at this great moment for him and the Russian revolution—he himself was amazed at his imperious voice:

"What shall I be called? The Soviet's emissary?"

"The commissar for oversight," Chkheidze said.

"Fine. Write the warrant"—and he recited from something unseen, squinting: "Seize all military and civilian power in Tsarskoye Selo . . . for the execution of the especially important . . . especially important act of state entrusted to him!"

Act! This could mean anything. Both any and all measures to isolate the Tsar and, of course, inspection of the conditions of his detention. But also any and all measures—for his execution. Today even, right there. . . . The commissar himself had not yet decided exactly, he didn't know, but it was an act of state.

Not wasting a minute, he rushed off to prepare. Inwardly he had already grown. But he lacked outward regeneration. He was at least wearing a military uniform and an officer-style greatcoat—but without epaulets, and only a quartermaster pin. He had been a librarian, a civilian, not a soldier; he was wearing the uniform and greatcoat illegitimately. To questions of who he was, he would reply: "Maslovsky, no rank." *No rank*—that could have been understood as high-level, as if not getting into officer ranks, but it could also be understood, unfortunately, as a low rank, a private.

There was no fixing this now, but while the warrant was being printed, Maslovsky found a solution to the situation: he asked a certain Kuban Cossack officer in the Tauride Palace to lend him his redoubtable tall Caucasian fur hat and short fur coat without epaulets until day's end. The coat gave him a martial, wild, irregular look straightaway, so that no one would even think to ask his title. And the tall hat was marvelous, black lamb, with lots of wiggling snake-curls, which also tripled the size of his head—truly it was like the head of a gorgon with snakes.

He checked himself in the gilt pier-glass in the EC's room, having also strapped on someone else's sword. Quite frightening! Quite expressive! (Only the mustache was but a civilian brush, as though his face were bare.)

And a Browning in his coat pocket! He felt it in himself: a revolutionary spirit beyond all recall. Even he was frightened by this sweep.

The warrant was ready, signed by Chkheidze. Yes, but not entirely so: "seize all military and civilian power in Tsarskoye Selo"—yes, but the Mensheviks had shied away from "act of state," and instead: "assignment of special importance.". . .

Well, this, too, covered . . .

A motorcar was waiting at the entrance. His suite consisted of two republican officers: Staff Captain Tarasov-Rodionov, a machine gunner; and the quick-witted ensign Lenartovich with the expressive face, whom he already knew.

Supposed to be waiting for them at the train station were an assembled company of Semyonovsky Guards and a company of gunners from the 1st Regiment. Indeed, they were. The Semyonovsky Guards in a rather dissolute formation; attached to them, two unconfident officers. The gunners were more menacing due to their gun mounts, on little wheels. (Not really a company, but they had seven machine guns.)

Gvozdev greeted them delightedly on the train station steps to hand over the hateful command and to go about his own business. It was true, his looks, so white-blond and naïve, were simply not suited to a great revolutionary task.

On the platform, idlers watched the soldiers rolling the machine guns onto the suburban train. Some newspaper correspondent on his beat latched on: Who were they? Where were they going? What for? But Maslovsky was not so guileless as to confide in a correspondent. The soldiers themselves got angry and drove him off.

They got going.

The staff captain suggested discussing tactics, but Maslovsky, who kept growing and growing under his awful tall hat, would not deign to discuss anything with him. He was above epaulets, and that elevated him above the staff captain, too.

His warrant was infinite.

En route, a Semyonovsky officer didn't even report but let drop, just like that, in the current revolutionary manner, that the Semyonovsky Guards were traveling with empty rifles, they had brought hardly any bullets. They hadn't wanted to bring them, carry around that weight, and no one had been able to persuade them.

Oh ho! . . . And then what ammunition did the machine gunners there have? They were slackers, too, of course.

[5 2 5]

Today was taking inexpressibly pleasant shape for Pavel Nikolaevich. Early this morning, at his ministry near the Pevchesky Bridge, he had scheduled his first meeting with newspaper correspondents. In the afternoon—in view of the special occasion, in the Mariinsky Palace—the entire government was to accept recognition from a foreign power, the United States of America. The great United States had had the daring to recognize the Russian revolution officially and in full, and moreover wanted to be sure to be first. (To this end, Milyukov had willingly entered into a minor conspiracy with the American ambassador, Francis, allowing him to beat out the other Allies.) In this afternoon ceremony, Pavel Nikolaevich also was both the honoree and the leading figure, both as Minister of Foreign Affairs and due to his special ties to America, where he had been the first popular elucidator of Russia and the first prophet of the Tsarist regime's fall.

And so, early that morning, in the ministry's luxurious hall with the tall windows, its gray-green drapes pulled back, and to match them a frog-green carpet—in armchairs with high, oval, old-fashioned backs, representatives of the Petrograd and Moscow press took their seats, about twenty people.

Pavel Nikolaevich had always had a keen love for the press, the vitally responsive nerve of society that expressed its very soul. In some respect, in one of his functions, as an editor for the Kadet *Speech*, he himself belonged to it, though not in the sense of being a reporter, naturally. The society of newspaper correspondents, exceptionally receptive and keen, was for Pavel Nikolaevich perhaps the most interesting, more piquant than the sometimes boring professorial gatherings or the occasionally pallid assemblies of the Kadet Central Committee. When between Duma sessions Milyukov was surrounded by correspondents, their stirring understanding often extracted the best formulations from his lips. Here today, well acquainted with the majority, but for the first time having grown to his genuine dimensions, he met them as the master, maintaining both an amiably understanding tone and an awareness of the incomparable responsibility he bore.

To start, two correspondents, rising from their chairs, congratulated Pavel Nikolaevich as Russia's first public Minister of Foreign Affairs. This was perceived as their shared celebration and hope that now relations between the ministry and the press . . .

Oh yes. Pavel Nikolaevich thanked them. Yes, their meeting was catching the government chosen by the Russian revolution at the end of the first week of operations. He himself would like to run his ministry in keeping with the grandeur of the present moment. As leader of Russian foreign policy, he intended to listen closely to the voice of public opinion expressed most sensitively by the press.

Milyukov had not written his statement in advance; all these thoughts were so organic to him, so fully matured that they could not cause him any difficulty in exposition.

"Gentlemen," he said, taking pleasure in speaking specifically to them, "I believe that my first task is to strengthen and stabilize the close bonds that link us with our Allies. Up until now, we have had to blush in shame before our Allies over our government. Our Allies were themselves ashamed. We could not even be certain that the Russian government would be faithful to its Allied obligations. Now, as a result of the great overthrow, backward Russia has pulled even with the leading Western democracies, and now an alliance with us cannot compromise any of them. Up until now, Russia was the sole black spot in the entire anti-German coalition; it hung like a dead weight on the Entente. Now, however, we do not have to be ashamed of ourselves and can act fully aware of our dignity. Now no one can doubt our sincerity. We have gained the right to discuss the war's highest liberation goals—to put an end to German dreams of hegemony and not to lose sight of liberating the peoples of Austro-Hungary."

The conversation's amiable warmth overpowered its official nature. Pencils and automatic pens moved joyously, gustily, over notebooks, not always keeping up.

"Here is a striking sign of the change for you. Just now, this morning, I received a telegram from someone known as Russia's bitterest enemy—the very prominent American banker Jacob Schiff. He writes, and I will allow myself to read from it: 'I was always an enemy of tyrannical Russian autocracy, which mercilessly persecuted my coreligionists. Now, however, allow me to congratulate the Russian people on the great deed they have so wonderfully accomplished. Allow me to wish you and your colleagues in the new government complete success.'"

The correspondents asked to be given the telegram in full later.

"You see, gentlemen, the old regime acted as a brake on the United States. Now, all our Allies have immediately taken the side of the new regime in Russia. They intend to officially recognize the new order with unusual speed. Naturally, though, they are counting on the swift strengthening of our military discipline, and it is our duty to do everything we can to justify this confidence. Maintaining our military might is especially important for us now. We must put an end to such acts of wavering discipline as the unfortunate Order No. 1. Thankfully, there will be no further excesses of any kind, I hope."

But what is the impression in Germany from our coup? the correspondents asked.

This was not a simple question. It made sense to answer it twofold, thereby extracting twofold benefit.

"On the one hand, the Germans count on taking advantage of the temporary weakening of our military might in order to carry out a powerful offensive on the Northern front. German reinforcements are already coming this way, in fact."

They scribbled quickly.

"Therefore, any citizen who does not want a new triumph by the Germans must assist in restoring military discipline. The danger is great, and the Russian army must prepare to deflect it. This is a matter of the Russian people's honor. And in the interests of our newly won freedom."

(This point was extremely important to spread widely.)

"On the other hand . . . On the other hand, a false notion has spread in Germany that the Russian revolution expresses the victory of pacifism, that now it can incline Russia toward a separate peace. I do not have to tell you, though, gentlemen, that this bizarre interpretation can only make us smile. The pacifist movement among some of our Social Democrats should not be overstated. I consider it my duty to warn"—his voice steeled, and the specter of his own steeliness, a repeat specter of his famous November speech, rose in the roots of his hair—"that the people who brought down Stürmer for his desire for a separate peace will definitely not agree to any separate peace."

Thus he had spoken directly about himself. Not only that, but more firmly—reaching for the holy grail:

"In particular, the elimination of the Turkish state now fits even more so into our national objectives. For five hundred years, this state, created through conquests, was unable to shift to a civil society, was unable to achieve the level of the modern cultured states—and it cannot exist!"

Milyukov's pince-nez gleamed brightly and firmly.

They wrote this down as something sensational.

Also about this and that. They asked about the war's possible continuation.

"Without a doubt, the war is already on the wane, gentlemen, we are closing in on the denouement. The enemy's forces are decreasing in a greater proportion than ours. By mid-summer, we can set the war's end with confidence. The war will end in the triumph of law and justice. If discipline is maintained, if we cope with ourselves—we will cope with the enemy. A beautiful future for our renewed Russia will be secured!"

The conversation quickly wrapped up in a warm, even affectionate atmosphere.

Since Pavel Nikolaevich, anticipating the diplomatic reception, was already wearing his tailcoat, he had only to drink a cup of coffee, sign a dozen submitted documents, and, continuing his triumphant day, travel from the Pevchesky Bridge to the Blue Bridge.

In the Mariinsky Palace, in the luxurious rotunda, with its thirty-two columns and thirty-two chandeliers in two tiers, a gilded molded ceiling under a light-filled cupola, preparations were already under way for greeting the American ambassador, but various complications had arisen, in particular, what flag to decorate the side of the Provisional Government, since they were without a flag of their own now.

After giving one, another, and a third instruction, Pavel Nikolaevich headed for the office of Prince Lvov. He now did not let slip any opportunity to meet with the prince alone, in order to guide him more surely. It was not all that easy to catch him without Nekrasov, without Tereshchenko, without . . .

But right then the prince was alone, and he could sit for a brief meeting with him.

Pavel Nikolaevich intended to inform the prime minister about yesterday's rather unexpected turn in the conversation with the English ambassador. Given the spiritual closeness that had arisen now between democratic Russia and democratic England, and considering that Buchanan had agreed to support the government in opposing Nikolai Nikolaevich's appointment, Milyukov in no way could have guessed that the Provisional Government resolution printed yesterday in the newspapers, about the arrest of the royal family, could give rise to such agitation in the English embassy. Buchanan had even insisted on guarantees that all measures of caution would be taken to protect the person of the abdicated Emperor—the English king's cousin. Milyukov had replied that this was actually not an arrest but merely a provisional restriction of his freedom. As before, the Provisional Government wished (and would be relieved) to see the royal family go to England—but were preparations already being made in England for their reception? "Not yet. There is still no agreement in principle," the ambassador stated. "Wouldn't Denmark or Switzerland be a more appropriate place for the Tsar?" "No, no," Milyukov spurned that idea and asked, on behalf of the government, and with urgency, that this haven be offered as soon as possible, and that the Tsar not leave England before the war's end.

But before he could tell Lvov all this (in order to convince him that right now what would be the least trouble was to send that entire family gaggle to England), the prince displayed total dismay (expressed in a certain moistening of his heavenly eyes):

"Oh, Pavel Nikolaevich, this is precisely the matter that has become significantly more complicated!"

"What's this, Georgi Evgenich?"

"You can't even imagine. The Executive Committee is in a rage! Someone spread the malicious rumor, and the Soviet believed it, that we did not in fact arrest the Emperor but are secretly conducting him abroad."

Although this almost did coincide with Milyukov's confidential proposal (indeed, did someone from the government, informed and unfaithful, spread it?), but in the stormy stream of the Executive Committee's indignation, also the criminality and impossibility of such a plan was revealed to the prince. How could he himself not have seen this?

"Oh no, Pavel Nikolaich, we must be irreproachably loyal to the Soviet. This entire scheme . . . Oh no, we must cast it from our minds. Can you just imagine, truly, how this would look from the Tauride Palace?"

It really did look counterrevolutionary.

"They want more. They want to lock up the Emperor in the Trubetskoy Bastion. I have been at pains to convince them to leave him at Tsarskoye Selo and reinforce the guard however they like. Post commissars from the

Soviet, if they like. It would be good, too, if they agree. What do you think, Pavel Nikolaich?"

Actually, what did Pavel Nikolaevich care? He and Nikolai II weren't exactly standing godfather to each other's children. Certainly, the tensions with the ambassadors was unpleasant, but they could not be compared with the Soviet's frantic zeal. Why provoke the fiery river of Acheron to flow again?

"Come, come, Georgi Evgenich. . . . You may well be in the right. In any case, we need to slow things down."

"But won't your position yesterday leak out, through the ambassadors?" the prince sought with worried eyes.

"No, no," Milyukov reassured him. "I specifically asked Buchanan to keep the matter in strict secret and in no event announce that the Tsar's departure was the Provisional Government's initiative."

"Oh! Oh!" the limitlessly good prince was in torment. Even looking at him was agonizing. He had always been extremely quick to get worked up but very slow to calm down. He cracked his knuckles. And searchingly, as if Milyukov were the prime minister: "Pavel Nikolaich! But if one considers well, then what good is this to us? After all, we are forming the Extraordinary Commission of Inquiry right now. And it is going to uncover serious crimes of state, the preparation of a separate peace. . . . Does this mean only the ministers are going to be held accountable while we let the Tsar go abroad? How are we going to look then? Where is the logic?"

The prince looked searchingly, and with all the pain only a Russian intellectual could summon:

"I'm afraid the Soviet is right—even in essence," he whispered.

Pavel Nikolaevich himself was beginning to discover this fully. Yes, given an eventual trial . . . Surely he did not want to don the cloak of a defender of the bloody tyrant and the whole dynasty? The democratic powers' ambassadors had simply knocked him off course. Because if people find out that . . . But in general . . .

Right then Nekrasov, of course, drilled into the room, with his impenetrable but ever suspecting look.

The conversation continued in a wholly official way, that Nikolai II should remain imprisoned.

In walked Tereshchenko, also wearing a tailcoat.

The government had begun to gather for the ceremonial meeting with the American ambassador.

Pavel Nikolaevich went to check on final preparations.

The day's second delight had come, an even more vivid one.

He had his tirade all prepared, and he knew what he was going to say:

"We thank the great trans-Atlantic republic for its recognition of our new order of affairs! You see how broadly and fully our country has shared the overthrow's lofty ideas! During the last few days I have received many congratulations from prominent men in your country. Permit me to . . ."

The warmest memories of his brilliant tours and lectures in America flooded Pavel Nikolaevich, and genuine gratitude for the American figures who had always been supporters of the Russian opposition.

". . . I have been more than once in your country and may bear witness that the ideals of free Russia are the same as underlie the existence of your own country. I hope that this great change which has come to Russia will do much to bring us closer together than we have ever been before."

Documents – 19

GHQ. 22 March

FROM GENERAL ALEKSEEV TO GENERAL JANIN

The Russian Army cannot go on the offensive in late March or early April. The prolonged winter, with its abundant snows, promises an extended mud season, when the roads are nearly impassable. Storms and severe drifting have disrupted the work of our railways, and our institutional stores have not been replenished. . . . Finally, the disease that the state is suffering through must be taken into account. The overthrow could not help but reflect on the completion of all operations.

Our offensive can begin only in the first few days of May.

[5 2 6]

Everything had collapsed. All around, everything was continuing to collapse. Everything was ominously dark, like Judgment Day.

Heaven had also sent consolation, however: together at last! At last, clinging to each other—it was inexpressible! Least of all in words. God, my God, how You separated us during these tragic days!

All these sundered days—how Nikolai had borne the exhausting armor of self-possession: not once, nowhere, in front of no one but his Mama, not even while saying farewell to GHQ officers, had his face ever expressed his sufferings, shown his sorrow, despair, and dismay, even his words had displayed only mild concern. He had been in front of people so much these past few days and had not broken in a single sentence, had not given himself away. He hadn't even complained to Alekseev, had not opened up in his wrenching, gnawing pain, even in that passionate moment when he had asked to return the throne to Aleksei. (Might it not have been possible . . .?)

Sunny! Sunny! Why wasn't I allowed to touch your strength during these days? Together, might we have found something better? But I wasn't able to. Understand and forgive me! I was felled by how swiftly telegrams arrived from them all and their unanimity. These telegrams—I have them all with me. You can read them now. And Nikolasha is first among them. I decided that from where I was I could not see something that everyone was seeing. I could not do better. I could not find other ways.

The kind of crippling force that kept everything under control for a week is the same irrepressible force with which it had surged up now, breaking through the prohibitions, the barriers, and with tears of penance, tears of despair, tears of liberation—and surged toward Sunny, he himself kneeling before her, his face buried in her lap, exactly as his soul desired.

He had laid down the burden of the past few days and given it up for her judgment.

He had been harassed by his tormenters and only now was released. He had been acting like a sleepwalker and only now had his mind cleared.

Oh, never have I been sent success! I always knew I would never succeed.

But my God, for twenty-two years I tried to do only what was best. Did I really never do that?

There is no justice among men!

This was in Alix's pink boudoir. She was sitting on her pink couch; he was kneeling on the carpet. In the room there was a delicate, fading, no, already faded scent—from the mass of wilting lilacs at the window—always supplied fresh from the South, but since the disturbances began they had not been replaced, nor had the hyacinths, none of the flowers.

From the moment the valet Volkov had suddenly announced: "His Majesty the Emperor!" Alix rushed to him at a half-run, as fast as her legs could carry her—and saw an unrecognizable old man—drab, with dark shadows under his eyes and many wrinkles that hadn't been there two weeks before, graying at the temples, and with a step—not his former step of a strong, young man but a lost, weary, uneven step. Could she, could she cast a single reproach at him, no matter how many mistakes he had made?

In this emotional breakdown, in this final decline—could Alix reproach him? For the fact that at many times only her firm advice had led him out onto the correct road? For the fact that he had declined the advice of the man of God and had listened to impure, unfaithful men like that Alekseev—whose betrayal he still did not see?

Perhaps only now that he had been freed was Nikolai fully aware of his overthrow for the first time. His humiliation. Cast down from all pedestals, he needed something to hold onto at least.

Guessing this, she responded to him, gasping:

"Nicky! Nicky! You are dearer to me as husband and father than as Emperor!"

This was and wasn't the truth, it was and wasn't so—but at that moment, that was what she felt, or at least she could not express it any other way.

His inconsolable sorrow—was it any different from hers? Had their hearts ever been disunited?

My farewell order to the army, my heartfelt farewell with my soldiers—even this they banned, blocked. Why?

My God, how Baby has been waiting for your arrival! He's been counting the minutes.

Does he know? How did he find out?

"I had Gilliard tell him: 'Your father will not be going to Mogilev any-more. He no longer wants to be Supreme Commander.'"

Was he distressed?

"Of course he was! He so loves the soldiers and the Army! But a little while later Gilliard added: 'You know, Aleksei Nikolaevich, your father no longer wants to be Emperor.' He got very frightened: 'What happened? Why?' 'Be-cause he is very tired. He has been through very trying times in recent days.' 'Ah, yes, Mama told me. Didn't they stop his train when he was coming here? But will Papa be Emperor again?' Gilliard explained that he wouldn't and that Mikhail had abdicated. Aleksei's face darkened. He thought and thought and said nothing about his own rights, but: 'But how can there be no Em-peror? If there isn't an Emperor anymore, who is going to rule Russia?'"

I did do the right thing, didn't I? Oh, how I hesitated! Leaving Aleksei on the throne meant separation from us. That is what *they* all would have liked: to take Aleksei away from us and for them to rule in his name. And then I changed my mind: return Aleksei to the throne. I did make an attempt to change the Manifesto, but Alekseev said that was just not practicable.

You did the right thing, you did the right thing, my dear sweet husband! How could we go on without our Sunshine? If you had seen what a disgrace and blow it was when the Guards Crew fled the palace. . . . But the Convoy behaved quite nobly! Quite. They alone could do nothing, though. I myself stopped any bloodshed and wouldn't let them fight. And your Combined Regiment! What heartbreaking wonders of loyalty! Yesterday, after the ar-rest was made, they refused to allow themselves to be replaced at their posts all day. They stayed all through the night, too. They themselves wanted to meet your arrival with appropriate honors! They rolled out the machine guns—and didn't want to let the new guard past the palace grating. But it was I who called in their colonel and said: "Do not repeat the climate of the French Revolution!" And they conceded, and only now, right before your arrival, did they leave.

Oh, this example was encouraging! Our holy people will yet not aban-don us.

And which regiment replaced them?

The 1st Guards.

That means they are ours, too, some of our most loyal!

Still in memory was the look of the last review of them Nikolai had made, that winter.

You know, Nicky, Kornilov is also a decent man. During the arrest he be-haved very decently.

This entire so-called arrest was like a moot point, an extra weight on a hard place, he was insensible to it—in fact, it had given him his freedom! The possibility of being together with Alix, alone with Alix, at last!

And pour out his grief to her. And confess. And complain.

In addition to this, they still had prayer, the limitless expanse of prayer. They prayed.

And wept again.

Oh, Nicky, let us put ourselves in God's hands! Oh, Nicky, the Lord sees his righteous! That means there is a reason why all this happened this way. I believe, I know, that there will be a miracle! A miracle will be revealed over Russia and us all! The people will open their eyes from their errors and will raise you up once again! Reason will return, the best feelings will be aroused.

And all this might even happen very soon.

Arrested, or not—but what isolation surrounded their conjoining! Something in the world there was rolling along, happening, but now they were together, and this no longer affected them. Now they would strengthen each other with love—and bear everything.

Shall we go see Baby? The children?

I can't with eyes like mine. I'll frighten them. Better I take a walk through the park. That always helps me.

Go on, then, and I'll be watching you through the window. And here is what . . . well, not all at once. Lili and Benckendorff persuaded me I had to burn the diaries, letters, and papers—so that *they* didn't take possession of them and use them for harm. I've already burned a lot.

Oh, what a shame!

But what could we do? . . .

Nikolai couldn't take in too much of what was going on here at once— he was practically still at GHQ. And the two Pskov evenings had sunk their claws into him. He and Dolgorukov left through the garden door—and went for a walk.

Quickly now, cross through a lot of the park—and he would relax, and dry out, and his face would brighten. So many gloomy misfortunes he had calmed with his vigorous lengthy walking.

As always, he walked five paces ahead of Dolgorukov. Down the broad, shoveled palace path, Nikolai headed toward the great allée. He did see the soldier cordon but understood it as a new type of protection for the palace, or, rather, he didn't understand at all, his thoughts were elsewhere.

All of a sudden, two soldiers stood before him and barred his way with bayonets, and one of them shouted defiantly:

"You can't go here, colonel, sir!"

Nikolai didn't even understand. Who was this colonel he was talking to? (He had always worn colonel's epaulets, but he had never heard this form of address!) He kept walking, not looking at the dissolute soldiers.

Then a few more ran up to him.

"Go back as you're told!" they shouted at him.

Or even:

"Go back, you!"

All this took half a minute. He saw a few simple soldier faces that had always frozen so gloriously still at inspections. This was the 1st Guards Riflery!

The Emperor couldn't think, understand, or object. He stood, lost, and looked at the angered, disrespectful soldier faces. He had simply never seen Russian soldiers like this!

Right then an officer hurried up—but a young one, not a career officer, with a poor bearing and lacking all respect. Without saluting, he said:

"Colonel, sir, you cannot walk in the park. Only in the palace."

The Emperor looked at him—and at the soldiers—and at the park's spreading, inviting branches.

And understood.

[5 2 7]

The machine guns rolled down the platform at the Tsarskoye Selo train station with a rusty squeal—the platform had been scraped free of snow, down to the asphalt. The Semyonovsky men's bayonets swayed over their shoulders under an overcast sky.

Maslovsky did not have precise instructions and had not worked out a precise plan, but one thing was clear: force and pressure! Accomplish something grandiose!

He ordered the telegraph and telephone offices occupied immediately. While he himself, with Lenartovich as his adjutant, burst in on the station chief and from the threshold announced:

"You are under arrest!"

His tall fur hat, felt by his whole crown, pushed too far forward, too big, and Lenartovich's tense and ready look left no doubts.

The station chief was struck dumb:

"Excuse me, but what for? . . . Who? . . ."

Seeing there would be no resistance here, Maslovsky graciously reconsidered:

"The arrest is secret. You will stay where you are, but an ensign will be assigned to you at all times to monitor your actions. You are required not to allow any military forces whatsoever pass through your station. Report to me immediately of any danger."

"But the station has a military commandant . . ."

(Ah, he was in the wrong place . . .)

"Arrest the commandant as well!" (This to no one.) "On the same conditions!" Nothing could stop or surprise Maslovsky anymore.

Where was the chief of the Tsarskoye Selo garrison?

Nearby, in the town hall.

He decided on the spur of the moment to go without his detachment, leaving them here at the station, in the passenger waiting rooms—and take

Tarasov-Rodionov and a couple of soldiers straight to the town hall! No one would detain them. They wouldn't dare! He had the Soviet behind him! He who takes the initiative seizes the day; they were all distraught and unprepared.

However, leading Lenartovich away, looking into his decisive face:

"If I'm not back in an hour and don't send orders—ensign! Take the entire detachment to the barracks of the 2nd Riflery Regiment, the most revolutionary one here, rouse the gunners and move on the palace. . . ."

And also, confidingly, but with full expression:

"And at *any* cost . . . I repeat, *any* cost, safeguard the revolution from the possibility of a restoration!"

The ensign's eyes opened wide, and his courageous face was trembling but understanding.

"Depending on circumstances. Either take the entire arrested family to Petrograd, to the Peter and Paul Fortress. Or . . . eliminate them. . . ."

"*Eliminate* them?" The clear-eyed ensign straightened up. His voice shuddered slightly.

He felt a stirring in his hair. Only the hair stirring—but he couldn't feel himself. What a destiny! Everything had fallen to him! He had taken the Mariinsky citadel—and now? . . . How much further had he been borne down the fiery track of revolution? . . . A hunt for the king? Take him where? To the guillotine? Sasha was quite possibly prepared—yes, he was!—but he would have liked to understand the fateful instruction with exact precision.

Maslovsky's penetrating, predatory gaze read everything that the ensign was going through on his clear face. He envied him! How could one hand off such a striking act to anyone else? No, he had said this so that he himself could calcify into a statue. Instantly, right now, in front of the ensign. But for now, he was on his way to the town hall, certain of success. He would be back in under an hour.

"*Eliminate the issue*"—on the spot, in Tsarskoye Selo. By setting a reliable guard. By ensuring the Soviet's oversight.

He and Tarasov-Rodionov took the motorcar readied for them. On the running boards, their bayonets dashingly set, were two revolutionary Semyonovsky men.

The Tsarskoye Selo town hall, which recently must have been quite gleaming, had now been seriously disfigured. The formal staircase and parquet floor of the window-flanked hall had been fouled with butts and muddy boot prints. The soldiers had lost their battle look and were sitting in silk armchairs with rifles, holding cigarettes in their teeth, or roaming unsteadily in loosened greatcoats.

This was good! This was the breath of our victory and weakened *them*.

Those for whom Maslovsky had come. On the second floor, there was a hastily cobbled together headquarters and in it two colonels: one, the commandant of all Tsarskoye Selo; the other, appointed garrison chief just yesterday, Kobylinsky, who had already been a participant in the Empress's arrest, so he was apparently on our side; everything was getting mixed up.

How many of these senior Army officers had Maslovsky seen during his service in the Academy! He knew their weaknesses: harnessed to the service but with no impulse, no initiative; it was always easier for them to do as they were told. How much anger had he boiled with all those years between the two revolutions when he was their hostage. He spent those years giving them books. He despised these colonels, and all their stars, and was certain that right now they wouldn't be able to withstand the pressure.

He entered like the wind. Without saluting, he slapped his terrible warrant down on the table.

Read it, read it . . . "All military and civil power"!

The colonels exchanged alarmed glances. They had something in common—not just their size, not just the St. Vladimir each had, but also the service one could read across their bald heads:

"Forgive me, but we obey the Provisional Government, not the Petrograd Soviet. And your document does not bear the government's stamp. Does that mean it was done apart from them?"

They were asking. . . . They themselves weren't certain. They themselves were wilting, they didn't understand what "Soviet of Workers' Deputies" meant.

Maslovsky's voice soared:

"Am I to understand that you do not intend to reckon with the resolutions of the Soviet of the revolutionary garrison and revolutionary workers of Petrograd??!"

The colonels shied away. The times were untested, and so were his methods. They exchanged glances again.

"Oh, not at all. Naturally, we know that the Soviet has been recognized by the Provisional Government. But you are a military man and must understand that any order is carried out only following direct subordination. We are subordinate to Lieutenant General Kornilov, who commands the District's troops. Fine, we will call him to the telephone right now."

The brown box was hanging on the wall.

No, if he let them telephone Kornilov, it would all fall through: Kornilov would call the government, who would call the Soviet, and the Mensheviks would get cold feet. Chkheidze had written out the entire warrant in a flurry—so he had to fly on the strength of the warrant:

"Leave Kornilov out of this! If I needed General Kornilov I would have brought him or his signature with me. But at the present moment I have no plan to take the command away from you, by force of this warrant. What is required of you"—oh, how much might in his voice, trembling to the point of pleasure—"is to hand over the Emperor to me immediately, and I will take him to the Peter and Paul Fortress!"

"The Emperor?" The colonels were shaken. "That is utterly impossible. It is formally and very strictly forbidden to allow anyone to see the arrested Emperor!"

The serviceman's desperate resolve! The one resolve they had, when they were directly compelled to violate their oath. (Oh, he'd gone wrong, gone too far. He shouldn't have skipped straight to the fortress.)

But he was still going to try. Menacingly:

"So you are refusing to obey the Soviet of Workers' Deputies??"

He knew these rams, they were not hardened in politics. They could withstand a battle but not a civilian clash:

"I am not refusing," Kobylinsky said slowly. "But I must have General Kornilov's order."

The telephone was right there, inviting him. Craftily, and thus even more menacingly, Maslovsky softened his voice:

"Listen, gentlemen. You perhaps have already been told that I came here with a machine-gun company. Instead of wasting time on conversations with you, shall I raise your entire garrison with a single battle signal?"

It was plausible. This they knew: their own garrison could be roused by any passing agitator at any moment and in any direction, this had already been proven. They commanded the garrison only insofar as the garrison agreed to be commanded.

They faltered.

All right, one more push! One more! The spirit of the moment, which was breeding giants. A desperate and elegant maneuver was spinning around in his head. Arrest me if you dare!—until my machine guns come to my rescue. And if you don't, I'll put you under arrest. You'll be stripped of all responsibility and I'll take the Emperor away!

Through the years, though, he had grown used to caution. No, that way he might overplay his hand.

"Gentlemen, if I don't raise the garrison now, it is only because I'm certain I will carry out my assignment, and with your consent. In the name of the revolutionary people! And so? . . ."

They exchanged distraught glances. He knew it! Had he won?

"You have to understand," Kobylinsky said slowly, not knowing how to address this man. "I don't have the right. . . . Only by order of the lieutenant gen—. . . ."

The pathetic slave of an outmoded duty! He was mumbling about official subordination while sitting on a powder keg.

"Fine, colonel! The blood that is about to be spilled will fall on your head!"

The colonels were pale.

But there was the sense that nothing more could be squeezed from them. He had neutralized them, in any case. For now he could move calmly through Tsarskoye Selo.

"Have a good time!" Maslovsky saluted them without regard to their rank—and nearly blundered, nearly turned across his right shoulder. No, the left, and a little more adroitly, even clicking his boot heels.

Tarasov-Rodionov was waiting in the motorcar, oblivious to the whirlwinds of battle.

The Semyonovsky men hopped onto the running boards and pointed their bayonets forward, Petrograd-style.

"To the Aleksandr Palace!" the emissary commanded, looking like some kind of Stenka Razin.

[5 2 8]

War! The issue that trumps all others. Let everyone else totter, just not the Bolsheviks. Shlyapnikov was keeping to what was most radical, and the most radical was also the simplest. A war had begun. We had declared: "Down with the war!" Now there had been a revolution, but it was still "down with the war!"—all the more so, even.

Previously, though, both the bourgeoisie and the opportunists thought they could let the Tsarist government worry about it. Now, after the revolution, everything had changed instantly.

For the bourgeoisie, it was understandable. It seemingly had come to power, but it did not have, as the Tsar had had, any real power to drive the troops to attack. All it could hope for was to capture their minds. For this purpose now the entire bourgeois press was singing out about loyalty to the homeland and the necessity of vanquishing Wilhelm. Instead of the priest's sermon about defending the Orthodox faith, they were now presenting new types of deception—freedom, land, liberty—anything to drive the soldier toward the barbed wire. Forget all the domestic insults, forget all the party and class differences, they said. The worker question would come after victory, the land question after victory, but for now, move toward the barbed wire for the sake of the fatherland, to wit, the money sack. And of course, they had no choice but to depict "down with the war" as a betrayal of the homeland. They depicted it as if the whole revolution was the result of the Tsar's military failures. All the soldiers wanted to win, but the Tsar and the court hadn't let them.

But this whole bourgeois fairytale was rootless. The revolution didn't happen because of any military failures but simply because they were tired. That was the starting point for the real revolutionary actions.

In all Russia, *Pravda* alone had fearlessly waged antiwar propaganda against the thousands of bourgeois newspapers. For the first time in Russia, the Zimmerwald resolution was printed openly. And it printed the Kienthal one. (No one else had the nerve.) And called for open discussion of the war question, which the new Russian democracy could in no way avoid.

But the Soviet's *Izvestia* had passed over the war in silence for eight days, as if there were no war at all. Their brother socialists found all kinds of things to express an opinion about except for that little something called war. The Mensheviks' *Workers' Gazette* began coming out—and was also roguishly silent. But there was already a slogan going around from mouth to mouth: "The revolution has the right to a defense." As they had recognized the government, so they had recognized the war: to go on, the way they all go on. They set their policy's shaky legs on the fact that the people had agreed to continue fighting. Not only did they decline to seriously discuss the war question and print articles about it—on the contrary, they were also reproaching the Bolsheviks, saying that their bald-faced "down with the war" was now introducing a schism into the unity of revolutionary democracy and playing into the Black Hundreds' hands, that's how far they went! They proposed keeping silent for the sake of the revolution's success.

But this was wild! What had Zimmerwald and Kienthal been for, then? What had changed? Why give it up now? That all Russian socialists were drawn to betrayal—that had been so throughout the war, and all the European ones were the same. No, one had to have the firmness to continue "down with the war!" no matter how it was met. It was for the revolution's sake that the question of war had to be posed even more acutely!

The fact that people were snapping at *Pravda* on all sides was unsurprising. What was surprising was that even in the party itself there were intellectuals who grumbled that they had to get rid of "down with the war" as a slogan, saying that it did virtually nothing for stopping the war. On the other hand, this slogan was very much to the point and agitated everyone. Go find another like it! Are we really supposed to slobber over "patriotic duty to the country" the way they're putting forward on all sides?

But it was discouraging that the slogan had met with weak support among the workers, too. In many plants, they listened glumly to "down with the war." They had succumbed to the nationalistic contagion.

And not only there! The soldiers had taken it badly, too. They were the ones for whose sake the war should be abolished, but they, out of backwardness, fooled, not realizing their own benefit, replied that only German agents could call for that. There were also instances when soldiers refused to take part in a demonstration if someone was going to carry "Down with the war." Naturally, they'd heard the same thing on all sides—from the bourgeoisie and the defensists—and they'd been scared off by the Bolsheviks. The defensists threatened the Bolsheviks with the "fury of the revolutionary people," and indeed, they had to be on their guard. They couldn't go just anywhere to speak, and when they did go, they couldn't say everything. Shlyapnikov himself had not been allowed to speak in a cavalry regiment, they'd shouted him down. Nearly driven him out. Other Bolsheviks, too, in recent days.

Shlyapnikov had the feeling that he had arrived at the most urgent question both for the entire revolution and for the party. He felt in his core that he was right. But he was short on brainpower. And getting resistance from all sides rather than support—who wouldn't falter? His confidence had melted away. What if something was wrong?

The Bureau of the Central Committee met once again, and so did the Petrograd Committee. Would the party keep this point in the platform or not? The transformation of the imperialist war into a civil war—what reason was there to remove it? What about defending the fatherland? Under what circumstances might we agree? Or never? Saying "never"—didn't that mean losing the soldiers for good?

Meager minds, they nevertheless managed an answer: we would defend the homeland only after we established a revolutionary dictatorship of the proletariat and peasantry. For now, demand that the Soviet of Deputies appeal to the proletariat of the warring countries to fraternize at the fronts.

You couldn't push against that: fraternizing was to the Russian soldier's liking.

What was important was holding onto the Soviet's propaganda work. Who went to what regiment to agitate was assigned by the Executive Committee's Propaganda Commission, and without its knowledge and permission not a single agitator was supposed to have access to any barracks; everyone had been warned. They would not allow agitators who were monarchists or enemies of the revolution to have access to the troops—but they did pick so that only defensists went. Fortunately, Shlyapnikov was on the propaganda commission and here he exercised his right fully. He had collected many of those forms, already with seals, and had himself filled them out and signed them for all his people. (With those forms, one could travel to agitate even to a zone close to the front.) The Executive Committee did not like this—but was afraid to confront Shlyapnikov head on.

What was he on this commission for if not to prevent them from putting a bridle on the Bolsheviks (and the Interdistrict men, to work out an agreement with them)? He attended this commission more regularly than he did the Executive Committee itself.

And today, arriving at the Tauride Palace, Shlyapnikov did not go to the EC to sit for a while but went to the large Duma hall to stand (there was nowhere to perch) and watch the session of the Soviet's soldiers' section.

This was instructive, taking in with just his eyes and all at once basically the entire garrison of Petrograd—the same garrison that astonishingly was not receptive to the Bolsheviks, who alone had defended its interests. Taking it in so as to understand how it could be taken. How were these soldiers to be led, and by what?

In his favorite steady pose, his legs spread slightly and his arms crossed at his chest, Shlyapnikov had a look and listen.

They were trusting, and mostly toward the greatcoat. Anyone wearing a soldier's greatcoat was one of them, even if it was a mobilized lawyer serving in the chancellery who would lead them against their own interests. They couldn't see that.

Actually, politics wasn't what they talked about in the soldiers' section. Their entire policy was that of course they would stand for the homeland, and their entire discussion here was about barracks life, how they were to get along in their units today, so that serving was easier. The Executive Committee's leaders had sent Boris Bogdanov here as chairman. A mass of soldiers, if only they could be drawn aside, this would end well.

Today they were reading loudly and slowly the readied Declaration of the Rights of the Soldier and listening to voices for and against, as people shouted back and forth and voted on each point.

The term "lower rank" was abolished. Also abolished were "yes, sir," "no, sir," "sir, I do not know," and "willing to do our best." Also abolished was "attention." (They debated—and agreed to leave that last one as transitional, impossible to go without it, but so that no one was held at attention for long.) All forms of punishment were abolished. On the contrary, any official who punished a soldier would be handed over to trial.

The debates were about trifles, albeit meticulous, albeit with invective, but the main thing was that the soldier mass was moving as one to seize its rights!

And Shlyapnikov thought: marvelous! This was the real course of revolution, seizing one's rights! There was no stopping this.

Right here and now, in this Declaration of the Rights of the Soldier—though in fact no one understood it—the Bolsheviks had won! The wise defensists from the Executive Committee had miscalculated, to say nothing of the bourgeoisie! "Down with the war"—this they categorically forbade, but "democratization of the army"—this they could not reject. That would be indecent. And what was the democratization of the army if not just that: down with the war!

It was simply ridiculous the racket they were making everywhere about how an elective army would give rise to battle capability, discipline would strengthen, and the army would be conscientious! It was going to fall apart, as sure as two times two is four.

And that was how we would be freed from the war!

So let's have democratization, that's what we need, work for our benefit! Six of one, half a dozen of the other—our side would win. It didn't matter that today the soldiers weren't letting us speak. All this was working for our benefit! And we won't abandon "down with the war!" No!

In the closeness of the bourgeois parliamentary hall, jostling with greatcoats, smoke on all sides—Shlyapnikov stood for a long time, not wearying, his eyes sparkling gaily at the presidium.

Documents – 20

22 March
FROM GUCHKOV TO GENERAL ALEKSEEV

Top secret.
Private and confidential.

. . . The current state of affairs is this:

1) The Provisional Government possesses no real power, and its instructions are being carried out only to the extent allowed by the Soviet of Workers' and Soldiers' Deputies . . . the troops, railways, post and telegraph are in its hands. One can say outright that the Provisional Government exists only as long as the Soviet of Workers' and Soldiers' Deputies allows it.

2) The initial degradation of reserve units is progressing—and there can be no question of sending a significant number of personnel reinforcements to the army in the next few months.

3) Equally hopeless is the issue of reinforcing the army's mounted component. The requisitioning of horses has had to be curtailed so as not to exacerbate the populace's mood.

4) . . . All the new artillery and other formations cannot be implemented by the dates set.

[5 2 9]

Prince Lvov's paramount principle for living was belief and trust. Belief in people, all people, our holy people. And trust in each and every person. (Only if a person had been put in bad conditions could he betray that trust.)

When the prince's trust was betrayed, or he himself wasn't believed—that hurt especially badly. Himself decent and honest to the highest degree, he did not allow for a lack of decency in others.

So when this afternoon a delegation from the Soviet stopped by unexpectedly to see the prime minister—Chkheidze himself and with him Skobelev and Nakhamkes—with an ominous question—what kind of flight has the royal family embarked on and how could the Provisional Government have so treacherously betrayed the Soviet—the prince's gentle soul was deeply wounded. He felt bitter to the point of tears.

"My dear fellows," he asked sorrowfully, "my dear, my good men, how could you think such a thing? How could you think such a thing of us? If we made you a promise, if we kept you advised, could we really betray you? Of course the royal family has been arrested!"

Fortunately, he could now tell them the latest news, that the former Emperor's train had arrived safely at Tsarskoye Selo and the Emperor himself had been taken by motorcar to the palace under guard. And the family hadn't budged the whole time.

The workers' deputies, sprawled in the velvet armchairs, still had not asked all their questions, still did not believe, then believed it.

You mean there are no plans to go to England?

Oh no, no, my friends!

And the government promises not to move the former Nikolai II without the Soviet of Deputies?

Oh, of course!

So the family would be arrested in Tsarskoye Selo ahead of the choice of a new, stricter place of incarceration?

Fine, so be it.

Moreover, a special commissar from the Soviet of Workers' Deputies must take part in the supervision of the former Tsar and his family.

The magnanimous prince had no objections whatsoever.

And Nikolai Nikolaevich? He cannot be admitted to the command!

Perfectly just! The prince had already sent the grand duke a letter of clarification about this.

But where was he? Where was he traveling?

We're hoping to intercept him en route.

He must not be at GHQ!

And he will not remain there!

Thus the prince was able to mollify his stern overseers. Both sides heartily agreed that these kinds of meetings would be useful in the future as well, regularly. The Liaison Commission, which they comprised, chosen by the Executive Committee, would come to the Mariinsky Palace every other day or two, and here they would openly exchange thoughts on further policy.

Very good! This was simply magnificent!

This truly did rescue the prince from many unnecessary and agonizing hesitations: agree on everything, coordinate everything, conciliarly, amicably!

He saw his guests out—and allowed himself to walk around his luxurious office for a while. More and more, the prince's fifty-six-year life appeared to him like a handsome construction. He had never sought out power, had done nothing for that. He didn't even like politics. More than anything he liked practical zemstvo work surrounded by good men. He had only always been irreconcilable to the abuses of imperial authority. And now certain powerful forces, whom he had not summoned, whom he didn't even know, had stood on every side to help and elevate him—the Russian public, or, even more broadly, the Russian people themselves, had elevated the prince as their chosen favorite—and now the prince could hardly hope to find what other loyal service he could offer to show his gratitude and vindicate their expectations. But for this he did not need to issue decrees or orders. Based on his experience of living in gloomy imperial Russia, he could not stand bureaucratic instructions from above that crushed human initiative; there should be an end to that kind of power in Russia. Rather, in every locale everywhere, the intelligent, creative movement of intelligent people should come to life and self-generate, and the sole task of the country's leaders should be not to interfere—and in this way Russia would achieve unprecedented glory among the enlightened peoples!

Meanwhile, in the marble, gilt, and parquet silence and comfort of the Mariinsky Palace, despite the incursion of 12 March barely disturbed by the revolution, where the noiseless, stately footmen in embroidered liveries and white stockings, themselves grander than the grandees, today served the new ministers and dignitaries tea, coffee, and cookies, and the government gathered for its daily session—in the room next to the formal reception room, behind rosewood and nacre doors. But the ministers were tired, to the point of exhaustion, even.

They took their seats at the polished oval table—with Prince Georgi Evgenievich at its head. The previous days the prince had been grieved that two, three, or four ministers were always absent, busy with their own affairs, of course—but their participation in the sessions was missed. Today, though, every last one of them had gathered, although Guchkov was about to leave, intent on going to the front. Guchkov's face had been vexingly sullen these past few days; it had not corresponded to our revolution's generally bright and smiling spirit. On the other hand, Milyukov today was beaming, and for good reason. The trans-Atlantic republic had been the first to shake hands with the first free Russian government! The prince sent a verifying gaze across their faces, and took a special look at Kerensky, in whom he sensed with every passing day a mounting energetic strength and for whom he felt a mounting respect. Kerensky placed his unopened briefcase on the table and set his long head at a slightly pensive tilt. Evidently, he had no objection.

Right then the disheveled Shingarev, who was always half-absent at sessions, and who had buried himself in his spread papers, insisted on being given the floor urgently. He began to speak agitatedly, without looking at notes, his freed eyes seeking understanding in his colleagues. And here is what he told them. He had just now been informed about the third and fourth instance of a group of armed soldiers at train stations detaining food supplies on their way to the army—and requisitioning from that food as much as they wanted for themselves, even entire freight cars. The instances occurred at different stations in the rear zone, stations unconnected to each other, so that it was looking as though a mass movement of seizing food trains by revolutionary units had begun. So what . . . what was to be done? The Minister of Agriculture was asking for decisive measures.

Ah, decisive measures again! Ah, "decisive measures," that's not our language, it is unworthy of a free alliance of free people. My dear fellows, why so ominous? Could Andrei Ivanovich be exaggerating? Where did he get the idea that there was the threat of a mass movement? Oh no, the anarchy will settle down, it already is, healthy common sense will take the upper hand, the people themselves will settle everything in the best way, the people themselves know everything as well as we do.

But Shingarev anxiously insisted on *measures,* he was so worked up.

What could the government actually do in this instance? Release an appeal to the soldiers saying such actions were impermissible. A draft had to be written up and presented. This would be most convenient for Aleksandr Ivanovich to do, obviously, since it was soldiers, which meant his ministry.

Guchkov sat in gloom. He did not write that down.

But Shingarev wasn't finished yet. Overall, he did not have any confidence that they would be able to supply the army with bread during these spring months, when the mud was everywhere. He raised the question of the desirability of reducing the per capita consumption of bread in the army.

If the Tsarist government had said such a thing a month ago, the Zemstvo Union and Prince Lvov himself would have delivered thunderous speeches about how the government was preparing to starve our gray heroes to death. In the present situation, however, to fortify the revolutionary situation—all right, maybe. . . . Well . . . let the Minister of Agriculture reach an agreement with the Minister of War very soon.

Guchkov glowered in silence, not moving.

But Shingarev wanted more. He had an idea. In order to increase the influx of grain from remote Russia, couldn't they write one more appeal— directly from the Army!—to the entire population—with a view to inspiring it to increase its supply of food for the army?

Guchkov shrugged and glowered in silence.

Reluctant to step through this glowering veil, the prince politely suggested that Shingarev himself write up a draft for such an appeal.

Of course, all kinds of appeals were useful because they cultivated communication between people.

But Shingarev also had directly material concerns: giving permission for fishing in the Caspian Sea with seines dragged toward the shore, something usually forbidden in this season. This could substantially aid army provisioning.

Why not? That was possible. The Caspian Sea was rich, wasn't it, gentlemen? It wouldn't be any the poorer?

But Shingarev could not be stopped: there was also sowing the fields.

Now the Minister of War jumped in. Here was an unpleasant piece of news, falling somewhere between three ministries: there had been agrarian disturbances in recent days in Kazan Province, pogroms on estates and agricultural holdings. There had been instances here, as well, in Petersburg Province. So who was going to undertake what?

Ah, what bitter recollections this brought for Lvov! Rural pogroms under Tsarist tyranny were understandable and forgivable, but why now, when the people had gained their freedom? . . . This was some kind of absolute misunderstanding!

Use weapons? Oh no, no, everyone present understood that well. In the given situation? At the present time? Oh no!

The Minister of War was more likely to suggest that the Ministry of the Interior concern itself with organizing new local police to replace the disbanded ones.

Inasmuch as the prince himself could no longer keep up with running his own Ministry of the Interior, he turned to Shchepkin. But Shchepkin had this to propose: let the Minister of Justice confirm to the prosecutorial inspectorate the necessity of calling the pogromists to criminal liability.

It was harsh, of course, going straight to criminal liability, but since the police did not exist, what could save the situation if not prosecutorial oversight?

As before, Kerensky sat pensively, squinting, not having opened his briefcase, not having spoken out for or against.

Had they so resolved?

But here's what, here's what—and the prince livened up, and with him others: in Kazan Province, go to the local public organizations and individuals who enjoyed the population's trust and ask them to use their influence to make the peasants see reason and calm down!

This was wonderfully conceived! This was best of all! We can wait on criminal liability.

Shingarev had knocked down, spoiled the entire mood from the American ambassador. But here was Milyukov's problem: how was he to confer on officers of the English army the Russian decorations they had been conferred before, under the Tsar? Was this permissible?

And then, the Ministry of Foreign Affairs needed additional loans. (30 million rubles.)

Such an important ministry and such a respected minister could not be refused or haggled with.

The Ministry of the Interior had a request for 28 million rubles as well.

Approved.

Finally, Kerensky loudly clicked the locks on his briefcase.

Everyone turned around, especially Prince Lvov. He was expecting strong words from this strong man.

But Kerensky did not take anything out of his briefcase, he just clicked the locks. And smiled venomously with his long mouth, taking his revenge on Guchkov for interfering in his ministry's affairs. It follows that the Minister of War halt and even stop altogether the mobilization of indigenous laborers in Turkestan. The population there had no inclination whatsoever for military efforts, and we could not force them to work against their will. That would go against the principles of our newly won freedom.

[5 3 0]

Up to this very minute, Maslovsky had not decided exactly what he should do. The biggest thing would be to snatch Nikolai from these crows and spirit him away. If only he could! And in an hour Nikolai would be in the Trubetskoy Bastion, and there would be very different conversations with the Provisional Government, and let the franchised grit their teeth.

But he didn't have the real forces for that. The Semyonovsky men at the train station had no ammunition, and how the 2nd Riflery Regiment might respond there—they might not feel like dragging the guns around either. Of course, if he were to let it be known through Tsarskoye Selo that people were getting ready to put the Tsar back on the throne—then they could raise the garrison. But that went far beyond his instructions. The Soviet would be alarmed and all hell would break loose!

However, Maslovsky had a sufficient sense of the unusual nature of revolutionary situations. They are made so capricious that they don't obey the laws of a regular life, they pierce through ordinary life like rapiers and can poke out in the most unexpected places. His warrant was just such a rapier: an ominous and puzzling set of words reinforced by the greatest force, the Soviet.

Let's try!

They drove up. The Aleksandr Palace was incomparably smaller than the Great Palace—less a palace than a long, two-story landowner's house, two wings.

In the near wing—a grated iron gate. In front of the gate, a sentry.

"Let us through!" Maslovsky confidently waved his menacing arm as if he had driven through here many times.

It was forbidden.

He was shocked at this irregularity.

"Then the chief of watch!"

The sentry went to call him.

Now it all depended on who came out. You weren't going to break through anyone experienced. Success. Half the army right now was men like this: very green, an ensign, childishly pompous and looking extremely important. And:

"Under no circumstance, no one, categorically."

Then, as menacingly as he had voice and look for:

"I have been sent . . . and if the staff captain next to me is silent, then bear in mind that I myself outrank the captain. I have been sent on an assignment of special importance by the Petrograd Executive Committee!"

Yes but, under no circumstances, no one, categor— . . .

"Young man, trust my experience. No instruction can envisage all possibilities. Do you understand what the Petrograd Executive Committee is?"

He stood taller, straighter. He understood.

And half-disdainfully:

"Am I supposed to show you my documents? Here, in the freezing cold?"

The ensign shuddered. He invited him into the outside watch building.

Success! But a weakening simultaneously: the rest of his military force, the staff captain and two Semyovsky men, remained outside. Now his entire strength was himself, his tall fur hat, and his warrant.

Display more menace. Show him significantly: the warrant on the table, he himself turned to stone under his tall hat.

The young ensign read it, utterly distraught. Given all military power! And for an act of *special importance*.

"What do you need?"

Condescendingly to his greenness:

"You understand I can't speak with you about this, only with your superiors. Let's go inside."

"I'm sorry, but I didn't even have the right to let you in here. As for the inside watch . . . An order from General Kornilov himself . . ."

"There are orders higher than Kornilov's. In the name of the Revolutionary People!"

There it was: the piercing rapier.

"Fine. I will summon the palace commandant."

Someone was sent. In the watch room the guard commander stood at attention. The ensign was twitching, pacing. Maslovsky wondered whether he should perch somewhere. No, standing was more imposing.

In walked a rather intelligent-looking Uhlan cavalry captain.

"Staff Captain Kotzebue, palace commandant."

"Colonel Maslovsky, special representative from the Petrograd Soviet!"

So be it. The Tsar was a colonel and so was he: he wasn't going to pass for a general anyway.

And the warrant—back on the table. (The Soviet had a large seal, it was good they'd managed to affix that. And Chkheidze's signature—each letter was clear.)

Yes. . . . *An assignment of special importance.* . . .

"And what does it consist of, if I may know?"

Maslovsky froze with eyebrows raised.

"Let's go into the palace and I'll explain."

"That is impossible. The head of watch did not have the right to let you through the gate. We have strict instructions from the legitimate authority . . ."

Menacingly:

"Captain, what sort of talk is this? And the Soviet of Deputies, in your opinion, is not a legitimate authority? The head of watch committed no offense, but *you*, commandant! . . ."

The piercing rapier. And what to do? In times like this you can turn around and suddenly they accuse you and cut off your head.

He had just been defending himself:

"But the Executive Committee has to understand that people cannot be put in this kind of position. After all, the Soviet also recognized the Provisional Government. And we are subordinate to it. So it must . . ."

"What *must*, captain, the Executive Committee knows!"

What music was this "Executive Committee"! The People's Will, who executed Aleksandr II, also had an Executive Committee. It's been playing ever since.

The cavalry captain was shaken.

"Well, if I may . . . If . . . Although this is not by the rules . . . I will telephone General Kornilov right now. . . ."

"If you telephone Kornilov, I will view this as an insult to the Executive Committee. With me at the train station is the vanguard of the Petrograd revolutionary garrison, and if necessary, the entire garrison will move this way!"

They had seen just that a few days before, there was no need to convince them. Revolution! The music of the moment! Yes, perhaps, Maslovsky might have declared Kotzebue under arrest right now, he could. He decided not to. In any case, however, the entire combined palace corps de garde would not dare arrest an agent with his warrant.

A warrant that cut through stone walls. We might still take Nikolai alive!

He led him, though! Led him. The two went together.

Through dark passages. An underground corridor. A large underground barracks, with electric lights, overflowing with soldiers, a mixed hubbub of voices.

An idea! Straight to the people! Take the masses away from them! Only his voice was too small:

"Good day, comrades! Greetings to you from the Petrograd garrison and the Soviet of Soldiers' Deputies!"

Those closer heard him and shouted back discordantly. Some rose from their cots; others started coming closer.

The cavalry captain got nervous. Now he himself:

"Let's go."

Well, no! This was the only place to assemble an army:

"Comrades! The Petrograd Soviet has news of preparations for the illegal liberation of the overthrown Tsar! In order to put him back on the throne! Revolutionary Petrograd is counting on your support!"

Those close up answered back to the effect that they understood. But some stepped away. And people in back asked what this was about.

Right then, had he been allowed to agitate freely, they might have gone straightaway and taken Nikolai!

But now a sullen lieutenant took him by the elbow:

"Let's go, let's go!"

No, he hadn't managed to raise these men. And he didn't know whether they ever would rise up.

A well-lit room on the first floor. About twenty officers from the watch regiment, along with Kotzebue, had already heard, already knew, and were seriously agitated. They surged forward in a half-ring, vying with each other (Kotzebue had assembled his forces by revolutionary means, too!):

"God knows what this is!"

"Who are you, colonel? We don't know you."

"A military man shouldn't act this way!"

"We are all carrying out an order!"

"This is outrageous! The soldiers have just barely calmed down, and you're inciting them again?"

"Stir things up like you did in Petersburg?"

Solidly surrounded! The Executive Committee's emissary started to lose his nerve. In recent days, officers had been so timid, and he had not anticipated this unanimity. If they were all agreed, you couldn't break through them.

His eye wandered, wondering who to stop on, and all of a sudden he saw a familiar face among them. Yes, a familiar face! A middle-aged ensign— and leftist Kadet! They'd met before!

This was how it should be! Wartime officers aren't your former Sobake-viches.

And this one recognized him. And shouted:

"Gentlemen! One moment. Turns out we know each other! Allow us to speak confidentially?"

The hope of some sense. The officers quieted down. He and the Kadet moved into the next room.

"Sergei Dmitrich, that's right, isn't it? Your scheme is mad, give it up. The regiment won't let you for anything."

The revolutionary phrases had stopped piercing for some reason. The emissary sat down. And this ordinary "Sergei Dmitrich" seemed to rip off his menacing, tall snake-curl hat. They would find out he wasn't a colonel.

Though the Browning handle could be seen from his pocket.

"What scheme?"

"You want to assassinate the Emperor? Here, in his palace?"

"Wherever did you get that? Just because I'm a socialist revolutionary?" (The phrase had a wonderful sound these days.)

"But Captain Kotzebue says that your warrant . . . Will you allow me to look?"

"Please."

This presentation was the first ordinary one, not for effect. However, the impression on the Kadet was powerful:

"Your warrant's wording is **terrifying**. I can find no other word. What can one think?"

"Well . . . Take measures, do not allow escape. In the interests of deepen-ing the revolution, detention here is inadmissible. If necessary, then . . ."

"Then what?"

"Move him somewhere else."

"That is out of the question. That is an insult to the regiment."

The emissary had not fortified his position against these discussions. Everything got bogged down. They returned to the officers in the room.

Maslovsky surveyed their hopelessly loyal Guards foreheads: even the days of revolution had not shaken their doglike loyalty.

He explained. The Soviet had incontrovertible facts that the Tsar's escape was being craftily readied—for his restoration. And the authorities of the commissar (already more restrained) were to ward off this danger. It might be calmer to move the Tsar somewhere else.

A new outburst of officer indignation—and again unanimous:

"You mean you don't trust us?"

"Are you trying to remove our regiment?"

Actually—that would be good. But clearly it wasn't going to work:

"Gentlemen, what's this about a lack of trust? If I didn't trust you, I wouldn't have come here alone and would have led at least an entire corps right up to the palace walls! All sailor **Kronstadt** if necessary."

Kronstadt was like sabers across their eyes, like blood spurting in their eyes—and they staggered back.

"Kronstadt!" He'd drawn blood. We could make short work of you, just run and get the sailors. "But if I'm convinced the arrest has been made in all strictness, that his guard is irreproachable . . . Maybe, maybe . . ." he conceded disappointedly, no longer seeing, no longer believing in success, "we can get by without taking him to the Peter and Paul Fortress."

Kotzebue stood there with a firmly challenging gaze, his hand on his hilt. No, he wouldn't let him.

A thickset old captain replied somberly and firmly:

"We will not let you take the Emperor away, even if it comes to a fight."

Maslovsky whipped himself up, trying all the same:

"You know very well, gentlemen, that if it is found to be necessary, not only he but you and anybody else will be taken away to the Peter and Paul Fortress! But *maybe*, I repeat, we might get by without a clash. The Soviet definitely does not want a clash. That is why I spoke with the soldiers, to be convinced. . . . And I see that the soldiers are entirely loyal to the Soviet. But I want to understand with respect to you . . ."

The senior officers stepped aside to confer in a window bay. After this, one of them:

"We did not have an easy time of taking over the watch either. All night and up until this morning the Combined Guards Regiment refused to be replaced. They didn't trust us, nor we them. They'd placed machine guns, and it nearly got to the point of battle. So we haven't taken this post just to go away easily. As long as we're here, neither the former Emperor nor his family will leave these walls. We will guard them continuously. We can undertake that our replacement will not come about without the Petrograd Soviet's knowledge. Are you satisfied?"

"Without the *consent* of the Soviet? Did I understand correctly?"

Silence.

Yes . . . He would have to be satisfied.

And so? That was it? The emissary's entire trip, his entire historic warrant, his entire audacious onslaught—and this was how it was ending? Had he made the trip for nothing? Was he going back empty-handed? His revolutionary pride would not allow that. He was ashamed before the Executive Committee.

Already breaking off and rolling down from the height he'd reached, the emissary kept imagining all the various combinations. What could he seize upon? How could he save face?

And he came up with this:

"Besides the reliability of the guard, however, I have to be convinced that the person you are guarding is indeed here. You are going to have to produce the prisoner."

The officers shuddered. They darkened. Angrily:

"What do you mean **produce**?"

"What is the idea? Worse than this, after all . . ."

"He will never agree!"

"What kind of cruelty is this, and pointless, moreover? You cannot truly doubt that the Emperor is here. In your opinion, the regiment would agree to guard empty rooms?"

"We have all seen him. We give our officer's word of honor that the Emperor is here and shut in."

Once again they resisted, a group of twenty officers, in a tense semicircle.

But the more heatedly they objected, the more surely the emissary realized he had seized on this correctly. They considered it cruelty—because of the humiliation? Well, the monarch's humiliation was what was most needed! Humiliation was more important than the arrest itself. In a certain sense, humiliation was even better than the scaffold! This fact would be reflected in the newspapers. Everyone would learn of it. Magnificent! The Tsar will not agree? That's exactly why he must! This would be the breaking of his will!

"Yes, exactly, *produce* him! I cannot return to the Soviet unless I've been convinced with my own eyes. . . ."

What made our SR terror so striking was that it exchanged the mystique of "God's anointed" for the physiology of bloody scraps. Humiliating the anointed one—as an inspected prisoner, before the commissar of revolutionary workers and soldiers! An emperor demeaned through prison inspection—that would never be forgotten, while he was living or after he is dead.

"Yes, exactly, produce him!" Maslovsky proudly tossed back his head in his tall snake-curl hat. "Otherwise the fate of the Provisional Government and all Russia will once again be at stake!"

This he had put marvelously. More and more he saw that they could not refuse him. *Kronstadt* had only just happened and could happen again.

They sent for the regimental commander.

[5 3 1]

Only outside guards from the 1st Riflery Guards Regiment had been posted. Inside, the palace remained as it had been. All the corridors and doors were free, one wing tightly inhabited by the royal family, then the empty formal rooms in the middle, corridors along both floors with side rooms for members of the suite—and in the far wing the ill Anya Vyrubova and everyone fussing over her.

They were supposed to go see her that evening—but these first hours they were with the children, first with the Heir, in his light-filled room. Aleksei had already recovered. Then with their daughters—the older grand duchesses recuperating. Then with the youngest, Anastasia, who was still ill. And in the entirely dark room of the seriously ill Maria, in a fever. She could not take in clearly that her father had arrived, first confirmed that he had, then talked deliriously about him not coming, and about the frightening crowd coming to kill her Mama.

Only after being in these rooms could Nikolai feel what his beloved had gone through looking after all her patients at once, and in times like these.

But Olya and Tanya exulted at their father's arrival. Although they were still in bed, they assured him that they were all better now. For them, their father's arrival had solved all their misfortunes.

That was how they talked, fidgeting on their pillows: now that we're all together, we're not afraid of anything, Papa, Mama!

Nikolai embraced his son, who had also cheered up, and held him close, in silence, trying to hide how lost he felt; he found it hard to speak.

He thanked Lili Dehn, that unexpected angel who had shared the Empress's most difficult days. Lili began to weep.

In front of her, in front of Benckendorff, he tried to speak of inconsequential things—but all his self-possession and habit were not enough. Such a hollow ached inside him, he wanted only to shut himself away, close his eyes, and fall silent and numb. Only with Alix could Nikolai be alone now, incapable of showing any signs of life.

Once again they went down to their rooms.

Locked themselves in.

An outing was forbidden—Nikolai could regain some strength by spending a few hours with Alix, in silence, collapsed. He had to pass through this period of neither speaking nor moving if he was to be reborn.

Aleksandra tucked him in on the couch. She sat by his side, applying cool, damp cloths to his brow.

The Empress's chambermaid did not knock but peeked through the door: "Your Majesty . . . Count Benckendorff is so bold as to ask for you."

Alix rose quietly and went out.

Count Benckendorff—his narrow side-whiskers were trembling—confused and agitated, was going on incoherently. The Emperor had to appear before some new arrival, a commissar from the Soviet of Workers' Deputies.

"What do you mean, 'appear'?" The Empress was indignant, still feeling some strength inside, all the more responsible the less strength her most august spouse had. "The Emperor has not scheduled an audience with anyone!"

The count kneaded his fingers. As if he, an old courtier, didn't understand that! But the new palace commandant said there was no other way. Might Her Majesty wish to receive the commandant and let him explain?

As was ever her lot: a man's duties, a man's decisions. In the state Nicky was in, he was unfit to decide anything.

The Empress went into the green drawing room, still wearing her now usual sick-nurse dress, and received Staff Captain Kotzebue, who had already been given a favorable recommendation by Lili Dehn, and now looked intently at him with her pained, weary eyes. They, too, apparently, the last to hold up in the family, would soon cease to function.

In this state you cannot get a good look at anyone new. But Kotzebue held himself very respectfully and his tone was one of concern—like all their former fine officers around them.

He explained that he had no choice, he didn't have the forces to quarrel with the Petrograd Soviet. And the Soviet wished to ascertain that the Emperor was indeed here.

It was enough to make you choke!

"But where do they think he has gone? Where else might he be?"

Kotzebue would not retreat, though. If there were a clash with the Soviet's forces, that would not be good for anyone. With great difficulty, however, they had found a peaceful solution. This was a very minor procedure and would not be onerous for the Emperor. He did not have to receive or speak to this commissar. He did not even have to greet him. They had devised the following. At the intersection of corridors upstairs, where the picture gallery was, the Emperor would pass through without stopping, down one corridor, and this commissar would watch from the other, and that would be all. The commissar would be surrounded by armed officers from the watch regiment and so could not move or hurl an insult.

She had to agree, it seemed. Their status as prisoners did not allow for much choice.

However, the Empress knew what a weakened, mute state she had left the Emperor in. Was he in any condition to show himself?

Could they not postpone this procedure for a couple of hours? An hour at least?

Alas, alas, no, the staff captain was deeply worried. An hour might mean the loss of a peaceful outcome. Her Majesty could not imagine the dangers that had been averted.

It was obvious she would have to concede.

Aleksandra went to ready Nicky. He was lying on his back in a heavy doze, his mouth half open, groaning. Her heart was breaking. Why had this added suffering and humiliation been sent him?

Taking his head in both hands, she stroked and roused him.

He could not fathom it. Why? Where must I go? What for? But he believed her.

And with difficulty, great difficulty, he sat up. Hiding the traces of his weakness, she herself rubbed him down and washed him.

In the bedroom he changed out of his house robe and into his Life Guards uniform. He always changed clothes easily and quickly, out of military habit.

His eyes and the many wrinkles on his dark face were like pits.

Alix made the sign of the cross over him, and he went out to join Benckendorff and Dolgorukov—whether understanding or still in a gray state of not understanding.

Thank God, he did not have to say anything to anyone.

This was like a brief walk down the hall, since the park was now forbidden to him.

But how shameful to go for a walk dethroned! . . .

They went up to the second floor. Benckendorff respectfully explained to the Emperor where he had to go and how—as far as the room of the valet Volkov. And he had to remove his headgear.

Did he understand or not? . . .

He removed his hussar cap and placed it on the corridor window.

Benckendorff himself and Dolgorukov hurried forward to take their positions. The Emperor was supposed to wait a few minutes here.

Then he started—utterly as if in a swoon, as if asleep, as if he himself were neither present nor participating.

He himself opened the panel of the wide doors, and the farther he went, at the intersection of the corridors, under the glass ceilings, which faintly let through the light of the closing day, lamps burned brightly, all the ones that were there.

Nikolai squinted in pain.

He walked slowly and aimlessly.

Three steps from the intersection, the commissar stood—sideways, wearing the uniform of a military official but also a large, shaggy, tall Caucasian hat, one short leg forward.

Standing, guarding behind him were two tense officers with their right hands in their pockets, an unusual position, he could not fail to notice.

And also an Uhlan staff captain.

Neither he nor the other officers saluted, but they did stand at attention. So did Benckendorff.

But the commissar did not budge or remove his tall hat. He stood there with the same wild look, foot forward, as if he had started to move toward the Emperor. And no one told him—or was it too late already?—to remove his hat.

And no one could bring himself to knock it off.

It got so quiet you could hear the breathing.

The Emperor was walking not very precisely, not at all his usual steps, and with the faint, sonorous jangling of spurs. He was walking and his very walk expressed perplexity and ignorance of the right way for him to do this.

The lack of a cap was odd. And his head did not sit firmly, military-fashion.

A tormented look, enflamed eyelids, and bags under his eyes. His mustache drooped. How he had aged!

All he needed to do was to cross the intersection of corridors as quickly as possible, without looking back or sideways—and go, be done with it.

But the Emperor could not pass without noticing the tense group to the side. He naturally turned his head to those there—and then slowed down—and then changed direction—a half-step, and another half-step this way, looking at all the faces in confusion—for the first time perplexed. Why were they standing like that? In that combination? And who was this in the tall snake-curl hat?

Starker yet were his snake eyes, they burned with hatred. The commissar's face twisted, and he was shaking feverishly.

In front of this vivid appearance of malice, the Emperor stopped, woke up—and felt it. On his face, puffy with weariness, the meaning became apparent—as did his exhaustion.

He swayed a little from foot to foot. He jerked one shoulder. And was about to turn and go—but couldn't, out of politeness, not nod to the group in parting.

He nodded.

And walked away, his step unsteady—but rather than go very far forward, in the direction he had been heading, he went back to from whence he had come.

MAPS

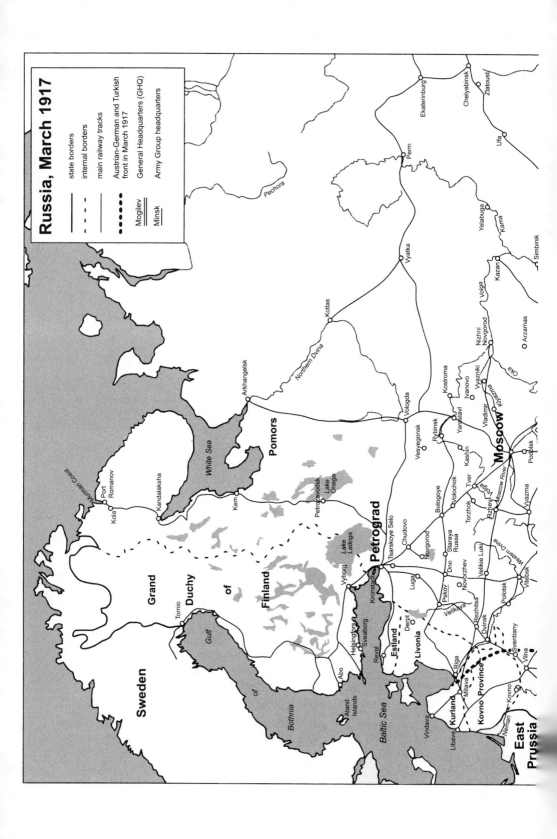

Russia, March 1917

	state borders
	internal borders
	main railway tracks
•••••	Austrian–German and Turkish front in March 1917
Mogilev	General Headquarters (GHQ)
Minsk	Army Group headquarters

Zlatoust
Chelyabinsk
Ekaterinburg
Ufa
Kama
Yelabuga
Perm
Simbirsk
Kazan
Vyatka
Volga
Oka
Nizhni Novgorod
Arzamas
Pechora
Kotlas
Kostroma
Ivanovo
Vyazniki
Kineshma
Vladimir
Northern Dvina
Vologda
Rybinsk
Yaroslavl
Moscow
Podolsk
Arkhangelsk
Vesyegonsk
Kashin
Moscow River
Pomors
White Sea
Bologoye
Volochok
Tver
Rzhev
Torzhok
Vyazma
Port Romanov
Kola
Kandalaksha
Kem
Petrozavodsk
Lake Onega
Staraya Russa
Dno
Velikiye Luki
Western Dvina
Murman Coast
Lake Ladoga
Tsarskoye Selo
Chudovo
Novgorod
Polotsk
Vitebsk
Petrograd
Luga
Pskov
Novorzhev
Rezhitsa
Dvinsk
Kronstadt
Vyborg
Grand
Duchy
of
Finland
Helsingfors
Sveaborg
Reval
Estland
Derpt
Livonia
Velikaya
Riga
Sventiany
Vilna
Sweden
Tornio
Gulf
of
Bothnia
Abo
Aland Islands
Baltic Sea
Vindava
Mitava
Kurland
Kovno Province
Kovno
Neman
Libava
East Prussia

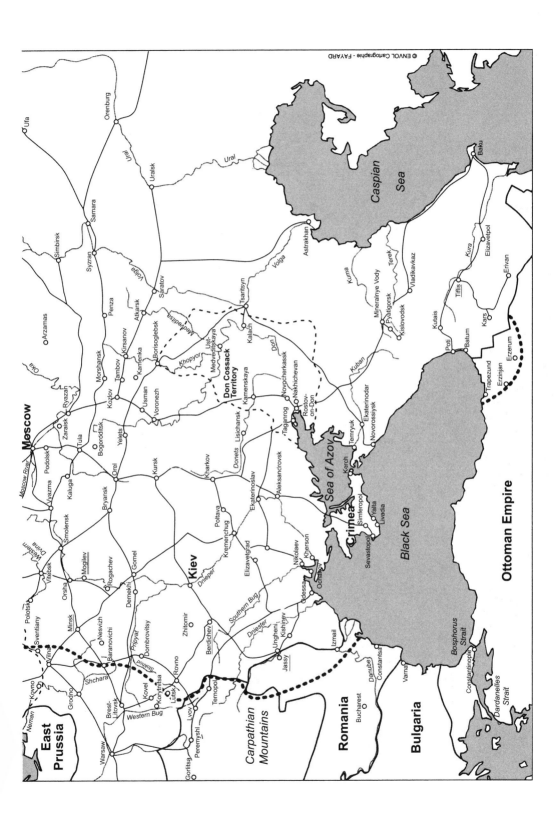

© ENVOL Cartographie - FAYARD

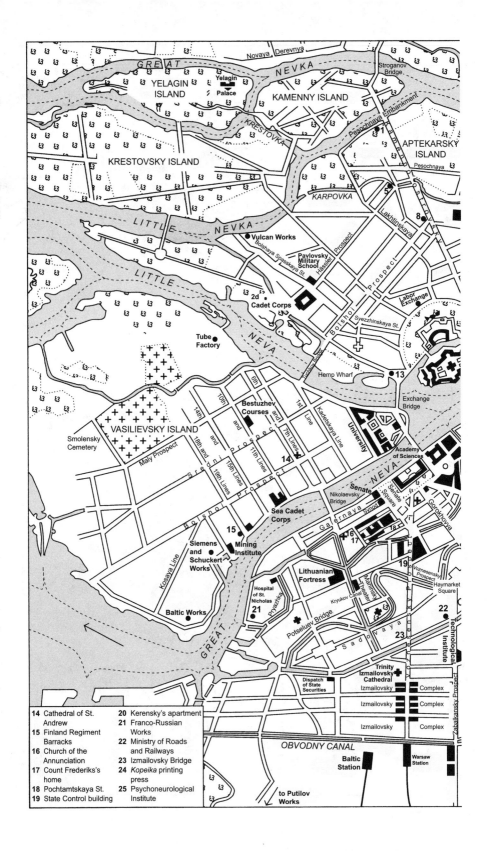

NEVKA

Novaya Derevnya

GREAT

YELAGIN
ISLAND

Yelagin
Palace

KAMENNY ISLAND

Stroganov
Bridge

Pesochnaya Embankment

1

APTEKARSKY
ISLAND

KRESTOVKA

Pesochnaya

KRESTOVSKY ISLAND

KARPOVKA

5

Lakhtinskaya

8

LITTLE   NEVKA

Vulcan Works

Bolshaya Spasskaya St.

Pavlovsky
Military
School

Hessler

Prospekt

LITTLE

2d
Cadet Corps

Bolshoi

Prospekt

Labor
Exchange

NEVA

Syezzhinskaya St.

Tube
Factory

Hemp Wharf

13

Exchange
Bridge

6th

Bestuzhev
Courses

10th

and

14th

16th and

19th Lines

11th Lines

and

Sredny

1st
Line

and 7th Lines

Kadetskaya Line

University

Academy
of Sciences

Prospect

VASILIEVSKY ISLAND

Smolensky
Cemetery

Maly Prospect

14

NEVA

Senate

Nikolaevsky
Bridge

Senate
Square

Synod

Gorokhova

Sea Cadet
Corps

Nikolaevsky
Bridge

Galernaya

Bolshoi Line

15

Siemens
and
Schuckert
Works

Mining
Institute

Koesaya Line

Lithuanian
Fortress

6
17

Moïsky

19

Voznesensky
Prospekt

Haymarket
Square

Baltic Works

GREAT

Hospital
of St.
Nicholas

21

Pryazhka

Potseluev Bridge

Kryukov Canal

Sadovaya

22

23

Technological Institute

Trinity
Izmailovsky
Cathedral

Dispatch
of State
Securities

Izmailovsky   Complex

Izmailovsky   Complex

Izmailovsky   Complex

Zabalkansky Prospekt

OBVODNY CANAL

Baltic
Station

Warsaw
Station

to Putilov
Works

14 Cathedral of St.
   Andrew
15 Finland Regiment
   Barracks
16 Church of the
   Annunciation
17 Count Frederiks's
   home
18 Pochtamtskaya St.
19 State Control building

20 Kerensky's apartment
21 Franco-Russian
   Works
22 Ministry of Roads
   and Railways
23 Izmailovsky Bridge
24 *Kopeika* printing
   press
25 Psychoneurological
   Institute

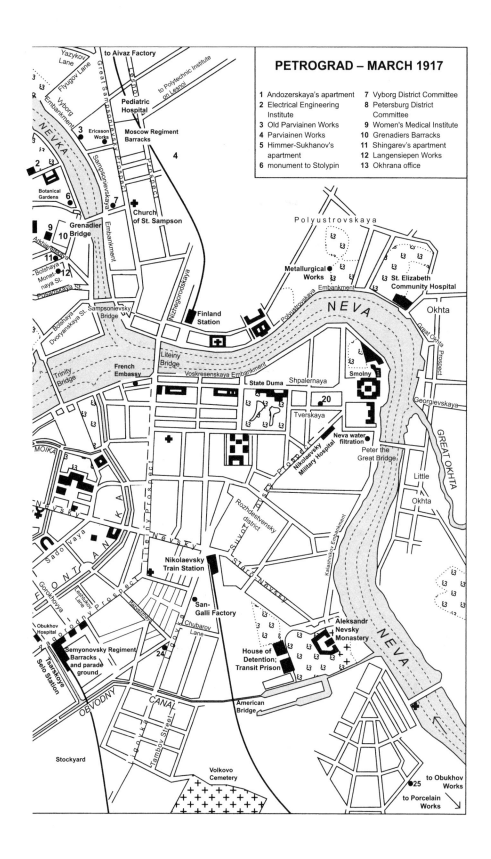

PETROGRAD – MARCH 1917

1 Andozerskaya's apartment
2 Electrical Engineering Institute
3 Old Parviainen Works
4 Parviainen Works
5 Himmer-Sukhanov's apartment
6 monument to Stolypin
7 Vyborg District Committee
8 Petersburg District Committee
9 Women's Medical Institute
10 Grenadiers Barracks
11 Shingarev's apartment
12 Langensiepen Works
13 Okhrana office

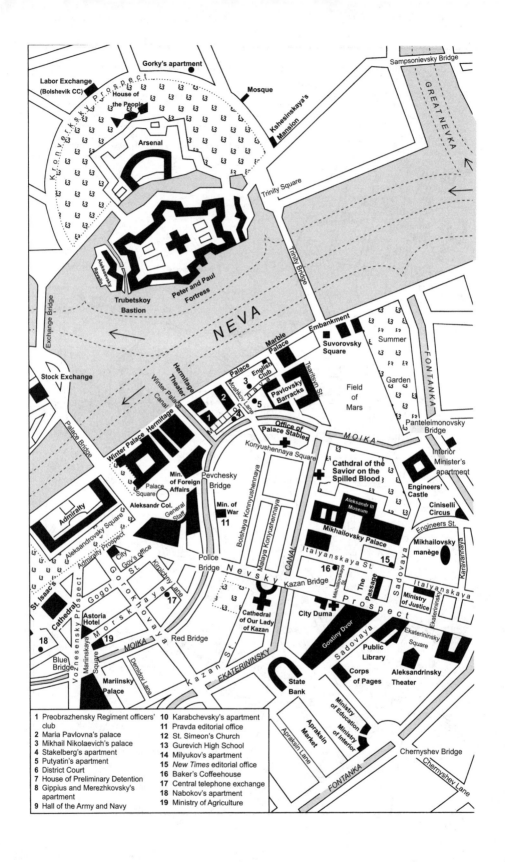

NEVA

Sampsonievsky Bridge

GREAT NEVKA

Gorky's apartment

Labor Exchange
(Bolshevik CC)

House of
the People

Mosque

Kronverksky Prospect

Kshesinskaya's
Mansion

Arsenal

Trinity Square

Peter and Paul
Fortress

Aleksevsky Ravelin

Trinity Bridge

Trubetskoy
Bastion

Exchange Bridge

Stock Exchange

Marble
Palace

Embankment

Suvorovsky
Square

Summer
Garden

FONTANKA

Palace Bridge

Winter Palace Canal

Hermitage Theater

Palace
Quay

English
Club

3

2

5

Pavlovsky
Barracks

Tsaritsyn St.

Field
of
Mars

Panteleimonovsky
Bridge

Winter Palace

Hermitage

1

Office of
Palace Stables

Konyushennaya Square

MOIKA

Interior
Minister's
apartment

Min.
of Foreign
Affairs

Pevchesky
Bridge

Cathdral of the
Savior on the
Spilled Blood

Engineers'
Castle

Palace Square

Palace
Square

Aleksandr Col.

General
Staff

Min. of
War

11

Bolshaya Konyushennaya

Malaya Konyushennaya

CANAL

Aleksandr III
Museum

Mikhailovsky Palace

Ciniselli
Circus

Engineers St.

Mikhailovsky
manège

Admiralty

Aleksandrovsky Square

Admiralty Prospect

City
Gov's office

Gorokhovaya St.

Kirpichny Lane

Police
Bridge

Nevsky

Kazan Bridge

Italyanskaya St.

16

The
Passage

15

Sadovaya

Italyaninsky

Karavannaya

Ministry
of Justice

Ekaterininsky

St. Isaac's

Voznesensky Prospect

Gogol St.

17

Cathedral
of Our Lady
of Kazan

City Duma

Prospect

Gostiny Dvor

Sadovaya

Public
Library

Ekaterininsky
Square

Astoria
Hotel

Morskaya

Marinskaya Square

19

MOIKA

Red Bridge

Kazan St.

EKATERINSKY

Corps
of Pages

Aleksandrinsky
Theater

18

Blue
Bridge

Demidov Lane

Marinsky
Palace

State
Bank

Ministry
of Education

Ministry
of Interior

Aprakisn
Market

Aprakisn Lane

Chernyshev Bridge

Chernyshev Lane

FONTANKA

1 Preobrazhensky Regiment officers' club	10 Karabchevsky's apartment
2 Maria Pavlovna's palace	11 Pravda editorial office
3 Mikhail Nikolaevich's palace	12 St. Simeon's Church
4 Stakelberg's apartment	13 Gurevich High School
5 Putyatin's apartment	14 Milyukov's apartment
6 District Court	15 *New Times* editorial office
7 House of Preliminary Detention	16 Baker's Coffeehouse
8 Gippius and Merezhkovsky's apartment	17 Central telephone exchange
9 Hall of the Army and Navy	18 Nabokov's apartment
	19 Ministry of Agriculture

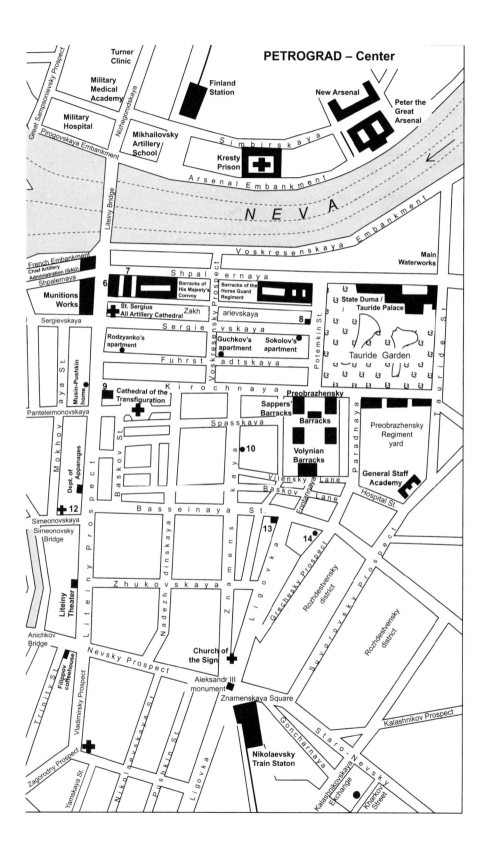

PETROGRAD – Center

Turner Clinic

Military Medical Academy

Military Hospital

Great Sampsonievsky Prospect

Pirogovskaya Embankment

Nizhegorodskaya

Mikhailovsky Artillery School

Finland Station

New Arsenal

Peter the Great Arsenal

S i m b i r s k a y a

Kresty Prison

Liteiny Bridge

A r s e n a l   E m b a n k m e n t

N E V A

V o s k r e s e n s k a y a   Embankment

Main Waterworks

French Embankment
Chief Artillery Administration (GAU)
Shpalernaya

Munitions Works

7   S h p a l e r n a y a

6

Barracks of His Majesty's Convoy

Barracks of the Horse Guard Regiment

State Duma / Tauride Palace

St. Sergius All Artillery Cathedral   Zakh   arievskaya

Sergievskaya

S e r g i e v s k a y a

8

Rodzyanko's apartment

Guchkov's apartment

Sokolov's apartment

Tauride Garden

Voskresensky Prospect

Potemkin St.

Tauride St.

F u h r s t   a d t s k a y a

Musin-Pushkin home

M u s i n - P u s h k i n a y a   S t.

Panteleimonovskaya

9   Cathedral of the Transfiguration

K i r o c h n a y a

Preobrazhensky

Sappers' Barracks

Barracks

Preobrazhensky Regiment yard

M o k h o v a y a   S t.

Dept. of Appanages

Baskov St.

S p a s s k a y a

Volynian Barracks

Paradnaya

General Staff Academy

10

Vilensky Lane

B a s k o v   Lane

Hospital St.

Fontannaya Lane

12

Simeonovskaya

Simeonovsky Bridge

B a s s e i n a y a   S t.

13   14

Nadezhdinskaya

Znamenskaya

Ligovka

Grechesky Prospect

Rozhdestvensky district

Suvorovsky Prospect

Rozhdestvensky district

Liteiny Theater

Liteiny Prospect

Z h u k o v s k a y a

Anichkov Bridge

N e v s k y   P r o s p e c t

Filippov coffeehouse

Trinity St.

Vladimirsky Prospect

Nikolaevskaya St.

Pushkin St.

Ligovka

Church of the Sign

Aleksandr III monument

Znamenskaya Square

Zagorodny Prospect

Yamskaya St.

Nikolaevsky Train Staton

Goncharnaya

Staro - Nevsky

Kalashnikov Prospect

Kalashnikovskaya Exchange

Kharkov St.

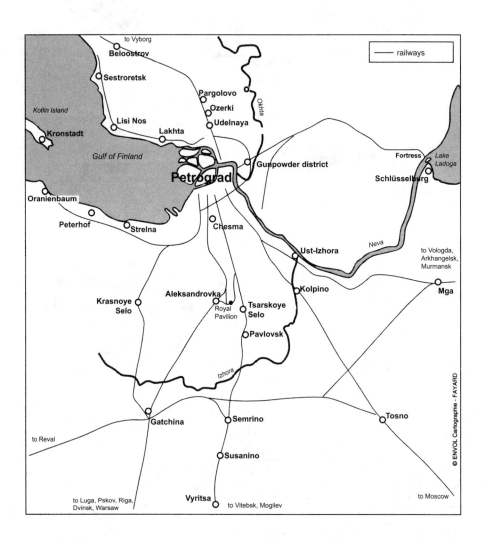

Index of Names

Abramovich, Aleksandr Emelyanovich (Shaya Zelikovich) (1888–1972): Bolshevik since 1908, he emigrated to Switzerland, then returned to Russia in Lenin's carriage. Collaborator of the Comintern.

Adrian: First name of Admiral Nepenin and his nickname among the "Decembrists of the Fleet."

Adzhemov, Moisei Sergeevich (1878–1953, USA): Deputy in Second, Third, and Fourth Dumas. Prominent member of the Kadet Party.

Akulia: diminutive and rustic version of the female name Akulina, "Aquilina."

Aleksan Mikhailych (Aleksandr Mikhailovich). *See* Krymov.

Aleksandr I (Aleksandr Pavlovich) (1777–1825): Tsar in 1801 following the assassination of his father; defeated Napoleon in 1812, entered Paris in triumph; his reign is known for promises of reforms that continuously went unfulfilled.

Aleksandr II (1818–1881): The "Tsar Liberator," presided over the emancipation of the serfs, the introduction of the zemstvo system of local government, modernization of the judicial system, easing of the burden of military service. Assassinated 13 March 1881 by members of the Narodnaya Volya (People's Will) organization.

Aleksandr III (1845–1894): Became emperor following the assassination of his father, Aleksandr II. Discontinued and in part reversed his father's program of reform. Father of the Franco-Russian Alliance.

Aleksandr (Aleksan) **Aleksandrovich** (Aleksanych, Sanych). *See* Rittikh.

Aleksandr Apollonovich. *See* Manuilov.

Aleksandr Fyodorovich (Fyodorych). *See* Kerensky.

Aleksandr Gavrilovich (Gavrilych). *See* Shlyapnikov.

Aleksandr Ivanovich (Ivanych). *See* Guchkov.

Aleksandr Mikhailovich ("Sandro"), **Grand Duke** (1866–1933, France): Grandson of Nikolai I, friend of Nikolai II in his youth. Married Nikolai's sister Ksenia.

Aleksandr Nevsky (ca. 1220–1263): Prince of Novgorod and then Grand Prince of Vladimir; conquered the Swedes on the Neva, and then German knights (1242); coexisted with the Horde; canonized.

Aleksandra Fyodorovna ("Alix"), **Empress** (1872–1918): Born Princess Alix of Hesse and by Rhine. Married the future Nikolai II in 1894. Nickname "Sunny" in letters with her husband. Murdered together with her husband and children by the Bolsheviks.

Aleksandra Mikhailovna. *See* Kollontai.

Aleksandrovich. *See* Dmitrievsky.

Alekseev, Mikhail Vasilievich (1857–1918): Infantry general, chief of staff, first on the Southwestern, then on the Northwestern Front. From September 1915, chief of General Staff. On sick leave 21 November 1916 to 7 March 1917. Advised the

Tsar to abdicate in March 1917. Supreme Commander until 3 June 1917. After the October Revolution organized the first White Army on the Don.

Aleksei ("Baby," "Sunshine") (1904–1918): Son and youngest child of Nikolai II and Aleksandra Fyodorovna, hemophiliac. Murdered together with his parents and sisters by the Bolsheviks.

Aleksei Maksimovich (Maksimych). *See* Gorky.

Aleksei Vasilich, Aleksei Vasilievich. *See* Peshekhonov.

Alix. *See* Aleksandra Fyodorovna ("Alix"), Empress.

Altfater, Vasili Mikhailovich (1883–1919): Veteran of Russo-Japanese War; rear admiral, joined Red side in the Civil War, was first commander of the Soviet fleet; doubts were raised about his official cause of death (heart attack).

Alyona: diminutive of Elena.

Anastasia (1901–1918): Youngest daughter of Nikolai II and Aleksandra Fyodorovna, murdered with her whole family by the Bolsheviks.

Andrei, Bishop (born Aleksandr Ukhtomsky, prince) (1872–1937): Bishop of Ufa; sympathizer of the Kadets; after February/March, he supported the provisional government; was an anti-Bolshevik. Chaplain in Kolchak's army. Returned to Ufa; trapped in the arrest-deportation-banishment cycle. Shot by the NKVD.

Andrei Ivanovich (Ivanych). *See* Shingarev.

Andrei Vladimirovich (1879–1956, France): Grand duke; cousin of the Tsar.

Andrew, Saint: This apostle is known in the Orthodox Church as "the First-Called" (cf. Matthew 4:18–20; John 1:35–40); patron saint of Russia, which he evangelized according to legend.

Anna Ioannovna (1693–1740): Empress of Russia; niece of Peter the Great; in order to ascend to the throne in 1730, she had to accept the leadership of the "Supreme Privy Council," which she quickly discarded.

Anna Sergeevna: Refers to **Milyukova** (née Smirnova), **Anna Sergeevna** (1861–1935, France), wife of Pavel Milyukov.

Anya. *See* Vyrubova.

Apraksin, Pyotr Nikolaevich, Count (1876–1962, Belgium): Master of the Court, chief of the private secretariat of the Empress, member of the ecclesiastic council of 1917; last mayor of Yalta, evacuated with Wrangel.

Armand, Inessa (née Steffen) (1874–1920): Bolshevik. French wife of the industrialist Armand and subsequently of his brother. Close friend and ally of Lenin from 1909. Buried in Red Square.

Astrov, Nikolai Ivanovich (1868–1934, Czechoslovakia): Important member of the Kadet Party; one of the founders of the Union of Cities; mayor of Moscow from March to June 1917; emigrated.

Asya: diminutive of Aleksandra. *See* Vyazemskaya.

Avilov, Boris Vasilievich (1874–1938): Left Menshevik; journalist; later worked in the government's statistics office on Five Year Plans; executed.

Baby. *See* Aleksei ("Baby," "Sunshine").

Balk, Aleksandr Pavlovich (1866–1957, Brazil): Major general, Petrograd city governor from November 1916 until March 1917.

Bazarov (pseud. of Rudnev), **Vladimir Aleksandrovich** (1874–1939): Social Democrat from 1896, first a Bolshevik but in 1917 a Menshevik Internationalist, like Himmer; perished in the purges.

Bazhenov, Vasili Ivanovich (1737/38–1799): Russian architect; many of his projects never came to fruition.

Bazili, Nikolai Aleksandrovich (Nicolas de Basily, 1883–1963, USA): Russian diplomat, drafted the abdication manifesto of Nikolai II, emigrated, author of books about the Soviet economy and posthumous memoirs, *Diplomat of Imperial Russia: 1903–1917*.

Beilis (affair): The trial of Menahem Mendel Beilis, accused in 1911 of the ritual murder of a Christian infant; he was acquitted in 1913 after a violently anti-Semitic campaign and a vigorous counterattack by the intelligentsia (Gorky, Korolenko).

Bekhterev, Vladimir Mikhailovich (1852–1927): Celebrated Russian psychologist, neurologist, and psychiatrist.

Belyaev, Mikhail Alekseevich (1863–1918): General. Vice Minister of War June 1915–August 1916. Minister of War January–March 1917. Arrested by the Provisional Government, liberated, arrested again and shot by the Bolsheviks.

Benckendorff, Pavel Konstantinovich, Count (1853–1921, Estonia): Cavalry general, general aide-de-camp, high chamberlain of the Court.

Blanc, Louis (1811–1882): French socialist politician ("Utopian"); participant in the Revolution of 1848 and exiled between 1851 and 1870; author of *The History of Ten Years*.

Bleikhman, Iosif Solomonovich (1868–1921): "Anarcho-Communist" leader; participant in February, July, and October 1917; arrested in October 1920; died soon after developing tuberculosis while in forced labor.

Bogdanov, Boris Osipovich (1884–1960): Menshevik, secretary of the Workers' Group, defensist; after the October Revolution spent forty years in and out of prisons, labor camps, internal exile.

Boldyrev, Vasili Georgievich (1875–1933): Quartermaster general of the Northern Army Group during the revolution; participant in various military White movements, fought in the Far East, arrested and pardoned in 1923, arrested again and executed in 1933.

Bonch-Bruevich, Mikhail Dmitrievich (1870–1956): Military leader who was the first to join the Bolsheviks after their coup, brother of the revolutionary Vladimir Bonch-Bruevich.

Bonch-Bruevich, Vladimir Dmitrievich (1873–1955): Publisher and publicist. Close to Lenin. Wrote for *Iskra*, specialized in history and sociology of religion. Many official functions under Bolshevik regime.

Boris (Boris Vladimirovich), **Grand Duke** (1877–1943, France): Major general, ataman of the Cossacks, cousin of Nikolai II.

Bosch, Evgenia Bogdanovna (1879–1925): Bolshevik. Nicknamed "the Japanese" because of her escape (with Pyatakov) from Siberia via Japan. Fought on the Red side in the Civil War. Accused of "Trotskyism," committed suicide.

their coup; president of a short-lived White government at Arkhangelsk during the Civil War; emigrated in 1920.

Chelnokov, Mikhail Vasilievich (1863–1935, Yugoslavia): Industrialist from Moscow, one of the founders of the Kadet Party; elected mayor of Moscow (1914–1917), chief representative of the Union of Towns, co-president of the Union of Zemstvos; emigrated after October.

Chenier, André (1762–1794): French poet; initially advocated for the liberal Revolution, he was arrested during the Terror; stigmatized Revolutionary excesses in his celebrated *Iambes*; guillotined a few days before the 9th of Thermidor.

Cherkassky, Mikhail Borisovich (Misha) (1882–1919): Rear Admiral (during March 1917, Captain First Rank). Supported the February Revolution but later joined the White Volunteer Army, was taken prisoner, and shot by the Bolsheviks.

Chernyshevsky, Nikolai Gavrilovich (1828–1889): Philosopher, literary critic, inspirer of populism, educator of several generations of revolutionaries. Arrested in 1862 for having participated in the writing of a revolutionary proclamation, he spent two decades in prison (where he wrote *What Is to Be Done?*), forced labor, or exile.

Chkheidze, Nikolai Semyonovich (1864–1926, France): Menshevik leader, deputy at the Third and Fourth Dumas; in February 1917, president of the Petrograd Soviet. After October, president of the Georgian Constituent Assembly. Emigrated in 1921, committed suicide.

Danilov, Yuri Nikiforovich (1866–1937, France): "Black" Danilov, to distinguish him from a red-haired namesake. Quartermaster general at Grand Duke Nikolai Nikolaevich's headquarters. Chief of staff of the Northern Army Group.

Dehn, Lili (Yulia) **Aleksandrovna** (née Smolskaya) (1888–1963, Italy): Close friend of the Empress. After emigrating, authored a memoir entitled *The Real Tsaritsa* (1922).

Demian Bedny (pseudonym of Pridvorov, Yefim Alekseevich) (1883–1945): Bolshevik poet; proficient author of satirical quatrains and fables.

Derevenko, Vladimir Nikolaevich (1879–1930s): Surgeon who cared for Tsarevich Aleksei and the royal family. Arrested for monarchist views in 1930. Not to be confused with Aleksei's "sailor-nanny" Andrei Dereven'ko.

Derzhavin, Gavriil Romanovich (1743–1816): Russia's greatest poet of the eighteenth century; celebrated for his triumphant, philosophical, and religious odes, such as the exuberant *Ode to God*.

Dmitri Pavlovich, Grand Duke (1891–1942, Switzerland): Son of Pavel Aleksandrovich, cousin of Nikolai II. Accomplice of Rasputin murderers.

Dmitrievsky, Pyotr (pseud. of Aleksandrovich, Vyacheslav) **Aleksandrovich** (1884–1918): Left Social Revolutionary, internationalist. Member of the Executive Committee of the Petrograd Soviet, later head of the CheKa (secret police); executed in July 1918 for participation in an anti-Bolshevik coup attempt.

Dobrovolsky, Nikolai Aleksandrovich (1854–1918): Senator, last Minister of Justice of Nikolai II. Executed by Bolsheviks during the Civil War.

Dolgorukov, Pavel Dmitrievich (1866–1927): One of the founders of the Kadet Party; émigré after the Revolution but returned in secret to the USSR in 1926;

of Bolshevik coup, but cooperated with the regime from 1919. Emigrated to Italy 1921, returned to the USSR in 1928, and became an apologist for Stalinism and the head of the Writers' Union established in 1932. Died mysteriously.

Gotz, Abram Rafailovich (1882–1940): One of the leaders of the Social Revolutionaries Party; returned from Siberian exile in March 1917; became an opponent of the regime after the Bolshevik coup, arrested in 1920 and condemned to death in 1922 (commuted to five years of detention); amnestied; re-condemned in 1939; died in the camp.

Grabbe, Aleksandr Nikolaevich (1864–1947, USA): Count, major general in the Emperor's suite.

Grabbe, Mikhail Nikolaevich (1868–1942, France): Student of the page corps; commanded various Cossak units; delegated Ataman of the Don Cossacks in 1916; emigrated after the Revolution.

Grigori. *See* Rasputin.

Grigorovich, Ivan Konstantinovich (1853–1930, France): Admiral. Battleship commander at Port Arthur in the Russo-Japanese War. Minister of the Navy 1911–1917. Emigrated in 1923.

Grinevich (pseud. of Shekhter), **Konstantin Sergeevich** (1879–?): Social Democrat, member of the Soviet of Workers' Deputies.

Groten, Pavel Pavlovich (1870–1962, France): General, hero of the First World War, briefly served as assistant to Palace Commandant Voeikov.

Gruzinov, Aleksandr Evgrafovich (1873–1918): Moscow nobleman, military officer, pilot. Embraced the revolution in Moscow, assumed control of the Moscow Military District; soon fell out with the Soviets, joined the Whites, died in the Civil War.

Guchkov, Aleksandr Ivanovich (1862–1936, France): Founder of the Octobrist Party. President of the Third Duma March 1910–March 1911. Chairman of the All-Russian War Industry Committees. Minister of War in the first Provisional Government, February–May 1917. Emigrated in 1918.

Guchkova (married Suvchinsky, married Trail), **Vera Aleksandrovna** (1906–1987, England): Translator. Became a Soviet sympathizer and agent, joined French Communist Party.

Gurko, Vasili Iosifovich (1864–1937, Italy): General. Participant in the Anglo-Boer and Russo-Japanese wars. After two years of fighting in the First World War, served as chief of staff during Alekseev's illness (November 1916–March 1917), returned to command Western Army Group March–May 1917. Dismissed and exiled by the Provisional Government.

Gutovsky, Vintsenti Anitsetovich (nom de guerre "Acetylene Gas") (1875–1918): Menshevik militant who wielded influence in the Workers' Group of Kozma Gvozdev.

Gvozdev, Kozma Antonovich (1883–1956): Worker, Menshevik leader, defensist, president of the central Workers' Group. Member of the Central Committee of Petrograd Soviet, then Minister of Labor under the Fourth Provisional Government. Imprisoned from 1930 on.

promoted to officer; but after October, when he joined the White forces against the Bolsheviks, was shot on the order of Aleksandr Kutepov.

Kishkin, Nikolai Mikhailovich (1864–1930): Doctor, one of the Kadet leaders, Minister of Welfare during the last provisional government, arrested in the Winter Palace and then released.

Kleinmichel, Nikolai Vladimirovich (1877–1918): Count; vice governor of Moscow in March 1917; shot by the Bolsheviks in Evpatoria, Crimea.

Kleinmichel, Vladimir Konstantinovich (1888–1917): Count, cavalry captain of the Guard, murdered by soldiers of the Luga garrison.

Klembovsky, Vladislav Napoleonovich (Vladimir Nikolaevich) (1860–1921): Infantry general; turned down Supreme Commander appointment in 1917, supporting Lavr Kornilov against Kerensky; was held hostage by Bolsheviks, then joined Red Army as a historian; arrested as scapegoat for Red Army's defeat in Poland; starved in prison.

Klyuzhev, Ivan Semyonovich (1856–1922): Deputy of Samara in the Fourth Duma; Octobrist.

Kobylinsky, Evgeni Stepanovich (1875–1927): Colonel; commanded the imperial guards; remained in this function until May 1918; entered the White Army; taken prisoner; was later tried and shot.

Kokoshkin, Fyodor Fyodorovich (the younger) (1871–1918): Jurist, one of the founders of the Kadet Party, member of the First Duma, signer of the Vyborg Appeal; Minister of State Control in 1917; arrested, murdered together with Shingarev at the Mariinsky Hospital.

Kokovtsov, Vladimir Nikolaevich, Count (1853–1943, France): Minister of Finance (1904–1905, 1906–1914), prime minister (1911–February 1914), banker; jailed in 1918, then escaped Soviet Russia; a notable émigré figure, left behind important memoirs.

Kolchak, Aleksandr Vasilievich (1873–1920): Polar explorer, vice admiral and commander of the Black Sea Fleet, which he was able to keep in order throughout the spring of 1917. Exiled by Kerensky, Kolchak returned via the Pacific during the Civil War and from 1918 to 1920 led the White armies in Siberia, was recognized by all White forces as the supreme ruler of Russia. His advance against the Red Army was stopped at the Volga, his armies were pushed back, and he was captured by the Bolsheviks and executed at Irkutsk on 7 February 1920.

Kollontai, Aleksandra Mikhailovna (1872–1952): Menshevik; companion of Shlyapnikov. Theorist of "free love." Novelist. In 1917, member of Bolshevik Central Committee. In 1920–1921, with Shlyapnikov, one of the leaders of the "Workers' Opposition." From 1923 to 1945 a Soviet diplomat.

Kolomiytsev, Nikolai Nikolaevich (1867–1944, France): Seaman; arctic explorer; hero of the Battle of Tsushima (1905); arrested repeatedly in 1917 and 1918. Escaped to Finland over the Gulf ice, fought for the White forces. Emigrated.

Kolya, Kolka: diminutives of Nikolai.

Konovalov, Aleksandr Ivanovich (1875–1949, France): Industrialist; deputy in the Fourth Duma. Leader of the Progressive Bloc. Vice chairman of the War Industry

Committees. During 1917 held commerce and industry portfolio in the Provisional Government.

Konstantinovich grand dukes: Six sons and two daughters of Grand Duke **Konstantin Konstantinovich** (1858–1915), distinguished poet, president of the Academy of Sciences. Three of them, **Ioann** (1886–1918), **Konstantin** (1891–1918), and **Igor** (1894–1918), were murdered by the Bolsheviks.

Kornilov, Lavr Georgievich (1870–1918): Infantry general in March 1917, then appointed Commander of the Petrograd Military District; in July became Supreme Commander. His attempt to forestall the Bolshevik coup was frustrated by Kerensky. Kornilov was arrested but succeeded in escaping to the south, organized the White armies after the death of Alekseev. Killed in battle in the Civil War.

Kornilov, Vladimir Alekseevich (1806–1854): Vice admiral, aide-de-camp, hero in the defense of Sevastopol, killed in the Crimean War.

Korolenko, Vladimir Galaktionovich (1853–1921): Journalist, short-story writer, humanitarian activist, publisher; opposed Tsarist strictures and then Bolshevik repression.

Kotlyarevsky, Nestor (1863–1925): Well-known specialist of literary history; academic; first director (1910–1925) of the "House of Pushkin" (Institute of Russian Literature, Russian Academy of Sciences).

Kotya: diminutive of Konstantin.

Kozlovsky, Mechislav Yulievich (1876–1927): Militant of the Russian, Polish, and Lithuanian Socialist Parties; held leading posts in the Soviet legal system.

Kozma Antonovich. *See* Gvozdev.

Krasikov, Pyotr Ananievich (1870–1939): Old friend of Lenin, Bolshevik, lawyer, member of the Executive Committee of the Soviet in March 1917. After October, played major role in Soviet legal system.

Krieger-Voinovsky, Eduard Bronislavovich (1862–1933, Germany): Railroad engineer who served as the last Minister of Roads and Railways of the Russian Empire; led an association of Russian engineers in emigration; published memoirs.

Kropotkin, Pyotr Alekseevich (1842–1921): Geographer, revolutionary, theorist of anarchism. Emigrant from 1876 to 1917.

Krotovsky (pseud. Yurenev), **Konstantin Konstantinovich** (1888–1938): Socialist, leader of the Interdistrict group from 1913, joined Bolsheviks in 1917, became a Red Army commissar in the Civil War, then a Soviet diplomat. Executed during the purges.

Krupskaya, Nadezhda Konstantinova (1869–1939): Lenin's wife. Teacher by profession. Active as educationalist after the 1917 Revolution. Avoided being noticed under Stalin.

Krymov, Aleksandr Mikhailovich (1871–1917): General. Corps commander, associate of Guchkov and the Octobrists. Committed suicide in September 1917 after the failure of General Lavr Kornilov's attempt to forestall the Bolshevik coup.

Ksenia Aleksandrovna (1875–1960, England): Younger sister of Nikolai II, married her paternal cousin Grand Duke Aleksandr Mikhailovich ("Sandro").

Kshesinskaya, Matilda Feliksovna (Mathilde Kszesinska, "Malechka," 1872–1971, France): Ballerina of Polish origin. Girlfriend of Tsarevich Nikolai Aleksandrovich before his marriage and ascent to the throne as Nikolai II; then of Grand Duke Sergei Mikhailovich; then wife of Grand Duke Andrei Vladimirovich. Her private mansion in Petrograd, of refined and modern architecture, was requisitioned by the Bolsheviks, who made it their first headquarters.

Kuba. *See* Hanecki.

Kuropatkin, Aleksei Nikolaevich (1848–1925): War minister, unfortunate commander-in-chief during the Russo-Japanese War; served in World War I; finished his life as a primary school teacher in his village.

Kutepov, Aleksandr Pavlovich (1882–1930): Colonel (as of 1917), later General. Fought in Russo-Japanese War and First World War. One of the few officers who tried to lead organized resistance to the February Revolution; then fought in the Civil War on the side of the Whites, being one of the last to evacuate from Crimea in November 1920. In emigration, led the Russian All-Military Union, an anti-Soviet veterans' organization; was kidnapped by Soviet agents and killed.

Kutuzov, Mikhail (Golenishchev-Kutuzov), **Mikhail Illarionovich**, Prince (1745–1813): Field marshal, leader of Russian armies in the Patriotic War against Napoleon; died in Silesia pursuing the Grand Armée westward. His monument stands outside Kazan Cathedral.

Kvetsinsky, Mikhail Fyodorovich (1866–1923, Norway): Served much of his career in the Far East; then in the First World War at the Southwestern and Western Fronts; in 1917 took a soft line on military discipline and was dismissed; later briefly led White forces in the Russian north, evacuated in 1920.

Lafarge, Paul (1842–1911): French socialist; son-in-law of Marx, whose theories he spread and popularized.

Lashevich, Mikhail (1884–1928): Social Democrat from 1901; Bolshevik from the very beginning; pushed into the background three times; at the front, 1915–1917, injured. Participated in the February–March Revolution; central participant in October coup d'etat. Important military functions; partisan of Trotsky; excluded from and then reintegrated into the Communist Party; sent to Harbin, China, undoubtedly in disgrace, as vice president of the Chinese Eastern Railway; committed suicide.

Lavr Georgievich. *See* Kornilov.

Law, Andrew Bonar (1858–1923): British politician; Conservative deputy; rapprochement with David Lloyd George (1916), who gave him the leading position in his war cabinet.

Le Bon, Gustave (1841–1931): Doctor and sociologist; pioneer of the psychology of crowds.

Lebedev, Yuri Mikhailovich (1874–after 1917): Deputy to the Fourth Duma, representing the Don Cossack region, member of the Kadet Party and the Progressive Bloc. Fate after 1917 unknown.

Lechitsky, Platon Alekseevich (1856–1921): Priest's son; enlisted in 1877; climbed the ranks by merit alone; infantry general in 1913; commander of the Fourth Army from the war's start; freed from his command for reasons of health in 1917; arrested and died in prison.

von Münnich, Burkhard Christoph (Christofor Antonovich) (1683–1767): Military officer from Oldenburg in the service of Russia since 1721; field marshal; career fortunes shifted across various monarchs.

Muravyov, Nikolai Konstantinovich (1870–1936): A prestigious lawyer involved in all the great political processes before 1917; in March 1917, president of the Extraordinary Commission of Inquiry. After October, worked again as a lawyer in the processes started by the Bolsheviks against their opponents; resigned from the Moscow bar in 1930; died of natural causes.

Muravyov-Vilensky, Mikhail Nikolaevich (1796–1866): In 1863, punished the uprisings in Lithuania and Belarus with such intensity that he earned the nickname "Muravyov the Hangman."

Muromtsev, Sergei Andreevich (1850–1910): Professor of law at Moscow University. One of the founders of the Kadet Party. President of the First Duma, signatory of the Vyborg Appeal in 1907.

Nabokov, Vladimir Dmitrievich (1869–1922, Germany): Lawyer. Active participant in Zemstvo congress 1904–1905; one of the founders of the Kadet Party. Signer of the Vyborg Appeal. Secretary general of the Provisional Government. Emigrated, assassinated by a Russian right-wing extremist. Father of the writer Vladimir Nabokov.

Nadya. *See* Krupskaya.

Nakhamkes (Steklov), **Yuri Mikhailovich** (1873–1941): Early Social Democrat; from 1903 close to the Bolsheviks, contributor to the *Social-Democrat* and *Pravda*; after February, a "Revolutionary defensist," then returned to Bolshevism; after October 1917, active in journalism and historical works; died in the purges.

Nakhichevan, Khan of, Hussein (1863–1919): General aide-de-camp (the only Muslim to attain that position in the history of the Russian Imperial Army), cavalry general; one of the rare generals of March 1917 that put his unit at the disposal of the Tsar; shot by the Bolsheviks in St. Petersburg.

Nakhimov, Pavel Stepanovich (1802–1855): Admiral, hero of the siege of Sevastopol; fatally injured in battle.

Nansen, Fridtjof (1861–1930): Norwegian arctic explorer, winner of the Nobel Peace Prize for his work on behalf of refugees; introduced the "Nansen passport" for stateless persons.

Naryshkin, Kirill Anatolievich (1867–1924): Childhood friend of Nikolai II, member of the Emperor's suite. Arrested by the Bolsheviks, died in prison.

Natasha: diminutive of Natalia.

Nebolsin, Arkadi Konstantinovich (1865–1917): Rear admiral, commander of the second squadron of line vessels of the Baltic Fleet in Helsingfors-Sveaborg, assassinated by his crew in March 1917.

Nekrasov, Nikolai Vissarionovich (1879–1940): Kadet deputy in Third and Fourth Dumas. One of the organizers of the Zemgor. Held ministerial posts in the Provisional Government, left Kadet Party and allied with socialists. Arrested in 1930, worked as a hydraulic engineer building canals and dams; freed; arrested and executed in the purges.

during the war, a defensist; unitarist; played only a symbolic role after his return to Russia in 1917.

von Pleve, Viacheslav Konstantinovich (1846–1904): Headed the Police Department in the 1880s, put down the terrorism of the People's Will organization; in 1902 was named minister of the interior and pursued a hard line against revolutionaries; murdered by a Socialist Revolutionary.

Pluzhnikov, Grigori Naumovich (ca. 1887–1921): one of the leaders of the Tambov peasant uprising of 1920–1921.

Pokrovsky, Nikolai Nikolaevich (1865–1930, Lithuania): Last Foreign Minister of the Russian Empire. Banker. Emigrated, taught finance at Kaunas University.

Politikus: pseud. of Mikhailov (Yelinson), Lev Mikhailovich (1872–1928); Bolshevik publicist, diplomat, secretary of the Society of Old Bolsheviks.

Polivanov, Aleksei Andreevich (1855–1920): Infantry general, close to Guchkov, dismissed by General Sukhomlinov; Minister of War 1915–1916, overcame the munition crisis, offered his services to the Red Army, died of typhus.

Polovtsov, Pyotr Aleksandrovich (1874–1964, Monaco): Lieutenant general, commander of troops in the Petrograd Military District in the summer of 1917. Escaped Russia in 1918; later lived in London and was a director of the Monte Carlo casino.

Potapov, Nikolai Mikhailovich (1871–1946): Lieutenant general; president (under Guchkov) of the Duma's military commission; joined Bolsheviks in 1917 and worked as a Red Army instructor.

Potemkin, Grigory Aleksandrovich, Prince (1739–1791): Field marshal and Russian politician, favorite of Catherine II, who named him the Prince Tauride for his conquest of Crimea and Tauride Province and offered him a palace by the same name. Unoccupied after his death, the palace was refurbished in 1906 to house the State Duma of the Russian Empire.

Potresov, Aleksandr Nikolaevich (1869–1934, France): Social Democrat from the beginning; Menshevik leader, defensist; in 1917, one of the writers of the journal *The Day*; leader of the party's right wing ("Potresov Group"); ill, he was authorized to leave the USSR in 1925.

Pozharsky, Dmitri, Prince (1578–ca. 1642): With Kuzma Minin, leader of the popular militia that dislodged foreign invaders and marauding armies during the Time of Troubles and cleared the way for establishing the Romanov dynasty. In 1817 Minin and Pozharsky were honored with a monument in Red Square that stands to this day.

Prokopovich, Sergei Nikolaevich (1871–1955, Switzerland): Economist, then independent socialist, minister in the last provisional government; exiled in 1922; author of important works on economics.

Protopopov, Aleksandr Dmitrievich (1866–1918): Deputy in the Third and Fourth Dumas, Octobrist, vice president of the Duma in 1914; accused of spying for Germany. Last imperial Minister of the Interior; incarcerated by the Provisional Government, shot without trial by the Bolsheviks.

Purishkevich, Vladimir Mitrofanovich (1870–1920): Monarchist, right-wing leader, deputy in the Second to Fourth Dumas, where he was known for oratory flare and outrageous behavior. Co-murderer of Rasputin. Joined White Volunteer army, died of typhus.

Putyatin, Mikhail Sergeevich (1861–1938, France): General of the Emperor's suite, administrator of the Imperial residence at Tsarskoye Selo.

Putyatin, Pavel Pavlovich (1871–1943, France): Colonel, equerry of the Imperial Court. His apartment on Millionnaya 12 would become the site of the dissolution of the Romanov dynasty. Died in emigration.

Pyatakov, Grigori Leonidovich (1890–1937): Anarchist, then from 1910, Bolshevik. In 1917 chairman of the Kiev Soviet. In 1918 headed the Soviet government in Ukraine. From 1918, supporter of Trotsky. Executed in the purges.

Pyotr Akimovich: the engineer Obodovsky. Listed under non-historical characters.

Pyotr Nikolaevich, Grand Duke (1854–1931, France): Brother of Grand Duke Nikolai Nikolaevich, husband of Militsa, sister of Nikolai Nikolaevich's wife Stana (the Montenegrin sisters).

Radishchev, Aleksandr Nikolaevich (1749–1802): Russian writer, a father of Russian social thought, great ancestor of the intelligentsia. Arrested for having printed, in 1790, the *Voyage from Petersburg to Moscow*, which was judged subversive for the way in which it condemned the principle and practice of serfdom; deported for ten years to Siberia, pardoned in 1796.

Radko-Dmitriev, Radko Dmitrievich (1859–1918): Bulgarian general who served in the Russian Army, commander of the Twelfth Army on the Northern Front. Murdered by the Bolsheviks.

Rafes, Moisei (Moishe) **Grigorievich** (1883–1942): A leader of the Jewish Labor Bund, revolutionary; joined Communist Party, was an overseer of Soviet cinema; arrested in 1938, convicted, died in labor camps.

Ramishvili, Isidore Ivanovich (1859–1937): Georgian Menshevik leader; 1918–1921; member of the government of independent Georgia.

Rasputin, Grigori Efimovich ("the Friend, Our Friend, man of God, Grishka") (1864–1916): Siberian peasant; self-proclaimed as a mystic with healing talents and ability to predict the future; a humble holy peasant at court, preaching and practicing licentiousness outside it. Met the imperial couple in 1905 (through the Montenegrin sisters) and eased the hemophiliac heir's suffering, probably by his hypnotic powers. Exerted growing influence in 1915–1916 over the imperial family and affairs of state; murdered in December 1916 by Yusupov and Purishkevich.

Rein, Georgi Yermolaevich (1854–1942, Bulgaria): Surgeon, member of the State Council, general administrator of public health from October 1916, a position that the Duma obstinately refused to upgrade to minister. Ceased to exercise his functions in March.

Rengarten, Ivan Ivanovich (Vanya) (1883–1920): Captain First Rank. Supported the February Revolution; taught in the Naval Academy from 1918, died of typhus.

von Rennenkampf, Pavel Karlovich (1854–1918): General. Distinguished himself in Boxer War. His inaction in East Prussia was held responsible for the loss of Samsonov's army in August 1914. Equally ineffectual at Lodz in November 1916, he was dismissed. Shot by the Bolsheviks in 1918.

Shekhter. *See* Grinevich.

Shingarev, Andrei Ivanovich (1869–1918): Physician and head of a zemstvo hospital. Deputy to Second, Third, and Fourth Dumas. Member of Kadet Party leadership. Minister of Agriculture in the first Provisional Government, then Minister of Finance in the second. Imprisoned by the Bolsheviks, murdered together with Kokoshkin at the Mariinsky Hospital.

Shlyapnikov, Aleksandr Gavrilovich (Gavrilych) (1885–1937): Born into a family of Old Believers. Bolshevik from 1905. Worked in factories abroad, 1908–1914. Collaborated closely with Lenin during the war, returned clandestinely to Russia via Scandinavia on various occasions, oversaw the work of the Bolshevik Russian Bureau. Trade union leader; first Commissar of Labor after the Bolshevik Revolution. One of the leaders of the Workers' Opposition movement in the Party, 1920–1922. Expelled from the Central Committee in 1922. Held minor posts subsequently. Excluded from the Party in 1933, arrested 1935, executed.

Shnitnikov, Nikolai Nikolaevich (1861–1940): Lawyer, former member of St. Petersburg's municipal duma; Populist Socialist.

Shulgin, Vasili Vitalievich (1878–1976): Duma deputy, leader of the right. Member of the Progressive Bloc. With Guchkov, received Nikolai II's abdication. Emigrated, made a clandestine trip to the USSR. Captured in Yugoslavia in 1944, spent twelve years in a prison camp, welcomed by Khrushchev, lived out his days in the USSR.

Shutko, Kirill Ivanovich (1884–1941?): Bolshevik from 1902, active in October Revolution; held posts overseeing cinema, culture. Friend of the painter Kazimir Malevich. Arrested in 1938, executed.

Shuvaev, Dmitri Savelievich (1854–1937): Infantry general; intendant general of the armies. Minister of war, March 1916–January 1917. Served, taught courses in Red Army after the Revolution. Retired after 1927; arrested in 1937 and executed.

Siefeldt, Arthur Rudolph (1889–1939): Estonian from Tallinn, joined Bolshevism; 1913–1917, in Zurich. Left Switzerland in 1917 with the second transfer of émigrés through Germany; arrested, died in labor camps.

Sklarz, Georg (1875–?): Supplier to German military; German agent; associate of Parvus; assisted Lenin's "sealed train" into Russia; scandalous legal process in Germany after the war.

Skobelev, Matvei Ivanovich (1885–1939): Social Democrat from 1903; Menshevik, deputy in the Fourth Duma. Patriot during the war. Minister in Second Provisional Government July 1917. Joined Bolshevik Party in 1922. Worked in foreign trade organization. Expelled from the Party in 1937; died in the purges.

Skobelev, Mikhail Dmitrievich (1843–1882): Infantry general; distinguished himself in particular in the Russo-Turkish War (1877–1878); liberator of Bulgaria; conqueror of Turkmenia. His statue stood in the square in front of the governor-general's home (today's city hall), and the square was known as Skobelev Square before 1917.

Smirnov, Vladimir Vasilievich (1849–1918): Infantry general, Commander of the First Army. Killed while held hostage by the Bolsheviks at Pyatigorsk.

Vladimir, Saint (d. 1015): Prince of Kiev; converted to Christianity and then converted his people in 988; one of the main imperial orders under the Romanovs was named after St. Vladimir, with medals and crosses awarded for both military and civil service.

Voeikov, Vladimir Nikolaevich (1868–1947, Sweden): Palace Commandant, General of the Emperor's suite, son-in-law of Count Frederiks, chairman of the first Russian Olympic committee. Had the reputation of a capable but self-serving organizer. After the Revolution lived in Finland.

Voevodsky, Stepan Arkadievich (1859–1937, France): Naval minister (1908–11); emigrated soon after Revolution.

Volkov, Aleksei Andreevich (1859–1929, Estonia): Empress Aleksandra's valet; he accompanied her to Tobolsk and then Ekaterinburg, where he was arrested; transferred to Perm, where he succeeded in fleeing just before being shot; published memoirs of his service to the imperial family.

Volodya: diminutive of Vladimir.

Vyazemskaya (née Shuvalova), **Aleksandra Pavlovna** (Asya) (1893–1968, Italy): Spouse of Dmitri Vyazemsky.

Vyazemsky, Boris Leonidovich, Prince (1883–1917): Personal secretary of Stolypin, heir and owner of the exemplary Lotaryovo estate, which was destroyed in September 1917 by revolutionary mobs, who beat Prince Boris to death.

Vyazemsky, Dmitri Leonidovich, Prince (1884–1917): Younger brother of Boris Vyazemsky. Organized a field hospital and treated wounded during the First World War. Was killed in Petrograd in March 1917 by a stray bullet.

Vyrubova (Taneeva), **Anya** (1884–1964, Finland): Lady-in-waiting to the Empress. For some years her closest friend and intermediary between the imperial couple and Rasputin. Victim of a railroad accident in 1915, arrested in 1917, liberated, rearrested, emigrated.

Wilhelm: Wilhelm II (1859–1941), the Kaiser, emperor of Germany, king of Prussia (1888–1918).

Wilhelm, Crown Prince (1882–1951): Son of Wilhelm II; renounced his rights to the German throne in December 1918.

Witte, Sergei Yulievich (1849–1915): Minister of Finance 1892–1903. Urged civil reforms and modernization. Prime Minister October 1905–April 1906, when he resigned (replaced by Goremykin). Author of an important memoir.

Wrangel, Pyotr Nikolaevich (1878–1928, Belgium): Cavalry captain in 1914; by 1917 he was a general and St. George medalist, division commander. Participated in the White movement beginning in August 1918; had serious disagreements with Anton Denikin, whom he ended up replacing after the defeat of the White forces in the Russian South. For most of 1920, Wrangel not only held on to the Crimean peninsula but also sought to create there a viable economy based on private land ownership by the peasantry. Wrangel's Crimea was recognized by France as the de facto Russian government but was overrun by the Red Army in November 1920. Led the orderly evacuation of 120,000 people from Crimea to Constantinople. While he was an emigrant, he created the Russian All-Military Union. Died in Brussels, buried in Belgrade.

Zenzinov, Vladimir Mikhailovich (1880–1953, USA): Hailed from a family of wealthy merchants. Member of Social Revolutionary party, active in 1905 Revolution. Elected to Constituent Assembly, opposed Bolshevism, emigrated. Worked as a correspondent.

Zhordania, Noe Nikolaevich (1869–1953, France): Leader of the Georgian Mensheviks; head of the government of independent Georgia (1918–1921); emigrated after the Bolshevik occupation of Georgia.

Zinoviev, Grigori Evseevich (pseud. Radomyslsky, Ovsei-Gershon Aronovich, born Apfelbaum, Hirsch) (1883–1936): Bolshevik from 1903. Chairman of the Petrograd Soviet after the October Revolution, Politburo member, leader of the Comintern. Helped depose Trotsky, then was deposed by Stalin, expelled from the Party, tried and executed in 1936.

Zubatov, Sergei Vasilievich (1863–1917): Minister of police, encouraged workers to collaborate with his administration.

Principal Non-Historical Characters

Adalia and Agnessa: Aunts of Aleksandr (Sasha) and Veronika Lenartovich, who brought them up after the death of their parents. Deeply populist, to the left of the Kadets, Aunt Adalia did not belong to any political party; Aunt Agnessa, however, was an anarchist, at times a maximalist, had been in prison and in Siberia, and was entirely devoted to the Revolution. The two sisters symbolize the Russian intelligentsia united by its hatred for the aristocracy, its scorn for police, and its desire for freedom of the people.

Alina. *See* Vorotyntseva.

Andozerskaya, Olda Orestovna: She was said to be the most intelligent woman in Petersburg. Professor of world history, she nonetheless supported the monarchy, a rare case in learned circles. In November 1916 she met Colonel Vorotyntsev, who was passing through Petrograd. They began a passionate affair, which continued through correspondence during the winter of 1916–1917.

Blagodarev, Arseni (Senka): Sergeant; peasant from Kamenka whose wife (Katya, Katyona) and two infants (Sevastyan and Proska) await him at home. Worked wonders in combat in August 1914. In 1916, his commanding officer, Sanya Lazhenitsyn, obtained for him permission to return to his village for leave. March 1917 finds him at the front lines.

Bruyakin, Evpati Gavrilych: Shopkeeper in Kamenka. In 1916, seized by a bad presentiment, he envisioned closing his business.

Bruyakin, Kolya ("Kolya Satych"): Son of Evpati. Adolescent, he was mostly interested in women.

Chernega, Terenti: Sergeant major in Sanya Lazhenitsyn's artillery battery. He is worldly, the happy warrior, one who sees life in simple terms, in contrast to Sanya's intellectual and spiritual quests.

Kharitonov family (based on a real-life family, the Andreevs): **Aglaida Fedoseevna**, stern headmistress of the best high school for girls in the Russian south, in Rostov, holder of progressive views. But her children defy her: older son **Yaroslav (Yarik)** by becoming an officer; daughter **Evgenia (Zhenya)** by marrying **Dmitri Ivanych Filomatinsky** while pregnant with their daughter, **Lyalka**; younger son **Yurik** dreams of becoming an officer like Yaroslav when, aged 14, he encounters the Revolution.

Korzner, David: Well-known Moscow lawyer, progressive, member of the municipal duma. When disorder began to capture Moscow, Korzner decided to propose the creation of the Moscow Provisional Revolutionary Committee.

Korzner, Susanna Iosifovna: Wife of a well-known lawyer in Moscow, David Korzner. Jewish, she militated for the improvement of the life of Jews in Russia. Specializing in "lectures and proclamations," Susanna forged a friendship with Alina, who offered to become her page-turner for musical concerts for the troops.

Kovynev, Fyodor Dmitrievich: Originally from the Don, he lived in Petersburg. His prototype is Fyodor Kryukov, believed to be the real author of the novel *And Quiet Flows the Don*, whereas Soviet officialdom ascribed the novel to Mikhail Sholokhov.

Lazhenitsyn, Sanya (Isaaki): From the North Caucasus, a student before the war, he was seduced by Tolstoy's ideas. In 1914, he fought in eastern Prussia, where he met Colonel Vorotyntsev and Arseni Blagodarev. He was still at the front when the troubles of March 1917 erupted. Sanya Lazhenitsyn is the prototype of the author's father, Isaaki Semyonovich Solzhenitsyn.

Lenartovich, Aleksandr ("Sasha"): Student, enrolled in the army at the beginning of the hostilities. Raised by his aunts in the revolutionary tradition of the intelligentsia and in respect for his uncle Anton's memory, he militated against the aristocracy and was opposed to war. In August 1914 he met Colonel Vorotyntsev at the front, where he did not display courage or military valor.

Lenartovich, Veronika (Veronya): Sister of Sasha Lenartovich. Although brought up in the family revolutionary tradition, she escaped its influence and showed no interest in politics. Eventually, however, she became a fierce militant, to the great satisfaction of her aunts and her brother, which led her to drift away from her school friend Likonya.

Likonya (Yelenka, Yolochka): School friend of Veronika Lenartovich, although their friendship was broken. A devotee of the arts, she is the opposite of the ideal of revolutionary militancy. Nonetheless, Sasha Lenartovich was charmed by her.

Lyoka. *See* Varsonofiev.

Obodovsky, Pyotor Akimovich (modeled closely on the historical character Pyotr Akimovich Palchinsky): Mining engineer, charged by the All-Russian Union of Engineers to form a committee of military technical assistance in the central War Industry Committees. A revolutionary, prosecuted twice, he was imprisoned, exiled, and even managed an escape abroad, always faithfully supported by his spouse, Nusya (Nina). Although he did not give up on his ideas, Obodovsky did not believe the revolution should take place before the end of the war.

Olda Orestovna. *See* Andozerskaya.

Pavel Ivanovich. *See* Varsonofiev.

Tomchak, Ksenia Zakharovna: Daughter of self-made landowner Zakhar Tomchak. Completed her secondary studies in Rostov-on-Don at Kharitonova's high school, where she discovered a thriving intellectual environment. Ksenia Tomchak is the prototype of the author's mother, Taisia Shcherbak.

Varsonofiev, Pavel Ivanovich ("Stargazer"): Aging thinker, seer of enigmatic dreams, whose meetings with Sanya contain riddles, and some answers, about duty, war, society, revolution, the fate of Russia, and the meaning of hope. Divorced from wife Leokadia (Lyoka), who repeatedly haunts him in his dreams.

Vera (Vorotyntseva, Vera Mikhailovna): Sister of Colonel Vorotyntsev. Lived in Petersburg with their old nurse. Worked at the Public Library. Fourteen years younger than her brother, she spent her childhood without him and was very influenced by the traditional peasant world of her nurse. In love with the engineer Dmitriev, she led a solitary life, while he was embroiled in a complicated love affair.

Vorotyntseva (née Siyalskaya) **Alina:** Wife of Colonel Vorotyntsev. Trained as a pianist, she devoted herself entirely to her husband's career during the eight years of her marriage preceding the 1914 World War. When he was sent to the front, Alina, who had no children, was left alone in Moscow and became extremely active, organizing concerts for the troops. During the war, she felt she had come alive again as a person, until she learned that her husband was having an affair with a famous woman from Petrograd.

Vorotyntsev, Georgi Mikhailovich: Graduated at the top of his class from the military academy. Colonel. After his studies in Petersburg, he and his wife Alina lived in garrisons in the Vyatka region until he was sent to Moscow. After a brief rise that took him to GHQ (General Headquarters), he was sent on a mission in East Prussia. He escaped the encirclement of the Samsonov army at Tannenberg in August 1914. Eventually he was "exiled" to a regiment because of his positions on war strategy. In early November 1916, on a mission in Petrograd, he met Professor Andozerskaya and they began a passionate affair.

Zinaida (Altanskaya): Former student of Fyodor Kovynev, when he was teaching in Tambov. She shared with him a passionate and complex love affair.

ABOUT THE AUTHOR

Aleksandr Solzhenitsyn (1918–2008) is widely acknowledged as one of the most important figures—and perhaps *the* most important writer—of the last century. A Soviet political prisoner from 1945 to 1953, he set himself firmly against the anti-human Soviet system, and all anti-human ideologies, from that time forward. His novel *One Day in the Life of Ivan Denisovich* (1962) made him famous, and *The Gulag Archipelago*, published to worldwide acclaim in 1973, further unmasked communism and played a critical role in its eventual defeat. Solzhenitsyn won the Nobel Prize in 1970 and was exiled to the West in 1974. He ultimately published dozens of plays, poems, novels, and works of history, nonfiction, and memoir, including *Cancer Ward*, *In the First Circle*, and *The Oak and the Calf* (a memoir that is continued in *Between the Millstones*). Few authors have so decisively shaped minds, hearts, and world events as did Solzhenitsyn.